HER GENTLE

Divine Creek Ranch 2

Heather Rainier

EVERLASTING CLASSIC

Siren Publishing, Inc.
www.SirenPublishing.com

A SIREN PUBLISHING BOOK
IMPRINT: Everlasting Classic

HER GENTLE GIANT
Copyright © 2011 by Heather Rainier

ISBN-10: 1-61034-276-3
ISBN-13: 978-1-61034-276-6

First Printing: January 2011

Cover design by *Les Byerley*
All art and logo copyright © 2011 by Siren Publishing, Inc.

Currington, Billy. Lyrics. "She's Got a Way With Me." *Doin' Something' Right.* Mercury Nashville. © 2005.

Wicks, Chuck Lyrics. "Hold That Thought." *Hold That Thought.* Sony Music Entertainment: RCA Records Label Nashville. © 2010.

Printed in the U.S.A.

PUBLISHER
Siren Publishing, Inc.
www.SirenPublishing.com

DEDICATION

For my husband, who has taught me more than he realizes about living life with no regrets.

ACKNOWLEDGEMENTS

Thanks to Rebecca, Dana, Lisa and Kayla for believing in me.

Thanks to Christie, Jennifer and Tonya for their contagious enthusiasm.

Thanks to incredible beautiful, graceful pole dancing specialist, Leigh Ann Orsi of Be Spun, for the inspiration she provided with her beautiful moves. I never thought to include something like pole dancing in my story line until I was doing related online research for a bachelor party scene. Wish I could move like that.

And my sincerest thanks to Diana, Alison, Caroline and all the wonderful staff of Siren Publishing, and cover artist Les Byerley who brought Eli and Rachel to vivid life.

Warning: Adults only. This is a work of erotic romantic fiction. It includes elements which some may find offensive, including scorching hot M/F love scenes with very little left to the imagination: from the first shiver, to the last contented sigh. Anal play, anal sex, light bondage, bondage play, sex toys, spanking, pole dancing and stripping, as well as love scenes involving a committed polyamorous foursome M/M/M/F separate from the main characters. This novel is not intended for young readers and was written for of-age adults, and should not be left out where young eyes might see it.

HER GENTLE GIANT

Divine Creek Ranch 2

HEATHER RAINIER
Copyright © 2011

Chapter One

August…

Rachel Lopez slid her laptop into its carrying case and zipped it closed. The work day was finally over, and she looked forward to a bubble bath, leftovers, and a DVD. She hadn't accomplished very much on her manuscript at lunchtime and hoped to get a little done before bedtime. She cleared her desk and lifted her purse from the drawer she kept it stashed in. Her head throbbed, and she remembered the other reason she needed a warm bubble bath. Her headache had persisted all day, and she was ready to relax.

"Rachel? There's someone here to see you."

Rachel looked up into the grinning, obviously curious face of her coworker, Bernice Williams.

"Who is it? Did they give you a name?" *What now?* Rachel was just about ready to walk out her office door. It was late Thursday afternoon and she wanted to slip out of her high heels.

Bernice smirked and leaned against the doorjamb. "Eli Wolf ring any bells?" She eyed her perfect manicure before crossing her arms in front of her, adding in her Texan drawl, "He asked for you by name."

Rachel groaned softly and laid her purse and keys on her desk, trying to ignore the thrill that ran through her body at the mention of his name.

This is not good. This is not good. Stop getting your hopes up. He'll give up and then you'll see. It's not worth the trouble, or the heartache, or the misery—

Her boss, Thorne Grogan, stuck his head in her door, interrupting her mental litany. "Hey, Rachel? You know there's some big hulking dude out there asking for you?"

"Yes, Mister—Sorry! Thorne. Sorry. I'll be right there."

Mr. Grogan rolled his eyes at her and headed down the hall. At her former job with the local newspaper, the dress and conduct code had been strict, and she'd gotten used to it. It was going to take her a while to adjust to the more laid-back environment of Grogan Home Theater, Inc., where she now worked as bookkeeper.

Bernice whispered, "He brought you flowers, Rachel. Is he your boyfriend?"

Lamely and with reluctance, Rachel said, "No. He's a good friend of mine. Is he waiting in reception?" She wondered why he'd brought her flowers.

Because he still wants me to go out with him after two months, and I keep telling him no. Because I'm a dumbass.

"Yeah, want me to send him back?"

In the last two months since she'd met Eli, Rachel sometimes felt like she had an angel sitting on each shoulder. Good Rachel knew only trouble would come of dating a bouncer in a nightclub, especially a scrumptiously delicious-looking bouncer like Eli. Good Rachel wanted to play it safe and avoid getting hurt. Naughty Rachel wanted Eli anyway and was ready to kick the ass of any woman who dare lay a hand on him or approach him to flirt. Naughty Rachel wanted to get laid. Whether she kept herself at arm's length or dated him, or worse, fall in love with him, she had a feeling she was going to have regrets.

Naughty Rachel tapped her shoulder.

He's right outside waiting for me with flowers. He's been so persistent. How can I say no to—

"Earth to Rachel?" Bernice passed her hand in from of her face.

Rachel grinned sheepishly and said, "Right. Tell him he can come on back."

Bernice grinned and scooted back down the hall to deliver her message.

Rachel gathered her things in her arms and stacked them on the front of the desk. She figured it would be best if she walked him out, and if he asked her out, she would turn him down in private. She knew Bernice might be eavesdropping on her conversation. Rachel liked Bernice, but she was nosey.

Her head throbbed again, and she remembered she'd dropped her bottle of Tylenol in her desk drawer when she'd taken a couple that morning. Instead of walking around the large oak desk to pull open the drawer, she stretched across the thick glass top and hooked the drawer handle with her thumb, opened it, and reached for the Tylenol.

Several things happened at once. As she stretched to reach the drawer handle, she began to lose her balance, and she heard a knock on her open office door. The slick bottoms of her new red high heels slid right out from under her on the carpeting, and she flopped ungracefully forward, knocking her breath from her as she landed on her large purse and her laptop case, which began to slide toward the edge of the desk with her on top of it. Rachel knew she was moments away from sliding off the desk and landing flat on her ass. Her fingers made useless slipping sounds as she vainly tried to get a hold on the slick, empty desk top. Clutching her laptop to keep it from hitting the floor, she sought a foothold with her pumps, and her pointed toes hit the carpet, slid sideways out from under her and she did the splits.

Her head pounded painfully, and she whimpered as she tried to get her feet back under her. In the two seconds it took for this scene to play out, she imagined she looked utterly graceless and then heard movement behind her. Large warm hands caught her in a strong grasp right before she slid off the desk, grasping her precious laptop in her arms.

"Whoa, angel!" Eli Wolf said as he caught her around the waist, keeping her and her laptop from hitting the floor. She'd never felt like a bigger klutz in her whole life, and he, of course, never looked more gorgeous.

"Oh, damn." She released her laptop when he took it from her and put her hands to her temples and whimpered again. Eli turned her to him and leaned down to look in her red-hot face.

"Rachel, are you okay?"

She looked up into his luminous gray eyes, which were filled with concern. Falling forward on her purse and laptop case had knocked the wind from her, and she felt a little nauseated on top of her pain and embarrassment.

He brushed her hair from her face and directed her to sit in one of the chairs in front of her desk. "Sit and catch your breath. What were you doing?"

She pointed to the open desk drawer. "I was reaching for my Tylenol. I've had a headache all day and what just happened didn't help it any. I'm sorry you saw me...like that." She envisioned her ass stuck up in the air with her feet flying out from under her, Lucille Ball-style, while she flopped around, and cringed again.

Want to get away?

He stepped around her desk and found the Tylenol in the open drawer and brought the bottle of water that had rolled to the edge of her desk in her clumsy scramble. As he stepped back over to her, she noticed a bouquet of vivid orange roses lying on the floor.

He noticed where she was looking and lifted the bouquet from the floor. "I brought you flowers," he said as he placed them in her hands.

Rachel took a few seconds to enjoy their fragrance, noticing that a single bright red rose was nestled in the center of the bouquet. He hadn't picked these up at the grocery store. These roses had come from Merritt's Florist, judging by the tissue paper that bore the florist's logo they were wrapped in.

"Thank you, Eli. They're beautiful. What are you up to?" she asked as she laid the roses in her lap. She opened the bottle of Tylenol, and he handed her the water.

"I came by to see if you had plans for this evening. I'd like to take you to dinner." He hesitated and looked down for a second as if he were bracing himself. "If you'd like to, that is."

I can't do this, I can't do this, I can't do this—

She heard Bernice speaking to another employee in the hallway. She didn't know if Bernice would return to her desk behind the reception counter and knew she could not turn him down within the hearing of her coworker.

"Let me get my things and I'll walk out with you, okay?" she asked softly. She hadn't told him yes, but the happy smile that lit his face made her heart do another flip-flop.

Oh, yes I can, oh, yes I can, oh, yes I can!

She contemplated the slippery slope she was on as she lifted her purse from the desk. He watched her carefully, as if making sure she was all right to get up from the chair, and lifted the laptop case strap to his shoulder. Her head throbbed, and she wanted that bubble bath something fierce, but she found that she also wanted to say yes to this knight in shining armor. If she let him, she knew he could charm her socks off. Heck, he could charm her panties off, for that matter.

"I'll go tell my boss good night."

He smiled in understanding. "I'll wait for you in the lobby."

Carrying the roses and her purse, she followed the hallway down to the end and stopped in her boss's open doorway. Another man sat conversing with Thorne, but Thorne looked up and grinned when he saw her. "Headed out for the evening?" he asked as he glanced at the roses she held. Her cheeks warmed a little, and she nodded.

"Did you get the e-mail I sent you?" she asked.

Thorne nodded. "Yes, and I saw the discrepancies you were telling me about. I can't go into detail about it, but I appreciate your diligence in getting to the bottom of the matter. I knew I made a good move when I hired you, Rachel. Good work. Enjoy your evening." His smile was broad, and he glanced at the roses with speculation in his eyes.

"Good night, sir—sorry! Good night, Thorne." She did it again. He rolled his eyes and propped his cowboy boots up on the corner of his big oak desk.

"G'night, Rachel. Have a good evening."

She nodded at the other man who had turned to see whom Thorne was speaking to and made her way back down the hallway.

Eli stood near one of the front windows looking out but did not appear focused on anything outside. Light from the windows shone in and illuminated his pale gray eyes. He was dressed in his leathers and a T-shirt and, as she approached, she could detect his clean, spicy scent. He looked good enough to eat with his shiny, long black hair streaming down his broad back. Underneath his T-shirt, every muscle stood out in relief, and the short sleeves lay snug around his bulging biceps. Her fingertips twitched with the desire to reach out and stroke him.

He must have finished early with his tower climbing job and gotten cleaned up to go to work at The Dancing Pony. He worked three or for days a week for the local electrical cooperative as a subcontractor doing some of their tower climbing work. To listen to him talk about it scared her. The thought of climbing three hundred feet or more in the area gave her the heebie-jeebies.

Eli looked up when he heard her heels click on the ceramic tile in the waiting area. Her heart flip-flopped when a broad, sexy smile spread over his face. His gaze warmed her as he looked appreciatively at her from head to toe. Her earlier humiliation at being seen in such an awkward position was salved by the admiration in his gaze now. He was used to seeing her in western wear, but for work she dressed in skirts, blouses, and heels. Today, her long brown hair was pinned up in a clip.

She turned to Bernice, who was currently ogling Eli from behind her reception counter. Bernice's facial expression mirrored those of many other women Rachel had seen gazing raptly at Eli over the last two months. The receptionist was his senior by at least ten years, although she was still in great shape, but Bernice was happily married with two kids, so Rachel didn't feel like gritting her teeth at her perusal quite so much.

"Good night, Bernice," Rachel said as Eli moved to hold the glass door open for her.

"G'night, sweetie! Y'all have fun!" she called in her high-pitched, reedy twang.

The sun hit her full in the face as she walked through the door. She held her fingers to shade her eyes and groaned at the excruciating pain in her head. A feeling of disappointment began to grow in her heart. She was definitely weakening under Eli's charm because she knew she would have said yes to a supper date this evening if not for the pain in her head.

Eli moved to block the sun from her face and put the palm of his hand to the back of her head. "It's pretty bad, huh?"

"Mmm-hmm. The brightness is killing me," she murmured.

"Come on, angel. Let's get you to your car." He put his arm around her shoulders and walked her to her vehicle, which was thankfully parked under a tree in the shade. She glanced up and noticed his big Dodge pickup was parked beside her car, dwarfing it. She used her remote to unlock it, and Eli opened the door for her. She sighed in relief as she sat down in the driver's seat. He put her laptop case on her back seat and then squatted down beside her as she sniffed her roses again.

"These are beautiful Eli, but I—" Should she tell him she would have gone out with him tonight? Should she encourage him?

At the sound of clicking heels, she looked up as another member of Mr. Grogan's staff walked down the sidewalk toward them. It was the big-busted blonde in her early twenties who worked in sales. Rachel saw the moment the girl laid her eyes on Eli. A sexy smile spread across her bright red lips, and she immediately exaggerated her wiggling walk, twitching her skinny ass as she approached. When she was even on the sidewalk with Eli and in his full view, she dropped her car keys then made a big production of retrieving them from the sidewalk, giving him a generous and slow-moving view of her big-busted cleavage in the process. The girl never even looked at her as she smiled invitingly at Eli and proceeded around the corner to her car.

Bitch.

Rachel fumed at the interruption of their moment and the slutty forwardness of her coworker. She glared at her then looked back at Eli, to find he was completely focused on her.

"You don't feel well at all, do you?" he asked, his brows knitted together. Rachel hesitated for a second, and he continued, "Would you have said yes, otherwise?"

Rachel reached back and rubbed her neck as another wave of pain brought on by the heat and brightness made her groan. The nausea from earlier returned as well. She looked at him and said, "I don't know. Maybe?"

Her answer seemed to satisfy him, and he stood. "I know what you need. Why don't you go on home and, if you don't mind, I'll swing by in a few minutes."

"What are you going to do?" She wanted to get in her bubble bath as soon as she got home, but he'd piqued her curiosity.

"I'm going to bring you something that will help. Don't worry, I won't stay because you need your rest. I'll see you at your apartment." He fished his keys from his pocket and closed her car door for her after she buckled her seat belt. She fished in her purse for her sunglasses, wondering why she hadn't thought to slip them on before leaving the building.

Maybe because I had six feet, nine inches of man-candy distracting me?

Eli allowed her to back out of her space first, and she noticed as she pulled out of the parking lot that he headed the other direction, farther into town. She made the short drive home and was standing in her kitchen gazing into one of the cabinets, trying to figure out which was the least unappealing choice, when she heard him knock.

When she pulled open the door, a delicious aroma wafted to her nostrils as Eli stood there holding a paper bag and a to-go cup. He had a warm smile on his face as she let him in.

"I brought the cure for what ails you."

Oh, baby, you have no idea. If I wasn't feeling like hammered crap, I'd let you cure me good!

"What is it?" she asked as she closed the door and followed him into her kitchen.

He opened the bag and removed the Styrofoam bowl and plastic spoon and handed them to her. She pried the plastic lid off the bowl and discovered the origin of the mouthwatering aroma.

"Have you ever had Rudy's Chicken Poblano and Habanero soup?"

"Yikes. Habanero? No, I can't say that I have." The one time she'd tried a habanero pepper, on a dare at summer camp, she'd gagged and coughed for an hour afterward. She could still taste it the following day, and her digestion hadn't liked it very much, either. Rachel wanted to keep her tongue in its current uninjured condition and was about to thank him graciously before refusing his offering.

"That is the look of someone who has eaten one whole," he said with a chuckle and she nodded sheepishly.

"Rudy removes all the seeds from the habanero before mincing it, so you get all of the flavor and none of the fire. The poblano pepper is mild. The soup will help to open up your sinuses a little. This," he said holding up the tall to-go coffee cup, "will also help. Rudy brewed it double strength for you. It's his cure for a headache, especially migraine headaches. He says he hopes you feel better, too."

Standing there with the steaming bowl of soup and cup of coffee, Rachel looked up at him humbly. He no longer cared about taking her out. He just wanted her to feel better.

She'd held this man at arm's length for two months refusing, for various reasons, every time he asked her out. Her reasons were starting to sound weak even to her own ears.

"If you ask me out again sometime, I'll go out with you."

A wide grin split his face, and he closed his arms around her after she went into his solid embrace. "Angel, you can count on the fact there will *be* a next time. Let's get you out of those killer high heels and comfortable so you can eat then I'll get out of your hair."

Eli led her to the couch and slipped her shoes from her feet. He rubbed each arch for a few seconds then propped her feet on her coffee table and said, "Okay, you go ahead and eat. Don't forget to drink that coffee. Remember, it's gonna be stronger than what you're used to."

"I will, then I'm gonna take a nice long bubble bath and go to bed."

Good Rachel tapped her shoulder and said, *Now why did I tell him I'm planning on taking a bubble bath?*

Naughty Rachel responded, *Because I want for him to think of me nekkid in my bubble bath, silly! Why else?*

Eli's piercing gray eyes were warm as he gazed at her, and she had to wonder if he wasn't already imagining it. He smiled and said, "I guess I'll leave you to it, then." He patted her knee and rose from the couch. She put her soup down and followed him to the door. Being out of those heels was helping her feel better, too. He turned to her as he opened the door of her apartment and said, "I hope you feel better soon. I'll call you sometime and see about cashing in my rain-check for our date."

Good Rachel rolled her eyes and shook her head while Naughty Rachel did a jiggling happy dance. "Okay."

He gave her a sexy grin and bent down to kiss her cheek. His spicy aftershave flooded her nostrils, and she was filled with the sudden desire to taste him, all over.

"Enjoy your bubble bath."

Rachel ate her soup, which was delicious, and filled the tub with hot water and bubbles as she sipped her coffee. It was incredibly strong but very flavorful, and she sipped on it as she soaked in the tub. She added warm water a couple of times, and after an hour or so, she finally let the bath water out. Her head felt much better, and she knew Eli's remedy must have helped.

All the peppers in the soup did open up her sinuses, and the extreme caffeine jolt had her feeling ready to take on the world. Rachel placed the vase containing the sweet smelling roses on the nightstand then settled in bed. She thought about Eli as she looked at the flowers and wondered at the significance of the single red rose in the center.

She recalled there was an old poem that spoke of the different sentiments behind rose colors and wound up googling the meanings of each color. A florist's website provided the answer and she felt her cheeks warm as she read it. Orange roses symbolized strong passion. Orange was a blending of red, which signified love, and yellow, which symbolized friendship. Orange roses could serve as a bridge between the two, signifying the desire of the giver for more than friendship with the receiver. Then there was the single red rose amongst the orange ones. Rachel could only use her imagination about what message he was sending with it.

After working on her manuscript until late into the evening, Rachel fell asleep. She nearly jumped out of her skin when someone woke her from a sound sleep pounding on her front door.

Chapter Two

Eli felt like his head had just hit the pillow when the cell phone on his bedside table began whistling and vibrating. Rubbing his eyes, he looked at the display before he answered. Mike Esparza, close friend and fellow bouncer at The Dancing Pony, was calling him at three in the morning and that couldn't be good. He answered as he sat up and flung the sheet and blanket back.

"Yeah."

"We're headed to Rachel's. She just called. Her apartment building is on fire."

Eli went cold. "Shit! Is she all right?" He turned on his lamp and reached for his leathers.

"Yeah, she was warned in time by neighbors. Her parents are out of town, and she hasn't been able to reach them. When I talked to her, she asked me to call you. Bring your truck."

"I'll be there in three minutes." He ended the call, zipped his pants, and slung a T-shirt on. Shoving his feet in his heavy leather boots, he was out the door in less than thirty seconds. He jogged past his Harley parked under the carport and jumped in his truck. He backed out of the duplex's driveway and laid a track of rubber, not worried about waking any neighbors. The other side of the duplex was vacant at the moment.

He turned the corner and saw the source of the orange glow he'd been watching in the sky for the last couple of minutes. Fire trucks and ambulances lined the street in the residential neighborhood. Hoses crisscrossed the barricaded street, so he parked along the curb behind Mike's pickup truck. The firefighters and police were keeping residents and onlookers from getting too close, and most stood in the yards across the street.

Being six-nine and 275 pounds paid off again because he could see over every head there. Everyone got out of his way instinctively as he moved through the crowd looking for Rachel. He found Mike and Rogelio Flores, the other bouncer at The Dancing Pony, where they stood with her on the curb. She seemed so tiny and vulnerable, standing next to the two very large men, and her beautiful, sooty face was strained with tension as she watched the flames lick from her living room window. A draft stirred ash in the air, and he felt the heat of the fire on the wind as it ruffled her long, tousled hair. He stepped off the curb and blocked her view momentarily as she looked up at him, and her lower lip trembled.

* * * *

A parade of emotions flashed through Rachel's mind as she looked up at Eli. She had steeled herself for what was happening as much as possible. If she fell to pieces, how was she going to capably deal with the aftermath of the fire?

She fought her tears as she looked up at Eli, his eyes partially hidden in shadow when the flames leapt into the sky behind him. He looked down at her with tenderness and compassion as his fingers wiped at the soot on her cheeks. He looked like a dark avenging angel with his long coal-black hair loose behind his back. Her view of the burning building was completely blocked by his massive, muscular shoulders and extreme height. Backlit by the glow from the fire raging across the street, he seemed even larger.

The flashing lights of a police car illuminated Eli's face for a second and revealed the tanned beauty of his features, part Native American warrior and part enormous Viking. His eyebrows were drawn together in concern for her over his gray eyes.

He put his arms out, and Rachel reached for him, wrapping her arms around his waist. She pressed her face to his chest, and a sob shook her body. As the dam on her tears broke, he didn't shush her, just let her cry. The feel of his hard body supporting her did strange things to her chest. This was a place she had fantasized about being numerous times, but never under these circumstances. She held on tight and hid her face against his muscular chest as she sobbed. He rubbed her back and smoothed her hair. He felt so good, but she needed to get a grip before her tears got out of hand. There would be time enough for that later.

Rachel needed to find a place to store the things she'd saved, which a firefighter had been kind enough to help her move across the street. That was one of the nice things about living in a small town. She'd piled them in front of her apartment until the fire department had arrived and warned her not to go back in again. She'd have to call her insurance agent so she could file a claim on the renter's insurance. Rachel tightened the grip on her emotions and wiped her face on the cuff of her robe, which probably made her sooty face even messier.

"Well, boys, it would appear I am temporarily homeless. I need to store my stuff somewhere until I can find a place to live. Any suggestions?" she asked matter-of-factly, standing there in her bathrobe, nightgown, and fuzzy slippers. The men went into action and gathered up her belongings in their arms.

"We can take your things to my place, Rachel," Eli offered. "You can store them in my second bedroom and stay with me if you'd like. The other half of my duplex is vacant right now, and I could put a good word in for you."

She looked skeptically at him.

"Honey, we could always take you out to your folks' place," Mike suggested. "You know they wouldn't mind if you moved in until you got back on your feet."

She shook her head decisively. "No, I'm not moving back home. I have some money saved and should be okay. I like having my independence. I know they wouldn't mind, but I would."

"You could stay with me and Rosa," Mike said, searching for other options.

"No, it's asking too much of Rosa. She has her hands full with the kids and her mom. Things are pretty crowded already. No offense, Mike."

"None taken. I think it's too crowded sometimes, too. What about Rogelio? You know he'd watch out for you." Rogelio nodded but looked a little doubtful, and Rachel knew why.

"Rogelio would definitely look out for me, but I think that would be a bad idea. Christina would not understand, and I don't want to mess things up between the new lovebirds. Plus, where would I put my stuff?" she asked.

Rogelio lived in a tiny travel trailer on twenty acres of land while he saved up money to build his own house. He'd only just begun dating Christina, and Rachel could tell that they were falling in love. She didn't want to take a chance on screwing up that little romance. If anyone deserved happiness, Rogelio did.

"Then I guess you're coming home with me, angel," Eli said as she piled more stuff into his arms.

"All right. But are you going to behave?" she said, chuckling as she tried to look serious. She was *so* on a slippery slope there.

"I promise I'll behave. But you don't know what you're missing," Eli replied with his usual charming persistence.

The week after Angel Martinez and Ethan Grant were shot by Patricia Ramirez at The Dancing Pony, Eli asked her out on a date, with Mike and Rogelio's permission, she found out later. Mike and Rogelio had known her since Rachel was a girl, having worked on her family's cattle ranch as ranch hands for a time. She'd turned Eli down flat. When he asked her why, she said she didn't know him well enough to go out with him.

A week later, Eli asked her out again, and again she turned him down for the same reason. He asked her out again the next week, and she said she knew him better and liked him but saw how the women threw themselves at him at the club. She told him flat out she was the *very* jealous type and would only make him unhappy with her territorial nature. Since then, she had told him she liked him as a friend, but that was the extent of their relationship. One thing about Eli she'd learned in the ensuing weeks—he was persistent. Her resistance to him had weakened dramatically last evening, but she still knew it was a bad idea. Good Rachel congratulated her for her wisdom while Bad Rachel thought she was being a chickenshit.

When she was at The Dancing Pony, Eli never returned any of the attention that was lavished on him by the women who frequented the club. Mike had mentioned to her privately that was the case *anytime* they worked, not just when she was around. She appreciated that fact, but she was aware of Ethan's policy of no domestic strife in the bar and knew she'd rip the eyes out of any woman who laid a hand on what she had claimed as her territory. It was better this way, she'd told him on several occasions, just to be friends.

"Stop teasing, Eli. You know I'm right. It's better this way. Given your line of work you need someone who is less jealous. You and I would be trouble from the get-go."

Rachel wished she was wrong about what she could handle, but she knew she wasn't. She knew how she felt when women put their hands on his body *now*. They were so casual about it, sliding a hand along his thickly muscled biceps or fingering his long, thick black hair that made her hands twitch with the desire to run her own fingers through it. Sometimes they would place a hand on his abdomen as they talked to him or hooked a finger in his belt loop.

One lucky woman had actually caressed Eli's thick, muscular thigh through his leathers. He'd promptly risen from the barstool he was perched on at the door, stopping her hand before it could slide up farther. The effect on her body was the same every time. Her blood was like ice water in her veins, while at the same time, she felt a strong desire to do bodily damage. She was tempted to go to these women and tell them to remove their damned hands before she ripped every hair out of their heads.

How would it be if they were together and those things happened? Right now, she only felt attraction toward Eli. What if they started dating and she became more intimately attached to him, or worse, fell in love? That thought always sent a thrill through her, but she knew someone would get hurt for sure. The thought of being intimate with him and then having to share him with the female horde at the club was asking too much.

He was always a perfect gentleman to all the ladies, even when he was removing their hands from his person. He had to be subtle about it so he didn't offend them and lose his employers their business. It was a narrow line he had to walk, and she understood. Thus, they were at an impasse because he still asked her out on a regular basis.

Rachel remembered that *she* had asked Mike to call Eli tonight. There was some deep part of her that needed him, which she was desperately trying not to acknowledge. His presence tonight comforted her so much. His arms around her and his chest to cry against made her feel so safe and secure. It was a losing battle she was fighting. If she looked into the vacant half of the duplex and considered becoming his neighbor, she knew the temptation to be with him would only grow.

"My car is parked down there now." She gestured toward the end of the block. "I moved it after I couldn't go in the building anymore."

"We'll load everything up, and you can follow me out to the house," Eli said. She walked over to get in her car and pulled it down to where Mike and Eli's vehicles were parked.

Rachel came to Mike and Rogelio and hugged them in turn then thanked them for running to her aid. They hugged her hard and promised to be there if she needed anything. More tears would do no good right now, and so Rachel kept a lid on them. She could fall to pieces later. She turned to Eli.

"I've never been out to your house before." This was a big step, and she knew it. She didn't doubt that he wanted to help her. Being honest with herself, she knew she wanted him as much as he wanted her, and this moment was going to change things. She needed to get a handle on her vacillating emotions and desires before they gave her whiplash.

"My place is less than five minutes away. Just follow me." There was a purposeful light shining in his eyes like there was every time he asked her out. She nodded and climbed into the driver's seat of her car and waved at Mike and Rogelio.

Eli got in his truck, and she followed him out of the chaotic scene, leaving it behind. The flashing lights and cacophony of sound had done a number on her nerves, and the insulated quiet of her car was deafening. She turned on the CD player and set the volume down low, listening to Nickelback as she followed Eli home.

Rachel thought back to the first time she'd seen him, his first night working at The Dancing Pony. She'd been sitting at a table talking with a friend when he'd walked in with Mike and Rogelio. His hair had been very long and he'd worn it loose, which had done all kinds of warm, fuzzy things to her insides. His features were incredibly handsome and exotic, like a Native American warrior's. Black eyebrows arched over his sensuous eyes, which she'd found out later were an arresting shade of pale gray. His great height and strongly athletic build reminded her of a character out of a Viking romance novel. He was clad in leathers and a simple white T-shirt, and his face and body were simply drool-worthy. He had exuded an air of calm and self-confidence, which she'd assumed was the reason women were drawn to him.

The club had been fairly busy when they'd come in and started their evening's work, and she'd realized that he must be a new hire. It had been hard to look away, and her gaze had repeatedly returned to him. She'd watched the way his thickly muscled biceps bulged when he shook hands with someone. She'd noticed she wasn't the only woman in the place who had been mesmerized by him as many of them had begun to make their not-so-subtle way over to him to introduce themselves and flirt with him.

Rachel couldn't have blamed them for striking while the iron was hot. Prime male gorgeousness like his was a hot commodity. He had maintained a friendly but uninterested demeanor and had spent his time talking to Mike and Rogelio, probably focused on learning the way things were done at the club.

Fascinated by his extreme height, Rachel had pined over the idea of being able to look *up* into a man's eyes instead of straight into them, or, worse yet, down into them. She was tall for a woman and full-figured. That was another reason she didn't date often because she hated feeling like she was bigger than her dates.

He'd chatted with customers and the other employees and she'd liked that he didn't put out a "big tough guy" image like he'd needed to impress everyone. He'd been head and shoulders over almost every man in the place.

Rachel had glanced over at him again, for the hundredth time, to see Ethan introducing Grace to him. Only a moment before he'd had a twinkle in his eye, and then, he'd seemed much more serious. A bleached blonde dressed in an almost non-existent scrap of spandex and five inch stiletto heels had approached him, sliding her hand up his thick biceps, over his shoulder and around his neck. Rachel had wondered if the woman might be a late arriving girlfriend, but that theory had been proven wrong when he'd risen from his stool, dislodging her grip on him.

She'd wondered what it must be like to go home from his job with the scent of all the perfume those forward women had doused themselves with on his clothes and his skin. Would he have liked that? Or would it be like the cigarette smoke, something that had to be washed off his skin and out of his hair.

With his long, shiny black hair, Eli had been very different from the other men who came in the club, although that hadn't seemed to deter him from fitting in and socializing well with the clientele and employees.

Later in the evening, after she'd gotten a load of that freaking-hot shelf bra that Grace had showed her and her sister, Charity, in the ladies' room, the three of them had danced together to a Big & Rich song. Rachel absolutely loved to dance, and sometimes it didn't matter if she had a partner or not, or if they were male or female, some songs she *had* to dance to. "Save a Horse, Ride a Cowboy" definitely topped her list of *must*-dance songs.

Grace and Charity had evidently felt the same way. They'd gone out on that dance floor, and all three had shaken what their mamas had given them, leaving the men at Grace's table slack-jawed and glassy-eyed with lust. It'd been almost comical.

Rachel had thrown her head back and laughed from the pure joy of moving to the beat and happened to look over and had caught that handsome new bouncer staring *straight* at her with what she could only call intense interest. It had been obvious in his body language. She'd almost been able feel the heat of his gaze on her body. She'd glanced his way again as she'd turned, moving her hips in a sensual rhythm, and had seen that his eyes were still on her. Boldly, Rachel had danced the rest of the song for him, sliding her hands around her hips to her ass and then up her rib cage and into her hair. Unfortunately, the song had to come to an end.

More groups had filtered in through the door, and he'd once again focused solidly on the job. The evening had ended abruptly, thanks to that crazy heifer, Patricia Ramirez.

Rachel noticed his place was a little off the beaten path as she followed him down a dark, sparsely populated country road. Eli pulled into the driveway and parked next to his Harley. She parked behind the truck and popped her trunk. He immediately started to unload her belongings, most of which she'd hastily thrown in garbage bags. It was all a hodgepodge of clothing, shoes, papers, her laptop, and mementos she could grab in a hurry. There was also a box that she kept for such a purpose where she stored priceless old photographs, paperwork, and documents that would be hard to replace.

After Eli had all her belongings unloaded and sitting on the living room floor, he gave her a quick tour. She recognized the difficulty right off. This duplex was a two-bedroom, one-bath unit. The smaller of his two bedrooms was set up as an office, with a desk and a loveseat, plus all the other junk that usually wound up in spare rooms. His king-sized bed dominated the master bedroom, the sheet and blanket flung back in disarray from when he climbed out of it after getting the call from Mike. The comfy sofa in the living room was probably where she would bed down because the loveseat was not nearly long enough for her five foot-nine-inch frame.

Rachel took a look at herself in the hall mirror and asked Eli if she could use his shower. She hadn't saved anything from her bathroom at all. Not soap, shampoo, razor, or curling iron, and, dammit, her birth control pills had gone up in flames, too. Shit.

He stood in the hallway with her, smiling tenderly down at her. She wanted nothing more than for him to fold her into his arms. "Of course you can take a shower, Rachel. Make yourself at home."

"I don't have soap or shampoo or any of that stuff."

He reached into the bathroom and turned on the light. She followed him in as he opened the linen closet.

"That's okay. You can use mine. Here's a towel and a fresh washcloth, too. You're welcome to what I have." When he said it, she had a distinct feeling it pleased him to provide those items for her use. "Whatever you need, you can use. There are even fresh razors in the cabinet if you need one. Angel, make yourself at home." Her cheeks warmed at the softly spoken endearment, and her heart beat a little faster when her body responded to it as well. He reached out a gentle finger to wipe at a smudge on her cheek, and her skin tingled where he touched her.

"Thank you," she said softly. "My robe and gown both smell like smoke. I'll see if I have something I can sleep in." Rachel went to her bags to look but knew she hadn't grabbed much in the way of clothing. He returned from his bedroom with a black T-shirt and held it out to her. She thanked him, found the bag she she'd thrown panties into, and found a fresh pair. It occurred to her that the pretty camisoles she slept in had been hanging in her closet. Dammit. She closed her eyes and sighed, mourning the waste. His hand was gentle on her shoulder.

"Are you hungry, Rachel? Is there anything else I can get for you?" His thumb gently rubbed above her shoulder blade.

Smiling up at him, she said, "No, Eli. I'm beginning to remember things that I didn't think to grab before it was too late."

"I'm sorry. I can only imagine how hard that must be."

"It's such a waste. I'm going to take my shower. Would you mind if I use your hairbrush?"

Eli smiled at her, and she thought he looked awfully happy about her using his hairbrush. She felt silly having to ask. "Sure. Take your time, angel."

Once the water was warm enough, she stepped into the shower and let the hot water run over her hair and stood under the spray for a few minutes, warming herself. Standing outside in the middle of the night had left her chilled. It was probably mild shock from the whole experience affecting her now that she could relax a little. She felt a little disconnected from it all.

Rachel washed her hair then bathed with his bodywash. After she was done, she dried off and slipped into his long T-shirt that came to just above her knees and put on her black thong. She chose not to analyze why she'd picked a thong over something with more coverage. Naughty Rachel did a fist pump at the thought. The T-shirt was on the loose side because Eli was very broad through the chest, so she thought it would be all right to not put the smoky-smelling robe back on over it. Plus, the T-shirt was black, so it didn't reveal much. She scrubbed her teeth as best as she could and left the bathroom.

He was reclining on the couch, waiting for her. "I'll sleep on the couch, and you can have my bed, Rachel. You're welcome to it for however long you stay." He got up and led her into the bedroom. He'd changed into a pair of black sweatpants, and he was now bare-chested. That was the first time she'd ever seen him shirtless, and he was...incredible. Massive and beautiful. It was a struggle not to simply stand there and stare at him. Then she remembered what he'd said.

"I don't want to run you out of your bedroom, Eli. I don't mind sleeping on the couch."

"It's no trouble, Rachel. The bed is more comfortable, and I'd rather you slept peacefully. I insist. I don't mind taking the couch."

"Are you sure?" She should feel guilty for taking his bed, but her heart pounded a little at the delicious thought of curling up in a bed with sheets and pillows that smelled like this handsome man. She'd wallow in them the first chance she got. He leaned down to her and kissed her cheek gently. She felt her cheeks heat up at the unexpected affection, quivering inside at the warmth that spread through her at his gentle touch.

"I'm sure. I put a glass of water for you on the bedside table. I'll bet you're really thirsty right now. Drink it and get some rest. I normally sleep in the morning after I work at The Pony, so sleep as long as you need to."

She nodded. "Goodnight, Eli."

"Goodnight, angel." The endearment rolled so easily from his lips, and the light in his eyes when he said it was hard to miss. Eli returned to the living room and lay back down on the couch, and she wondered if he normally wore sweatpants to bed. She attributed her random lustful thoughts to sleep deprivation and shock.

Sitting on the bedside, she greedily gulped down the glass of water he'd placed there for her. Thoughtful Eli. She turned off the lamp and slid in between the cool black sheets. Pulling one of his pillows to her chest, she laid her head on the other one. She was soon awash in the heady fragrance that was pure, undiluted Eli. She breathed deep and felt cocooned and secure in his bed. Amidst those safe and secure feelings was another stirring deep in her body, a tingling, throbbing sensation that she did her best to not examine too closely.

Rachel knew if she called out to him, he'd come to bed with her, and if she asked him to, he'd make love to her. That would be stupid and foolish on too many levels. She shouldn't make decisions like that when under such monumental stress, and it couldn't happen, anyway. She'd only bring him trouble in the long run and plenty of heartache for herself. But thinking sane thoughts like that did nothing for the desire that bloomed within her for him. She could keep trying to talk herself out of the growing closeness between the two of them, but she knew she was fighting a losing battle. She pressed her nose to his pillow and inhaled deeply, trying to will herself to sleep.

* * * *

Eli listened to her get into his bed, clearly hearing his sheets rustle as she settled herself into his pillows. The thought of her in his bed, even though she was alone there, filled him with satisfaction. If only she would welcome him into the bed as well. He couldn't understand her reluctance to draw closer to him because he could sense that the attraction between them was not one-sided.

He knew she was reluctant to place her heart on the line because she said she was the jealous type. Rachel had an understandable problem with the way women approached him at The Pony. He was always clear with them that he did not welcome their advances, but that didn't stop the more aggressive ones. He believed once the word got out that he was dating Rachel the advances might cease or at least diminish in number. She remained concerned, but that didn't mean he'd give up on her. He contented himself with the fact that at least she was in his bed, regardless of the circumstances.

When had she emerged from the bathroom, she'd turned this way and that, searching for him in the dim light, before spying him on the couch. He'd seen her lush curves in perfect profile as she turned, the full swell of her delectable breasts, and the tight peaks of her nipples had been visible as she turned. Normally, she wore denim everywhere she went, so he had seen much more beautiful leg than he normally did.

What he wouldn't give to run his hands up the backs of her curvaceous legs, to suckle on those delicious little peaks under his T-shirt, to have the rest of what lay hidden beneath that T-shirt under his tongue. His thoughts served only to make his pulsing erection throb even harder against the fleece of the sweatpants he wore. Normally, he slept nude, but he'd donned these for her benefit, hoping his erection hadn't been too noticeable earlier. He did his best to get comfortable, but his cock twitched again at the sound of her soft, contented sigh.

Chapter Three

Eli woke to the sound of sobs coming from his bedroom. It wasn't loud, but it didn't need to be. That heartbroken sound would have awakened him from a coma with its forlorn intensity. Reality must have set in at some point, or perhaps she'd had a bad dream. Whichever the case was, he couldn't leave her to cry alone. If she kicked him out of the bedroom, fine. He'd understand and accept that, but he had to at least offer his comfort to her.

Rachel sat up on the side of the bed, her face in her hands, looking so small and vulnerable. He whispered to her so he wouldn't startle her as he knelt in front of her, slipping his arms around her waist so she could put her head on his shoulder and cry, which she did, for a few minutes.

"Did you have a bad dream?"

"M–my…m–my poor fish. My aquarium. It's awful. They probably suffered." She wept softly. "And my grandmother's turkey platter and my antique china. My o–o–old teddy bear." She whimpered and sobbed. "My hope chest that my grandpa made for me was in my bedroom. My *orange roses!*" She sobbed loudly at last, letting it out.

She held on to him and poured out her heart on his shoulder. The orange roses had certainly made an impression if she remembered them among all her other precious possessions. He lifted her in his arms, laid her on the bed, and climbed in beside her. He sternly reminded himself this was to comfort her and not to get his hopes up. He was going back to the couch after she returned to sleep. Dammit.

* * * *

The thought of her hope chest lying in ashes under the rubble of her apartment building broke her heart, not only because of what it contained, but because of who made it for her. Her grandpa was laid to rest in the Divine cemetery in town three years before. There was no way to replace it. Her link to him was the love in her heart, but that tangible link, something made especially for her, had been precious to her. Tucked away inside it, wrapped in tissue paper, was a hand-crocheted tablecloth that had been made by her grandmother as well as the christening dress both she and her mother had worn as babies.

It hurt and on some level renewed the loss of her grandparents, who had passed away within six months of each other. She could remember as a little girl watching her grandparents interact with such love and affection for each other. It was not uncommon to see them kiss each other and hold hands. All her life, the deep and abiding love they felt had been a real and living testimony to her of how a marriage should be, a tradition her parents had continued.

Sometimes her mom and dad were nauseating with their affection. After she moved out on her own, she'd learned the hard way not to use her key and walk right in. Her parents finally had the house to themselves after raising her and enjoyed making full use of every room, she'd discovered much to her embarrassment one day. She hoped she lived to have that kind of ageless, profound love with her future husband, the kind that embarrassed her kids and made them roll their eyes and laugh. The thought cheered her, and the tears stopped abruptly.

What the hell is wrong with me? If she didn't know better, she'd say love was staring her right in the face, and what was she doing? She was running from it, afraid to take a chance because of a little adversity. Her parents had not raised her to run from a challenge. Eli did not strike her as the type to shrug his shoulders at the obvious difficulty she had with her jealous nature. He'd been both sympathetic and unfailingly persistent. He had not dated anyone else she knew of since he'd begun pursuing her.

For crying out loud, Mike and Rogelio had even given their thumbs-up to them dating, and the good Lord knew how protective the two of them were. Her father had even met Eli in the bar one night. He said nothing to her, but she'd heard from Mike that her father approved of Eli. She wouldn't have been a bit surprised if Mike or Rogelio had told her father about Eli pursuing her and he'd come in to check Eli out for himself, to size him up and see if he was good enough for his little girl. She knew he would have had plenty to say if Eli had not measured up.

Rachel lay quietly, tucked into Eli's side, and wiped her eyes with the sleeve of the T-shirt she wore. Her heart was still heavy with the loss and the stress of the fire, but she knew she had moved through a barrier of some sort and dealt with feelings that had been building up for a while. The fire had just provided the catalyst.

"Better?" Eli asked as she laid her head back on his chest. No longer curled in a defensive little ball, she stretched out beside him and took stock of her current position. She tentatively placed her hand on his bare chest under her cheek. Lord have mercy, but he smelled good. All male. Woodsy and clean.

"Yes. Much better." Her fingers splayed out and skimmed across his chest, sifting through the smattering of hairs there over his nipples. She heard his slight intake of breath, and the sound of his heartbeat increased in its rhythm. The accelerating beat made her smile, the sound so solid and reassuring. Rachel snuggled to him and allowed her thigh to drape over his just a little as her hand slid to his abdomen, but no lower, as she listened for a reaction from him. She didn't have to wait long.

"Rachel?" He sounded a little breathless as her fingertips gently but deliberately caressed his abdomen. "Should I return to the couch?" His voice had a deeper husky tone than usual. His large warm hand gently slid over her forearm. Beneath her ear, his heart pounded. They were poised on the brink of something that would change them both.

"No," she whispered shakily, and her breath hitched from her crying spell. Her body ached to feel his touch. Her clit throbbed, and moisture surged in her aching cunt as her body prepared to receive a lover. "Please don't go." All this emotion and sensation had been held back for so long, and now it surged forward as her body clamored to be consumed by his.

His arms surrounded her and held her close as his body trembled almost imperceptibly and a soft sigh escaped his lips. Her thigh became entwined with his as she drew closer to him. She reached across the wide expanse of his chest and pressed her lips to his muscled pec. Encouraged by that offering, he easily pulled her on top of him so that she would have straddled him had she opened her thighs. Palming the back of her head, he kissed her for the very first time on the lips. It was a gentle kiss, which seemed to silently beg for her trust, then quickly became more passionate and demanding. Parting her lips, Rachel accepted him as he sought entry to her mouth, his warm tongue stroking hers. She felt a sudden rush of moisture between her legs and a more intense throbbing in her clit. Her body begged to be taken.

"Are you sure, Rachel?" Eli's voice was deep and steady. "I want to make sure you want this. If something happens between us, I don't want to go back to the way it was. I also don't want you to regret it later."

She could hear the emotion that ran deep in his voice. His fear of being hurt was just as strong as hers. *How* had she ever resisted this gentle giant so long? Was she crazy?

"Eli, I'm done running. I'm done fighting the way I feel about you." She rested her head on his shoulder, under his jaw. "Yes, I'm stressed out and emotional, but I trust you. And if I trust you, I should give us a chance. I know now that I'll regret it forever if I *don't* give us a chance." She lifted her head and looked up at him in the pale moonlight that shone through his bedroom window.

* * * *

Eli looked into Rachel's eyes, illuminated by the moonlight. Her face was still damp with her tears, and his heart skipped a beat at the trust and vulnerability he saw in her eyes. His fingertips drifted up to her cheekbones and traced them before sliding into her silky brown hair, strewn over his chest in shiny waves. He kissed her again as he caressed her back and her thighs. He pulled her closer to him, unworried now that she would feel his growing erection against her belly. She gasped in shaky breaths as she came into contact with his rock hard shaft. Gazing into her eyes, he felt her capitulation as her thighs finally parted over his hips. She straddled him, opening to him. He stroked the backs of her smooth thighs, and let out a pleased growl when his hands came into contact with her bare ass cheeks, but he held himself in check.

"Angel, you feel so good, but it's torture having you this close. I want you so much right now it's painful. I want to feel you beneath me and be inside you. But I need to make sure in the morning you won't regret it. I can't believe I'm saying it, but maybe I should go back to the couch," he said uncertainly. Shit! This was happening so fast now, and he didn't want to screw it up.

Rachel smiled down at him. "One question. Do you have any condoms?" Damn, she wasn't making this easy. She arched up to look down at him, and when she did, her sweet body applied more pressure to his eager cock.

"Yes, and I always use a condom. I don't do bareback. I was tested the last time I went in for a physical. But I want to make sure you're ready."

With a soft, shuddering breath, she shifted on him and reached down to pull at the ties on her thong. He bit his lip as he realized what she was doing. She sat up and slid the thong out of the way, gently took his hand, and placed his fingers where, up until now, he'd only fantasized about going.

"Why don't you tell me if you think I'm ready?" Rachel gasped breathlessly as she pressed his fingers against her pussy. Eli groaned as they slipped through the abundant hot, silky moisture there. He gently slid a finger into her tight entrance before easing up to rub her clit, which made her cry out in pleasure. Another rush of arousal wet his fingers more. There was no longer any question about her readiness.

"I'm on the pill, though I'll need to run to the pharmacy in the morning for a replacement pack. We can use a condom if you prefer," she said, stuttering as he repeated the motion. "It's been a long time…since I've been with a m–man." He was instantly addicted to the hot, slick feel of her pussy under his fingertips and the soft sounds she made as he touched her. "And I've never been with anybody as big as you." She finished her sentence on a moan as he pressed his erection to her pelvis and gripped her satiny smooth ass. "There has only been one man. It was a terrible mistake, and it only happened once. I was stupid."

Only once? He'd love to replace that bad memory for her.

"Not stupid. Beautiful and trusting. If *I* made love to you, Rachel, I'd show you how it *should* be. I'd be gentle and make it good for you." He slid his hands over her thighs, which were still straddled over his hips. Her belly rested against his throbbing cock. "You wouldn't look back on this time with regret because it's only the beginning. It would be very good between us, angel."

Eli's conscience warred with his natural instinct to use whatever means were at his disposal to get her writhing beneath him. But what about her doubts and fears? They'd still be there in the morning if he didn't make sure this was what she wanted tonight.

The vulnerability and trust he saw in her eyes strengthened his resolve to prove himself worthy of her.

"Don't break my heart, Eli. I couldn't bear it."

"Your heart is safe with me, Rachel. Please trust me."

* * * *

"I need you." Rachel lowered her lips to his for another kiss and held on when he rolled her under him on the big bed. She could tell he kept most of his weight off of her but pressed his heavily muscled torso lightly into her as he continued to kiss her. His weight and his immense physical presence were unspeakably comforting and arousing, by turns. Still dressed in his sweatpants, he settled his hips between her open thighs and pressed his hard erection into the cradle of her body. Her head fell back on his pillow, and she moaned quietly at the feel of his hard length pressed to her. She secretly wondered how it would all fit. Resting on an elbow, he began to inch the shirt up her thighs.

"I'm craving my first look at your bare, luscious curves and then a taste of your sweet pussy. Would that be all right, Rachel? Would you let me do that?" He licked tenderly at her lips and nuzzled her jawline.

Whoa. She looked into his eyes. "You *want* to do that, Eli?" Rachel was truly hesitant, not understanding why that would turn him on. She knew about oral sex, but she thought that the only men *really* interested in pleasuring a woman that way were the heroes in erotic romance novels.

Her experience was limited to one disastrous encounter that had been all about the guy getting what he wanted. That encounter with Reese McCoy had not made her afraid of men but merely confused about what it was they wanted and were willing to give in reality, not fantasy.

Eli wanted her like that?

"More than you could possibly imagine. I fantasize all the time about the beautiful body under your clothes. I imagine what you would taste like, and I wonder how you'll sound when you come that way."

Rachel's cunt clenched and became wetter, begging to be filled. Uncertainty about her inexperience made her want to apologize.

"If you're sure, but I've never done that before. I don't know what you want me to do, Eli. I'm sorry." She felt like an inept teenager.

"Never be sorry for that. I'm sorry I wasn't your first lover, but I can be the first to taste your sweet pussy, to show you what real pleasure is. Did you come for your other lover?" She caught a glimmer of jealousy in his eyes.

Come for that rat-bastard Reese McCoy? She shook her head. "No, it was over right after it began. It wasn't a good first experience." She thought that was the fucking understatement of the year. "I never even got close. It never came close to feeling anything like this." She held on to his shoulder as he lowered his lips to her collarbone, above the neck of the T-shirt. Butterflies took flight in her stomach as he brushed his knuckles over her abdomen, and thoughts of Reese McCoy faded away. He looked up at her, and she saw the tender reassurance in his gaze as he slid the T-shirt up slowly.

"I'll go slow for you, Rachel and I'll stop if you need me to." Her body wept at his tender words and begged for him. Pleaded to be filled. She panted softly when his lips followed the hem of the T-shirt as it was lifted over her rib cage. His tongue slid along the underside of her breast, which made her insides quiver.

"Mmm, like velvet." His warm mouth closed over her tightly peaked nipple, wringing a high-pitched moan from her. She was strung as tight as a bow. He gently spread her thighs and knelt between them. He slid his hands under her waist, arching her back and drawing her to his lips. She felt so claimed and knew she would feel that same sensation to a greater degree before long and reveled in the knowledge. His long black hair slid forward, over and around her, forming a dark curtain as he suckled hungrily on her flesh. His lips made their slow, tantalizing way to the other nipple before kissing up to her collarbones and the hollow at the base of her throat. As he worked the T-shirt over her head, he spoke of how he'd longed for her, that the wait had been worth it, and how delicious she was.

Eli settled her back on the bed and began to slide his lips and warm tongue down her torso, and her panting increased substantially, knowing where he was headed. Rachel's body sang for him with her arousal.

He paused to look up into her eyes. "Will you let me love you?"

"Yes, I want you to." She moaned as he made his way to her navel.

"I love the feel of your skin, Rachel, how curvy and soft you are. You're beautiful here." He slid his face over her abdomen and licked into her belly button, making her shudder breathlessly.

"I'll be your slave soon if you keep telling me things like that." She placed her palm on his cheek and jaw.

"I'm only telling you the truth, but if you'll be my slave, I promise to take good care of you." He chuckled softly as she moaned at the feel of his tongue at the dip below her hipbone at the top of her thigh. Her heart was hammering a rapid rhythm, and she could already feel the tightening sensation in her pussy that always preceded an orgasm. Her clit throbbed, begging for one gentle touch, one little flick, and she'd go off like a rocket.

He reached up and quietly, with one long sweep of his arm, spread open the drape covering the window over his bed. She looked questioningly at him. "So that I can see you. I want to see you the first time I taste your pussy. I want to watch your beautiful face when I make you come." His lower lip brushed against the flesh to one side of her mound as he maintained eye contact with her, teasing her.

Rachel had no idea he'd say such things to her. His loving, erotic words made her breath hitch as she gazed back into his pale gray eyes, anticipation robbing her of the ability to speak. Keeping eye contact with her, he slowly lowered his mouth to just barely above her wet slit, and his warm breath wafted over her for a few seconds. Rachel shuddered in ecstasy, her cunt tightened like a bowstring, and she thought she might scream.

Eli slid his warm hands up her inner thighs, which she spread wide for him. His fingers gently touched her mound, pausing for what seemed like an eternity, allowing her tension to build. Her breath came in racing gasps as she waited. She looked into his eyes, and every muscle in her body tensed. Finally, he looked down on the most intimate part of her body, and she realized he'd played out the moment for himself as well, allowing his anticipation to build for the first sight and taste of her. His fingers gently parted her outer lips, and he groaned softly.

"I could die and go to heaven now. So pretty and pink. You're wet and swollen. The waiting must be unbearable for you. I'm going to lick you, Rachel, and finally know what your sweet pussy tastes like. Would that be all right?" he asked softly.

Like he needs to ask!

"Yes, I need you." Her hands slid into his hair, which moved like a silken drape along her thighs. Eli's callused fingers splayed out over her inner lips, sliding over the wetness there but not touching the one place she wanted him to. One finger slid a little into her entrance, and her back bowed off the bed. He placed a gentle hand on her abdomen to keep her in place as he gazed up at her and slid his tongue into her wet slit.

Heat to spread through her like a raging wildfire at his approving growl. The tension built to unbearable levels, and the muscles in her pussy clasped almost painfully. He slid his tongue into her entrance and then upward over her clit. She began to moan and shake as he carried her to unbelievable heights with each gentle touch. A fresh rush of moisture flowed from her at his masterful playing of her body. His skilled tongue flicked up and down on both sides of her clitoris.

Rachel sobbed as the tension suddenly released, and she came completely undone and she wailed his name as he continued to lave her clit with his warm tongue. Her hips rode every wave of her orgasm until she felt like nothing more than a warm, trembling puddle in his arms. He continued to gently kiss her and lick her, as she recovered. She breathed out a contented sigh as he looked up at her.

Eli was practically beaming with masculine accomplishment as he kissed her inner thigh, looking very satisfied with himself. "Angel, you're even sweeter than I imagined you would be."

Rachel stretched, arching her back, and asked, "Was it all right? I mean, did you really like...the way I taste?" She wanted to know, but she didn't want to know. How could it be good? Since she'd never thought to taste herself, she wouldn't know.

Eli closed his eyes for a brief moment before they opened and made her still-galloping heart skip a beat with the love she saw there. *How* had she been so foolish to think she could resist falling for him?

He chuckled before saying, "Rachel, besides your kiss, I've never had anything that delicious on my tongue before. I'd stay here for hours licking your pretty pussy if you'd only allow it."

Funny, she'd never cared for that word before, always considered it vulgar and insulting. But the way he said it made her feel...powerful. It sounded sweet on his lips when he said it. It was like a secret they shared. He sounded almost reverent, like he was grateful she'd allowed him to taste her and found that part of her delectable. The word didn't bother her at all between the two of them.

"Eli, I'm not very experienced, but that was so beautiful. Thank you."

He lay down beside her and stroked her hip. She turned to him and snuggled to his chest as he tilted her chin up and kissed her deeply. Her clit throbbed in response when she tasted herself on his lips and tongue.

"Now you know why I persisted, Rachel. I've dreamed of the chance to show you how good it can be between us." She lay there in his arms, completely bare and open to him, knowing he was right.

"Will you make love to me, Eli?" As she stroked his cheek with her palm, he lifted his wolf-gray eyes and looked into hers. She could see the emotions that warred inside of him.

"Angel, I have condoms but no lubricant. For your first time with me, and until you become used to me, we should use a lubricant. I don't want to hurt you." He wanted her badly. She could tell as much by the hot, huge erection that pulsed against her hip. Her pussy should be clenching in fear of it, but all she could think of was how badly she needed to feel him planted deep inside her.

"But I'm so wet for you. Couldn't we at least try? You haven't come, and I don't want to leave you hanging like this." She tentatively rubbed her fingers over his shaft and balls. He groaned and shuddered a bit.

Rachel bit her lip as he gazed at her and then nodded, evidently willing to agree with her on that point. He quickly shed the sweatpants, and his erection sprang free, huge and rock solid. She wondered again how it would all fit as she touched him. He hissed when she closed her hand around it, gently stroking back and forth.

He turned on his side and palmed her breast, suckling at the tight little nipple. She moaned, enjoying the feel of his strong, hard body over hers. Her pussy wept for him, and the throbbing returned to her clit as her arousal began to grow again. He slid his forearm under her neck and tilted her lips to him for a kiss. She wanted his mouth everywhere on her body. She wanted him to possess every inch of her.

He reached for the drawer in his nightstand, and she said, "Eli, if you're sure you're safe, we could skip the condom. I'm clean, too, and I'm on birth control pills. I want to feel you inside me, with no barrier," she murmured, emboldened by her words and thoughts. "Would you like that?" She giggled when he was suddenly on top of her, his lips on hers. He was demanding but gentle, and his movements graceful and strong as he kissed her.

He rose above her and knelt between her thighs. Looking at him sent a thrill of lust through her. He was just so…huge and larger-than-life. The kicker was the love that glowed in his hypnotic eyes. Her body completely surrendered to him.

He slid his hands over her inner thighs and parted them with slow reverence. He raised her left thigh and hooked it over his right forearm, lifting it slightly as he placed the head of his big, swollen cock at her entrance. Her body trembled at his warm, intimate touch. He gazed into her eyes, waiting for permission. She nodded, reaching out to him. He leaned over her, bracing himself on an elbow, and kissed her, allowing anticipation to build within them again.

She felt the heat of his cock at her pussy, and the rippling sensation began again. He probably wouldn't even be all the way inside her before her next orgasm slammed into her. She slid her hands up his thighs and felt him flex into her just a little. She gasped as her lips stretched tautly around him.

He shuddered and whispered, "I'm going to take this slow, baby, so it's good for you. I don't want you to be sore. You feel so good."

"You're not hurting me." She kissed him as she opened herself to him. As he began to flex and push forward, his phone whistled and hummed from the living room.

Chapter Four

Rachel groaned in frustration at being interrupted. His head fell, and he let out a gusty sigh. He pulled away from her without ever entering and said apologetically, "That's Mike's ring. I'd better get it."

"The battery on my phone is dead. My parents may have called him when they couldn't get through on mine," she replied with a deep sigh. He was right. Rachel didn't want Mike or her parents to worry because they'd decided not to answer the phone so they could continue with their lovemaking. It would have been sweet, but even sweet lovemaking under duress was not what she wanted for their first time.

"Yeah." He returned to the bedroom with his phone to his ear and climbed onto the bed. "She's fine. No, she's awake. Here, I'll let you tell her. It's Mike." He handed her his cell phone.

"Hello?"

"Hi, Rachel. Your mom and dad called me. They got your message and tried your phone and got voice-mail. I told them you said the battery on your phone was running low."

"Were they upset, Mike?'

"A little maybe, but I think they're mostly worried about you. They'll wait to hear from you in the morning, which technically it is now. They want to know if you need them to come back early. I told them I'd let you know. You'll need to tell them where you're at when you talk to them, okay?" The unspoken message in his words rang loud and clear. It was up to her to tell her parents she was staying with Eli.

"Of course. Did they expect me to move back home?"

"Didn't say one way or another, but I think they trust you to make good choices. Don't worry. They just want to make sure you're all right. Are you and Eli okay?" he asked gently, not prying.

"Yes, Mike. We're fine." She looked up into Eli's eyes. He leaned forward, and his lips descended along her jawline.

"Then I'll let you go. I didn't give them Eli's number so call them by mid-morning or they'll begin to worry," Mike said then wished her sweet dreams and ended the call. She handed Eli the phone, and he placed it on the bedside table and lay back on his side.

Propping his head on his palm, he gently slid his warm hand over the lower swell of her breast, drawing a shaky sigh from her. She put her forearm under her head and raised the other one to draw her fingers over his warm lips. He kissed her fingers, pressing them to his mouth with his hand. The mood had shifted even though they were both back in the bed, still naked. It almost felt like her dad was looking over her shoulder. Eli looked at her with understanding in his eyes.

"Rachel, I've kept you awake when you should be resting. It will be morning soon, and you need to sleep some more. Would you like to wait? We can make love later if you want to, but I feel kind of selfish for wanting you, knowing your parents are worried about you and waiting for you to call them." He covered her with the sheet.

Rachel looked up at him and was surprised once again by his thoughtfulness. There was no way in hell she would have turned him down if he'd wanted to pick up where they left off before the phone rang. He'd noticed the shift in her mood and had acted accordingly, not forcing her to tell him no. There was nothing quite like parental worry and the guilt that followed for dampening the ardor. She admired and respected him for putting her needs and her parents' needs before his own, knowing he had to be in real need of a release.

"What about you, Eli? I wanted you to feel good, too," she said softly.

"We can make love later, after you've had a chance to call your parents and ease their concerns. Will you tell them you're staying with me? Tell them I'll keep you safe?" he said. "You could call them now while I take a shower if you want to. That way you'll have some privacy."

"Are you taking a cold shower?" she asked sympathetically.

"Maybe." He grinned ruefully and handed her the phone. "I doubt that they will mind if you call. It's already six. The sun will be rising soon. Then we can decide what to do today."

"Wouldn't you normally sleep in today since you have to work tonight?" She mentally tallied the amount of sleep he lost that night.

"Yes, I would. But if I have you near me, I don't want to sleep. I want to spend the time with you. If you want a nap later today, we can take one, but I'll be fine for tonight. I don't go in until seven on Friday evenings."

"A nap later would probably feel good. Right now I'm wide awake. But, Eli?"

"What is it, baby?"

"Later could we make love?"

"Sure, angel. Maybe we'll have a chance to stop somewhere and pick up a bottle of lubricant. I don't want to take a chance on hurting you."

"I need to call my pharmacy, anyway, because my birth control pills were in my medicine cabinet in the apartment. I'll need to replace them as soon as possible this morning."

"All right. Why don't you call and leave a message and that can be our first stop. I'm gonna to take my shower, and then I'll make you some breakfast." He dropped a tender kiss on her lips as he climbed naked from the bed. She ogled his ass as he got up, and he chuckled when he caught her at it. It was so hard she bet she could bounce a quarter off it, and some primitive part of her wanted to take a bite of it. Her cheeks felt like they were flaming as she picked up his phone and dialed her dad's cell phone number.

Her parents were on their annual camping trip in Big Bend National Park. They always went by themselves, packing only the basics.

"Dad? Hi, it's me."

"Hi, princess. Are you all right? Mike told us what happened to your apartment."

"Yes, I'm fine."

"He told me everything he knew. It's hard for this dad to not be there when you need me. Do you have your emergency fund built up?"

"You taught me well, Dad. One thousand dollars plus about four months' worth of expenses in the bank, easy to get to. I'll file my renter's insurance claim later today."

"Good. Do you need to come home until you can find another place to live?"

"No, I already have my eye on a place. It's quieter and in a safer neighborhood."

"Where are you staying until you can find out if it's available?"

"With Eli Wolf. He lives in a duplex, and the other half is vacant. I'm going to talk to the landlord today to see about getting into it." She listened to the long pause on the line as her father decided what to say next.

"Are you thinking about moving in with him?"

"No, Dad. Eli brought me home with him because it was the logical choice at the time. It was three in the morning when Mike called him, and he was there in less than five minutes. He had room for my stuff, and he knew he had a vacancy next door. It made sense to stay with him. He has been very thoughtful and considerate."

"We raised you right, princess. I trust you to do what's best for you, but I'm curious."

"About what?"

"Do you have feelings for Mr. Wolf?"

"Yes, Dad, I do. I have for a while now. He's a good man."

"I know. It's just hard seeing you as a grownup, making your own choices. I want to hold on to my baby girl. Be careful and take things slow."

"I promise. Dad? I'm always going to be your little girl."

"I know, princess, and I love you. Do you need for us to come home?"

"No. I think everything is going to be all right."

"All right, then we should be home on Wednesday night. Were you able to get much out of your apartment before you left?"

"I threw a bunch of things in garbage bags, plus my box of important papers. But, Dad, my hope chest and Grandma's tablecloth were in my bedroom."

"Will they let you go back to salvage?"

"I don't know."

"Have Eli check with the fire department. They're probably investigating the fire right now, but they may let you go in unless the structure is unstable. I'll look into it, too, when we get back."

"All right. I love you, Dad. Can I talk to Mom?"

"Love you, too. Here she is."

Her mom's dulcet voice came on the line. "Hi, baby. You okay?"

"I'm okay. I haven't slept much, but otherwise I'm fine."

"So…you're staying with Eli Wolf?" Rachel smiled at the happy curiosity in her mother's tone.

"Yes, Mom. Temporarily. He said not to worry. He'd watch out for me and keep me safe."

"You have feelings for him, don't you?"

"Yes, Mom, I do. I fought them for a while because of his line of work. But he's kind to me and thoughtful. He was there for me last night when everything went up in flames, and he slept on the couch last night and let me have his bed. He says I'm perfect, Mom. How can I fight that?" she asked as she fought the lump in her throat.

Her mom's voice cut to a conspiratorial whisper. "I say why try? It sounds to me like he may be in love with you. *You* sound like you're in love. Don't tell your father I told you, but he said he approved of Eli. He thinks he needs a haircut, but otherwise he seems to have a made a good impression on your father. Long hair, huh?"

"Trust me, Mom, his hair is perfect the way it is. Thank you for telling me that. It'll be our little secret. The other half of his duplex is open, and I'm going to see about leasing it today."

"That's good. You know you'll be safe with him nearby. If you need any furniture once you get settled, you can always come see what's in the storage barn."

After she ended the call, she placed a refill order on her pharmacy's automated refill line. She'd just finished when Eli came out of the bathroom with a bath towel wrapped around his hips. The towel didn't leave any doubt as to whether or not the shower had alleviated his arousal. It hadn't.

"Sorry, baby. I forgot to take clothes in the bathroom with me."

"And you're used to walkin' around nekkid, aren't you?" She giggled.

He peered out of the closet at her, wry humor on his face and in his voice as he replied, "As a matter of fact, yes, I do walk around naked after a shower. Though I'm not usually in the condition I currently am when I do."

"Which would be?" she asked, giggling some more.

Emerging from the closet with a fresh pair of jeans on, he answered, "Hard, achy, and a little needy." He sat on the edge of the bed, putting a pair of socks on and then his boots.

"I have a game plan," she said as she propped herself up with pillows.

"Whatever it is, I'm at your disposal."

"I'll get ready, and we can eat an early breakfast. I need to call Mr. Gran and tell him what happened and take the day off. Then I need to run to the Wal-Mart on the Interstate. I need to get some clothing and other stuff. We can come back to the pharmacy for my pills and the lubricant. We'll call your landlord while we're on the road, and Dad asked if you would call the fire department about the possibility of checking for things that might be salvageable. Once we've done all of that we'd have the day to ourselves. *Then* maybe I could tend to your *neediness*." She said the last part to him softly as she sat up in his bed and tucked the top sheet under her arms.

He smiled cautiously at her. "You know, there's no hurry about you moving, Rachel. I'd let you stay here as long as you wanted." He leveled his gray gaze at her. "Even let you stay permanently." She crawled to him, bringing the sheet with her, and put her arms around his shoulders.

"That's very sweet of you, Eli, but I won't live with a man I'm not married to. I don't want a live-in arrangement. What you and I have is so new. I wouldn't want to rush into something like that, although under the circumstances, it is very tempting. My parents would take a dim view of it, and I don't want to damage the good impression you've made on my dad."

His eyebrows arched in surprise. "I made a good impression on your dad?"

"You sure did, but he thinks you need a haircut," she said and chuckled.

He turned a mischievous grin on her. "What do you think?"

"I think your hair is perfect the way it is. I love it." She nuzzled her nose in the damp strands.

He pulled her into his lap with the sheet all twisted around her. "You knew I would offer to let you move in, right?"

"Yeah, I figured you would. You knew I would have to turn you down, right?"

"Yeah, I did. So we're okay?"

"Yes, and later we'll have the afternoon to spend doing whatever you'd like."

"I think we both know what that would be." He smirked as he caressed her fingers on his chest.

"I think we'd both *agree* what that would be."

Chapter Five

After breakfast, the first item on Rachel's agenda was calling her boss. Mr. Grogan was surprised and very sympathetic, offering her whatever time off she needed. She told him she would see him bright and early Monday morning. At the store, she found what she'd need to tide her over for a while as far as clothing and toiletries were concerned.

Eli called his landlord and arranged to meet with him at the duplex right after lunch and talked to the fire chief while she ran into the pharmacy and picked up her birth control pills and the lubricant. The fire chief told him the structure remained intact in the rear portion of the building. Only the front of the structure around the porch had collapsed, so they could probably get in through the rear door to check for any salvageable belongings once the investigation was over with.

The fire chief said the preliminary investigation indicated that faulty wiring was the cause of the fire, and asked Eli to wait until they were completely finished before attempting to get into her apartment. The chief also recommended that Eli not go alone or allow her to go in alone. Eli called Mike and Rogelio, who were more than willing to come help the next day.

They stopped for a quick early lunch and got back to his place shortly before his landlord arrived. Charlie greeted her and gave her an application to fill out, which she did after she did a walk-through of the duplex. She could envision the space, a mirror image of Eli's, with a minimum of clutter, potted plants and a new aquarium. She needed to find a bed and a couch and other smaller pieces. The closet had a large built-in dresser so she'd need a mirror for her bedroom, but that was it. The price was right, and they shook hands on it. He told her he needed to run a background check on her, which was a formality, and he'd be in touch with her that evening to get the keys to her. After he left, she turned to Eli, and his eyes twinkled playfully as she wrapped her arms around his neck and allowed him to lift her off her feet and hug her.

"Hello, neighbor," he said huskily before he kissed her deeply. She melted in his arms, and her lips fell open under his onslaught. His warm tongue stroked hers as they stood on her soon-to-be front porch. They were interrupted by the sound of a truck door slamming and a wolf whistle.

"Hey, you two, get a room!" Jack Warner called out as he came around the front of his SUV to open his wife's door for her. Eli released Rachel with a sigh and a little whimper. She giggled up at him but hoped this didn't mean that their time alone together was about to evaporate before her eyes. Rachel stepped off the porch to go and greet them. She hugged Grace Warner, who looked completely radiant as usual.

Grace looked into her eyes with concern. "Rachel, I heard what happened last night. I'm so sorry! I'm glad you're all right. I brought you some stuff. Hey, Eli," she tugged on Rachel's arm and pulled her toward the SUV, "Rachel and I need some girl talk for a minute. I'll be right back, honey. Come here, Rachel. Let me show you what I brought you!"

Grace pulled her around to the rear doors of the SUV, which was full of shopping bags. Had Grace gone to the mall in Morehead to shop? Grace turned to her conspiratorially. "I never saw two people more meant to be together than the two of you. That lip-lock he had you in was very impressive!" she whispered. "Did you spend the night here last night at his place?" Grace's enthusiasm was undeniable.

"Uh-huh!"

"Is he a good kisser?"

"Uh-huh!"

"Did you fool around last night?"

"A little."

"A little?" Grace snorted a little in disgust. "Did you get laid or not?"

Rachel laughed out loud. "You sound more like Charity every time I see you, Grace. We fooled around, but we haven't made love...*yet.*"

"Yet?"

"We were headed that direction when you pulled up."

Grace's eyes opened wide, and she grimaced then turned to grab shopping bags. "Crap! Sorry. Let's get this stuff unloaded, and we'll get out of your hair. Why were you on the other porch?"

"Because I'm renting out the other half of the duplex. Eli and I will be neighbors."

"For *now*," Grace said with a smirk. "You were meant to be together."

"I'm not moving in with a man I'm not married to. Uh, no offense, Grace," she added, hoping she had not offended her friend who, for a short time, had lived with her three husbands prior to marrying them.

"Oh, none taken. They knew I wouldn't settle for a live-in arrangement, either. The damage to my house moved me in a little faster than we anticipated, but it never occurred to me to go anywhere else but to them."

"I felt the same way, Grace. Last night when he told me about the duplex and offered me a place to stay, I knew I needed to go with him. I've been fighting the attraction I feel for him since I first met him. I'm not gonna do that anymore."

"I can't believe it took so long for the two of you to get together."

"You know why I couldn't go out with him."

"Why the hell not? I mean, look at him!"

"Yes, I know, but I've also seen the way women throw themselves at him in the club. Grace, I'm the jealous type, and I don't think I'd react well to them doing that if we were together. I was afraid I'd only cause him trouble at work. I know Ethan and Ben's policy about no domestic strife in the bar."

Grace grew thoughtful. "Rachel, they mean no fighting between couples if one is employed there. As in, don't go in there and squabble with *him.* Ethan would understand if you had to ask someone to keep her hands off Eli. You remember that crap with Patricia the night I met you? That happened because she wouldn't keep her grubby hands off of Ethan. Ethan had no problem with it because I was a lady when I did it. That's all he asks, Rachel. No hair pulling or cat fights." Grace peeked through the inner window of the SUV to see where the men stood a short distance away, talking, before she continued.

"*Look* at him, Rachel. He's so purty I don't see how you could stand it the last two months. Believe me. I know adoration when I see it. He adores you. I think Eli would also set any women straight who laid their hands on him if he *knew* he was yours. It's obvious from the way his eyes follow you he *wants* to be yours. He wouldn't tolerate someone upsetting you anymore than my men would. You need to give him a chance."

Rachel ogled Eli through the window and prayed that Grace was right. "I hope it works out the way you say. We're going to spend some time alone this afternoon."

"Mmm, 'time alone.' Two of my favorite words." Grace sighed as she lifted another bag from the back of the vehicle. "Let's get these things inside, and we'll leave you alone. You can call me later with all the details, though, okay?"

Rachel chuckled and shook her head as she lifted bags out. "You sound more like your sister every day."

"Thank you, Rachel. That's sweet of you."

"Speaking of details, I haven't heard all about the honeymoon and Grand Cayman Island."

"We'll get together sometime soon and talk about everything, but this is the short version. We went snorkeling, got laid, went swimming with dolphins, had a foursome, went shopping, got laid some more, visited Hell—which is a real location on the island—had another foursome, which was heavenly, by the way, went dancing, gave great head, and got laid. There. That's what I did on my honeymoon." She burst out laughing at the dazed look on Rachel's face.

"You really do that, Grace? Have foursomes? Like…" If ever there was going to be an opportunity to assuage her curiosity, this was it.

"All three at the same time?" Grace whispered breathlessly, giggling. "Oh, hell yes! I absolutely *live* in heaven. Can you imagine," she spoke softly, looking around to see if the men were listening, "having three handsome, thoughtful men tend to your needs? All loving you and paying attention to you at the same time, murmuring sweet words in your ear, and kissing you all over, making love to you? When someone loves you like that, you'll do anything you can to make them feel loved in return, and that's the truth, Rachel."

"Some time, if you wouldn't think it's too weird, I'd like to get some pointers from you, since you're the *voice of experience.*" Rachel's cheeks went red-hot as she glanced over at Eli.

"I'll help however I can. Ask me *anything,*" Grace replied with a twinkle in her eyes.

* * * *

While the girls busied themselves with their gossip, Eli shared all the details with Jack about what happened the night before.

Jack said, "Grace went to the store and picked up all kinds of stuff for Rachel. Some household things and also some girly stuff. I don't know what all."

"That was nice of you to do that for her, Jack. She lost most everything, especially the basics."

"Grace adores Rachel and hates to see people hurting. Matter of fact, it's sort of how the four of us got together, over a pot of homemade stew she brought to the house after my mom passed away back in May." Jack lowered his voice and leaned a little toward him. "Hey, were we interrupting you earlier? I didn't know you were an item."

Eli grinned happily. "That's sort of a new development. Rachel is going to move in next door and be my neighbor."

Jack smirked at Eli knowingly. "How long you reckon *that's* gonna last?"

"She says she won't live with a man she's not married to," Eli replied with a shrug as he gazed at her through the SUV's tinted windows.

"Sounds familiar. Good luck with that and let me know when you need the name of a good jeweler," Jack said, chuckling.

"So how was the honeymoon?" Eli grinned at the slow, satisfied smile that spread across Jack's face. "That good, huh?"

"Better. We are three lucky bastards, I'll tell ya. Grand Cayman is beautiful." Jack smiled and shook his head. Grace and Rachel came around, carrying shopping bags. Jack quickly went to take them from Grace. "Here, darlin', let me have those. Let us bring them in. Just tell us where you want them, Rachel."

Rachel looked at Eli, and Eli smiled back at her. "I guess in the living room with the other bags for right now since she'll have her own place soon. We'll move her in later today or in the morning, depending on when Charlie brings the keys."

They brought all the bags inside, and Rachel thanked Grace and Jack again, promising to call Grace soon. Grace spoke something in Jack's ear that made him smile, and they said their good-byes

* * * *

Rachel slipped off her shoes and tucked her feet under her as Eli came and sat beside her on the couch. Nervous butterflies took up residence in her stomach at the warm look in his eyes. He took her hand in his and kissed her knuckles.

"Are you happy about becoming my neighbor?"

"Yes, but I'm happier about being here with you on this couch." She sighed happily as he kissed her palm.

"Could I be more than your neighbor, Rachel?"

"You mean like a boyfriend?" she asked as she allowed him to pull her into his lap.

"Yes, but more. Could I be your lover, too?"

She answered softly with a nod. "Yes, but I want...more, too."

"Tell me what you want, and I'll give it to you." "I want more than your lovemaking. I want your heart and your soul as well. I want all of you, even the rough edges." She asked for her heart's desire. Might as well go for it. "No regrets, right?"

He grinned and kissed the tip of her nose. "That's right. I love your straightforward honesty. But you've already claimed all those things, and I think you just haven't realized it."

"When did that happen, and how could I not know this?" She was confused. Prior to last night they'd only been friends to each other.

"It happened the first night I worked at The Pony when I saw you dancing with Grace and Charity. You stole my heart and soul from me in that moment, and they have belonged to you ever since."

She looked into his eyes, a little surprised. "You know, I remember seeing you watch me from the door. All the women kept approaching you. I didn't think I had a chance with competition like that. But," she looked down at her hands and felt her cheeks tingle with warmth, "from the moment I noticed you staring at me, I danced for you, moved for you. It was my secret until now."

Eli nuzzled her cheek. "I loved the way you moved. So beautiful and sexy. I couldn't take me eyes off of you."

She laid her head against his shoulder and traced a pattern on his chest. "What about you? What do you want from me? Can I give you what you need?" she asked softly. His clean smell invaded her nostrils, so she turned her face up into his hair, wallowing for a second in it.

Eli smiled and chewed his lower lip, giving that some thought. "What do I want from you? I want your willingness to try a relationship with me. I want you in my life, everyday. I want you in my bed, tucked into my side, safe and warm, and I *even* want your jealousy."

She drew her eyebrows together and looked at him quizzically. Crazy man.

He continued on. "I want your beautiful body, and your passion, and your cries of pleasure when I make you come. I want the naughty twinkle in your eyes and your kisses. I want your sexy, swaying hips and that succulent, sweet ass when you're walking away from me. I want your silky-soft hair draped across my shoulders and my thighs when you make love to me, and I want the heaven that I know lies inside your heart and between your luscious thighs." He grinned at her astonishment when her lips fell open at his words. He evidently had given this some thought.

Then he added, "*That* would be enough until I discover all the other little things about you that I want. By the end of that first night, I was half in love from watching you. Then I got to know you better. I love you, Rachel," he murmured, tilting her chin up to kiss her.

She could hardly even speak. She was so stunned she began to tremble. Is that how he saw her, how he felt about her? He was absolutely amazing to her. Like a Viking warrior poet. He loved her?

"You love me? Our first kiss was only this morning. How can you be so sure?"

He chuckled. "Silly girl, I didn't fall in love at your kiss. I've been falling in love with you a bit at a time over the last two months, even though you kept turning me down."

For once, she spoke the words that came into her mind without first filtering and editing them. He spoke from his heart, and she did the same for him. "I fell in love with you last night when you showed up at the fire and held your arms open to me, and when I slid between your sheets last night and felt enveloped by your presence. And when you touched me and told me I was beautiful. I fell in love with you only last night. Before last night, it was purely physical attraction. What does that say about me?"

"That you were scared and didn't want to be hurt. Everybody's different. Adam Davis told me at the wedding that he fell in love with Grace the very moment he laid eyes on her. I fell in love with you by degrees, and maybe you might have, too, if you hadn't been fighting it so hard, you know?"

She smiled at him and nodded. She knew he was right. "One fact remains the same."

"What?"

"I do love you." She turned to him and parted her lips as she kissed him. "Are you sure you can handle me?"

"You mean your jealous nature?"

"Yes, we should probably talk about that at some point rather than waiting for it to rear its ugly head. Given the change in our status, how would you handle a woman who threw herself at you?"

"I wouldn't wait for them to do that. Ethan has invited you to sit up front with us any night you come in while I work. They would all see that you were my girlfriend, and that would stop the more decent ones. I want people to see you at my side. You could even kiss me if you wanted," he said with a little bit of a grin. "We could also dance during breaks. That's something I've never done before because I didn't want to encourage them, but I'd dance with you as often as I could. Let's focus on us and deal with those situations as they arise."

"When did Ethan tell you I could sit up front with you? How does he know about us?" It had been less than twenty-four hours.

"He asked me one night why you hadn't given into my charm yet. I told him about it. It was his suggestion that you sat with me to send a message to them."

"Oh. I hope I'm worth the trouble." She let out a big yawn.

"Come on, angel. Let's put you in bed," Eli said as he yawned also. "We need a nap." He stood with her still in his arms, and she let out a startled squeal and held on.

"What about..."

"Making love? You're too worried about being jealous. We're both preoccupied, and the mood isn't right. It's one o'clock right now. Let's wait and see how you feel after a nap. When I make love to you, it's going to be worth the wait." He carried her into his bedroom.

Nap my ass! What? Am I two years old? Naughty Rachel tapped her shoulder, ready with a plan.

She smiled innocently at him and asked, "Would you mind if I slipped out of my jeans? I'll be more comfortable that way." Rachel pictured Eli weighing his options. In one hand, he had his conviction that she needed a nap and maybe he did, too. In the other hand, he had a half-naked woman about to climb in his bed and snuggle with him. She felt safe in predicting the outcome. Pretty smug, actually.

He set her on her feet. "I want you to be comfortable here, Rachel. No pressure, whatever helps you relax." He removed a large woven throw blanket from the closet, big enough for both of them to cuddle together under. Dang, he seemed okay with that.

After she removed her jeans, she climbed onto the bedspread, wondering if maybe she should be a good girl. Naughty Rachel rolled her eyes. He spread the blanket over her and climbed in under it with her. She yawned, which caused him to yawn again, and they both laughed. He turned toward her on his side, and she snuggled up close to him, resting her head on his biceps as he pulled her close in his arms.

He chuckled deeply and murmured knowingly, "I see the sparkle in your pretty blue eyes, Rachel Lopez."

Shit. She pressed her lips together and tried to not giggle, failing miserably as soft laughter escaped her. *Dang, his bed is comfy.* "I can't help it. I'm impatient."

"Me, too. But what you need right now is—"

"—I get it," she pouted. "No nap, no cock."

"Well, I wouldn't have put it quite like that, but yeah."

"That's some impressive self-discipline you got there, Mr. Wolf." She yawned and allowed him to tuck her against his chest. He smelled so good.

"Well, thank you, angel. But I can see that you're running on nerves and adrenaline right now. If you'd lie quietly for a minute, you'll see that I'm right."

"And when I'm still awake in ten minutes?"

"*If* you're awake in ten minutes, I'll make love to you until you lose track of how many times you come," he murmured in a sexy voice. "But you have to rest quietly for ten minutes first."

She yawned and heard him chuckle quietly to himself.

"Deal," she said smugly. She was *totally* getting laid. All she had to do was lay on his comfortable bed snuggled to him for ten minutes. What a hardship.

Chapter Six

Rachel woke slowly. Her eyelids slid open, and she became aware of the steady thumping noise under her cheek. She was relaxed and warm, content to soak in the quiet. Well, quiet except for the sound of Eli's heartbeat, which she could hear because he'd rolled onto his back and pulled her along with him. She was now sprawled across his torso. How she'd gotten in this position without waking up testified to how tired she'd been. Still motionless, she glanced over at the clock on the bedside table, which read four o'clock. They'd slept for three hours.

Yes! Shoot. He was right.

She lay there for a minute and took stock of her position. Her left forearm was under her at his side, her hand curled under his shoulder. Her right arm was stretched across his chest. She lay on her left hip on the bed, and her right thigh was tucked between his. She smiled softly when she noticed the very hard ridge that lay against her thigh and wondered if he was still asleep. His respirations sounded very deep and even, and his heartbeat was the same steady beat. She didn't move for fear of disturbing his sleep and then felt the almost imperceptible slow caress of his fingertips on her ass through the blanket. She wondered how long he'd been lying there awake, watching her sleep.

She slid her hand down his abdomen and noticed a subtle increase in his heartbeat. She laid her palm on the denim covering his cock and slid it down to cup his balls and then back over his hardened shaft. He was so long and thick, and the thought of him sliding his cock into her made her pussy lips begin to swell with desire. Her body sang for his, longing to feel his possession. The gentle contact caused him to arch his back and press into her hand. A soft hiss escaped his lips.

Slowly, she slid her hand over him again, taking time to caress his balls through the denim of his jeans. She smiled at his soft gasp. Never ceasing the contact with his erection, she arched her back and stretched like a well-contented jungle cat, tilting her head back to look up at him. His eyes were half open, smoldering with desire. He must have been like that for a while, lying there hard and ready, allowing her to get her rest. He was so thoughtful. How had she ever managed to find a man who was gorgeous and considerate of others?

He cupped the back of her head as he kissed her and pulled her over him. Her legs splayed over his hips, and he cupped her ass in his hands, pressing her to his erection.

"Did you sleep well?" he asked, kissing her chin and her cheeks and her nose before plundering her mouth. His voice was deep with arousal.

"I slept so well, I feel much better. And you?"

"I haven't had a nap that good in a long time. Then I woke up to find an angel in my arms," he murmured, pressing her to him again.

Her cheeks warmed at his sweet words. "Have you been waiting for me to wake up long?"

"Only a little while. I like watching you while you sleep. It's very relaxing."

She smiled softly, loving the slow burn growing inside her. Simple touches and soft words encouraged the embers back into flames. "You liked watching me sleep?"

"Yes, very much. It's satisfying to have you here, to know you trust me and feel safe with me. It feels right." His other hand slid into her hair, fanning it out around her and over his chest. She rose slightly, bracing her hands on his shoulders, and gently tilted her pelvis against his erection, rubbing over him. His eyes fluttered closed, and he groaned as his head fell back on the pillow.

"Angel," he drew the endearment out in a whisper, "I've got to know what it feels like to be inside you."

She leaned forward, breaking contact with his cock, and kissed him tenderly.

He pulled the throw blanket off of them, tucked her to him, and rolled her under his immense, strong body. She tentatively reached down and undid the button of his jeans and pulled the zipper down partway. Her fingers strayed inside, and she sighed happily at the contact with his silky, hardened shaft. Hissing softly, he pulled the zipper down and rolled over to remove his clothing and then returned to her, kneeling beside her on the bed.

He was so beautiful this way. His broad chest narrowed down over his abs to a trim waist and lean hips. His cook jutted out at her, so immensely long and thick. She had never seen such a beautiful thing. That was the only word she could use to describe it as she wrapped her hand around him. As Eli softly groaned, Rachel looked up into his eyes, and was filled with awe and admiration. He gazed at her, sitting back on his heels so she could see all of him. He had to be all of nine or ten inches in length and incredibly thick.

"You're so big, Eli. So beautiful like this. I want you so much, but…" Rachel's fingertips traced the vein on the underside of his cock. He closed his hand over hers and eased her hand back and forth in a gliding stroke and groaned in pleasure. After he released her hand, she eased her panties down over her thighs and slipped them off. She looked up at him through a haze of desire, her body clamoring for him as she glanced again at his enormous size.

He came to her and stroked her arms before reaching for the hem of her top. She was so wet she wasn't even sure he'd need the lubricant. He drew the shirt over her head and slid his arms around her to unhook her bra. For that moment, she nestled against his chest and let him take care of it.

He laid her on his pillows and sat back on his heels, watching her with eyes that radiated desire. She drew her knees up with her feet flat on the mattress and opened her thighs to him, inviting him in. Retrieving the bottle of lubricant from the bedside table, he devoured her with his eyes as he slowly came to her.

He squeezed some onto his fingers and smoothed it onto his cock. He slid his wet fingers through her pussy lips, lubricating her entrance as well. She wanted to thank him for his thoughtfulness but was unable to speak, gasping when his fingertip found her clit.

Eli's voice was husky with desire as he murmured, "Angel, you're so warm and wet already. Do you want to feel my cock?"

"I want you to fill me with it," she said softly, her voice shaking a little.

He once again lifted her left thigh and laid it over his forearm. She felt so vulnerable in this position, his gaze unspeakably intimate, knowing he could see all of her opened up to him. He groaned as he positioned himself at her wet, swollen pussy. Her breath came in panting gasps as the head of his cock pressed there, seeking access, but not inside her yet.

"So beautiful," he whispered shakily as she looked up into gray eyes filled with adoration. She was buffeted by the emotion she saw there and the powerful vulnerability she felt in her current position, about to be possessed by him. His left hand traced over her pussy lips, parted them, then gently rubbed over her clit. His touch elicited a low moan from her as he pressed into her, the broad head of his cock sliding in slowly. She was consumed by the sensation of his huge cock filling her so tightly.

"Angel, you are so tiny, so tight. Your little pussy is…" He groaned softly.

"Eli, it's so good." She whispered softly, panting as her body allowed him to slide in farther. His cock was so hard and so silky at the same time, and she was filled to bursting by his thickness. It was a wonderful plundering.

"Can you take more? Are you all right?"

She chuckled softly as she flexed her hips and relaxed as much as she could for him. "I'm so all right I could scream, baby. I want some more."

Eli looked down, still holding her thigh over his right forearm. He ran a fingertip through the lubricant on her lips and slid it over her clit, and she trembled and moaned. He slid a few more inches of his beautiful cock into her before beginning a slow, sensuous rocking motion.

With each gentle thrust, he gained more ground, and she watched the pleasure on his face as he moved in her. His cock was enormous and filled her cunt tightly, leaving no sensitive spot untouched. On each downstroke, he tilted his pelvis, stroking a part of her pussy that created a sensation of intense pleasure and almost unbearable tightening every time he stroked over it. He seemed to know what he was doing to her as he gazed down on her, watching her take her pleasure. She'd been horribly robbed the first time she had sex, and Eli was making up for it in spades with his careful attention to her needs.

She looked down and smiled as she watched his cock, coated with her juices, slide into her cunt all the way. "Baby, you were right. It does fit. So *beautifully.*"

"Mmm, baby, you feel good, and you're so hot." He braced his hands by her shoulders and leaned in to kiss her, never missing a beat, before kneeling over her. Grasping her hips with his big hands, he lifted her slightly and tilted her to him in a way that created an increased friction on her clit. How did he know to do these things to her? Pure genius.

"Amazing, it's amazing. You're so big and hard, but so gentle with me. Eli? I want—"

"Tell me what you want, angel. I'll give it to you. Whatever you want."

"That spot inside me you keep stroking, do it harder, please." She slid her hands over his.

He pulled out then thrust back in, tilting and pulling out harder and a little faster with every stroke. "That one?"

Every muscle in her body tightened down, out of her control. "Ooooh! Yes! Eli! Ba—by! Yes! Eli…I'm…Harder! Don't stop. I'm coming!" She screamed as she flew apart in a million pieces, every ounce of tension in her whole body suddenly shattering. Grasping her hips, he thrust hard one final time and groaned in ecstasy as he came, his body vibrating with passion. He held her tightly to him and ground his hips against hers, sending her into a wave of aftershocks, and all she could do was hold on to him.

As the storm passed, she looked up at him in awed bliss, trying to catch her breath. For the moment, he was upright, his head tilted back, recovering from his release. His features were relaxed, though the muscles in his arms and chest rippled as he held her tightly to him. She reached for him, and he lowered his massive upper body to hers. He gathered her in his arms and rolled them over so she was on top, their connection unbroken. Breathing hard, she laid her head on his chest and smiled at the sound of his pounding heart.

"Are you all right, Rachel?" He smoothed a hand over her hair. It was his gentleness that released a rush of tears from her eyes. Their lovemaking had been amazingly intense and even more beautiful than she'd imagined.

"Yes, Eli. Thank you," she murmured, not knowing what else to say as she snuggled into him. She had never experienced such a powerful orgasm before. She released a breathy, satisfied moan and sniffled.

"Look at me, honey." He touched her cheek, and she lifted her face to look at him, making eye contact. His worried gaze became tender when he saw that she smiled at him through her tears. "Am I hurting you, still being inside you?"

Her eyelids slid closed, and her smile widened a little. She shook her head and laid it back on his chest with a thud, no longer able to hold her head up.

"No, you feel so good inside me. Don't leave until you want to."

He chuckled, squeezing her ass playfully. "I'd never *want* to. Was it as good as you hoped it would be?" She could hear the concern in his voice.

"*Infinitely* better than I could have imagined. I wish you'd been the first. I'm sorry you weren't," she whispered softly. She felt remorseful for rushing into that first time and basically throwing away something more precious than she could realize. She regretted even more all the emotional fallout that resulted from the night she lost her virginity.

She tilted her head up to look up at him as he murmured, "Don't apologize. Life is what it is. We're here together now, loving each other, so there can be no regrets. I love you, Rachel." He kissed the top of her head.

"I love you so much, Eli. I'm glad you didn't give up on me." She wiped away another stray tear and sniffled a little.

"There's no one else for me but you, Rachel. No one could make me feel the way you do, the way you've captured my heart."

"When you say things like that to me, it makes my heart ache, but in a good way. I'm very happy. You're going to think I'm crazy, Eli, but I think in a way the fire was a good thing. It forced me to realize how much I needed and wanted you. I've gotten used to being independent and self-sufficient. But I know now I need you so much. Whatever we have to go through with those horny women at the club is worth it to me."

"Remember that it's *you* that I need, Rachel. It's *only* you that I want touching me, no one else." He glanced at the clock. "We lost track of time. Why don't you get yourself ready for tonight and I'll take you out for supper before we go in? It's five p.m."

Her head shot up. "Five o'clock? I completely lost track of time. I'll take a shower and get ready. What should I wear?"

"Whatever you're comfortable in. I'll bet there's something pretty in one of those bags Grace brought from Macy's."

"Macy's is Grace's favorite place to shop, besides Hips and Curves," she said, grinning as she sat up while still straddling him.

"Hips and what?" he asked.

"Hips and Curves dot com. Plus-size lingerie."

"Mmm, interesting. Does Rachel like Hips and Curves?"

"Mmm-hmm. Rachel likes a lot." She gasped as he pulled out of her, noticing he'd started to get hard again. Eli groaned and smiled at her.

"I'll probably be hard all evening, getting to be close to you."

"Maybe if I'm good, you'll give it to me again when we get home." She chuckled as she climbed naked from the bed to retrieve the Macy's bag and brought it back to bed.

Home? She'd said home. Her words echoed in her mind, and she looked up at him in concern. Subconsciously, she already considered this home.

"I wish you'd consider this your home, Rachel, regardless of where you live. Nothing would make me happier even if we're taking this slow, like we agreed."

He gave her a hug and a kiss. They were interrupted by the doorbell. "I'll bet that's Charlie with the key." He pulled on his leathers and T-shirt before quickly closing the door.

She slipped into his robe, which hung on a hook in his closet, and began to pull clothing from the Macy's bag. Dang it. Grace had removed all the price tags. Rachel was going to have to do something special for Grace because she knew Grace would never accept repayment. She'd guessed pretty accurately on sizes, and Rachel loved her style.

They were all in bright colors and sexy styles. Empire waists with low-cut necklines, sexy, slinky V-necks, sheer sleeves and beading. There was also a long derriere-hugging denim skirt she could wear with her boots. She chose the skirt, a blouse with a deep overlapping surplice neckline and a built-in halter top underneath, a black push-up bra and, bless her heart, a black satin G-string. Man, she loved Grace!

She gathered everything up and listened at the bedroom door to hear whether or not someone was still there. She didn't hear anything, so she opened the door and took the new clothing to the bathroom. The house was quiet, and she assumed he'd stepped outside to talk to Charlie. She walked to his living room window and peeked out.

Eli was outside in the front yard, talking to Charlie. Charlie pointed at the roof and at something located on what was now her side of the duplex. He must be planning repairs. While they spoke, a Toyota sedan pulled up along the curb. Curious, Rachel stayed at the window to see who it was. She was not overjoyed when an unfamiliar young woman got out of the car. She had short, curly jet-black hair, and she was tiny. She was also very pretty in a pixie-like sort of way. Rachel focused on Eli. He shook hands with Charlie, who was making his exit as this new visitor arrived.

He turned, his back to the house, with his big muscled arms crossed over his chest. His stance was wide and unmoving. Then he tilted his head to the side. Rachel wished she could see his face. The young woman held her hand up to shade her eyes from the late afternoon sun and smiled sweetly at him. She stood in the open door of the car and removed an overnight bag and placed it on the trunk of the car.

Oh. Hell. No. Not so soon.

Chapter Seven

As Rachel watched in growing trepidation, the young woman slung another bag over her shoulder and walked around to the other side of the car. Oh, no. The second bag was a *diaper* bag. This was going to be interesting. She placed it on the trunk also and opened the passenger side door and leaned in momentarily. When she stood back up, she held a newborn infant in a fuzzy blue sleeper against her chest. The baby also had jet-black hair and was snuggled up to the pretty young woman, fast asleep.

Rachel's heart began to pound, and the muscles in her throat refused to work, so she couldn't swallow. A cold chill skated over her skin, and she willed herself to breathe deeply, knowing it was just adrenaline. She trusted him, and there had to be more to this than what she saw.

The young woman spoke to Eli from the open door of the car. As she spoke, she became emotional. By this point, Eli had walked slowly to the car and then gently enfolded the young woman and the baby in his arms. She cried while he held her and patted her back. He spoke to the young woman and gestured with his hand toward the house. The young woman wiped her face with one hand and smiled at him.

Rachel watched, her heart aching as he took the tiny little infant boy with shiny black hair from his mother. He snuggled him up high on his chest, under his jaw, held him with one big hand, and gently guided her to the duplex before he grabbed the two bags off the trunk and closed the car door with his boot.

Rachel turned and hurtled into the bathroom, stripped his robe off and quickly turned on the shower, jumping in even before it was warm, gasping at the shock of the cold water on her skin. She needed a few minutes to process this latest development. Was that his baby? Was that an old girlfriend? She had cried and looked so vulnerable. He comforted her like someone who was emotionally invested in her. He had not acted unhappy to see her. He might have been surprised but not unhappy.

As she bathed, she was reminded that she and Eli had made love earlier. She was very sensitive, though not all that sore. He'd been so sweet to her and so careful with her. She knew he wouldn't take her trust and the intimacy they now shared for granted in light of this new visitor. At least, she hoped not. Whatever the case, whoever she was, it was too late for Rachel. Her heart was lost to him, and when she thought of it, it beat a hollow rhythm in her chest.

There had to be a reasonable explanation for this young woman's presence. He had gestured to the house like he wanted her to come in, even knowing Rachel was there. He was not trying to keep this woman and her baby a secret from Rachel. She wanted to kick herself remembering that *he* was the one she trusted. She had no reason, and he had *given* her no reason to distrust him.

Her problem was with the women who threw themselves at him in the club. In the club. This woman wasn't throwing herself at him. She also didn't seem like the barfly type. Maybe she was—

She leaned against the tile and allowed the spray from the showerhead to run over her hair. She put her head on her forearm and tried to calm her breathing, feeling foolish for thinking this could possibly work out between them. She should have known it would be too complicated. She should have known she'd find all this out after her heart was completely open to him. She should have known something this magical, this fantastical couldn't be real. Her breath hitched in her throat, and she jammed her lips shut, trying unsuccessfully to contain the small sob that shook her whole body before they heard her.

Eli's warm hand on her shoulder made her shriek and practically jump out of her skin. She looked up at him through overflowing eyes, waiting for him to lower the boom. His head tilted in concern at her obviously upset state, and then he smiled at her compassionately. "Rachel? I'm sorry I scared you. My little sister is here. She drove in from Abilene with my new nephew. I want you to meet them. I should have brought her right in, but I was surprised by their arrival. Breathe, baby, are you all right?" he asked, looking into her eyes with concern.

She put her hands to her face, feeling like an utter dumbass. "I'm so stupid. I need to work on my trust and jealousy issues. I'm such an ass, Eli. I'm—"

He smiled softly at her and leaned forward to kiss her shoulder. "So beautiful, naked and wet in my shower? Sexy and dripping like a marooned mermaid? Yeah, you are all that, but stupid or an ass? No, I don't think so. Her husband shipped out for Afghanistan two weeks ago, and she's missing him and having cabin fever. I can't believe she drove all the way here by herself with the baby. Why don't you finish up and come meet Kelly and Matthew. They're dying to meet you." He slid his hand down her wet back and over her ass cheek, squeezing gently. "Everything else all right? Feeling okay?"

Her relief was so great, she shook a little with it. "I feel fine," she replied, looking up at him as she rinsed the rest of the shampoo from her hair and reached up to squeeze the water out. The action tipped her breasts up to him invitingly, a temptation he didn't resist. He smiled mischievously as he cupped her breast in his hand and rubbed his thumb over her tight nipple, making her sigh in pleasure and wish for more.

"You're not sore?" he asked as she turned off the water and he wrapped a towel around her.

"No. I feel more sensitive, like I've been with you, but want *more*," she murmured as he grinned down at her. "I'll hurry and get ready so you can take your shower," she said, toweling her hair as he slipped from the bathroom.

Kelly and Matthew were both precious. Kelly was like a little sprite. She laughed and teased Eli when he took them to supper. Matthew was a precious little sleepy baby who napped through most of supper. Rachel even had an opportunity to hold him once she talked him out of his doting uncle's grasp.

As she watched him with the baby, she thought she remembered hearing him say something about visiting his sister in Abilene a few weeks ago, right after she'd had a baby. Later, she caught Eli's warm gaze when she looked up from cuddling the baby and saw the tenderness in his eyes as he watched her. Her cheeks tingled with heat, realizing what he was probably thinking. He didn't look away but blushed a little himself. Kelly thoroughly enjoyed teasing him about the way they made goo-goo eyes at each other.

He was due at the club in less than half an hour when he dropped Kelly off at the house. "I'm going to get us both ready for bed and lay on the couch and watch television. You go have fun. Good luck with the floozies, Rachel," she called as they left for the club.

Eli helped her back into the truck because of her long, narrow skirt. His hands rested on her thighs after she was settled. "I haven't told you how pretty you look in this sexy skirt, have I?"

"Nuh-uh," she replied quietly, nuzzling into his neck as he reached over and buckled her seatbelt for her.

"It does delicious things for your derriere, and that top...*Mmm*." He slid his finger over her bare collarbone and down between the open neckline and the inner halter top. "It's very pretty on you." He caressed the upper swell of her breast with his fingertips. His touch left a warm tingle behind as he stroked her. Leaning into him, she kissed him and squeezed his hand. After a scintillating minute of that, he released her and closed her door and went around to the driver's side door. He grinned at her as he climbed in on his side of the truck. "I wonder what people will think when they see you sit with us at our table by the door."

"I'm proud to be seen with you, Eli."

"Same here, baby."

They got to the club at ten till seven to find that Ethan had brought another chair over for her to sit on, right next to Eli's usual spot. Excusing herself, she sought Ethan out to thank him for doing that and for understanding her concerns.

"Sweetie, remember what it was like when Patricia was after me?" Ethan asked. "The first time Grace saw Patricia put her hand on my arm I was worried she'd get mad at *me*. When she confronted Patricia, she handled herself like a lady but essentially told Patricia to fuck off at the same time. I know it may not be easy creating boundaries for some of the more *friendly* women, but Eli is probably worth whatever trouble you go through. He only sees *you*, honey. I'm glad to see you came to your senses." He chuckled when she feigned outrage at his last comment.

"Yeah, I know," she agreed. "I was a little slow on the uptake. Is Grace coming in tonight?"

"Once she heard you were going to be here, she said she would. I'm saving a seat for her next to Bill, just in case."

"Why Bill?"

"He watches out for her like an old spinster aunt. Sometimes guys that don't know any better still hit on her. He provides a buffer when I'm not in close proximity, and of course the guys watch over her, too."

"I need to thank her for all the things she brought over for me today."

"I was about to say how pretty you look in that outfit. Is that something she picked out for you?"

"Yes, your wife has great taste."

"She does, doesn't she? Listen, you stick close to Eli tonight and see how things go. I think that will send a pretty clear message all by itself. All I ask is that if you have to set anyone straight, you do it without drawing a lot of attention to them or yourself."

"I'll remember that, Ethan. Thanks again." Rachel turned to go back to Eli's table and let out a heavy sigh.

Two women chatted with him very flirtatiously. This was how it always started, then one of them would reach out to his hair—*there* she went. Rachel watched as Eli stood and put up a forearm to block her reach, a very subtle but very clear communication that he didn't want to be touched. He glanced at her over their heads and winked at her when she smiled at him.

The women were on either side of the chair he leaned against, well within the boundaries of his personal space. It would be rude to verbally tell them to go away, but she could remove their reason for being there in such close proximity without saying anything. As she walked up, Eli slipped into the tall bar chair and spread his knees, an open invitation. She stepped right into that opening and reached for his hair, taking two generous handfuls of it at his shoulders. He slid his hands up her ribcage and laid a big, happy, wet kiss on her as the two women looked on in surprise.

Word would spread quickly now, and the grapevine would no doubt be put to the test. Releasing her from the kiss, he nuzzled her cheekbone and the sensitive flesh under her ear. "You are the most beautiful thing I've ever seen, Rachel. I love you."

The words were truly meant only for her, but she felt sure that at least one of the two women had overheard him. She hugged him. "I love you, too, babe. Thank you." She rested her hands gently on his thighs and looked at the woman on his left and said, "Hi, would you excuse me? I'd like to sit in my chair." She indicated the tall chair the woman was currently blocking.

The women made their excuses and reluctantly walked off to the bar, their heads together, chattering to each other. Eli took her right hand in his left, clasping their fingers together. They sat there chatting quietly when Mike and Rogelio rolled in and stopped short, gaping at the two of them. Mike turned to Rogelio with an I-told-you-so look and pointed at them.

"What did I say, Rogelio? I thought something was up when I talked to them earlier." The very large man looked at Mike, grunted and nodded without saying anything else, so Mike continued, "I had a feeling this might bring the two of you together."

"Yeah, it's amazing how sometimes a bad thing can bring about good results," she replied, hugging them both before she returned to her seat.

"So besides the obvious turn of events, how did everything go today?" Mike asked as he settled in at the door.

Eli stroked her palm with his callused fingertips as he said, "We talked to my landlord and got her set to move in next door. We're still planning on going over to Rachel's old place tomorrow morning to see about getting into her bedroom."

While Eli explained about Kelly and Matthew, Rachel thought about how odd it was to think of her burned-out apartment as her old place. It had only been a day, but it felt old already. She felt removed from the situation. She needed to update her parents and try to make a trip out to the storage barn to see if they had any furniture she could use in the new place.

As more people came in the front door, Eli left his chair and stood next to Mike, helping him check IDs. Rogelio made the rounds to check on the restrooms and the seating areas. The music got louder, and more people moved onto the dance floor.

Grace arrived later in the evening. After hugging Rachel and greeting the bouncers, Grace promised to get right back with her. She made a beeline for Ethan, who was at a table talking to a couple of local ranchers. He saw her approach and excused himself, drawing her into his arms for an adoring kiss. Rachel smiled as she watched them.

Somehow Grace handled the inherent challenges of Ethan being a co-owner in the club, so Rachel knew she could survive the challenges involved in being with Eli.

For the short period of time she sat with Eli, no one else had approached him. She could not recall that ever happening before. Unless he was actively working the door, there was always a bevy of eager women clamoring for his attention.

Morbidly curious to find out what would happen, she gathered her purse and told Eli she was visiting the ladies' room and would be right back. She glanced back as she sashayed away and caught him ogling her ass. He looked up and smiled hungrily at her. Blowing him a kiss, Rachel gave him the show he wanted. She found Grace seated in Ethan's lap at another table.

Grinning, Rachel said, "Come on, bathroom buddy!" Grace kissed Ethan, and he released her. She slipped out of his lap, jerking around suddenly when Ethan goosed her fanny. Giggling, she followed Rachel into the bathroom and checked the other stalls for company. They were alone.

Grace leaned against the counter while Rachel checked her lipstick. "That outfit looks every bit as sexy on you as I thought it would. Did Eli like it?"

"He likes it very much. I can't thank you enough."

"Oh, come on. What did he *say*?" Grace asked and giggled delightedly when Rachel told her. "How was your afternoon?"

"It was wonderful. We napped." She grinned at the disappointed look on Grace's face. "He said I was too tired from everything last night, and he didn't want to make love to me when I felt like that. So we took a nap, *then* we made love."

"Oooh! How was it?" Grace asked, blushing a little. Rachel didn't say anything at first, just looked up at Grace. "Oh, damn, it was *that* good? I know that look. I've worn it many times in the last few months. You are *so* in love! I'm so happy for you, Rachel. You deserve a good man like Eli. You can tell he's smitten by the way he watches you when you're not looking."

"What do you mean?" Rachel asked, looking at Grace's reflection in the mirror as she fluffed her blonde hair.

"He doesn't *look* at you, he *drinks* you in. Anyone can see he absolutely adores you." Conspiratorially, she continued, "I've been listening this evening, and everyone is talking about the two of you."

"What do they say?" Rachel asked. At Grace's doubtful gaze, she added, "Come on, you can tell me. That's part of why I'm in the bathroom with you. Nothing will surprise me at this point."

"Ethan overheard a table full of single women in the back planning to wait for you to go to the bathroom before making a move." Rachel's eyes shot up, and for a split second, she saw red and almost sprinted to the door. Grace laid a gentle hand on Rachel's arm and deterred her from leaving.

"I heard two women talking. One of them planned to come over and spill her drink on you *accidentally*. While you're in the bathroom cleaning up, the other one will give him their numbers and offer him a threesome. She said she knows where he lives and everything. Before you ask, she said she followed him home one evening, curious where he lived. Ethan said you handled yourself well with the same women earlier this evening, so you'll know what they're up to when you see them coming."

"Ethan said that?"

"Yeah, listen to me, okay? *Don't* rush out there ready to do battle. Give him a chance to prove to them he is not interested. Up until tonight, they all thought eventually he'd take an interest in one of them. You'll both need to show them that he is permanently off the market, but you have to be subtle about it. That doesn't mean you can't make your message crystal clear, just don't let them upset you.

"Remember how catty women can be and that their best strategy may be to try and get the two of you fighting. Don't let that happen with your guy. If you love him, *always* give him the benefit of the doubt. *Always*. Roughly half the customers in here are women. In here, he has to be kind to them, allowing their flirtations to a *very* limited extent. Now that you have cut off their supply of 'Eli love,' they may become bolder, trying to get with him and get *by* you."

Rachel nodded, seeing the wisdom in Grace's words. "When you're not with him, your trust is going to have to be absolute. But the upside is that if you are with him outside the bar and he is approached, you can be much more persuasive in warning them off. Just remember, Eli sees you as a lady. And speaking of being a *lady*, I think we need to go ask Ethan to play something so you and I can dance for our men. Let's show them that there's more to us than *that* waiting for them when we get home tonight. Whatya say?" she asked with a sexy, crooked grin.

"I say you are an evil genius, Grace. Thanks for talking me down off the ledge. I was getting pretty defensive there for a minute, but what you say makes perfect sense. I'll be watching for those two with the spilled drink plan. Let me fix my hair and we can go."

"Get ready because that table full of women should be at it by now. Strut that fine ass out there and work it. That's how you thank him for having eyes only for you. Make it worth it to him to turn down all the free pussy that's being flung at him right now. What?" she asked innocently, her big blue eyes popping open. "Call a spade, a spade. Give him a little sample of what he gets to taste tonight," she said, adjusting her cleavage for maximum affect.

"Grace, you talk dirty in bed, don't you? Those words roll off your lips like you get practice." Rachel was surprised, but also a little awed, at the transformation in Grace. She could remember the first time she laid eyes on her in this very restroom, squaring off with Patricia Gonzales over Ethan. She'd looked a little unsure of herself back then. This woman was self-confident and knew where she stood with her man and every other female in this club. Self-confidence was a remarkable attribute in her, and damned if she wasn't wearing that same pair of great dance shoes, only in dyed pink snakeskin this time.

"Grace, those shoes are *kick ass*!"

"I know! June called Adam to let him know that she'd seen them in a new color. I told her how much I liked them the last time we saw her, and he surprised me with them. They like seeing me in pink." She snickered, showing Rachel the pink waist band of her satin thong, giggling.

"You are so naughty, Grace! I love that about you."

Grace sassily held up two fingers. "My rule number one is seize the day, and my rule number two is live life with no regrets."

"Words to live by. Give me five minutes to fight off the floozies, and then you and I can go shake our moneymakers."

"Deal. That will give Ethan a chance to look forward to me dancing for him. Sometimes the anticipation is the best part." Grace said with a chuckle.

"Don't I know it," Rachel murmured, thinking about that afternoon when she thought she'd die of anticipation. Rachel pulled open the restroom door, and slowly exited, walking through the club with Grace like their fine asses owned it.

Chapter Eight

Rachel snickered as she watched Grace settle herself back into Ethan's lap. Cheekily giving him an extra little wiggle, she winked at Rachel as she spoke softly to him. The ear-to-ear smile on his face at Grace's words told Rachel what she wanted to know.

She continued sauntering through the club, getting a glimpse of Eli amongst all the bleached and highlighted heads currently surrounding him. She smiled, sympathizing with her poor handsome baby. She took slow, deep breaths, asked Ben at the bar for a club soda, and glanced over to see how Eli was doing.

From her location, she could see him standing in front of his chair, literally surrounded by women. She noticed that he did not sit down in his chair when they did this and came to the realization that, if he sat, it gave them easier access into his personal space and they were more likely to put their hands on his legs or in his hair. When he stood, most of them had to back up so they could gaze up at him adoringly.

He smiled, making friendly conversation with them and other bar patrons as they came in the door. She pulled a maraschino cherry off its stem and chewed it thoughtfully as she truly observed him this time. Before, she supposed that she'd spent most of her time glowering at the women and never spent much time noticing how he handled their advances. They sure were a pushy lot. She had the sense that he was uncomfortable and noticed he kept looking over at the restroom door. He must wonder what kept her, or maybe he was concerned about what she would do when she saw all the women gathered around him.

She peeked over again and saw him raise a forearm to gently block another woman's reach as she made a move to touch his long, silky hair. Poor thing. Rachel couldn't blame her. She could barely keep her own hands out of his hair when she was with him. He jerked back suddenly as though someone had touched him in an inappropriate way. It was time to rescue her lover from his groupies, she thought with a determination. She was very proud that she remained calm rather than becoming angry and jealous.

Ethan came to stand beside her and chuckled, saying, "He's been doing his best, Rachel. But they've been very persistent ever since you left. You're making me proud of you the way you've handled all of this. I know it's not easy for you." He turned to his partner, who was behind the bar at the moment. "Hey, Ben. How about a shot of Crown for Rachel and 1800 for Eli. He looks like he needs the fortification. Put them on my tab." Ben came over, grinning, and poured two generous shots for her.

Ethan turned back to her. "Time to go rescue your man from his admirers," he said with a smirk.

She smiled gratefully. "Thanks, Ethan. You're a peach."

"So Grace tells me," he said. "I'm looking forward to the next set of dance music. We've got two of your favorite songs coming up, back-to-back," he said meaningfully, his eyes twinkling.

"Enjoy," she murmured with a grin and backed away from the bar. She approached the front of the club and made sure she was in clear view of Eli as she sauntered slowly to where he stood, completely blocked in by female bodies. His discomfited face split into a wide grin as he made eye contact with her over their heads.

Mike elbowed Rogelio, watching with avid glee as she approached. They both looked thoroughly amused by the scene playing out before them. She winked at Eli, held up the shots, and didn't slow her approach. The relief on his face was almost comical.

In her friendliest stewardess voice, she piped cheerfully, "Oh, hi! How are you all doing?" Like they'd come to see and talk to *her*. "Careful, ladies, don't want to spill the shots. Watch out, I *love* that dress!" She sliced with surgical precision right through the group, never so much as bumping anyone aside. They all moved back a bit in surprise at her smooth, unimpeded advance through their ranks.

She offered the shot to him. He took it, slammed it, and placed the glass on the table. He gently pulled her to him, wrapping her arms around his neck, breast to chest, as he sat down in his chair.

* * * *

Damn, but Rachel knew exactly how to ease him. Eli couldn't sit in the presence of these women because if he did, they'd invariably slide their perfumed hands up his thighs, which always led to other things. In another life, he'd have loved it, but he despised that they all knew he was here with Rachel and still felt as though they could act that way around her. She made it all worth it. The slow, seductive smile she'd given him as she strutted across the club, holding those drinks up, sent a shot of lust straight to his groin. He was rock hard by the time he pulled her into his arms, and judging by the look in her eyes, she knew it, too.

"Is that a gun in your pocket, or are you just glad to see me, big man?" she asked, giving him a sultry smile and her best seductive imitation of Mae West. He held her tightly pressed against him.

Her eyelids slid closed over her gorgeous deep blue eyes, and she looped her arms around his neck. It sent a pleasant tingle up his spine when she threaded her fingers through his hair, something he knew she liked to do. It was a small way she could put her mark on him because he never allowed anyone else to touch his hair. He was glad she liked it long and loose the way it was.

She tilted her head up to him and laid a warm open-mouthed kiss on his lips. There were disappointed sighs and moans from the group of horny females, and he had to grin as he kissed her. She shook with inner laughter as she stroked his tongue with her own and drew all his attention back to her. By the time she was done kissing him, all the groupies were gone in search of greener and, hopefully, more available pastures.

"Hi, beautiful," he murmured as he slid his hand gently down her back. He stopped at the upper swell of her ass, showing her respect in front of Mike and Rogelio by not continuing farther south in their presence.

"Hello, my lover." With a breathy sigh, she laid her head against his chest. "Do you mind if Grace and I dance in a few minutes?" she asked as she bit her lip. She had no idea how much that simple little gesture affected him. Add to that the mental image of watching her dance and his cock was hard as a rock.

He grinned crookedly at her. "Not at all. Why?"

"Grace requested a couple of songs for us." Rachel smiled innocently at him.

"I see."

"Grace told me she overheard the two women that were on you earlier. They're planning to give you their phone numbers and offer you a threesome."

Holy crap, where did these women come from? "How do they plan to do that?" he asked, amused at her nonchalant description of an event that should have her seething with fury.

"One will spill a drink on me, and while I'm in the bathroom cleaning up, the other will slip you their phone numbers and make the offer. She's got it all planned out, even knows where you live."

"Knows where I…How?"

"She's followed you home before."

"I never—"

"I know, honey. Can you try to watch out for them, though? I don't want my new outfit to get messed up," she replied, contentedly hugging him.

"Don't worry, baby. The only thing happening to this pretty outfit is gonna be me slipping it off of you later tonight. And if we get messy, we can always take a shower afterward." He grinned at her sudden delighted gasp when he quickly pulled her up onto his lap.

"I'm keeping you from work, sitting in your lap like this." She put her arm around his shoulder. He held her to him tightly, enjoying the feel of her delicious curves in his arms. His cock was equally appreciative, if a little unsatisfied. If he was going to be tortured with her delectable nearness all night, he might as well enjoy himself.

"The front is quiet. Everyone's having a good time, and no one's fighting, so you're right where you're supposed to be. If I have to get up in a hurry to help break up a fight, I'll put you in my chair first. Don't worry, Rachel. You're *right* where I need you. I love having you in my lap. Drink your shot. I think I see Grace headed your way. She looks very pleased with herself. She must be ready to dance."

"That girl does love to dance." Rachel waved at Grace as she approached.

"Hi, Grace," Eli said, giving her a friendly hug. "Thanks for watching out for Rachel. I appreciate it. It's amazing the levels some people will go to."

"You're welcome, Eli. Believe me, Rachel has done her share of watching out for me, too. You mind if we go dance?" she asked, her blue eyes wide and innocent.

"You go right ahead, Grace. I think I hear your song playing." He grinned as Big & Rich began pounding out "Save a Horse, Ride a Cowboy" over the sound system. Grace blew a kiss to Ethan, who was up in the DJ booth. He waved at her and put his hand over his heart, watching as she sashayed over to the dance floor. Eli kissed Rachel's knuckles and released her.

Ethan left the DJ booth and came down to the front where he could see Grace better and stood next to Eli and the others.

"I shouldn't be watching this, man," Mike muttered, transfixed. "She's like my little sister or something."

Rogelio groaned and started checking his fingernails.

Eli heard Ethan exhale and murmur, "Damn, watching Grace move like that never gets old. We may not even make it home first," he added softly, groaning as she slid her hands suggestively over her ass then her thighs.

Eli was hypnotized by the swaying rhythm of Rachel's hips. He never took his eyes from his woman as she began to move to the pounding rhythm of the song. He knew it was nothing more than mental gymnastics, but he swore he felt her movements on his cock. He was as hot and hard as he'd been earlier that afternoon before entering her tight, silken cunt. Watching her now was akin to waving a red cape in front of a bull. Her every movement enticed him and drew him in.

"Man, she is *gorgeous.*" He watched her hips roll and dip. The snug skirt hugged her luscious derriere as she shimmied and rocked. The backs of her fingertips trailed over her rib cage then strayed up the sides of her breasts, over her collarbones, and into her hair. The movement caused her breasts to tip forward invitingly.

Eli hissed at his painfully twitching erection, which throbbed to be inside her, pounding into her along with the rhythm of the song. Making eye contact with him across the room, she licked her lips and smiled seductively at him, and he freaking moaned *out loud*! Ethan looked over at him sympathetically as the song drew to a close. Another one requested by Grace followed along on its heels—"Steam" by Ty Herndon.

Oh. Hell. No. More teasing and tantalizing torture.

"Uh, boss?" Mike interrupted. "We got things under control here if…y'all want to take a break and dance with your ladies."

Ladies. They were definitely *not* being ladies right now. Like moths to a flame, both Ethan and Eli were drawn to the dance floor. Rachel saw him coming and smiled playfully, crooking her index finger at him. Eli gently collided with Rachel and spun her around on the dance floor, pressing his erection against her belly. "See what you've done to me, angel? I'm so hot for you right now I may explode."

Coming out of the turn, Eli grasped her hand and hip, then gently pulled her to him. Her long hair sailed around him in a dark cloud. Her intoxicating scent filled his nostrils and made his mouth water and he softly said, "I can't wait to make love to you again."

She gasped happily as his hand brushed her breast as they moved. He pulled her to him again after spinning her, and he groaned when she very deliberately swiveled her hips into his and undulated against his rock-hard cock.

"I can't wait, baby," she said softly as she shimmied against him.

Eli grinned and looked over as Ethan and Grace spun by on the dance floor. Ethan held Grace's hands and let her dance for him. Her silky skirt swished around her thighs as she shimmied for him. He spun her then pulled her back to his front, and she gyrated against him, giggling as he spun her again and pulled her to him face-to-face and did a very suggestive cha-cha-cha. Grace smiled, and her eyes closed when he whispered God-only-knew-what in her ear. It must have been to her liking because her eyes glittered, and she laughed suggestively. The look on Ethan's face could only be described as primitive lust. Someone was getting laid *but good* tonight.

Up to that point, the four of them had only had eyes for their partners, but as the song drew to a close, Eli realized they were on the dance floor alone, surrounded by loud applause, raucous cheering, and loud catcalls.

"Ladies and gentlemen, Ethan Grant and Grace Warner, Eli Wolf and Rachel Lopez. Let's hear another round of applause for the happy couples. Now go get a room, guys!" the DJ announced as they laughed and kissed each other, exiting the dance floor.

Rachel noticed pointed stares directed at her and Eli from several tables around the dance floor and had to laugh. As she turned to him to kiss him, he swept her up into his arms. She wrapped her arms around his shoulders, feeling tiny and petite. That got them more cheers and catcalls. He set her down, and they walked back to the table at the front. She took her seat to catch her breath.

Eli leaned over her, palm against the wall above her head, and tilted her chin up to him. She leaned into him breathlessly as he gave her a sweet, gentle kiss intended to make her knees melt and her spine tingle. She held on to his biceps, closed her eyes, and moaned softly. He released her lips after only a moment. "I am so lucky."

* * * *

Rachel was about to disagree that she was the lucky one when they were interrupted by a sudden commotion and the sound of a fistfight on the other side of the bar. Eli murmured to her quickly, "Duty calls," and vanished in an instant. Rogelio appeared next to Rachel and said, "Stay right here, sweetheart. I'll be right back." Both Eli and Mike had waded in to separate the combatants while others moved the women out of the way and returned overturned chairs to the bar. Three men who had been sitting at the bar were involved in the confrontation—Brice Huvell and two other men she recognized but did not know personally.

Every woman who came into The Dancing Pony on a regular basis knew who Brice Huvell was because he'd used the same inept pickup lines on all of them, including her. Brice was kind of sleazy with his come-ons but basically harmless. Once a woman told him *no* a time or two, he generally left her alone, which was why Rachel placed him in the harmless category. More than anything, Brice needed a makeover and someone sympathetic to take him in hand and teach him some etiquette.

Ethan left Grace with Rachel and got involved in the fray, helping to separate the three men, and then had pointed words with all three of them. Eli, Mike, and Rogelio bodily dragged the three of them to the door, away from the customers at the bar and away from listening ears. Grace stood with Rachel as Ethan listened to what Brice had to say.

Brice angrily pointed a finger at one of the men. "This *bastard* asked if she was the one newly married to Jack Warner, and I said yes. He said she was acting like an adulterous whore dancing with some other man like y'all were dancing and that she ought to be ashamed."

He gestured angrily at the other man and said, "His friend said maybe she'd like to dance like that with him, or maybe *both* of them, and I couldn't take no one talking about your Grace like that. I had to kick the shit outta them. Grace is a happily married *lady* and wouldn't have *nothin'* to do with the likes of you *sorry bastards*," Brice said through gritted teeth and threw another punch, landing it squarely on one of the other guy's jaws before Eli restrained his arm from landing another blow.

The other two both had bloody noses and the beginnings of black eyes. Brice was on the small side, but he evidently fought dirty because both guys were bigger than he and hadn't done more than bloody his nose.

Grace let out a quiet sigh at Brice's narrative, making sad eye contact with Ethan. Hands on his hips, Ethan made eye contact with Eli, Mike, and Rogelio and pulled out his phone. After speaking no more than ten soft words, he hung up. He spoke to Eli and Mike and gestured to the back exit. Eli released Brice, patted his back, and took hold of one of the others. Rogelio returned to his post at the door, stoic as ever.

"Jack and Adam should be here in a few minutes," Ethan explained to Eli and Mike. "Hold them and I'll be out in a couple of minutes."

"You got it, boss," Eli said, winking at Rachel. "Back in a few minutes, angel." He had a fierce gleam in his eyes. The two men glanced nervously at each other as the two bouncers began to walk them to the backdoor by the collars of their shirts. One of them resisted for a moment, and Eli jostled him by his shirt collar and Rachel heard him growl, "Yes, *please* fight me, asshole."

People stared at the men as they were escorted across the club and out the backdoor.

Ethan turned to Brice and held out his hand. Brice shook it and smiled at him, blood dripping off his chin onto his white dress shirt. Ben poured a shot of Cuervo 1800 and put it on the bar for him. Ethan took it and offered it to him. After tossing it back, Brice softly said, "It was the least I could do, Ethan, to make up for being such an ass."

"You're not an ass, Brice," Ethan replied, grinning. "We need to work on your pickup lines, that's all. Grace wants to thank you, I think," Ethan said, indicating her where she stood behind Brice, next to Rachel.

Grace also held out her hand to him. "Thank you, Mr. Huvell, for defending my honor. I appreciate that, and I'm sorry you got hurt in the process,"

Brice blushed and couldn't even make eye contact with her as he shook her hand. "It was the least I could do, ma'am, for making such an ass of myself with you a few months back."

"You are a man of worth, Mr. Huvell. Never doubt it," Grace replied. Grace had told Rachel a couple of months before about the pickup line Brice had used on her the first time she'd visited Ethan at The Dancing Pony. To say Brice employed shock value with his choice of icebreakers was putting it mildly. Rachel had laughed out loud and told Grace he'd used the same line on her.

Rachel watched Brice's rounded shoulders straighten and his head come up as he finally made eye contact with Grace. He didn't say anything else, just politely nodded, put his cowboy hat back on, and wiped his bloody chin on the back of his hand, smiling broadly. Rachel looked on, smiling, as something about Brice Huvell was transformed in that moment. It was true that *everyone* had a story to tell.

Ben held out a clean bar towel filled with ice for Brice to put on his face. Gradually, the hubbub died down, and the music played on. Waitresses delivered fresh drinks, and the noise of the club returned to normal levels. Ethan sat Grace in a chair next to Rachel and looked at his watch.

He smoothed his palms over Grace's thighs as she settled in the chair and said, "Stay here with Rachel, all right?" Grace nodded and tried to smile at him. Ethan tilted her chin so she looked directly into his eyes. "Don't worry, Gracie." He gestured with a thumb to the backdoor, referring to the men who had disappeared through it. "They have opinions they feel like sharing, they can answer for them to Jack. I'll be back in a few minutes. Rogelio will watch over you both." After kissing Grace gently, he turned and stalked purposefully toward the back of the club.

Rachel tilted forward and looked at Grace, who sat distractedly watching as Ethan disappeared into the dim hallway that led to the emergency exit. "You okay, Grace?"

Grace shrugged. "Yeah, this is not the first time something like this has happened. They have a very strong need to defend me from people like that."

"Does it bother you that they feel the need to do that?"

She looked at Rachel and shook her head with a soft smile. "No, they can take care of themselves, and it's a fact of life for us that not everyone appreciates our choices. That doesn't bother me so much. People can think whatever they want, but it's when people begin to say or *do* things to offend me that they take matters into their hands. It is what it is," Grace said matter-of-factly. She told Rachel the short version of her confrontation with a busboy in Rudy's restaurant, the day Jack, Ethan, and Adam proposed marriage to her back in June.

"Is it worth it?" Rachel asked, grinning at the thought of not one, but three men defending Grace's honor.

Grace smile warmly. "To be *with them*? Totally."

Chapter Nine

Eli held one of the men by the back of his collar as the black SUV pulled to a halt by the backdoor of the club. Jack and Adam climbed from the vehicle and walked over to Ethan, who quietly gave them the synopsis of what happened. Eli and Mike stoically held both men as one cursed the other for getting him into this mess. He didn't even know who Jack was, for crying out loud.

Jack and Adam reacted predictably to Ethan's words, simmering with anger. Ethan spoke a few more words, and Jack nodded before he and Adam walked over to the two men. Eli and Mike released them and stepped away, crossing their arms over their chests.

"*Adulterous whore?*" Jack quoted to the unlucky bastard who'd been dumb enough to utter the words and then applied his fist to the man's jaw.

Adam took the other man by his shirt collar and yanked him forward and up to eye level. "You insulted the sweetest, gentlest woman on this planet, and now you're gonna to regret it. Brace yourselves. This might *hurt* a little," he grated as he applied his fist to the other man's face.

"But she—"

Jack cut the man off, shaking him by his shirt collar. "She what? What? Danced with a man who has been my best friend my whole life? She dances with Adam, too, with my approval. Dancing with us makes her happy. We love to see her happy. Right now she's *not* happy, and if she ain't happy, we ain't happy. You caused that unhappiness, and now you're going to regret it. *No one. Insults. My. Wife*," he ground out before he dropped the man on the ground.

"Sorry, Jack, I didn't know—"

Ethan dropped a Ziploc bag filled with ice on each of their chests. "You'll be a damn sight *sorrier* if you ever insult her or come near her again. Don't judge people you don't know, Jim, Roy. You might want to ice that."

"Can we apologize?" Jim offered. "We don't want to get banned." The Dancing Pony was the only decent nightclub for miles.

"What do you think, Jack?" Ethan asked. "Should we ban them? Or let them sacrifice what's left of their self-esteem for the evening to avoid getting banned?"

Jack replied, "Yes, but only if they march their asses back through the club and make it a public apology. And then they'll need to leave for the evening."

Judging by the change in his expression, Jim had been hoping for a less public apology, which would have been a little easier on his ego, but he'd offered, so now he'd have to man up.

The noise level in the bar dropped a little when the men re-entered through the backdoor, minus their dignity. Ice packs to their faces, they cautiously approached Grace after Jack nodded to them to say their piece.

"I'm very sorry to have insulted you, Mrs. Warner. I spoke out of turn, and I hope somehow you can forgive me," Jim said as clearly as he could around his swelling sinuses.

"I accept your apology," Grace replied softly.

The other man offered a similar plea for forgiveness, and after she accepted, they both made their way to the traditional exit of the club, the front door. As if on cue, the DJ started another song, and club patrons left their tables and headed for the dance floor as Grace and her men excused themselves and made their way back to their table on the other side of the bar.

Eli returned to Rachel's side, doing his job, carding a few people who had come in the entrance. After Eli was done, the group entered the club, and he returned to Rachel. She looked up at him curiously.

"You okay, Rachel?" He looked into her deep blue eyes.

"I'm sorry that our little moment was interrupted, but, yes, I'm fine, Eli."

"Why so serious?"

"I was thinking about the fight. It's not uncommon for fights to break out in here. I've even watched you break a few up over the last couple of months. Most of the fights are *over* a woman, but I can't recall ever seeing someone fight *for* a woman, to defend her honor.

"*Every* woman wants a man that will deal out reckoning like that in her defense. Maybe it makes me sound a little bloodthirsty, but I was turned on by it when you winked at me then carried that son of a bitch out the backdoor for his beating," she said, stroking his chest as she looked up to him with eyes filled with admiration.

"Mmm, are you a bloodthirsty wench? Does it turn you on that I might someday have to rip some stupid bastard a new one for offending you? Because the defensive feelings I have for my boss's wife are *nothing* compared to the feelings I have for you. If someone ever hurt you, I might not stop at beating them to a bloody pulp. I might have to put them in the hospital...or worse. I'd fight to my last gasp defending you, angel." Eli cupped her cheek and then trailed a hand down her back.

"I can't begin to tell you how much it pleases me to know you're my defender," she murmured, reaching for him. He leaned down and let her wrap her arms around his neck as he wrapped his around her waist, hugging her. He kissed her lips again, and they were right back in their romantic moment from before the fight.

"Uh-oh, watch out, baby, here come the Bubblehead Twins," he chortled, grateful to Grace for the heads-up.

"The what?" She looked around his biceps. "Oh, them!" She chuckled. "Are you sure you don't want to try two women at the same time?" She snickered. "Especially a *sure* thing like them?"

He picked her up and gently sat her in her tall chair. "You're *all* the woman I'll ever want. You have more beauty and sex appeal in your little pinkie finger than they do in their entire silicone-implanted bodies."

She laughed out loud, then said, "You won't let them get me wet, will you?" She waited for his response to her double meaning. He did and grinned devilishly then spoke softly so Mike and Rogelio couldn't hear his words.

"Oh, you're going to get wet, all right, but it will be under my touch and my tongue, not from some barfly's drink. Watch me work." He winked.

By this point, the women were almost upon them, one armed with a full drink, the other carrying a folded bar napkin that no doubt had their phone numbers written on it. Rachel settled back in her chair and crossed her legs, watching the drama play out. Eli moved forward, and he smoothly caught the first blonde by the wrists as she "tripped," miraculously never spilling a drop of her drink on Rachel.

"Whoa! Careful there, ma'am. Are you all right? You almost took a tumble, didn't you? It would have been terrible if you'd spilled your drink all over my girlfriend's lap. I think there's been enough drama for one evening, don't you?" he asked, looking seriously into her embarrassed face. She smiled uneasily and apologized then backed away from him.

Not to be deterred so easily, her friend tucked the napkin in the front pocket of his leathers, perilously close to the semi-erect shaft Rachel had inspired with her earlier words. He gently extricated her hand, which held the napkin.

He took the napkin from the woman and opened it up and looked closely at it. "What's this? Sorry, I have a girlfriend, and I don't think she'd appreciate you offering me your phone numbers. I'm a *one woman* kind of man, ladies." Eli emphasized the last part clearly but softly. He slipped the napkin back into her palm and gently closed her fingers over it. "Would you excuse me?" he asked kindly.

"Sure. Sorry," she said grudgingly before walking away with her friend, a little red-faced but with most of her dignity still intact.

Eli returned to Rachel, grinning. She looked up at him with amusement, a very sexy smile on her sweet lips.

"Disaster averted. You're *good,* Mr. Wolf. I was a little worried when she slipped her fingers in your pocket, though. I have *big* plans for *that* and have a *huge* problem with another woman putting her fingers where I plan to put my *lips* later," she murmured, subtly holding her index fingers farther and farther apart with each emphasized word, snickering when he groaned. "Despite all the drama, tonight has been wonderful and not nearly as difficult as I thought. You make dealing with all these persistent women almost fun."

"I'm glad it's not as difficult and that it's worth it to you to go through all this trouble to be with me, Rachel."

"Totally worth it. I admit I hate it when they put their hands on you, but I've always felt that way."

"You have?" he asked incredulously, surprised that she'd paid that much attention to his social challenges.

"Yeah," she said sheepishly. "I remember watching you get groped, thinking it must not faze you that much because you were so cool in how you handled yourself. I didn't realize until tonight how much it bothered you when they felt free to touch you. I mostly focused on how it felt to watch them act that way."

"I wish it had been your hands that were put on me. I wouldn't have minded that at all."

"When they did that, did you go home smelling like their perfume?" she asked, and he liked that she spoke in the past tense.

"Sometimes. That's one of the reasons I didn't like it when they touched my hair. It's too close to my face, then I'd have smell them on me the rest of the night. But I love that you put your hands in my hair, run your fingers through it. It feels good when you do it. I'll also admit I like it when you do that in front of the others. They see that I let you do what I always stopped them from doing."

"Oh, baby. I love to hear that so much," she said enthusiastically to him as he sat beside her

"Hey, lovebirds, check out Brice Huvell on the dance floor. He got a little cutie to dance with him," Mike said, standing beside them, grinning.

"You know, I've never seen anyone dance with him before." Rachel smiled as she watched Brice scoot the cute little blonde around in a surprisingly efficient two-step.

"I think Brice's stock went up a little while ago," Eli said.

Mike chuckled and said, "Look, she's flirting with him. Oh, man, I hope he doesn't say—"

"*Don't say it*! We don't want to jinx the poor guy." Rachel giggled.

"Say what?" Eli asked.

Rachel leaned forward and gestured to him to come close. She cupped her hand to his ear and said, "His favorite pick-up line used to be, 'I don't normally beat around the bush,'" she snorted, "'I prefer to beat *in it*. Wanna go somewhere more quiet?'"

Eli sat up straight and looked at both of them. "No, really? Did it work for him?"

Rachel clapped her hand over her mouth to cover her laughter. "It didn't work on any woman I know! Thank goodness Ethan seems to have taken him under his wing."

While he watched the dance floor, Eli noticed Jack and Grace doing a slow, graceful two-step. Ethan and Adam stood off at the edge of the dance floor, watching them.

"Grace is so beautiful," Rachel said as they watched Grace's slow, languid movements, allowing Jack to lead her.

"She makes them very happy," Eli replied softly, wishing he could lead her out on the dance floor for another dance, but the club was busy, and he needed to stay focused on the job. "I'm going to make the rounds and check the restrooms. I'll be right back."

* * * *

Rachel wondered how many women would attach themselves and require removal before he made it back. She was proud that she could joke with herself about it. Up until tonight, she didn't think that was possible. It was just like Grace had said earlier. It was worth it to be with him, totally worth it.

Mike sidled up to her after Eli left the front. Rogelio was standing right beside him. Mike didn't say anything, just arched an eyebrow at her.

She grinned, her cheeks warming a little. "What? You're not surprised, are you? I've been running from him for two months. I finally stopped running," she said with a little shrug. She didn't begrudge him this conversation at all because he was like her older brother or something. As a matter of fact, she'd expected it the moment Eli left her side.

"I have one question. Is he treating you, well, with respect?" His fists were on his hips, looking like a big brother would.

"Of course he is, but you tell me, Mike. Has he done anything to disrespect me in your sight? It's you he needs to impress with how he treats me because he knows you'll tell my parents, who already know, by the way. I already have a key to the other side of the duplex, and I'm going to move in tomorrow."

"So you staying with him isn't a permanent thing?"

"For one more night. Tomorrow, I move in next door. You know me better than that, Mike. I'm not gonna live with him. He's made a good impression on Daddy, and I don't want to mess that up."

"You look happy, Rachel. He looks happy, too. He deserves a good woman like you," Mike said before he sat down in his chair. "You should go ask him to dance. He's due a break right about now," Mike added with a chuckle.

Eli had been intercepted by three Spandex-clad beauties, one of whom immediately attached herself to his arm and pressed her breasts against his biceps. They tried to pull him to the dance floor, and the body language of the other two suggested that they all wanted to dance with him. What was it with Eli and multiple women? Part of her wanted to laugh at their tenacity, and part of her bristled at the sight of another woman's fingers and body parts stroking his biceps.

He smiled and placed his hands on his hips and looked down at them. He gestured to other tables, filled with men ready to dance with them. The one clinging to his arm pouted, which Rachel thought was not a very pretty look for her. Eli detached her hand and pointed toward the front of the club, indicating that he was working. The girls looked her way, one of them nodded, and they released him to continue on his way, unimpeded, back to the front.

"What did you say to them that they gave up so easily? The ladies don't usually peel off that easily," Mike said, grinning at his expense as Eli returned to Rachel's side.

"I said the woman I love was waiting for me to return. I asked them how they would feel if they were in love with someone and had to watch other women putting their hands on him all night. They wanted to dance, and I told them I'm saving all my dances for Rachel. At least they were nice about it and backed off. Some of the women think I'm playing hard to get and figure that if they grope me, I might change my mind. Blech." Eli sniffed his arm. "Do I smell like perfume?"

Smiling, she sniffed him, giggling. "Not much, but if you'll take your break and dance with me, I'll do my best to erase it for you," she said as she looked over at Mike.

"Y'all go ahead. Things are slow up here, and you've got a break coming to you, anyway. You never take your breaks, so I think you've got a little extra time. Go dance with your woman." Mike grinned as he made a shooing motion with his hands toward the dance floor.

Eli helped Rachel from her chair. "Thanks, man. I owe you."

"Yeah," Mike called, "and I know how you can repay me, too." Eli grinned and nodded but said nothing more about it.

Grace was on the dance floor with Adam, enjoying another slow dance. Her head was tilted back as she looked up into his eyes, speaking softly with him. Rachel looked away from the intense love she saw radiating from Adam's eyes. Rachel's respect for the four of them grew as she realized the love and unselfish devotion that was necessary to balance their marriage. Grace laid her cheek against Adam's chest and wrapped her arms around his waist as he slowly danced her around the hardwood floor.

Eli turned and embraced Rachel on the crowded dance floor. He expertly guided her through the throng. She leaned against his massive body, her breasts pressed close to him. She was conscious of the warmth increasing inside her as her sensitive nipples rubbed against him. His gentle hand on her back pressing her close to him told her that he enjoyed the contact with those tight little points as well. She relaxed against him, allowing him lead her around the dance floor. She loved to be wrapped in his warmth and sighed happily at the thought of going home with him tonight.

"You sound happy," Eli murmured in a deep, husky voice that made her shiver with desire for him.

"I am," she replied softly, nodding against his chest. "Very happy not to be running anymore."

He cupped the back of her head, and she tilted back to look at him. His eyes were soft with adoration as he leaned down and kissed her so tenderly, so gently, she moaned in response to his light but intoxicating touch.

"I want you, Rachel. I need you. I wish tonight was not the last night you'll be staying with me." His gaze was intense, searching.

"I know, Eli, but I'll only be next door. You know I'll be there safe, right next to you." She knew the only thing that would satisfy him was her under his roof. He loved her, and that was a wonderful beginning. She knew she loved him, but she was used to having her own space, and she didn't want to jump into such a monumental decision on the spur of the moment.

"I would prefer you right next to me in my bed." He slipped his fingers through the hair at her nape. When he was with her like this, it was so tempting to say yes, but she remembered her parents and tried to keep their opinion of him in the forefront of her mind. This move was as much for his sake as it was for hers.

"Eli, you know I'll be over all the time. The same would go for you. My door would always be open to you. My parents' opinion of you is very important to me."

Changing the subject, Eli said, "Have you ever been on a motorcycle before?"

"Yes, I went once with Mike for a short ride. He rode like a grandma, and we never got over twenty miles per hour. It was very disappointing." She laughed, remembering him giving in to her begging and pleading. Rosa had finally talked him into it. As slow as he went, she should have saved her breath.

"Well, I would be worried for your safety, too. But I'd like to take you for a ride out to the lake on Sunday. By then you'll be all settled in next door. Would you like that?"

"I would, very much."

* * * *

Eli held her in his arms as they danced across the floor and tried to steady his breathing so she wouldn't know she affected him like he was a teenage boy. He wanted to kick himself for pushing her so hard about moving in permanently. He knew in his heart it was only a matter of time before she'd be ready to make a permanent change in status, but she needed this time, and he needed her to see he would honor her parents' wishes.

Holding her like this and spending this time with her was so sweet. He grinned, knowing what he owed Mike for the extra-long break. He looked over her head and noticed looks from some of the women and girls who had approached him tonight. Some looked bitter or disappointed, but he also noticed a few who smiled at him as he danced with Rachel, admiring them as a couple. Not all of them had been loose women. Some might have been genuinely attracted, and he hoped there was someone else here who would feel the same way about them that he felt about Rachel.

He ran his hands down her back, coming to rest on her waist. He nodded to Brice Huvell when he glided past him with another of the girls from the large table who had visited with Eli earlier in the evening. It was good to see the little dude finally score a few hits. The smile on the face of the girl he danced with was genuine.

Another in a series of slow love songs played. Eli looked up in the DJ's booth and saw Ethan watching the dance floor. It was then that Eli realized Ethan was dictating what songs were being played for Grace's benefit so that she could enjoy a few slow dances with Jack, Adam, and Ethan. The look in Ethan's eyes as he watched Grace move was tender and protective, giving her what she needed.

Eli felt totally outclassed by him, by the three of them, in the way they loved their woman. The way they raised the standard, though, gave him something to aspire to with Rachel. He wanted her to feel loved the way that Grace felt loved.

Chapter Ten

Eli noticed a man watching them from a corner table by the bar. At first, he thought he was mistaken, but as they moved in a slow circle, he watched from the corner of his eye. The man's eyes never left the two of them. Eli's senses sharpened as he continued to watch the man. He was very tall, though not as tall as Eli, and very lean, hardened, and tough.

Feeling as territorial as the wolf his surname brought to mind, Eli lifted his head from nuzzling Rachel's ear and kissing her cheek. He made direct, unmistakable eye contact with the tall stranger. He kept his body relaxed and never missed a step in the dance, but in the way he enveloped Rachel protectively with his own body, he sent a clear unmistakable message.

Mine.

The tall stranger gave a slow challenging grin to Eli from across the room, and Eli wondered what the fuck this was all about. Did Rachel know him? The man continued to stare at them, for all the world looking as though he simply relaxed with a beer and watched the crowd, when in reality, he was observing them.

"Eli? What's the matter?" He looked down into her concerned eyes. He thought he'd done a better job of hiding his reaction from her. "Is there trouble brewing?" She looked around her.

"No, everybody is fine. Someone I've never seen before has been staring at us for the last few minutes, watching the two of us. He's in the corner by Ethan's table, black T-shirt and leather jacket. Do you know him?" Eli asked as he slowly turned her so she could look over at the man.

"No, I've never seen him before. Which one of us do you think he's staring at?" she asked as she snuggled in closer to him. He couldn't stop his soft growl of gratification as she snuggled closer to him, seeking him.

"I think he's staring at you."

"Well, he can stare all he wants. I've only got eyes for you, Eli." She gazed up at him as she palmed his cheek. "Ignore him, and I will, too." She reached for him, and he leaned down to kiss her tenderly as the love song ended. "How much longer do we have?"

"I should get back soon. It's been at least thirty minutes we've been out here."

"Wow, it amazes me how fast time flies when I'm with you."

"Funny, I feel the same way about you. Do you need to go to the ladies' room? With that guy staring like that, I'd rather walk you over and wait for you before going back to the door."

"Yes, I do. Maybe you should mention it to Ethan. He'd want to know if something was suspicious."

Eli walked her to the restroom and turned to the task at hand, only to be surprised and a little dismayed. Grace and Jack stood at the man's table, talking with him as if they were friends. Grace even leaned in and gave him a friendly hug as she held Jack's hand. It appeared that all four were acquainted with this stranger. Eli made his way over, intent on speaking with Ethan, curious now to know who this man was who had issued such an obvious challenge to him. Better to take the bull by the horns, his father would say.

"Hey, Eli, I want you to meet a friend of ours," Ethan said, indicating the stranger. Eli walked up to him and put out his large hand to shake. "This is Ace Webster. He works in private security and investigation. He helped us out a few months ago when Grace's ex was harassing her. He's thinking about settling in the area and came in for a visit. Ace, this is Eli Wolf. He provides security for the club. The two of you have something in common."

Ace quirked an eyebrow and grinned crookedly as he shook Ethan's hand. "I'd say you're right, Ethan." Ace grinned as Eli caught his double meaning. "Good to meet you, Eli. It's always good to meet people in the same line of work."

"Good to meet you, Ace. See something you like earlier?" Eli asked straightforwardly but not with animosity.

"That's a beautiful woman you were dancing with. Is she spoken for or here on her own?" he asked, friendly but challenging. They were keeping it light for the sake of the mutual friends and employers.

"Rachel is my girlfriend and *definitely* spoken for," Eli said with a smile. The message again was unmistakable. Mine. Eli felt a tightening in his chest as he made eye contact with Ace and had to suppress the urge to snarl.

"Well, in that case, you're a lucky man, Eli. I had hoped to ask her to dance with me."

"I don't know, Ace," Ethan countered, evidently sensing the undercurrent between the two men. "Eli is very territorial about Rachel. As territorial as she is about him. There are plenty of other women here who'd take you up on that offer. Rachel's been beating them off Eli like pesky mosquitoes all night." Grace caught Eli's eye and smiled. She felt it, too.

"I'm going to go check my lipstick, honey. I'll be right back, okay?" Grace said, patting Ethan's chest lovingly then slipped away after Jack kissed her and released her hand. The men changed the subject and continued talking at the table.

* * * *

Grace slipped into the restroom, hoping it was empty, as Rachel exited one of the stalls. After a couple of women left the room, Grace dropped all pretense of fluffing her hair. "Eli is getting acquainted with your new admirer at our table."

"My *what*?" Rachel asked, surprised by how quickly things had moved. "What do you mean, acquainted?"

Earlier, when she'd looked up at the man sitting at the table, he'd made eye contact with her. Dressed all in black with sleek, short black hair, he had a bad-ass cool alpha vibe going on. He must have just gotten there because no women hovered near his table yet trying to get his attention. That thought had relieved her in a funny way. Maybe some of the floozies in the bar would be drawn to him and would give it a rest with Eli.

"Ace is a good friend of ours. He watched out for me when Owen kept pestering me back in June. He's here to testify in that drug trial, and he's thinking about leaving San Angelo and settling down here. He seems to have taken a fancy to you. I don't think Eli is very happy about it. It's interesting, actually. The shoe appears to be on the other foot now."

Rachel's eyes narrowed, not understanding. "What do you mean?"

"Eli is definitely showing *his* jealous nature. He's sending out all these territorial vibes and innuendos, trying to warn Ace off of you. It's very sweet to watch, seeing him struggle to be nice to our friend when he really wants to kick his ass for staring at you and wanting to dance with you."

"He said he wants to dance with me?" Rachel asked softly as another woman came in the restroom.

Grace nodded and pulled Rachel into the corner by the door. "Eli did not like that *at all*, but he didn't say anything. He doesn't want to offend Jack. Ethan was trying to smooth things over and told Ace that he didn't think that was a good idea but that there were lots of other women who'd love to dance with him here tonight. Isn't *that* the truth! But *then* Ethan also told him that you'd been beating the women off Eli like mosquitoes all evening, so he may not want to dance with any of them if they were after Eli first." Grace rolled her eyes as if to say, "Men."

"Well, I don't want to dance with anyone but Eli."

Grace shrugged like it was all very simple. "So just say you're here with Eli. Ace will understand, although that doesn't mean he won't try to ask you. It's probably a good thing we got our girly dances in early because you dancing with me to those songs while Ace is in here watching would be like a red flag to Eli's bull. Not good."

"So you're my informant?" Rachel asked, grinning. "Or are you in here trying to buy Ethan time to smooth things over between the two of them before I show up?"

Grace snickered, evidently amused by the whole situation. "Both! I'm watching out for my friends, plus stalling a little to give Eli and Ace a chance to get on friendlier terms before you make an appearance. Eli is probably watching for your return by now." She paused and became serious for a moment. "Remember, he's probably feeling pretty territorial right now. If you love him, follow his lead." She grasped the door handle and pulled on it.

Eli made his excuses and stepped away from the group when she appeared, and he met her outside the hallway. She looked up at him and allowed him to lead her away to the front of the club. Evidently, he was not feeling magnanimous enough to take her over and introduce her. He didn't say anything about the man, just helped her into her chair before sitting beside her. He was attentive as ever, though he seemed distracted. A few times she noticed him staring at the other end of the bar.

* * * *

Toward closing time, Eli noticed when Ace rose from the table across the bar and made his way to the front of the club, probably ready to call it an evening. Eli had known this moment would come and that Ace would not be the kind to miss an opportunity. Ace stopped in front of him and stuck out his hand to shake Eli's again, his eyes drifting to Rachel expectantly.

"Eli, it was a pleasure," Ace said with a grin. It was not lost on Eli that Ace left the statement open-ended, leaving no question as to which part of the evening had been a pleasure for Ace, no doubt observing his beautiful Rachel as well as antagonizing him in the process. Eli shook his hand, matching his grip but unwilling to embark on a pissing match in front of Rachel.

"Yes, it *has* been a pleasure." *All mine, you son of a bitch.* "Rachel, this is Ace Webster, a friend of the Warners', and Ethan and Adam. He works in security and investigation. Ace, this is my girlfriend, Rachel Lopez," Eli said politely, though it sounded as stiff as he felt.

"I was admiring you on the dance floor earlier, Miss Lopez," he said as he shook Rachel's hand gently. "You move beautifully with your partner. It's a pleasure to make your acquaintance. You're a lucky man, Eli." He released Rachel's hand and moved away toward the door.

Eli watched him as he stalked casually out the door. He looked over at Rachel, perturbed that Ace had made mention of watching her on the dance floor and had felt the need to hold her hand so long after shaking it.

Her hand was held out in front of her awkwardly, and when she turned it over, he could see the business card in her palm. It lay on her palm and she didn't even close her fingers over it, holding it out to him to take instead. Worry showed on her face, like she was afraid he'd be mad at her for accepting the card.

Gently taking Rachel's hand in his, Eli lifted her palm, took the card from it, placed a soft kiss where it had been, and then pulled her to him.

"I can't believe he did that, Eli. I didn't mean to take it from him. He slipped it into my hand," she said, her eyes searched his face. She seemed worried he was upset with her.

Eli slipped the card into his back pocket. "I know, baby. I can't blame him for trying, though. Eli tried to see the humor in their role reversal. Rachel had been shooing women away from him all evening. Turnabout was fair play, he supposed.

Additionally, she'd been dealing with it all evening from *multiple* sources, and he'd only had the one to deal with. Still, he knew they hadn't seen the last of Ace. "He's right. You are beautiful, and I can recall being hypnotized by the way you move a time or two." He grinned at her dark blush. "But that doesn't mean I take kindly to him slipping you his card right under my nose."

Her hands slid slowly up his torso, distracting him with her soft touch. "Eli, you do know I'm not a bit interested in him, right?"

"Yes, I figured you weren't, but it's good to know for sure. I guess we each know how the other feels receiving unwanted attention tonight."

"Yes. Yours is the only attention I want. This has been an interesting evening."

"Yeah, it has. I hope you weren't too bored, sitting up here with me."

"Bored? No." She chuckled. "Bored would have been me sitting at the bar, waiting for you to come over during breaks. I spent the whole evening with you, and we even got to dance quite a bit. It was not a boring evening. Plus, I have later on, after we get home, to look forward to," she reminded him softly as she looked up into his eyes.

He looked down at her and trailed his fingers over her cheekbone. "I know. I'm hard just thinking of it."

"Remember, you have company, so we're going to have to be very, very quiet."

"That's fine, because I was planning on making slow, sweet love to you, anyway. I was rough today, and I want to take it easy with you tonight."

In a subtly aroused reaction to his words, her eyelids fluttered at his words, and she licked her lips and he wondered if she was imagining what Eli had just described. His hardening cock eagerly jumped to attention.

Glancing up at him, Rachel smiled. "You didn't hurt me, Eli. But slow and sweet sounds heavenly." She rested her head against his chest, sighing when his hand slid over her back. "How much longer?"

"The club closes in fifteen minutes. One of us usually stays to make sure all the waitresses get to their cars and safely on their way, but it's Rogelio's turn to do that, so I'll be good to go in about thirty minutes. Think you can hang on that long?" he asked, looking into her blue eyes that were now soft with desire. Slowly, a playful, yet seductive, smile came to her lips, and she chuckled.

"I don't know, Eli," she murmured suggestively. "That's a *long* time, it's *very hard* for me to wait, but if I get to *come* home with you, I think I can *take it*." She giggled delightedly when he groaned and rolled his eyes.

"Bad girl." He nibbled on her ear and hugged her when she squealed.

"Hey, are you two going to be like this every night from now on? 'Cause, it's downright nauseating," Mike muttered from his chair.

Chapter Eleven

When they arrived home that night, Rachel stepped inside the front door after Eli opened it for her. She noticed that Kelly and Matthew were snuggled sweetly together on the couch. Matthew was dressed in a fuzzy yellow sleeper, curled up in the crook of his mama's arm. Kelly was curled inward on the couch, forming a nice little cocoon for the baby to sleep in. Both were out cold. Only a dim light shone from one of the lamps, left on by Kelly, undoubtedly, so they could find their way through the house. Eli turned the lamp off, and they made their way back into the bedroom on silent feet.

"Do you want a warm shower?" he asked.

"That sounds nice. But won't it disturb Kelly?" She wanted to get the smell of cigarette smoke off her skin and her hair before she made love with him. A slow burn began inside her pussy.

"No, she's a heavy sleeper, and she says Matthew is, too. I don't think we'd disturb her as long as we're not too noisy." He stood before her, his hands gliding down her arms.

"We? You want to take a shower together?" The thought sent a delighted thrill straight through her.

"Don't you?" He slid his arms around her, and his hands glided over her derriere, squeezing firmly. She loved the feel of his big hands sliding over her body like that.

"Yes."

After he grabbed his robe from his closet, they slipped into the bathroom and undressed while the water heated up. She brushed her long hair out while she watched him remove and fold his leathers, placing them on the long counter then adding his white T-shirt and knit boxers to the pile. She boldly gazed at his hard-muscled body from head to toe, desire smoldering within her. He stepped into the shower, affording her a glimpse of his sculpted ass, and held out his hand for her so she wouldn't slip as she followed him in. He doused himself under the spray and moved aside so she could do the same while he reached for the bottle of shampoo.

She enjoyed his heated gaze even more than the hot water sluicing down her body. The water collected and ran in rivulets over and between her breasts. She reached up to squeeze the hot water through her hair, which caused her breasts to lift up to him in a playful invitation. She gasped softly when she felt his warm mouth close over one of her nipples. His tongue played with the tight peak, drawing on it before releasing it with a soft pop from his lips and moving to the other one and giving it similar teasing attention. He released it only because he needed to rinse the shampoo from his hair and to allow her to finish bathing. She lathered her hair and rinsed then took his washcloth and poured bodywash on it.

After they had both lathered and scrubbed, Eli poured more bodywash in his hand and murmured, "I think you may have missed a spot, Rachel."

"Where?" she asked softly, and she lifted her arms helpfully, clasping her hands in her hair. "I don't see it." She looked at his hands as he rubbed them together, getting them slippery with the soapy gel. "Maybe you could help me?"

* * * *

Eli's cock twitched hungrily as he smoothed his wet hands over the upper swells of her breasts, evoking a soft moan from her at his questing touch. He cupped her full, round breasts tenderly, smoothing his hands down her ribs to her abdomen, delighting in her panting gasps, before sweeping over the gentle swell of her hips to her ass and her thighs. He kissed the pulse in her neck and laved her silky skin with his tongue and could feel how quickly her heart was beating. She took bodywash in her own hands and paid him similar attention before he pressed her body to the cool tile wall with his own. The hot water sprayed down on them, rinsing the soap away as they kissed under the shower head.

He wanted to lift her to him and lower her onto his cock right now, but he wanted a slower buildup to their lovemaking and didn't want to take a chance on waking the sleeping baby. After the soap was all gone, he shut off the water and reached for a towel to wrap her in. He squeezed the water from her hair with a towel then dried himself off. As she combed her hair and used the blow dryer, he noticed a blush on her cheeks as his cock grew harder and thicker. She licked her lips, and his cock bobbed enthusiastically at the thought of her going down on him.

Eli wrapped a towel around his waist and held his robe out for her as she hung the towel up to dry. She slipped her arms into the robe and closed the front as he opened the bathroom door. He switched off the light and then turned to her in the dark. He lifted her from her feet and gently carried her into his bedroom, softly closing the door behind them. She snuggled to him as he stood there by the bed with her, enjoying the sensation of her cuddled in his arms.

"I love you." He climbed onto the bed with her in his arms. Her warm hand swept along his cheek, and her fingers slipped slowly into his hair. Eli recalled Jack telling him earlier that he knew a good jeweler, and he squeezed Rachel to him gently. He'd never be able to sleep in this cold room alone without thinking of her. He wasn't sure why he hadn't noticed how minimalist it was before now. Maybe it was because his life was so full now that she was a part of it. He noticed the chilliness because her warmth was in his life now.

"Eli, I love you. I–I adore you," she said, her voice husky with the depth of her feelings, sounding like she was holding back tears.

He'd known how he felt about her for weeks, and it was dawning on her, as well, how right for each other they were. He could count on the fact that Rachel would be practical and knew that was the reason for her moving next door. It was the reason why she wouldn't consider moving in with him, even though she knew she was in love with him. She needed a little more time, and he'd gladly give her whatever she wanted. He'd use that time wisely and work on increasing that good impression he'd made on her folks. Being on their good side could only help his cause. He'd get that phone number from Jack tomorrow. A good craftsman would need time, too.

Kneeling in the center of the bed, he held her, unwilling to let her go even for a moment. She tilted her head up to him, and he kissed her sweetly, reverently. He nuzzled along her throat and kissed and licked her, sucking on her earlobe. Wanting his hands free to roam over her warm silky body, he laid her down on his pillow, fanning her long mahogany locks across it. He kissed her blushing cheeks as his own hair fanned out around them, blocking out the cold white sterility of his bedroom. He pulled back the covers, allowing her to shift onto the sheet with a little help. She removed his robe as he did likewise with his towel and tossed it on a chair and climbed under the covers with her. He settled his big body over her warm, curvaceous form.

She smiled up at him, and her eyes fluttered closed with a contented-sounding sigh. He pressed his body to her, smiling tenderly at her as she looked up at him so trustingly. "I love being like this with you. I feel safe and protected." She paused, and her eyes grew shiny with unshed tears. "Eli? What if I hadn't given in to your persistence? What if I'd convinced you that I was too jealous and not worth the trouble? What if we missed this, here, right now? How would I know to regret it every day of my life? This moment with you is everything to me now that I know. I could have missed it if I'd kept running."

"No regrets, right? My dad says, 'Live life with no regrets, nothing left undone or unsaid, because you never know how long you have.'" He caught a tear with his thumb as it slipped across her temple.

"Thank you for understanding. I'm sorry I'm so emotional tonight."

"You're in your heart, which is a good place to be. I feel the same way, honey," he murmured, his voice shaking a little.

He slid his lips in a slow, brushing trail down her quivering torso. She moaned softly as he lifted her hips gently to him and pressed his lips to her soft abdomen, just inches above her mound. He lifted one of her thighs and placed a gentle kiss on her silky inner thigh at her knee before working his way down to her pussy. He pressed his lips at the dip between her inner thigh and her outer labia, and his black hair streamed across her pussy. She moaned softly in frustration as he skipped over the area where she evidently wanted his mouth most and worked his way once again from the other inner knee and slowly down her thigh.

"You torture me, Eli. Please, I need your mouth on me. I need you so much it hurts," she murmured in a shaky, husky voice filled with need.

He lifted her thigh so he could look into her eyes as he smiled down at her, slowly placing one kiss after another in a damp, slow trail that led straight to her pussy. She whimpered as he came closer and closer, flicking with his tongue so she'd know what else he would use on her. Her breaths came in rasping pants, her chest rising and falling rapidly. He caressed her abdomen, soothing her with gentle hands.

His hair slid over her abdomen, and he took a thick lock of it and gently trailed it over her wet, open pussy lips. She tilted her head back on her pillow, a whimper coming from her as he slid it up, ever so softly, over her engorged clitoris, tickling her mound with the very ends before drawing the lock over her lips once again. He could tell she was actively trying to hold her orgasm off, trying to wait for him, swallowing convulsively, her breathing now staccato panting.

Judging by her sounds, she needed his touch desperately, and as he reached the base of her thigh, his tongue dragged over her wet pussy lips. She was coated with her sweet juices, so ready to receive him and so hot for him. She tried to keep her noises quiet, moaning softly and sighing his name over and over again. He kissed her lips and slid his tongue into her opening again and flicked up gently and slowly to her clit, feeling it the instant her tension broke like a bowstring pulled too tight and finally released.

She sobbed as he laved her swollen clit then slid into her entrance again and tasted the sweet cream that flowed from her powerful orgasm, licking each drop from her lips. Eli slid his hand up her outer thighs and over her hips and rib cage, soothing her as he was overcome by a feeling of utter masculine possessiveness toward her. He felt pride in his ability to give her such pleasure and loved to see her blushing and moaning beneath him in the absolute height of ecstasy.

Her sobs quieted to soft moans, and he felt dazed by her response to him. He looked into her dark blue eyes, and a profound peace filled him. "My angel." He closed his eyes, so overwhelmed was he by his emotions. He kissed her inner thigh before settling himself in the cradle her body formed for him, giving ease to him, innocent to the deep way she affected him.

Maybe tomorrow at the lake he could explain to her why he reacted to her this way, the peace she brought to him. Maybe he could explain the painful place inside him that she alone had been capable of healing with her love, her smiles, and her acceptance of him. Right now, all he could focus on was being inside her and feeling her silken warmth caress his hardened shaft. He wanted to fill her and claim her as his one true love. His angel.

"Would you open yourself for me?" Eli knelt over her, gazing ravenously on her gorgeous curves. Smiling radiantly, Rachel nodded then stretched under him, arching her back, spreading her hair out on the pillow. Gazing at him, she lifted her feet one at a time, pointing her toes and sliding each calf slowly, sinuously in blatant invitation over his forearms, which would allow him access to whatever part of her he wanted to explore. It was a clear message of how vulnerable she was making herself for him.

She curled her forearms and wrists on either side of her head and allowed her thighs to fall completely open to his stare. The blood rushed to his cock, and he hardened further at the sight of her engorged lips and the fresh honey that moistened her entrance.

He allowed the anticipation and tension to build as he held her, drinking this beautiful sight in. She moaned in need, wanting that first touch as much as he did. He gazed at her open pussy and licked his lips, noting the fresh arrival of honey in her entrance as her body responded to him, begging for him to fill her. His thickened cock twitched in eagerness to get inside her. He tortured them both with anticipation.

Remembering the need for lubricant, he opened the bottle and applied some to her pussy lips. He wanted to make it as easy for her to receive his cock as possible. He smoothed more over his cock, knelt in front of her. She slid her feet and calves around his hips, and he planted her feet flat directly behind him. She allowed him to position her to his liking and gasped as he reached for her. He lifted her with his hands under her back, holding her upright in his arms, her feet braced behind him, so that she could watch for herself as his cock slid into position at her entrance.

Rachel held on to his arms as he lifted her slightly to gain the perfect angle and then allowed her to control the speed at which she slid onto his long, thick shaft. He helped her take it slow, finding tremendous satisfaction in the ecstasy that flooded her face at the sight of his stiff cock disappearing inside her hot, slippery cunt.

Looking up at him with almost childlike joy on her face, Rachel closed her expressive blue eyes briefly. She pushed against the mattress with her feet, rose off his cock, and moaned as she slid back down. He could see her juices smeared over her inner lips as they stretched around his thick girth. He rumbled deep in his chest as she reached between them to rub her clitoris and slid again on his hot, hard shaft.

"I love watching you touch yourself, angel. Do you like being able to watch my cock slide into you?" He groaned at the sensation of his cock sliding into her sweet tight cunt.

"I've never seen anything as beautiful as this, you gliding into me so hot and big. It still amazes me that your huge cock will fit. I love the way it fits. You're so strong." Her eyelids slid shut for a few moments, and her head fell back as she rode his cock with increasing fervor.

"I want to hear you when you come again. Say my name when you come for me," he whispered as her fingers strayed to her clit again. He held her securely in the cradle of his arms and pumped into her in an achingly slow rhythm that had them both groaning and panting for air. Eli took his time, dragging his cock almost all the way out of her pussy before sliding in to the hilt. She began to softly beg him to go faster, harder, but he stuck to this slow rhythm. He was in no hurry this time and planned to give her what he promised—a slow sweet release.

"You feel so good. It feels like you're getting even bigger and harder."

"It's because you feel so good. You make me so hard and hot. Don't hold back. Come for me." He held her tightly as he began to pump into her a little harder, giving her every inch on each pass. She arched her back and whimpered his name.

"Eli, oh, Eli, I'm coming, baby. Oh, baby, Eli! Eli!" She moaned as she pumped over his cock, his name slipping from her lips over and over. She came to rest with his cock fully seated in her. He groaned as the last of her rippling orgasm pulsed around his cock, and she raised her head to look in his eyes. She grasped his shoulders, pulling herself upright into his trembling arms. Clinging to his neck, she began to softly gyrate her hips over his cock. She gradually quickened the pace and rode him for all she was worth. He grasped her hips in his large hands and helped her ride his long shaft in smooth, sweet abandon.

"Damn, woman, you feel so good, so hot and wild. Spread your legs wide. I'm going to change positions." She opened her legs wide for him, and he laid her on her back and pushed her legs up to her chest, slowing the pace but riding her deep, stroking her G-spot as she struggled valiantly to remain quiet. He stroked her to another hot, gushing orgasm, keeping control of his own release, and pulled out. She had a look of momentary shock as he grinned lustily down at her. "Hands and knees, woman."

She grinned saucily at him and eagerly complied. He leaned over her as he reached between her legs and fingered her clit. "You've never been taken by a man this way, have you?" His other hand trailed around to her breast, rubbing the nipple between his fingers, dragging on it. At the negative shake of her head, he turned her chin to face him, and he kissed her, his approach gentled, no longer as rough. "I'm glad I'll be the first."

She whimpered, the anticipation evident in her shaky voice. He rose up behind her, spreading her legs, smoothing his hands up and down them as he did. Her juices dripped in translucent droplets down her thighs as he tilted her hips so her pussy was completely bared to his gaze. He gently pressed her lower back so that she arched toward him.

"Damn, you are beautiful. Your pussy is wet and swollen. Do you want to feel my cock inside you, taking you from behind like this?"

"Oh, baby, more than you can know."

"I love the sight of you so ready, needing my cock so much," he murmured as he slid a finger slowly into her entrance. "Mmm, I can feel you quivering around my finger. Are you close, baby? Do you need to come?"

"Yes, Eli, I want to feel you inside me. I want you to fill me. Give me your cum," she whimpered and gasped when the head of his cock pressed into her pussy. He swept his finger into her juices and swirled it around her asshole, and she gulped, stiffening a little.

"Don't worry, baby. I wouldn't hurt you for the world. Just relax for me, okay?" He rubbed her juices around her ass with his thumb, pressing inward. She arched her back and tightened the muscles in her pussy around the head of his cock, causing him to hiss again at the tightness.

"So you like that, I guess?" At her nod, he slid his cock into her a little more, groaning at the different sensation from this angle and from feeling the tightness of the ring of muscle at her ass. She whimpered and moaned under him and tried to take more of him. "You're so tight, baby. He could tell by her sounds that she was close and not content to take it from him slow, but that's how he was going to give it to her.

Her soft whimpers increased as he slid a little more of his thick cock into her, her hips reflexively grinding on him, making him groan as well. He pressed the pad of his thumb more firmly against her asshole feeling the muscles there begin to give way as she gasped softly. He'd be willing to bet she wanted to scream right now.

Grinning devilishly, he slid the rest of his cock slowly into her hot, tight cunt, and his thumb pressed gently until, with a shuddering whimper from her, the tight muscles in her asshole gave under the pressure, and his thumb entered her ass. Her head flew up, her hair sailing around her, and she was utterly silent. Her body told a different story, though, as she quivered and shook. Her body flushed all over with heat, and he felt a fresh gush of honey from her pussy. He could no longer keep himself from stroking into her sweet, slick heat, and she moved with him. He reached around with his other hand and heard her muffled cry as he stroked her swollen clit.

"I want to fill you with my cum, baby. See it dripping from you when I'm done. Do you like the way my finger feels in your ass?"

Her whole body vibrated with tension in his hands.

"Oh, Eli, yes!" Her soft voice shook, and he knew she'd come soon. "You're close. I can feel those little spasms on my cock as I pump into you. Come for me, baby. I want you to feel good. Let me give it to you." He continued to stroke slowly as she begged him to take her harder and faster. He continued the same rhythm but also began to stroke his thumb into her ass until he was up to the top knuckle, pumping in and out in the same rhythm in both openings.

The tension building in her body must have been unbearable, and he murmured, "Let go for me, angel," plunged into her hard, and gave her several deep, fast thrusts. She moaned blissfully, her pussy was tight as a vise on his cock as she came. His release gathered momentum until it felt like his whole body might explode, then he did. Eli had no idea how much noise he made as he came hard, his cum pulsing into her in long hot streams. The relief after so much tension was overwhelming and sent chills up and down his spine.

She cried out softly and her arms collapsed beneath her. The only thing holding her up was his hand clasping her hip tightly to him. He leaned over her, resting his forehead between her shoulder blades.

He withdrew his finger from her and wrapped his arms gently around her hips, listening as she tried to catch her breath. He breathed in her clean, womanly smell and rubbed his cheek and forehead in the damp sheen of sweat that had formed on her back. On impulse, he licked her and smiled at her shuddering gasp and the taste of her sweet saltiness on his tongue. There wasn't a place on her that didn't taste good.

"Are you all right?" He groaned with her as he slowly withdrew from her silken, warm cunt, once again aware again of the chill in the room. As his softening cock withdrew from her, he experienced a moment of simple, primal satisfaction as his cock left her pussy dripping with his cum. His seed, mixed with her cream, trickled from her opening and ran down her thigh, and he smiled at her satisfied, feminine sigh. He glanced up and caught her watching him over her shoulder. She seemed to enjoy his close scrutiny of this beautiful part of her. She truly did have the prettiest pussy he'd ever seen.

He helped her roll over on her side and covered her up. "I'll be right back, angel." He went to the bathroom and soaked a washcloth in warm water and retrieved a towel. After washing up, he returned and, despite her protests that she could do it, he cleansed her of the sticky residue from the lubricant. He returned to her warm, sleepy form curled up in his bed and slid between the sheets, pulling her back to his chest.

"Are you all right?" She nodded as she yawned, snuggling against him. He'd fucked her harder than he'd intended, unable to hold back at the last.

"You didn't hurt me, Eli. You're always very careful with me," she said sleepily before giggling softly. "Even when you're fucking me good and hard like I asked, you're still my loving, gentle giant." She yawned again.

"I love you, Rachel. You own my heart." He squeezed her warm, languid body to his.

"I promise to take good care of it." She stroked his forearm then clasped her fingers in his before falling deeply asleep.

Later, they both were awakened by the brief sound of his infant nephew crying. With Rachel curled up against his chest, Eli smiled at the sound of Kelly cooing to Matthew. Her dulcet words calmed him while she must have been changing his wet diaper. Matthew's fussing abruptly ceased, and Eli grinned, thinking that he must have gotten what he was squalling for. Rachel shook with soft laughter against his chest.

"A nice nipple in the mouth can solve a world of problems, regardless of the man's age I guess," Eli said, chuckling.

"I'll bear that in mind, big man." She snuggled closer. "Matthew is a precious baby and Kelly is very good with him. She must miss her husband something fierce right now."

"He's a good man. He counts himself lucky he has her in his life. The woman is a saint. They're both grateful he was here for Matthew's birth because they knew Chris was leaving soon. They just didn't have a date. Every day he spent with them was priceless." He cuddled her closer, trying to imagine himself in the same shoes as his brother-in-law.

He thought of Rachel, large with his child, and the mental image stole his breath away. He could see her as she held an infant with dark hair in her arms, and it made his chest swell with a myriad of emotions, pride and love being predominant. His hand strayed to her smooth abdomen, and she slid her hand over his. He kissed her shoulder softly. "I would be the happiest man in the world, Rachel."

She turned to him, and he could tell there were tears in her eyes as she looked up at him.

Chapter Twelve

Rachel carried Matthew through Stigall's Department store as she and Kelly looked for linens and felt her cheeks flush a little at the memory of Eli's soft heartfelt words during the night. She'd been so overwhelmed she'd been unable to speak for fear of bawling like a baby. Eli evidently understood and had comforted her until she fell asleep.

Rachel could picture herself pregnant with Eli's baby, his gentle hands resting on her swollen belly as the baby kicked and squirmed within her. She could also picture Eli making love to her with the intent of making a baby. She smiled at the thought of his intensity, momentarily distracted from what Kelly was telling her as more telltale warmth spread over her cheeks.

"What? I'm sorry, Kelly. I didn't hear that last part you said," she confessed as they walked through the department store. Rachel had invited Kelly and Matthew to go shopping with her for kitchen items, which she held no hope of finding salvageable because the kitchen had been in the front part of the apartment which had suffered the most damage. She also planned to get fresh linens for her bedroom and bathroom.

Kelly's eyes twinkled merrily as she stared at Rachel. "Wow, girl! You have it *bad* for my brother, don't you? He put that blush on your cheeks just thinking about him?" Kelly laughed as Rachel's cheeks flamed even hotter. Rachel giggled and put her hand to her cheek as she cuddled Matthew against her chest.

"Maybe."

"He's pretty wonderful, isn't he?" Kelly asked as she reached for Matthew so that Rachel could look for a set of sheets and a comforter in the bedding department.

"He really is."

"You're in love. I give it two months, and you'll be married," Kelly predicted smugly.

"Think so?"

"I *know* so. It's in Eli's eyes. He adores you, and rightfully so. It's good to see him so happy, not lonely anymore. He's always been too solitary."

"I love him, too."

"I can tell. Are you gonna say yes if he asks you to marry him?" Kelly looked at her expectantly. Her little pixie face was bright with hope, and she looked like she was about to start bouncing on the balls of her feet.

Teasing her, Rachel asked, "How is it that Eli is like a giant and you are positively elfin? Huh? I see the resemblance in your eyes and the color of your hair, but the similarity stops there." Rachel laughed at Kelly's disappointed pout.

"Eli got his height from our dad, but our dad is blond and blue-eyed, very Scandinavian roots there. I got my stature and build from my mom, and we got her eyes, too. Can you imagine," Kelly snickered, "what it must have been like trying to get it on? Like *climbing a tree*! *What*? Am I wrong?" Kelly laughed, watching Rachel break out in a fit of giggles.

"I know two gals you have to meet while you're here, Kelly. You would fit in so well at our get-togethers. Do you like to dance?"

"I love to dance, just not much opportunity lately." Kelly smiled and pointed at the baby.

"I have two good friends who are also sisters. Grace Warner and Charity Conners. Eli is friends with Charity and her husband, Justin."

Kelly's eyes sparkled. "I remember them from before we got stationed in Abilene! Charity is a *nut*. I absolutely love her." Rachel smiled at Kelly and thought there were probably very few people whom she didn't love. "My husband and Justin grew up together and were friends with Eli. Eli introduced me to Christopher. They all used to ride together all the time. So has he taken you for a ride on his Harley yet?"

"Well, we've only been together a couple of days, if you count today and yesterday," Rachel answered.

Kelly looked genuinely horrified. "You mean I horned in on your first night together?"

"Well, technically no, because we got to his duplex during the night on Thursday night, but it's all right. We've known each other for a few months, and he's been asking me out since the moment we met."

Rachel told her the whole story while she picked out a set of ivory-colored sheets in a luxurious Egyptian cotton and found a pretty wedding ring patchwork quilt. She wasn't sure why she picked that particular quilt pattern over the others and didn't want to analyze herself too much. She picked out some towels with help from Kelly, who had been surprisingly mute through the whole wedding ring quilt selection process but had looked like she was dying to say something. As Rachel picked out a stack of dark blue bath towels, she couldn't keep quiet any longer.

"So, are you gonna say yes?" Kelly asked expectantly.

"To what?" Rachel asked, nervous at this line of questioning. She didn't want to sound desperate.

"When he pops the question, silly!" *When*, she had said. Not *if*, but *when*.

"Kelly, we've only been a couple for a couple of days."

"Yeah, but you've been in love since you set eyes on each other two months ago!"

"Nuh-uh!"

"Uh-huh! He's going to ask you, and I bet you're married by Christmas. *Ooooh!* A Christmas wedding, how romantic! Oh, Rachel, can I help you pick out your dress?" Now Kelly *was* dancing on the balls of her feet. Matthew squeaked in her arms and drifted back off to sleep.

"Oh, so now you're planning my wedding?"

"Ooooh! *Can I?* I'm excellent at planning weddings and parties! You should totally let me do that. You would love it! So? Are you gonna say yes?" She settled down long enough to ask again.

Rachel looked at her and smiled, finding Kelly's enthusiasm contagious. What would she say if he asked her to marry him? Oh, hell yeah. She'd say yes.

"I would say yes, Kelly, but I need a little time, and he told me we would take it slow. I don't know about your Christmas wedding scenario. I mean, he hasn't even hinted at that. I can't believe I'm talking to you about it. We only just got together." Rachel felt like she was jinxing herself, putting the cart before the horse.

"But you do love him?"

"I adore him, Kelly. If I had any idea how good it was going to be, I wouldn't have said no to him for as long as I did. All I could see was all the women hanging off of him every night. I didn't think I could deal with that."

Kelly laughed. "He's a total *ho* magnet, isn't he?"

"Kelly! He's your brother. He can't help it."

"Yeah, he can't help it he's yummi-licious."

"You *do* know Charity Conners! Did you say your brother is *yummy*?"

"What? I'm not blind! He's got that whole badass biker dude-slash-gentle giant thing workin' hard for him. Worked on you, didn't it?"

"Only totally, bad girl. Only I find him to be more of a cross between an Indian warrior and a Viking." Rachel chortled and looked around them to see if anyone was listening to their conversation. Kelly gave her a salacious thumbs-up and then got a startled expression on her face.

"*Wait a minute*! You're friends with Grace! Are you the one who saved her ass? You are, aren't you! Oh, I have so got to meet that Hot Mama. Three freakin' husbands. She must be a *dynamo*!"

"Shhh! You maniac! Sure, I'll introduce you, but you gotta ixnay on the ee-thray usbands-hay! Grace shops here, honey. She used to work here, too."

"*Oops*, sorry, big mouth here." Kelly patted Matthew's back gently. "I've gotta meet her!" she said more softly.

"Help me pick out a shower curtain and rings. I'm anxious to get back home and see how the guys did at the apartment. That was thoughtful of him to not want me to go over there. Facing all my burned up stuff would not be near as much fun as shopping with you."

Originally, she had intended to go, but Eli had talked her out of returning with them to the burned-out apartment. The fire chief had said that while they were welcome to come and salvage they should not hold out much hope of finding much more than ash and charred remnants of her belongings. They would bring whatever they could to her, be it a little or a lot. Rachel was thankful she'd invested in the renter's insurance policy because everything was covered, and her claim was already being processed.

Kelly asked, "Did he say if they recovered much?"

It sounded to Rachel like they'd made some progress, maybe even found a few things that weren't ruined that she could still use, but they didn't give her any specifics.

"No, just that it looks even worse over there in the daylight. I'm not holding out much hope, but it would be nice if a few things were salvageable. Which one do you think I should pick?" Rachel asked, gesturing to the shower curtain samples.

"Well, you picked blue towels, and your rugs are blue. Not going very girlie here, are we?"

"Blue is my favorite color, but I wanted things that Eli would feel comfortable using if he came over."

"Okay, but go more girlie on the shower curtain. Stuff like that doesn't bother him near as much as you might think. You're going to need a king-sized comforter on your bed. With Eli under the covers, it will be too small, and you'll freeze."

Rachel snickered. "Trust me. I don't worry about freezing in bed with Eli."

"Like a sick kitten to a hot brick, huh?" Kelly said suggestively. "Still, you should get the king size. You can use it on his bed after you get married. Lemme have it. I'll be right back. Don't get the *paisley* shower curtain, get the girlie white *lace*, and make sure and get the clear liner and a window curtain to match for the bathroom window. Be right back."

Rachel smiled, watching Kelly as she scampered away. Talk about dynamos. She picked the white lace shower curtain and got the clear liner and plain white hooks. Kelly came back with another wedding ring quilt in a king size, but with brighter colors and fewer muted shades.

"Is this one all right? The colors are a little different but very pretty. The ivory background will match your sheets. You done?"

"Yes, that's fine. I think I like it even better than the one I picked out. You've got a good eye, Kelly. I like your style."

Kelly brightened up, not missing the opportunity to self-promote. "See? You should let me plan your wedding. You would be so happy!"

They arrived home as the men were unloading Eli's pickup into the entrance of the garage, setting everything inside for when she settled down enough to go through it all. Mike and Rogelio came over, grinning, to help her carry in all the shopping bags. She carried the first bags she'd picked up to the porch then turned to look up at Eli standing in the truck bed. He looked down at her from his tremendous height, his thick, muscular arms crossed over his broad, powerful chest.

Rachel asked, "What are you up to, Eli?"

With a big grin spread across his face, Eli jumped out of the truck bed, landing beside her. Feeling instantly enveloped in his massive presence, she looked up at him, smiling into his twinkling eyes.

He reached over the bed and said, "I found something of yours." Then he yanked a dirty blanket off her cedar hope chest.

She let out a loud yelp and jumped into his arms. One leap and she was clinging to his neck, holding on tight. He laughed and put his arms around her hips as she wrapped her legs around his waist. She kissed him, thanked him, and cried a little because she was so relieved it was okay. Finally, she released him, and he set her back on the ground and helped her into the bed of the truck.

"It's got some pretty bad burn marks on the side nearest your bedroom door, but I think a refinisher could probably remove or repair that damage, and it would be good as new. It's very well made, and the lid has a nice tight fit on it. I think you're going to be happy."

She reached to press the latch and lift the lid. Everything inside it was untouched, with no evidence of smoke creeping in around the lid. The fresh scent of cedar was the only aroma to rise from the interior of the hope chest. She paused as she gently touched the contents of the chest then closed the lid carefully, looking at the three men standing there.

"Thank you for being willing to go back there, for going to the trouble for me. It means a lot to me. I gave up hope there was anything left. Can we put it in the garage for now? I'll empty it out and store everything inside while I work on it. I think I can remove that blistered varnish and sand it down and refinish it myself. I'm so happy. Thank you." They lifted it down, and Kelly looked on smiling as Eli came back to Rachel, put his arms around her, and hugged her before helping her back down.

"I found your wristwatch on the floor by your night table. It must have gotten knocked off in the rush," he added, reaching in his pocket to hand her the undamaged wristwatch her father had bought for her twenty-seventh birthday last year. She accepted it from him and hugged him again.

"Oh, lunch is getting cold. I got us all sandwiches at Rudy's." Rachel opened the takeout bag and began handing out sandwiches. The men didn't stay in the duplex long because the smell of soot and ash permeated their clothing and boots. They ate on the front porch and the girls joined them.

They drove out to her parents' ranch to pick up some furniture. Back at the duplex, they unloaded everything and she showed them where she wanted everything placed, smiling as Eli assembled a pretty oak bed for her. They unwrapped the mattress and box spring, and she groaned when she realized that she'd forgotten to buy pillows.

"Rachel, you can borrow one of mine tonight," Eli offered.

Rachel remembered that tonight he'd be sleeping alone, most likely. That thought didn't exactly sit well with her.

Kelly sat in Rachel's rocker with Matthew and said, "I could sleep over here tonight with the baby and give the two of you some privacy. It's the *least* I can do." She winked at Rachel. "That way you won't have to make a special trip for pillows. I'll even help you get settled tonight before you go in to the club."

"All right, Kelly, you've convinced me. Be my houseguest."

Eli had to go in at six o'clock that evening, along with Mike and Rogelio. Rachel made arrangements for Grace and Jack to swing by and pick her up on their way to the club later that night, and then she'd simply ride home with Eli at the end of the evening. Doing this would give her time to unpack everything and begin getting settled. She hung her clothing in the walk-in closet, grimacing as she thought of all the ruined clothing in the boxes in the garage. She smiled again, though, remembering Eli's boyish grin as he'd jumped down from the truck bed earlier.

Eli got cleaned up and offered to take the girls for an early supper. They took him up on the invitation, and after they ate, he dropped them back off at the duplex and headed to The Dancing Pony.

Rachel made up the bed and hung her new shower curtain, which was perfect in contrast to the dark blue towels. The quilt Kelly had chosen for her was beautiful on the bed, and she was right about the size issue. After everything she'd saved Thursday night and all her new things were put away, she started getting ready for the evening.

She decided to go all out and surprise Eli now that she had more clothing options. It was time to climb out of the denim jeans rut and live a little. Kelly had talked her into a little black dress she had spotted earlier at Stigall's, along with a rather expensive pair of strappy four-inch black high heels. Grace would definitely approve when she saw the outfit.

The dress reached to just above her knees and had a deep V neckline with a gathered bodice. Underneath, she wore the black satin plunging neckline bra and a black satin G-string, both courtesy of Grace Warner and her excellent taste in men and lingerie. Rachel slipped the strappy heels on, inspected herself in the mirror, and liked what she saw.

She rolled her hair and applied foundation and light eye makeup. Her coloring was dramatic enough, and all she needed was a little extra sparkle. She was styling her wavy brown hair when the doorbell rang. She applied perfume and listened, smiling, as Kelly introduced herself. Rachel smiled at the fuss Grace made over meeting Kelly and admiring Matthew. Rachel emerged from the bedroom and made her way down the hall and watched them, hoping to gauge the effect she'd have on Eli in this outfit.

Grace's eyes popped wide open at the sight of her, and Jack's jaw dropped for a split second before he recovered himself. That was all she needed to know, and she smiled happily at them, hugging both. They chatted for a few minutes with Kelly while Rachel transferred the items she'd need that night to her evening bag, which had been one of the inexplicable things she'd grabbed in her mad last-minute dash through her apartment.

"Ready to go?" Grace's eyes twinkled as she took in Rachel's fresh new look.

"More than ready." Rachel hugged Kelly and patted Matthew. Kelly had her pillow and a good book and was going to settle down for the night after she bathed the baby.

"You look stunning, Rachel!" Grace said as Jack walked them out to the SUV. "Doesn't she, Jack?"

"Absolutely gorgeous," he replied with a twinkle in his eyes. "I want to see Eli's jaw hit the floor when he gets a look at you tonight."

"You think he'll react that strongly?"

"Oh, I don't think, I *know* he will," Jack said with feeling and reached for Grace's hand. "You both are real stunners tonight. I love that pink on you, darlin'," Jack murmured as he stroked Grace's hand.

"I love that slinky, sexy dress, Grace. Pink is your best color."

"Thank you, it's very comfortable," Grace said. As she turned to look at Rachel, she added, "The print is *very* camouflaging so no one can tell what I have on underneath it, or not." She giggled and gave Jack a sideways glance as he tried to keep his eyes on the road. Rachel heard a small groan from the driver's seat.

"Where is Adam tonight?"

Grace replied, "It's his grandmother's birthday today, and he wanted to take her out to eat."

"Aw, that's so nice of him. I'll bet she loves all that attention."

"She does." Grace said, then giggled. "I think she was going to try and talk him into taking her to a movie afterward. She's wants to go see the new Nicholas Cage movie."

"But isn't her eyesight failing?"

"Uh-huh, but she's a big Nicholas Cage fan."

"I see. You never know, huh?"

Rachel climbed from the cool SUV and stepped onto the still-hot asphalt of the parking lot. Jack walked them both up the sidewalk, one on each arm, and made a show of escorting them through the door of the club.

Ethan stood right in the entryway, blocking their progress. He had a big grin on his face as he looked his lovely bride over. Grace did a sassy turn for him then hugged him and gave him a long kiss. Once again, Rachel heard that barely audible groan from one of Grace's men and knew there was more than met the eye in tonight's outfit. She'd find out at a bathroom-buddy break. Grace was the owner of lots of delightfully wicked lingerie, and there was no telling what was under that dress.

With a hand resting on Grace's hip, Ethan gave Rachel a friendly hug and said, "You look lovely tonight. Eli is going to have heart failure when he sees you in that pretty dress. I wanted to warn you. Dinah Cooper is here tonight and about as weirdly tenacious as she's ever been. He's doing his best, and I was about to step in myself when you walked in. Want me to peel her off of him, or would you like to do the honors?"

"Let me try first, but thank you for the thought. I trust Eli to not allow her to take liberties."

"He's trying, anyway. She's planted herself in your chair. I'll give it a few more minutes for you to help her understand, and then I'll try and distract her if I can," Ethan added, patting her shoulder. Grace kissed his cheek and left him to his work and followed Jack to a table.

Rachel walked into the entryway of the club and was greeted by a loud wolf whistle from Mike, of all people.

"Get a load of the supermodel! Rachel, you are hot stuff tonight," he said as she approached. As she hugged Mike, he quietly said, "Dinah is in rare form. Go easy on him. He's done his best."

She nodded and smiled at Rogelio, who grinned and gave her a favorable once-over. Then she walked over to a very distracted Eli. He hadn't even turned at Mike's loud whistle.

He hadn't seen her entrance because he was too busy keeping an eye on Dinah's hands. Rachel knew he had to move faster than she did, or her hands would be on his thighs, in his hair, or worse, his front pocket. She had not been in the club the night before and would need to be educated firsthand like all the ladies last night.

Rachel smoothed her hand down Eli's shoulder and biceps. He jumped and cringed without looking over at her. Wow, this *had* been a rough night for him when his reactions were that reflexive and abrupt. She wondered what exactly Dinah had been up to tonight and stepped around Eli's massive form, slipping her hand gently into his. He glanced down at her and had an instantaneous reaction to her appearance.

"Hot, holy hell, angel, you look amazing!" He looked both relieved to see her and surprised at her fresh look. He reached an arm out and wrapped it around her and pressed his lips to her forehead, still very distracted. "Honey, you look beautiful. I could eat you up." She felt her cheeks heat up.

From the chair which had been placed there for Rachel, a sultry, deep woman's voice said, "Why don't you start with me and let's see how far we get. Who needs an *appetizer*, anyway."

Eli rolled his eyes and jerked reflexively again, and Rachel watched as long red fingernails curled around his other biceps and slid up into his snug shirtsleeve.

Chapter Thirteen

"Your hand is on my boyfriend," Rachel said firmly, making direct and unmistakable eye contact with Dinah Cooper. She was dressed in a red spandex dress that barely covered her ass and her boobs. Her red hooker heels had to be at least six inches high.

"In that getup, Dinah, I'd say you have an excellent chance of finding someone who is interested in you, but Eli is off the market." Each word from Rachel's mouth only seemed to spur Dinah on, and she grinned at Rachel in challenge.

"It didn't seem that way before you got here, Rachel, when he let me sit down in *your* chair. Maybe you need to get here earlier in the evening if you want to stake a claim. Early bird gets the *worm*, so to speak." Yet again, Eli jumped and reached for her hand that had slid behind him.

Eli's eyebrows drew together in irritation. "Dammit, Dinah, I asked you not to do that, and I did not invite you to sit in my girlfriend's seat. You helped yourself."

"Baby, you were so much *friendlier* before she showed up," Dinah said through pouty red lips. "What? Are you afraid of her?"

Rachel tried one more time. "Dinah, I'd appreciate it if you would get the hell up out of my seat and get your damn hands off of my boyfriend."

"No. When I see something I want, I don't give up," Dinah said proudly as she lifted her mixed drink to her lips.

If her demeanor were different, she could probably pull off the getup she was wearing quite well. Dinah had an abrasive, hardened personality and was rather intimidating to a lot of the men in the club. She was tall, thin, and muscular for a woman, probably two inches taller than Rachel in her bare feet. In tonight's outfit, she was almost eye level with Eli. Rather than play down the more androgynous and unfeminine aspects of her image, she seemed to capitalize on them with her choice of revealing clothing. Why she came into a country and western nightclub instead of one of the more urban clubs in Morehead where she would fit in better was lost on Rachel.

"Dinah, why is it that you are so determined to get with Eli? Why are you so fascinated with him?"

"In strength and build, he's my equal, Rachel," Dinah said, using her name condescendingly. "We'd be incredible in the sack. The question in my mind is why he has this passing fancy for a chubby thing like you?" Foolishly, she didn't lower her voice when she said it.

Ethan placed a comforting hand on Rachel's shoulder blade. "Hey, Eli. Things are quiet right now, so why don't you and Rachel take a break?" He'd heard the entire conversation. "Dinah and I are going to have a talk. I'll help watch the front. You go ahead," Ethan said, giving Eli a communicative glance then smiling sympathetically at Rachel.

Eli took Rachel's hand and led her away to the dance floor. Rachel could see the tension in the rigid set of his shoulders, but he was gentle as he led her away. He turned to her, and his face was unreadable. She coasted into his embrace, her torso pressed against his, his thigh between hers as he quietly guided her around the dance floor. She placed her cheek against his pectorals and smiled softly when his warm, heavily muscled arms slid around her shoulders and down her back, his hands coming to rest at her hips. He felt so powerful and immense wrapped around her like this.

She could hear the frustration in his voice when he spoke. "I'm sorry she said that to you, Rachel. You're not chubby. You're perfect." He kissed her temple.

"I had a feeling she would be very difficult to deal with once she got wind that we had gotten together, and I suppose I'm not surprised she wouldn't back off. There was no graceful way for either you or me to handle her, and I probably should have let Ethan deal with her before I even walked up. Did you notice how she tried to manipulate you into getting mad at me? That's her style. Divide and conquer."

"Emphasis on the conquer. She's pretty scary."

"Sex with her must be like a competition," she said, giggling at last when Eli had a full-body shudder.

"I did not need that image burned into my brain. Thank you very much."

"I love that we can see the humor in this situation. She's definitely the worst of them, though."

"You're right. I'm sorry she hurt your feelings, Rachel. All I can think about now is how right and beautiful and sweet you felt in my arms last night before I laid you on my bed. You're not chubby. You're voluptuous and womanly, and you feel perfect in my arms." He looked into her eyes with such adoration it took her breath away and made her heart pound.

She gasped quietly when he pressed against her, and she noticed his hardened shaft against her belly. A low ache began in her pussy and her panties became damp. She closed her eyes and experienced the slow burn that was so much a part of being in close proximity to him.

"You, too?" He smiled knowingly at her.

"So much, Eli," Rachel replied with feeling, pressing herself to him, tightening her arms and gripping his broad, hard back with her hands. "I feel like I could combust right on this dance floor." Rachel smiled as Eli begin to relax under her hands. The next song began to play, one of her new favorites by Chuck Wicks, called "Hold That Thought." Rachel smiled at Eli seductively, thinking the DJ had excellent instincts picking music.

"Close your eyes and picture this
Lying in bed in the candlelight
We start to kiss"

"I love this little dress on you. Very sexy." He slid his hands on the clingy knit fabric over her hips. "Other men in the club are watching you right now. Did you know that?"

She didn't bother looking around, just gazed into his eyes. "Well, I hope they know I'm yours."

"Pulling your body in close to mine
Now picture us
That moment before we make love"

She held on to him more closely and gasped as his big hands slowly, purposefully slid down over her ass, squeezing gently as Mr. Wicks continued to croon.

"Now hold that thought
Hold it right there"

"Oh," she uttered softly as her cunt contracted suddenly. Her panties grew even damper as his hands lingered there for a moment. He dipped his head and kissed her, inhaling her panting breaths. His hands slid back over her hips, coming to rest again on her lower back, but this time one of his long fingers settled into the cleft at the top of her ass in a clear mark of possession.

"You do that again and I might make a fool of myself right on this dance floor," she said shakily, wondering if that had been a mini-orgasm she'd just experienced.

A wolfish grin spread across Eli's face. "Oh? Wouldn't that be something?"

Rachel felt her cheeks flush and whispered, "I think I just came…a little."

Eli smiled tenderly as he nuzzled her temple. "And the evening has only just begun."

"Mmm, I know. I wish there was something I could do for you, to return the favor," she said with a giggle.

He groaned softly. "I'll have to look forward to when I get you home. I need to check the restrooms while I'm on this side of the club. Need to slip in the ladies' room for a few minutes?" He maneuvered to the edge of the dance floor closest to the restrooms.

As they approached the doors he said, "Take your time. I'll wait outside the door for you and walk you back. Ace Webster is here again. He must have come in while we were on the dance floor."

"I'll see you in a few minutes. Don't rush," she replied as he kissed her gently on the cheek and pushed open the door for her before stepping down the hall.

As she entered one of the stalls, the restroom door opened and clicking heels tapped on the restroom tiles. She grinned, guessing correctly who had joined her in the restroom.

"Grace, is that you?" Rachel asked.

"Yep, we're alone, for now. Are you okay? You looked a little shaky when Eli brought you to the door."

"I'm fine. Is Eli waiting outside for me?"

"No, not yet. Ethan told me that Dinah warned to allow the bouncers to do their jobs and leave them alone. He told her specifically to leave Eli alone. He's so thoughtful to do that."

Rachel exited to stall. "I know. I should have let him deal with Dinah from the very beginning. I probably only aggravated her."

Grace shrugged. "I'm anxious to see how you do with all the other groupies. Ace Webster was asking how long you've been an item. I think he wants to dance with you."

Rachel shook her head. "I'm not dancing with anyone but Eli tonight or any other night. He seems very nice, but I'm here with Eli. I would be very upset to watch Eli dance with another woman, and I know he'd feel the same."

"If the opportunity comes up, I'll mention of that. The one thing I can tell you is that he is a decent guy. Persistent maybe, but decent. If you tell him flat-out no, he'll back off, I'm sure."

"I hope it doesn't come to that." Rachel fluffed her hair and opened her evening bag to fix her lipstick as she eyed Grace. "All right, time for show and tell."

"Hmm?" Grace asked innocently as she ran her fingers in her hair, rumpling it.

"You said earlier your dress is very camouflaging so no one knows what you do *or don't* have on under there." Rachel arched an eyebrow. "I have to see. I'm dying of curiosity."

"It's a very sexy teddy with a built-in underwire bra. It's very sheer and matches my skin tone, so at first glance, I look naked in it. The sexy thing about it is that it's a thong, and the entire torso is dozens of little tiny strips of the sheer fabric all crisscrossing. I'm not sure I should show you because it's like I'm *nekkid*."

"Oh, come on! I'm like another sister. You'd show Charity, wouldn't you?"

Grace snickered. "She'd give me no choice!"

"Please? I wanna see."

So Grace showed her. Giggling, she stepped into the handicapped stall and motioned Rachel to come in, too, and she closed the door in case someone came in. The sheer fabric had a slight sheen to it, and it did match her skin tone perfectly.

"Do they know this is what you have on underneath your dress?"

Grace smiled and nodded with a naughty twinkle in her eyes. "Yeah, I hinted to Jack, and Ethan figured it out when we came in and he put his arms around me. Adam should be here any minute, and I told him earlier I was going to wear it tonight."

"It's beautiful on you, Grace."

"I think you would look pretty in it in black with your dark hair and lashes. Maybe I'll get it for you for a bridal shower gift."

"Grace, he hasn't proposed. Do you know something I don't?" Rachel asked, surprised by Grace's comment.

"Only what I see, Rachel. He is so in love with you. I'll bet you're hitched by Christmas!" Grace predicted.

"Kelly said the same thing today when we were shopping."

"Oh, isn't she the cutest little thing you ever saw? And that baby boy with jet-black hair. He's as sweet as he could be, like a little sack of sugar! Maybe you would have black-haired babies, too! The two of you would make gorgeous babies!"

"Well, let him propose first before you start planning baby showers, okay?" Rachel laughed and let Grace get her dress straightened out before they exited the restroom stall.

"Ethan and Jack are probably looking for me. I'll see you out there, okay, sweetie?"

"Sure. Grace?" Rachel called out. When Grace turned to look at her, she said, "Thanks for looking out for me. I appreciate it."

"What are friends for? Love ya, babe!" She sashayed through the door, smiling. Rachel returned her lipstick to her bag and washed her hands.

Slipping out of the door into the dark hallway, Rachel bumped into a tall, hard body. In the dark, she thought it was Eli and relaxed, putting out her hands to steady herself. She made contact with a hard chest and washboard abs as strong, warm hands grasped her upper arms and kept her from stumbling.

A second later, she knew it wasn't him because his scent was totally different, a dark, spicy fragrance mixed with the clean smell of an unfamiliar soap. Her hand brushed a butter-soft leather blazer, and she knew instantly whom she was holding on to. Ace Webster. She released her hands straight away and tried to back up, expecting him to do the same. Instead, his hands remained, gently holding her upper arms, and he leaned in closer, effectively pinning her to the wall in the dark, narrow hallway.

His voice was soft and husky. "Miss Lopez, how nice to see you again. I noticed you dancing earlier, and hoped I might talk you into dancing with me this evening." He leaned in close to her. "Your scent is beautiful, womanly." He dipped his head to nuzzle her hair. Her heart pounded, and she shrank from him but backed into the solid wall.

Grace had assured her he was a decent guy. Rachel felt like *intense* might be a better description at the moment. Before Eli had come into her life, she probably would've enjoyed this attention, his spicy, clean scent and the solid strength that he emanated. Right now, she did *not* enjoy his close proximity and certainly not the way he inhaled her fragrance. Good gracious, would he be able to detect her recent arousal? She vehemently hoped not because that felt like an invasion of something sacred between her and Eli.

She breathlessly placed a hand on his chest to stop him and spoke quickly. By her tone, she made sure to leave nothing to his imagination concerning what she thought about his offer and advances. "Mr. Webster, I thank you for your kind invitation, but I can't dance with you. I am very deeply in love with Eli Wolf. Grace and Jack brought me in so I could be with him tonight, and I'll only dance with Eli. I'm sorry to disappoint you."

"Loyalty like yours is rare in today's culture," he said, but his actions led her to believe he was unconvinced. He hadn't backed away and continued to breathe in her scent. As her eyes adjusted to the dim light, she could see his eyes and the lust and desire that smoldered there. "I hope someday I am lucky enough to have a woman who is as loyal to me as you are to Mr. Wolf. It's my loss." Rachel cringed inwardly and balled her hands into fists as he leaned even closer. She feared he might try to kiss her before he looked to the side and grinned. "Mr. Wolf, nice to see you again," he murmured.

Chapter Fourteen

Rachel was filled with relief. "Your hands are on my girlfriend, Mr. Webster." Eli asked harshly. His eyes glittered dangerously as Ace backed away and released her arms.

"Rachel and I bumped into each other in the hallway as we passed," Ace replied, holding up his palms in surrender. "I didn't want her to fall." He turned to Rachel and kindly said, "Miss Lopez, a pleasure to see you again. Have a good evening." He continued down the hallway to the men's room.

Eli approached Rachel and hugged her. "You're pale. Are you all right?"

She nodded, clinging to him briefly. "The hallway was dark. I bumped into him and thought for a second it was you. He asked me to dance with him." Ace had sounded as though he wanted to offer a lot more.

"I know, I heard what you said. Thank you, honey, for those sweet words. I didn't like seeing his hands on you."

"I know. You looked very angry." She trembled in his embrace, soaking in his warmth and strength. A minute ago, if she could have backed through the wall away from Ace, she would have.

"Not at you, at him. Do you think he took no for an answer?" he asked as he escorted her down the hallway back out to the club.

"His attitude changed after I told him I was in love with you. Maybe he'll respect that and find another dance partner."

"He looked like he was about to kiss you when he noticed me standing there," Eli said, sliding a hand over her shoulder.

"I thought so, too. I'm relieved he noticed you there when he did. That hallway was a bad place for a fight."

"If I had felt the need to use my fists, I would never have done it in such close proximity to you. I'd have taken him out the backdoor. I sort of wish I had, so we could settle this once and for all."

"He seems like a decent enough guy, if a little persistent. I hope he finds someone else to pay attention to." Changing to a safer subject, she said, "Grace said Ethan warned Dinah to leave the bouncers alone."

"She reminded me a little of what Ethan has told me about Patricia Ramirez."

"I'm sure Ethan was probably thinking the same thing, since he was on the receiving end of Patricia's obsession back in June. It's rare for Ethan and Ben to ban someone from the club, and they wouldn't do it without good reason."

During Patricia's days hanging out at The Dancing Pony with her friends, she'd gotten involved in some pretty sordid affairs and tried to intimidate some of the single women that came there. Patricia was a master manipulator and she'd spread a rumor that could have gotten Grace hurt and that wound up being the reason she got banned from the club.

They returned to the front where Mike and Rogelio carded a group coming in the door. Eli helped Rachel into her seat and checked in with the other two bouncers.

Rachel sat quietly for a good part of the evening, doing her best to let Eli focus on his job. She felt that he'd had enough distractions for the night. She'd been there an hour when he leaned over to her, concern in his eyes.

"You're awfully quiet. Everything okay?"

She looked up at him and sighed inwardly at the masculine beauty of his face. His massive presence next to her, coupled with his gentle but confident strength, made her heart do flip-flops. The tender look in his eyes made her melt inside thinking about what had happened on the dance floor.

"I'm trying to not distract you and let you do your job. Since we got together, I feel like I've kept you from working when I'm up here with you."

"Are you bored?"

"No."

"You seem withdrawn. Ethan does not mind that you sit up here with me, and he doesn't expect you to sit quietly in your chair. Since you started sitting up here with me, I'm less distracted because there is no longer a stream of women who come to the front trying to get my attention. Mike said the same thing earlier. Honey, you being up here is a *good* thing. I don't want you to think you distract me from my job." He twined his fingers in hers and pulled her from her seat.

"I don't want you to regret having me up here with you."

"No regrets, remember?" He drew her arms around his waist and kissed her sweetly.

"Thanks. I'm trying to figure out how I fit in up here. Last night was so busy with other distractions that I didn't have a chance to contemplate it."

"It's been nice to be able to work without the constant distraction of giggling females hovering around me, but I don't need for you to sit there quietly. When you're up here with us, it's okay to be involved in conversations. It's also okay if you want to mingle around the club. There must be people here you know tonight. Of course, there is always Grace. I thought you would have danced at least one dance together by now."

"She and I thought it would be best if we didn't because of the thing with Ace. We both agreed that might be asking for more trouble. And I don't want to dance with anyone else but you. I'm content to wait until you have a break later on tonight."

"The club is so crowded now he may not even see you. I'll stay where I can see you, and I'll intervene if he approaches you. I know that's a sticky situation, but it's not anything I can't handle, honey. I don't want it to keep you from having a good time when you come in. This is supposed to be fun for you, and you already know how I feel about watching you dance."

He said the last sentence with a bit of a growl in his voice, and it sent a thrill down her spine. "You'll stay where you can see me?" she asked coquettishly, pressing her breasts against him.

"Mmm, I wouldn't miss a second," he replied, smiling devilishly. He kissed her again and released her as she went in search of Grace.

She found her at Jack and Ethan's table, perched in Jack's lap, talking with Ethan and Ace Webster. Grace beamed and did a little rocking motion with her hands and hips, much to Jack's delight and distraction. Evidently, that was body language for, "Do you want to go dance?" Rachel nodded as Grace leaned over to whisper in Ethan's ear. A wide grin split his face, and he excused himself from the table and made his way to the DJ booth. Grace kissed Jack on the lips and spoke quietly to him as Rachel glanced over and caught Ace gazing steadily at her. So much for this being a covert operation. There was no chance of them going unnoticed by Ace now. His gaze was friendly but not flirtatious. He stood, leaning slightly in her direction as Grace rose from Jack's lap. His eyes were apologetic, and his smile was conciliatory.

"Rachel, I'm sorry if I've made you uncomfortable. You're very beautiful, and I was overzealous earlier. I hope you'll forgive me. I was out of line when I slipped you my business card last night as well. I suppose I was hoping things were not as serious between the two of you as they obviously are," he said sincerely, every bit the gentleman.

Rachel smiled and sighed in relief. "Of course, Ace. No offense was taken. In other circumstances, I would have taken you up on your offer for a dance, but I'm very committed to Eli and no longer dance with anyone else. Thank you for understanding that," she replied, relieved to get on less personal footing with him.

"Eli is a very fortunate man. I wish you both the very best," he said graciously before sitting back down. Grace hooked her arm in Rachel's and pulled her toward the dance floor.

"Ethan is going to play some good songs for us. I'm glad you came over when you did. Ace feels badly about your confrontation in the hallway. He mentioned it to me, and I told him a little about you and Eli. He has no desire to come between two people who are genuinely committed to each other. Some of the other women have been hovering, trying to attract his attention. He seems a little put off by women who approach him, so I'm going to try to introduce him to Rosemary Piper's friend, Kathleen. Remember her? Tall, voluptuous, sexy, and mysterious redhead? She's not here with anyone tonight, so I'm going to invite her and Rosemary to the table."

"Whoa, Grace. Wes and Evan are here tonight. Do you think that's a good idea?" Rachel asked, chuckling at Grace's attempts to match make for *all* the people she cared about.

"Hmph! Maybe it's just the kick in the *ass* they need. Wes and Evan didn't bring her here tonight, and if they've laid claim to her, maybe they ought to let *her* in on it, ya think?" she asked sarcastically. "Sometimes I think those two couldn't find their asses with both hands and a road map, much less find true love when it's staring them straight in their handsome faces."

"You're going to get yourself in trouble with your men over this if you're not careful."

Grace smiled mischievously at her. "Yeah, and if I play my cards right, I might *even* get a *spanking* out of it." Grace laughed out loud when Rachel's eyes and mouth opened wide in shock.

"You're serious, aren't you?" Rachel wasn't even sure why she was surprised.

"By the *right* hand, there's nothing I'd enjoy more," Grace replied, giggling and blushing as she blew a kiss to Ethan then looked at Rachel and winked. Rachel's eyes got big, and her lips popped open in surprise. She should have known.

She mouthed silently, "Ethan?"

Grace nodded dreamily. "Baby, yes! That man owns me body and soul. They all do. You can ask me any question you want to about that *in private*," she said to Rachel as "Sweet Home Alabama" started to play.

Grace laughed and got caught up in the music as they took the floor. Rachel glanced over toward the front and found Eli standing halfway between the front door and the dance floor. Anyone watching him might have thought he was standing in the midst of the club, surveying the tables and the dance floor to see if all was well security-wise. But once she began to move, his eyes rested only on her, watching her move to the beat of the song. As she turned, she made eye contact with him and was warmed by his gray gaze even from that distance. She delighted in it, pleased that he enjoyed watching her dance so much.

The Dancing Pony mostly played country and western dance tunes, but they liked to shake things up sometimes and play some rock and popular music as well as some of the popular line dance tunes. Once Skynard was finished, Duffy's "Mercy" began to play. The mood changed on the dance floor, and couples began to gyrate to the heavy dance beat, Grace and Rachel included.

* * * *

Eli crossed his arms over his chest, which swelled with pride in his woman's beauty as she moved. She paid little attention to the other couples, staying by Grace as they both danced for the men who watched them. Eli glanced up at the DJ booth and saw Ethan in a similar stance, his eyes trained with intensity on Grace, causing Eli to smile.

Eli looked over to where he knew Ace sat at Jack and Ethan's table, involved in a conversation with Jack. Ace looked up and gazed momentarily at Rachel before he looked over at him across the club. Ace raised his beer bottle and nodded at Eli. Eli nodded in reply and, satisfied, resumed watching Rachel as she moved gracefully to the music, laughing with Grace. The dress Rachel had on hugged her curves and revealed just enough of her generous cleavage to leave him wanting more. He glanced around, noticed other men in the club watched her and Grace, and instinctively moved closer to the dance floor.

Wilson Pickett's "Mustang Sally" played next, and the tempo on the dance floor slowed down. Eli could tell that Rachel had held back on the dance floor tonight, probably more conscious than she wanted to be that Ace might be watching, but she must have liked the song because she let the worry go.

When the song ended, Eli was at the edge of the dance floor where he waited to escort them both. He noticed Ethan standing beside him, same as the night before.

"They're like spontaneous combustion on the dance floor, aren't they, Eli?"

"Damn good analogy, boss."

"We'd better escort them. Otherwise, every randy stud in here is going to be all over them. It sure is good to watch them have fun, ain't it?"

"Absolute torture," Eli replied, trying for reasonably straight face.

Ethan laughed out loud, clapping Eli on the back. "That, too!"

Grace slipped into Ethan's embrace as he leaned down to kiss her. Rachel joined Eli as a young man stepped up to Rachel and opened his mouth to ask her for a dance. He took one look in Eli's eyes, slammed his mouth shut, and backed away to go in search of another dance partner. Rachel looked after him apologetically and smiled up at Eli as he walked away with her.

* * * *

Rachel noticed Wesley and Evan sitting at a corner table, both of them facing the club. They made a handsome pair in their Wranglers, dress cowboy boots, and Stetsons. They didn't look like tourist cowboys who dressed in full cowboy regalia they'd bought at Cheaver's Western Store for an evening out at a cowboy nightclub. They looked like they might have been on the back of a horse or hefting a hay bale before getting cleaned up to go dancing and drinking. They were the real deal sitting there, looking slap-your-grandma gorgeous.

Wes was dressed in a starched white western dress shirt, unbuttoned at the neck, leaving his tanned throat visible. Evan was dressed in a jet-black dress shirt also unbuttoned so that a bit of his chest hair was visible. His usual brooding bad-boy stare was there, but the set of his shoulders and hands would lead any observer to believe that it was more than an act. Evan looked decidedly pissed off, while Wesley looked heart-broken.

She turned to watch the object of their sad perusal. Rosemary Piper and her friend Kathleen walked with Grace and Ethan to their table. Rosemary looked adorable in bright red Wranglers and a silky white shirt that barely hinted at the thin lace camisole beneath it. Her black boots were polished to a gloss, and she wore a belt that glittered brightly with rhinestones. Her long, curly coal-black hair was pulled back in a jeweled headband that echoed the sparkle in her belt. The image of a happy cowgirl out with friends having a good time would have been complete until Rachel saw her eyes. The hint of a broken heart lingered in the poignant sadness there. Kathleen looked like her usual sophisticated self, dressed in a sleeveless black mesh sheath dress with a hint of sheerness to it and a black lace slip beneath. The neckline dipped into a deep V in the front and back, revealing her generous, ivory-toned cleavage and the curve of her spine. She wore a delicate crystal necklace that dipped between her breasts and also dangled halfway down her back, swaying with her every movement. Her stockings had seams up the back, hinting, for those astute enough to observe, at the garter belt that rested around her hips. Her high heels were a mass of glittering crisscrossing straps covering the insteps. Kathleen was tall and had stunning dark red hair. She carried her shapely curves with confidence and grace, moving across the room as though she were aware half the men in the club were watching her, and she didn't mind a bit. Her elegant but not haughty air practically invited their gaze as she moved.

Rachel observed as Jack and Ace got up when the ladies arrived at the table with Ethan. Grace introduced Rosemary and Kathleen to Ace, who greeted them graciously, his appreciative gaze moving over both of them. Ace offered Rosemary his seat, as Ethan pulled up another chair for Kathleen. Grace contentedly resumed her perch in Jack's lap, his large hands coming to rest on her thigh and lower back.

Rachel smiled, noting that Grace always seemed to take joy in every moment she had with any of her men. She never took their presence for granted. She snuggled up to Jack and spoke quietly to him. He obviously loved having her so close and smiled at whatever she said and nodded and kissed her. The love and satisfaction on his face were obvious.

Rachel glanced again in sympathy at Wesley and Evan Garner. Wesley was having sharp but indistinguishable words with Evan as Evan slouched over his beer unhappily. He muttered a few words in Wesley's direction, and Wes bit back a harsh reply, his big, strong hands knotting into fists. Rachel looked back over to Ethan's table and happened to catch Rosemary watching Wes and Evan, looking distinctly torn. She turned away to look up at Ace as he spoke to her and smiled at him. Rachel looked up at Eli.

"Would you mind if I went over to talk with those two idiots for a minute?"

"No, I'm sure they could use all the wisdom they can get their hands on. Be gentle. Or not." Eli shrugged then smiled when she tucked her fingers in the waistband of his leathers, stroking his lower back.

"Be right back, honey." Rachel turned to saunter over to the Garner boys. They looked up as she approached. She felt a little sad for them as they tried to put on a happy face for her visit to their table.

Wesley got up and held out a seat to her, which she took, and he asked, "I know you're here with Eli, but do you want a drink, sweetheart?"

"No, thank you, Wesley. I appreciate it. I want to talk to you."

She looked back and forth between the two of them, struck yet again by the contrast in these two brothers. Wes was tall and lean, at least six feet three inches, hard-muscled, and tanned. His hands were big and hardened from his line of work as a custom furniture craftsman. His wavy, sandy-blond hair peeked out from the back of his white Stetson, curling slightly at the nape.

Evan was stockier and had a shorter, thicker build, at five ten. Despite being shorter than his brother, he was no less powerful. His dark brown hair was barely visible under his hat, and he grew a soul patch beneath his bottom lip, which Rachel secretly thought was sexy as hell on him. She wasn't normally much for facial hair, but that little patch of hair was almost lickable on him. His shoulders were broad and thickly muscled as were his arms and legs. His hands were also work roughened and calloused.

The shapes of their faces were unique to each of them, as well, taking after different sides of the family. Where Wes's features were lean and angular with round, deep-set green eyes, Evan's features were broader, his jaw square, and his cheeks dimpled. She hadn't seen the dimples make much of an appearance lately because he smiled so rarely. His eyes were more of an almond shape and chocolaty brown. They were warm and inviting when he was happy, changing to dark and unreadable when he wasn't, like right now.

"What's on your mind?" Wesley asked, glancing beyond her in Rosemary's direction again. His green eyes were filled with soulful longing.

"We've been good friends a long time, right, guys?" Rachel's voice grew husky as an aching lump formed in her throat for the pain she saw in their eyes.

Wes smiled. "Ever since we beat Bobby Joe Booker up for pushing you off your bicycle when we were all six years old."

"You were my heroes that day. You helped put the chain back on my bike and cleaned up my skinned knee, too."

"I'm not sure spit counts as cleaning, sweetheart," Wes said with a halfhearted chuckle.

"My knee healed up fine, and Bobby Joe finally left me alone after that. You fixed all that for me because you cared."

"What are you trying to say, baby?" Evan looked sadder than an old hound dog.

"You're friends with Grace, right?"

"Sure! Good friends with all four of them. Why?"

She knew she had their full attention. "If the two of you have unresolved issues or questions, you should get together with them *soon*. When you look back, are you going to be proud of causing her all this pain before you let her down for good? Or will you thank your lucky stars that you wised up and grabbed hold of the best woman to ever come your sorry way. I don't know what happened with her, but I'm willing to bet *someone's* alligator mouth wrote a check their hummingbird ass couldn't cash." She placed a soothing hand over Evan's. "Sorry, honey, but you know it's the truth. You both tend to let your mouths get the better of you. Either forgive her and start over, or let her go. Remember this is about Wesley, too."

"I know, Rachel, but he's asking *too much*," Evan replied, his voice husky with emotion.

"What? Asking for you to get over yourself is too much?" Rachel said softly. "You told me once a long time ago, you don't have it in you to hold a grudge against someone you love so much. I don't understand what's holding you back."

"She'll only pull the same shit again. Not *all* women are manipulators, I know that. And Grace seems to make her men very happy—"

"*Seems to?*" Wesley asked incredulously. "Talking to any of the three of them is like conversing with a man who has died and woken up in heaven. We deserve a chance to be happy, too."

"Yeah, see, that's just it. I'm not going to be able to make her happy," Evan muttered.

"You don't know that, Evan," Rachel replied for Wesley. "But you'll never know if you don't give her a chance. She's all grown up, in case you haven't noticed, and she's *nothing* like your ex-wife, Evan. Boy, Rita worked you over good."

"You got that right," Wes muttered. To his brother, Wes said, "Rachel's right. If we don't work things out soon, Rosemary's going to give up, and I can't have that. I *love* her. I've *always* loved her, and this is what she *wants*." Wes's voice was soft but full of emotion. They'd been in business together since the beginning, and it would be a tragedy if Evan left Divine. It sounded to Rachel like he might have been thinking about that.

"Maybe it'd be easier if I left."

"For who? She loves you, too. If you do that you'll just hurt her some more? You love her, too. You're too damn stubborn and unwilling to trust her or anyone else. She doesn't like it when you try to control her. You backed her into a corner today, and she reacted the only way she knew how."

This debate had raged on since their college days. Leaving Divine to go to school may have broadened their horizons, but it had been devastating for their relationship.

Rachel sighed at their back and forth bickering and finally broke in. "A word from someone who knows, guys. That man she's currently talking with is rather charismatic and charming, not to mention totally gorgeous. He's also persistent. If he's interested in her, *he* won't waste any time letting her know. Fortunately, he is also a gentleman. He's talking to Kathleen now, but he was speaking very solicitously to Rosemary earlier and gave her his chair. I'm telling you this because I love you guys like you were my brothers. That's *your* chance at happiness right there, and she's fixing to slip away." She patted their shoulders before she slipped from the tall chair. "Just thought I would encourage you."

"Thanks, sweetheart, we appreciate it," Wesley replied.

"Thanks, Rachel." Evan looked even more miserable. He slipped off his hat and raked his fingers through his thick hair, looking as though he wanted to yank some out in the process.

Rachel walked away, having done what she could. The rest was up to them. She groaned to herself when "Cowboys Like Us" by George Strait began to play. Looking over at Grace's table again, Rachel watched as Rosemary rose from Ace's chair. Ace led Rosemary by the hand to the dance floor and began to waltz gracefully with her. Rosemary *loved* to waltz. She looked over at Wesley and saw he had risen from his seat, his spine ramrod straight. She returned to Eli, stepped between his knees, and leaned against his chest as he sat in his tall chair at the door.

"It's like a car wreck," she said softly. "I can't look, and I can't *not* look. Tell me what's happening." She closed her eyes and pressed her cheek against his chest. She enjoyed listening to his steady heartbeat and the deep vibration there as he chuckled and gave her a play-by-play description of the events as they unfolded. She sighed happily as he took advantage of the opportunity to gently stroke her back.

"Wesley's headed to the dance floor. Later, Evan!" he called. "Evan just walked out the door, but he doesn't look unhappy. Wesley asked to cut in."

"Did she let him?"

He paused and sighed. "She told him no. He took off his hat. He's asking again. Man, she said no again, but now she looks upset. Ace is talkin' to her. Now he's talkin' to Wesley. They're off the dance floor. Ace's talking to her some more. She's shaking—no, she's nodding her head. Wesley's shaking hands with Ace. Ace is walking away. Damn, I'll bet he's had his fill of being the Good Samaritan and deferring to other men. Oh, now Kathleen is pulling him on the dance floor. Good, she seems more like his type."

"I can't stand it. I have to look." She watched as Wesley slid his hands up Rosemary's arms. She pulled away from him and spoke indignantly to him, poking him in the chest with her index finger, then turned to walk away in a huff. Wes snagged her arm, pulling her gently, but firmly, to his chest. She glared up at him angrily but also like she wanted to cry. She didn't say anything else. He leaned down to her and said something to her very gently. She nodded and looked up at him like she was about to break down.

Rosemary left Wesley's side and went to her girlfriends' table and got her purse. She stopped at Grace's table, hugged her and spoke quickly to them, then returned to Wesley. She looked up at him, and he took her hand and led her to the front door. She gave a little wave to Rachel and Eli as she trailed behind Wesley then mouthed, "Thank you" to Rachel.

"Wow. Everyone has a story, don't they?" Eli chuckled as they watched them leave.

"Yeah. I hope those two don't blow their chance."

"Me, too."

A waitress delivered a shot of Crown and another of Cuervo 1800 to their table. "The gentleman in the leather jacket sent these over for you with his compliments. Ethan said this is what you'd like."

Eli raised his shot glass to Ace. All was well.

What a relief, Rachel thought as she drank hers.

"You're not much of a drinker, are you?" Eli smiled at her as her eyes watered a little.

"No, I'm a lightweight, but I'll take a shot of Crown Royal on occasion," she replied. "I want to go powder my nose. I'll be right back." She picked up her evening bag from the back of the chair where it hung by its strap.

"Want me to walk you?"

"No need. I'll be careful in the hallway." She smiled up at him as he kissed her knuckles before releasing her hand. As she made her way around the bar, she heard a lot of female voices coming in the door behind her, but she didn't turn around.

Chapter Fifteen

Rachel walked into the restroom, checked her makeup in the mirror, and fluffed her hair. Several women she had not seen that evening came barreling through the restroom doors. They must have just come in the club but looked like they'd already had a few drinks. She reapplied her lip liner as they talked loudly from the stalls and the lavatory.

"Did you see the big hard body on that bouncer? I would love to take him for a test drive, or three."

"Shoot, he could probably take us all on at once. I love all those strong muscles and that hair." Several of them cackled and snickered.

"I'd love to run my fingers through it. He smelled good, too."

"He didn't look very interested in any of us. Maybe he's gay?" said a petite brunette as she fluffed and scrunched her hair.

"Maybe he didn't look interested in y'all, but I definitely got a closer look."

"Yeah, dummy, because he was checking your ID."

"Oh. Well, I don't think he's gay. Did you happen to see that hard-on he was sporting?" a blonde said as she left the restroom stall.

"He must be huge. Maybe he has a break coming up in a little while. I noticed this bathroom door has a lock on it," said a particularly predatory-looking blonde with super-short hair.

"You *would* think about doing him in the bathroom, you nasty thing."

"Did any of you guys pause to consider he might have a wife or girlfriend?" This comment came from the same brunette who sounded like the designated driver for the group.

One of the younger women turned to Rachel. "You come here often?" At Rachel's friendly nod, she continued, "Does he have a girlfriend?"

"Yes, he does." She tried to maintain a straight face, surprised she was laughing inside instead of seeing red at their ribald comments. That shot of

Crown must have kicked in. She had to put her hand to her mouth to stop herself from snickering as she pretended to check her lip liner for smudges.

"She wasn't up there. I say we go for it," the sporty blonde said as she reapplied her lipstick.

"Who is *we*?" the fluffing brunette asked skeptically.

"We as in *me*, honey. I didn't see anyone laying claim to him. If he was my man, I'd stay by his side all night long, except to pee occasionally."

"I'm going to tell your boyfriend how you've been acting."

"Hey, this is a bachelorette party. Whatever happens at The Dancing Pony stays at The Dancing Pony. Isn't that right, miss? You won't say anything, will you? To his girlfriend, I mean?" Rachel was liking this blonde less and less by the second.

"Oh, no. Mum's the word." Rachel made the motion of locking her lips and throwing away the key. She powdered her nose and tried to keep from laughing at their drunken banter. She adjusted the rear strap on her high heels.

"Hey! Those are some great shoes!" the fluffing brunette squealed.

"Oooh! They're pretty. I'll bet they cost quite a bit."

"Not too bad. I found them at Stigall's here in town." Rachel experienced a surreal moment conversing about her shoes with women who had earlier talked about fucking the man she loved.

"So, what's his girlfriend like?" one of them asked her conspiratorially. "Is she a total dog? Paper-bag ugly?"

"No, she's not too bad. He seems to like her a lot. She's a great dancer, too. I know for a fact that she's here tonight, and she's *super* jealous. He's *really* a nice guy. Very thoughtful and honest."

"Is he?" one of them said dreamily.

Rachel nodded helpfully. "Yes, supposedly he's an incredible lover. Very *considerate*, if you know what I mean," she added with a leer.

"Really?" another woman asked breathlessly.

"And *huge*!" she stage-whispered dramatically as she held her fingers a good distance apart to their stunned gasps.

"But be careful because his girlfriend usually sits in that chair right next to him. And he *only* dances with *her*."

"Damn!"

"You are so sweet to tell us all of that. What was your name?"

"Rachel."

"Right, Rachel. Hey, if you want to join us at our table, we're having a bachelorette party for Mandy. She's getting married next weekend. It's her third try, and we're all hoping it *sticks* this time," fluffing brunette told her.

Rachel heard braying laughter from one of the restroom stalls, and a whiney blonde popped her head out and said, "I heard that! You should totally join us, Rachel! Maybe you could point his girlfriend out to us. He'd make a *perfect* going away present for me," she added drunkenly.

"That sounds great. But I'm here with my boyfriend, and he's probably wondering where I am right now. But I'll see you out there."

"Do very many decent guys come in here?" one of them asked.

"Oh, lots of them. I met my boyfriend here, as a matter of fact."

"So they mind their manners in here?"

"For the most part. My boyfriend asked me out the night I met him, but I turned him down for two whole months before finally saying yes. Very persistent, but, yes, lots of great guys come in here, some I even know personally."

"I wish you could sit with us, point out the available ones to us," Mandy whined.

"Sorry, my true love awaits," Rachel said as one of them sighed. She almost laughed.

"Okay, later! Later!" several of them called out as she made her exit, fighting back laughter. She sauntered over to the bar and spoke to Quinten for a moment before returning to Eli's side.

"Angel, it's about time I took a break. Would you like to dance?" he asked her as she hugged him. She watched as the group of bachelorettes made their way to a large table.

"I'd love to. That's a *fun* group of gals over there. You would not believe what they were talking about in the restroom."

He groaned and ventured a guess. "I don't know. The hot bouncer guy with the long, pretty black hair?"

"The one and the same. *Oooh!* The things they want to do to you, honey!" Rachel grinned evilly and rubbed her hands together.

"How many eyes did you blacken?" he asked jokingly but his eyebrows knit together a little, showing he was only partly kidding and was now a little worried.

"Oh, none. They're all drunk, and I played along with them. They asked me all about you, and I shared *helpful* information and warned them about your *super* jealous girlfriend. I hope they aren't too upset with me when they see us together. I ordered a round of drinks for them from Rachel to soothe their disappointment that they won't be fucking *or* sucking you in the ladies' restroom." She cackled in glee at his shocked look.

"No more Crown Royal for you. You're an evil woman, Rachel Lopez. Shall we go dance and give them an eyeful?"

"Let's wait until their waitress comes to take their order and discover the first round is on Rachel, and then we can dance and even go say hi if you want to." She giggled when he rolled his eyes at her suggestion.

Eli looked down at her and raised an eyebrow. "What *kind* of helpful information did you share?"

Rachel chortled as she slid her hands over his thick biceps. "I told them what a sweet, honest guy you are. And that I've heard you're a very *considerate* lover. *Oh*, and that you're *huge*. You should have seen their eyes." Eli groaned, and Rachel chortled as she watched the waitress venture over to their table after they were seated.

A few minutes later, she walked with a chuckling Eli to the dance floor after he let Mike and Rogelio know he was taking a break. She wrapped her arms around him as they glided smoothly over the hardwood floor as Gary Allan's "Nothing On But the Radio" played. Eli leaned down to give her a kiss, and she slid her arms around his neck. His hands glided down her spine, settling on her lower back as his fingers gently caressed the upper swell of her ass. A tingle shot over her skin where his fingers stroked, and she let loose a feminine sigh of pleasure when he squeezed gently.

They both looked up at the sound of loud braying laughter and shouting. They were near the table of bachelorettes, and Mandy had spotted them. Rachel clung snugly to Eli with one hand and waved at the ladies as they all began laughing at her practical joke, or almost all of them. The blonde who had noticed a lock on the ladies restroom door looked a little peeved and disappointed but cheered up when her drink arrived. They all raised their glasses to Rachel and Eli in toast.

* * * *

After the club closed, Eli walked Rachel to his truck and helped her get in. He buckled her seatbelt for her, brushing his cheek against her fragrant, firm breasts as he leaned past her to reach the latch. She chuckled and ran her fingers into his hair. He paused and looked up at her.

"I like that you let me do things like this for you, Rachel."

"Well, then I'll always let you, honey." She hummed softly as he kissed the upper swell of her breast before closing her door.

Coincidentally, the Chris Young song "Getting You Home" was on the country radio station as they drove back to the duplex. A few minutes later, they *were* walking in the door, and that little black dress *did* hit the floor.

He started the shower so the water could warm up. He knew she liked to go to bed clean, not smelling like cigarette smoke. She used some of his shampoo and lathered her long brown hair. As he bathed, he remembered a moment earlier in the day when they had loaded his truck with the salvage from the apartment.

He'd bent over in the bed of the truck, wrapping her cedar chest in a blanket, and then had moved it closer to the cab so it wouldn't be damaged any further. A sudden breeze had blown through his hair and billowed it into his face a little. His hair had brushed against his face again, and he had caught her familiar scent from that part of her he loved so much. He had recalled the delighted sounds she'd made when he had teased her pussy and clit with his hair the night before.

He rinsed the shampoo from his hair and scrubbed his body, watching as she did the same. The sight of the water as it rushed over her curvaceous figure caused him to reach out to touch her gently, startling her a bit. She ran her hair under the showerhead with her eyes closed. His hands slid down her rib cage and made her gasp again, and her lips curved in a sensual smile. She seemed to like not being able to see, maybe because it heightened her other senses.

When she was finished, she smiled up at him and stepped from the shower, quickly dried off, and toweled her hair. She handed him a towel as he stepped out, and he wondered at the secret smile on her face. She hung up her towel and led him, nude, from the bathroom into his bedroom. She lit a few candles and turned off the lamps. The normally sterile, plain, white-walled room was bathed in warm, flickering candlelight. The effect on her was stunning. Her damp, pale, olive skin glowed and glistened in the shimmering light. The natural light bathed the walls in warmth, and tonight, his room didn't feel so cold and barren.

She turned down the covers and led him to the edge of the bed. She tossed a pillow at his feet, and he caught his breath as he realized what she wanted to do. There were lots of things he'd hoped to do with her but, given his size, had not expected any of them. He knew he was intimidating and did not want her to feel obligated. She knelt between his feet and looked up at him.

He ran his hands over her soft shoulders. "You sure?"

She gazed at him, and a slow, sensual smile spread across her soft lips. That smile held promises in its soft warmth. He had a feeling this was not going to be the standard three-minute blowjob.

Rachel took his hands and placed them slightly behind him so he could lean back. She nudged him to scoot forward to the edge of the mattress. She gently splayed his thighs wider so she could slip in between them. His cock was now rigidly erect, stiff and straight up against his abdomen, extending past his navel.

A shaky sigh of anticipation left Eli's lips, and he closed his eyes, eagerly awaiting her touch.

She scooted in close and spoke in a silken voice. "I've wanted a taste of you all night, especially after you made me come on the dance floor. I fantasized about unzipping those sexy black leathers so I could put my lips on you. I want to suck on your big cock until you come, and I want to swallow every single drop."

Her gentle fingers sent chills racing all over his skin as they slid up and down over his cock and balls. With his eyes closed, the sensation grew and intensified. His head fell back a little, and he gulped and swallowed shakily at her words and her tender touch. His insatiable cock strained toward her, and he ached for the feel her warm lips on him.

* * * *

Rachel admired his handsome face as she smoothed her hands up his inner thighs, leaned in, and blew a stream of warm breath over his balls. He moaned softly, and she felt his thighs tense until they were rock hard. She licked her lips and leaned in to his sac. She lapped at one ball smoothly and then tongued it, smiling at his gasping moan. She hummed softly to him in return. He tasted and smelled clean, like his soap, and the nest of curly hairs around his cock tickled her nose a little. She laved her tongue over his testicles and this time took one of his balls in her mouth. She gently sucked it as his hips flexed toward her. He made a noise that was a toss-up between a wail and a groan.

Grace *said* he would probably love this, she thought gleefully.

She gathered some of her saliva that slid down from his balls and skimmed her finger along the center line of his perineum, between his balls and his rear opening, and he *did* wail. *He must not have expected that.* She sucked his balls and slid her finger over that center line again, enjoying the sound of agonized pleasure coming from his lips. She slid all the way back and circled his rear opening. He cried out loudly and sucked in a loud gulp of air. His breath sounded more like panting now.

She circled his opening again, and his hips gyrated smoothly with her movements. He groaned in ecstasy. The moment was undeniably erotic as she was reminded how immense he was. An echoing flood of moisture rushed to her pussy at the feeling of power that engulfed her. His body bucked slightly under her mouth, and a sob slipped from his lips. She paused.

"Are you all right, Eli?" she asked softly, sliding her other hand over his abdomen, making him shudder again.

He panted and spoke in a voice gravelly with tension. "No one's ever taken the time to do what you're doing for me. I'm fixing to explode, and your lips haven't even touched my cock yet."

"Do you need a minute? Or would you like me to do it some more?" she asked softly, caressing his perineum again.

He moaned softly, flexed against her hand, and groaned. "More, angel. Don't stop."

Rachel lapped at his balls again and watched his face. Her fingertip swept over his rear opening, pressing gently in a circular motion one more time, making him moan loudly, uninhibitedly.

She gently wrapped the fingers of her other hand around his cock. His startled gasp made her smile, and he sat forward a little to give her full access. His warm, work-roughened hands smoothed over her arms and her back, and heat emanated from his torso, which was covered in a light sheen of sweat. He leaned forward and kissed her, and his long black hair fell around her shoulders in a dark curtain. The cool, silken strands tickled as they slid over her collarbones and teased the upper swell of both breasts, causing a pleasant shudder to ripple through her.

Rachel licked her lips, stroked his shaft smoothly, and admired his length and girth. She glanced up into his hooded, stormy gray eyes, pressing her wet lips to the underside of his cock, and ran her lips back and forth. Each time she took pleasure in his moans of delight. She lifted his cock from his belly and gently tilted his length toward her lips. He panted ecstatically in anticipation.

He loved to build the tension and anticipation, so she lightly flicked the head of his cock with her tongue and breathed gently on him. His abs rippled in the candlelight, and he sounded like he was in ecstasy, waiting for that first touch. His hand caressed her shoulder and slid into her hair. She remained motionless, breathing, flooded with ecstasy herself. She listened to him and waited for the right moment.

His cock grew harder within her grasp, and his breathing deepened. He gazed down at her with glittering eyes and growled softly. Silently licking again, she pressed her closed lips to the head of his cock and slid them gently over the head.

"Holy fuck!" He groaned loudly as her lips slowly parted for him. He cried out again as the head of his steely-hard cock popped into her mouth and her tongue swirled slowly around him. She could taste the droplets of pearly fluid that had appeared at the slit on the head moments before she touched him. He tasted slightly salty, a combination of his essence and pure maleness. Her mouth watered for more, and she allowed more of his cock to slide into her mouth until he touched the back of her throat.

Rachel glanced up and saw him watching her, lying back on his elbows. Her cheeks tingled with warmth, and her eyelids slid closed as she focused on his pleasure. She sucked on his cock and slowly slid her lips up to his head then back down again. She slid her fingers around his shaft at the base, and she began to stroke him with the same rhythm she used with her lips.

He said little but was certainly not silent as her smooth rhythm began to take him higher. She stroked his testicles as she sucked him and then slid gently back over his perineum, feathering closer and closer to his rear opening again. His body tightened powerfully at the added sensation.

"Oh, angel, you're going to make me come doing that." He whimpered and moaned anew as she increased the slow smooth rhythm again, moaning softly with him at times as she sucked on his cock and feathered her fingertips in a sensual caress of his ass. She knew he was close when his balls began to tighten and draw close and his hips began to rock.

Breathlessly he said, "I'm going to come soon. It's so good, you'd better stop soon or I'll come in your—Oh, baby, what are you doing? Angel! You're going to—"

I sure am.

Stroking with her mouth, reveling in his shouts of absolute ecstasy, she slowly, but firmly, stroked his ass in that sensual circling motion that echoed the rocking of his hips. She carefully turned that hand palm down and curled her index finger so it was bent at the second knuckle and continued the stroking motion against his ass. She caressed her knuckle against all the nerve endings in that tight opening, and the tension broke in his body. He roared when he came. His cum jetted into her mouth, and she began to swallow.

He cried out in tormented ecstasy as she gently stroked his release from him then licked him clean as he shuddered and panted. Grace had told her what to expect because Rachel had never swallowed cum before. It didn't bother her in the least to swallow his, and she failed to see why so many women refused to do that for the men they loved. Grace promised that if she took her time and listened to how much he enjoyed it that it would be every bit as pleasurable for her as it was for him. Grace had been *so* right.

She stretched out next to him and listened as his breathing returned to normal. He gathered her warm body to his, lifted her chin, and kissed her slowly and tenderly.

"Angel," he whispered reverently. She loved it when he called her that. Each time he said it, she thought there was more to that word than just a sweet endearment for him. It went deeper than that. "No one could love me like you, angel."

She wrapped her arms around him when his immense body trembled a little. "Are you chilled?"

"No, I'm...I'm in awe of the way you took your time with me." He stroked a lock of her hair between two fingers. "You enjoyed what you were doing and swallowed when I came."

"I loved listening to you come. I imagined how good it must have felt to finish that way."

"Angel, you are something else, full of surprises. I certainly didn't expect that one." Eli's callused hand slipped down over her breast, and he kissed its peak before his fingertips slid over her abdomen to her hip and stroked her. "Are you wet for me?"

She silently nodded and slid her foot up the mattress, opening so he could see the evidence for himself. His fingers slid down over her mound and then smoothly slipped into her wet slit.

Chapter Sixteen

Rachel melted like warm butter and moaned when he growled again. She loved when he made that sound. He slid his finger over her clit and rubbed in smooth, fluid strokes.

His eyelids were hooded as he looked into her eyes. Like his hands, his gaze was hot with desire. Her body trembled, and her pussy pulsed with need for him.

"Mmm, your sweet lips are so warm and silky."

He kissed her tenderly, and her body felt like it was liquefying as he slid a finger into her entrance, his thumb resting over her clit as the other began to stroke her G-spot. She couldn't help but move against him.

"Is that the right spot?" he asked in a sexy, deep tone.

She moaned in response and clutched his massive shoulder. Curled up in his arms like that, she felt completely enveloped in his strength as he stroked her pussy with as much care and enjoyment as she had with him earlier.

"Oh, Eli! Don't stop, please," she whimpered as her movements became completely reflexive and out of her will or ability to control. He added another finger to the one already stroking her G-spot. The sensation was unbelievably pleasurable as the tension in her body began to mount. Moving with his fingers inside her, she listened to him murmur love words to her. She heard the smooth, wet sounds her pussy made as she rocked on his fingers and lost every inhibition. The tension increased inside her, and her pussy flooded with a fresh rush of her moisture. He groaned deeply as she moved with him in fluid grace.

Her body drew up tight inside, as he stroked her firmly without pausing. She tilted her head back, and came with a loud, sobbing scream. The hot cream from her orgasm gushed over his hand and soaked them both as she rode each ecstatic pulse of her climax. Her head fell to his shoulder weakly, and she panted and trembled in his gentle arms.

He licked her juice from his fingers like it was the sweetest honey he'd ever tasted while she watched with deep contentment. After he finished, she palmed his cheek. He reached down and grasped her ass and pressed her mound against his hot erection. He hissed in pleasure and looked down into her eyes and nuzzled her cheek.

Rachel laid her head on the pillow, and he caressed her thighs as he knelt between them. She opened her legs wider for him and slid a finger over her clit as he watched. She felt powerful when she saw the lust and enjoyment in his eyes as he watched her impulsive fingertips.

"I like to see you touch yourself," he said in a deep, smooth tone, stroking his big, warm hand up and down her inner thigh. Her pussy trembled at the sound of his sexy voice and clamored for him to fill her.

"It feels even better with you watching." She gasped as she stroked a finger slowly over that favorite spot. She was swollen and hot, and with him avidly watching her, she knew she'd go off soon.

"Do it more if you like how it feels. I like to see your fingers slide over your wet lips." She shuddered in pleasure while she listened to the wet sounds her fingers made when they slid through her soaked pussy lips. "That's right, touch your clit. Are you almost there? Don't come yet. I want to feel you come on my cock this time. That's right. Such a *good* girl, saving your orgasm for me." He stroked his long, hard shaft. "I can't wait to stroke into your hot, wet pussy, honey. It's like sliding into warm silk," he murmured as she continued to stroke her clit.

Rachel breathed in bursting pants and held her orgasm back. She traced her fingers over her inner lips to give her arousal a chance to come down a notch. She didn't dare slip a finger inside because she knew she'd lose control given the way her pussy pulsed in longing to be filled with his massive cock.

"Baby, I want you," she whimpered as her fingertip slid once again over her clit. She looked up into his beautiful eyes and begged, "Please!"

He rose over her, his eyes filled with love and passion. With a tender kiss, he positioned his cock at her swollen, aching entrance and pressed his cock into her just a bit. She moaned and cried out in need, wanting him seated to the hilt *now*.

Eli began to rock into her a little at a time, taking more of her with each firm stroke until he was pumping all the way in and out. She braced her feet on the bed and rocked her body against his, her hips undulating in sinuous rhythm as her orgasm built and finally shattered into a thousand pieces. Riding each electrifying pulse, she heard him cry out as he found his release. His cock pulsed inside her as he filled her with his seed. They grinded together in ecstasy until all desire to move had ceased.

"Are you all right?" He smiled in breathless satisfaction. "Am I squishing you?"

"Yes. No. Don't pull out yet. I want to feel you inside me a bit longer, please," she murmured against his chest as she held on to his hard buttocks.

He rolled them over so she was now on top of him, their intimate connection unbroken. He groaned, and his cock pulsed inside her as she settled into the new position. He still felt hard inside her. Her heart literally brimmed with satisfaction, and if it were possible, she would have stayed this way with him all night, filled to the brim with his cock and wallowing in his love.

"Was that good?"

"Woman, that was so good I saw stars. Five minutes and I'll be hard for you again." His large, gentle hands stroked lazily over her ass, and pleasant shivers and aftershocks made her pussy quiver around him.

"Really?" Her cheeks warmed as she looked at him with dazed eyes. "That soon?"

"Yes, I'm feeling it already. Being inside your sweet, warm body is like a drug to me," he murmured as he flicked his tongue playfully along her throat. He arched his back under her, pressing his cock deep into her wet pussy, and she felt an answering pulse in her clit.

She turned her head and pressed kisses to his throat and suckled on his thick, muscular shoulder. "Can we? Again? I mean?"

He swept his hands up her back, under her hair. "Yeah, but it'll take longer, and I don't want you to be sore. Rest for me. We'll see what happens, okay?"

"All right," she said with a contented sigh. She rested her head on his chest, listening in bliss to the sound of his heartbeat under her ear. She gently pressed her hips to him, enjoying the feel of him inside her, delighting that every time she did his heart rate sped up a bit and he felt thicker and harder. He gently stroked her back and her ass, and his hot hands left a trail of warmth over her skin.

She flexed her hips again and moaned when she felt him thrust gently into her, pressing on her clit as he did. She braced her hands on his shoulders, lifted her chest off of his, and began to move, slowly grinding and rolling her hips over him. She was in the perfect position, her clit brushing his pubic bone with each stroke as he thrust into her throbbing, wet pussy.

"You feel so good. I love you, angel, so much."

His hands slid down her back again, and he closed his eyes as the tension in his body began to crest. She moved wantonly over him, dragging her clit over his cock again and again. He grasped her hips, and he began pumping into her fiercely. His face looked like he was in agony, and coupled with the groans coming from his chest, she might have thought he was in pain.

She propped herself up on him and rode his cock hard, her breaths rapid and high-pitched as her orgasm began to build up inside her. A smile crossed her lips as she experienced that beautiful moment of certainty that she was about to come. He gripped her ass firmly and pumped with several short strokes, and they both cried out at the same moment as he tensed under her, flooding her pussy again with his cum. She cried out again as multiple aftershocks raced through her before she collapsed, writhing on top of him.

Once they'd recovered, he gently lifted her and pulled out. His seed and her cum from her earlier orgasms leaked from her cunt onto him.

"I got you all messy, honey," she said with a contented sigh as she snuggled back onto his chest.

"Do you want another shower?"

She lifted her head. "No, I want to stay this way with you, right now. In the morning I'll bathe again." She yawned sleepily as she curled closer to him, her head back on his chest.

After falling asleep, she must have rolled off of him because she woke during the night with him spooned behind her. She was curled in a ball with a pillow between her knees, and her head rested on his warm biceps. He'd gathered her to him and had fallen asleep holding her this way. Snuggled into his warmth, she felt safe and secure. He'd even pulled the covers over them. She clasped her fingers in his, relaxed in sleep. As he continued dreaming, he unconsciously squeezed her hand, and she closed her eyes and fell back asleep.

Chapter Seventeen

Eli ran along the cold white-tiled hallway in his fuzzy blue slipper socks. The cast on his left arm bumped against his sore ribs. Tears flooded his eyes as he sobbed quietly and stopped running, momentarily disoriented. The nurse's station was ahead of him, and he knew if he went that direction the sweet nurses would see him and return him to his room. He needed to find the little church where he could feel better and chase away the nightmares. The bandage over his right eye was damp from his tears and had started to come loose. He wanted to pull it off, but his eye hurt, and the nurses told him to not pull it off or he might hurt himself worse. They were so sweet and doing their best to help him feel better. He didn't want to upset them, so he left it alone and tried to ignore the sodden feel of it.

He turned back on silent feet and padded back down the hall, took a left turn, and found the familiar room. He'd missed it earlier because of his cry-baby tears. He silently pushed open the door because there might be someone in here and he didn't want to be seen. Someone sat hunched over a pew in the front, a man. He silently dropped down to his hands and knees and crawled along the back wall, keeping away from the quietly sobbing man. He crept to the darkened back corner and curled up in a pew. There was a Bible sitting on the seat, and he placed his hand under his cheek and rested his head on it, waiting for the man to leave. He listened as the man sobbed softly and thought he sounded like his heart was broken. Maybe he had bad dreams, too.

He prayed to God and asked him to help Mom feel better so they could go on to Grandma and Grandpa's. He asked God if she was hurting to fix her or heal her and make her feel better. He woke in a daze as soft hands smoothed his hair and touched his cheek. He looked up into deep blue eyes and knew he was dreaming again. "You can't stay here, Eli. Come with me so you can rest." Gentle arms picked him up, and he was lovingly carried back to his room, tears spilling from his eyes. Soft lips touched his cheeks, kissing the tears away. A gentle hand feathered in his hair, speaking words of comfort to him.

Eli slowly awakened, clasped snugly in Rachel's arms, his cheek against the gentle swell of her breasts, which were damp. His chest ached, and he realized he'd had that familiar dream again. It was not unusual to wake from the vivid dream crying, and he prepared for the gut-wrenching heartache that came when he relived that loss. She pulled his hair back from his face and wiped the tears from his cheeks. The pain was still there, but he felt comforted this time, just as he had in his dream. He felt the loss, but he no longer felt like he was alone in his grief.

He rested his cheek against her shoulder for a moment before sitting up in the bed. It was already daylight outside, and the clock on the night table read nine o'clock.

"Wow, we slept hard," he murmured, sitting up and wiping his eyes with the heels of his hands. She gathered the sheet around her and straddled his thighs. Her eyes were full of concern for him. She brushed her fingertips over his jaw then leaned forward to hug him.

"Eli, you were dreaming. You cried as if you were in pain. Are you all right?" she asked as she looked deeply into his eyes.

"Yes, it's a recurring nightmare. I don't have it very often anymore, but when I do, it hits me hard. It's very vivid." He tried to smile for her.

"I didn't know what else to do, so I woke you up." She tenderly stroked his big shoulders.

"Thank you." He was grateful she woke him so he didn't have to relive the whole experience.

"Want to sleep some more?"

"No, you?" He nuzzled her throat and squeezed her curvy hips through the sheet.

"I'm good. Are you hungry?" She wrapped the sheet over her breasts.

"Starving. Did you still want to take a ride with me?"

"Of course!" she responded enthusiastically.

He grinned wickedly. "Then we'd better get out of this bed before I take you on a different sort of ride. Are you sore from last night?"

"I feel fine. A tiny bit tender maybe, but I feel wonderful, and I'm sure the shower will help. Do you want to talk about the dream?" she asked, looking into his eyes again, not with pity but with obvious concern for him.

He shook his head reluctantly. "Still too fresh. Maybe later, okay?" Changing the subject, he grinned devilishly as he reached for her. "Right now, you'd better either climb off or climb on."

She giggled and shimmied backward. "Nuh-uh! I need a shower! You can't possibly want me first thing in the morning, all sleep crusted and morning breath-y."

"Baby, I'll take you any way I can catch you first thing in the morning." He reached out like he was going to grab her and pull her back under him. She squealed loudly and stripped the sheet from the bed as she raced for the bathroom, giggling loudly.

The doorbell rang, and he let Kelly and Matthew in. His sister had considerately brought Rachel a change of clothing with her. He hugged Kelly and patted little Matthew's back then took the clothing from her and went back to the bedroom. Rachel had just slipped back in, dressed in his bathrobe.

"Here are your clothes, babe." Eli caught her around the waist. "Although I like how my robe looks on you," he murmured as he pushed the bedroom door closed softly. She smiled invitingly up at him, letting the front of the robe go to reach out to him. He slid his hands smoothly inside the robe, around her waist, and nuzzled her throat as she pressed against him.

"Mmm, you smell good. Feel better?"

"Cleaner, yes." She sighed happily as he stroked her derriere and pressed her against his semi-erect cock.

"Wanna get messy again?" he asked playfully, growling as he nibbled her throat.

"Don't you have company?"

"Yes, dammit." He smacked her behind lightly. "Why don't you get ready and I'll take my favorite girls and nephew to brunch?"

"Sounds great! Give me a few minutes."

Eli took them to brunch at Rudy's and had fun talking with the girls and held little Matthew while Kelly ate.

Eli took a closer look at his sister. "You look tired, sis. Was the baby fussy last night?

"Did you not sleep well?" Rachel asked. "Was the mattress not comfortable?"

Eli thought he recognized the devious little smirk on Kelly's face. "Oh, yes, when I was *allowed* to sleep." She cooed at Matthew, giving Eli a significant look, which Rachel totally missed as she took a bite of eggs. *Oh, shit.* Eli felt his cheeks grow warm with embarrassment as he looked in Kelly's eyes and shook his head, asking her silently to not say anything else.

Kelly grinned devilishly. "Yep, a little black-haired angel kept me awake last night. Just when I thought he'd settle down and let me rest, he'd start back up again with his hollering and wailing. Frankly, he was so loud I was afraid you might even hear him next door. But I did eventually get to sleep. He was right back at it this morning." In a short fit of giggles, she actually snorted.

My sister knows what I sound like when I get a blowjob.

Crap. Eli's mortification was complete. Not only had Kelly *heard* them, she could make out the endearment Eli used for Rachel. Kelly smiled innocently at Eli. "Is it hot in here to you, Eli? You look a little flushed."

Eli cleared his throat and replied, "Yeah, maybe so."

"So was your last neighbor an elderly person, Eli?" Kelly asked naughtily.

Eli groaned quietly and allowed her to have fun at his expense. "Yeah, he was. His children had to move him into a nursing home."

"Was he in ill health?" she asked, the picture of concern.

"They worried about his safety. He was…hard of hearing." Eli gave her a look that promised retribution as she snickered. Rachel looked at them quizzically.

"Am I missing something here?"

Attentively, Eli replied, "No, honey, how's your breakfast?"

"It's good. So what were your plans for today, Kelly?"

"I'm headed over to Charity and Justin's in a few minutes. They haven't seen the baby yet, and it's been a couple of years since I've seen their kids. What are you going to do today?"

"Eli is going to take me on a ride out to the lake."

"How romantic," Kelly said approvingly. "You're so perfect together. Did you know there's a chance of rain this evening?"

Eli replied, "No, but thanks for letting me know. We'll make sure and watch the skies. You're full of all kinds of *helpful* information, aren't you, sis?" he asked sarcastically.

"Yep, helpful me!" she said, smiling innocently. "Don't wait on me for supper. I may stay and eat with them."

* * * *

Rachel pulled her long hair back and braided it then allowed Eli to help her put her helmet on. She slipped her arms into his big leather riding jacket, which he insisted she should wear. He climbed on and started his Harley then held it steady while she climbed on behind him and got settled.

"You all right? Ready to go?" Through the small speaker inside the helmet he asked, "Hear me okay?"

"Yes, honey. I'm ready." She scooted toward him and slid her arms around his waist and couldn't resist rubbing her breasts against him playfully.

Eli chuckled and rubbed back. "Damn, do that as much as you want, angel. Hold on to me." He turned the bike in the driveway and pulled out. She pressed against him and held on tight. The vibration of the motorcycle traveled through every fiber of her body. She felt the throaty roar as he accelerated down the road and experienced a rush of adrenaline at the openness and freedom as the wind blew around them. He eased the bike at low speeds through town to get her used to being on a motorcycle and then rode out on the state highway that led out to Bowie Lake farther up in the hill country.

Rachel knew Eli took the ride easy for her sake, staying well within the speed limit. She also noted that he would occasionally rub his back against her breasts and figured he took the ride slow and easy for his own sake, as well. She made sure he enjoyed the extra few minutes of her snuggled up so close to his back as she held on around his waist. It was a perfect day.

They rode on the lake road that looped around the shoreline before they stopped at a rest area that was close to the water and perfect for taking a walk. He helped her off, and they strolled down to the shore. Holding hands, they walked along the water's edge. She was very quiet, lost in thought as he stopped at a weathered log on the shore and took a seat. She sat down beside him and picked up a sun-bleached stick and began poking the rocks with it. The sunlight sparkled off the water as a breeze blew across it, and the water lapped at the shore.

She removed the elastic band from the end of her braid and slowly ran her fingers through the plait. She'd braided it at Eli's suggestion because having long hair blowing about while riding on the back of a motorcycle was never a good idea. The wind would turn it into a knotted mess. She felt a little bereft for some reason. She attributed it to the Sunday afternoon blues and to being out of her usual routine. She didn't care whether her laundry and oil change got done today or tomorrow, but she was a creature of habit, and finding a new rhythm with Eli had her a little off kilter.

"You okay, angel?" Eli looked over at her, and his pale gray eyes showed a little concern.

Rachel shrugged. "Yeah. The real world will encroach on us again tomorrow. I've gotten comfortable in our little bubble, and I wonder how we'll work out seeing each other. I'm going to need to stay home tomorrow night and do the laundry. I need to finish settling in."

He slid his arm around her reassuringly as he said, "Our schedules are a little mixed up, but if we give it time, we'll find a new routine. We'll find time to be together because I'm not letting you go."

She smiled up at him and felt her cheeks grow warm. "Good. Thank you for understanding. How are you feeling?"

He smiled slowly, looked down at her, and she snuggled close beside him. He slipped an arm around her shoulders and slid the other under her knees and lifted her into his lap. When he did things like that, it made her feel less like an Amazon, and more petite and precious to him. "I'm feeling about as satisfied as a man can be." He kissed her tenderly. Then he laid his ear against her chest and listened to her heart throb. "Your heart is pounding."

Rachel chortled, and the blue feeling dissipated miraculously. "Of course it is, when you say things like that to me. I feel better already. I guess I was just down from the thought of having to go back out into the real world. This weekend has changed me."

"For the better or worse?" he asked seriously.

"The better, of course." She smiled into his silver-gray eyes.

"The real world has been with us all along, I think. It's just taking on a new form. I'm the same man I was Thursday night, maybe better for you being a part of my life now, but it's still me, and you're still the same beautiful woman you always were. All the other stuff will work itself out."

"You're right. I need to stop over-analyzing everything. Can I ask you about your dream? Do you feel like talking about it?" She didn't want to push him any further but give him an opportunity if he wanted it.

"I lost my mom when I was four years old. In the dream I sort of relive the events that led up to her death. Her death was very hard for our family, and sometimes I think I'll never be over it."

"I'm so sorry, Eli. I didn't mean to pry. I'm sorry you lost your mom at such a young age. Do you remember very much about her?"

"Yeah, I do have some great memories of her. I know she would have loved you."

"Really?" Rachel was touched that he thought so. She didn't ask him any more questions, and he didn't offer any more information. They got up and walked farther down the shore then returned to the motorcycle.

Eli gazed off in the distance and said, "We'd better get back. I don't want your first ride to include riding home soaked to the skin."

At home, he grilled steaks for the two of them while she prepared a salad and baked a couple of potatoes. While the steaks cooked, they laughed together and rearranged the patio furniture on the covered back deck so that everything was in the middle, even moving the grill to the center space between their backdoors. They traded keys so they could come and go as they needed to.

They ate outside, drinking from a bottle of red wine she'd picked up at the store along with a few groceries. They enjoyed the evening off and the chance to spend some more time alone. After cleaning up the mess, they went back over to his place, since Kelly would be staying until Tuesday morning, and watched a movie. It felt early to go to bed, but Rachel knew she'd be a zombie Monday morning if she didn't, so she got up and took her shower while he made sure both places were locked up for the night and that Kelly had made it home all right

She sighed happily when he joined her in the shower. She was awed by his immense size and masculine presence. "You are so incredibly handsome, Eli Wolf," she murmured as she rinsed off under the spray.

"You are very beautiful, Rachel Lopez." He leaned forward to kiss her. "Want me to scrub your back?"

"I'd love that." She handed him the body wash and washcloth. She lifted her clean wet hair over her shoulder and turned her back to him. He lathered the washcloth and gently scrubbed her back as she leaned against the shower tiles. "Mmm, that feels good. You're giving me goose bumps." She arched her back to tempt him to slide his hands over her ass and around her hips.

His hands were gentle, and she felt the telltale ache begin as her pussy engorged and tingled. He slid his hands over her hips to her abdomen and pulled her snug against him. His skin slithered against hers because of the soap. She sighed and bit her lip when his cock slid along the cleft of her ass. His callused hands slid up her ribs to cup a full, round breast in each hand and squeezed them gently, which made her moan softly in pleasure. She lifted her hands to his shoulders, slid them up his neck, and pulled him to her for a kiss.

She turned to him. "Can I bathe you?"

At his nod, she reached for the soap and washcloth and worked it into a lather while he wet his hair. She smiled up at him and started at his shoulders. She scrubbed them gently then down each arm and over his wide chest. She let out a sigh of feminine appreciation as she admired his assets. Her body was swamped with desire. But also mixed with it was a territoriality she would have been hard-pressed to explain. He was hers, all hers.

A little guilty for feeling that way about someone who was so strong and self-possessed, she glanced up at his face and saw a similar emotion in his eyes. Lust was there, too, unmistakably, but she also had the feeling he saw her as his, *all his*. She was good with that and smiled deviously at him as she slid the washcloth over his ribs and abdomen.

Instead of trailing farther south where he would have liked her to go, she slipped under his arm to his back and scrubbed it good and hard, just the way he liked it, judging by his groans of approval. He pulled his hair out of the way, and she scrubbed his shoulders and even under his arms.

Slowly ran the washcloth over one of his ass cheeks, she knelt on the tiles beside him. Her fingers slithered through the suds along with the washcloth as she tended to one long, muscular leg, then the other. She bent over and scrubbed his feet as well. Rachel stood with his help and gazed up into his clear gray eyes as she stood at his side and washed his ass cheeks. Her fingers and the washcloth slipped into the cleft and slid down. Eli gave a low soft groan as her fingers, covered in the washcloth, delved over that forbidden, sensitive region again and again. He tilted his head back, and he moaned quietly as she swept her finger gently over his perineum. It felt very naughty and sexy to do this for him, and she was turned on as she watched how it affected him. She swept over the whole area again with the washcloth before coming to stand in front of him at his other side.

His hand swept over her shoulder, and she asked, "Am I making you feel good?"

"Honey, you *know* you are. I'm still tingling," he murmured huskily.

She lathered the washcloth again and smoothed soap over his lower abdomen. Her touch made his abs ripple as the washcloth slid lower. With great care, she washed his balls lovingly, but thoroughly, until he was panting for breath and murmuring her name over and over again.

"Will it hurt if I use the washcloth here?" she whispered sexily as she ran a finger slowly up the underside of his very rigid cock.

"No, just be gentle when I'm hard like this or use your hand if you want. Or bo—th," he replied shakily as she gently washed the short, crisp hairs around his cock and then smoothed the washcloth along his length, wrapping her hand in the washcloth around him. After a few strokes that way, she rinsed the washcloth quickly and said, "You can wash your hair while I finish this, can't you? Then we can get in bed."

She applied more bodywash to her palm and lathered her hands. He poured shampoo in his hand and watched her movements as he began to lather his hair. She knew he always took a couple of minutes to wash his hair very thoroughly. Once he closed his eyes and began scrubbing, she wrapped her fingers around his hard cock. He gasped again.

"Did I startle you?'

"No—o—o. Feels good. I love your hands on me, everywhere. Ah, that stroking is nice," he murmured as he moved within her hands. The soap made her hands slip up and down smoothly over his shaft. She swirled her palm softly over the head before sliding down again. He placed his big, warm hand over hers and stopped her motions. "If you keep doing that, I'm going to come in the shower. I want to be deep inside you when I finish."

His words made her giddy at the mental image of him doing exactly that. "I'm done. I'll let you finish." She climbed out and reached for her towel. After drying off and combing her hair, she used his blow-dryer and dried her hair and then went into his bedroom. He'd already lit the candles and turned down the bed, so she set the alarm on her cell phone and placed it on the bedside table then slid between the cool sheets.

He came into the bedroom totally nude, his cock stiff and erect against his abdomen. He stood at the end of the bed and motioned to her to come to him. She rose off the pillow and crawled on her hands and knees to him, delighting in the dark lust she saw in his gaze. He was ready to play, and she wasn't surprised by how quickly her body responded to the look in his eyes. She grew wet with desire before he'd even said a word.

When she reached him, he slid his big, muscular arms around her shoulders and allowed his hands to glide down her back to her hips. Grasping her soft curves, he tilted her body to his. With her on her knees, the height of his bed allowed for an advantageous alignment of his cock with her wet slit. She shivered in delight, thinking how well they would fit together if she turned on her hands and knees for him right now.

He'd taken her from behind before, with both of them in the bed, but there was something more...dominating about kneeling in front of him, wide open as he stood over her and took her from behind. The thought made her feel small and vulnerable. She knew his heart and trusted him completely, so she wanted to be that open to him and allow him that kind of control.

He tipped her chin up to look into her eyes. "I want to ask you about something. Yesterday, you said you might like to try anal sex with me. Is that still true for you, or were you merely caught up in the moment?"

Chapter Eighteen

Rachel gulped nervously and remembered how she'd felt the previous day when he'd slid his thumb into her ass. The wildly erotic sensation had convinced her she'd try anything he wanted. But there was a big difference between his thumb and the huge cock he'd been blessed with. Did she want to try *that*?

She looked up at him. "I liked what you did yesterday, and I would like to try it again, but I don't know if I can handle it."

"The difference in size?" he asked, and she nodded, grateful that he understood and didn't seem put out by her trepidation. "I wouldn't start there. We would have to work up to that. I would do a little shopping, get some things for you that would help you work up to the point where you could comfortably take my cock in your ass."

A ripple of pleasure shot up her spine at the thought of whatever it was he would get and how he would use it to get her ready to receive him. "That sounds like fun," she said shakily, but she smiled up at him with enthusiasm. "What kinds of things?"

He grinned at her, evidently pleased by the anticipation that must have shown in her eyes. "Well, you'll just have to wait and see. I don't have to go in to The Pony until eight o'clock. That gives me time to drive into San Antonio tomorrow and find what we need and get back to you after you're off work. We can play for a while in the afternoon."

"Mr. Grogan said I could have a half day off tomorrow. I have an important meeting in the morning and then I'll be home by noon."

She slid her fingers over his lean hips to his firm backside and squeezed.

"You and I are going to have lots of fun. You're shivering," he said when she trembled and broke out in goose bumps. "Are you excited?"

"Yes. I, um, I can't wait to see what you get. What are you going to *do* to me?" she asked softly into his chest. He tilted her chin up.

"I'm going to make it very good for you. But you're going to tell me if you need me to stop."

"I promise. Is it going to hurt?"

"At first it may," he replied honestly, "because you'll be acclimating to receive a big cock in a tight opening. But it will be pleasurable also, if I do it right. The last thing I want is to hurt you."

She felt a flutter in her belly, and her cunt tightened. Moisture seeped from her slit and caused her pussy lips to slide over each other as she scissored her thighs together. This conversation was having a dramatic effect on her body. Her heart pounded a little, and she hoped he might give her a foretaste tonight.

"Honey, I'm…"

"What is it, angel? You can tell me anything," he said, a small, knowing smile on his handsome face.

"I–I'm…"

"There is nothing I wouldn't do for you, angel."

"I wish we could start right now," she blurted softly and then brushed her lips over his chest. "I want to feel you in my ass tonight. Do something to me, so I know what it will be like, please?" she asked softly. Her pussy contracted and begged to be filled. "I want you in me, all over me. Please?"

Her pussy quivered with expectation when he smiled down at her, his gaze warm with tenderness, combined with that dark, edgy lust that she wanted to explore. "Turn on your hands and knees. I'll help you, baby," he murmured as he opened a drawer in the night table. He brought the tube of lubricant to the bed, as well as another lubricant in a bottle with a rounded end, and then went to the bathroom and returned with a hand towel. "Spread your thighs for me, baby." He smoothed his warm palm over her tailbone and trailed his fingertips over her cleft. "Arch your back and give me your ass."

She tilted her hips for him and arched, presenting her ass. Her breath caught in her throat at the sensation of vulnerability.

"Do you trust me, honey?"

"Of course."

"The diameter of this bottle is a good place for us to start with stretching you. I'm going to lubricate your opening and gradually slide it in. It's not as good as what I plan to get for you tomorrow, but I think you'll like it. Will you promise to tell me if it hurts too much?" he asked softly, smoothing his warm fingertips over her puckered opening.

"I will. I promise," she replied breathlessly, shuddering at the sensation of his callused fingertips caressing her asshole, exciting every nerve ending in her entire body.

"Relax the muscles in your bottom and let me work you a little. When I start to penetrate, I'll want you to gently push back, but not too hard."

"Do it, baby." She wiggled her ass at him. Chuckling at her enthusiasm, he smoothed a generous amount of lubricant on her ass in a slow circular massage. She groaned as the sensation sent tingles straight to her clit, which began to throb.

She squealed in surprise when his warm tongue lapped playfully at her swollen cunt and the juices that trickled from her opening onto her thigh. He chuckled devilishly. "Waste not, want not. Angel, you're so wet already. You're going to love this."

"I already do," she crooned as she pushed back against his fingers. The sensuous circular motion of his thumb continued, and her body hummed in pleasure, ready for his invasion. "Eli, that feels so good. I can't wait."

He pressed more firmly, and she felt a little burning as her ass began to give him access until the tip of his thumb slid into her bottom. She gasped then sighed at the sensation. It burned slightly, but it felt incredible also. She arched her back, opened to him, and gave him as much as she could.

"Good?"

"Oh, yeah."

"How does it feel?" His voice vibrated with tension as his lubricated finger teased and swirled just inside her ass.

"*Very* naughty, but sexy, too. It feels hot and so tight, but I want more at the same time." She shuddered softly. Her whole body hummed with an erotic vibration at his invasion. As if it wanted to sing for him.

She moaned as he slid his thumb in farther and began to gently pump the entire digit in and out. He lubed his fingers again, and this time, his index and middle finger slipped into her ass. She hissed at the pinch and added tightness, relaxed her bottom, and tried to not clench. He thrust his fingers farther into her, pumping in a slow, gentle rhythm that made her whimper in pleasure but also at the tiny bite of pain that was somehow part of the pleasure.

He reached around her hip with his other hand and slid his fingers through her pussy lips to her clit, rubbing along her favorite spot. She groaned as he coupled that caress with the parting of the fingers in her ass to stretch her a little farther, pumping in and out. His tender attention to her clit had her soaring, and she moaned as he removed the fingers from both places momentarily.

He lubricated her opening again and the rounded end of the bottle. He even smoothed a little over her clit as he stroked her again. He positioned the rounded end of the bottle at her rear opening and began to push and withdraw rhythmically. The loosened muscles gave way, and she pushed back with her bottom as he pushed forward very carefully, his fingers still flicking her clit. She groaned as the hard plastic began to enter her ass. There was a hot pinch as the muscles there stretched, but it was balanced by a tingling pleasure that was wild and overwhelming.

"Okay so far?"

"Yes. Oh, honey!" She felt like she was soaring.

"Like it?"

"I love it, but I need to move. I need to come."

"I'm going to give you a little more, and then I'll help you come. Angel, we are going to have so much fun tomorrow."

"Oooh! I can't wait. Eli, that feels so good." She moaned as he slid the tube in a little, pulled almost all the way out, and then slid it in again. He gradually gave her more until she was easily taking the entire length with no problem. She arched and moved up and down the bottle as he held it for her, letting her set her own pace. She needed more. It wasn't quite enough.

She whimpered softly. "It feels so good, but I want you inside me, please!"

He positioned his cock at her cunt, gripped her hip in one hand, and slowly drew her back onto his rock-hard length. Rachel threw her hair back as she began to gyrate and pump faster on him as he thrust into her. Her soft moan gradually grew into a wail as she lost control. The overwhelming sensation of being taken in both openings drove her into a frenzy of motion as she came undone, curving and arching her back, taking every inch offered to her in both places. He gripped her tightly and pounded into her, groaning as his release exploded inside her. He thrust deep several more times then stilled and held her to him, and she reveled in his embrace.

Rachel's breathing hitched and slowed as her arms collapsed under her, and she laid her face against his comforter, breathing heavily. His hand massaged the hip he'd held on to so tightly as he slowly withdrew the improvised sex toy from her ass. He laid it aside on a towel and drew her hips back against him, his cock deep inside her, and she delighted in the ways he found to give her pleasure.

"That was amazing, Eli. I can't wait for what you have planned for tomorrow."

He chuckled huskily. "I'm glad you liked it. You're a wild thing when the mood strikes you, Rachel." He withdrew from her gently and paused to stroke her entrance. He knelt behind her and licked her clit, making her mewl like a kitten as her thighs quivered.

He growled softly in appreciation. "I will *always* love that sight."

"Hmm? What sight? Tell me?" she asked, having a feeling she already knew.

He patted her fanny as he stood. "The sight of your pussy, fresh from lovemaking, filled with my cum."

"Oh." She sighed ecstatically, liking the thought herself.

Chapter Nineteen

Eli pulled into the driveway on his Harley, his saddlebags filled with all kinds of goodies for Rachel. The sight that greeted him brought a big, wide smile to his face and caused all the blood to leave his brain and flood his rapidly expanding cock. She must not have heard him pull up, which was surprising because the vibration could have been felt it in the ground when he rode up on his Harley.

Kelly looked over at him from the flowerbed between their respective porches and grinned. The baby lay in his bouncy seat in the shade, sucking his fist, while she planted small, colorful flowering bushes in the freshly turned soil.

Rachel squatted in the yard, working on his lawn mower. She wore a pair of faded cutoffs that were cut a little too short. White straggly fringe from where they were cut hung down in light tufts around her bare thighs. She had sneakers on and a body-hugging tank top. Pink earbuds dangled from her ears down to the tiny, hot pink MP3 player clipped to the top edge of her bra and the tank top.

Sweat glistened on her lower back where her tank top rode up, exposing her light olive skin and the waistband of the G-string she wore under the cutoffs. Her hair was pinned up on the back of her head in a clip, and loose ringlets hung down around her shoulders. The lawn mower was running, which explained why she hadn't heard him, and the MP3 was probably playing, too. Kelly waved a hand at Rachel, and she looked up through her wraparound sunglasses as Kelly pointed at Eli. A slow, sexy grin crossed her beautiful face as she turned off the mower. Eli noticed the secret smile on Kelly's face as she returned to her work to give them their privacy.

Rachel stood, wiped her hands on her cutoffs, and sauntered over to him. He got even harder watching her hips sway until she was only inches away from him where he sat on the bike. He leaned toward her as she removed an earbud and turned down the MP3 player, then asked, "Do you have any idea how sexy you are in those cutoffs and that tank top, bent over my lawnmower?"

"Yuck, I'm sweaty, gross, and covered in grass clippings." She chuckled and slipped off the sunglasses.

"Well, I see you've been very busy on your afternoon off."

"Yes, I have been. I told Mr. Grogan my visit to the insurance agent would only take a little while, but he told me I could have the whole afternoon. So I figured I might as well be productive."

The landscaping looks good," he said, gently placing his hands on her hips. "Charlie will like what you've done. All I do is keep the lawn mowed and trimmed."

"Now it will look homier with some color and foliage."

"Next time I'll help you, and we'll get it done together. Maybe you'd like to plant another flowerbed in the backyard. I could help you dig it up if you like."

He felt like he was coming *home* when he pulled up today rather than just coming back to a house. The difference was *her* and the little things she had done. He noticed an outdoor chair on her porch and saw that there was one on his porch, as well. He grinned, thinking his new goal was to get both of those chairs onto the same friggin' porch. Or better yet, place them together on a new porch somewhere else where the walls weren't so thin.

She leaned into him and kissed him deeply as his hands squeezed her hips and slid over her ass. She sighed. "So? How was your day?" she asked quietly, but he could hear the excitement vibrating in her voice.

"I had good luck finding all the fun things on my list, plus a few surprises for you. I also bought another set of sheets."

"That's good. I washed the sheets from your bed and the towels earlier today. It's all put back now, and I made your bed up, too."

"Thank you for doing that, angel."

"Mmm, knowing you were going shopping for fun stuff, I felt like it was the least I could do for you." Her body quivered as she added, "I *can't wait* to see what you got."

"Baby, you're trembling. Have you looked forward to me getting home all afternoon?" he asked, already knowing the answer. Holding her close like this, he could smell her arousal. He pressed her closer, and she relaxed into him.

"*All* day long," she said slowly as he nuzzled her breast.

He glanced over at Kelly to find she still worked with her back turned. He wondered briefly what she would think if the two of them disappeared into his side of the duplex for a few hours.

"Tell you what. I'll bring in the shopping bags. You take a shower at my place, and I'll tell Kelly we're going to spend some time alone."

"I hate to leave her alone working out here."

"It's the heat of the day right now. She's probably planning to go inside any minute. I don't think she'll mind. I'm going to take you both to supper later, before I go in. We have several hours to play before then. Would you like that, honey?"

"Yes, Eli," she responded quietly as he got off the bike and opened both saddlebags and removed several shopping bags from the roomy compartments. He carried them in as she followed him into the house. She didn't say anything else, but the excitement she was feeling was palpable to him, as well. While she got ready for her shower, Eli went back outside. He stepped off the porch and walked over to where Kelly knelt, wiping the dirt off her gloves.

"Hi, Eli! I'm going to take a little break now that it's so hot. Matthew needs to cool off, too, so I think I'm going to go in and lie down with him on the loveseat for a little while. Do you think Rachel will mind? I can't go as long as I used to before I had him. The heat zonks me out."

"Are you drinking plenty of water?" He squatted down to help her up.

"Yeah, Rachel reminded me to drink, too. I have my bottle right here." She held up a sweaty bottle of cold water.

"I think Rachel and I are going to take a break, too. You don't mind if we take some alone time, do you?"

"Of course not, Eli! If Christopher was here, *we'd* take some *alone time*, too," she added devilishly.

"I'm going to take you both out for supper before I go in at eight o'clock, so don't make any supper plans, okay?"

"'Kay. Go have fun. See you at…"

"Six thirty?"

"Perfect. See you then, big brother. I'm going to go nap with Matthew on the *loveseat*, in the *living room, away* from the bedroom. Go have fun." She snickered.

"You're a riot, sis, a regular comedian," he commented sarcastically as he turned to go back inside.

"Love you."

"Love you, too," he replied as he walked back to his front door. There wasn't a better little sister anywhere, devious though she was.

Since Rachel had finished cutting the lawn, he put the mower away in the garage, along with the weed eater and his shovel. He closed the garage and went in the house.

The bathroom door was open, and steam floated in the air from the shower. He opened one bag and went quickly through its contents. Everything would need to be removed from its packaging and washed and put away, but for now, he removed only the things he would need for today. He laid a dish towel on the counter, and after the shower turned off, he ran a sink of warm soapy water. He removed the wrapping from the items he needed and placed them in the warm water.

He removed other items from another shopping bag and cut off the tags. He left the items in the sink to soak a bit longer so that they would be nice and warm when he removed them. He walked back to the bathroom and smiled at her in the mirror as she combed out her damp hair.

"You have time to dry your hair if you want to, honey. I need a few more minutes before we get started. I bought something I think you might like." He placed the satiny bundles in her shaky hands. "You're trembling. Are you excited?"

She caught her bottom lip between her teeth and nodded mutely, her eyelids sliding shut momentarily. Her chest glistened with droplets from her shower, and he couldn't resist leaning down to kiss one on the upper swell of her breast above where the towel rested. His tongue flicked out to lick it up and caused her to gasp softly and sway toward him a little.

He placed another small bundle in her hand and said in a low, husky voice, "Put this on after you've dressed and wait for me here. I won't be long." He kissed her cheek and left her to dress.

* * * *

Rachel couldn't wait to put it on and hoped it would fit as she checked the label to see what size it was. The sleek black satin nightgown was trimmed in silky-soft ivory lace around the neckline. The same lace adorned the hem line and the deep slits on the side. The bodice was held up by thin black spaghetti straps.

She smiled, discovering the gown was a plus-size extra large, exactly what she would need. She noticed the manufacturer's label and realized he had made more stops than just an adult toy store today. This was an expensive designer gown he must have shopped for in an upscale department store. He'd probably talked to Grace because Grace knew all the best-kept secrets for where to shop for sexy plus-sized clothing.

She gathered up the gown and slipped it over her head. She stifled a gasp as the cool satin slithered over her warm skin, falling in a smooth sweep to her shins. The lace was as soft as silk, another sign that this was not a cheap nightgown. She moaned softly as she picked up the matching bundle made from the same silky-soft material. Holding up the robe as it unfolded, she slipped her arms into the deep sleeves. The satiny fabric caressed every inch of her body it touched, and she closed her eyes, wrapped her arms around her middle, and felt beautiful and precious. She knew that had been his intention, and she was surprised by the arrival of tears behind her eyelids. She wiped them quickly away and smiled again, not wanting her eyelids to become red-rimmed.

She reached for the other small bundle and unfolded it. Her lips popped open as she realized what it was. A black satin blindfold with satin ribbon bindings. She used the blow-dryer quickly and brushed out her long hair. With shaking hands, she placed the blindfold to her eyes and tied the ribbons at the back of her head. She straightened and stood there waiting for him. She could hear him moving back and forth between the kitchen and bedroom, then after a short time, he stopped at the bathroom door and knocked softly.

A couple of stuttering breaths passed over her lips as he asked softly, "Are you ready, angel?"

Her breath rushed from her lips. *"Yes."*

She smiled, thinking it sounded more like she whimpered than actually spoke. She knew if she didn't get her pounding heart and raging hormones under control, she would go off like rocket the first time he touched her intimately. She took a deep breath as the door knob turned and opened with a metallic whisper. Blindly, she turned to him and smiled softly at the sound of his breath as it caught in his throat.

"Rachel, I've never seen anything more beautiful in my life. I swear," he said in a husky, strangled voice that sent shivers straight to her clit. Her breath caught in her throat when his warm hand made contact with the exposed flesh above the lace bodice and slid just a little inside the robe. Her abdomen quivered, and the strong pull of desire raced through her body.

"The blindfold is heightening all my other senses, Eli. Your hand...it feels so warm and gentle. Thank you for the lingerie. It feels so soft on my skin." Every nerve ending in her body tingled as he slid his other hand alongside her breast and over her ribcage to her hips. Wherever he touched her, the satin caressed her body, sending her senses that much closer to overload.

Rachel reached out and her hand landed on his broad chest. He had changed out of his clothing into his robe, judging by the feel of soft fleece under her fingertips. She came close and laid her cheek against his chest as he slid his arms around her and enveloped her in his warm, woodsy-scented warmth.

"Does the blindfold bother you?" he asked as he slid a fingertip over her cheek then down to her lower lip. Without thinking about it, she licked her lip and caught his thumb with the tip of her tongue.

"No, it doesn't. I–I like it, actually."

"Good. Come lie down on the bed with me." He slid his big hand into hers and led her carefully to the bedroom. He lifted her in his arms and crawled with her to the center of the bed, laying her on the cool sheets and fanning her long, wavy hair on the pillow. She lay completely still as she waited for him to settle down beside her.

"Rachel?"

"Yes, Eli?" she asked in a shaky voice. He sounded unsure of himself.

"You would tell me if I was...overwhelming to you, wouldn't you?" He brushed a stray lock of hair back from her cheek.

"Overwhelming...how?"

"My height and my size mainly, but in other ways, too. Physically, I know I'm a lot to handle, but I also mean timewise. You said you needed to stay home to finish settling in, and I respect that. But if you're feeling overwhelmed by me, like you need more space or time, I don't want you to feel rushed."

She wished she could see his face and look into his eyes right now, but she understood that with the blindfold on, it might have made him more comfortable being that open. He was certainly the first man she'd ever known who could drop the "playing it cool" act long enough to show that he *had* some vulnerability.

She reached out carefully and her hand came into contact with his throat and moved up to his cheekbones.

Caressing him, she said. "Honestly, what I needed to do tonight is already mostly done. I was trying to give you a way to have a little time away from me because I didn't want you to get burned out on *me*."

He sighed and rested his forehead gently against hers as she continued, "As far as the rest of you is concerned? Your body is…beyond my wildest dreams. You don't just take what you need from me, you *give* so much. So, yes, you overwhelm me, Eli, in all the best ways. And, no, you don't overwhelm me in the ways you were worried about."

She could hear and feel his heart pound as he held her close. His hands seared her through the satin of the gown and robe.

"Rachel, I adored your beautiful body from the moment I first saw you on the dance floor. I'm glad, and a little relieved, that what I have to offer is pleasing to you. I'll be honest and tell you that you bring out the caveman in me, the territorial and possessive part of me that wants to beat his chest and tell everyone else that you're *mine*. Sometimes *he* brings out the worst in me."

"Like with Ace Webster?"

"Exactly."

"I'm all yours, Eli." For as long as you'll have me, she thought to herself. "And I don't feel rushed."

"The blindfold?"

"Leave it. I enjoy feeling at your mercy, so long as you don't…"

"So long as I don't what?" Eli asked curiously.

"I was going to teasingly say, 'so long as you don't tie me up or anything,' but then I reconsidered. I, um, wouldn't mind that, either."

"Really?" he replied with avid interest. "What else is going through that decadent mind of yours, hmm?"

"Well…"

"You can tell me anything, Rachel. You're safe with me."

"If I was naughty, you might need to spank me, occasionally," she replied breathlessly.

"If you were naughty? Should I plan on you being naughty?"

"I might not be able to avoid being naughty sometimes. I would need a thorough spanking on my bottom," she said in a shaky voice, her bottom lip caught between her teeth.

"And how would you like me to tie you up? Faceup or facedown?"

"Oh, definitely both. Facedown you could put me on my knees and I'd be at your mercy. Faceup you could spread my legs wide and tie them down, too. You could do all sorts of things to me," she replied in anxious anticipation. Denied visual input, her imagination was even more vivid.

"What would you want me to spank you with?" he asked in a husky voice.

"Oh, only your hands, please, Eli. Nothing else. And I wouldn't need to be tied down for that. You could put me right over your knee and…" A pleasant little shudder ran through her as she imagined being turned ass up over this big man's powerful thighs.

"Turn your sweet ass pink?" he asked, and she nodded eagerly. "If I was to inquire the most effective means for delivering a spanking that had the desired effect, could you suggest the name of someone I might want to talk to about that? The last thing I want to do is hurt you, Rachel."

As if he could ever hurt her. He proved he couldn't by being humble enough to ask for a name. "I have it on good authority that Ethan might know a thing or two about such matters," she replied softly. "Please don't think I'm a freak," she squeaked out. "Grace let on last weekend that a spanking by the right hand was a good thing, and ever since then, it's been brewing in the back of my mind."

He laid soothing fingertips on her collarbone and stroked her as he pressed gentle kisses over that spot. "Does it turn you on to think about it?" His hair slipped off his shoulder, and the cool, silken strands slid over her shoulder and her chest, leaving a tingling trail in their wake.

"Yes, it does, Eli. But, Eli, that doesn't mean whips and chains are next on my wish list, okay? I'm fairly sure we've plumbed the well on my interest in mild pain play. I think what I really like is the idea of you having total control of me in that way."

"That's good to know," he chuckled, "because I don't think a black patent bodysuit would be a good look for me."

"I don't think it would be for me, either," she replied. "Although I doubt that the majority of people involved in that lifestyle dress that way. Now, *you* in black leathers, bare-chested and wielding a whip...hmm. I'd wear your collar, baby. So you'll talk to Ethan?"

"Sure, he's cool. We have the rest of the afternoon to ourselves. I told Kelly we would be ready to go to supper at six thirty."

"What time is it now?"

"Don't worry about that. We have plenty of time. I told you once already, but, honey, you look amazing in that gown and robe. Just beautiful."

"Thank you. I love it. I'll get a thrill every time I put it on, the way it slides over my skin, and the way your hands feel through the satin when you put them on me." She stretched luxuriously in his arms and trembled slightly as his big, warm hand slid down her torso until it was mere inches above her mound.

"I hope you'll wear it for me on a regular basis."

"Of course, if you'll promise to take it off of me on a regular basis."

"Undressing you is a pleasure no matter what you have on." He rose up and knelt in front of her. He took her hand and drew her to him so she knelt facing him. She allowed him to remove it, and then he lifted the hem of the gown. She raised her arms over her head and shuddered as he allowed the gown to slide slowly over her skin as he removed it.

With the blindfold over her eyes, her other senses became more acute. She could hear the satin as it slid over her skin and hair. Her nerve endings were in overdrive, and gooseflesh formed on her skin at the slippery, silken touch of the gown. She heard Eli's soft breathing and the slight sound of his movements as he placed the gown with the robe. The bed dipped again as he returned to her.

Feeling gooseflesh on her arms, he asked, "You cold?"

"A little, but you can warm me." She smiled as his hands slid over her shoulders again. His lips brushed her hair as he came closer and enveloped her in his arms, surrounding her with his warmth.

"Nervous?"

"A little. Just wondering what will happen next."

"You seem a little tense, so we're going to start with a massage. I've laid out a towel for you on this side of the bed. Come over here to me as I lead you. Damn, but you're beautiful, baby," he murmured. She moved toward his voice as he held her hand.

He helped her lay down on the towel so that no massage oil got on the fresh sheets. The light scent of jasmine floated on the air.

He spread the oil over her back and shoulders. He took his time smoothing it over her skin, down to her buttocks. He maintained constant contact with her as he gently spread her legs so he could smooth the oil all over them. She gasped when his fingers strayed near her wet pussy lips. He teased her and made her groan when his hands moved away without touching her. He continued to massage her legs then worked his way back to her buttocks.

Her flesh was warm now, and between her legs, her pussy blazed. He massaged the cheeks of her ass firmly. His thumbs strayed now and then to her rear opening, smoothing oil over it. He patiently worked his way up her back and finished by gently working her shoulder muscles, which were tense from pushing the mower and turning the soil in the flowerbed.

Finished with her back, he helped her turn over. She moved her hair out of the way over the pillow and lay still for him. He smoothed more oil over her upper chest and gently massaged over her shoulders, chest, and arms. He smoothed the oil in gentle upward strokes over her breasts, taking his time and gently tweaking her nipples into hard points. She moaned softly at the stimulation. His hands swept up the underside of her breasts, cupped them, and squeezed gently. Rachel noticed his breathing sounding a little rough. The throbbing in her cunt increased as he dragged each nipple between his fingers one more time before moving on.

Eli caressed her ribs and abdomen and rubbed the oil into her skin. Her breaths came in little pants as his hands moved lower and separated before reaching her mound and glided down her legs. He was thorough in the massage he gave her and even rubbed the soles of her feet. Her heart began to pound in an erratic rhythm when he started to work his way back up her legs to the only spot on her body he had yet to touch. He spread her thighs gently, and every sensation seemed magnified somehow. The heat of his touch, the feel of his breath on her skin, and the gentleness of his hands all united to set her senses on fire.

Her clit throbbed incessantly, keeping time with her hammering heart. Rachel moaned low and panted as he gently spread her thighs wide and knelt between them. He spread his fingers gently over her mound and outer lips, and little ecstatic cries erupted from her throat. With a firm but gentle touch, he smoothed the lubricant over her pussy, gradually working his way to her opening. Her lips felt swollen, and more moisture welled from her pussy as he smoothed his fingers over her wet lips.

He pressed his fingertips into her opening and slowly slid his fingers to her clit, which made her cry out and shudder as he made contact with that bundle of pleasure-inducing nerve endings. His fingers swept around again. His thumb came to rest on her clit while two fingers slowly and torturously slid into her opening, which felt feverishly hot. She gave a delighted gasp as he sought and found her sweet spot, applied light pressure, and began to strum her body.

Rachel felt turned inside out. Her body had been so loose and relaxed, but now as he began to stimulate her G-spot, the incredible tension built inside her cunt and spread through her torso to the rest of her body. Thanks to his tender attention, her pussy felt like it was on fire. His fingers filled her tightly as he stroked her sweet spot over and over again.

"How does that feel, Rachel? Am I getting it?"

"Yes, Eli, it's perfect. Please don't stop. I love it!"

"Feel for me, baby. I won't stop." His thumb stroked her clit while his other hand slid back over her abdomen and gently massaged above her mound. The tension increased, and she panted and rocked her hips, moving with him as her orgasm loomed closer and closer.

"You like it, don't you, baby? I need to taste your sweet honey." He lowered his lips to her pussy and laved her clit with his tongue then sucked it between his lips. She hissed at the sensation, and her back bowed off the bed. Her head fell back on a wailing scream, and her pussy clamped down on his fingers and pulsed wildly as her orgasm rushed over her and the tension in her body broke free. She sobbed her release as the cream flowed fresh from her pussy. When she was done, he removed his fingers from her, and she faintly heard him growl in pleasure as he licked and kissed her.

Chapter Twenty

By this point, Eli's cock was a twitching, throbbing, rock-hard steel fucking *pole* pressed up against his belly, but that monster would need to wait a bit longer. Soothing her, he caressed her inner thigh as she came down from her orgasm.

"Was that the mother of all orgasms?" he asked and chuckled as she stretched and nearly purred for him. She looked so decadent, spread before him like this. The blindfold was still in place, her arms were flung over her head, and her thighs spread wide open for his appreciative gaze.

She sighed blissfully. "I'm *very* all right. Thank you, honey. You have *magic* fingers."

"I'm only just getting started." He rose over her and kissed her tenderly. "Ready for more?"

"Mmm, yes, more!" she said enthusiastically and reached for him.

Taking her hand, he said, "Come here to me, then, on your knees. I'll guide you. Still like the mask?"

"Yes!" she replied as he helped her down to the end of the bed. She was hesitant at first and seemed a little disoriented. She reached out a hand to feel the bed.

He caressed her shoulders and held her upper arms gently. "Don't worry. I'm placing you in the center at the end of the bed so you face the headboard." He helped her turn and back up and drew her ankles toward him. "There. Can you feel the edge of the mattress with your foot?"

"Yes, now I feel better. It would be very embarrassing to fall off the bed," she murmured with a chuckle.

"I won't let you fall. Now back toward me a little at a time. That's fine." He smiled broadly as she arched her back and presented her ass and pussy to him in invitation. "Now *that* is a pretty sight. You must be ready for this to offer yourself to me without me even asking."

"Tell me what you'll do to me, Eli." Her voice vibrated with arousal, and he could see the juices that dripped from her opening as he gently traced his fingers over her pussy lips. "You've made me so wet. I'm so ready."

"I've bought you a series of plugs to stretch your ass. Each one is bigger than the next, and you'll work up to the largest, which will enable you to handle my cock with ease. You'll wear them for an hour or so around the house each day. They'll help stretch you, and you'll also become accustomed to the sensation of being entered here." He pressed a thumb to her rear opening. "You'll also learn how to relax these muscles to allow entry."

"How long before you'll give me your cock?"

He loved her eager tone of voice, and his overeager cock bobbed in twitching agreement. "Let's give it a week or two. I'm going to try a few of them today to see what you can tolerate for now." He slid his hands over the gentle swell of her hips then up the sweet curve of her back. "That's not the only thing I got you, though. I have other surprises for you that I'll show you later." He opened the warmed lubricant, placed some on a finger, smoothed it over her rear opening, and applied gentle pressure.

She released a slow, velvety sigh. "You're always so gentle with me, Eli."

He stroked her derriere as he continued massaging her anus. "I love you, Rachel, and I want you to enjoy what we do together. Remember, I'll stop if you tell me to."

"I want you to do everything."

He removed the smallest plug from under the warmed towel and applied a little lube to its end. The plugs were all made from a soft jelly-like material, maybe four inches long, including the handle. The ends were all tapered, widened at the center, then tapered down again to the handles. The widest part of this one was three-quarters of an inch at the most. She arched her back again slightly, eager with anticipation. He slid his hand over her cleft to prepare her for its touch.

"This is the smallest plug, baby. I'm going to slid it in, all right?"

"Yes, please." She wiggled her ass at him, and he smiled at her enthusiasm. She gasped delightedly at the slippery invasion of the jelly plug and moaned softly as it slipped inside her ass. The jelly material and the lubricant made it easy to take, and she flexed her hips and moved with him as the plug slid with relative ease into and out of her bottom. He pumped it several times, satisfied that she could move on to the next. He placed it on another towel spread on the dresser next to the bed where he would collect what they'd used to be cleaned later.

"This one is bigger, honey." He lubricated the tip and smoothed more on her opening. He'd do everything he could to minimize her soreness. The tip slid easily into her well-lubricated opening. He twisted as he pumped it back and forth and listened to her pant as she tried to relax for him.

"How does it feel?"

"It feels good and naughty at the same time."

"Mmm, are you saying you're being naughty, Rachel?" Eli asked in a deep dark voice. Her head came up, and her lips parted with a happy sigh.

"I may get much naughtier before we're through."

He almost got sidetracked with fantasies about how she might get naughtier and shook his head to clear it then patted her fanny lovingly. "We'll see about that. Relax, baby, I'm going to slide it all the way in."

The plug slid easily enough, but there was more resistance this time as the widest part slid in, and she gave another aroused sigh as he pumped it in and out like the other one. So far, so good. He pushed gently on it once it was all the way in and enjoyed the sound of her ecstatic moan. He gently removed it and laid it aside in favor of the next size up.

She handled this well. The playtime last night must have helped her. She did not visibly work to relax to allow for a tighter fit, so he continued to the next one. This one was longer and wider at its thickest point. The jelly was very flexible, which was why he'd chosen these, so she would be able to move comfortably, relatively speaking, while she was at home.

He lubed the tip and length. Before he placed it at her opening, he looked down at Rachel and thought she might like to be in a more relaxed position. He placed his hand on her lower back.

"Rachel, why don't you relax your arms and legs. Pull your knees under you. Yes, like that, and cross your forearms and rest your forehead on them or the bed. There, now you can relax a little more. I don't want to rush through this process."

"Thank you, honey," she murmured quietly, sounding totally into their play. He stopped to gaze at her appreciatively, enjoying the sheer eroticism of the moment and her sweet, submissive posture. The trust she held for him was obvious in her relaxed, vulnerable position.

He placed the broader tip at her entrance and slowly pressed inside. She breathed out slowly. The tight ring of muscle resisted a little over the intrusion but allowed entry after only a little gentle pumping. She hummed lightly at the sensation then let out a startled gasp as its extra length slid into her ass, and she hissed at the end of the stroke.

"Does that hurt, Rachel?" Eli asked attentively as he pumped it into her ass several more times.

"No," she said simply.

"Are you sure?"

"No. Eli?"

"Yes, baby?"

"I…"

"Tell me." He sensed what she was feeling and continued to pump in a steady rhythm with the plug.

"I–Is there another one?" she asked in a shaky voice.

"Yes, one more is the most I'll give you today."

"Can I have it, please? Right now? I *want* it." His cock responded sympathetically to the tension in her voice, weeping a tear from its slit. The greedy bastard wanted to commiserate, too.

"You can have it, baby." He released the one inside her, lubed the next, and readied for a trade. This jelly plug was the same length but thicker through its length then tapered again by the handle. If she could grow accustomed to this plug with little discomfort, it wouldn't take long to be ready for his cock. He didn't want to rush her through the process. He wanted it to be about her pleasure and not a means to an end. His cock screamed and twitched incessantly, wanting to be useful, too.

She held still for him and waited patiently. He pumped the plug already in her and began the rhythm again that she liked. The larger plug was ready in his hand. Rachel moaned as he slid one out of her, placed it aside, and immediately positioned the tip of the other in her quivering opening. Eli placed his fingertips at her swollen pussy lips. He rubbed gently then stroked upward to her clit. Rachel reacted with a stunned gasp at the added sensation. Eli pressed for entry with the fourth anal plug, and she moaned loudly as the thick part began to crest at her opening.

"Ogodogodogodogodogod," she murmured but kept it at a low level.

She didn't sound like she was in pain, so he continued to press it inside her a bit more until about one-third of the length was inside her. He reached beneath the towel and removed the silver egg. Still warm, he gently placed it over her wet pussy lips so she would know something was about to happen.

"Wh–what is that?" she asked after shuddering again.

"It's a little gift. One of my surprises for you."

"Wh–what are you going to do with it?"

"For now, I'll hold it against your clit, but later I may place it deeper inside you. It's a small vibrator, and I'm turning it on now."

It was the perfect size to hold between her lips and over her clit. He turned it on with the remote and held the egg to her damp pussy as she began to quiver and cry out. He began pumping the anal plug again as she writhed, returning to her hands and knees. Her juices seeped through his fingertips, and he felt her thighs tremble hard as she whimpered.

Finally, he was plunging all seven inches into her ass, glad he'd used extra lubricant as he pushed the plug to the hilt and it slid into place with the handle against her opening. He released it and parted his robe and shrugged it from his shoulders.

"Do you like the little egg?"

"Yes! Oh, Eli, yes! I love it, but will you *please* fuck me now?"

"Would you like me to remove the plug first?"

"Oh! *No*! Leave it, please, Eli. Leave it and slide that big cock in me now, please! I'm going to come. I can't hold it off any longer! Oh, god, Eli, please!" she wailed.

He positioned his steely cock thrust home with one gentle stroke into her tight, hot cunt. She let loose a high-pitched wail as she began to buck under him. He fucked her with his answering thrusts as her orgasm rushed over her. He loved the tightness of her pussy as she rode his cock to another tumultuous orgasm on the heels of the first and showed no signs of stopping or slowing down.

"Ooooh! Eli! Fuck me hard! Oh, yes! Harder! Oh, fuck, *yes* that's perfect! Ah! Don't stop!"

He continued to thrust into her, giving her exactly what she asked for, pleased with her wild abandon. He chuckled. "My baby feels like talking dirty. You sure are being naughty, Rachel. I guess I'm going to have to see about disciplining my naughty little girl. What do you think?" Eli grinned as her breathing turned into raspy cries and fresh honey flowed over his cock, which confirmed what she thought of that idea.

"I think you definitely need to deal with naughty behavior. It could get *worse*, out of hand. Oh, *Eli*, what you do to me! I'm so wet just thinking about it."

Pumping continuously into her pussy, he asked, "The plug feel okay?"

"Oh, hell, yes! I feel so full, so tight. I feel like I'm on fire!"

"Where is the fire, baby? Can you tell me?" He slid a finger into the handle of the plug, ready to show her something new. His cock throbbed, aching for release.

"My–my ass and…"

"Where, baby?" he asked softly and slowed the pumping of his hips a bit. She groaned in frustration as he slowed down. "Where?"

"My ass and my pussy."

"Yeah?"

"Yes!" she howled. "Eli! I'm so close. Don't stop now!" She wailed in dissatisfaction as he slowed further.

"Don't worry, you're going to come hard for me."

She swallowed convulsively and whimpered, "What are you going to do?"

He slid almost the entire length of the anal plug from her ass, leaving only the tip inside her. As he slid it out, he slid his cock back in to the hilt then reversed and gave her every inch of the plug as he pulled his cock out until only the head remained inside her. He continued the seesawing rhythm as she moaned softly and grasped a handful of the comforter in each hand. Her hips began to softly undulate with his movements, finding her place in the rhythm. Her back arched, and she glanced back at him over her shoulder.

"How's that feel?"

"Amazing! So naughty. Like being fucked in both places at once. I love it!" She howled as her movements became more forceful.

"This is as close as we'll ever get to a threesome, baby. I could never share you, but you can have this anytime you want." He increased the pumping rhythm, pleased she enjoyed it so much.

"I only want you, Eli. Only you. Give it to me hard!" she pleaded. She laughed as he growled in reply.

He gently pushed the plug back in to the hilt and released it. He grasped her softly curved hips in his hands and pistoned hard into her soft heat. The sound of damp flesh smacking together filled the quiet of his bedroom.

"Come for me, Rachel. Oh, yes, yes! You're so tight and hot."

His hand left her hip and returned the little silver egg to her clit. Three seconds later, she let loose with an earsplitting howl he was certain that Kelly would hear even with the bedroom door closed on the other side of the duplex.

Her hips thrust back against him as her pussy clamped down on his cock and squeezed him like a fist, taking him along with her. His head fell back as a shivering tingle radiated hotly down his spine. He shouted his release as it poured from him. Her breath came in ragged sobs as she collapsed under him.

Still inside her, he kissed her back and her shoulders. He pulled the tie on the blindfold loose, smoothed her hair back from her face and listened as her breathing gradually returned to normal. She remained motionless.

"Damn, baby. Are you all right?" he asked, concerned for her.

"Yes, I can't move. I think I'm dead."

He pulled out slowly and helped her crawl up to her pillow to lie down. He removed the towel from the sheet and covered her with the turned-down sheet and blanket. He left the plug in place for now and gathered everything else in the other towel to wash and put away. He sat down on the edge of the bed facing her, and she drowsily opened her eyes and gazed up at him from deep pools of blissful blue. He smiled tenderly and stroked her cheek.

"Go to sleep, baby. I'm going to wash all of this and put it away, and then I'll lay down with you. Do you feel all right with the plug in place, or should I remove it?"

"How long should I wear it each day?"

"Only for an hour, maybe two. We'll remove it before we go eat."

"I can handle that. Hurry back," she murmured sleepily.

He sat there, watching her for a moment as she fell asleep. Her cheeks were rosy from her orgasmic blush, and he marveled at her stamina. He stroked a lock of her hair, which was spread out in wild disarray on his pillows. He couldn't wait to come back to bed and rest his cheek on the silken strands and breathe her scent in as he drifted off for a nap.

Chapter Twenty-one

The scent of jasmine evoked memories of their play earlier that afternoon as Rachel pulled back the covers on Eli's bed. The scent rose in the air, and Rachel smiled, not surprised by the warm thrill that raced through her body. Knowing she had work to do out in the garage, she'd decided to stay home that night and thanked Eli for the invitation, and he'd understood completely.

The main hurdle for the evening was the one she'd dreaded a little.

She walked out into the garage and opened the automatic door. The enclosed space reeked of smoke. What was left of her old life filled a stack of boxes the size of a small car. Having laid Matthew down for the night, Kelly followed her out into the garage.

"Want some company?"

"Sure." Rachel could have put this off for a few days, but she felt driven to put the whole experience with the fire behind her as quickly as possible. It was late, but she'd had a nap earlier and didn't feel sleepy.

Rachel noticed that Kelly had a roll of paper towels and a bottle of spray cleanser and a three-gallon bucket full of sudsy water. "If you find any clothes worth saving, they can soak overnight in this."

"Thank you," she said quietly as she lifted the lid on her cedar chest. Lifting the tissue-wrapped tablecloth and christening dress and several other similarly wrapped bundles from the chest, she handed them all to Kelly, who took them inside the duplex for safekeeping. She re-covered the cedar chest with the old blanket to protect it and carefully moved it out of the way.

Pulling the Dumpster over to the stack of boxes, she opened the first box. The sharp, acrid odor hit her in the face and transported her back to the moment when she realized she had to grab what she could and run.

She grimaced and said, "Would you mind getting that box of trash bags from the kitchen, Kelly?"

"Sure." Kelly hopped up and returned quickly with them.

Rachel looked in the box that was full of her clothing, now coated in a layer of smoky soot. Kelly opened a trash bag and held it while Rachel made quick work of sorting the contents of the box into the trash bag or into the bucket of hot, soapy water. She sorted all the boxes of clothing first, most of which went into the Dumpster, she noted with a disgusted sigh.

Rachel removed photographs from frames and tossed the grimy, soot-smeared frames in the trash. The knickknacks and collectibles that were cleanable Kelly worked on with the paper towels and spray. Kelly handled each item with care, taking them inside to wash in a sink of soapy warm water after removing most of the soot out in the garage. The last thing Rachel needed was for her new home to begin to smell like smoke, and so she was choosy with what she attempted to salvage.

It was eleven when she stopped for the evening. Kelly said goodnight and took Matthew back to her place to get some sleep. She'd be leaving in the morning to return to Abilene. Rachel hugged her and thanked her for all the help, glad for this chance to have gotten to know a member of Eli's family. Rachel took her shower then smoothed on a little of the jasmine-scented lotion Eli had purchased for her.

* * * *

"Thanks, Ethan. I appreciate your advice," Eli said as they left Ethan's office at The Dancing Pony. It was after closing time, and the evening had been slow, which gave Eli the opportunity to talk to Ethan privately. He'd broached the subject of Rachel's earlier statement as delicately as he could, knowing that Ethan would not want it widely known that he knew much about the topic of erotic spanking.

"I hope that helps, Eli. Remember, if you put her needs first, you're both going to be satisfied with the outcome. Take small steps and let her responses be your guide. It's very considerate of you to look into this for her," Ethan said, dropping his keys in his pocket.

"I felt awkward asking you because I didn't want to take a chance on offending you." Eli looked him in the eye as Ethan stopped and turned to him in the dimly lit hallway.

Ethan grinned and shook his head, reassuring Eli. "I know. Grace and Rachel are close. If Gracie feels all right talking to her about it, then I should feel equally comfortable talking with you about it. My door is always open. I appreciate your discretion, though. You heading home?" he asked.

"When all the ladies are in their cars safely, yeah. I'll be headed home. Kelly is going back to Abilene tomorrow."

"Wish I could have met her. Maybe next time. Has Rachel been staying with you?" Ethan asked.

"Yeah."

"How's that working out?"

Eli couldn't fight the sappy grin that spread on his face. "It's been great having her there, but she'll be over at her place after tonight. Kelly's been staying there the last few nights."

"Rachel's independent."

"That she is. I came home today to find she had landscaped and was working on my lawnmower."

Ethan chuckled. "Sounds about right. She's independent in a good way, which comes from being on her own for a few years. So you like having her over there?"

"It's like coming home, where before it was just a place I rented." Eli imagined Rachel asleep at that moment, soft and warm in his bed. The caveman in him growled softly.

"Word of advice?" Ethan asked. At receptive Eli's nod, he continued. "Give her whatever space she needs, but let her know you want her with you. If she's anything like Grace, don't expect a permanent arrangement unless you plan to make it official."

"Gotcha, boss. I'm already on it." Eli grinned broadly.

* * * *

Eli didn't just inhabit her dreams, now he tucked himself in behind her and pulled her against his warm, muscular chest as if she were weightless. Rachel shifted and turned to him, opened her legs, and wrapped her thigh and calf around his hip. She was already warm and wet from her dream as she snuggled deeper into him. She rubbed her nose and cheek against his pectoral muscles. Smiling contentedly, she slid her hand over his forearm and biceps. Her thigh slid over his hip, and when it registered in her mind that it was bare, she pressed her hips to his and felt the heat of his erection. He hissed softly as she did that, and his big, warm hand slid down the curve of her back over her derriere and pressed her to him with a yearning groan.

"Hi." She'd been mute up until that point because no words had been necessary between them.

"Were you having sweet dreams?" His thick fingers gently caressed her pussy and found her slick and hot. He dipped a finger into her wet opening, and her desire flared at his deep groan.

"I was dreaming of you." Her hand slid down his abdomen slowly, seeking and finding his stiffened cock. His breathing was ragged as she stroked his length within her soft grasp.

"Angel, are you sore from our earlier play?"

"My ass is still tingling a little from the plug, but the rest of me is fine. I want to make love to you, Eli." She sat up on her haunches. She leaned to him and kissed him, moving over his hips and straddling him. Languidly, she lay atop him, caught up in their unhurried kiss.

His large hands slid soothingly over her back as he pulled the sheet and blanket up over her legs and hips. She sat up, and her damp pussy pressed against his hardened length, getting him wet with her juices. His eyes closed in pleasure, and he moaned at the sensation. She slid down his length then back up again, delighting in the panting sounds he made.

"Does it feel good?"

"I want inside you. As good as this feels, I want to slide all the way into you and feel you all around me. I want all of you, angel. Let me help you."

She rose over him, and he lifted her as though she were weightless. He positioned her with his cock at her entrance but, once again, let her control the slide. They both moaned aloud as the blunt tip of his cock slid into her slick, wet entrance. She loved the feel of him as he breached those tight muscles beyond her lips, stretching her deliciously. She looked down and gasped in renewed awe at the sight of his huge cock sliding slowly into her slippery cunt.

"Beautiful." He lifted her slightly, so they could both see the honey that now coated his cock and flowed so freely from her for him. "I love to watch my cock fill your pussy, Rachel. I love seeing your cream covering it even more."

"Me, too," she whimpered quietly as he gained more ground then slid almost all the way out.

"Does it bother you at all that I call this beautiful part of you that?"

"I thought it might, but it doesn't, Eli. When you say it, it's not derogatory, like you're making fun of me. It sounds…"

"Reverent and respectful, Rachel. That's how I feel, when you allow me to share this part of you. I feel humble that you allow me inside you."

She slid down more of his length before she rose up again, leaving only the head inside her. "My gentle giant, Eli. I love being with you. When we make love, I feel like I belong to you. Like I am," she shuddered as she slid all the way to the hilt, "*yours*. Claimed. Marked. Loved." Punctuating each word with a gentle downward twist of her hips, Rachel reveled in the glow that seemed to come from his light gray eyes as she said these things to him. "Does that make you happy?"

"You have no idea how much." He growled as he gently grasped her hips and thrust inside her. "I want you to feel claimed, to *know* you are mine. I want to take care of you, love you, and protect you."

She moaned softly in pleasure as she clasped her hands with his. "I feel safe when I am with you. I love that feeling." She glided back up almost off his cock and looked down between their bodies. "But I also feel a little wild and uninhibited with you because I trust you not to judge me."

"I think you're incredible."

The only thing she felt incredible about right now was the turn her life had taken in the last few days. He slid his feet up and raised his knees until she slid all the way onto his cock and leaned forward over him, bracing herself on his chest as he rose up from the bed.

Damn, he is strong!

In a quick maneuver, without breaking the connection, she found herself on her back.

She raised her knees as he looped his forearms under her thighs and spread her legs wide so he could see every inch of her as he slowly pistoned into her depths. Each time he entered her, she felt it all the way to her toes as he dragged over that sweet spot inside of her. Taking her ankles, he placed one at each of his shoulders, freeing his hands to roam over her heated body. He squeezed her ass cheeks before sliding his hands up to her breasts as they swayed slowly with his movements.

"Eli?"

"Hmm, baby?"

He reached down and wet his finger in her juices and rubbed over her clit, making her crying out and buck in pleasure. In her current position, he was in control of how much she could move.

"Take me so I know I'm yours. *Show* me I'm yours."

He pulled out carefully, left the bed, and went to the closet. He opened the door and carefully positioned it then returned to the bed where he sat on the edge and reached for her. She began to climb into his lap facing him, but he faced her away from him and pulled her back onto his lap, impaling her on his long, thick cock. She gasped at the different sensation as he entered her from the different angle, and then he did something that she didn't expect.

After she was seated on his lap, his cock buried to the hilt inside her, he slid his hands to her knees and parted them. He laid her thighs open over his, and her calves draped on the outside of his calves. She perched there, feeling tiny, in stunned silence at the unspeakable eroticism of the pose she found herself currently in. He spread his knees, splaying her open even wider. She softly wailed at the wild sensuality of the moment, and the desire to move was driving her crazy, but she couldn't get any leverage. She would need his help for that, but he sat still and quiet.

"Look." He pointed at the mirror on the inside of the closet door.

Oh, Lord have mercy.

She was splayed so that they could both see. A fresh rush of moisture came to her burning pussy, and he growled deeply in his chest. He slid his big, warm hands down her calves and lifted her ankles until her feet were flat against the side of the mattress. He slid his hands down to her shins and cupped them gently to support her and give her leverage of a sort. He kissed her temple as she watched in the mirror, and she turned her head to kiss his warm, full lips and stroke his chin.

"Do you want to ride me, or do you want me to help you?"

"Hold me tight, okay?" she asked unsure of herself. This was new.

He squeezed her shins gently and encouraged her. "I've got you. Push against the mattress and lift at the same time. I'll hold you steady. Look in the mirror."

Rachel looked in the mirror and moaned at the image of the two of them locked together like this. She could clearly see the hilt of his cock pressed inside her, her swollen pussy lips glistening and stretched around him. Yes, she felt completely taken and marked.

All his.

He held her shins with her feet stable against the bed and balanced over his thighs, and she began a slow rise and fall motion over him, gripping his forearms, her shoulders against his chest, watching the entire time. Oh, it felt good, and watching like this made it even more exciting. His cock glistened when she lifted over it, and she could see her juices smeared all over the length of his shaft as she rose over him and glided back down.

As she found her balance, her hands slid to her breasts, and she played with her nipples, dragging on them with her fingertips, pinching them. As she was swept away by the rhythm, she slid her hands into her hair, rising in an arch and falling over and over. She watched the way his face showed his pleasure, his cheeks darkening and his features becoming so tense and focused. His hair was a black pool behind him on the bed as he tilted his head back slightly.

She realized the sound she heard was her moaning loudly. The muscles in her pelvis had begun to tingle and jump, a certain sign of an impending orgasm. She looked in his eyes, and he smiled at her.

"I feel it, baby. Touch yourself for me. Yes, that's right, baby. If harder and faster is what you want, do it. I've got you."

"Yes! Oh, Eli! Look at us!" She whimpered as she slid her middle fingers through her slit, focusing on that spot alongside her clit that loved stimulation. She slid her clit between two fingers and pinched slightly, her breathing nothing more than high pitched panting.

"Are you mine?" he asked in a soft guttural voice.

"Yes!" she sobbed loudly. *Yours.*

"Do you see that you are mine?"

"Yes!" *Yours.*

"See how perfectly we fit together?"

"Yes!" she wailed. Her orgasm began to pulse through her. Her mind screamed again, *Yours!*

"You're *mine*, Rachel. *Mine*! Oh, god! Mine! *Fuck*!" He roared as his orgasm was brought on by hers. She rode each pulse, milking his cock as it twitched and pulsed inside her.

"Yes, Eli. I am. *I am*," she whimpered softly. As he reached forward, his fingers slid in over hers and gently rubbed alongside the bundle of sensitive nerve endings. Her head fell back to his chest as her feet now dangled outside of his, her legs quivering as he held them open with his own. She whimpered when she realized he wouldn't be content until she'd come again for him.

His other hand settled around her waist and pressed her back to his chest and abdomen, giving him control of her body. He slid his hand up to her breast and tweaked the nipple as he gently rolled her clit between his fingers. With his cock planted deep inside her, she undulated against him, reaching up to hold on to him from behind. He began to rub over her lips and strum her clit at the same time. Feeling very wanton, Rachel arched her back and began to pump on him in sinuous, smooth strokes. She locked her gaze with his in the mirror and came undone again as he held her tightly to him.

"Yes, angel. Yes. I love listening to you come. You're so beautiful when you lose yourself like that. You've got me hard again." He lifted her off his cock with a groan, and she allowed him to position her on the bed on her hands and knees.

"Oh, angel, I love your pussy so much." He shoved his cock home again. She moaned as she raised her ass to him.

"Do it, honey. Give it to me good and hard." Rachel answered his thrust with one of her own. The sound of flesh smacking flesh was loud in the room as he pounded into her. She turned her head and gaped at the sight of him fucking her with his huge cock from behind in the mirror.

It was the perfect viewpoint from the side. She could see his cock ram into her, smeared with her cum and his, pistoning perfectly into her feverish, swollen pussy. Her muscles clamped down on him, and he reached forward and flicked her clit hard. She groaned rapturously and came again.

He growled deeply in his chest, and a shiver and a thrill shot up her spine at the animalistic sound. Eli suddenly stilled and snarled. She felt his cock pulsing as his seed jetted from his cock, bathing her pussy yet again. Wrapping both arms around her torso, he gently pulled her upright against his chest. His cock still pulsed deep inside her as Rachel placed a hand over his forearm across her hips. She slid her other hand into his hair behind her as he wrapped the other arm under her breasts. Floating with only his solid form to keep her from drifting away, she turned her head and met his gaze in the mirror as they looked at the reflection of their joined bodies. Her thighs were splayed wide on either side of his, on her knees before him, her body languorously draped against his torso.

"Beautiful." He kissed her temple.

"Yes. Beautiful."

Chapter Twenty-two

Eli enjoyed the tempting sight that greeted him when he came home from work the next day. Kelly had loaded up Matthew and her stuff and had left early that morning, so Rachel was home alone. After Kelly left, he'd gotten ready and gone to work.

Two or three days a week he did tower work for the local electrical cooperative. It was very dangerous, but Eli loved the exhilaration of being that high in the air. He had assured Rachel that he never climbed without a harness and all the requisite climbing gear. She'd had a full-body shudder and wrapped herself around him, quivering. He liked that part of her reaction.

He sat in the truck behind the steering wheel and watched her bent over the fender of her car. A streak of jealousy shot through him as he glanced around to make sure no other men were in the vicinity also watching her. There were no houses close by, and the nearest neighbors were at work. Her current position was his to enjoy alone, he noted with caveman-like satisfaction.

The hood was up. She was wearing a pair of cutoffs and tank top. He was willing to bet there was a G-string under those cutoffs since he'd told her how much he'd liked the one from yesterday. He could see the bright pink wires of her earbuds connected to her MP3 player, which explained why she had not noticed him yet. She was doing something to her engine. He saw a pan underneath the car and realized with amazement that she was changing her own oil. Damn. She really was independent to the core. He debated about whether it was worth it to tell her that was his job. Maybe she'd accuse him of being a chauvinist. He grinned evilly and thought giving her a hard time might be a lot of fun.

* * * *

Rachel watched him surreptitiously from behind her wraparound shades as she unscrewed the plug to let the oil drain from her engine. She kept her face carefully passive, unobservant as she watched him. He seemed to enjoy watching her current position, and she wondered if he might have even been a little surprised that she could change her own oil. She fought a grin and leaned in a little farther, stretching her leg muscles. For good measure, she even tilted her ass up a *little* bit more and widened her stance. Perfect!

She saved herself thirty bucks every time she did this. But watching the expression on his face change was priceless. He was up to *something*. The loud thump of his truck door slamming told her she was in for it. A chill went up her spine as his evil smile turned to a scowl. Her pussy leaked moisture at the look of intent on his face.

Oh, goody! I am so in for it!

No one was around to see them. Otherwise, she would never have draped herself over her fender like this. She felt like one of those models on the cover of a hot rod magazine. She couldn't believe her cheekiness as she subtly arched her back and presented her ass even more plainly to him and peeked over at him from behind her wraparound sunglasses, pretending to look at something in the engine.

The cutoffs Rachel was wearing today were shorter than the ones she'd worn yesterday, so Eli was getting a great view of upper thighs and maybe even a little ass cheek. Giving free rein to naughty side, she lifted up on her tiptoes in her little thong sandals.

How's this for an invitation to a spanking, big boy?

Surely he knew she was aware of him charging across the little lawn over to her. She glanced at him again through her shades and kept her face carefully passive, shivering with anticipation at the feral intent in his gray eyes. If she didn't know him for the sweet, gentle giant that he was, she would have been tensed up and shaking in her…sandals, she supposed. As it was, her body loosened and relaxed, more moisture flooding her cunt as she braced herself in anticipation of whatever he had planned for her. She yelped loudly as his hands grasped her hips hard, then the collision of his big hard body against hers pressed her to the warm fender of her car.

"Doing a *man's* work again, angel?" he grated in mock anger at her as she braced herself over the air filter. She grinned devilishly. This was how he wanted to play it? *Awesome!*

"Hey! Anyone could change their own oil!" she hollered back as she *struggled* against him and tried to back away from the warm fender, rubbing against his rock-hard erection.

"Maybe. But not just anyone looks the way you do right now with this beautiful body on display for the whole world to see." He gently shoved her back against the fender.

"There's no one around."

"Anyone could see as they drive by."

"We live at the end of a dead end!" she growled, trying not to laugh as he rubbed his cock against her denim-covered ass. *This is freaking fun!*

"That's beside the point. You could hurt yourself working on your car while no one is home. No one would know if you needed help."

"That's bullshit. How am I gonna hurt myself changing my—"

"*Also* beside the point." He gripped her ass cheeks again and then yanked her hips to him hard. "What if you *did* hurt yourself with no one around, and how about the way you put yourself on *display* with no one around to keep you safe from strangers? That's two ways you've endangered your safety."

"Huh?" *Where is he going with this?*

Eli elaborated. "Ethan says that if Grace puts her safety in jeopardy knowingly, she gets a *spanking*. He lights her little bottom up until it's a glowing bright pink."

A shiver raced over her skin. She so loved Ethan right now! "All I did was—" she began in a *very* sassy tone. Maybe sassing him would get her a few extra swats.

"You got two strikes against you already, Rachel. Ethan says back-talking him gets Grace *extra* licks."

Ooooh. Extra licks sound good.

In a very sassy tone, Rachel retorted, "Ethan can kiss my *ass*."

Oops! Looks like my ass is grass and Eli's the lawnmower!

She thought that Eli did well at adopting a shocked tone. "Cursing from those pretty lips, Rachel? Such a shame. More sassing and foul language. That's definitely extra licks." He pulled her to a standing position. He bent, put his shoulder to her hips, and lifted her over his shoulder. She squealed loudly and tried not to giggle, *much*. She beat on his back with her fists and struggled to be put down. He gave her a solid pop on her bottom that didn't even sting a little.

"Oh, come on. Is that the best you can do, you big brute?" she sniped.

He mounted the steps to her porch, barged through her apartment, and dumped her on her bed. His sheer strength was breathtaking, and she could have sworn she experienced a small orgasm.

Without giving her a chance to brace herself or get her balance, he swiped the thongs from her feet and yanked at the button on her cutoffs. She struggled to turn away from him, determined to not make it easy for him, but he got the button undone and the zipper down as she tried to get her long hair off her sweaty face. He yanked the cutoffs down her legs, and she allowed him a split second to appreciate the little G-string she wore. It was pink with little skull and crossbones printed all over it. It was cute because all the skulls were pink and had little bows on top. Very girly. She could tell he liked it a lot because he was careful not to rip it as he tore it from her body in the next split second.

"Careful, that's my favorite!" She howled as it shot across the room and landed on the curtain rod.

"Ordering me around? You really want to add to the list of offenses?"

"Offenses my *ass*! I'm the one offend—Hey!" she yelled as he gently but firmly grasped her around the waist and slung her torso over his knees.

"When Grace misbehaves, Ethan says he puts her right over his lap, like this." He methodically got her into position. Her head and upper body dangled over his thigh, and her ass was within his easy reach. He spread his legs a bit until her mound was seated firmly against his thigh and spread her thighs enough that she was sure he could see her sopping wet pussy lips between her legs. She was barely balanced on her tiptoes.

Rachel bit her bottom lip as another thrill shot through her when his big hand rubbed hard over her bottom, barely tracing over her parted pussy lips.

Struggling again for good measure, she said, "Ethan can *kiss my ass*, and so can *you*, Eli. Don't you *dare*—Ow!" She screeched as his big hand came down over the fleshy part of her ass cheek. That stung a little. "Is that the best you can do, you big bully?"

Her ass began to warm against his palm. When he popped the other cheek, the sting was followed by a tingling, warming sensation. Ooooh, she adored Ethan. Eli must have taken notes.

She wiggled her ass, careful to keep her mound pressed against his thigh as he popped her again, this time on the other cheek in a new spot. Each smack sent a thrill to her clit and reduced her struggles until she could barely move for the pleasure she experienced. She forgot she was supposed to be struggling. She shrieked in surprise when the next pop made contact with her outer lips.

The next light tap landed full on her pussy, and she moaned in ecstasy. A few more light pats landed on her ass then a few more to her pussy that were more like light thumps that vibrated through her clit. His hand sounded wet as he spanked her again, and she knew she must be leaking. She heard his guttural growl and felt his erection at her waist.

The thudding vibration of each tap sent her higher and higher until she was moaning and crying out from the little bite of pain mixed with pleasure.

His other hand slid down to gently part her lips. She opened her mouth to gasp in surprise and wailed instead when the next few light taps made direct contact with her clit. The tension increased, and her back arched more with each impact. On the third tap, she screamed and came hard, undulating on his lap as he rubbed her clit, helping her ride the pulsing waves before she melted against him. When she came back to herself, he was rubbing and caressing her ass. She even felt his lips kissing her there.

"Oh, Eli." She sighed blissfully, lying limp over his thighs. His hands smoothed down the backs of her thighs then up to gently massage her ass again. He was silent as he let her slip to her knees. Her ass throbbed and tingled. She rested her forehead on his thigh for a second and caught her breath.

When her strength returned, she climbed into his lap and looped her arms around his neck. She straddled him and laid her head against the juncture of his throat and shoulder. With her warmed face buried there, she found the button to his jeans and unzipped the fly and pushed them down with a little help.

Lifting up, she positioned his rock-hard, weeping erection at the entrance to her pussy and sat down hard on him, making them both cry out. She lifted her chin and looked into his eyes, holding his cheeks in her hands as she rode him. Eli groaned loudly when she gripped him with her pussy muscles and bounced up and down on his cock. She brought them both to a quick, simultaneous, exploding rush of pleasure. He surged into her depths, filling her to the brim with his cum.

"Damn." He nuzzled her throat, kissed his way to her jaw, then behind her ear, sending goose bumps zinging over her flesh. "You all right?" he asked as he caressed her tingling butt.

"Uh-huh." She melted against his warm, muscular frame, his cock still deep inside her. She was completely content to stay there with him like that for a few minutes. He gently tipped her chin and looked down into her eyes and smiled playfully, his eyes warm with love for her.

"I suppose that will teach you to misbehave."

"Yes, it *will*. I'll be misbehaving all the time, if that's what I can expect." She chortled. He rubbed her ass gently.

"Your ass is a nice bright pink and hot, too."

"I take it you talked to Ethan?"

He nodded. "He made some suggestions and told me what Grace likes best. *Next time*, you get the plug in your ass *first*." He grinned evilly at the way her eyes got big, and her lips popped open. "The *biggest* one, so you have something to look forward to."

"Oh, baby. I feel more misbehavior coming on soon." She gasped as he gently lifted her off of him.

"Talking about this while I'm inside of you is going to get me hard again."

"And that would be bad *because*?" she asked as she stood up on shaky legs and went in search of her cutoffs and removed her G-string from the curtain rod.

"No, angel. I've been pushing you hard physically the last several days."

"Eli, I'd let you know if I didn't feel up to it." He shook his head gently and smiled at her, caressing her ass again.

"I know. But I'm imposing some rest on you, whether you want it or not. We'll continue with the plugs. Did you wear one today?" he asked as he reached for the bottle of scented body lotion on her night table and poured some in his hand. He patted the bed beside him and nudged her to lie down on her stomach.

Smiling mischievously, Rachel nodded. "Uh-huh, while I was at work." She snickered at his surprised expression. "The *big* one, too."

She'd felt incredibly daring leaving the plug in place for an hour or two that morning while at work. Every time she'd risen from her desk, she'd felt it shift inside her, and she'd fantasized about having Eli take her ass someday. Her panties had been drenched by the time she'd removed it.

"I thought about you all morning, and I was turned on the *whole* time." She wiggled against his hand, practically purring at his gentle touch to her throbbing ass.

"Damn, woman. You are motivated, aren't you?"

"Like you read about, baby!" She giggled as he leaned down playfully and blew on her lotioned butt. He surprised her when he pressed his lips against her butt cheek and blew a raspberry on her ass before smoothing lotion on that cheek. She cackled loudly and then sighed in pleasure when he laid sweet kisses all over her ass. She sighed at the pleasant tingle. "I need to run out to my folks' house and check their mail and see if UPS left a package they were expecting this morning."

"Tell you what. Since I interrupted your oil change, why don't you let me finish it for you? You take a shower and get ready while I do that. While you run out to the ranch, I'll shower and get ready and then I'll take you out to O'Reilley's for dinner. Tonight is my night off from the club, so we have the whole evening in front of us. We can go dancing or to the movies if you want to."

"I'd like that. You're sure you don't mind finishing my oil change?" She laughed when he rolled his eyes at her. "I know, *men's work*, right? The oil filter is on the front seat," she added as she sauntered naked into the bathroom, chuckling at his groan of appreciation.

* * * *

After Rachel put the mail and the cardboard box on the kitchen counter, Rachel locked up her parent's house and trotted out to their storage shed. She unlocked it and went in, flipping on the light switch. She must have overlooked the tall floor lamp inside the doorway when they were there a few days ago. It would be perfect in her living room. She found a box filled with assorted picture frames and carried it and the lamp out to the car. After

Rachel removed the heavy glass shade and laid it on the back seat, she disassembled the lamp and put both sections on the back floorboard. She placed the box of picture frames on the front passenger seat. She waved to the ranch foreman as she passed him in his truck on the driveway.

As she pulled onto the state highway, she tuned the radio to a country station where a popular love song was playing. She sang along with Lady Antebellum and agreed that she just needed him now.

As she approached the river bridge, Rachel noticed movement to her right. One second, she was thinking that it was a little early in the year for the deer to be chasing as a young doe raced out in front of her car, followed closely by a large buck, evidently intent on mating. The next instant, she heard screeching brakes as an oncoming SUV attempted to avoid colliding with both deer as well as her vehicle. Slamming on her brakes, Rachel sent a prayer heavenward.

Chapter Twenty-three

Ace Webster held tight to his steering wheel as the doe ricocheted off his front grill then into the guardrail. His SUV slammed into the red sedan as it lost control upon impact with the big buck. His vehicle came to rest against the guardrail. Ace shook his head, gathered his wits, and peered out his side window, searching the road for the little red car. He realized it was no longer on the road at all and slung his door open in time to hear the horrible crunching sound as the little car finally stopped rolling down the steep incline. Both deer lay in the roadway, dead. He turned on his flashers and descended at a dead run down the incline to the river bottom, thankful the car hadn't been in danger of rolling into the water. Praying hard, he threw open the driver side door.

The sight before him took his breath away, but he kept his wits about him. He ripped out his phone and prayed he had a signal down there. He hit the speaker button and went to work as fast as he could. He tore off his dress shirt and undershirt and started ripping them into pieces. As the 911 operator picked up the call and inquired the nature of his emergency, he found his voice. He mopped with the shredded cloth trying to find the worst sources of bleeding.

"My name is Ace Webster. I'm out on FM 709, south of the river bridge. There has been an accident. A vehicle has rolled down into the river bottom. I'm with the injured driver. It is a young woman, and she appears to have severe lacerations. Without moving her, I'm trying to determine where the worst bleeding is. The vehicle rolled numerous times. Judging by the debris in the car, it looks like she was cut by objects loose in the passenger compartment."

"Is the driver conscious, sir?"

"No. She's unconscious. There is a large sliver of wood piercing her side. A lot of glass shards embedded as well. Lots of blood." The coppery scent of blood permeated the humid air around him as he palpated her torso, trying to determine the worst bleeds and doing his best to staunch the flow with the makeshift bandages.

"Please do not remove the piece of wood or the glass, sir. Is she buckled into the seat?"

"Yes."

"Leave her that way."

"Yes, ma'am. Oh, God!" Ace moaned as he wiped at her face with a fresh rag. "Oh, no. Rachel!" He gasped, horrified that he had been squatting here for several minutes with someone he should have recognized. There was so much blood. He redoubled his efforts.

"Sir, I have emergency services on their way. They're about five minutes away from you right now. Do you know the driver, Mr. Webster?"

"Yes. It's Rachel Lopez. Can you call her boyfriend for me?"

"Yes, sir, I'll take care of it. His name?"

"Wolf, Eli Wolf."

"Yes, please don't hang up, sir. I'll see that he is called. Is the driver still unconscious?"

"Yes."

"Will you check her pulse without shifting her at all?"

"Pulse feels weak, but regular."

He found several wounds beside the one at her ribs that were bleeding heavily and gently pressed the cloths to them. He didn't want to push the glass in farther, but knew the bleeding needed to be stopped. He looked around at the destruction of the interior of her little car. Shattered plate glass was everywhere as well as little pieces of wood, ceramic, and metal. His eyes came to rest on a small wooden frame in the floorboard. He realized what must have happened. He saw a heavy glass lampshade on the front passenger floorboard. It looked heavy, and he prayed she didn't have a head injury from it. He could hear sirens in the distance and checked her pulse again.

Still there, but weak.

He held her hand and said, "Hang on, Rachel. Help is coming."

* * * *

Eli's phone started ringing and vibrating as it sat on the bathroom counter. Caller ID read unknown, and he answered it on the second ring.

"Eli?"

"Yeah."

"Hank Stinson here."

Eli's heart jumped a little in his chest, and a cold chill went up his spine. This was not Hank's usual friendly part-time co-worker chit-chat voice. This was his sheriff's department business voice. "You need to run on up to the hospital. Rachel's been involved in an accident."

Another cold chill skittered across every inch of his skin. Adrenaline dumped into his bloodstream, and his skin prickled and felt hot and frozen at the same time. Rachel? No! Not his angel. An accident? Not *again*.

"What happened?" he asked, trying to stay focused and calm. He sat on the end of his bed, pulling his boots on quickly. He grabbed his truck keys and ran out the door.

"The other person involved in the accident says they hit some deer. He recognized her and asked for you to be called. I'm pulling up to the scene right now."

Eli could hear the muffled sounds of a seatbelt being released and a vehicle door slamming and the sound of Hank running down the asphalt. There was also the sound of a siren in the background and distant yelling.

His heart hammered as he yanked the door open on his truck. He was torn between wanting to know where she was so he could go straight to her and knowing he needed to get to the hospital where they would take her.

"Where is she?"

"South side of the river bridge on FM 709. Get to the hospital, Eli. They'll have her there in a few minutes. Damn. Yeah, looks like they hit a big buck and a doe. I'll see you up at the hospital, Eli. Gotta go."

"Thanks, Hank," he replied and ended the call backing out of the driveway. The thought of her little car and a white tail buck mixing it up on the bridge with another vehicle caused chills to race up his spine. He tried to take deep breaths to calm himself and floored the accelerator.

A familiar old pain made its ugly presence known in his chest along with a feeling of powerlessness and fear. He recalled another car accident and another woman he loved beyond belief being injured. Just like this time, he'd been unable to help her. He put aside that powerless feeling and focused on what he could do. He prayed the whole way to the hospital. Beating the ambulance to the emergency room, he ran to the information desk and checked with the receptionist. The door opened behind him, and Grace and Adam ran in, making a beeline for him as soon as they saw him.

* * * *

Ace heard Rachel moan weakly. She moved in the seat and attempted to lift a hand to her seatbelt. He caught her hand and delicately put it back in her lap.

"No, Rachel. Don't move, sweetheart. You've been in an accident."

She whimpered in response. She tried to speak and cried out, reaching for her throat. A long, nasty looking shard of glass protruded there. She reached up and cried out again as she touched it. He gently immobilized her fingers and held them in her lap.

"Rachel, you've been hurt in an accident. Don't try to talk or move. EMTs will be here in a minute to help you. The 911 dispatcher has called Eli for you. I'm sure he'll be waiting for you at the hospital. Try to be still for right now. Careful, you'll cut yourself if you keep feeling around. There's glass everywhere." He heard the technicians removing gear from the ambulance. He stood and hollered up the incline, "Down here!" They came hurrying down the incline with a stretcher, emergency medical kit, and a backboard.

He squatted down to her to reassure her again, but she was unconscious. Freeing her from the seatbelt, the EMTs carefully removed her from the vehicle, stabilizing her back and neck on a backboard. When they moved her, the bleeding started again. They discovered several other splinters lodged in her torso and under one arm as they checked for the worst sources of bleeding. Another ambulance showed up, and the EMTs rushed down to help. One of them checked Ace out, cleaned and bandaged the cut on his forehead, and recommended that he get checked out in the ER as well. They quickly loaded Rachel on the stretcher. Ace found her purse in the back seat and gave it to the EMTs. He climbed up the steep incline to find that a sheriff's deputy was also there, examining the scene on the bridge. He'd met Hank Stinson a few months before, working on a private investigation case for Jack Warner. Ace and Hank stood there looking disgustedly at the deer on the roadway.

"There is a metaphor for life here somewhere," Ace muttered, eyeing the buck and the doe, "but I'm not going to go there now. Should I call Grace? She'll want to know."

"I already did when I heard it was Rachel. Grace sounded pretty upset. Adam was bringing her in. She'll probably beat them there, same for Eli." He walked over to the damaged guardrail and looked down the steep incline. "*Fuck!* I hate when stuff like this happens, and it's worse when it's someone you know well. She didn't look good," Hank muttered, scrubbing his callused hand over his face before putting his cowboy hat back on.

Ace would not have voiced his opinion if Rachel or anyone else who knew her was around, but he muttered, "She's lost a lot of blood, from a lot of places. I'm pretty sure one of her arms is broken, too."

"Damn deer," Hank mumbled and walked over to the carcasses and dragged them off the road as a tow truck pulled up on the shoulder.

"Hank, I'm driving up to the hospital. If you need me, that's where I'll be," Ace said then he turned to his damaged SUV.

"That's fine. I'll come up there in a few minutes to get your statement. Gotta have everything documented for the insurance companies. Your SUV running okay? It took a hit, too."

"I'm pretty sure it's superficial damage."

"I'll be behind you in a few minutes after I check in with Dave," Hank said as he turned to go talk with the tow truck driver.

* * * *

Eli stood at the window, waiting anxiously. Someone entered through the sliding doors, and before they closed, he heard the sound of a siren growing closer. His heart began to pound, and his lips moved silently in prayer. Grace stood beside him and held his hand, her eyes closed as she prayed, too. Adam's heavy hand came down on his shoulder as the ambulance came to a screeching halt outside the emergency department unloading bay.

The doors swung open wide, and a doctor and a nurse ran out as the ambulance doors popped open. An EMT jumped quickly out of the back and reached for the stretcher, giving the doctor the run-down on her condition. The stretcher slid out with Rachel on it, feet first. She was partially covered in a blanket, but her upper torso was uncovered as the other EMT climbed out, working to help her breathe. The pretty blue top she'd put on earlier was now drenched in blood, and her arms were covered in blood. There was blood all over her face, and she was clearly unconscious.

A wild, guttural cry welled from his throat. He turned to run out of the waiting room doors to her and felt like he was moving in slow motion. His eyes slammed shut over tears of fear and frustration as Adam's arms locked around his torso, holding him in place. He opened his eyes and looked down into Grace's face but couldn't hear her over the pounding of his heart in his ears. She shook her head and put her arms around him, pushing him back with her shoulder as he struggled against Adam.

"No, buddy. You have to let them help her. You go out there now, and you'll just delay her getting the help she needs," Adam said, struggling to hold on to him. "I know. I'd feel the same way. You gotta let them do their job, Eli."

Afraid of accidentally harming Grace, Eli ceased his struggles and looked out the window again. He prayed this wasn't the last time he'd see Rachel alive. Her long hair billowed off the gurney in the hot wind before they wheeled her in the double doors. He allowed Grace and Adam to direct him to a chair, where he sat down heavily and put his head in his hands. Now the torture of waiting without knowing began. This had been the worst part years ago. It was even worse now waiting for news because the image of Rachel lying bloody and unconscious on the gurney kept flashing in his mind. Eli felt like he might come unglued.

Ace entered the waiting room from the ER trauma room area. His left temple was bandaged, and his eyes were narrowed like his head hurt. Eli knew whoever had been in the other vehicle knew Rachel and had asked to have Eli called. He hadn't expected it to be Webster.

Eli approached Ace and held out his hand in gratitude. "You were in the other vehicle?"

"Yeah."

"Hank told me you asked the dispatcher to call me. Thank you."

"Hey, no problem, Eli. It was the right thing to do."

Hoping for a hint of good news, Eli asked, "Did you see her?"

"Yeah, seemed like everything was gonna to be okay," Ace replied.

Grace went to Ace and gave him a hug. "Ace? Are you all right?"

"It's nothing much, sweetheart, just a little cut. A couple of Tylenols is all I need."

"Does your head hurt?"

"Yeah, I banged it pretty hard. They checked me out in there and the doctor said there is no sign of concussion, so I'm good to go."

Suddenly, they heard someone yell from inside the emergency treatment area and a loud crash. Everyone outside in the waiting room became quiet and listened to the muffled, rapid-fire sounds of doctors giving orders. Eli longed to know what was happening on the other side of those doors and went to where the loading bay was visible from the side windows. There was no ambulance sitting there. The new activity was for a patient already in the ER.

Grace gently led him back to a chair, and she made him sit down, then sent Adam to check with the receptionist. She told Adam the doctors were with her right now. Eli put his head in his hands and tried to breathe calmly. He didn't even try to make sense of his prayers, just released all the fear and panic to God, begging for her to be okay. His heart pounded in his ears but he felt so cold he would have sworn there was no blood running through his veins warming his body. He barely noticed the hand on his shoulder or the murmuring around him. He tuned it all out.

A little while later, Grace grasped him hard by the shoulders and got right in his face. "The doctor needs to talk to you. Rachel's parents aren't here yet." She grasped his hand and pulled him from the chair. That was good, he supposed. If it was bad news, they would be asking him to sit down, right?

The doctor quickly filled Eli in on what was about to happen. "Mr. Wolf, we've taken Miss Lopez into emergency surgery. She had internal bleeding. Which we caught in time. Her spleen is ruptured and may need to be removed. We'll take good care of her, Mr. Wolf. She'll have X-rays as soon as possible, and we'll be setting her fracture and checking for other broken bones as soon as we can. She's in good hands." The doctor assured him that he'd let him know how the surgery went as soon as it was over.

After that conversation, Eli began to focus better. Rachel was alive. That was enough for the moment. Eli stepped into the hall and called Rachel's parents, who were still a couple of hours away, to give them an update. When he came back, Ethan, Jack, Angel, and Mike were all sitting in the waiting room. There were a few others he didn't know by name, but he thought he recognized her employer, Thorne Grogan, in the group. A lot of people cared about Rachel.

Eli was talking to Ethan and Mike when the doctor he'd spoken to earlier came and asked for him and Grace. This time, he was smiling. For the first time since the phone call, Eli felt like there was a little warmth in his body. The doctor explained Rachel's complicated condition to them. It had been possible to repair the damage to her spleen, and they'd caught another bleed that had gone undetected from one of the large shards of glass that had penetrated the abdominal wall. She had a concussion, and they'd already set the broken bone in her left arm. They would keep her for several days, watching for signs of a blood clot or infection. She was sedated and would be for at least another day while they waited for signs of complications. The rest of her scans looked normal. The doctor said he was optimistic for a full recovery.

"When can I see her, Doctor?" Eli heard a slight tremor in his voice.

"They're moving her right now, Mr. Wolf. A nurse will come and get you," the doctor told him before excusing himself.

The relief in the room was palpable. Grace's men took her to get a bite to eat, and the others dispersed. Eli walked along the hall until he found what he was looking for. Stepping into the quiet, softly lit chapel, he approached the front. He was no longer a child crawling on his hands and knees in the hope no one would notice him.

He sat in the second pew and rested his forehead in his hands and broke into quiet sobs. The tension leaked from his body with his tears as gratitude poured forth from his heart. He prayed in thanks for her continued presence in his life and asked for the chance to spend his life loving her and keeping her safe. As he prayed and wept, he felt enveloped in a warm, calming embrace. A memory of soft hands and deep blue eyes holding and comforting him as a little boy came to him from many years before. An angel had been sent to him back then, and surely that angel was with him now. But he had been blessed even beyond that consolation. Another angel waited for him somewhere in this hospital, hurt but *healing*. He smiled, and another sob broke from him as he wiped his eyes.

Chapter Twenty-four

Rachel woke to the sounds of quiet voices in the distance. She recognized her father's voice, then her mother's. They were speaking so softly she was unable to make out what they were saying.

She tried to swallow, and her throat was pierced by a stabbing pain. Reflexively, she tightened her hand into a weak fist and became aware of the large, callused hand holding hers. Only one person she knew had hands that big and warm. Blinking, she tried to turn her head, but *that* hurt excruciatingly. She grimaced and opened her eyes then slammed them closed again as the room spun around her. Nausea churned her stomach.

Her brow creased as pain affronted her from many different levels. Rachel's head pounded with a nauseating rhythm, her throat burned, and the stabbing pain surged when she tried to swallow unsuccessfully, and the whimper that escaped her throat made it worse. Her stiff body felt like she'd been bludgeoned with a cinderblock, and sharp pain lanced her from more points than she could assimilate. Her left arm was stiff and unmoving. Tears leaked from her eyes, and one of her cheeks began to sting like crazy. Breathing even hurt.

Rachel tried to open her eyes again, slowly this time, and focused on the soft soothing voice that spoke to her. The room spun a little but began to settle as Eli moved into the center of her vision, bent over her bed. A *hospital* bed. Oh, this *couldn't* be good. In confusion, she looked at him, as he settled carefully on the edge of the bed where she could see him.

He spoke softly, which helped with the pounding in her head. "I've never been so happy to see those gorgeous blue eyes of yours, Rachel. We were all so worried about you."

Eli looked like he hadn't slept in days and his eyes were very bloodshot. Had he been crying? What in the hell had happened? How long had she been in the hospital?

He evidently saw the confusion in her eyes and softly began to fill her in. "You were involved in a car accident two days ago. It's Thursday morning. Two deer and another vehicle. Ace Webster was driving the other vehicle and called 911. He helped control your bleeding until EMS got there."

Two days? Ace? Did she see Ace? In a flash, she saw the deer and remembered a screeching sound. The other vehicle. Ace? The longer Eli talked, the worse she felt. She must be in bad shape.

The other voices came closer and entered her room as Eli stood and moved to the foot of the bed where it was easier for her to see him. Her mom and dad and a man she didn't know came in, all with eyes on her. Her parents looked tired but relieved. Gingerly, she reached with her right hand, and her mom took it, rubbing it on her cheek and kissing her knuckles. Rachel smiled at her, trying to not pull at the bandage over her cheekbone. She looked at her dad and pointed at her throat.

He nodded and said, "No talking for a little while, honey. That needs time to heal."

She motioned with her fingers, and he reached into her night table for a pad and pencil.

Eli caressed the top of her foot and said, "Angel, I'll give you a few minutes while I go get something to eat real quick. I'll be back soon."

Showing she was a trooper, she smiled and winked at him, blowing a little air kiss. He teared up and mouthed, "I love you," before exiting. Her heart lurched a little at the vulnerability in his eyes, and tears welled in her eyes, too.

* * * *

Utterly exhausted, Eli leaned against the wall out in the hallway, uncaring that someone might see him in such an emotional state. He put his head in his hand for a moment before pushing off and going once again to the little chapel down the hall. Prayers of praise came from his lips, tears slipping from his eyes as he remembered her winking at him, such a simple little thing, yet so powerful. That feeling of peace and comfort overtook him, and he knew they would get through whatever came next. His angel would be all right, but she was in some very real pain, so he prayed for her to feel better.

By the time he returned, the doctor was gone, and her parents remained only long enough to thank him for the tender loving care he gave their daughter. Humbled, he thanked them both and returned the hug that Mrs. Lopez gave him and shook Rachel's dad's hand. After they left, a nurse brought in another large fresh flower arrangement then checked her vitals. The nurse injected a pain reliever into the port of her IV line.

"She's going to get sleepy soon, but she should feel better within a minute or so, Eli. You need anything?" she asked as she walked to the door.

"No, thanks, Eva, I appreciate it." He smiled at the nurse that had gone to great lengths to make his stay in the hospital over the last two nights as comfortable as possible. He looked over at Rachel in time to catch the irritated scowl she cast at the door. He put his hands on his hips and raised an eyebrow at her. She tried to scowl at him and even raised a weak fist at the door before smiling sheepishly at him.

"Jealous much?" He came to sit down in the chair and held her right hand. "You have nothing to worry about, angel. My eyes see only you. She made my stay more comfortable here by finding me a folding cot, blanket, and pillow, that's all. How do you feel now?"

She scribbled on her pad then showed him. *Better, but sleepy now.*

"Good, the more rest you get the better. Are you thirsty?"

No, Mom helped me earlier. It hurt, but it was wonderful, too. My throat was very dry. Getting woozy. She dropped the pencil and looked at him with a dreamy serene smile on her face.

"Good drugs?" He chuckled, watching her eyelids slide closed as she nodded happily then conked out. He tucked the blanket around her, kissed her forehead, and settled back in the chair.

To see her in so much pain earlier had torn him up. Almost as much as seeing her when they unloaded her, unconscious and helpless, from the ambulance, drenched in her own blood. They had waited anxiously for the last day and a half until she regained consciousness. He had tortured himself in those hours spent waiting, especially when he had tried to sleep, with a contrasting image of the two of them making love, the wild ecstasy that had turned to sweet tenderness on a dime. What if last time had *been* the last time?

The doctor opened the door and motioned to him to come out so their conversation would not disturb her. Out in the hall, the doctor leaned against the door frame and said, "Listen, I don't know what your circumstances are, but now that Rachel is past the critical point, you'll need to think about what to do until she's fully recovered. I want to keep her here for a few more days to watch for complications. Once those dangers pass, she won't need such intensive care. She'll need someone to prepare and serve her meals and make sure she is eating properly, help her get around, and she needs to be someplace she can rest. I can recommend an intermediate recovery facility, but that's not the only option you have available."

Eli cocked a knowing eyebrow at the doctor. "How does *she* feel about a facility?" Eli could not picture her staying in a hospital setting that long.

The doctor chuckled. "She doesn't think she needs it. But she hasn't tried to move around yet, either. She's going to need the extra time, but it doesn't have to be in a hospital setting. Peter and Renata have offered to let her come home and stay with them for a while. She was opposed to that, not wanting to 'move back home' was how she put it. You could encourage her to either option, but they want you to know that they offered, for her sake, and not because they want to have her dependent on them. This must be a big deal to her."

"Doc, you have *no* idea."

The doctor nodded and smiled wistfully. "I'm married to one of those types, too. It's a good thing with the hours I keep. Speaking of which, that's the main reason that I'm recommending intermediate care. I know you keep some strange hours, too. She needs someone at home around the clock to watch over her. We don't want her to get up to use the restroom by herself rather than bother anyone and wind up falling and breaking her other arm."

Eli cringed, not liking the sound of that. The ache in his chest grew at the thought of how much he'd miss her.

"How long?"

"Four weeks. I'd like to see her then, evaluate her progress and determine whether she needs any physical therapy or not." He gave Eli a knowing grin. "Absence makes the heart fonder, right?"

"You're an intuitive man, Doc. Anyone ever tell you that?"

"All the time. You see what I'm getting at, though? She needs more than a few days to recover, and she needs to do that with others around her.

If she likes being on her own, it will probably drive her crazy, but that will motivate her to work toward her recovery."

"Rachel won't want to go home, but I doubt she'll agree to go to a facility because she won't want to offend her mom. I'll talk to her and help her to see she needs this. Can she get up at all?"

"She can sit up in bed and sit on the edge of the bed. No walking unless someone is holding her because she's going to be dizzy. In another day or so, I'd like to see her moving around in the halls. Will you talk to her, Eli? Peter and Renata both seem to think she'll listen to you."

"I'll talk to her. She'll see reason, but she won't like it."

"Good luck with that," the doctor said dryly and shook his hand. "Let me know what she agrees to."

* * * *

A week later, Rachel carried her favorite flower arrangement in her lap as Eli wheeled her out of the hospital exit to his waiting truck, parked in the shade under the portico. He opened the door, and she smiled at the comforting blast of frigid air. The September heat was absolutely stifling. He lifted her effortlessly into the passenger seat, and she had to stifle a chuckle as she watched the two nurses who carried flowers out to the truck for her. One's mouth popped open, and the other couldn't help the dreamy sigh that escaped. She couldn't blame them for their admiration as they watched him buckle her seatbelt for her.

He handed her the arrangement she'd brought down, a squat vase filled with exotic-colored roses from Merritt's Florist. He took the other two arrangements from the nurses and thanked them graciously then placed them in a cardboard box on the back floorboard. She waved at the nurses, who smiled and waved back then turned the wheelchair and took it back into the hospital entrance.

Rachel hadn't been happy with this arrangement when Eli had first brought it up, saying she was perfectly capable of taking care of herself at home. The first time he helped her to the restroom after they removed her catheter, she changed her mind. That one little adventure out of bed had used every bit of strength she had. She had asked him to call the nurse to assist her, but he'd helped her up and pulled up her panties himself, without batting an eyelash, then helped her back to bed. Rachel knew then that he was right. She did need help. She'd laid back down on the bed in a cold sweat, completely wiped out by the short trip.

Now here she sat on her way to her parent's ranch feeling like an invalid. It galled her that she would need someone to help her with the basics for a while, but that wasn't what caused the pain she was in right now. She felt like a big baby.

Tears filled her eyes, and she caught him look over in her direction with concern in his eyes. A hitching pain clenched in her chest.

"Angel, you can do this. It won't be for long, and then you can be on your own again. Your mom promised not to hover. She knows you like your independence. It'll be okay." He covered her hand with his, where it lay on her lap, restrained by her cast. "I took your laptop out to the ranch, with your clothes and other stuff earlier. If you feel like it, you can do some writing later. Time's going to fly. You concentrate on resting and healing, and you'll be back in your own place before you know it."

"It's not that, Eli," she said softly, still hoarse from the wound to her throat. It was deep but had not damaged her vocal chords and was healing nicely. The doctor said the hoarseness might linger and would persist if she used her voice too much.

"What is it, angel? Do you need a pain pill?" He reached for the meds her doctor had prescribed for her pain.

"No. I mean, yes, when we get to the house I'll need one, but that's not what's bothering me." She turned carefully. The tears spilled from her eyes, and she said, "I'm going to miss you so much." Her lips trembled, and a sob escaped. She gingerly wiped the tears away before they soaked the bandage over her cheekbone.

Because she'd been self-conscious of all the wounds and lacerations she'd suffered, he'd helped her look under all the bandages. She had been able to see for herself that they were all healing well and that she wouldn't look like Frankenstein's creature when the healing process was through. Eli had reminded her with tender kisses that he was just grateful that she was all right and would recover fully.

He pulled over to the shoulder of the road and slid across the seat to her. He gently cupped her cheeks in his hands and said, "Angel, I'll miss you, too. *Especially* at night. I haven't slept worth a damn since I've been sleeping alone. But I'll be out there all the time when I'm not working. Your dad and mom will probably get sick of seeing me all the time. *You'll* even get sick of me. Don't worry. You'll be back on your own in no time," he said, smiling down at her. She sobbed painfully, and more tears spilled over her cheeks. He looked confused and said, "Rachel, what did I say? I didn't mean to upset you. Tell me."

"I don't care about being on my own. I need you. I'll never be able to sleep if you're not there," she whispered hoarsely.

She felt silly and ashamed as she looked into his eyes, unable to get a better handle on her emotions. She couldn't believe what a ninny she was being. His face registered a mixture of surprise and sympathy and something else she couldn't quite pinpoint.

His fingers were gentle as he lifted her chin. "I want you with me, too. Promise me you'll be good and work hard on recovering for me and then we *can* be together, just the two of us. Will you do that?" he asked, beaming down at her. Rachel looked into his eyes, and what she saw there made her feel hopeful. She smiled up at him and wiped away her tears.

"I love you, Eli. I'm so in love with you." She rested her forehead carefully on his chest and sighed shakily, her breath hitching a little from her tears.

"If you only knew what you do to me. I love you so much my chest hurts." He leaned down and kissed her tenderly on the lips then brushed his lips over her uninjured cheekbone. She sighed contentedly and wrapped her good arm around his waist.

"Let's get you settled." He released her and slid back behind the steering wheel, buckled in, and continued down the road. "I talked to my dad yesterday."

"Oh, yeah?" Rachel replied, sniffling as she dried her eyes with the back of her hand. Her heart felt much lighter, like a burden had been lifted from it.

"He's coming for a visit around the end of October."

"I hope it cools off for his visit."

"I do, too. Maybe by then you'll be home?"

"I'm planning on it, big boy." She smiled when he said "home" like that. Yeah, *he* was her home.

Chapter Twenty-five

Rachel was the best convalescing patient *ever*, even when she thought the process would drive her crazy. She spent a little time every day moving around, pushing herself to do things when she could do it in safety while her mom hovered nearby. She did not want to elongate her stay at home.

A week into her recovery, she could no longer stand the thought of the work piling up at her job and called Mr. Grogan. Bernice put her on hold, and after a minute, he came on the line.

"Young lady, you may not return to work."

"But—"

"I'm sitting at your desk right now. The bills that need paying are getting paid, anything else pressing is coming directly to me. The other stuff you can catch up on when you come back. Get your butt back in bed and get better." Rachel could hear him chuckling as she gasped in surprise, and then she did something very uncharacteristic as she made a face at her phone and blew a raspberry at it.

She put the phone back to her ear in time to hear him say, "I heard that. Now, see? I told you that you'd fit in just fine around here."

"But you could send me everything electronically. I can do that from bed."

"But that's not restful or healthy, now is it?"

"I'm bored!"

Thorne chuckled deeply. "Tough shit, sweetheart. We miss you around here. You kind of 'class' the place up a bit. But I don't want to see you here or have you working for at least another three weeks. That's what your doctor says, right?"

Begrudgingly she replied, "Yes, how did you—"

"A little bird told me." She looked at her phone and stuck her tongue out at it then put it back to her ear in time to hear him say, "So there you have it, sweetheart. Rest and heal, and we'll throw you a party when you come back. In *three weeks*."

"I like working. I'm not a baby."

"I know. You should work on that book you're writing instead of pestering your poor old boss. Three weeks, not a moment sooner."

She set up her laptop and spent time each day working on her manuscript. In a way, the accident had provided her an opportunity to work on it consistently. Writing helped to pass the time.

Eli often spent his evenings off at the Lopez ranch and came to visit her in the afternoons, on the nights he had to work at The Pony. Her parents never tired of his visits and always seemed curious about his work and his plans. Her father was especially observant of Eli, and she wondered what was going through his head when he watched Eli and the way he was around her. She was glad to see they had become friends. Several times she'd observed them deep in conversation and wondered what they found to talk about.

Her mother's eyes always twinkled when Eli was around. She quickly found out what his favorite foods were and cooked them for him. She approved of the way he treated Rachel and always made a point of complimenting his manners and personality to Rachel. Mike and Rogelio came to visit her, and, of course, she saw Grace or talked to her on the phone almost daily. That helped because Rachel always laughed when she talked with Grace.

Her one difficulty regarding her recuperation was sleeping. She struggled with insomnia and nightmares of the accident, but she refused to take sleeping pills. She dreamed of being trapped and unable to talk or get out of the car, of being in pain and not being able to move. One time, she even dreamed she was the doe being chased and struck by the SUV. She always woke bathed in sweat, sometimes screaming, which scared the crap out of her poor parents.

Once she had the nightmare, she had a hard time falling back to sleep. Some nights she wasn't troubled by bad dreams, but she still couldn't fall asleep, her mind filled with thoughts of Eli. She didn't worry about him on the job. She just missed him. Eli was having trouble sleeping, too, because he'd told her about it one night when she mentioned that he looked tired. He told her he needed her, that was all. Her heart felt full at his words.

She would lay there in the dark and remember what it felt like when he surrounded her with his big, strong arms and cuddled her against his broad chest and she used his biceps as her pillow. Sometimes she'd go for full-on torture and think about making love with him, clinging to his warmth as he slid his stiff cock into her and stroked her to a hot, moaning orgasm. If she fell asleep thinking of those times, she woke with her body clamoring for his, wet and ready. Once she woke as an orgasm inspired by her dream washed over her, but it felt unsatisfying when she realized she was alone with no warm arms to hold her and help her come down from it.

By the fourth week, she was getting around much better but had dark circles under her eyes from lack of sleep. Her mom came to her and sat down at the kitchen table with a bottle of Tylenol PM. She showed her the label. Non-addicting.

Her mother tapped the bottle on the table. "I talked to your doctor. You'll take these tonight, tomorrow night, and the next night. You've got to get some sleep, or you'll never fully recover, sweetheart. I think Eli is what you need now, not more sitting around," she said with a twinkle in her eye. "Be a good girl and do as I say, and I'll help you pack on Friday and take you to your duplex."

Rachel grinned and said cheekily, "Tonight, tomorrow night, and you take me home on Thursday. I want to surprise Eli, so don't say anything to him tonight when he comes over."

Her mom tried to hide her smile with a grimace. "Always negotiating. I think we should tell him."

"No, I want to surprise him. Please?"

"*All right*. Take one now and go lie down for a nap. It's early enough, and I'll wake you so you don't sleep too long." She handed Rachel a tablet and a glass of water. Rachel smiled and took it obediently, excited at this development. Restlessness had plagued her the last few days and she knew that was because she was getting better. Rachel knew she needed Eli if she wanted to sleep. She knew he needed her, too.

She did succeed in taking a nap that morning and then applied herself into completing the novel. Wednesday night, they all watched a movie together. After taking her Tylenol PM, she laid her head in his lap, and she fell asleep twenty minutes into the movie. She woke a bit as he carried her gently in his arms to her room and tucked her in after sliding her slippers off her feet. She turned to him half asleep as he kissed her cheeks.

* * * *

Thursday morning, Rachel watched her mom close the backdoor on the Escalade her dad had given her as an anniversary gift a few months before. "Grab your laptop, Rachel. I have everything else loaded. Do you need to check and make sure you haven't forgotten anything?"

Rachel stood in the doorway. Three weeks ago, the laptop had felt like it weighed a ton. Now, she could lift it in its carrying case with hardly any effort.

"No, I already have. Let's go."

Her mom chuckled as Rachel carefully climbed into the driver's seat. "Aren't you an eager beaver? I already stocked your kitchen with groceries, and I've packed some things I cooked for you, so all you'll have to do is reheat food in the microwave. It can all go in the freezer, so you should have enough to last a week, at least." As her mom drove down the long drive way, she looked over at Rachel and patted her thigh. "You'll call me if you need me, right?"

"Of course, Mom."

"I know Eli will take excellent care of you, but you can call me during the day if you need me while he's at work."

"Thanks, Mom, for taking such good care of me. I'm glad you like Eli so much. It means a lot to me."

"Well, I see how happy he makes you and that he loves you, too."

While her mom got her unpacked and settled, Rachel took a warm shower and washed her hair. She slipped into a fresh pair of pajamas and settled into her bed, a little strung out from the move and the excitement of being home. Her mom talked her into taking another Tylenol PM and kissed her cheek. She brought Rachel her cell phone in case she needed it and let herself out, locking up behind her. Rachel cuddled up to her pillows and fell asleep.

A noise woke her later, and she sat up, feeling disoriented. The sun was gone from her bedroom window, and she realized she must have slept into the afternoon. She heard the sound again and realized what it was. Eli must

be home because the noise that woke her was the sound of a Harley pulling
into the driveway.

She stretched carefully, testing how she felt, and smiled at the butterflies
in her stomach. Even though she wasn't medically released for
"extracurricular activities" like sex yet, she was giddy at the thought of
being alone with Eli. Two more weeks, the doctor had said. Torture. That's
what she thought of his recommendation. She'd be surprised if they made it
two more weeks without attacking each other. It'd been easy at her parents'
house because they were never alone, but she was feeling better now, and
they were *so* blessedly alone.

Her thoughts were interrupted by the sound of a door slamming on the
other side of the duplex. Dang. She'd never noticed that before. The walls
were—thin. The blood ran cold in her veins as a muffled male laugh came
through the wall, followed by a feminine giggle. She fell flat on her back as
the adrenaline rush slammed into her. She turned on her side, intending to
go see what the hell was going on over there.

Before she could pull on her robe and slippers, she *knew* exactly what
was going on next door. Gooseflesh covered her skin as she listened to the
unmistakable sounds of boisterous fucking coming from Eli's side of the
duplex. She tried to stand, but the strength had left her legs.

The sounds of female arousal, begging to be fucked, even the sound of a
loud slap and a moan were clear and unmistakable. Even with her hands
over her ears, she could hear the joyous sound of a woman getting her brains
fucked out. Rachel listened, utterly mystified and hurt. She couldn't believe
she was listening to Eli fucking another woman. Filled with confusion, she
couldn't reconcile this with his solicitous behavior at her parents' house.

Rachel lay there listening as the pace of the noise next door increased in
tempo. She heard loud moans and wailing as Eli evidently satisfied the fuck
out of the woman he was screwing and then a loud yell as he got off, too.
She curled on her side as it grew quiet next door except for a giggle now and
then.

Pain lanced through her from her injuries, and she knew she must have
been tensing up too much. She lay there *praying* that they were finished.
She'd give herself a few minutes to recover and then call her mother to
come get her and take her back home.

No, she couldn't do that. She had a place of her own now. She couldn't run home to Mommy and Daddy even though that was what she wanted to do. She'd screwed up royally taking a place right next door to Eli. Now she'd lose her deposit when she moved for breaking the lease agreement.

This was one gigantic fucking mess. Had this been going on the whole time she had been at her parents'? He must have gotten tired of going without sex and one of those sluts at the club had seized her opportunity. Better to know this now before her heart was fully committed.

What a dumbass. Who am I kidding?

Her heart had been committed from the moment their eyes had locked across the dance floor. This was going to hurt, no matter how she candy-coated it or tried to rationalize it.

She pulled the pillow over her head and tried to calm her breathing and figure out what to do next because she couldn't stay there. She'd make some calls in a few minutes and try to find a hotel room for the night and then start searching for a new place from there.

Rachel nearly came out of her skin when she felt a big hand on her arm.

"Angel? What's the matter?" His soft voice sounded alarmed as he removed the pillow from her head.

* * * *

Eli knelt down at the side of her bed. Her hair was stuck to the damp trails of her tears, and her pillow was damp, too. How long had she been like that? A cold chill went through him at the stark pain in her eyes.

"Are you hurting? When was the last time you took a pain pill? Do you need one? Your mom called me. She knew you wanted to surprise me, but she started to worry and decided to call me and let me know you were here."

She stared mutely at him, hers eyes full over misery and pain.

He whispered softly, "Angel? You're scaring me here. What's the matter?" He sat on the edge of the bed and helped her sit up carefully, but she inched away from him. Fresh tears tracked down her cheeks, and a fresh painful sob rasped hoarsely from her throat. The sound made his heart kick up a notch.

She stared at him as if she didn't know him. Her brows knitted together when she looked into his eyes. Furiously, she swiped at the tears as he continued to stare at her, waiting for her to say something. She brushed her hair back. Eli became more baffled by the second as she looked at him coldly, her hands trembling. He was so *glad* to see her and ached to take her in his arms and fix whatever was troubling her, but she wouldn't speak to him.

"Baby, what is it? Is it your throat? Are you in pain?" He gently grasped her upper arms and pulled her to his chest as her body began to shake, racked with soundless sobs. He felt tears in his own eyes at the pain and confusion he saw in hers. "*Angel*, please tell me what is wrong."

Angrily, she pushed back from him and knocked his hands away, flinging herself violently to the other corner of the bed out of his reach. He stood and walked around the bed, frightened that she would re-injure herself.

He spoke softly to her to calm her, his heart breaking at the way her shoulders shook and the rasp of her soundless sobs in her chest. She held her hand protectively over the surgical site on her abdomen, really scaring him now. He held both palms up, trying to calm her. Clearly, touching her only upset her now.

"Angel, tell me *what's wrong*. I came home right after your mom called me to let me know you were here. Has something happened?" She glanced at the denim work shirt and jeans he wore for his tower climbing work and seemed to become even more bewildered.

"I *heard*."

"You heard what?"

"I heard *you*…and *her*," she gasped, her voice vibrating with anguish.

"*Who*? I just got home. I came straight in here to check on you. Angel, tell me what's wrong."

Fresh tears overflowed her tumultuous, dark eyes, and she trembled as she repeated, "I heard you…and her. It's no use, Eli. I *know*." Her voice had all but deserted her. She hung her head and sobbed breathily.

"Baby, I'm confused, I—" he began, then paused and looked at the wall that adjoined his bedroom.

He let out a long groan because now they could *both* hear it. The unmistakable sound of a squeaking bed frame and a soft moan. He cringed as understanding dawned on him even as the bewilderment deepened in her eyes. She looked mystified as he shook his head and held up a finger, pulled out his phone, and dialed a number.

She looked on in bemusement as, through the wall, a cell phone rang. The squeaking persisted for a moment before finally ceasing while Eli waited for an answer. He put his palm to his forehead as the easily identifiable voice answered the phone.

"Yeah, man."

Eli suppressed a chuckle, thinking Mike sounded a little pissed.

"Hey, Mike. It's Eli. I'm just checking in."

Rachel put her hands to her red-hot face, and he watched as realization dawned on her who it was she'd heard having hot sex next door. He could not imagine how it must have felt to think it was him she was listening to. "I'm going to be home in a few minutes and wanted to make sure the coast was clear."

Mike's voice was gravelly with frustration. "Oh, yeah. Um...we just got here a few minutes ago. How long do you think?"

"Maybe thirty or forty-five minutes."

"Oh, that would be great."

"Hey, Rachel's coming home with me."

"Oh, yeah? That's good news. We'll stop over there and bring you the key. We would have been long gone, man, but Rosa got called in to work this morning."

"That's fine, Mike. Don't worry about it, man. I'm sorry you were delayed. See you, man." Eli finished the call and slid the phone back into his pocket and held his arms out to her.

Holding her abdomen, she slipped from her perch on the bed, and he pulled her gently into his lap. As the squeaking of the bed next door resumed, he lifted her and carried her into the living room, pulling the bedroom door closed softly, and then sat down with her on the loveseat.

"I thought..." She laid her head weakly on his chest.

"I know," he replied softly.

"I'm sorry I didn't trust you."

"Don't be sorry. I should have explained before now. You know how tiny Mike and Rosa's house is, right? They've got five kids and her mother living with them, complaining about every little thing. Mike was starting to look a little desperate, so I offered my place to them to…take the edge off, you know? They had no idea you were over here."

She nodded and closed her eyes. Then she sat up and turned to him and said, "*Oh, crap*! Kelly heard us when we made love while she was here, didn't she? Oh, no!" She hid her red-hot face as Eli chuckled.

"Yep, but she handled it with her usual good humor. She teased me quite a bit when you weren't within earshot, so don't feel too bad for her. Let me get you something to drink. You're hoarse."

"Thank you," she whispered as she climbed from his lap and curled up, still looking tense. He brought her a glass of water, which she drained and set on the coffee table.

"Come here, angel." She resumed her perch in his lap, and he caressed her shoulders. "You're wound too tight. Lie back against me and let me hold you. Relax, I've got you," he said as she laid her head against his chest. He pressed his lips to her hair and breathed in her clean womanly scent and the fragrance of her shampoo.

"I felt so weak earlier when they first got started. I couldn't even stand up to walk away from the bedroom so I wouldn't hear it anymore. Then, you came in looking so worried and concerned I thought I was losing my mind." She shuddered against him, and he gently wrapped his arms around her and held her snugly. "I'm not going to be able to look Mike or Rosa in the eye for a while."

Eli chuckled while he rubbed his palm up and down her back soothingly. "Angel, now is not the most romantic time to tell you this because I can still hear them on the other side, but let me tell you anyway. This love I have for you is *it* for me. There could never be anyone else that holds a candle to you. I felt so powerless when I thought of you hurt on the side of the road, maybe even dying, and I couldn't get to you. I saw you when they unloaded you from the ambulance, baby, and I thought for sure I'd lost you. You were *bathed* in blood. I had to be held back."

"Grace told me about that." She quivered in his embrace.

"I thought I'd lost my one chance at a happy life. Being back in a hospital setting brought back painful memories and I felt like I was reliving them all over again as an adult."

"Something like this happened to you before?" Rachel asked softly, her voice full of sympathy.

"I told you my mom died. But I never told you how. I also never told you about my own experience in the hospital as a four-year-old not understanding what had happened. My family was involved in a very serious car accident right before Thanksgiving. My mom was holding a cookie sheet with my toy magnets on it in her lap. I'd just made a picture with them for her, and she was going to make one for me, but I fell asleep. She was holding it on her lap when the accident happened."

"I never knew you were in a car accident. Is that how your mom died, internal injuries?"

Eli nodded. "The official term is 'unsecured objects within vehicle,' but the collision forced the cookie sheet into her abdomen, doing catastrophic internal damage."

Rachel looked straight into his eyes. "Eli, you know what happened wasn't your fault?"

In theory, yes, he knew that, but it hadn't eased him at all the day he found out years later when he finally had gotten the nerve to ask his father about it. His memories were sketchy of the time after the accident, but he remembered clearly the time leading up to it.

"Yes, I do. But it didn't make it any easier to bear. Ace told us about the lamp and the picture frames. It was like reliving that nightmare all over again."

Eli told her his story as he was transported back in time to those painful memories. He took long pauses here and there, and she rubbed his back comfortingly with her good arm. Her warmth seeped into him and eased the telling, buffering the pain of the memories as he shared them with her.

Chapter Twenty-six

Eli wanted to go see his grandma and grandpa. His grandpa said they were going to eat turkey and jellied cranberry sauce until they both popped then they would take a nap. He wanted to see Aunt Becky and tell her about his Legos and give her the picture of the helicopter with the monkey piloting it that he'd drawn especially for her. He wanted to play with her long, long blonde hair and coil it until it looked like a long snake and loop it around his arm.

He wanted to climb Grandma's tree in the backyard with his other boy cousins and hang upside down from his favorite branch. He hated sitting in his car seat for hours, but it was totally worth it when his grandpa would grab him from the car and hoist him up over his shoulder and give him a piggyback ride.

His grandpa was big and strong like his daddy and super tall like a big mountain, and when he laughed, it made Eli feel like the air shook around him. His grandmother would take him from Grandpa, and he'd loop his arms around her neck and wrap his legs around her waist as she held him and hugged him hard, and then she would say what a big boy he was getting to be and how he'd be tall someday like his daddy and his grandpa. She always made him feel special and important, and he hoped she was right about getting tall because right now he just felt short.

Mom had buckled him in his car seat after he'd gone to the potty and gave him his favorite big animal picture book and a cookie sheet with bunches of magnetic figures stuck all over it. That was his special toy she saved for long car trips. His daddy loaded the luggage in the car while she buckled his baby sister into the car seat next to him and tucked a fuzzy blanket around her and adjusted the neck on her fuzzy sleeper.

He looked over at his baby sister, and she grinned sleepily at him and blew a bubble with her spit. He loved when she did that because it was so gross and awesome. He loved gross stuff. His mother playfully called him the King of Gross and said she always wondered what she'd find in his pockets on laundry day. She'd gotten on him the day before about the earthworms, but he thought it had been totally cool when she showed him the bits and pieces they'd become in the load of laundry she'd just done. She didn't think it was so funny, but he thought she hid a smile behind her hand when he told her he loved gross stuff. She'd shaken her head and sent him outside.

After sis was loaded and he had all the magnets off and piled in his lap, his dad started the car and they were on their way to Grandma and Grandpa's. He made a picture with the magnets and handed it to his mom so she could look at it. He settled down to look at his big animal book, and she said she would make a picture for him with the magnets.

He woke up hurting badly, and people had been talking and shouting all around him. It was too much, and he fell asleep. He woke up again and hurt even worse. It was dark, and he couldn't see at all. He began to cry and scream because he couldn't see right, and someone picked up his hand and held it. A baby was crying loudly, and he thought it sounded like his sister. He thought that his mom would never let her cry like that and reached out to pat her, but she wasn't next to him anymore.

He fell asleep and woke up, feeling woozy, in a hospital bed. An old lady he'd never seen before sat next to him, holding his hand, and she looked up from her book when he moved. He realized he was all bandaged and it was nighttime. He could see now, but one of his eyes was all covered up. When he moved, his chest and sides ached bad. The old lady got his dad, who thanked her nicely, using her name like he'd known her forever. He leaned over and kissed him on the cheek, and he saw the terrible hurt and pain in his daddy's eyes. It frightened him to see that. He looked like he hadn't slept in days and days, and tears spilled from his eyes as though he hadn't seen Eli in as long.

Daddy said they had a crash and Mom and Sissie were hurt real bad, and so was he. Daddy said he was going to pray and would he like to come along? He went with his dad and that was how he found out that hospitals had little churches inside them. Once he knew it was there, though, he liked coming alone better. When the nurses discovered him missing from his room, they always came there first. He only saw Dad a few times, but each time he looked worse and worse.

He went every time he could to pray for Mom, Dad, and Sissie. He promised God that if he could see them, he would be so sweet to Sissie and kiss her and hug Mom's neck and kiss her, too. He even promised to not be gross anymore if it would make Mom happy.

He went up where it was brighter from the soft lights and kneeled down on the steps to pray. He cried until the carpet was wet with his tears because Mom wasn't getting better and he was scared. He prayed to God, asking him to help her feel better so they could go on to Grandma and Grandpa's.

He woke in a daze as soft hands smoothed his hair and touched his cheek. He looked up into deep blue eyes and knew he was dreaming again.

"You can't stay here, sweetheart. Come with me so you can rest."

Gentle arms picked him up, and he was carried back to his room, tears spilling from his eyes. Soft lips touched his cheeks, kissing the tears away. Hands as soft as butterfly wings swept over his cheeks, soothing him as strong arms laid him on his bed and covered him with his blanket. He looked up at the tall angel with the cool white-feathered wings and smiled, thinking this must be a really cool dream and how he felt a little better now. The angel smiled down at him and stood watch over him as he fell asleep.

His daddy came in his room and found him alone on his bed. His father had been crying and, holding back sobs, told him that his mom had gone to heaven, and she didn't hurt anymore. Terrible pain seized his chest, and he began to breathe hard, sobs ripping through his chest as his dad held him.

The next day, his father looked like a ghost when he saw him, but the nurses told him Sissie was doing better. He snuck back to the chapel again even though they told him not to go alone, and he curled up on the steps in front of the pews again and prayed. He thanked Jesus for helping Sissie get better and asked Him to take care of Mom and help him be a good little man and help his dad to not feel so sad. How was he gonna do this? His mom had always been there for him.

Then he sobbed and sobbed until all his tears were gone. He laid his head on the carpet and felt the tears run from his eyes endlessly. Soft, warm arms lifted him from the steps and cuddled him close. He opened his eyes and looked up into the same deep blue eyes again.

"Sweetheart, I'll watch over you for her."

He turned his face into soft, silky, dark hair and put his hand over his face and shut out the world, safe in his angel's arms as she sat with him in the pew and rocked him, comforting him with a soft tune. He woke in his hospital bed as Grandma and Grandpa came through the door, looking tired and much older. They packed his few personal belongings in a small suitcase, and Grandpa carried him gently from the room. He never had a chance to go back and thank the angel for watching out for him and hoped maybe she could come with him now or visit him later.

* * * *

Eli felt like a ton of bricks had been lifted from his chest after relaying the story to her. "Sometimes I dream about her holding me while I cried. Those aren't bad dreams, though they used to make me sad, but not anymore. You know why?" he asked, tears welled in his eyes.

"Why?" she asked softly, wiping her own eyes as the tears spilled.

"You have her eyes. Deep midnight-blue and sweet. I noticed them when Mike first introduced us to each other. I already knew I wanted you, but your eyes were the reason I asked you out the moment I met you. Now all I want is to wake up each morning to your beautiful face after sleeping cuddled up to you all night." He squeezed her soft form to him gently as she blotted the tears from his cheeks with her tissue. "I'm sorry I never told you that I let Mike and Rosa use my place when they need some time alone."

"I'm sorry I didn't trust you more."

He shrugged. There was no reason for her to apologize. He'd had good intentions, trying to help out a friend. Sometimes good intentions backfired. "The assumption you made was a pretty safe one, considering that's my place and my bed next door," he replied, chuckling. "No one could love me the way you do, angel. I'm ruined for all others. That bed belongs to you now, and Mike and Rosa will understand about needing to find another place to be alone."

"Will you stay with me tonight?" she asked softly.

"Need a little distance from this bizarre situation?" He nuzzled her throat.

"Just a little." She grinned as she tilted her head for his kiss.

"We're having more company this Saturday."

"Oh, yeah?"

"Dad is driving in from San Antonio. He says he can't wait to meet you. I hope you don't mind, but I told your mom, and she invited us all over for supper on Saturday night."

"Oh, that will be fun. He and my dad will have plenty to talk about." She laughed.

"Government, taxes, and healthcare?"

"Once they get started, we'll never get them to shut up. How did your dad cope all these years?" she asked.

"Well, we kept him pretty busy growing up, and there was always work. He dated a few times, but he told me once that no one could hold a candle to my mom. I reckon there's someone out there for him. They just have to find each other, I suppose."

"Is he tall and handsome like you?"

"He's tall like me, but I take after my mom in my coloring and features. She had Native American blood in her. When I was little, I used to imagine him in a horned Viking helmet and wrapped in furs with long blond braids. He cut his hair a long time ago, but he always reminded me of Thor from the Marvel comic books. You'll have to judge for yourself whether or not he's handsome. Maybe I should call Kelly and invite her down, too. They could stay over here if you wouldn't mind staying with me."

She chuckled. "I don't know. You might have to twist my good arm, honey. Remember what the doctor told us?"

"I'm trying." He shifted her on his lap and tried to make more room behind his zipper for the erection that was now pounding for release. "But having you in such close proximity makes it hard."

She snickered. "I've noticed."

Shaking his finger at her in mock threat, he said, "Back to what we were talking about. I'll call Kelly and invite her and Matthew."

While they talked, the doorbell rang. Grinning knowingly at her, Eli answered the door while she tried to hide her laughter.

Mike and Rosa were holding hands and looking rather rosy-cheeked themselves. "Hey! We were in the neighborhood and thought we'd stop in and say welcome home, Rachel," Mike said as Rosa smiled gratefully at Eli and surreptitiously handed him his house key, which he slipped into the pocket of his denim workshirt. She hugged him then went to hug Rachel.

"It's good to see you back on your feet, Rachel. Mike and I were so worried about you. We can't stay. We need to pick the kids up from school and check on my mother. We just wanted to say hello."

They spoke for a couple more minutes and took their leave, and then Eli hustled Rachel back to bed, tucking her in with her laptop. "I'm going to run some errands. I'll call Kelly and invite her for a few days and let Dad know that they can stay here. You rest and don't write too long. Take a nap if you can, and I'll be back in a couple of hours."

"Why don't we invite Grace and the guys? They know my mom and dad pretty well now. Mom and Dad will say the more the merrier."

"I think that's a terrific idea. You call her and invite them. I'll let Mike and Rogelio know, too."

He sat on the edge of the bed and reached for her hand. "We had some scary moments in here earlier this afternoon. We'll erase them and make new ones tonight."

"But the doctor—"

"Trust me?"

Her smile dazzled him when she replied, "Yes, Eli."

"Then rest for me. I'll be back."

When Eli's feet hit the porch, he was flying high. He pulled out his phone and dialed while he started his truck. He made phone call after phone call, saving Grace for last to give Rachel a chance to call her first. She screamed so loud Eli's ear hurt. Kelly's reaction was a not-so-distant echo of Grace's. Within the next two hours, he had all the arrangements made. He returned with take-out food for supper and fed her from his own plate, sharing a glass of tea with her.

After eating their supper, he took a warm shower then returned with her hairbrush. His hips were wrapped in a dark blue bath towel, but his massive erection was plainly visible. She grinned suggestively at him, obviously game for whatever plans he'd made for this evening. Unfortunately, they only had until seven thirty when he needed to go in to work at The Pony.

He helped her sit up and turn so that he could brush out her long, silky hair. She sighed in obvious enjoyment, and his cock twitched in response. He ran his fingers through it as he brushed enjoying the feel of it, then laid the brush aside.

He reached down and slid her pajama top carefully over her head. Her hair fell back and settled in shining waves down to the small of her back. Facing her, he slid his hands over her shoulders and through her hair to her hips. He slid his fingers into her waistband, and she rose on her knees so he could lower the bottoms. Then he helped her recline on the bed as he removed the bottoms and her panties from her legs, leaving her completely nude. The only thing covering any part of her was the cast on her left arm.

All her scars were exposed now, and as he laid her down, he kissed them all gently one by one, kissing her left shoulder and hand last before leaning over to kiss her lips. A shiver rippled delicately through her frame as she touched him. Her soft fingertips drifted through his chest hair then over his shoulder and into his hair, causing him to shudder in pleasure at her touch. She looked up into his eyes and kissed him. Her lips were so soft and lush, and he savored the delicate brush of her tongue against his.

As he kissed her, she lowered her hand and ran it lightly over his erection, still covered by the bath towel. His shaft responded eagerly, and he knew he'd better get a hold on that response or this would be over too quickly. Loosening the towel, she drew it off his hips then gently stroked his cock, which was so hard it was painful.

"Angel, it's been so long, and I've missed you. If you keep doing that, I'm going to come before we even get started." He backed away from her reach. He helped her lie down with her head on a pillow and then positioned her to his liking. She looked up at him, breathless and trusting, her eyes telling him she needed his touch as much as he needed hers. He caught the scent of her arousal, and his cock responded, pulsing with eagerness.

"Doc was concerned about strenuous sexual activity when he told you to wait two more weeks, but that doesn't mean we couldn't gently love each other and bring each other release. You'll have to wait two weeks more for harder and faster, but I'm going to give it to you slow and sweet right now, angel. Try to stay still, okay?" he asked as he put a pillow beside each knee.

He began by kissing the arches of her feet then moved over her instep and up her ankles. He teased her with soft, warm kisses but stopped at the juncture of her thigh and hip then started with the other foot.

He noticed she made a concerted effort to do as he asked, but he could tell by the soft sounds she made how difficult it was. He drew his fingers up and down the back of her thighs in a light tickling touch that made her whimper in pleasure. As he finished with each long leg, he positioned it on the pillow he'd placed on either side of her. Her cast lay resting on the bed with her left hand lying over her abdomen. He lifted that hand, kissed it, and felt her tremble.

"Comfortable?" he asked softly.

"Very," she replied, the need evident in her shaky voice.

Kneeling between her knees, he stretched over her and kissed her again, deeply, stroking her velvety soft tongue with his in slow tender caresses.

He slid his hand over her shoulder and collarbone to her breastbone. She closed her eyes and sighed in contentment. His hand cupped one full, lush breast and sucked at its tip before sliding to the other and teasing the nipple mercilessly until she was breathless and then switched and suckled on the other nipple.

Her fingertips slid down his bare chest, and he backed away before she could reach his cock again. He kissed his way down her abdomen, pressing his lips gently to the skin beside her new surgical scar. She gasped, and gooseflesh rose under his lips for a few seconds. He dipped his tongue in her belly button, and she giggled. He continued his slow descent, and she opened herself wide for him, perfectly at ease in his arms with only his hair covering her from his view. Dipping down again to the juncture of her upper thigh and hip, he kissed his way down to her inner thigh, and she moaned happily as he nuzzled her fragrant, damp outer lips with his lower lip. He gently spread her open.

"Mmm, angel. You are so wet, and your honey smells so sweet it's making my mouth water. You must be *very* ready for me to be inside you." At her enthusiastic nod and whimper, he continued. "I'll give it to you soon, but first, I need a taste of your pretty little pussy. Would you like that?"

"Y–Yes, Eli, please!" Her voice shook softly.

She moaned at the touch of his fingers at her opening, and then his tongue slid over her wet slit. He growled in pleasure as he tasted her fresh cream and slid his tongue deeper, evoking a strangled cry from her lips. His tongue swirled over her swollen clit repeatedly, and her body began to respond to his rhythm. He slid a finger into her quivering opening and stroked inside her.

"Angel, I've missed your tight little pussy." He slid another fingertip into her opening, and both fingers slid in together and went deeper, filling her tightly. He found her sweet spot and stroked that excited bundle of nerve endings.

The moment he found that spot, her eyes flew open wide and her ascent began. He thrummed that spot inside her until she was poised on the verge. Continuing the same rhythm, he licked her clit. Her moans became a soft, keening wail, and as her orgasm crashed over her, she cried out his name, sobbing her release. Her hips rocked with each loving stroke of his fingers as her orgasm gushed from her in a warm, wet wave. He licked up every drop before he gently withdrew from her.

"I wish I could go down on you."

His sweet, greedy vixen. He growled in approval. "I wish you could, too. I've missed your sweet little mouth, but it'll have to wait two more weeks. After this cast comes off," he said, tapping her arm.

"I know, but I've missed it, too. I want it now."

"Bad girl, you'll have to wait two weeks. If we use the plugs, your ass might also be ready for my cock by then," he said grinning at the pleasure that statement obviously gave her.

"Ooooh! Yes, I want that, *too!*" she chortled and wiggled her luscious ass in anticipation.

"You are a greedy girl. Ready for my cock?" he asked as his fingers slid over her inner lips, soaked with her cum and fresh arousal brought on by their conversation.

She nodded eagerly, and he slid his knees under her thighs, bracing his hands on either side of her. Resting his weight on them, he positioned his twitching cock at her silky, wet entrance. He gently stroked her clit with his thumb as he slowly entered her. She began to undulate the moment he slid in a little.

He stopped and groaned in torture at the feel of her silky heat slithering over his shaft. "Angel, you have to be still. I don't want you to hurt yourself. Feel it as I slide my cock into your tight pussy, but don't move."

"Honey, you feel so good, I can't help myself. I feel every inch of you. Oh! Eli!" She groaned as his length glided slowly into her until each glorious inch was eased inside of her. He arched over her, his lips nuzzling her throat as he shuddered, struggling for control himself.

"Angel, it's been a while, and once I start moving, I'm not going to be able to slow down. Damn, I can feel those little rippling spasms inside you."

His whole body shuddered, trying to control the almost undeniable urge to pound into her fiercely. He gritted his teeth and thrust gently.

"Eli, please let me move just a little, let me rock on you a bit, please. I'll be good, I promise." She showed him what she needed, gently rocking her hips. He reached between them and slid his finger gently along her slit and found her swollen, wet clit and began to stroke it as she whimpered and moved slowly.

They both gasped when fresh moisture increased the slick pleasure created by her rocking rhythm. "Eli, that feels so good. I need to come." He slid from her depths and gently stroked all the way back in, his cock glistening with her juices. "Yes!"

Grasping her hips to keep her motionless, he began to stroke into her with a tender but firm thrusting motion. Her panting turned into a keening wail as her orgasm built higher and higher, waiting to rush over her. He stroked her clit between his fingertips several times, and her release came in another surging wave, her hips moving gently in his hands.

The inner fight to thrust gently and carefully intensified the storm gathering within him. He kept a tight hold on the caveman who was so glad to be back inside her and channeled that energy into the care he took with her. The struggle heightened the pleasure as his whole body tensed. He thrust one last time and felt his nervous system explode with volcanic ecstasy. A loud howl erupted from his lungs as his cum jetted deep inside her silky heat. Once he stopped surging into her, he curled over her for a moment.

He rested his forehead on her shoulder very lightly before slowly pulling out of her and lying down beside her. He hated to withdraw so soon because he knew she loved it when he stayed inside her afterward, but he knew he'd be hard for her again inside of five minutes. Once was enough for her tonight. He didn't want to regret the decision to make love to her later.

"Do you feel okay, angel? Any pain?" He stroked a hand over her warm, bare hip. The warm, sated look in her languid eyes and the adoration on her face took his breath away.

"No, honey. I feel so good. You take such good care of me," she murmured in bliss.

"I was trying hard not to get carried away. You feel so good, and I missed making love to you so much," he said with a heavy, satisfied sigh. "I feel like I can't get close enough to you sometimes, even when I'm inside you." He lifted her hand to kiss it. He moved the pillows back to the headboard and covered them both with the sheet and blanket then curled up to her. He traced his fingertips over her shoulders, arms, and throat, sending little shivers through her. When he told her he needed to clean up and get ready to go to The Pony for the evening, she nodded slightly.

"Do you feel all right?" He kissed her shoulder before rising from the bed and tucking the sheet and quilt around her.

"Mmm, yes. I feel good, just tired. Will you stay with me tonight?"

"Yes, angel. I'll be home around one, I think. I'll be thinking of you."

"Wish I could come sit with you."

"Your chair is waiting beside mine for when you're all better."

Chapter Twenty-seven

Rachel lay in bed restless and wide-awake for several minutes. She picked up her cell phone and dialed Grace's number. "Hello, Adam. It's Rachel. Yep. I'm home now. Can Grace come over and play?"

Thirty minutes later, the doorbell rang twice in quick succession, and Rachel opened the front door. Grace stood on the front porch, her arms full. "I have microwave popcorn, chocolate truffles, Big Red, and movies!"

Rachel laughed and took the chocolate and DVDs from Grace and closed the door after she entered.

"What time does Eli get home?"

"Sometime around one."

Rachel watched as Grace slipped her cell phone from her pocket and pushed a button. "Mmm. Three handsome hunks on speed dial." Grace put the little phone to her ear and waited then spoke in a soft, sexy voice. "Baby? He'll be home around one. Pick me up around twelve thirty? I love you so much, Adam. You spoil me rotten." After a long pause, Grace blushed and chuckled suggestively. "You will? You are? *Baby*, the pleasure would be all *mine*," she replied softly, her voice tender with love. "See you then. Thank you." Grace ended the call, slipped the phone back in her pocket, and sighed dreamily.

"Did Adam drop you off?" Rachel asked, not sure what to think. Was that sweet or overprotective?

"Yes. He's worried about me driving home by myself so late at night. He's going to come pick me up later," she said in a dreamy, breathy voice.

"Overprotective much?" Rachel asked as they went into the kitchen and opened the popcorn and got out glasses.

"We're not going home after he picks me up," she replied in that same dreamy voice.

"Oh, yeah?" Rachel asked, her curiosity piqued. "Care to share?"

"All I know is we aren't going home till *later*. He's planning a surprise for me."

"Details later?"

"Maybe," she replied softly, almost hesitantly. "Adam is special. They all are. He likes to plan surprises like this. He knows I love it when he does. But something about the time I get alone with him is a little sacred, and I— It's not that I don't want to share the details. It's just—"

"Sacred. I totally get that," Rachel finished for her. "You don't have to tell me anything. I was watching you dance with him one night at The Pony. He looks at you like you are the *only* woman in the world. He adores you in the truest sense of that word. I wouldn't want you to feel obligated to share about your time with him. I don't think I could if I were in your shoes. We have so much fun gabbing, but I don't mean to intrude."

Grace cracked open a Big Red with a smile. "Ready for a movie? Or do you want to talk about *other stuff*?" she asked, arching an eyebrow.

"Other stuff?"

"Come on, Rachel. We never had a chance to talk at your parents' house because your mom was always bustling about. I'll bet you're *dying* to ask me all kinds of questions."

"But—"

"It's not *all* off limits, only certain aspects. Adam's heart is so tender, and I'm reluctant to reveal much about our relationship, but I think there are plenty of other questions that I could answer for you without betraying his confidence."

Rachel's cheeks grew warm. "I've read my share of ménage romances, but what's it *really* like?"

Grace laughed softly and explained how it worked for the four of them, and Rachel got an inkling of the magic in their relationship. What others found sordid or forbidden based on hearsay, gossip, and tacky Internet porn was a sacred and beautiful thing for the four of them, shared in mutual love.

Rachel didn't mind when Grace would pause, become introspective, and then skim over some details. She did tell Rachel that Adam was the first of them to be intimate with her, although they were all there with her at the time.

Grace blushed hard, and her eyes took on a far away, shiny quality. They laughed over the story about the boudoir portraits and how they'd managed to keep it a secret from each other.

"Can I see them someday?"

"Some of them, yes. I have three beautiful black and whites hanging on my bedroom wall. I'd love for you to see those. When you get engaged to Eli, we are going to see my photographer friend and have her do the same thing for you. That was a life-altering experience for me, posing for them like that. I felt different afterward. More confident and sexy. Comfortable in my own skin."

"He hasn't asked me yet, Grace. It's a little early to—"

"Nonsense. I can see it in his eyes when he looks at you. He's going to, and you'd be crazy if you didn't say yes. He's hardworking, loyal, financially stable, fun, absolutely gorgeous, and freaking huge!" She giggled. "He'll always watch over you, provide for you, and protect you. Did I mention he's gorgeous and freakin' huge?"

"I love all those things about him," Rachel said softly, remembering his self-restraint earlier as he made love to her.

"So you'd say yes?"

"Grace, you know I would. How could I turn away such love and sweet devotion? I just hope I'm worthy."

"Worthy? You're perfect for him, and he's no fool. I'll bet you're married by Christmas."

"I dunno. I don't want to say anything and jinx it," Rachel replied nervously.

Rachel shared with Grace about the outrageously hot spanking Eli had delivered to her the day of the accident. Grace clapped and snickered.

"I *told* you, didn't I? By the right hand, there is nothing hotter than a good spanking."

"It was incredible and...*fun*."

"Good. Ethan told me Eli had asked him about it, and I was hoping you would share."

"Grace, I'm curious. Do you ever feel overwhelmed by dealing with the needs of three different men?"

"They don't allow it. They work out all that stuff on their own."

"You mean prioritizing?"

"Yeah. They have good instincts for my energy level and desires. Sometimes I ask for more because they don't want to push me too hard. It's all about balance."

Rachel giggled. "So you aren't swinging from the chandeliers on any given night?"

Grace laughed in reply. "Nope, chandeliers are swinging only on the second Tuesday of every month."

"So," Rachel concluded, "spankings for naughty little girls are every first Monday night?"

"Yep! But with Ethan only."

"Jack and Adam aren't into that?"

"No, they don't have an interest in it the way Ethan and I do. That's a part of my relationship with Ethan," Grace said in all seriousness. That surprised Rachel. "There are parts of our relationships with each other that are completely private, that are only between me and the individual man in question. Ethan is a more open man about certain parts of our relationship, and I operate within those parameters. Adam is different and more private, which is why you'll have to use your imagination. Same with Jack," Grace added softly. "Like I once told you, they're worth it." Her hand shook a little as she wiped a little tear away carefully with the back of her hand.

"Thanks, Grace. I'll always be careful to not violate your trust." Rachel reached over and gently patted her arm. For a while, they quietly watched the movie in companionable silence, each lost in her own thoughts. Rachel switched the DVDs when one movie ended and the next began.

Later, a soft knock sounded at the door. Rachel opened the door, revealing a handsome and devilish looking Adam Davis on her stoop. Grace appeared to melt on the inside at the sight of him.

"Ready to go, baby?" he asked affectionately as Rachel invited him in.

Grace slipped on her sandals, hugged Rachel and thanked her for inviting her over, then went straight into Adam's big, strong arms. They departed soon after and Grace laughed when Adam scooped her up in his arms as he walked down the sidewalk to his truck. Grace waved one last time to her before Rachel closed her front door.

Chapter Twenty-eight

Saturday evening, Rachel squealed when Eli pinched her on the ass as he passed by, his hips wrapped in a towel after he dried off from his shower. She stood in front of the mirror at the long bathroom counter, putting on her makeup, dressed in a black mesh thong and a black lace demi-bra. The play of muscles in his upper body and biceps drew her gaze as he brushed his long hair, and Rachel didn't think she'd ever tire of looking at this handsome giant. She sighed as the familiar ache began in her pussy. Anytime she was near him, her body yearned for his.

He'd made love to her several times in the last two days but would not allow her to move strenuously or participate to the extent she wanted to. She was pining for a good, hard fucking but was going to have to wait for it, or so he'd told her several times with a hint of devilish gleam in his eyes. Her eyes roamed hungrily over a hard bicep and shoulder to his handsome face, directly into his smoldering gray eyes.

"See something you like?" he asked in a sexy voice that always got her wet and ready.

She gulped and swallowed at the invitation in his eyes. They didn't have time, and she *knew* it. He'd take his time with her, and they'd wind up being late. Eli stroked his hand down her back, smiling seductively at her hiss and shudder as he stroked sensitive nerve endings, finally reaching the curve of her ass.

One long finger stroked over her cleft before it thrust gently against the plug lodged deeply in her ass. She braced her hand and her hips against the bathroom counter and flexed against his finger, thinking she'd need to change to a dry thong before they left the house. Small price to pay. He'd wanted to remove the plug earlier before the shower, but she'd wanted to wait, enjoying the sensation too much. He'd snickered and called her a naughty girl, and she'd reminded him what naughty girls needed.

No dice. Dammit.

"I'm going to get dressed, angel. You finish in here, and when you're done, we'll see about removing that plug and taking care of the need I see in your beautiful blue eyes."

A warm, decadent shiver traced over her skin. "We'll be late," she murmured weakly. She felt like a junkie in need of another fix when her clit began to throb and her damp pussy lips swelled and throbbed a bit.

"Not that much, and I'd feel bad if I removed the plug, which I know you find stimulating, and then left you frustrated. Being on time is not worth leaving you like that. Finish up and I'll call your mom and let her know we may be a little late. She won't mind."

"But your dad—"

"Is watching a race over at your place and playing with Matthew. He's not going to care. I *need* to, okay?" he added softly, kissing her shoulder.

Her cheeks tingled with heat, and she nodded with a breathy sigh. How could she resist that entreaty? The low-level hum in her body turned into a buzz. She lined her eyes lightly and applied her mascara. She planned to leave her hair down around her shoulders. After she dried it and brushed it out, she left the bathroom and found Eli on the bed, naked. She unconsciously licked her lips, and her gesture inspired a grin from Eli as he enjoyed her obvious, lecherous perusal of his assets.

"Come here, angel," he murmured and reached for her.

The muscles in her ass clenched at the thought of him removing the plug and the pleasure he'd promised her afterward. He rose from the bed and led her to the end of it. He unclasped the pretty demi-bra and removed it then slid his thumbs into the waistband of her thong and slid it over her hips and down her thighs and calves. He steadied her as she stepped out of it, and then he laid it aside on the bed.

Missing *nothing* about it, he said, "Your thong is soaked, angel. Are you wet for me? Ready at the thought of me touching you?"

"Eli, I get wet at the sound of your *voice*." She laughed softly as he helped her onto the bed on her knees. He held her gently until she was balanced on her right hand. He was always cognizant of her needs with the cast on her arm. He moved back, and she gasped slightly when he grasped the soft handle. He pushed and pulled gently on it, drawing a shaky whimper from her. Her arousal was approaching the point of no return. He left the plug in her ass for the time being and slid his fingers down her cleft to her dripping wet opening.

"Mmm, you're dripping wet." He leaned forward to kiss her cheek as she tilted her head back. Her hair slid over her shoulder and softly collided with his fragrant black hair where it draped across her back, sending ticklish shivers down her spine. His other hand slid over her abdomen and down to her mound, and a finger slipped through the curls there to her slit. His fingertip slid past her clit to her lips, gathered moisture, then returned alongside it in the tender caress she loved. He'd learned her body so well and knew just how she liked her clit touched, when to be gentle, and when not to be. His lips sought hers in a warm, wet kiss as he stroked her clit, teasing her.

"Eli, you're so good to me. Please, honey. You know what I need."

"Yes, angel. You want the plug and my cock at the same time, don't you?" he asked in a husky voice, driving her even higher with his touch.

"Couldn't we try? I feel fine. Let me have it, please!"

His gentle hand rested on her left shoulder. "How's your arm? Shaky?" She shook all over, but it wasn't from fatigue.

"No, it's fine. You know it won't take much. You can feel how wet I am." She flexed her hips against his fingers and shuddered when waves of pleasure washed over her at his touch.

"Okay, but we're keeping it short and sweet. I don't want you to be sore later." He stood to his full height behind her at the foot of the bed.

Knowing he was behind her watching as she rubbed her pussy against his hand had her already on the verge. The thought of his tremendous strength and how vulnerable she was before him was a powerful aphrodisiac. He was being so gentle and careful with her right now, but one day soon, he was going to release that stored potential on her. She couldn't wait.

His fingers continued to stroke her clit, and the other hand swept over her open thighs, finding the honey that overflowed from her pussy. He gave a low growl of satisfaction as his fingers slid to her lips again and opened them gently. She moaned, knowing she was seconds away from feeling his cock against her opening. Her pussy clenched in eager anticipation of his invasion. She whimpered when she realized he'd paused to enjoy the anticipation and the erotic sounds she made. Rachel knew how much he loved listening to her.

She panted softly and said, "Remember your dad and sister can hear us."

He chuckled evilly. "Mmm-hmm, it's going to be hard to not scream when you come, won't it?" he teased as she squirmed, frustrated and ready to be fucked. Her pussy contracted in agreement.

She'd opened her mouth to softly beg for mercy when the thick head of his cock pressed at her throbbing, wet entrance. She panted softly and pressed back against him.

He leaned down and whispered, "Angel, I need to be able to hold you steady, so the plug is going to stay in place once I enter you. I know how you love this, so hold still a minute. My cock is right there if you want to move a bit, but not too much." He slid a finger into the handle of the plug and pumped gently in small in and out motions. Gradually, the plug was sliding in and out over the sensitive nerve endings in her ass, which grasped it uncontrollably. She took up the rhythm and began to move on the head of his cock, squeezing him with her pussy muscles.

One hand moved the plug, and the other stretched beneath her torso to support her in case her right arm gave out. If he hadn't been so big and tall, they never would have been able to fool around like this, but she felt completely safe and at no risk of hurting herself. Taking advantage of that security, she thrust her pussy against the head of his cock and heard him gasp as she took more of his stiff cock inside her. She threw caution to the wind and thrust her hips back onto him and heard his groan as she slid forward on his cock and then slammed back all the way and took his long, thick rod to the hilt.

"There. That's more *like it*." She whispered triumphantly.

Rachel almost purred in satisfaction at the full feeling. A wave of really bad naughtiness come over her, and she moved as hard and fast as she wanted to, regardless of his warning growl. Giving in to her wild, wanton movements, Eli pushed the plug back in and released it. He grasped her gyrating hips in each strong hand and pumped into her over and over. Her head flew back, and her lips popped open on a silent scream. She came in a great, silent, undulating wave, stifling a gasping sob as he followed her to his release and groaned in the throes of ecstasy, trying to be as quiet as possible.

His arm slid beneath her sweat-dampened torso, taking the weight off her arm, supporting her as he helped her into an upright position. Nuzzling her throat as they both caught their breath, "Bad girl. You know how to bring out the caveman in me, don't you?"

"Mmm, I love that guy."

"He loves you, too, angel."

She turned to him and kissed his warm lips and looked into his eyes. Leaning back against his shoulder, Rachel sighed ecstatically as he stroked her swollen breasts. He cupped them in his hands and caressed the undersides before smoothing his hands over her abdomen to her hips and thighs. He shifted and gently withdrew from her pussy and she sighed in satisfaction as he removed the plug.

"I wanted to wait at least the two weeks before being that rough with you, Rachel."

She snickered in response but made no other comment.

"I'm going to have to take you in hand if you think you're always going to get your way that easily."

She snickered louder. "You may just need to. Wouldn't want me to become too headstrong and spoiled now, would we?" She waggled her ass at him.

He grinned. "You may even need a spanking, I think."

"Ooooh! Yes, I think so, too!" she replied enthusiastically. "I've gotten out of hand and need to be shown the boundaries."

She showered quickly and chortled as he did the same, wondering if the occupants next door were wondering why they could hear the shower running *again* through the equally thin wall in the bathroom.

She put on a fresh black lace thong and her demi-bra with his help. He slid his hands down her right arm and paused, gently kneading her bicep, which trembled slightly.

He kneaded it gently. "I hope your arm isn't too sore tomorrow."

"If it is, it will have been worth it, Eli. I needed that so much." She kissed him, then added, "I'll get dressed and be ready to go in a minute."

She sauntered out a few minutes later, dressed in embellished blue jeans, a silky, deep blue V-neck blouse, a glittering rhinestone studded belt, and her cowboy boots.

Eli was dressed in a pair of fresh new blue jeans, boots, and a white T-shirt stretched over his sexy chest. His big biceps stretched the sleeves with no mercy whatsoever. She handed him a necklace and turned her back on him as he commented, "Well, aren't you the sexy sparkling cowgirl tonight?"

"Do you like it?" she asked as she turned and faced him, adjusting the necklace so the sparkling gems dangled down to the top of her lush cleavage. "Too sexy?" she asked, smiling into his territorial gaze.

"Perfect, angel."

She smiled and thanked him then turned and sashayed back into the closet and came out with the matching dangling earrings on. "I'm ready!" she said enthusiastically.

It was her first evening out since the accident, and she was brimming with happiness, ready to get back into the swing of things.

"You might want to grab a jacket in case we're outside this evening. The temperature is supposed to drop into the fifties overnight."

"Ooooh! That's perfect." She retrieved a sexy leopard print fleece from her closet. She got her bag, and they headed over to Eli's place so he could grab his jacket. When they came in, they were greeted by a squeal from Matthew, who was sitting on his proud grandpa's lap. Kelly was flitting here and there with the phone in her ear, looking beleaguered but excited.

Elijah Wolf stood as they entered, and Matthew squealed again as he was lifted much higher than he was used to in his tall grandpa's arms. Rachel smiled up at him, seeing clearly where Eli had gotten his height and body structure. Elijah was in his early fifties, blond and blue-eyed, but otherwise, it was obvious they were father and son. Rachel could not help but tick through the list of single women she knew who would love to meet him because Elijah was a looker, plain and simple.

* * * *

Rachel enjoyed snuggling next to Eli as everyone sat around on the back deck, laughing and sharing stories as the sun went down. The common denominators for the gathering were Rachel and Eli, so they were the subject of most of the stories. He drew her close, and she reveled in his gentle touch as he caressed her knuckles and stroked his fingertips over her hand.

The air that evening had a light chill to it, so her dad had lit the fire pit in the center of the back deck earlier, and they were all grouped around it to enjoy the night air and conversation.

Grace reached over and refilled Rachel's glass of sangria. At the moment, it was Rachel's turn in the hot seat as her dad told a story about her. Rachel gestured to her father to have at it, and he grinned and told the story in all its Technicolor glory.

"I found out from Rachel's mother that a certain young man had asked my daughter out on her first date. The point was up for debate and still is," he said, smiling and winking at Rachel, "but at the time I felt very strongly that if a boy wanted to date my daughter, he needed to come and ask *me* first before asking her out. Call me crazy, *I know*," he spoke aside to the men as they shook their heads in commiseration.

Rachel remembered being horrified that her father planned to give the third degree to the boy who had asked her out. She could look back on it with humor now but recalled being terrified that once it got around school she'd never be asked out ever again.

"So I asked her about him and discovered that he worked at the Exxon station in town. The last station in town with full-service pumps. An honorable job," he stated in concession. "I liked that he was working already, and Rachel said he was mannerly."

Rachel laughed. "That *should* have satisfied you, too. You didn't need to go interrogate him."

"I wanted him to know she had a daddy who cared. So I paid him a visit at the station and had a chat with him. He seemed like a nice enough guy for my daughter. I told him I'd see him when he picked her up. He seemed *fine*." Her father shrugged innocently, and Rachel rolled her eyes. She could recall the rather wide-eyed look on the poor boy's face when he told her about it the next day at school.

Eli slipped his arm around her shoulders and squeezed her consolingly, obviously enjoying the tale of how her father terrorized her first date.

"So the big evening came. Rachel and her mother were upstairs for two hours doing hair, twittering, and primping. When he pulled up, I went out front to greet him." Her dad lifted his hands as though he'd done nothing wrong.

"Nuh-uh, Dad," Rachel interjected, fighting hard to not laugh. "Tell them *how* you greet him."

"Did you prefer that I leave him out there?" He laughed, obviously enjoying the verbal sparring with his daughter.

"Tell them *how* you greeted him."

"It couldn't be helped. I heard him pull up from the backyard. You were upstairs. You might not have heard the doorbell. It wasn't a big deal."

"Tell them, Peter, before I do!" her mom said, laughing behind her hand. "Tell them how you were *dressed*."

"It was deer season! How was I supposed to be dressed? I'd just gotten home from the deer lease, princess."

Her father had arrived home only a couple of hours before from the tract of land he leased every year during deer hunting season from a good friend, two hours south of the Lopez's ranch.

"Yes. After two days with no bath," her mom added, giggling.

Rachel was about ready to fall out of her chair they were all laughing so hard.

Her dad continued, "I'd bagged my limit, and I needed to deal with them before it got dark. You weren't complaining over all the deer sausage that winter, I recall."

"You were *gutting a deer*, Daddy!" She turned to Eli and said through her laughter, "He came around the side of the house with his rifle in one hand and the bloody hunting knife in the other!"

They all erupted in hysterical laughter at the vivid mental image of her father greeting her nervous date in full hunting camouflage, a gun in one hand, and hunting knife in the other, stinking to high heaven. Elijah and her dad bumped fists as Kelly and Rachel looked on in disgust before bursting out in laughter again.

"I was about to put the gun back in the gun safe. Safety with firearms is a *priority* for me," her dad said with all innocence, raising his hands like he was surrendering.

Rachel took up the thread of the story then. "He looked like a mass murderer. There was blood on his camos, and you know what it *smells* like when you gut a deer," she said with a grimace. "The boy at the door had never been anywhere *near* a deer blind. He was new in town. He took one look at Daddy and got a whiff of him, to boot. Want to know what happened? He passed out on the porch." The laughter erupted again over the poor city boy's reaction. "It would have helped if you had offered an explanation for your appearance."

"I did!" Her dad said with a snicker. "After you revived him with *smelling salts*." He laughed so hard he had tears in his eyes.

Rachel wiped her own eyes as she said, "He was so embarrassed, he asked if he could leave and go home. He never did go out with me, and it took six weeks to get him to even look me in the eye, much less talk to me again."

"Yeah, but word got out, didn't it?" her father said, sagely nodding and raising a finger like he had a point to make.

Rachel grinned. "I guess it did."

"What do you mean, Rachel?" Eli asked.

"That boy told everyone how Daddy answered the door, and all the boys from around here knew what *that* meant. They always came and asked permission to date me before they asked me out. During the fall for several years, Daddy had a new hunting buddy, and we always had deer sausage in the freezer because they knew he liked it. And they all knew how to use a gun and a knife. I felt like a two-for-one deal for years. Date me and get a chance to go to my dad's deer lease in the fall. And *none* of them ever laid a hand on me."

"Good Texas boys, all of them. Mitchell brings sausage every once in a while."

Rachel smirked. "Ah, he just wants to know if you still have the same deer lease."

"The two us are talking about going on a hog hunt next month," her father said in passing. Rachel rolled her eyes, but her father's statement had Eli's attention.

"You're planning a hog hunt?" Adam asked, interest clear in his eyes.

"Yeah, over at a friend's ranch in the hill country. You ought to all come. Heaven knows there are enough of the damned things to go around."

Feral hogs multiplied prolifically and could lower land values and damage crops with their destructive habits.

"Think we might take you up on that offer," Ethan replied, tipping his beer to his lips.

"Goody! You know what that means!" Kelly squealed. "Girl time!"

"That's right!" Grace said. "You could all come out to the ranch and we could have a girls' weekend. Goodness knows we have enough space!"

Rachel looked at Eli for confirmation, and when he nodded, she said, "It sounds like we have a plan."

"They would be safe out there." Jack said, grinning at Grace's enthusiastic response.

"Then I'll let you know when I get all the details," her father said.

"Isn't the sunset pretty tonight?" her mom commented.

Rachel had to agree as she admired the fiery hues. The setting sun cast the last of its rays for that day, shades of pink, orange, and purple over the puffy little clouds that filled the sky.

* * * *

Eli's heart galloped as he made eye contact with Rachel's father. Peter grinned at him and nodded his head. Renata sat next to Peter, and Eli noticed her lips tremble when she looked away from the beautiful sunset and wiped a tear that trickled down her soft cheek. She smiled at him and looked lovingly at her daughter.

Eli stroked Rachel's upper arm as she snuggled to him. "Yes, Renata. The sunset is beautiful tonight, but not nearly as beautiful as your daughter."

Rachel looked out at the sunset, watching the colors fill the sky, but Eli could plainly see the rosy blush that swept across her cheeks.

The velvet covered box had rested in his pocket all evening as he waited for the perfect moment. That moment had arrived.

Chapter Twenty-nine

"Beautiful." Rachel gazed out to the horizon, quietly admiring the sunset with the others.

Someone shifted behind her, and Rachel heard a distinct feminine sigh. Eli stood from his seat beside her and Rachel smiled at him, assuming he was getting another beer from the cooler. Looking into his eyes, Rachel could see the love and purpose in their gray depths as he got down on one knee in front of her chair.

Good Rachel and Naughty Rachel perched on her shoulders and broke out in the Hallelujah Chorus.

Rachel sat there in shock, and a small squeak escaped her lips. Her body went limp in the chair as she gazed at him. For several seconds, she stayed that way, memorizing the moment and waiting for him to speak, reveling in the gleaming emotion she saw in this gentle giant's luminous eyes.

Close by, one of the women sobbed softly. It sounded like her mom. Eli placed his callused hands over hers, which now rested on her thighs. She smiled happily at him and stroked the undersides of his wrists with the knuckles on her fingers.

"What are you doing?" she asked quietly.

He smiled and whispered softly back, "What I've dreamed of doing for months now." He took her right hand in his, kissed her palm, and stroked it with his warm fingers. His touch sent a rippling thrill up her arm and through her body.

"When I laid eyes on you the first time, I recognized what was missing from my life. I asked you out, and you turned me down, but I understood why. I kept asking you out, and you kept turning me down. The blows to my pride were worth it if eventually you'd say yes." He kissed her palm again and pressed it to his cheek. She listened in awed silence.

"When the accident happened, I was so afraid I'd lose you. In such a short time, you'd become everything to me. Now, here you are, almost healed up from all your injuries, and I don't want to waste another minute. Will you marry me, angel?" He gently wiped the tears trickling down her cheeks with his thumbs.

Trying to frame a reply equally as romantic as his proposal, Rachel was momentarily distracted as he removed a box from his jacket pocket and opened it so she could see the ring inside. She let out a sound that was a cross between a whimper and a wail. All the women gasped when he removed it from the box and they could see, too. Suddenly, all the women were talking at once. She placed her hand in his, and he slid the engagement ring onto the ring finger of her right hand

He brushed her knuckles with his warm lips. "You haven't said yes. Will you marry me?"

Conversations came to a halt, and all eyes turned to her.

"Of course I'll marry you, Eli!" She wrapped her arms around his neck, careful not to club him in the head with the cast on her left arm, and promptly burst into happy tears. "Yes! I'll marry you! Yes! Yes! Yes!"

Everyone laughed as he wrapped his arms gently around her back and under her knees and stood with her. He cradled her in his arms and kissed her like no one else was there, oblivious to the clapping, laughing, and chattering going on around them. He smiled happily at her and tilted his forehead to hers.

"When?" he asked softly as she rubbed her nose against his.

Not fast enough, big boy! "As soon as Kelly and Grace can help me pull it together."

"Good, because I don't want to wait any longer than we have to."

"Your sister and Grace were both betting we'd be married before Christmas. Did you know that?"

"They both made mention of that, yes," Eli replied with dry humor.

"Kiss me again and leave the details to me, honey." Rachel squeezed his shoulder and held up her hand to admire her ring. "My ring is perfect."

Made from platinum, it had a round one carat stone surrounded by swirling flourishes and inset with tiny diamonds.

"Let us see! Let us see!" came the chorus of female voices as they all clamored to see the ring.

Rachel scoffed before allowing them to ogle the ring. "Oh! Like you haven't already seen it. You all knew Eli was planning to propose tonight, didn't you?" She didn't see a repentant face in the bunch as she continued. "Well, girls, looks like we have a wedding to plan!"

Rachel and Eli both cringed as Kelly and Grace shrieked and jumped up and down, hugging each other.

Eli and Rachel chuckled and kissed again as the other women put their heads together and started making plans without her. Eli released her lips and murmured, "So your old boyfriend is going to be on this hog hunt next month, huh? Do I need to kick his ass?"

"Don't you dare. Mitchell never laid a hand on me and was always a gentleman. Like I said before, if he behaved himself, he got the added bonus of going to my dad's deer lease. He's a nice guy and considered a family friend." Rachel giggled and gave him a crooked little grin before adding, "But I don't mind if the caveman wants to beat his chest a little."

Eli grinned, and a deep chuckle rumbled in his chest. Finally, he released her and allowed her to stand up

"It's too bad Mike and Rogelio couldn't be here to see you propose," she murmured, missing her two old friends. "Especially since Mike introduced us."

"You ought to go out to The Pony and show off that rock," Ethan said, winking at Rachel. "Show 'em he's *officially* off the market."

"You should all go!" Renata echoed. "You, too, Kelly. I can watch Matthew for a couple of hours for you. He's so sweet, and it would be no trouble at all."

Kelly looked torn, hopeful but doubtful at the same time, glancing from her dad to her brother. Because of his age, she had not left Matthew with a babysitter yet.

"Sis, I think a couple of hours of dancing and having a good time would do you good. You know Matthew will be perfectly safe with Renata—"

"Mom," her mom said softly, correcting Eli.

"With Mom," he said, looking gratefully at her mom, "and I think Christopher would approve of you having a little fun tonight. It's a celebration."

"I think the break would be good for you, honey," Elijah said. "I'll come along, too, and whenever you feel ready to go, I'll bring you back to get him."

Kelly patted her hair. "I think I will, if it's truly no bother, Renata?"

"None at all. I would have been up late, anyway. Peter, you could go, too, if you want?"

"No, no. I'll leave that to the young. I know my daughter is in good hands."

Rachel smiled contentedly as her dad held out his tanned, work-roughened hand to his future son-in-law.

* * * *

Mike whistled admiringly when Rachel showed him the ring, and tears prickled in her eyes when he hugged her and told her he was proud and happy for her. The Dancing Pony was packed almost to capacity by the time their group arrived.

"Quick announcement, ladies and gentlemen," Ethan said through a microphone in the DJ booth. "For all of you who know Rachel Lopez, you are aware she was involved in a serious car accident last month, and we want to welcome her back tonight."

Cheers came from around the room because she *did* know almost everyone there.

"And many of you know our most recent addition at The Dancing Pony, Eli Wolf." There were many more whistles, shouts, and even a few shrill wolf whistles. "Eli proposed to Rachel tonight, and she said yes. Sorry to all you single ladies. He's officially off the market. A round of applause for Rachel and Eli!"

Eli put his arms around her gently, encircling her in his protective embrace, and he kissed her tenderly during the din and roar of applause and cheers.

Rogelio hugged her and congratulated Eli. She held on tight to Eli's hand, not wanting to be passed around the room away from him, but well-wishers crowded in on them. Nodding at his dad and sister, he carefully led her forward to the dance floor.

In the DJ booth, Ethan requested a special song for them. Eli took her in his arms as "I Wanna Make You Close Your Eyes" by Dierks Bentley began to play. She happily wrapped her arms around him, careful of the cast on her left arm, and rested her head against his chest. As they danced around the big dance floor, other dancers patted him on the back or congratulated her as they passed.

"How are you feeling, angel?" Eli asked, his hands sliding down her back to the swell of her hips.

"I feel terrific, Eli. So happy." She slid her be-ringed right hand over his hard biceps. Eli pointed to his dad and Adam, both taller than almost everyone else there, as their group of friends claimed a recently vacated table.

After the song ended, he led her from the dance floor and helped her into the tall cushioned chair, saying, "Rest for one song, angel. Then we'll dance again. I want you to pace yourself." There was concern for her in his eyes. She'd already had a lot of excitement, and this was her first night out since before the accident.

She knew he was right and nodded in understanding. The men closed in behind her so that she was not completely surrounded by well-wishers, of which there were many. A thick knot of friends and acquaintances soon formed around their table.

Eli stood behind her chair, his gentle hand on her arm or shoulder stroking her. Luckily, the table and chairs they sat at were tall. Otherwise, Rachel would have felt a little claustrophobic with the press of bodies. Everybody was shaking their hands and wishing them well when it occurred to her why they were flanking her so protectively. Rachel felt a lot stronger, but she didn't think she could take too many slaps on the back or hard hugs before she'd be hurting. She glanced up at Eli and reached for him. He leaned down to her.

"Thank you."

"For what, angel?" he asked, smiling at her.

"For protecting me. I know they mean well. Thank you, Eli," she said, watching the crowd.

"Sorry Rachel," Ethan murmured from the other side. "Maybe I shouldn't have made the announcement."

She shook her head. "I don't mind at all, Ethan. It's good to see them again after so long."

Adam said, "We'll stay here right beside you until the crowd thins out, sweetheart. By then you'll probably be ready for another dance." There was laughter in his voice. He knew her well.

She did get her next dance a few minutes later and a few more after that. At one point, a friend cut in, asking to dance with Rachel, and Eli reluctantly allowed it. He stayed near the dance floor as others cut in also to watch her for signs of fatigue or a signal that she was ready for him to cut back in. She did eventually look over at him and nodded slightly for him to come to her rescue. As her current partner released her, she came into Eli's arms and hugged him close. He steered them across the dance floor to the table.

"How are you doing, angel?" he asked.

"A little tired, but mostly just thirsty. I need water or a Coke." Eli looked up for the waitress, but Ethan patted his back.

"I'll be right back with it, Eli. Sit tight, Rachel."

Looking concerned, Grace patted Rachel's hand. "Rachel, you feeling okay?"

"I feel fine, but my stamina isn't back at full strength yet. I'll probably sit the next few out. Where is Kelly?"

"She's dancing with her dad. She looks like she's having a good time. Oh, Lord. Look who just cut in on them," Grace added. Rachel looked and, to her surprise, saw Kelly dancing and chatting with Brice Huvell. Brice was looking sharp, dressed in new Wranglers and a freshly pressed white dress shirt and sporting a new black Stetson. He'd even polished his cowboy boots.

Ethan walked up behind them and placed Rachel's Coke on a napkin in front of her and said quietly, "I told him he should."

Grace turned to look her handsome husband in the eye. "You did?"

He grinned down at her and said softly, "Brice and I have been talking lately. I've been helping him understand how women like to be talked to. He asks lots of questions, receives what I've been trying to pass on to him, and uses it. Things have changed a lot for him socially since that bar fight. I didn't want him to miss out on Miss Right because he gets nervous with small talk or overlooked basic hygiene. I told him Kelly was here with us, taking a little break from the baby grind, and that her husband is serving over in Afghanistan right now. You should have seen his little chest puff up."

Rachel grinned up at Eli, who was smiling also, watching Kelly as she chatted with Brice on the dance floor. He was every bit the gentleman and danced two dances with her before he returned her to their table. He'd also obtained permission to dance with her again later on.

"Having fun, sis?"

"I sure am! I'm so glad you talked me into coming out for the evening. Brice was so nice and polite, and he's a pretty good dancer, too. He said he's a friend of yours, Ethan."

"That he is, Kelly. That he is," Ethan replied.

Rachel recalled the fierce look on Brice's face the night he had defended Grace's honor against two other men who were bigger than he. Yeah, he definitely was a good friend.

"He's a good friend to all of us," Jack said quietly as Grace and Adam nodded in agreement.

"Ready for another dance, angel?" Eli asked after Rachel finished her Coke. She nodded enthusiastically.

"I'd love to. But I'm pacing myself, and nobody cuts in this time, okay?"

"I have you all to myself and don't have to *share*? I can deal with that. The caveman doesn't like when other men cut in."

"Was he beating his chest earlier?" she asked playfully as he squeezed her ass when he helped her down from her chair.

"He wanted to throw you over his shoulder and take you back to the cave."

"And do what?" she murmured seductively. "Fuck me by the fire pit on his animal skins?"

He chuckled and drew her close to kiss her temple. "Holy shit, you paint a vivid mental image. I'm getting stiff thinking about it."

"There's only one problem with my fantasy."

"What's that, sexy?" He pressed her hips against his as they turned to each other on the dance floor.

She placed her hand over her mouth at his ear. "The caveman has to be very quiet as he fucks me by the firelight so that the caveman's father doesn't hear him in the next cave."

He grinned and snickered. "Me caveman. Me no care!" He growled as he slid his big, warm hands down over her ass and pressed her to his tremendous erection.

"Baby," she whispered, very impressed, "you're so big and so *hard!*"

"And ready to slide right into you, angel." He licked her earlobe and nuzzled the soft skin beneath her ear. "I can't wait. But this is your first night out in a long time, and I don't want to cut it short because I have the self-restraint of a freaking Neanderthal."

Rachel was instantly wet picturing him dressed in animal skins, standing in the flickering firelight reflected off the walls of a cave. He looked down at her with a knowing look on his face, and she bit her lip and grinned sheepishly. "I would be your cavewoman in a heartbeat, Eli. I am *right there* with you."

"Easy, now. I could still put you over my shoulder."

"Your shoulder, your knee, it's *all good.*" Rachel laughed when he groaned and rolled his eyes.

"Let Me Down Easy" by Billy Currington began to play, and Grace and Adam joined them on the dance floor, followed soon after by Ace Webster and Kathleen Stevens, who seemed lost in their own little romantic bubble.

Kelly and Elijah eventually took her leave after Kelly thanked Brice Huvell for his hospitality and thanked the others for convincing her to come along.

"Are you going to dance with Grace this evening?" Eli asked as he helped her back into her chair.

"I was wondering the same thing myself," Ethan added, standing beside Grace's currently empty chair.

Rachel shook her head. "I don't think it would be safe with this cast. It would feel awkward, and I might hurt someone with it. It's pretty hard." She rapped her knuckle on it.

"I could see where that might be a problem," Ethan tapped it with his knuckle as well. "When does it come off?"

"Two weeks. I can't wait." She waggled her eyebrows at Eli while Ethan watched Grace on the dance floor.

"Well, it looks like you've got lots of help lined up planning your wedding." Ethan smiled and chuckled. "Grace has been chomping at the bit for weeks, doing Internet searches and talking with Renata on the phone.

She was afraid she'd give the surprise away before he could pop the question."

Rachel turned to Eli, and asked, "How long have you been planning this?"

Eli chuckled and grinned at her. "I asked your father for permission to propose when I brought you to your parents' house to recuperate."

Ethan said, "Grace has had a good feeling about the two of you for months. She loves weddings and planning events like that."

"I look forward to hearing Grace and Kelly's ideas." Rachel leaned into Eli a bit and held on to the arm he wrapped around her. There would be plenty of time for that in the coming days, but for now, she wanted to revel in the fun and joy of this moment.

A while later, Rachel and Grace were standing at the table taking a sip of their drinks and catching their breath from their latest trips to the dance floor. Eli and Jack were standing near them doing the same. The club was quite crowded by that late hour, and the mood shifted as the upbeat country rock song that had been playing gradually changed into a slow, romantic love song. It was one of Rachel's favorites because of its acoustic guitar sound and vaguely erotic lyrics. It certainly put her in the mood to dance with Eli. He'd been taking every opportunity to whisper naughty, sexy things to her as they danced until she was simmering inside.

Grace gave her a knowing grin as Rachel put her glass down and turned to Eli. Both women watched incredulously as an extraordinarily beautiful tall brunette gracefully walked up to Eli and slid her hand over his pecs and around his shoulder. Pressed from hip to breast against him, she asked him if he'd like to dance. Rachel saw red and nearly growled out loud but Grace put her hand on Rachel's forearm.

She watched as her fiancé immediately backed away and gently extricated him from the brunette's grasp. He said a few succinct words to her, and her body language changed. She glanced over at Rachel and Grace standing three feet away, shrugged, and said what sounded like "sorry" to Eli before walking away, just as gracefully, with her dignity intact.

Feeling like she was going to get whiplash from her emotions, Rachel was actually glad Eli didn't make a bigger show of rejecting her invitation. Glancing around, Rachel saw that men all around them were eyeing the unfamiliar brunette. Rachel was willing to bet she'd have a dance partner before the song was over.

Eli turned to her and smiled and seemed relieved when she smiled back. He held out his hand, and she allowed him to lead her out onto the dance floor.

"She said she was new in town and wanted to dance."

"I didn't recognize her. If I was new in town, I'd go for the most handsome guy in the place, too."

Eli chuckled and kissed her forehead, and she pressed herself as close as she could to him. He kept her on the dance floor for another song and whispered to her about how well *he'd* make her feel at home if she were the new girl in town. He intoxicated her with his nearness and the deep timbre of his voice.

On two other occasions as the night progressed, Rachel was surprised to watch other women approach Eli and invite him to dance. One of them was another unfamiliar face, but the other woman should have known better and gave Rachel a catty look before walking away. Both times, Eli dealt with them, smoothly rejecting the offers.

There came a point when he drew her to him, standing at the table, and didn't allow her to leave his side anymore to deflect any other comers with her mere presence. In her present mood, she knew if any other women approached him tonight the cavewoman was going to be the one dealing with them.

"Angel? Are you all right? You're so quiet now."

"It's nothing, just that old jealousy rearing its ugly head."

"Feeling territorial?"

"Very."

"How about we dance?" He smiled down at her, and for some reason, she thought her words met with his approval.

Eli guided her onto the dance floor with Grace and Ethan for a sexy slow dance when Ethan requested "Just Got Started Lovin' You" by James Otto to be played for them. Rachel proved, cast or no cast, she could still hold her man. She earned a few dirty looks from women around the club. Rachel didn't care in the least.

Chapter Thirty

Eli made it as far as the last long stretch of road that led to their duplex. Rachel slid her hand along his thigh as she sat beside him. Her fingers strayed farther and farther up until she was skimming the length of his cock with her fingertips on each pass. He groaned at the stimulation, and when she smiled seductively at him, he placed his hand over her much smaller one and pressed it to the large, hardening bulge.

He pulled over to the shoulder of the road, ready to tear her clothes off. "Angel, you're playing with fire. I need you. Hard and loud. I don't think I can be quiet for our houseguests right now."

He gave a heartfelt groan when she wrapped her fingers around what she could of his denim-covered cock and squeezed gently. He could smell her sweetly aroused scent in the confines of the truck cab, and it was making him crazy. She was about to get fucked but good, and he hoped and prayed he would be gentle enough in his current state.

"Fuck me, then, honey."

Eli shut off the ignition and the headlights, ripped open the driver door, slammed it behind him, and came around to her side of the truck. He jerked open the door.

Rachel turned, and he pulled her to him, kissing her until she was breathless. He unbuckled her rhinestone belt, jerked her boots off, unzipped her jeans, and pulled them and her thong right off of her, dropping everything on the floorboard. Standing in the open doorway, he grasped her thighs and pulled her to him, pressing her gently to lie back on the seat as he buried his face in her pussy. She yelped in surprise at his zeal and he growled his approval when she draped her legs over his shoulders.

Damn, but she had the sweetest tasting pussy he'd ever had the pleasure of eating. She was perfect, sweet, slightly salty, and purely decadent. The muscles in her cunt quivered and grew taut under his tongue as she moaned and whimpered, crying out his name. Her hips thrust against him, and he felt her gentle fingers slide through his hair as her sounds became more high-pitched and urgent.

His tongue slid through the silken flesh of Rachel's pussy lips and moved up to her clitoris as she began to pant. He circled her clit with the tip of his tongue several times then zeroed in on that swollen little bud. Pressing his lips around it, he suckled as he simultaneously slid two fingertips into her hot, slick cunt and went to work on her G-spot. Her body tightened up, and she froze then screamed as she came in a warm, wet gush on his tongue and his fingers, giving him more of her sweet, creamy cum. With one hand, Eli unbuckled his belt, freed the button on his jeans, and then he lifted her hips and helped her slide back so he could climb in the truck and shut the door.

* * * *

Rachel trembled from her orgasm, sliding over as he climbed in and sat in the passenger seat then she eagerly straddled his lap. Careful not to smack him in the head with her cast, she pressed her body to his immense physique, kissing him until she couldn't breathe anymore, tasting her cum on his lips. Their combined scents filled her nostrils and felt like a siren song, pulling her as close to him as she could get. He hit the locks on the door and tilted the leather seat back so he was reclining slightly.

She moaned, unable to speak, and fumbled with his fly. He lifted up and slid his jeans down, and then he helped her into position over him while she held on to the headrest for stability. When she felt the broad, thick head of his cock at her opening, she slid down onto him in one smooth, wet stroke. Rachel panted as the tingling, jumping muscle spasms in her pussy began again almost immediately. She twisted her hips and rose up again and began a pumping motion that lasted less than a minute before they both howled as they came hard, clinging to each other.

Breathless, he stroked her back as she lay sated against him. Small aftershocks ran through her as she responded to his light touch across her back. Bathed in sweat, both of their bodies began to cool as they caught their breath.

Eli murmured, "Feel all right?"

"Mmm, yes. Perfect." She arched over him and kissed a line from his collarbone up to his jaw, squeezing his cock gently with her pussy muscles and making him groan and thrust gently into her again. "Did I give it to you good?" She chuckled softly.

"Hard and loud. Just like I asked for. I get so worked up when I'm with you, angel."

"Me, too, honey. Help me up?" He lifted her hips and pulled out gently, and she noticed he was still semi-erect. She made sure he saw her lick her lips. Eli laughed and tapped her bottom, saying, "Bad girl."

He opened the passenger door, and cool air rushed into the cab. After zipping and buttoning his jeans, he helped her put her thong back on then slip back into her jeans and her boots. He looked down the road, which appeared quiet and ordinary. "I probably could have pulled in the driveway and gotten you inside naked without anyone seeing you."

"Ooooh! But we'd never live it down if your dad or sister caught us like that, not in a million years. At least we got to be as loud as we wanted, right?"

Eli climbed in and drove the rest of the way down to the duplex. All lights were out, and it was quiet on her side. He helped her down and set her gently on her feet.

"Okay?" he asked.

"Yes, baby." She gazed up at him and wrapped her good arm around him. She pressed her cheek to his chest, feeling the ache inside her for him begin again. His big, warm arms felt so good, so solid around her, she never wanted to leave his side.

"I'll bet you'd love a nice hot shower, wouldn't you?" she asked as he put his arm around her and they went inside.

"Will you be in it with me? Nekkid?" He opened the door for her. Soft candlelight flickered off of the white walls around the living room and on the marble bar leading into the kitchen and dining room.

"Kelly must have done this for us after she got home, the little minx," Eli said, smiling at his sister's thoughtfulness.

"They go all the way back into the bathroom and bedroom. Where did she find all these candles?" Rachel said as they followed the trail which led to the bedroom. More candles were lined up on all the flat surfaces, the air warmed by so many small flames. The comforter and top sheet were turned back on the bed and the pillows fluffed. The walls of his bedroom were bathed in a soft, flickering, golden light. "She is going to be so cool to have as a sister."

"Yeah, she is."

* * * *

"Good morning, angel." Rachel loved the sound of his gravelly, rough voice first thing in the morning.

She stretched slowly, humming in delight at the feel of his fingertip as he stroked her nipple. "How long have you been awake?"

"A while. I've been watching you sleeping."

"You have? Did I drool or snore?"

"No. It was like watching a beautiful angel sleep. Peaceful. You smiled in your sleep. It must have been a good dream."

"You were probably in it. I dream about you all the time."

"Good dreams?" he asked huskily, his hand sliding around to stroke her breast.

She caught her breath at the warm touch. "Yes, but frustrating, too."

"Oh, *that* kind of dream?"

"Yes, frequently. I got left hanging quite a few times, and the one time I came in my dream, I woke up feeling let down. The orgasm was real enough, but you weren't there to hold on to, you know?"

Eli stroked along her ribcage down to her hip and back with two fingertips, sending warm shivers over her skin. "While you were in the hospital, I hardly slept at all. Once I started sleeping here at home again, it was nearly impossible to fall asleep. I slept alone all those years, and it took me less than a week to get used to you pressed against me. It's like I didn't know I was cold until you came and warmed me. Then when you couldn't be there, I was more aware of how cold I was."

Sliding her right hand over his bicep, Rachel smiled at the sight of his ring on her finger. She looked up into his handsome face. "Last night really happened? It wasn't a dream?"

Rolling her onto her back, he fit his immense body to hers with his hard cock cradled against her wet slit. "You said you'd be my wife." He sighed as she slowly wrapped her legs around his hips and opened herself to him.

He lifted his hips and hissed softly as the head of his cock found home and slid into her quivering entrance a little.

"I did," she said in a shaky voice, "and I've never been so happy." Her eyes swam with unshed tears. Her head fell back in ecstasy as he slid more of his length into her until he filled her completely.

"You are so warm, Rachel." Eli nuzzled her temple with soft strokes of his lips. "So tight." He pulled all the way out and thrust back in, and she groaned in pleasure, tingles racing up and down her extremities. He did it repeatedly, pulling all the way out and then gently sliding back in, until they were both tortured by it.

He lifted her thighs over his forearms and began to slowly stroke her pussy over and over. Eli's chest, abs, and thighs were massive bunches of muscle rippling over her. He slid his hand to her slit and stroked her clit rhythmically with each thrust of his cock until her muscles contracted around him and her orgasm broke free. She took him with her as her pussy pulsed around his cock. Both of them moaned softly in ecstasy as he fit his hips tightly to hers, and he thrust deeply one last time then stilled, breathing deeply. In the aftermath, he held her to him and petted her until she thought she might purr.

"Your sister and father are probably wondering what's keeping us," she murmured softly and writhed as his fingertips stroked over her spine in a light, tickling touch.

"We *hope* they are wondering and that we haven't removed all doubt." He chuckled softly as he rose from the bed in all his naked Viking-Indian warrior glory.

"I thought we did admirably. Sex that freaking good can't be completely silent," she said with a little snicker as she rose from the bed. "Come on, big boy. I need sustenance if I'm to plan a wedding." Rachel watched with territorial pride as he strode naked into the bathroom to turn on the shower.

Mine, mine, mine all mine.

"I'll bet Kelly and Grace already have it planned between the two of them. They probably even have your dress picked out and a date set," he said, laughing.

Climbing into the shower with him, she said, "I'm not much for planning big events like that. I may agree to show up and be their Barbie doll just so I get to marry you when the day comes."

They found out later that Elijah, Kelly, and Matthew had left the house early and were out visiting and running errands so their attempts at being quiet were for naught. Rachel and Eli met them at Taquería Gomez for breakfast. Kelly was ready and waiting with a notepad and wanted to know what elements were the most important to Rachel.

Rachel held up her hands. "I get final say on my dress and your dresses. You know how much I want to dance and that I want to get married as soon as the budget and the arrangements can be worked out and a date set. Have at it."

At the word budget, the men joined the conversation, and Eli told Rachel, "Your father has been saving for your wedding for years. I didn't want him to pay for it, but he said it was a point of fatherly pride. He said whatever you don't spend can go toward a down payment on a house. He asked me how I'd feel if we had a daughter getting married, and I agreed with him. So the honeymoon is on me, angel."

"Great, then all we have to do is set a date. Where are you taking me, Eli?"

"I haven't decided yet. Is there some place you've always wanted to go?"

"The Grand Canyon," she replied easily. "I've always wanted to go and never have."

* * * *

The coming days were fast, productive ones for Rachel. Mr. Grogan set it up for her so that she could work from home since she wasn't cleared to drive yet. When she wasn't working on his books, she was working on her novel. True to her word, she left the wedding plans up to the experts. She checked in with her dad occasionally about the budget, but he said the girls were doing fine and he had no complaints.

Grace heard from Maudie about the dresses, and Kelly planned another trip down from Abilene for dress fittings. In a great leap of faith, she left Matthew for the afternoon with Eli, who promised to call if he had any problems. Rachel's mom made the shopping trip with them to try on mother-of-the-bride dresses.

Maudie seemed confident that Grace and Kelly would love their dresses and enthusiastically unwrapped the two gowns, both in a gorgeous, silky fabric in sapphire. It looked and felt sumptuous, and all three sang Maudie's praises for her good instincts. Grace and Kelly tried the gowns on and sighed along with Rachel as they got a look at themselves in the mirror.

"Jack, Ethan, and Adam are going to flip when they see me in this dress, and it's perfect with the shoes!" Grace exclaimed. "What do you think, Rachel?" They turned so she could see them from all sides.

"Wow. Um, Maudie? Is something like that available in white?" Rachel asked, looking at Maudie's grinning countenance.

"I thought you might ask me that question, so I checked. Yes, it is, and, yes, I have one that is similar in white for you to try on. It has a beautiful crystal beaded embellishment at the waist and neckline." Grace and Kelly cheered and hopped up and down. "But I have three other gowns for you to try on as well."

Grace and Kelly were like giddy little school girls. Rachel smiled, relaxed, and watched them have fun. She'd dreaded this excursion a little, but it had turned out to be a lot less stressful than she thought it would be. Maudie was so easygoing and only let her try on things that specifically fit her requirements.

Rachel said, "Maudie, these are great, but I want to try on that white one that's similar to Grace and Kelly's."

Maudie grinned. "I saved the best for last. Let me help you, sweetie. Have a seat ladies, and prepare to be *amazed*," she said in a sing-song voice. She ushered Rachel into the big dressing room. Rachel squealed happily once the dress was on and she got a look at herself in the mirror.

"What?" Grace called out.

Kelly sounded impatient. "What?"

Grace asked, "Is it that good?"

"Get out here, Rachel!" Kelly called in a bossy tone.

Her mom sobbed melodramatically and said, "My *baby*!"

Rachel and Maudie snickered together but stayed in the dressing room, building the suspense. "You are truly lovely." Maudie's little chin wobbled a bit. "You look like a princess."

Kelly hollered. "Either you come out or we're coming in, Rachel!"

Grace laughed and said, "We're dying out here, Rachel! Kelly, stop being so bossy. She'll only make us wait longer."

"My *baby*!"

Kelly called, "The suspense is killing us!"

Rachel stepped through the dressing room door and made her way with stately elegance to the raised pedestal and smiled at them.

Kelly and Grace screamed in unison. "Aaah!"

"My *baby*!"

Then they were silent, in awe as Rachel twirled for them.

Grace smiled. "I know *just* what you need to go with that perfectly gorgeous dress."

Kelly turned to her conspiratorially, and said, "What?"

"My *baby*!"

Grace had a mischievous twinkle in her bright blue eyes. "She needs sheer white lace-edged stockings, garters, a white silk G-string, and the *wickedest* looking silk corset we can find!" They all cackled.

"Well, Grace," Maudie began, "I have basic white foundation garments here, but you know where you might want to look for great plus-size bridal lingerie? Hips and—"

"Curves.com!" Rachel and Grace cheered together.

"You've heard of it?"

"Like you read about!" Kelly snickered.

"You know what would be fun?" Grace asked Rachel and Kelly. At their questioning looks, she added, "A lingerie shower! You can *never*, ever have enough lingerie! You need things for the honeymoon, and every woman should have *everyday* lingerie, not just underwear and bras," Grace said cheerily.

"Grace, you are a hoot. Fine, plan me a lingerie shower." Rachel laughed, feeling her cheeks heat up when Maudie efficiently wrote down all her measurements and sizes for Grace on a card.

"Goody!" Grace squealed as she placed the information inside her pocketbook.

"She's like a force of nature!" Kelly laughed good-naturedly.

"She's more like her sister all the time," Rachel quipped with a smirk.

"You say the sweetest things, Rachel!" Grace laughed.

Chapter Thirty-one

Rachel found Eli on the covered back deck upon their return after dropping her mother off at home. Matthew was in his bouncy seat, chewing on his fist and listening to Uncle Eli play his guitar and sing for him. Rachel was surprised by that. She didn't know he knew how to play the guitar, or sing, for that matter. He seemed a little embarrassed to get caught at it, so she didn't ask him to play more while the others were there.

She bent down and gave him a kiss over the guitar. Speaking so the others couldn't hear and blocking their view, she gasped seductively and said, "Oh! Would you look at that? You can see right down my shirt."

He grinned handsomely and pressed his face to her cleavage for a second before kissing her there. She sure loved that smile.

"Did you have fun?" he asked as he laid his guitar aside. "Have any luck with the dresses?"

"Did we ever! Maudie is amazing! We accomplished everything we set out to do today," Grace replied as she cooed to Matthew in Kelly's arms.

"So that means you found your dresses?" he asked.

"You should have seen Rachel, Eli. She is going to be a vision!" Kelly said triumphantly. "This is going to be the best wedding *ever*," she said softly to the baby as she nuzzled him.

"I just changed him, sis. Matthew was really good for me. We even took a little nap together."

Rachel smiled at him tenderly when an image of her gentle giant napping with the tiny little baby on his chest popped into her mind.

"Thank you, Eli. You're the best." Kelly hugged him around the waist.

"No problem, sis. We did great. You all want to go eat? I have to go in at eight tonight, but I can take you to O'Reilley's for supper and still be there in plenty of time. Jack and Adam said they could meet us up there at six o'clock, Grace. Ethan's already up at the club. Sound okay?"

Grace nodded. "That sounds great."

"We have plenty of time if you want to rest for a little while," he said as he held the back door open for them so they could go inside.

He slipped into the bedroom to put the guitar away in the closet. Rachel followed him in and kissed him thoroughly.

"I didn't know you could play the guitar."

He smiled self-consciously and simply said, "Yep."

"You have a beautiful singing voice, too."

"Oh, you heard that, huh? My croaking?"

She rubbed her hands across his chest, enjoying the feel of his hard, warm muscles. "Don't say that. I think you have a beautiful singing voice."

"Thank you, angel. That means a lot. Matthew seemed to enjoy it."

Kelly came down the hallway. "Hey, if we're gonna go soon, I'd better nurse this boy. I'm about ready to explode here."

"Yeah," Eli said dryly, "thanks for sharing, sis,"

"Hey, at least I'm not flopping it out right in front of you, big bro," Kelly quipped, sticking her tongue out.

"Thank you for that mental image—"

"Burned into your brain. Yeah, I know, smartass." She laughed and carried the baby into the other bedroom.

* * * *

Eli noticed something was on Rachel's mind as he drove her and baby Matthew to the restaurant, arriving as Jack and Adam pulled up in Adam's truck. Grace and Kelly pulled in beside them.

"Eli, you know what I need to do?" Rachel asked.

"What's that, angel?"

"I'm cleared to drive after next week when my cast comes off. I need to shop for another vehicle."

"We can look tomorrow, if you want. What do you think you want this time?"

"I remember what it felt to look that deer straight in the eye the second before I hit him. I think I want a truck this time."

"I don't blame you. Are you coming up to the club later?" he asked as he parked on the other side of Adam's truck.

"That depends on Kelly and Matthew. I'd like to come up, though. I want to sit with you up at the front. I've missed doing that."

"Me, too, but I'll understand if Kelly wants to stay up late talking." He unlatched the harness on the baby's car seat and carefully lifted his infant nephew out of it. "Oh, your dad called with info on the hog hunt at the end of the month."

"Are you looking forward to going hunting?"

"Yeah, I haven't been in several years. I'm also looking forward to meeting your old boyfriend." Eli tucked the tiny baby under his chin and tickled her ribs as he put his arm around her waist. Matthew squeaked, snuggled closer, and fell back asleep.

"I wouldn't exactly call him my old boyfriend. Remember, they were all a little in awe of my dad and didn't want to piss him off. Mitchell is just an old classmate who I dated a few times."

"Well, I love hunting, and I like your dad, but I never would have been able to keep my hands off of you if I'd dated you in high school."

"Yeah, Daddy definitely would have met you at the door with his hunting knife and shotgun. You have trouble written all over you," she snickered. "But I admit I might have tried sneaking out my bedroom window to see you, if he hadn't let me date you."

Eli looked shocked. "Did you sneak out of your bedroom window to date boys?"

"Never. None of them ever motivated me enough to get the guts to try it. The one mistake I made in dating was after I was already on my own when I was nineteen."

"Your parents let you move out at nineteen?" He was surprised Peter had allowed her to move out that young.

She nodded her head, grinning. "Eighteen, actually. I worked evenings at Cheaver's Western Store during my junior and senior year, so when I graduated, I already had three thousand dollars in the bank and a steady job, plus I did ad sales for the *Divine Courier*. I went to college online and got my degree in accounting while I worked. When I wasn't working, I was studying, so I didn't have many opportunities to get into mischief."

"I'll bet your parents worried about you a lot."

"They did, but they raised me to be independent and taught me to manage my money well. Plus, I've been lucky in my friendships. Selling ads, I felt like I knew everyone in town. I enjoyed that job, but the office environment at the paper was not to my liking. Too many catty women in each other's business. I prefer the laidback atmosphere at Grogan Home Theatre much more. Plus, I'm working in the profession I chose as their bookkeeper."

"You are something, Rachel. I'm learning all kinds of new things about you."

"Hope you're not easily bored." She laughed as they joined the others in O'Reilley's courtyard.

Dinner was a festive occasion. Jack introduced Eli to several friends who came to greet them, and Matthew got passed around the whole time until they all had a chance to hold him and play with him. Grace especially enjoyed holding the baby, and Rachel noticed Adam and Jack's soft smiles when they watched her cooing to him. Grace glowed with happiness, and Rachel wondered if they were planning on having kids any time soon. The food was excellent as always, and Grace and her men thanked Eli graciously when he picked up the tab.

Eli drove Kelly, Matthew, and Rachel back to the duplex and went on to work. Kelly and Rachel composed wording for the wedding invitations and e-mailed it to Grace for her input. At Kelly's enthusiastic urging, Rachel got herself dolled up, and Kelly drove her to the club.

"Grace and I have monopolized your time this weekend. I don't mind at all. Matthew's already had his bath, so I'll put him down when I get back to the house, and then I think I'll watch a movie."

"You sure you'll be all right by yourself?"

"I'm positive. I've meant to ask you how your novel is coming along."

"Oh! It's awesome! With all the downtime I had while I was at my parents, I accomplished a lot. When it's finished, I'll let you read it. That probably won't be for another few weeks, depending on how much time I get with it."

"Is it romantic?"

"Very, and erotic, too. You may blush a time or two or three. Heck, you may even need a cold shower."

"Ah!" Kelly laughed delightedly. "So you're writing from experience?" She laughed out loud when Rachel's mouth fell open and her face went red-hot.

"Oh, my gosh! You *did* hear us that first weekend!"

"It's all right. You didn't know the walls were that thin. And don't worry. I haven't heard you at all since then. I assumed you must have figured it out on your own."

"Yeah, the hard way," Rachel replied and moved on. "So...yeah, my novel is basically smut."

"Oooh! Goody! So I get to read it when you're done?"

"Of course. You and Grace both get an autographed copy."

"I'll cherish it always. Grace tells me she's writing also. I can say I knew you before you were famous!"

"Whatever," Rachel said skeptically.

"Hey! It could happen. Here we are. Have fun in there, and I'll see you in the morning. Dance one or two for me."

Chapter Thirty-two

Grace took a deep breath and began hooking the hidden closure on the side seam of the corset. She made sure the ribbons were in two neat bows at the back and tucked the ends out of the way. Bending over, she adjusted her cleavage to the best advantage, her nipples almost peeking out of the top but still visible through the sheer black lace. Peeking over her shoulder in the mirror, she sighed happily and adjusted the strings on the G-string panty. She hooked the garters to the ribbon loops at the bottom edge off the corset and attached them to the sheer black stockings she was already wearing.

With her foundation garments all on, she slipped into the brilliant sapphire-colored dress. She was happy and pleased to see the corset gave her silhouette even more definition, pushing up her breasts and enhancing her cleavage. After zipping up the back, she put on the bridal jewelry Ethan had purchased for her. The platinum and diamonds were a beautiful touch in combination with the blue of her dress.

Winding her long, wavy blonde hair into a soft twist, Grace pinned it up with her jeweled hair clip. She touched up her makeup with a little powder, freshened her eyeliner and lipstick, then slipped into the new silver strappy sandals they'd found earlier that day and paused to take another look. Perfect.

Satisfied she had achieved the desired effect, she opened the bedroom door and called down, "I'm ready! Would you like to come up, or should I make an entrance on the stairs?"

Soft masculine laughter echoed at the bottom of the stairs. "Make an entrance, baby," Adam called in his deep sexy voice.

Grace tiptoed to the landing and stepped down the stairs. The hem of the dress draped prettily behind her, exposing the silver sandals.

She heard a soft whistle when her sexily-clad feet came into view. With a seductive smile, she moved slowly, knowing the skirt of the dress was now in view, softly revealing the curves of her thighs and her hips, which were greeted by a soft growl. *Definitely* Adam, she thought and felt a tingly shiver. A softly muttered oath could be heard as her corset-clad torso and upper body came into view until she was completely visible on the first landing, standing in the light.

Jack and Adam stood in the living room, gazing at her with intense expressions, drinking her in. Grace took a few more steps down the stairs until she reached the bottom landing. She stood at the bottom of the stairs as they both approached her. Releasing the banister, Grace stepped toward them, and turned slowly so they could see the outfit from all sides, knowing they'd enjoy the effect of the fabric softly clinging to her curves from all angles.

They each took a hand and kissed her knuckles. Jack spoke after a quick glance at Adam. "Darlin', words fail me. You are a vision," he murmured, looking her over hungrily.

"Baby, you dazzle me," Adam said softly. Neither of them said anything else, just silently looked her over, adoration shining in their eyes.

"So, you think it will do for the wedding?" Grace took their hands, drew them in, and kissed them both. She smiled as they both stroked their hands over her hips and waist.

"There's a little something extra under this dress, isn't there, baby?" Adam stated appreciatively.

"June sends her regards, Adam," Grace said with soft laughter as Adam grinned devilishly and traced one of the bones on the corset. The back of his hand grazed the side of her breast.

"Darlin'? You gonna model that for us, as well?" Jack asked softly while playfully nuzzling her throat.

"Mmm-hmm, just give me a minute to get upstairs and out of my dress." She backed away from them and removed the clip from her hair, shaking the wild blonde curls loose. With a crooked little grin, she inched back to the stairs. Jack and Adam glanced at each other.

"Grace wants to be chased, I think," Adam remarked in his sexy, deep voice and moved slowly toward her.

"I think you're right, buddy. What do you say we oblige her?" Jack made a sudden move for the stairs, where she'd paused on the bottom step. Grace screeched, gathered up her skirt, and ran up the steps, giggling loudly as they pounded the stairs behind her. A bone-deep thrill raced through her body as they chased her, and adrenaline gave her feet wings.

She stopped suddenly at the bedroom door and faced them, one hand upraised. They paused at the landing. "Tear this dress, and Rachel and Maudie will be furious with me," she said in warning.

Her pussy swelled and ached with need. Her juices dampened the midnight-blue silk and lace of her G-string, and because she wanted it off so badly, she reminded *herself* not to tear the gown when she removed it.

She crooked her finger, and Adam followed her into the closet while Jack texted Ethan. Adam caught her from behind in the big walk-in closet. He kissed her and growled softly when he groped her ass playfully and found the garters attached to her stockings. Adam loved her in garters and stockings. He pulled the tab on the zipper for her. Turning and smiling seductively as she peeled the sleeves and bodice of the dress off, Grace slowly revealed the sheer lace and silk of her undergarments. She lowered the dress over her hips, turned, and presented him with a full view of her bare ass as she stepped from it then pivoted to face him again. Adam's reaction delighted her as he stood there ogling her. Then with a muffled curse, he backed from the closet.

"Damn! *That* good?" Jack said from the bedroom.

Adam looked over at Jack and said, "I'm never gonna get tired of the way Grace surprises us. Get a load of this." He gestured at Grace as she slowly sauntered to the closet door and leaned against it, striking what she hoped was her sexiest pose. From the looks in their eyes, she'd succeeded.

"Damn, darlin', what's the fastest way out of that?" Jack asked, smiling at her in the latest addition to her growing lingerie collection.

"Why?" she asked, feeling sassy. "You don't like it? I haven't even properly modeled it for you. Yet."

"Model it, hell. I'm more in the mood for another striptease!" Adam said with a sexy chuckle.

With a grin, Grace softly said, "That's exactly what I had in mind. I love the way you think, Adam. Go sit down, big boys, and let me show you a thing or two...or three," she murmured. She gave them her best sexy saunter as she stepped into the bedroom while they sat in overstuffed chairs by the lit fireplace.

The soft warmth from the flames caressed her thighs as she followed them to the sitting area. Grace caught a glimpse of herself in one of the standing mirrors as she passed it. The glimpse made her smile and increased her confidence even more as the men sat down and gave her their undivided attention.

Turning slowly for them, Grace looked seductively over her shoulder, smiling as she watched their warm eyes roam over her indecently clad form. She slid her hands over her hips and the tops of her thighs before sliding them back over her ass cheeks. She grinned mischievously when Adam's hands tightened into fists. The men eased back into their chairs as she approached and placed a beautifully shod foot on Jack's knee.

"Jack, honey, could you help me with my sandal please?" she asked softly.

He obliged her, and then she switched and let him remove the other, as well, while she winked at Adam. Grace unhooked the garters that connected the corset to her stockings one at a time, smiling as their eyes closely watched her slow, teasing movements.

She caressed his cheek as Jack handed her the sandals. Laying them aside, she turned to Adam and said, "Adam, would you help me with all these little hooks?"

Grace raised one arm so he could see the hooks closing the side of the corset, and rested her hand on the back of her neck. Her other hand held the front of the corset to her as it came loose quickly in his hands. She moved away momentarily to lay it aside, turned back to them, and revealed her little surprise.

She wore a silver nipple and belly chain that was made from the same silver wire and crystals as on the clit clip she'd surprised them with right before their wedding. The nipple dangles were connected by a draping silver chain. Both the men leaned forward, pleased approval in their features.

Grace came close enough for them to reach out and touch her. Jack lifted one of the dangles, grazing her nipple lightly, and smiled at her soft intake of breath. Adam grinned and reached for the silver chain that draped between her breasts. He gently hooked it with his finger and tugged down a bit then set it to swinging. She gasped and felt her pussy flood with wet warmth as his hand slid down the extender to the silver length that was secured around her waist. He must have noticed that the end hung down until it rested inside her G-string. She whimpered as Jack's finger gently traced it down over the blue silk, finally ending against her clit. She saw him glance at Adam.

Adam stood and moved behind her. Her eyes slid closed, and she moaned softly at the sensation of his warmth. She opened her eyes, remembering she was supposed to be giving them the show. Grace smiled teasingly at Jack, still in his chair, and carefully placed a stockinged foot on the chair between his legs.

"Jack, could you help me with my stockings?"

Adams warm, soft lips slid over her shoulder, and he kissed his way up the side of her throat. She tilted her head back and closed her eyes at the dual sensation of his warm lips combined with Jack's gentle hands as he slid the stocking over her knee and down her calf. Jack helped her switch to the other foot and removed the other one.

One of Adams hands slid over her shoulder to her breast and tenderly stroked the weighted chain that dangled there, and she moaned again. His other hand stroked down over the extender, sliding all the way to the top edge of her now damp G-string. Engulfed in all the wonderful sensations, Grace left her eyes closed and allowed her men to take over.

Jack's hands smoothed slowly up her thighs and slid under the elastic waistband then gently drew down the scrap of silk. He leaned forward to tenderly kiss the juncture of her hip and thigh as he slipped the G-string from her legs. Adam's fingers slid down to her wet slit, where the chain dipped in, disappearing between her lips below the narrow strip of blonde curls but he did not seek entry, yet.

"Grace loves playin' hide and seek," Jack commented with a smile. He gazed up at her and caught Adam's attention and nodded.

"Good thing we love hide and seek, too, isn't it, Jack?" Adam asked conversationally as his hands slid to the backs of her thighs and he moved in closely behind her. She realized at some point he'd removed his shirt because she could now feel his hot, bare chest against her back. "Baby, why don't you put your pretty little foot on the arm of Jack's chair?"

Grace's breathing turned to panting as she did as he asked. She leaned against Adam and tentatively lifted her other foot. Adam grasped the backs of her thighs and leaned her against his naked torso as she placed that foot on the other arm, both knees bent so that she was spread, warm and wet before Jack, open to him. She slid her hands over Adam's strong hard-muscled shoulders, turning to his kiss as she tilted her head back.

"Darlin', you're so beautiful tonight. With your pretty little pussy spread open like this. Your scent is making my mouth water. I think I'd like a taste. Wonder what I'll find." Jack smiled at her whimper and leaned forward in the chair.

"Mmm, she sounds ready, Jack. I'm anxious to see what she's got hidden. Why don't you take a taste and find out?" Adam murmured huskily.

Jack's hands slid along her inner thighs, moving slowly toward the spot she most wanted to feel their touch but hadn't yet. Her body felt like it was vibrating with the power of the arousal they inspired in her. Using his index fingers, he gently opened her outer lips, humming in pleasure at what he found there. Grace answered with a moan. Her back arched at his gentle touch, parting her inner lips a little more.

Carefully, Adam spread her thighs for Jack so that he had better access, holding her gently but securely. "Do you love that Jack can see all of you, Grace? I'll bet your little pussy is on fire to be touched right now, isn't it?"

"Oh, yes!" Her body trembled in his loving grasp. Her clit throbbed where it was trapped in the clip, and the feel of Jack's gentle, questing fingers was bringing her close to the edge.

Jack kissed a path along her inner thigh to the trembling, wet flesh that lay beyond, eager for his touch. Her back arched reflexively when he slid the tip of his tongue into her opening, before he dragged it over her inner lips, lifting the heavy bead from its little damp nest between them. The movement of the bead tugged slightly at her clit, which was even more sensitive because the silver chain had been gently rubbing over it with her movements since she'd first put it on.

"Oh! Oh, Jack! I'm...Oh!" she yelled as he licked her clit over and over with the same gentle rhythm, giving her this orgasm fast and sweet as she cried out. She slipped right over the edge for him.

"Jack! Adam! Oh, I'm coming!" she wailed as the orgasm washed over her in a rushing tide. She panted heavily, her cheeks heating as she gazed down into his ocean-blue eyes, eyes that now reminded her of the waters around Grand Cayman Island, where they'd spent their honeymoon.

"Did you like that, darlin'?"

Sighing, still catching her breath, she murmured, "You know I did, Jack. I guess you won hide and seek." She turned her head to smile up at Adam. "I love to play with you. Want to play some more hide and seek?" She caressed Adam's jaw as she turned back to Jack. "This time you get to hide something."

Chapter Thirty-three

Eli stood in the foyer of The Dancing Pony, talking with Ethan, when Rachel walked in the door. Ethan saw her first and smiled, drawing Eli's attention to her. Eli looked up and sighed, drinking in the beautiful sight of her. Rachel was dressed simply in a snug long-sleeved black T-shirt and jeans and with high-heeled boots. She snuggled into his arms as he hugged her and all notions of *simple* went out the window.

Whatever the hell she had on under that top was *anything* but simple. It thrust her breasts up so her cleavage tempted him from the low-cut top and made him wish he could cup their lush, fragrant fullness in his hands right that moment. Her hair was pinned up loosely, and she was wearing large silver hoop earrings. Rachel smiled suggestively at him, evidently enjoying the appreciative once-over she was getting. Ethan greeted her with a kiss on the cheek, complimented her appearance, and excused himself. Rachel tilted her head up for a kiss from Eli. When she came up for air, she laughed because Mike and Rogelio were standing there dumbfounded.

Eli murmured, "Hey, beautiful, what do you have on under this T-shirt? Whatever it is, it feels sexy and naughty as hell."

"It's a little something I wore just for you," she replied softly in his ear before licking his earlobe with the tip of her tongue. The soft, warm touch sent shivers shooting down his spine straight to his cock. "I'll show you later."

"I can't fucking wait." He brushed his instant erection against her abdomen as he pressed her to him.

"Me, either." She smiled up at him seductively and then looked over at Mike and Rogelio, who couldn't hear them over the music.

"Okay, *hot girl*, who are you? And what have you done with my young, innocent friend Rachel?" Mike asked, hands on his hips. Behind him,

Rogelio rolled his eyes. Where Rachel was concerned, Mike tended to be a cross between an old spinster aunt and an obnoxious pit-bull...with tattoos.

Rogelio tapped him on the back of the head and spoke up for him. "I think Mike is trying to say you look beautiful tonight, Rachel. How is your arm doing?"

She patted her T-shirt-covered cast and said, "Oh, it's fine, Rogelio. My cast comes off next Wednesday afternoon. How are things tonight?"

"Not too bad," Rogelio replied. "I think Eli is due for a break if you'd like to go dance together."

"Thank you, Rogelio. I'd love to, if you don't mind." Linking her arm in Eli's, Rachel said, "By the way, how is Christina doing?"

"Oh, she's as sweet as ever."

"You ask her to marry you yet?"

He laughed. "You know I want to get my house built first. I want to be able to give her something besides a little travel trailer to live in. I'll be ready to start building next spring. I heard you set a date." The Lopez's pastor had called Eli while the girls were out shopping that afternoon and confirmed the date with him.

"Yes! The fifteenth of December. Make sure and tell Christina I want her to come, too. Tell her it would make me happy if she was there," she said as she squeezed Eli's hand.

"Will do. Now you go dance." Rogelio grinned, patted her hand, and winked at Eli.

Rachel kissed Rogelio's cheek and made him blush. Eli drew her to him and led her to the dance floor. The club was busy, the music thumping loudly, and the dance floor was full as he pulled her to him.

"Who's that man Ethan is with?" Rachel asked, gesturing over to the table by the dance floor where Ethan and a friend sat talking. "He looks familiar, like he's been in here before, but I can't place him."

"He's a friend of Ethan's from Morehead. It's been a while since he's been in."

The man glanced up from his conversation and caught Eli's eye. She quickly turned to Eli, snuggling to his chest as they danced together.

"Interesting guy, huh?" Eli looked down at her, stroking his fingers along her spine, feeling what was underneath the soft T-shirt. He grinned when he felt her soft, trembling shudder as she reacted to his touch.

"I suppose. Not as interesting as you, though, Eli."

He growled softly. "I'm glad to hear it. He keeps looking at you."

* * * *

"Then turn me so he can't see me," she said, clinging to Eli.

For some reason, she felt mildly intimidated by the man. He wasn't nearly as big as Eli, or as strong looking, but something about him made her feel vulnerable. Not weak as much as exposed. As if he could hear her thoughts. The man was dressed informally in jeans, T-shirt, and boots but had a distinguished air about him. Formidable and mysterious but also elegant despite his casual dress. His jet-black hair was short, but not too short, and slicked back, revealing a strong regal profile.

"He seems to have an interesting effect on women, at least some. Kerry, his waitress, is usually bubbly and talkative, kidding around with everybody, having a good time while she works. She gets quiet like that when she waits on him. Not like she's scared of him or anything, more like she's showing him deference. She doesn't look him in the eye unless he speaks and looks directly at her, and she fills his orders fast."

"Do you think she knows him outside of the club?"

"Probably. He asked if she was working tonight. She reacted the moment she saw him and went right to him without being asked to serve him. I'd be willing to bet they know each other well."

"He's talking to her."

"Yeah, watch her face," Eli whispered.

Rachel watched as Kerry returned with a drink for him, and the man spoke in a soft voice that Kerry had to draw near to hear. Her demeanor was almost reverent. As she carefully held her tray, her posture was alert, not servile at all, and her face seemed to glow with quiet contentment.

"Look."

Though unusual for someone like Kerry who was bubbly by nature, her attitude was not put on at all. She replaced his napkin with a fresh one and placed his mixed drink on it. He passed her a folded bill, and she thanked him respectfully. Her face had a serene quality to it.

"I'll bet you that was a one hundred dollar tip," Eli said. "I heard one of the waitresses say he always tips well if they give good service. But he seems to prefer for her to wait on him."

"My goodness. What does he do for a living?"

"Ethan told me he owns a club in Morehead."

"Oh, a nightclub, like this one?"

"Um, no. He caters to an exclusive clientele. You have to be a member or be invited by a member."

"Like a country club?" she asked, feeling like she was missing something.

"He is a Dom, angel," Eli said softly. "His club caters to the BDSM community in this part of Texas. But his club is exclusive. All members are carefully screened."

"Oh!" Rachel felt like a dimwit. She recalled Grace telling her Ethan had a friend who was a Dom. This must be him.

Rachel decided to not say anything. Grace had mentioned that was a private part of her relationship with Ethan only. Rachel wondered to herself how Grace would react if she were introduced to him. She glanced over at him once more and found him watching her again.

This was different from the time when Ace Webster had watched her on the dance floor with avid interest. He'd made no secret that he was interested in getting closer acquainted. This man seemed to merely observe, almost as if he were assessing her. She found it interesting that Eli was not throwing territorial vibes like he had with Ace. She wondered why and exactly how well acquainted with this stranger he was.

He never approached them, and Eli made no move to introduce her to him, but the man did nod to Eli at one point. Interesting. Ethan and he talked for at least an hour. During that time, when she could do it without being obvious, Rachel observed Kerry as she continued to wait on the intriguing customer. She wondered how Kerry knew him outside the club. Her behavior was out of the ordinary for her bubbly personality, but by no means strange, and she made no production of the way she served him. Rachel might never have noticed the subtle difference if Eli had not pointed it out.

Her mind began to wander, imagining the kinds of things that happened behind the guarded doors of this stranger's exclusive club. Thoughts of whips, chains, and ball gags did nothing for her, but she did ponder what it would be like to be tied up and spanked and then fucked to a screaming orgasm while strangers observed. The thought produced a startlingly palpable reaction as her nipples hardened and a warm ache began deep in her pussy. Need coursed through her, and her clit pulsed at the vivid fantasies floating through her mind.

Rachel imagined Eli, chest bare and glistening with sweat, restraining her aching body and teasing her, requiring her to withhold her orgasm until he commanded it. She might have been sexually inexperienced prior to knowing Eli, but that didn't mean she hadn't read about this subject in her erotic romance collection, before it had been reduced to ash, that is. She had a basic, if possibly patchy and glamorized, knowledge of that lifestyle.

The thought of serving Eli submissively, in a setting like that, with observers, affected her much more strongly than she might have thought it would.

Observers? Really?

She recalled their late-night detour the night of his proposal and how exciting sex on a deserted—but very public—street had been. In conversation, she'd confessed a willingness to be tied up, spanked and fucked. The incredible erotic spanking he'd given her came to mind, and her pussy clenched a little and she was unable to stop the gasp that escaped her lips. Eli looked down at her from his seat next to her.

"Everything all right, angel?" He smiled at her softly, and she knew he had to see her deep blush as it spread down her throat to her chest.

He didn't say anything else after she nodded breathlessly at him and felt more moisture gather at her entrance as the fantasies continued to dance in her mind. If she hadn't let that little gasp out, she might have come right there in her seat, thinking about him doing it to her again. Gosh, talk about being suggestible.

"You're flushed. Are you feeling okay?" When she nodded mutely and looked into his eyes, he smiled and leaned down to her. There was a compassionate, knowing gleam in his eyes. "I'll bet I can guess what you're thinking about."

The heat in her cheeks increased, and she leaned into him a little. "I'm that easy to read?"

"No, angel. I looked in your beautiful blue eyes, saw the need there, and I put two and two together. You've been uncharacteristically quiet since I mentioned the customer at Ethan's table to you. You and I both enjoyed the hell out of the hot spanking I gave you last month, and we've talked about other fun activities we'd like to try. You've been watching Kerry off and on all night, and I think her behavior is becoming more and more intriguing to you. It turns you on, doesn't it?"

"Your instincts are pretty good, Eli. You nailed it right on the head. Do you know him personally?"

"Ethan introduced me to him tonight when he arrived. Since I'd asked Ethan for some advice about spanking and other stuff, he thought I might like to meet him. I talked to him for a little while before you came in. His name is Joseph Hazelle."

"You had already met him? That's why you weren't throwing alpha male caveman vibes in his direction like you did with Ace?" she said, smirking at him.

"Something like that. I wondered if you were interested in learning more about…"

"Dominant/submissive relationships?"

"Yes, angel, and I thought I'd share a little information with you and let you determine if this was something you wanted to pursue later."

"Later?"

"Yes, I mentioned your accident. He suggested waiting a few months and using this time to explore reliable sources of information and determine what it is about that lifestyle that is striking a chord with you. He gave me his website address. I'm willing to look into it together, with one understanding."

"What's that, Eli?"

"I won't share you, nor do I care to be shared. Beyond that, I'm willing to explore and am more or less a blank slate. There might be something there that we like, or we may find that the occasional spanking is all we're interested in. Either way, I wanted you to know you have the freedom to explore it with me if you want."

"Will you be disappointed if that's all I want? Or if it's all that I can handle?"

"No, not if I still have your love."

"You're all I want, all I need." She reached to hug his neck as he wrapped his arms around her. He stroked her torso through the shirt again. "I can't wait to see what you have on under this. My curiosity is getting to me in a big way."

"Just a little something I threw on." She giggled. "I promise to show you as soon as we're alone."

Not a single female customer had approached Eli with more than the occasional friendly greeting all evening, and she decided to test the waters to see if there were any sharks lurking, waiting for an opportunity. Ethan had made it official the weekend before by announcing their engagement to the entire club from the DJ's booth. She decided she also needed a few minutes alone to process all this other information.

"Eli, I'm going to visit the ladies' room. I'll be back in a few minutes." She reached for her purse.

"Would you like me to walk you?" Normally, she'd say no, but there was a particularly rowdy group of men at a table near the doorway that led to the ladies' room. She thought an escort wasn't a bad idea.

"If you wouldn't mind. But you don't have to wait for me. I know you're working."

"I understand if you need a break. Take your time, and I'll keep an eye out for you," he said as she slipped her hand into his and followed him through the crowd.

As they passed near the tables at the edge of the dance floor, Mr. Hazelle and Ethan looked up and smiled at them. Rachel smiled back as Eli escorted her past them to the restrooms. The ladies' room was empty, and she took a seat in the chair in the corner.

Was this something she wanted to pursue? She shook her head and asked herself the most fundamental question. What was her core telling her to do? In her heart, she acknowledged there was a natural dominant and submissive component in her relationship with Eli. It warred with her need to be independent, which stemmed from her desire to please her parents, especially her father. Rachel was undeniably curious, and she'd never know if she didn't look into it.

She acknowledged the pleasure it gave her to turn control over to Eli, both in their relationship and in bed. She loved it when he took charge. She remembered making love sitting in his lap while they both watched in the mirror. He'd told her she belonged to him, and she'd gloried in that moment. She'd felt completely his, without reservation or question. It had nothing to do with him being in control of her but had everything to do with her exchanging that control for his protective, loving, and sometimes territorial care of her. Even the territorial part of him gave her great pleasure when he showed that side of his nature. The caveman, he called him. Rachel really *did* love that guy.

She did not have the in-depth knowledge needed to make an informed choice, but something resonated inside her at the thought of learning more. She was grateful for the open timeframe Eli had given her as she continued her recovery but secretly hoped maybe the opportunity to *play* again would come soon. First thing she needed to do was get released by her doctor, get the damned cast off her arm, and build the strength back up in it. Rachel plucked at her curls, fixed her lip liner and lipstick, then washed her hands and exited the ladies' room.

Rachel stepped from the bathroom and immediately heard a commotion outside the hallway. She stepped to the opening leading back out to the club, trying to determine the best path around whatever was going on. She stepped out and saw a fight in the process of being broken up. Rather than being caught up in the flux of people moving forward to watch and people moving back trying to get out of the way, she stepped back near the door and waited for the crowd to disperse.

She watched as Eli frog-walked a large, angry roughneck toward the dimly lit hallway where she stood. Not only did it lead to the restrooms but also to the back offices, a storeroom, kitchen, and the rear emergency exit, which they were evidently about to make use of. Eli's large hands grasped the drunken man by his shirt collar and the belt in his blue jeans, and the guy did not look happy about it. He struggled, and Eli's muscular arms and shoulders bunched and rippled as he maintained his hold easily. Entranced, she watched as Eli and his unfortunate cargo were followed by Mike and Rogelio with similarly cursing, drunken, sweaty, pissed-off friends in tow. A big, strong arm surrounded her waist and gently extricated her from the opening to the hallway as the troublemaker began to fight free from Eli.

Looking up, Rachel realized it was Ethan trying to remove her from the drunken fool's path before he trampled her. Eli muttered a soft curse and moved to obtain a stronger hold on the guy as his fists started swinging.

Three things happened all at once. Eli's attention was briefly diverted as he saw her in their path. The guy lost his balance and pitched forward, arms and fists flailing. Eli reached for him and caught him again, but not before the man's arms swung out in a wide arc, and one of his balled up, meaty fists barely missed striking Rachel in the face. If Ethan hadn't been there to pull her out of the way, she'd have been on the floor. Except for the loud music, which continued thumping, all movement and sound ceased in the immediate vicinity of the doorway.

"Are you all right, angel?" Eli asked quickly, gaining a viciously hard grasp of the drunk by the shirt collar and his long hair. By this point, he'd given up fighting to break free of Eli but continued to curse incoherently, unaware he'd nearly struck a woman in the face with his flailing fists.

Rachel nodded and found her voice. "I'm all right, Eli."

Eli looked closely at her as if assessing her for injuries. He looked up at Ethan, who stood behind her and, after a moment, nodded. She had not looked back at Ethan, so she didn't know what communication had passed between them.

"Come on, Rachel. Eli will be back in a few minutes. I want you to sit with us until he does. Are you sure you're okay?" Ethan asked as he escorted her away from the men but not before she heard a meaty thud and a groan.

"I'm a little shaky, but otherwise I'm fine. Wow, that was close, I think."

"I saw it happen. You have no idea how close you came to getting clocked by that dumbass drunk's fist. It's a good thing I saw you standing in the doorway and pulled you out. Otherwise, we might still be picking you up."

"Thank you, Ethan, for looking out for me," she said as he led her to his table.

"You're welcome, sweetheart. I'd like to introduce you to a friend of mine. This is Joseph Hazelle. Joseph, this is a close friend of ours, Rachel Lopez. Rachel is newly engaged to Eli Wolf, whom you met earlier."

"It's a pleasure to meet you, Rachel. I'm sorry that unpleasantness precipitated our meeting but glad to meet you all the same," Joseph said as he shook her hand. His hands were firm and strong. Not as rough as Eli's but not soft by any means, either.

"The feeling is mutual, Mr. Hazelle, believe me. It's a pleasure to make your acquaintance." Rachel attributed her bravado to the adrenaline rush and nerves because she was now completely at ease speaking with Mr. Hazelle, where before she had felt only intimidated by him. She smiled and thanked Ethan when he quickly returned with a Coke from the bar for her. She sat in the chair Ethan offered her and sipped her drink, gazing over to the hallway Eli had disappeared down a few moments before.

"Eli will be back in a minute, I'm sure. It was bad enough that bozo started a fight and needed to be removed, but he nearly injured you on top of that. I'm sure Eli is having a talk with him about that right now."

"A talk?" She grinned. "Kind of like that talk you all had with Jim and Roy? Your fists and their faces?"

Ethan nodded seriously and replied, "If it had been Grace standing there, I know what I'd be doing right now. I imagine he's doing the same. That guy came in here looking for trouble, picked a fight and he's earned whatever he's getting."

Joseph nodded in agreement.

"What caused the fight in the first place?"

"What's behind most of the fights that happen here?" Ethan asked, discreetly gesturing at a rather dejected looking woman as she gathered her coat and purse and was led from the club by a tall, handsome cowboy.

"A woman?"

"There are few other things worth fighting over," Joseph said quietly. Rachel wasn't quite sure what to make of his statement.

Speaking to Joseph, Ethan said, "Grace and Rachel are close friends. They've been busy planning Rachel's wedding, which is next month."

"That's good. Eli sounds like a happy man," Joseph replied.

They conversed for a few minutes, and during that time, neither Joseph nor Ethan mentioned Joseph's line of work, and Rachel didn't, either

"I got a text from Jack earlier that Grace tried on her dress and modeled it for him and Adam," Ethan said with a grin. "From the sound of things, you all must have had a good time this afternoon."

Rachel laughed. "We did. Your wife loves to shop."

Eli and the others returned from the hallway, looking cool and unruffled. At least that's how it appeared until she saw the feral gleam in Eli's eyes. Before she could rise from her chair, he was beside her.

"Are you all right?" His eyes were fierce as he gently checked every inch of her face, making sure for himself.

"Yes. Ethan got me out of the way in time. Let me see your hands." She turned them palm down so she could see his knuckles, which were red and a bit swollen. "Thank you, Eli. Sorry my reflexes weren't better. Then I wouldn't have been anywhere near him. I was a little awestruck, watching you."

He enveloped her in his arms and kissed the top of her head. "Were ya?"

She nodded. "You're very powerful. Very good at your job. Scary good." She snuggled up to him. Mike and Rogelio had already returned to the front.

"Did I scare you?"

She leaned into him and whispered softly, "You turn me on when you're like that."

He grinned knowingly but tried to control his expression.

Turning to his boss, who was already caught up in conversation with Joseph again, he said, "Unless you need anything else, Ethan, we'll head back up to the front."

"Will one of you check the parking lot? I want to make sure Heather and Sam were able to leave without being harassed. Jeremy was here with several guys, not just the two who got kicked out with him."

"Sure thing. Thanks for watching out for Rachel for me."

"It was our pleasure. I'm just glad she didn't get hurt." Ethan hugged Rachel back as she reached for him. "We've got to watch out for our girls, right?"

"You do a fine job, too," Rachel replied as Eli tucked her against him and they started to make their way back to the front. She turned back for a moment, "It was nice to meet you, Joseph."

"Likewise, Rachel. Likewise," Joseph said with a smile and a nod.

* * * *

Rachel watched with enjoyment as Eli lifted baby Matthew into his embrace for one last kiss on the cheek. Matthew squealed and grinned, showing his toothless gums. "Later, little buddy. Be good for Mommy." He nuzzled the thick black hair on top of Matthew's head and kissed his crown.

The way Eli was with Matthew made Rachel yearn to have kids with him. She wanted a few years to play with Eli, like she'd said before, but she looked forward to watching him with his own children. He was confident as he handled the baby and so openly affectionate. He was not the kind of man to maintain a tough guy image. On the contrary, he acted like a clown and talked baby talk with Matthew, which Kelly hated. She'd gotten on him several times about it.

The last time had been the evening before while she'd been packing.

"If you don't stop that, he's going to develop improper speech habits," Kelly had fussed at him.

"He's two and a half months old," Eli had said, defending himself.

"Yes, but if you're in the habit of baby talking with him, you'll still be doing it when he's a year old. When his kindergarten teacher contacts me and wants to talk about speech therapy, I'm going to call *you* first." She'd poked him with a little manicured index finger. Rachel thought watching the little pixie fuss at her big brother had been like watching a tiny kitten taunt a big, lovable mastiff.

"Come on, it's not that big a deal—"

"Stop it. Or I bring Rachel your baby pictures, including the nekkid ones the next time I come visit." She'd put her hands on her hips, and an evil grin had spread on her face. Rachel had a feeling Kelly was going to bring them *anyway*.

Eli looked genuinely horrified, quickly changed his tune, and had started backtracking. "*Never mind.* I won't do it anymore."

"What a minute, there are nekkid baby pictures of Eli?" Rachel had asked with a snicker. Her imagination had gone wild, trying to picture this big, formidable, sexy man as a little baby or toddler.

"It'll never happen again!" Eli had yelled in mock horror. "I promise!" He'd threw his hands up in surrender.

"I may carry them with me for insurance. Especially the one with the water hose," Kelly said then had laughed with an unladylike snort. "Rachel, you'd be amazed by how big those old-fashioned diapers would swell up with water before they finally *exploded*," she'd hinted with an evil gleam in her eyes.

"Sis, don't you dare!"

Wow, Rachel had thought, it must have been a really embarrassing picture.

Rachel had consoled Eli. "Oh, come on, Eli. Mom showed you mine, and you'll recall there were several nekkid baby pictures." She'd rubbed his chest and winked at Kelly. She had every intention of seeing *all* his baby pictures.

"Yeah, but you were a pretty little baby girl. And your mom promised no other boyfriends ever saw those pictures," Eli had reminded her.

Kelly had snorted. "Eli, you were as cute as you could be with that water hose stuck in your diaper. You looked like you were *really* enjoying it."

He'd glowered at his little sister. "It was hot! Come on."

"Aw! You thought I was a pretty little baby girl?" Rachel had cooed, pretending to disregard their argument.

Grinning at her, Eli had ignored Kelly like a bothersome gnat. "Angel, you were gorgeous! With your pretty *widdle bwoo* eyes and your cute *widdle* dimpled *heinie*," he'd replied as he nuzzled her neck then he'd whispered softly, "Luscious."

In disgust, Kelly had said, "Oh, you two make me wanna *gag!*"

"It's got more dimples now!" Rachel had giggled as he'd palmed her ass.

She'd hoped Kelly couldn't hear his reply. "I'd like to nibble your luscious ass right now."

She'd whispered back, "You only want to nibble it?"

The devilish look in Eli's eyes had led her to believe what other things he'd like to do to her ass.

Kelly had made a gagging sound and gestured like she was sticking her fingers down her throat before she'd turned to Matthew in his bouncy seat. "Don't worry, sweetheart. Mommy won't let Uncle Eli teach you any bad habits." Matthew had passed gas and blown a spit bubble. She'd frowned and said, "Too late."

All three of them burst out laughing at Matthew's well-timed humor.

"Remember, I have those pictures, *you*," she said, jabbing her finger at him in mock-threat, and then she winked at Rachel.

Yep, she's still bringing the pictures.

Kelly hugged them both hard and got on the road, anxious to get the three-hour drive over with.

At the Toyota dealership in Morehead, Rachel found a jet-black four-door Tundra that she fell in love with. It had leather seats, dark tinted windows, and a decent stereo. She negotiated with the salesman and got a great deal. Rachel wasn't jazzed about taking on a new car payment, but she'd had great luck with her last Toyota and knew this vehicle would be around for a while. Plus, it had four doors, so it would be great for when they had kids and car seats to deal with.

They decided before they got out of Eli's vehicle that if she found a truck she loved, she'd negotiate the best deal she could and then tell the salesman she wanted to take two days to cool off and make sure it was the right choice. The salesman didn't greet this announcement with enthusiasm, as predicted, and threw in an upgraded MP3 compatible stereo, premium floor mats, heavy-duty bed liner, and a maintenance package if they did the paperwork today.

"I don't care about those things. We'll upgrade the sound system with a stereo of my choosing, not whatever you have in inventory. The floor mats that are in it will last forever. I don't need ones that have the company logo on them, which is the only real difference. The heavy-duty bed liner is fine, but the maintenance package is really nothing but oil changes, which I can do myself," she said with a bit of a scoff. She smiled at the salesman, who was anxious that they not leave without a truck, and said, "Knock another fifteen hundred off the price you've already quoted to us and we'll sit down and fill out the paperwork right now."

The salesman excused himself to speak with his "supervisor," who Rachel knew was just another salesman in a different office. As they walked around the car, Eli surreptitiously caressed Rachel's ass. "You drive a *hard* bargain, Miss Lopez."

"I'm good at negotiating, Mr. Wolf. There's nothing I love more than *driving* a *hard* bargain," she said seductively.

Eli groaned softly and leaned over to her as she climbed in the driver's seat. She glanced at the salesman through the glass window in his office.

"What if he offers a thousand off?"

"I'll ask for twelve hundred and settle for eleven hundred if he makes the offer and doesn't waste any more of our time. It'll be suppertime by the time we get back to Divine, and I'll be hungry. Heaven forbid I should get cranky," she said.

The negotiations went as predicted. Eleven hundred *with* the stereo upgrade and bed liner. Rachel smiled when the salesman offered to deliver the vehicle since she was not cleared to drive yet. They were home with plenty of time to go by the store, get shrimp to put on the grill, and a buy bottle of wine to celebrate.

Crankiness averted.

Chapter Thirty-four

The following weekend, Eli's suspicions were realized when he drove Rachel to Grace's house and found Kelly there already. She made no secret of the big box on the dining room table, which he knew contained baby pictures. His mom and dad had taken lots of baby pictures. Lots and lots.

Hell, if it made Rachel happy, Kelly could show them every single one, even the really embarrassing ones. Renata and Grace's friend, and former co-worker, Teresa was also there. Eli pulled Rachel into the kitchen so he could talk with her in private.

He slipped his big hands over her hips and groaned softly as she pressed her soft breasts against his chest. "I slipped a little something for you in your makeup case and in your luggage."

"You did? A surprise for me? Will I like it?"

"I already know you like it," he hinted then grinned at her curious expression.

"I know you'll probably stay up late, but text me after you find them tonight."

"I have to wait?"

"Until bedtime. Text me when you go to bed."

"What if it's super late?"

"Angel, I only sleep well with you. I'll probably still be awake. Text me, and I'll call you back. Where are you sleeping?" Eli asked, looking around.

"I'm in Ethan's bedroom."

"Good, any roommates?"

"No. Everyone got their own room. We'll probably be down here in the living room most of the evening."

"Good, so when you go to bed you'll have some privacy."

"I should, yeah. Eli, are we going to have *phone sex*?" Rachel whispered, blushing a pretty rose color.

"You'll see," he said mischievously.

Everyone was talking in the living room and going in and out of the front door, loading up.

Ethan came in the kitchen. "Hey, Eli, can you help me for a second?"

Eli nodded then smiled down at her. "Be right back, angel. I'm not leaving until I get my good-bye kiss." He left her with Grace as she came in the kitchen.

Eli followed Ethan up the stairs to Grace's opulent master bedroom suite. Jack and Adam were downstairs helping load the two SUVs they were taking with them. Eli could tell how much Grace's men cared about her and how much they enjoyed spoiling her as he looked around at the beautifully furnished and decorated room.

"While they're all occupied, I wanted to show you something we did for Grace as a wedding present. Grace's sister arranged for these to be done. I thought I'd suggest you doing something similar that fits your relationship and your personality, for Rachel. Grace was floored when she saw these the first time. She really loves them. She told me if the house ever catches fire, she's grabbing us, these three portraits, and her laptop before she heads out the door." Ethan led him to each one and showed him the three outdoor portraits they had made for Grace as a wedding gift.

"Charity arranged this?"

"Yeah, she was a pivotal force in our relationship with Grace," Ethan said cryptically.

"I'll have to call her. These are awesome, man. I'll bet Grace loves them," Eli said. Looking around, he added, "Your house is nice."

"That's Grace. We did some major remodeling, but Grace has a touch that makes everything around her better," Ethan said then slowed on the stairs and turned to him. "It was just a house and then she came."

"I know what you mean, Ethan," Eli said, nodding. "Where would we be?"

"Cold and lonely, man. Cold and lonely," Ethan replied knowingly. "Thought I would share those with you. Food for thought. It would make a nice surprise for her."

"I'll call Charity. It's a great idea, and I know Rachel would love it."

"Charity would probably help you get it arranged since you've known each other a while. She's a hoot."

They returned to the hubbub downstairs. A few minutes later, all the men loaded up into Peter and Ethan's SUVs and left the girls to their fun.

* * * *

Rachel went out with the girls to Rudy's for supper. Rudy seated them at a large secluded booth in the corner and hand delivered complimentary appetizers to their table. He turned their service over to his best and most well-mannered waiter.

They nibbled on shrimp cocktail while they talked and looked over their menus. Remembering a few of the details Grace had shared with her about enjoying shrimp cocktail with Jack, Ethan, and Adam at Tessa's, Rachel leaned over to Grace and asked, "How's that *shrimp cocktail?*"

Grace laughed and nearly choked on her shrimp. "It's good, but I know a place where I get more *personalized* service," Grace said and jabbed Rachel in the ribs.

Grace had told her once that on their first date, Jack had held her in his lap while they fed her shrimp cocktail, and one thing had led to another right there in the private dining booth. Rachel hoped she got to visit one of those privacy booths at Tessa's someday. Rachel remembered Teresa was with them and she should probably keep the risqué references to a minimum. Teresa was shy and needed time to come out of her shell a bit before they brought out the bawdy humor.

"How are things at Stigall's, Teresa?" her mom asked politely. "Has business picked up much for the holidays?"

"It's fairly slow right now, which is why I was able to get this weekend off, but after Thanksgiving we'll be very busy."

The waiter returned and listed the evening's specials for them and took their orders then returned to refill their drinks.

Grace said, "Remember, Teresa, if you ever need to leave Michael with me at the house, you can," Grace said.

They'd talked Erin, Ethan's sister, into babysitting for them tonight. Erin would've liked to have gone out with them but was trying to pay her way through school and needed the cash, so had stayed home to babysit

Michael and Matthew. Michael was two and a half years old, while Matthew was two and a half months old. Having a babysitter would make it possible for them all to go shopping the next day because the moms could be completely unencumbered.

"Thank you, Grace," Teresa said, then added with a blush, "Angel also told me he could help out with Michael in the evenings if I needed him."

"What a great guy," Grace said, and Rachel noted the high color in Teresa's cheeks.

Rachel changed the subject, knowing that Teresa hated being the center of attention. They gabbed for two hours and lingered over their meal, enjoying the excellent food and service. Rudy served complimentary desserts to them himself.

After they got home, Kelly opened the box of pictures while Rachel's mom assembled the ingredients for homemade sangria, and Teresa helped her make it. Grace crooked her finger at Rachel silently and drew her down the hall.

"I had Erin put the babies in the office so I could show you something tonight without disturbing them." She paused outside of a bedroom door. "This is Ethan's bedroom, where you'll be sleeping." She motioned Rachel in and turned on the light so that Rachel could see. On the wall hung a large, tasteful, but undeniably sexy portrait of Grace dressed in a low-cut black top and high-cut black ruffled panties. The ruffled top edge of a demi-bra peeked from the low neck of the top. Otherwise, Grace was bare-legged and sporting a sassy grin in the portrait.

"Recognize that top?" Grace pointed, giggling.

"Like mine?"

"Yep. I love Hips and Curves."

"I'll bet Ethan loves this portrait. It's perfect for him," Rachel said, admiring her chutzpah for modeling barelegged.

"I modeled in clothing each of them ordered for me from there."

"Can I see the others?" Rachel asked eagerly.

Grace took her to Adam's room and showed her the picture of her curled up in the champagne-colored robe and teddy, appearing as though she were taking a nap but undisputedly sexy.

Slipping quietly across the living room, Grace led her into her old bedroom, now Jack's bedroom. There on the wall was the portrait of Grace in a pretty pink satin robe and nightgown, one sexy bare knee perched on the edge of a four-poster bed.

"I'll bet they flipped for these, Grace. They're beautiful. I've been wondering, do you think I should try and do something like this for Eli? Is there even time?"

"I talked with Carrie and Raquel this week about doing a family portrait of the four of us, and she said they had some openings. I'm sure they could fit you in, and I know they would appreciate the business. Things were slow for them this year, and their rates are reasonable. We'll call her tomorrow if you'd like."

Rachel nodded. "I think I would, very much. Thank you for showing them to me. Kelly and Mom will think they're beautiful, too. You know they love you all."

"Friends like you mean a lot to us. Do you have something sexy to model in? We could always take a look and see what's new at Hips and Curves."

Rachel chuckled and said, "I already have the perfect thing, but I want to take a look at Hips and Curves with you, anyway."

They went out into the living room to find the other three enjoying their sangrias. Grace turned on her laptop computer and pulled up the plus-size lingerie website.

"Ooooh, pretty!" Erin squealed softly, trying to be considerate of the babies she'd just left sleeping in the other room.

"Wow. That's just…wow," Rachel looked over Grace's shoulder at the computer screen.

"I know. Check her out," Grace said, pointing to a model. "See? It's all about angles. She's the same size as you, maybe a tiny bit shorter."

"Dang, she's hot! Gorgeous hair," Rachel commented, drawing her mom and Kelly's attention. Teresa rose from the couch and followed them over.

"Forget her hair, that's a great ass," Kelly said matter-of-factly. "She's plus-size?"

"You'd never know it. It's the way she carries herself. Look at this one," Grace said, navigating to another page. "Isn't that corset pretty? Yeah, those are real boobs, no silicone implants. They also have some beautiful gowns and robes. Everything I've ever bought through them has been of excellent quality. No cheap fabrics or scratchy lace, and their prices are reasonable. But I love this website because the lingerie is modeled on plus-sized models, so you can see what it will look like."

Kelly piped up and said, "Speaking of plus-sized models, *Mizz Lingerie Diva*, did you model your dress for your hunky men?"

Grace blushed and chuckled happily. "Did I ever! They loved the dress and shoes, and adored my new corset. Yep."

"That's all you're going to say?" Kelly said.

"Yep."

Kelly smirked and said, "That's *code* for they couldn't get it off of you fast enough and may have even torn some of it, isn't it?"

Rachel's mom snickered, Teresa blushed, and Rachel snorted her sangria.

"Maybe. Yep." Grace nodded seductively then giggled more. "I need sangria. Kelly, show me these precious nekkid baby pictures of Eli you've been cackling over."

Chapter Thirty-five

Rachel and the girls spent the rest of the evening looking at pictures of Eli at various ages, including the one Kelly had threatened him with. It was a black and white photograph of him at maybe one year of age. He sat on a shaded porch, dressed only in a diaper, and just as Kelly had described, he had a beatific grin on his cute little face. The garden hose was running full blast and gushing out of the front of his very swollen diaper.

There was another one taken the same day. He stood with his back to the camera, holding the hose up so that water sprayed up in the air. The waterlogged, swollen diaper was down around his chubby ankles, his plump little butt exposed as he grinned over his shoulder at whoever took the picture. Rachel laughed until she thought she might pee in her pants.

"I brought all of these pictures for both of you, Rachel, so you have them for your kids. I've already made copies of the ones I wanted to keep. Isn't that a cute little *bubble butt?*"

Kelly leafed through a stack, looking for one in particular. "There's a cute one of the two of us stuck in the bath tub together. Here it is!" She handed it to Rachel.

"Aww, look!" Rachel handed it to the others to look at.

Eli was sitting in the tub, and his hair was spiked and standing up in the requisite shampoo Mohawk. His chubby little toddler arms were wrapped around his baby sister, helping her sit up in the hip deep water. There was a soap bubble in her mouth, and both of them grinned for the camera.

"Ooh, Rachel! Look! Here's one of Eli when he was in Little League. Eli was a handsome little hunk!" Grace showed her a picture of Eli when he was twelve or thirteen in his baseball uniform. He was posed holding a bat, looking straight into the camera. His face was a preteen version of Eli, but when she looked at it, the handsome man he would one day become was clearly there, waiting to grow up. The man she loved was especially visible to her in the young boy's intense gray eyes.

"Here's one of him with his first motorcycle when he was seventeen." Kelly handed Rachel another photograph, this time of a teenaged Eli leaning up against a beat-up motorcycle. His hair was longer in this photo and more closely resembled the man he was today, tall and muscular for his age.

"Gosh, hunk is in his genes." Her mom popped her hand over her mouth. "Did I just say something inappropriate about my future son-in-law?"

Rachel rolled her eyes and laughed.

"Um, no. You said what we're all thinking." Grace snickered. "He's extremely photogenic, Rachel. I hope you have an engagement portrait taken together."

Rachel hugged her future sister-in-law. "Thank you, Kelly. I love that you did this for us. I'll always treasure these pictures."

"You're welcome. They belong to you now, part of your future kids heritage." Kelly hugged her back.

They started winding down around midnight. Grace and Rachel closed the house up and turned off most of the lights.

"I'll be up reading for a little while if you need anything, Rachel," Grace said as she made her way to the stairs.

"Is it hard for you to sleep without them, too?"

"Very. Most nights, I prefer to sleep cuddled up with all three of them," Grace said quietly. "You look like you've been sleeping better since you came home, too."

"I have been. I'm supposed to call Eli when I go to bed. He said he'd probably have trouble sleeping, too."

Grace grinned knowingly. "Well, don't let me keep you from your man. I have three texts of my own to send."

* * * *

Eli lay in bed with the light off, his phone beside him on the mattress. He could barely make out the sound of one of the other men snoring in the room next to his. He'd lucked out that the hunting lodge was large enough for almost all of them to have a room to themselves. Adam and Ethan had voluntarily roomed together. Eli's phone lit up and vibrated. He looked at it and grinned.

I found it, you naughty boy.
I'm wet. Call me if you're still awake.
R.

He dialed her cell phone number and she picked up on the first ring.

"Hello, handsome."

"Hello, angel."

"That was a sweet thing you did, slipping that little silver egg vibrator into my luggage. I found the black lace nightgown and robe in the suitcase, too. You're thorough as well as thoughtful."

"Did it feel good slipping into that nightgown?"

"I don't have it on yet."

"Are you ready for bed?"

"Uh-huh," she replied softly.

"Are you nekkid?" he asked in a husky whisper.

"For you, yes."

"Are you under the covers?"

"Yes," she replied silkily, and he could hear her sheets rustling. "How are you? Were you asleep?"

"No, I couldn't. I need you to sleep," he replied softly, missing her warmth and her scent next to him.

"Maybe I can help," she said softly. "So you were already in bed, under the covers?"

"Yeah."

"Pajamas?"

His cock twitched. "No. I brought them in case we bunked together, but we all have our own rooms. This lodge is huge." He was thankful because he hated sleeping clothed.

"Oh," she said in an achingly soft voice. "Are you hard, Eli?" The tone of her sexy voice made his cock twitch.

"Very, angel. Your voice does that to me," he murmured. He thought he dimly heard the sound of a phone ringing somewhere in the cabin but didn't hear it again.

"You know what I'd do right now if I was there?" Her seductive voice sent a wave of shivers down his spine to his cock as he imagined it.

"Tell me, angel."

"I'd wet my lips with my tongue, slide your big, hard cock into my mouth, and suck and lick you until you were panting. Are you stroking your cock yet?"

"I am now." He reached down and stroked his tingling, rock-hard length, and groaned. "Do you have the egg with you, angel?"

"Yes," she answered shakily.

"Are you nice and wet for me? Throbbing and aching for me?" he asked.

"You know I am, Eli. I wish you could touch me."

"That's why the egg was in your luggage. Pretend it's my fingers, and later it'll be my tongue. That's why I sent it with you. Turn it on and put it over your clit." He listened as she did as he asked, and she whimpered at the sudden stimulation. His shaft throbbed and wept a translucent tear at the sound of her arousal.

"Good, angel. Does it feel nice?"

"It's torture, Eli. I'm so wet it keeps slipping," she said with a soft, sexy chuckle. He wished it was his tongue that was doing the slipping.

"Mmm, my angel *is* good and wet."

"Y–yes. Are you stroking your incredible, thick cock for me? Can you imagine me sucking the head for you? I want to climb on top and suck your cock while you lick my pussy. Would you like some sixty-nine with me?"

"I'd pull you down on my face and lick you till you came, screaming my name." Eli imagined the feel and taste of her sweet pussy pressed against his face while she sucked his cock. "I'd lick your little pussy until my face was coated with your honey."

"Oooh, baby, I can almost feel that warm tongue of yours." He heard her moan low and soft.

"Are you stroking your clit yet?"

"Uh-huh," she whimpered softly.

"Slip that little silver egg just inside, between your sweet little pink lips. Pretend that's my tongue, angel. Feel it?" he asked in a strained, guttural voice.

Rachel did as he asked, and the sound of her soft whimpers increased. He could hear her rapid breathing. She sounded like she was already close to coming.

"Oh, Eli. I want you so much." She panted softly, trying to catch her breath. "After I'm done licking you, I think I want to turn and straddle those lean hips of yours. I want to stroke your hard cock with my wet pussy and just slide back and forth over you and get you wet with my juices. Do you want that, Eli?"

"I want all of you, yes," he hissed, straining against the mattress. "But I'm going to take hold of your pretty curvaceous hips and lift you onto my cock."

"Oh," she whimpered softly. Rachel sounded like she'd increased her stroking, and he groaned in response as he stroked his cock harder.

"Then I'd watch the head of my cock part your soft, wet, hot lips and slowly push into your sweet, lush pussy."

"Oh," she keened softly, "I feel you, Eli, sliding into me!"

He imagined it probably made her even hotter to have to be so quiet.

He groaned as he flexed his hips. "Then, *oh, god,* then I'd sink my shaft into your hot, tight little pussy nice...and...sl–slow. Oh, babe, are you close?" he asked, growling as he stroked his stiff cock firmly now, feeling his balls drawing up tight, ready to explode with his release.

"Mmm...Yes!" she gasped, sounding like she was ready to come. Her voice had that soft euphoric sound that told him she was just about there.

"Then I'd flip you on your back, lift your sexy, long legs high and pump into you nice and slow. I'd wait until you begged me to fuck you harder and faster. Then I'd give you *exactly* what you begged me for and fuck you until you screamed."

He could hear Rachel's sudden high-pitched exhalation. "Eli! I'm coming, I'm..." She panted softly as her orgasm overtook her, moaning low into the phone.

He fisted his cock and stroked twice more. "Then I'd fill your tight pussy with my cum until you overflowed with it. Oh, angel. Yes!" His voice shook slightly as he came into his hand and on his belly, catching it with a hand towel he'd packed for this purpose, not wanting to explain the mess later. "Oh, angel." He groaned, lying there panting for a minute, listening to her soft breath sounds as she recovered.

"Eli?" she said with a breathy sigh that brought a grin to his face. It was the sound of his woman, satisfied. He heard her shifting around a little, removing and turning off the vibrator, he guessed.

"Are you all right, angel?"

"Yes, Eli, and you?"

"The only thing missing that would make this perfect is if you were cuddled next to me now, trying to catch your breath and holding on to me. That would make this perfect."

"Yeah." She sighed contentedly. "I've never had phone sex before."

"That was my first time, too." He chuckled.

She laughed softly. "Aw, we were virgins."

"Are you flushing all over?" he asked, knowing that was a sign she'd come good and hard for him.

"Yes, I just felt it spread over my cheeks and my breasts. Mmm." She sounded like she was stretching, and the sheets rustled again. "You're the best, Eli."

"Thank you. Same goes for you, angel. Did you have fun looking at all my embarrassing baby pictures?"

"Oh, they were adorable, Eli! You were a precious little baby. I loved them all, including the one with the water hose."

"Ugh! Which was your favorite?"

"Honestly? The one of you when you were seventeen with your first motorcycle. But that's not a baby picture, I suppose. Probably the one of you sitting in your highchair coated in spaghetti sauce and chocolate pudding. I'll bet your mom had to scrub you hard to get that mess off of you."

Eli laughed. "Yeah, see what you have to look forward to, angel?"

"I'd love to have a baby boy or girl that looks like you, Eli. With your gray eyes and black hair."

"As long as I get a little angel who looks like her mommy, too. I miss you. Will you be able to sleep?"

"I have a better chance of sleeping now than I did before your call. I hope I can stay asleep. I miss you, too, Eli."

"I'd stroke your soft back if I was there. And tickle you with my fingertips just the way you like."

"I love it when you do that." She yawned, he noticed with satisfaction.

"I love it when you moan when I find the right spot above your tailbone."

"Mmm. You know right where it is, too," she replied languidly.

"You have your nightgown nearby?"

"Yes, it's on the chair by the bed."

"Why don't you put down the phone and slip into it and climb back into bed?"

"All right, honey. Hold on." She did as he asked, and he smiled when he heard her sigh contentedly as the heavy satin slid over her skin. She picked up the phone after she got back into bed, sighing happily. "Okay, I'm tucked in."

"Damn. Listening to you sigh like that makes me wish I was there. After you hang up, imagine the gown is me wrapped around you, snuggling you close to me, all right?"

"You were so thoughtful and romantic to pack this. Are you getting sleepy?"

He folded the towel up and used it to clean up a bit, laid it aside to take care of later, then slid back between the quickly cooling sheets. "Yeah, I think I probably could. I'll let you go on to sleep, angel. One thing?"

"Yes?"

"Press your index finger and middle finger to your lips for me?"

"Okay?"

"Good. That kiss is from me. Now put it wherever you want it." He chuckled at her soft giggle.

"Mmm, done," she said softly. "Guess where."

"Mmm. Someplace I plan on kissing a lot when I get you alone, angel. I love you."

"I love you, Eli. Goodnight."

Eli ended the call and placed the phone on the table by the bed. He gazed out the window opposite the bed and watched the stars twinkle. He could almost feel her soft, warm skin under his fingertips and smell her unique womanly scent. He rolled to his side and pulled the other pillow close to him and tried to fall asleep.

* * * *

Rachel and Grace were the first ones up the next morning. Grace made a pot of coffee, and Rachel joined her out on the back porch. The morning breeze had a slight chill to it, so they sat in their robes enjoying their coffee and a quiet conversation. Grace asked her if she'd managed to sleep last night.

"Yes, I slept well after I talked to Eli. It was good to hear his voice," she replied softly, her cheeks heating a little at the memory.

Grace chuckled knowingly. "Yeah, the *sound of Jack's voice* helped me sleep, too."

"You didn't talk to Ethan and Adam?"

"Oh, yes. I talked to all of them. This is the first time I've been apart from all three of them overnight. I couldn't sleep if I didn't hear their voices first, but Jack and I got to have a *little chat* last night. I slept well after we hung up, but I still missed them." She smiled at Rachel, blushing at her euphemisms. "We can call Carrie and Raquel later if you want."

"That sounds great. I'd like to get together with them soon if they have any openings."

"I'm sure they could work that out."

"How are the wedding plans coming for you and Kelly?"

"Great! Everything is coming together nicely, and your dad's budget has been easy to work with. He's a real peach to throw you a nice wedding like this."

"My dad's a sweetheart. He's a tough guy on the outside, with a warm, gooey filling on the inside, where me and my mom are concerned."

Later that morning, all the ladies climbed into Rachel's new truck and went with her to Clay Cook's to order Eli's wedding ring. The girls browsed the display cases with her mom while Rachel and Clay talked about Eli's ring and Clay took down her inscription. Rachel complimented Clay on the beautiful workmanship of Grace's wedding ring, for which he thanked her with a shy, warm smile. While they finished up, Grace stepped outside to make a phone call.

A few minutes later, she stepped back into the door of Clay's shop and crooked her finger at Rachel. "Carrie and Rachel's afternoon photo shoot had to reschedule on them. Do you want to run out to Morehead today and take some sexy portraits?"

Rachel was shocked but jumped eagerly at the opportunity. "But what about the others?"

Grace shrugged and grinned broadly. "They'll have a blast. Maybe we can talk them into posing for portraits, too."

"If they're game, I am, too!"

Rachel thanked Clay then said, "All right, ladies, here's the deal..."

Five minutes later, they were in the truck driving back to the ranch to pick up lingerie and then out of town.

As she buckled up, Kelly said, "That Clay Cook is a cutie pie."

Grace giggled. "I know. He's gorgeous with his blond hair and green eyes. So far, he's resisted my efforts to match make for him. I think he's rather shy."

"I got that impression, too. But he's very handsome," Kelly said appreciatively.

"That he is! I haven't given up yet. Just have to find the right girl to introduce him to." Rachel noticed Grace turn and wink at Teresa in the back seat and then heard Teresa chuckle.

Two hours later, after a light lunch, Rachel found herself dressed in her black lace nightgown and robe. Raquel carefully applied more eye shadow and eyeliner, giving her a smoky-eyed look, and then she helped Rachel pose seductively for the camera.

"Aren't you going to change and let me shoot you, too?" Carrie asked speculatively, eyeing the garment bag Grace had brought with her.

"Twist my arm, why don't you?" Grace laughed, rifling through it, looking for the perfect outfit.

Rachel's mom had a beautiful portrait made with her daughter as well as a sexy one with a feather boa and dark red lipstick for her father.

Kelly and Teresa were excited to have a portrait taken, as well. Teresa had loosened up and gotten into all the fun but blushed beet red at seeing Rachel and Grace dressed only in lingerie.

While her mom, Kelly, and Teresa took a break and got something to drink and snack on in the waiting room, Rachel allowed Grace and the two photographers to persuade her into posing for a very tasteful nude.

After they were done, Grace was excited, both over Rachel's enthusiastic approach to this endeavor but also over the nudes she did for her men, as well. Carrie assured them she'd call when they were all ready. They left the photography studio energized and euphoric.

"Am I high?" Rachel giggled as they headed down the highway farther into Morehead.

"It's endorphins, Rachel," Grace replied, fixing her lipstick and powdering her nose. "Stretching out of your comfort zone like that releases endorphins in your system, plus you feel beautiful because you've been dolled up and had professional portraits taken. You'll sleep like a baby tonight." She winked then pulled out her cell phone and sent a text, most likely to one of her men, as Rachel drove them to the large shopping mall in Morehead. Grace's phone vibrated in her hand. Looking at the display, she started giggling. "Oh, my goodness!"

"What is it?" her mom asked from the back seat.

"The great white hunters are scoring big time," Grace said. "They're already planning a pig roast and bonfire next weekend. It's a good thing we have big deep freezers, girls. We're going to need them. Don't worry, Kelly and Teresa, we're gonna keep you stocked to the eyeballs. Rachel, Adam says Eli bagged one that has to be at least four hundred pounds!"

Rachel's mouth popped open at that announcement, and then she grinned big. "Yeah, pan sausage!"

"Adam says they are hunting right now and that everyone has already gotten at least one decent-sized hog, some of them two. I wonder how they're planning to get all that home."

Her mother supplied the answer. "Allen has a flat bed trailer he's letting them use. They'll probably take whatever they kill today to a nearby processor and pick up the meat later. He's anxious to get those off his property. They moved in the last few years, and the population of white tail deer started dropping off. Plus, they've cause a lot of property damage."

"It sounds like they are definitely going to need that trailer," Grace replied, and then her phone buzzed again. "Adam says we should come up with them next time. They all have their own rooms, and the lodge is nice." The phone vibrated again in her hand, and she looked down to read the message and chuckled softly.

"What does he say?" Teresa leaned forward.

"Oh, that he loves me and couldn't live without me." Grace sighed breathily, to which she received a chorus of, "Aww."

"What exactly are they going to do with the pigs they bring home?" Kelly asked, as if the thought of dead animals hanging around the house had just occurred to her.

"They'll send them immediately to a processor," Renata replied. "Peter stopped bringing his kills home when Rachel was in college. I couldn't stand the stench and the gore anymore. Have you ever had wild pig before, Kelly?"

"I don't think so."

Rachel glanced at Kelly in the rearview mirror. "Honey, you are in for a treat. Do you think you can come back next weekend?"

"I'd already planned on it. I'm here more than I'm home on the weekends, it seems like," Kelly said with a laugh.

"Does your husband mind very much?" Rachel asked.

"No. He's encouraged me to spend time here with you when I can. Chris worries about me at home alone so much. He knows how much I enjoy being with you all and that I'm having fun with Grace, planning your wedding."

"Good, because we love having you and little Matthew," her mom said. "He travels so well, and he's the most easygoing a baby I've ever met."

Grace's phone buzzed again, and she chuckled softly but didn't say anything.

"I'm nosey," Kelly said. "Who's that from?"

"Jack."

"What's he say?"

Grace gazed at the screen. "It was for my eyes only," she replied with a soft, blushing smile. The others chuckled knowingly. Grace texted back and forth for a couple of minutes with him then sighed dreamily. "He's so romantic. He said they would all call us tonight."

At the mall, Grace and Kelly split from the group, in need of some time together to purchase reception decorations. Rachel handed Grace the keys to the Tundra, and they started off. Rachel, her mom, and Teresa went to have a little snack in the food court. The mall was decorated festively for Christmas already, and Rachel wondered out loud what the wedding decorations would look like.

"Well, judging by what I've heard Kelly and Grace say, it's going to be festive and colorful," her mom replied. "They are using a varied color palette, including the blue from their dresses. I always hoped you'd want to get married at home, out in the pavilion."

"I used to dream about it when I was little. I told Grace about some of my imaginings as a child, and she got a twinkle in her eye, which means she's got a little something up her sleeve. I'm so grateful I have two friends who love to plan things like this," Rachel said with a chuckle. "Where were they going, anyway?"

"We can't tell you, Rachel," Teresa said, grinning. "We were instructed to help you find a pair of warm, waterproof boots and a heavy winter coat, plus everything to go with it—hat, goggles, gloves, scarf, and thermal underwear. Whatever you want or need for being outdoors in the cold were Eli's instructions."

They took her to an outfitter in the mall and set her up with a heavy waterproof and insulated jacket in the hottest pink Rachel had ever seen.

"Grace will be pleased!" Teresa said, chuckling when Rachel tried it on.

They found a beautiful imitation fur hat that matched the fur that lined the hood on her jacket. Her snow boots were warm and comfy inside, and most importantly, insulated and waterproof. They found socks and silk thermal underwear at a great price, so she was able to get several pairs.

Several hours later, as it drew close to suppertime, they met Grace and Kelly, who now had the back of the Tundra loaded with sealed boxes.

Rachel yelped when she saw the stacks. "Dang, Grace! What have you been up to?"

"You'll see in four weeks." Grace snickered as she popped Rachel's hand when she tried to lift the flap on a box. "Absolutely no peeking. You'll see when it's time. How'd you do finding your coat, boots and other stuff?"

Kelly clapped her hands happily. "We lucked out and found lots of great deals and saved Eli a lot of money shopping the sales."

"Good, then we're done here. It's suppertime, and we have girls' night reservations," Grace announced happily.

Rachel looked in the bed of the truck. "What about the boxes?"

"Don't worry. Where we're going they'll be fine," Grace replied.

Grace directed her to a country road on the outskirts of Morehead. Rachel saw the restaurant tucked back amidst the trees and gasped happily when she saw the diminutive sign. "You're taking us to *Tessa's*?"

Chapter Thirty-six

Rachel looked over at Grace and arched an eyebrow, the question in her mind answered as they all squealed in unison, "Surprise!"

Grace laughed. "This is your lingerie shower, Rachel! There's a small party room reserved for us."

Rachel parked and noticed two other cars were pulling in next to them. Rosemary Piper and Charity Conners jumped out and crowed, "Surprise!" They all climbed out of the Tundra, laughing and hugging.

"Happy bridal shower!" Charity cackled, giving her a big hug. She opened her trunk and removed a large, heavy looking gift bag from the interior. Rosemary hugged her, too, looking particularly radiant and happy.

Grace said, "Come on. Tessa has a special room all set up for us."

Rachel noticed that Grace and the others weren't carrying anything. Grace really was a planner. Tessa greeted them at the door, hugged Grace and welcomed then all graciously. She was supermodel tall and gorgeous, but had an easy openness to her that was refreshing, not haughty at all. She sauntered down a dimly lit hall and led them to a small, intimate dining room. Candles and festive decorations, which perfectly blended the holiday season and the romance of a wedding, adorned the table as well as the antique sideboard and buffet.

"Tessa, it's perfect," Grace commented. "Thanks for all your help."

"You're welcome. I'll step out and send your servers in to you. They're the best. Enjoy," she murmured before excusing herself.

Gaily wrapped presents were arranged artfully on the buffet, to which Charity and Rosemary added theirs.

Rachel gestured to the decorations and gifts. "How did you..."

"We set this up in advance. The men dropped everything off for me yesterday after they left."

"So Eli knows about this?"

"Oh, yes, honey. We have his full knowledge and blessing. There may even be a surprise or two there because the men knew in advance what we were doing. As you've discovered, our men are just as adept at buying gifts as we are," Grace said with a chuckle. "Come sit, so we can get started."

Grace glanced over Rachel's shoulder and smiled mischievously. Rachel sat down in the chair Grace indicated and looked up into the clearest, greenest eyes she'd ever seen.

"Good evening. I'm Paul. I'll be one of your servers this evening."

As he assisted the ladies in seating themselves, Paul shared the list of culinary offerings for the evening. Bless their hearts, Rachel didn't think any of the women heard what he said. Paul was not merely handsome, he was…celestially handsome, a wondrous spectacle of masculine beauty. He had tousled, shoulder-length blond hair, beautiful green eyes, high cheek bones, and a nose that looked like it had been chiseled by Michelangelo's own hand. He had wonderful full, kissable lips and a *sexy-as-freaking-hell* soul patch below his lower lip. He was dressed in cowboy boots, blue jeans, and an untucked white dress shirt, which he had not bothered to button all the way up.

Guiltily, Rachel noticed her mouth was watering as she looked at him. He took their barely coherent drink orders. A couple of them switched to alcoholic drink orders midway through the process. When he strode from the room, Rachel could have heard a pin drop to the floor.

Kelly broke the silence. "Hot. Holy. Hell. Is he for *real*? Is he a waiter? Grace, is he a *stripper* you hired, pretending to be a waiter?"

Grace chortled happily. "You know our men, right? Strippers we don't need. That, dear hearts, is Tessa's younger brother, Paul. Isn't he positively luscious? He's a chef here, but for this special occasion, he was willing to serve us personally from the kitchen while the other chefs pick up the slack. He *and* his brother, Peter, will be serving us tonight."

"He has a brother?" Renata asked incredulously.

Grace grinned crookedly. "Mmm-hmm. And it gets even better." She paused for effect, waiting to be asked how.

"How could it get any better? Did you see those beautiful green eyes?" Kelly sighed.

"Paul and Peter are…*twins*."

"Oh, no. Oh, yes...oh, *boy!*" Charity whispered as both handsome men entered the room carrying their drinks.

"Hello, ladies. I'm Peter. I'll be helping my brother serve you tonight. Can I suggest an appetizer?"

Grace and Charity glanced at each other and Rachel, who grinned then felt her cheeks grow hot at their knowing smiles.

Grace turned to him and said, "Good evening, Peter. I think Rachel would enjoy your *shrimp cocktail*. I've been craving one, too. How does that sound, ladies?" At their assenting nods, Grace turned back to him and murmured, "A large shrimp cocktail?"

Paul left the room to turn in the order while Peter reiterated the evening's selection. He took their individual orders and then added, "The bakery delivered the cake, Mrs. Warner. As you requested, we haven't cut it but will wait for word from you. I'll turn in your order, and please don't hesitate to page either of us if you need anything at all. We're at your beck and call this evening," he said with a crooked little grin, "and we'll be right down the hall in the kitchen."

He leaned forward and handed Grace a small black cell phone, kissed her hand, then did the same for Rachel. "It's always a pleasure to see you again, Mrs. Warner," Paul added then excused himself.

They sat at the table, in shock for a moment. "They're so pretty they make my eyes hurt," Charity said.

"Exactly how often do you come here, *Mrs. Warner?*" Rosemary asked with a snicker.

"Her men spoil her rotten and bring her here at least *once a month*," Charity butted in.

"Wow," Teresa said softly. Everyone's attention turned to her. She burst out laughing, and they all laughed with her.

"Yeah, *wow*," Rachel agreed.

"Well, let's get started, shall we? They'll let me know before they bring anything else." Grace rose from her chair and went to the buffet. Touching this gift and that with a well-manicured fingertip, she lifted a square box wrapped gaily in blue paper with a frilly bow. She placed the gift in front of Rachel. "Why not start with your beautiful mom's gift?"

Rachel smiled at her mom and blew her an air kiss. She tore open the paper, lifted the lid, and gasped. From the box, she lifted a pair of high-heeled platform slides with clear acrylic heels. The first of many risqué giggles rippled around the room. She lifted out another tissue-wrapped package. The tissue revealed a filmy red babydoll nightie and matching G-string.

"Thank you, Mom! Wow!"

"I was shopping for a granny gown to keep you warm, and Grace suggested something more fun that might inspire *Eli* to keep you warm." Her mother laughed when Rachel gave her a goggle-eyed look and felt her cheeks heat up.

"Mom! This is a side of you I've never seen before! I like it! I love the nightie. Thank you." She would never have imagined her mother buying her sexy lingerie.

Grace placed another gift in front of her and passed the heels and babydoll nightie around to the others to see. "This is from Teresa."

Rachel smiled at Teresa, glad to know this demure friend of Grace's. They'd had a few chances to get to know each other since Grace's wedding and Rachel had visited with her on several occasions at Stigall's. Teresa once commented to Rachel that she appreciated her involvement in protecting Grace from Patricia. That confrontation hastened Patricia's expulsion from Angel's life, which was an added bonus for Teresa.

Rachel opened the gift and the women cooed over the sheer black mesh and lace gown, robe, and thong panty. "That's beautiful, Teresa, thank you so much."

Everyone commented appreciatively on how diaphanous it was. Rachel wondered what Eli would think of the sheerness and had a pretty good guess.

"You're welcome, Rachel," Teresa replied, smiling back at her.

"Kelly's is next," Grace said, placing it in front of her.

Rachel grinned at her tiny friend and future sister-in-law. Inside the gift-wrapped box was a pretty royal-blue satin nightie. It had a drawstring opening at the deep V-neck, and the sides were crisscrossing satin strings which held the front and back together, waiting to be untied. Inside was also a matching long, blue satin robe with flowing sleeves. The slithery fabric slipped and slid over itself as she lifted it from the box with a soft sigh.

"Gorgeous!" Her mom said as she stroked the silky fabric.

The phone Peter had handed to Grace vibrated on the table. She checked it and texted back then took her seat after she placed the opened gifts back on the buffet.

"Paul is bringing the shrimp cocktails now," she said moments before their lovely waiter tapped on the door and entered, carrying a tray.

After serving them, he refilled their drinks and took orders for refills on their cocktails. They chatted while they waited for him to return. "Your entrees will be ready in twenty to thirty minutes, Mrs. Warner. We'll let you know and wait to hear from you."

Grace thanked him, and he excused himself quietly. Grace rose again from the table and returned with another wrapped gift. "This is from Rosemary."

Rachel tore off the paper and lifted the lid, then opened the tissue. Momentarily puzzled, she lifted the delicate strips of fabric from the box and found the picture label that had been attached to the lingerie. "I can honestly say I've never seen anything like this. Wow, would you look at that?"

"Do you like it?" Rosemary asked uncertainly.

"I love it, but I can tell you Eli will absolutely *flip* for it. He loves a good mystery. I'm going to wear this under an outfit and let him wonder all evening." She lifted it up and passed the card around so they could see it.

It was a silky spandex chemise that could be worn four different ways. Forward, backward, upside down to the front and upside down to the back, strapless or with shoulder straps. It was a series of clingy straps and strategic cutouts that revealed curves but strategically hid or revealed other parts depending on which way it was worn.

Charity handled it. "Oh, yeah! If I know Eli, he will totally flip for this. Keep that card, Rachel, so you can wear it a different way every time and keep him guessing. I think I need one of these. Where did you find it, Rosie?"

"Oh, this great website, maybe you've heard of it? Hips and—"

"—curves.com?" Grace, Rachel, and Charity all laughed outrageously.

"That's the one! I *love* their lingerie!"

"We do, too!" Grace chuckled and handed Rachel another gift to open while the girls tucked the picture card back in with the chemise in its box and passed it around. This one was two boxes tied together. She opened the smaller box first and giggled in delight when she found a butter-soft front-lacing leather corset in it.

"Ooooh! That is *awesome!*" Kelly said. "I'll bet you get a lot of use from that. Eli loves that biker babe stuff! That's perfect for you, Rachel."

"See, it zips up the back, but you can tighten the laces in the front. It's a lot less work for you than reaching behind you to tie laces, and he can get you out of it in a hot second if he wants to," Grace said. "Look at what else is in there."

Rachel lifted out a leather throat collar with a large silver ring attached to the front of it, and all the women giggled uproariously. She laughed and unbuckled it then slipped it around her neck. It was thick but softly lined. She could not hide the pleasure she had at the thought of wearing it for Eli as her cheeks heated up. Laughing softly, Rachel thanked Grace for it, trying to not betray how much she *really* liked it. Her mom was in attendance, after all. No point going there. Rachel looked at Grace, and Grace spoke up for her.

"I'm sorry, Renata. The gifts kind of degenerate from this point," Grace said with a grin.

Rachel's mom batted her hands and said, "Oh, don't, Grace. I'm having so much fun. I'm a little more *liberated* than my daughter knows. Don't worry that you will shock me. Let me see that, Rachel. Is it lined? Oh! That's nice and soft." She rubbed her thumb on the lining.

Grace exchanged a relieved look with Rachel.

Rachel opened the larger box and found a truly kinky pair of high, chunky-heeled, black patent platform lace up boots. "Oooh! Hot mama! Look at these!"

Laughter erupted around the table when she lifted it out of the box.

Grace brought Charity's gift to Rachel and sat the gift bag in front of her. "This is from Charity. Guaranteed to be *adult eyes only*, if I know my sister!" She giggled and then added, "And we love you for it, sis."

Rachel reached into the bag and pulled out a...feather duster? Only, the duster was small.

At Rachel's confused look, Charity snickered and said, "It's a tickler. Keep digging. Eli is going to thank me." Rachel lifted out a bundle of red satin. She unfolded them and looked at Charity in confusion. "Those are eight-foot-long bondage sashes for Eli to *tie you up* with." Charity grinned as all the ladies giggled and Rachel's cheeks turned red hot.

The last thing in the bag was a pretty, black butter-soft miniskirt with zippers that ran down the front seams to the hem, and a matching leather G-string. "They will match that corset and those boots perfectly, don't you think? Then you'll have a complete outfit. Here's something else from me and Grace," Charity added the last part in a whisper and slipped her a gift card envelope.

Charity being discreet? Surreal.

Rachel peeked in the envelope and understood. It was a one hundred dollar gift card to a popular online sex toy website. She smiled at Grace and Charity, and they winked at her. She didn't pass that one around for the others to see. She caught Grace's wink at Kelly and realized the elf knew about it, too. She slipped the envelope in her purse at her feet.

The phone at Grace's seat buzzed. She looked at the display. "Our entrees are ready. Let's go ahead and eat, and then we'll finish afterward." She replied quickly to the text.

Rachel looked around the table. "Thank you so much for the beautiful gifts. I love all of them, and you know Eli will appreciate them as well," she said to a chorus of risqué laughter.

"You're welcome, Rachel." Grace gestured to the buffet, where several gifts sat waiting to be opened. "But you're not done yet."

"Huh?" She looked around the room and remembered opening every woman's gift. She looked up at Grace questioningly.

"Those are from some people who could not attend today since this is a *ladies* only event," Grace said as Peter and Paul tapped on the door and entered with laden trays. The handsome men made conversation as they solicitously served each lady her plate and refilled her water or tea glass.

"Mrs. Warner, will you page us when you're ready for the cake? We have it set out for you." Peter said.

"Thank you. I'll page you when we're ready for it, Peter. Thank you, Paul. We appreciate your special attention tonight."

"Thank you, Mrs. Warner," they murmured and sauntered from the room.

They enjoyed the excellent cuisine and talked about the wedding plans. They also teased Rachel about the variety of gifts she'd received and speculated on which ones would get the most use. She took all the ribbing good-naturedly, giving as good as she got where she could.

"Peter and Paul prepared our entrees themselves." Grace chuckled when they all smiled and got that dreamy look again.

At the ladies' eager urging, Grace paged them both to return and clear the table. Once again, they flirted outrageously as they worked. The women talked and laughed with the handsome men until everything was removed from the table and they left once again.

Grace laughed when Kelly released a disappointed sigh and asked, "Is there anything else they can come back for?"

"Oh, don't worry. They'll be back," Grace said with an indulgent smile. "Why don't we see what else is here?" She returned to the buffet, bringing Rachel a small, prettily wrapped box.

"Before you open these, Jack, Ethan, and Adam wanted me to tell you something. Over the years, they've always held you and your family in the highest esteem and value your friendship to them, but especially to me. They appreciate the way you defended me with Patricia, but also Eli's quick thinking in handling her the night of the shooting."

Grace paused for a second, perhaps reliving that night, before continuing, "Our lives would be very different if it were not for your friendship, Rachel. You're family, and we love you. These gifts are a small token of friendship for both you and Eli. Why don't you open Adam's first and let's see what it is."

Tears stung her eyes as Rachel picked at the pretty paper. She hugged Grace as she handed her a tissue, and Rachel opened the gift. Sniffling a little herself, Grace rose and brought two more small presents to the table.

Rachel lifted the lid on the box and gasped at the gift inside. Lifting it from the box, she looked at Grace.

Her friend said, "I helped him pick it out. It's a slave bracelet. You wear it on your upper arm." The heavy silver bracelet was a series of interlocking flourishes. It reminded Rachel a lot of the design of her engagement ring, which she held up to it.

"Clay made this?"

"Yep. Want to see if it fits?"

"Thank you." Rachel held it out to Grace to open and then lifted her sleeve. Grace opened a hidden catch and demonstrated how to adjust it at the hinge before closing it on Rachel's upper arm. "It's beautiful, Grace. Thank you. Make sure and tell him I love it."

Rachel unwrapped Ethan's gift. Inside was a bracelet made of the same heavy silver, only the flourishes were made into linking sections so it had more flexibility. It, too, was adjustable, which Grace showed her as she put it on her ankle. She modeled it for all of them and thanked Grace again.

She opened Jack's gift when Grace handed it to her. Inside was a pair of beautiful, intricate chandelier earrings done in the same intertwined flourish pattern, silver teardrops dangling in a row across the bottom edge of each one.

"Wow, Grace. I'm overwhelmed," Rachel said shakily, feeling like a ninny for being so emotional. "You didn't have to do this for me."

"Well, it would have been weird for them to buy you *lingerie*, right?" Grace snickered, trying to make light of the extravagance of her men's gifts. "You have one more gift to open though, sweetie. See?" She gestured again to the buffet, where a large, flat, wrapped package lay all by itself.

"Who's that from?" Rachel asked curiously

Grace retrieved the heavy box and laid it in Rachel's lap. She lifted the small envelope from the package and removed the card.

For the woman I've been dreaming of.
Love, Eli

After a few seconds, she read it out loud.

The ladies all exclaimed in unison. "Aww!"

She tore the paper from the box and lifted the lid. Inside was a sexy, black leather riding jacket. She lifted the jacket out, and they all cooed again. The jacket had fringe across the chest and the back and down the arms. Above each breast and in the center of the back was a pretty red rose inlay.

"Try it on," Charity said excitedly.

Rachel slipped out of the lightweight cardigan she'd put on to protect her from the evening chill. The fragrant leather jacket hugged her curves perfectly.

Grace pointed to the sides and the center of the lower back and said, "Look, it has drawstrings here and here so you can adjust the fit. How does it feel?"

"Like a dream. It's so soft inside."

Grace grinned and sent a message to their hot waiters. "I think it's time for cake, don't you?"

"I'd settle for another look at those handsome waiters," Teresa said then popped her hand over her mouth. "I said that out loud, didn't I? You're rubbing off on me!"

Paul and Peter returned with a beautifully decorated little bakery cake and cake plates and silverware. "Miss Lopez, aren't you a lovely sight in that leather jacket? If you weren't off the market, Paul and I might fight over which of us could persuade you to climb on the back of our Harleys."

"You're *both* bikers?" Charity asked, and then said unabashedly, "They are perfect, Grace."

"Perfect gentlemen, yes." Grace thanked Peter as he handed her the silverware and serving utensils.

"I don't know about perfect, but we both do ride in this area. It looks like we might run into at least one of you on a ride, maybe two? Do you ride, too, Miss…" Paul asked cheekily of Charity.

"Charity. Yes, I ride with my husband all the time."

"Maybe we'll see you around sometime. Mrs. Warner, are you sure you don't want me to cut and serve it for you?" Peter gestured to the serving knife.

At their eager looks, Grace said, "We—Yes, I'd like you to both stay and cut the cake and serve it. If you have time, that is. I know the restaurant must be busy right now."

"Tessa prides herself on the fact that we offer more than just the best food, but that our service is also exceptional. The kitchen is well staffed, and we are here to serve you," Peter replied as Grace handed him the serving knife.

He deftly cut the cake while Paul refilled their glasses and helped him get the cake on plates, which he then served to each woman.

Rachel picked up her fork, and her mouth watered from the luscious scent of it before the bite was even in her mouth. It was absolutely delicious.

"I love this cake."

"Good," Grace said. "If you like it, I'll be ordering it for your wedding cake."

"I knew there was a reason I put you both in charge of this stuff. This is wonderful."

After the ladies had been served and there was nothing else for them to do, Peter and Paul thanked Grace for asking them to serve her friends. They both kissed Rachel's knuckles and Grace's, as well, and wished Rachel good luck with her wedding plans.

After they'd left the room, Charity turned to Grace. "Wow. Just wow. You topped yourself, sis."

The others agreed.

Chapter Thirty-seven

It was almost ten o'clock by the time Rachel parked the Tundra in front of Grace's home. Rachel tried the whole leather outfit on for them, and Grace and Charity snapped pictures. Grace sent a picture e-mail to Eli's phone. While Rachel changed out of the outfit, her phone buzzed with an incoming text. She smiled as she unzipped her boot and reached for the phone to look at the display.

I love seeing you in leather.
I can't decide if I want you to straddle my bike, or me!
Call me as soon as you're alone.
Love you like crazy.

She started to put her clothes back on but thought better of it. She snapped a picture first and then sent it with a short text, giggling deviously.

Hiya, sexy! Did you eat yet?
Delete this picture after you enjoy it, pleeeeease!
Love you like crazy!

* * * *

The men sat on the back porch around the fire pit drinking a beer. Eli had propped his feet up on the porch rail and tilted his chair back on two legs. His phone buzzed back, and he smiled, expecting a text from his pretty woman. He grinned and lifted it to eye level. He did a double take and choked on his beer. He lost his balance and fell backward in the chair. All the men jumped up and laughed, telling him he'd had one too many. He stared at the display screen of his phone and grinned.

"Bet me it's a nekkid pic," Adam said to Ethan, grinning.

"Hey, her father is right over there!" Eli shushed him and pointed at Peter, who stood by the porch rail talking with Elijah. He looked one more time at the picture and grinned.

"Yep," Adam offered a hand to help him up, "nekkid pics." He snickered softly.

* * * *

Two minutes later, Rachel giggled happily when she received a picture of Eli's handsome face with his eyes bulging out and a two word text.

Dayum, baby!

"Yep." She chuckled as she zipped up her jeans.

When she came out of the bedroom, she found the others piled on the couches in the living room, watching *Braveheart*.

"Aren't you exhausted?" she asked as she came in the living room and stood beside Grace, who sat on the couch.

"We got our second wind and decided we had enough energy to take on William Wallace," she said with a pathetic Scottish accent. *"Ooh, yes, I'll marry ye, William."*

Rachel yawned. "I'm going to take a shower and go to bed."

"Okay, we love you, sweetie. Enjoy your phone sex!" Kelly called as Rachel left the room. She poked her head back in the living room.

"Hey, that's my mom sitting next to you!"

"That's okay, honey. I may call your father later," her mom said with a snorting laugh.

With her fingertips in her ears, Rachel hollered, "Lalalalala! I can't hear you! Thanks again, ladies. For everything," she added with another yawn.

Kelly yawned with her. "Poor thing, we wore her out."

After her shower, Rachel dressed in her black nightgown, climbed into bed and cuddled up to a pillow. She picked up her phone and typed a short message and sent it to her man.

Hi.

She opted for simple, considering the shock she gave him earlier. She hoped like hell he had deleted that picture.

Hello, my angel. You surprised me so much earlier I fell out of my chair.
Are you tired?
Feel like talking?

Rachel knew he had to have been up early that morning. To hear his voice for a few minutes would be enough.

I'm sleepy, but I miss you.
Call me?

Her phone rang thirty seconds after she hit the send key.
"Hi."

* * * *

As the afternoon dragged on, anticipation began to build in Rachel's body for her reunion with Eli.

Rachel looked forward to the feel of his big, strong arms wrapped around her and snuggling into his warm masculine embrace. She ached for his gentle fingers trailing over her torso in a tender, unhurried caress and his rugged, masculine scent wafting through her nostrils. She—

Grace waved a hand in front of her face. "Earth to Rachel."

Rachel felt her cheeks warm up and laughed with her friend, trying to pay attention to what Grace was saying. She strained her ears for the sound of vehicles pulling up. They were due home anytime now.

At five thirty, Rachel finally heard a vehicle pull up out front. Her heart did a quick double flip, and she shot from her seat on the couch, yanking open the front door.

He'd asked her last night on the phone what she wanted to do the moment she saw him. Chuckling, she'd told him she wanted to fling herself into his arms and have him catch her in a big bear hug. She didn't even hesitate, once he closed the SUV door and turned to her. He grinned with his arms held out wide.

With child-like glee, Rachel raced across the porch and leapt into Eli's big, strong, outstretched arms. When he caught her, she wrapped her legs around his lean waist and her arms around his neck. He held her close, and she breathed him in as she hugged him. He squeezed her tightly and hummed with happiness. She could hear amused male chuckling at their very public display of affection but didn't care enough to let go. Sinking her fingers into his long, silky black hair, Rachel kissed him for all she was worth.

"I missed you," she said sincerely when she finally came up for air. Someone coughed nearby and she recognized her father's voice, full of dry humor. "Hmm, so we gathered," he said as he opened the back of the SUV.

Eli walked away from the men milling around the vehicles with her still attached. "I missed you, too, angel," he murmured and nuzzled her throat. "You trusted me to catch you," he stated happily.

She hugged him tighter. "I missed you so much. Now I have you, I don't want to let you go."

"Your legs wrapped around my waist feel better than you can imagine, but I think we may be testing your poor father's tolerance."

Eli squeezed her back gently as she unlocked her ankles, and he set her back on her feet carefully. He kissed her once more and smiled down at her.

He stared into her face intensely and spoke in her ear. "I'm starving for you."

His lustful gaze made her feel self-conscious, but Rachel didn't look away, just pressed her body to his. Her eyes widened when she felt his bulging erection press against her abdomen.

"For me?" she whispered and licked her lips.

He groaned softly. "If you don't stop that, everyone is going to know what's on my mind."

She smiled. "I can't help it. Can I help you carry your things to the truck?"

"There's just one bag," he said, indicating the duffle bag lying on the driveway by her father's vehicle.

She glanced at the empty flatbed trailer still hooked up to Jack's SUV. "Are the hogs already at the processors?"

"Yeah. We just dropped off the two big ones Ethan and Adam got this morning at the butcher in Divine. They're going to prep and store them whole for the pig roast next weekend." She walked with him as he retrieved his bag and took it to her truck. "The processor near Allen's lodge is going to have a busy week processing all that meat."

"I heard you got the biggest one." She slid her hand into his after he put his bag on the back seat of her Tundra.

"Until last night at dusk. Your dad shot one that was a little bigger. You wouldn't believe the size of them."

Rachel shuddered, having a pretty good guess. "We have supper almost done. The steaks are seasoned and ready to go on the grill."

"Great, I'm starving."

Rachel noticed the others had already gone inside.

He lifted her knuckles to his lips and kissed them and said in a gravelly, soft voice, "We're going to behave for now, but when I get you home, I'm going to be all over you the moment the lock turns on the front door. I hope you're packed and ready to go."

Her pussy liquefied at his words, and her clit ached for his touch, all in a matter of seconds.

"I am," she said shakily. She loved it when he took charge like this and told her what he planned to do. "It's already in the truck. Carry me out of here when you're ready, if you want, big caveman."

He growled low, and there was a fierce gleam in his eyes. "So, you're feeling me right now?"

"Yeah, I'm *feeling you*, Eli," she agreed, then added in a seductive tone, "but I'll be a good girl and behave myself."

"Until I ask you to do otherwise?"

"Yes. Then I may misbehave very badly." He leaned down and kissed her hard and quick then drew her in the front door. She said, "I'm going to check in with Grace and see what I can do to help."

Turning to walk into the kitchen, she barely contained a gasp as he boldly caressed her ass. She glanced back and smiled with pleasure, too. His eyes followed her hungrily as she crossed the room. She hoped he never changed.

Grace and her men were ecstatic to be with each other again and practically fought over serving each other. The men convinced her to sit down in one of the overstuffed chairs and allow them to wait on her. They took every opportunity to kiss or caress her when they were near. Rachel had a feeling that both she and Grace were going to have an early night if their men had any say in the matter.

The men made plans for the pig roast the following Saturday night. The roast would be at the Divine Creek Ranch, and Adam and Jack were even planning on lighting a bonfire. The nights were chillier now, and they'd been looking for an excuse to burn a gigantic pile of mesquite brush they had cleared from a pasture the year before.

Elijah and her parents were deep in conversation and Kelly and Grace had their heads together, talking, when Eli and Rachel went from group to group saying goodnight, making good on their getaway plans. It looked like Elijah and Kelly might be at the get-together a while longer, which spurred them both on even harder to get home. Who knew how long the privacy might last?

When they got to the duplex, Eli shouldered his bag and helped her carry her bags and the gifts in the house. The deadbolt slide home and her heart pounded as he stalked her back to the bedroom.

He pulled her to him firmly, and his lips devoured hers in a searing kiss.

She threaded her fingers in his hair and held him to her as his hands worked with the buckle of her belt and the button on her jeans. She toed her boots off and raised her arms when he lifted her top over her head then helped him with his belt buckle and his jeans. He removed his flannel shirt and T-shirt.

"Want a warm shower?" he asked between slow, wet kisses.

"No, I did all that right before we expected you home. I'm completely ready for you right now. Did you want a shower?"

"I showered at the lodge right before we left. Let's get the rest of these clothes off of you. Mmm, look at these cute little britches you have on." He palmed her bare ass under her silver lace cheeky shorts.

"I found them when we went shopping yesterday."

He unclasped the matching silver lace push-up bra and kissed her lips greedily. Eli's kiss was demanding, and he groaned when she slipped her tongue in his mouth, clasping her arms around his neck. He skimmed his hands over her hips and slid her shorts down her legs.

"Did you fantasize about what you would do to me tonight? How did you take me?" Rachel asked as she caressed his abdomen and his thickly muscled chest.

Eli slid his hands up and down her back and over her bare ass then gripped her buttocks and pressed her to his rock-hard cock. He gazed at her with glittering eyes in the soft light from the candles as he looked into hers. "I want to sit on the edge of the bed, like we did before, and use the mirror to watch. But I want you to face me this time so I can kiss you and look into your eyes as you ride my cock. Then I want to make love to you slowly on your back, with your hair laid out over my pillow and your legs spread wide in my hands. Then I want to take your ass."

His words fanned flames that blazed into an inferno inside her. A soft, lustful groan fell from her lips at the vivid images he planted in her mind, and her pussy began to ache in a way only he could fix.

"If you'll trust me, I'll make it feel so good. I promise to go slow and stop if you need me to."

"Of course I trust you, Eli. I'm going to love it." Rachel put her arms back around his neck, and as he lifted her up to him, she wrapped her legs around his waist.

Eli opened the closet door and carried her to the edge of the bed, carefully sat down and scooted back. He helped Rachel onto her knees then held her hips when she rose over him, and her nipples rubbed against his chest hairs, drawing a shaky sigh from her. He positioned the thick head of his cock at her wet entrance, and she rocked her hips to take him in a tiny bit.

She paused and whispered, "Did you miss my pussy?"

"I missed your hot little pussy *so* much." He groaned as her slick lips kissed his stiff cock. Rachel took fierce pleasure in the way the blunt head stretched her open that first inch or two before her body acquiesced to his entrance.

"Like I missed this great big, hard, long cock. I'm going to slide down over you nice and slow, gloving every last inch of you." Rachel rocked her hips again, and the head was past the tight muscles of her entrance and engulfed inside her. She squeezed his cock as she rose again, tugging on his erection before sliding back down. Eli sighed blissfully, and his fingertips slid lightly up her spine, causing her hips to flex involuntarily, and his cock slid farther into her pussy with her movements.

Rachel gazed in the mirror and moaned at the sight she and Eli made. It was so erotic, and she relished the thought they'd only gotten started. His cock was barely half-way lodged inside her pussy. He watched their reflection, too, and reached forward, grasping and gently lifting the cheeks of her ass so she could see her glistening pussy better. The movement parted her lips farther, and she slid down over the rest of his hard length as their eyes met in the mirror. Rachel smiled at the ecstasy on his face as his eyelids slid closed and his head tilted back. Her hips flexed forward, and she took him deep until he was seated completely within her. He held her hips still for a moment. She closed her eyes and listened to the warm, deep timbre of his voice.

"Don't move, angel. I want to feel you. I missed you so much, all of you. This was what I wanted, to have you wrapped around me and me wrapped around you." His hands slid all over her body, touching her cheeks, her throat, and her shoulders. He kissed her collarbones and stroked her ribs and her hips.

Reaching behind her, Rachel stroked his testicles with her fingertips, taking him by surprise. She loved his moan of pleasure and the way he leaned his forehead against her shoulder, so vulnerable. She lifted slightly, tugging on his cock with her pussy muscles, and slid back down. Her honey coated his cock and made him slippery inside of her.

Eli lifted his head and looked in her eyes, and then they both watched the mirror. She arched her back in pleasure, lifted off him until only the head remained inside her, and plunged back down over him. She loved the sight of his thick, warm cock easily sliding into her wet pussy. Each time she did it, her hips were angled so that her clit received maximum contact on both the upward motion as well as the downward slide. Each stroke to her clit drew her closer and closer to climax.

Eli growled softly as his fingertips found her rear opening. The sensation took her by surprise, and her breath left her in a shuddering gasp. He smiled at her with a possessive gleam in his eyes as one of his fingers circled her asshole and pressed insistently at the tight ring of muscles but didn't enter yet. She turned and watched in the mirror as his middle finger slowly stroked that hole while she pumped up and down on him with a slowly increasing rhythm. Her juices flowed over him, and her clit dragged over his cock with each delicious thrust.

The finger at her puckered opening pressed insistently, and she whispered, "Yours, Eli, all yours."

"Mine," he growled as he cupped her ass and helped her ride him, that finger still pressed against her.

Those tight muscles gave way and relaxed for him as her orgasm loomed over her. Eli's finger slid inside her asshole and Rachel felt like her body shattered into a million sparks of combusting pleasure. She threw her head back and came with a long, rapturous cry of ecstasy and rode each pulse of her orgasm to utter satisfaction. He gripped her ass, thrust deep inside her and held her hips tightly. Eli's head fell back, and he let loose with a loud yell. She clung to him and kissed his throat and his shoulders, glorying in the feel of his immense cock pulsing inside her.

Rachel lay limply against him when he lifted her hips and pulled out. He helped her under the covers with her head on his pillows and went to wash up. When he returned, she lifted the covers for him, and he climbed right on top of her. He covered her with his immense, comforting heat and kissed her tenderly. His cock was already hardening again, and she joyfully spread her legs for him as she watched him stroke himself. The sight of his hands on his cock turned her on, and she reached down to spread her pussy open for him and welcome him inside her. *Yours.* He smiled at her warm invitation and positioned his cock and growled again.

In one slow, sinuous stroke, he impaled her, and she moaned in delight. She lifted her knees and offered herself to him. He held her ankles and gently spread her thighs open wide so he could watch as his cock slid out, dripping with her juices. He plunged back into her, growling with pleasure as he slid to the hilt. She held on to the headboard with one hand and slid the other down her abdomen. She stopped at the top of her mound and looked up at him.

"Yes, angel. Stroke your clit the way you like it. Mmm, I love the sight of those delicate little fingers stroking your pussy."

Her hips began to flex with his movements, and her touch at her clit had her on the verge of another orgasm. He released her ankles, grasped her hips and tilted them, and began thrusting against her sweet spot. Her eyes opened wide at the sudden onslaught of sensation, and she threw her head back, screaming as her orgasm exploded over her. She arched her back and fucked his cock for all she was worth and came again almost immediately. He grasped her hips tightly as he thrust deep one last time and growled as his release jetted from him.

"Oh, Eli." She sighed with a shaky breath.

He rested his head beside hers and nuzzled her as he settled carefully over her. She stroked his arms, entwined her legs with his, and loved his encompassing warmth.

Rachel was overwhelmed by the deep attachment and love she felt for him, and a soft sob shuddered from her throat. Tears slid from her eyes and ran over her temples into her hair. He saw them, lifted his head to look into her eyes, and gently thumbed them away.

He kissed her lips tenderly. "Happy tears?"

"Yes." She nodded. "Happy, joyful, ecstatic, and *in love* tears," she murmured as she pressed her forehead to his shoulder. "I'm so thankful you didn't give up on me when I kept turning you down."

"I wanted you in the worst way, Rachel. There was nothing for me to do *but* persist," he said with a soft chortle. "I'd still be asking you out today. The wait was worth it, angel." He wiped her tears as they fell, drew her trembling body to his, and kissed her.

After a few minutes, she shifted under him, and he groaned at the movement and pressed his hips to her. She was amazed by his stamina as his hardening cock stroked her pussy. He rolled onto his back and drew her with him, holding her against his chest.

Nuzzling his pec, she asked, "Will you still…"

"Claim this sweet ass of yours? Yes."

Chapter Thirty-eight

"How do you feel?" he asked as Rachel ground her pussy against him. The image of him taking her ass bathed her pussy and his still embedded cock in a fresh flood of hot moisture.

Eli chuckled softly and stilled her movements with his warm hands on her hips. "I guess that answers my question," he murmured pressing himself deeper inside her.

"I'm buzzing from those two flaming orgasms you just gave me." Rachel smiled contentedly as she received his kiss.

"Flaming, eh?" His fingertips trailed softly up and down her hip, raising goose bumps all over her body and making her shudder with pleasure. "I'm going to let you rest a little while. We have time." He nuzzled her warm throat.

Rachel snickered softly. "You're such a gentleman, even when it's about taking my ass." She felt his low rumbling laughter vibrate through his chest under her palms. He grasped her ass cheeks gently but possessively.

"I happen to love this sweet ass and plan to take good care of it. Rest for a little while and I'll stroke your back."

"I don't want to fall asleep."

"I'm not trying to get you to go to sleep, angel. Catch your breath and recover a bit. We'll play more, don't worry."

Eli lifted her hips and pulled out, then helped her to lie on her stomach and stroked her back and her ass while she relaxed. She noticed his play gradually focused more on her ass than her back, and sighed happily when his fingers stroked her cleft from top to bottom. A thought occurred to her.

"Do you think your dad and sister are back from Grace's yet?" What a time to have to worry about being noisy. Rachel knew she would be screaming like a banshee before he was done. She heard him chuckle softly.

"I've been a little preoccupied with the hot woman in my bed. I'll go check." Throwing his robe on, Eli left the bedroom for a moment then returned. "They aren't back yet." He removed his robe and climbed back into the bed.

He reached for the drawer in his bedside table and removed the tube of personal lubricant and another small pouch. Taking the velvet pouch from him, Rachel peered inside and grinned.

"Another little surprise?" she asked, arching an eyebrow playfully.

He grinned back at her. "I might want to use it on you while we play. Are you game?"

"Hell yeah!" She giggled and handed the pouch back to him and rose up on her knees. Rachel still buzzed from before, but the ache and need were intensifying. She'd looked forward to this for so long, and the moment was *finally* here. He climbed from the bed and went to the foot of it.

"Come to me here then we can use the mirror. You'd like that, wouldn't you?"

Eagerly crawling to him, Rachel turned, then backed to the end of the bed. She could clearly see her profile in the mirror, in perfect position and ready for him. Hot juices flooded her cunt, and the heat and ache got stronger. Tiny pulses rippled in her pussy at the thought of what he was going to do to her, and her ass tingled in anticipation. She couldn't stifle the little whimpering moan that escaped her lips. His warm fingers caressed her and then dipped into her wet cunt.

"Mmm, angel, your lips are swollen. Are you aching for me?" he asked in a seductive tone that got her even wetter as his fingers stroked her pussy lovingly.

"I want this so much, I *am* aching for you. Please take me."

"All in good time, angel."

He smiled at her in the mirror as she watched his hands. He opened the pouch and took out the stimulator. It was an oddly shaped jelly vibrator that tucked inside her pussy and stimulated both her clit and G-spot at the same time. She was getting wetter by the second at the thought of him using it on her tonight.

After lubricating it, he teased her clit with the jelly nubs on the head. A ripple of pleasure raced up her spine at the new sensation. Her pussy tightened up in excitement when he slid it inside of her and tucked it against her G-spot and her clit simultaneously. Then he turned it on.

"Oh!" She moaned deeply.

She was already so aroused she knew she'd come in less than a minute. The G-spot stimulator had a vibrating egg in it like the one he'd hidden in her luggage for her. It was nailing the perfect spot at the moment and sending delicious vibes to her clit, as well. She was glad nobody else was home because she was about to *scream*.

"Oh! Eli! I'm not going to last! Hold it for me!" Rachel squealed and pushed back against his hand holding the vibrator. She rubbed her clit against the nubs, and the friction brought her to the edge of insanity. The muscles in her cunt began to contract around it as she squeezed tightly and let out a loud, screaming wail. Coming hard on the *mother* of all orgasms, her pussy gushed over his fingers and hand. She rocked on the vibrator as he held it for her. "Oh, *fuck* yes!" She groaned.

"That is one good investment. Damn, baby, you are so hot." Eli's voice was strained with lust and desire.

"Oh, *that* is my new favorite toy. That was amazing." She sighed happily, still breathless.

"Ready for me to take your ass?" he asked, stroking her cleft from pussy to tailbone and back again.

"I'll beg if you want me to." Presenting herself in open invitation, Rachel arched her back and wiggled her ass at him.

"Eager, aren't you?"

"You know I am. I'm ready for you."

She watched in the mirror as he applied a generous amount of the lubricant to his hard, thick erection. Rachel remembered wondering how he'd fit that enormous monster inside her pussy. Now confident in her body's ability to handle his size, she knew no fear that he would fit and only a little trepidation when he penetrated her ass the first time. Her confidence in his gentleness went a long way to allay her nerves.

Her pussy pulsed with eagerness as she watched him stroke his shaft and then smoothed the same lubricated hand over her pussy. He applied more lube to his fingers and smoothed it all around her asshole and then applied more directly to the opening, pressing it into her tight channel. He removed another little toy from it's' pouch after wiping his hands off on a towel and placed it within easy reach on the bed.

"Ready for my cock, angel?"

"So ready, honey."

She looked in the mirror as Eli lovingly smoothed his hands over her hips. He trailed his fingers down in a light, trembling touch to the cleft of her ass. His fingertips slid through the lubrication to her asshole and swirled in a sensual caress of those overexcited nerve endings. Her pussy throbbed with excitement.

Eli circled her rear opening with one finger, and she closed her eyes and focused on the sensation. She relaxed those muscles and allowed him access to her virgin ass. He growled softly in approval when the muscles obeyed her and gave way to his pressing finger.

He pumped it in and out several times, applied more lubricant to her opening again, and got more of it into her this time. He slid one finger, and then a second, into her ass. Her bottom tingled at the additional stretching, but she accommodated his fingers after a few pumps with ease, sliding in and out with no problem. The tight achiness in her cunt intensified, and the urge to rock against him became insistent.

Rachel moaned in need when he removed his fingers again. He applied more lube inside her opening and slowly slid three fingers into her ass simultaneously. She gasped at the added fullness and the slight burning pinch as he pressed past the opening. Willing her body to accommodate him, she relaxed as he pressed in, twisted his fingers around to thoroughly lubricate her opening, and spread them out a bit. She knew the last thing he wanted was to hurt her, and she was happy he could now see she was ready for this experience with him.

When he slid his fingers from her ass, she tried to follow his hand. "My angel wants my cock bad, doesn't she?"

He pressed the nozzle of the lubricant bottle to her relaxed rear opening and filled it with additional lube to ease his passage deep inside her, as well. Her ass burned from all the intrusions, and her pussy and clit screamed to be invaded at one opening or the other. It didn't matter which.

She begged softly to him. "Eli, please, I need you."

In the mirror's reflection, Rachel watched as he stroked his stiff cock and placed it at her rear entrance. She moaned at the feel of his blunt head pressed against her there. He wiped his hands on the towel then gently grasped her hips and placed the pads of his thumbs on either side of her asshole.

Eli's voice trembled slightly. "It may hurt a little, angel. If you want me to slow down, I will. If you can't handle it, please tell me. I would never want to hurt you while making love to you."

Making eye contact with him in the mirror, she could see the intense desire and tenderness in his features. Smiling reassuringly at him, she said, "I love you so much I ache with it right now, Eli. You are the kindest, gentlest man I've ever known. You won't hurt me. I want this so much. Just go slow for my first time?" she asked softly, her cheeks flushing warmly.

"Of course, angel." His voice shook with emotion.

Rachel could hear his breath trembling as he struggled to hold back and not give into the urge to plunge forward, which she knew had to be strong for him. She arched for him to encourage him and willed her bottom to relax against his intrusion.

He gripped her hips and pressed for entry gradually. She watched his massive, proud form in the mirror as he slowly took her ass. Rachel hissed at the heart-pounding sensuality of his gentle pressure as he eased past the tight ring of muscles in her ass. The pain was mixed equally with a burning pleasure like she had *never* experienced when using the plugs. Eli had prepared her well, and she cried out softly in triumph when the thick head slid past the tight barrier.

"Oh, yes, Eli."

"Are you all right?" He stopped his advance and rocked against her gently.

"Oh, Eli, it's *amazing*. Please keep going."

He rocked in a little farther on the advance and pulled out a little, so he was deeper inside her with each thrust. She focused on the reflection in the mirror as he slowly slid into her ass, and like she knew it would, every glorious inch fit.

"Oh, fuck, that is beautiful." He growled deeply.

His huge cock slid in and out of her ass in a slick, sinuous motion as she watched in fascination. Eli's body vibrated with tension, and she could see his glorious muscles rippling with every movement in the mirror. On his features was a mixture of pure pleasure and agony as he loved her in this erotic way. The glorious sensation of her orgasm stirred within her, and she rocked back on him in a graceful, slow dance with him.

Eli reached over and slid his index finger into the tiny vibrator he'd laid on the bed earlier and flipped it on with a fingertip. He slid that hand over her hip and down to her mound and found her clit and began to stroke alongside it. His fingertip found the swollen, aching bundle of nerves, and the vibrations to her clit were heaven and hell all at once. All she felt was throbbing pleasure as she began bucking against him.

Rachel's cries echoed rapturously in the room and mingled with his. She was unable to stop the rising tide of sensation and unwilling to hold it back. She dove in as she was overcome by her orgasm. Her back arched and her hips rocked as he pumped his hot release into her ass, growling and softly cursing. He grasped her hips hard and thrust deep.

She lifted her head and threw her hair back and watched him in the mirror. Every muscle flexed and rippled powerfully, his head bent forward so his face was hidden by the black curtain of his hair. His big hands were strong but gentle as they held her upper thighs. She savored the pure ecstasy in the sounds he made and felt it, too. She was utterly consumed by him. Consumed *with* him.

Weakly lowering herself onto her elbows, Rachel rested her head against her forearms as he slowly withdrew from her throbbing ass.

He placed his hand on her lower back and helped her to rest on her side. "Stay still for a second, angel. I'll be right back." He came back with a hot, wet washcloth, which he pressed to her tender rear opening. It caused her to hiss in surprise at the heat, but it felt good. He cleansed her opening and wiped away the lubricant as well.

"Does it hurt, angel?" he asked softly, brushing a lock of hair away from her face.

"No, the heat feels good. It just surprised me. I don't think I can move. I have no bones." Her body hummed with satisfaction.

"It'll do that to you. You need to rest now. I'll bet you sleep like a baby tonight."

"I know I will. Now that you're home."

* * * *

Rachel smiled blissfully and moaned when Eli pressed his warm lips against the tender skin of her inner thigh. He palmed her leg open with his warm hand and stroked it soothingly. He licked a wet trail to her damp pussy. How long had he been playing this morning? While she'd slept, Eli had brought her to a full state of arousal, so he must have had plans for her that morning.

Rachel found out a second later when his talented tongue dipped into her wet pussy then licked her from one end of her slit to the other. He flicked playfully at her clit and grinned at her from between her legs. Eyeing her devilishly, he slid a finger into her wet cunt and rubbed that finger over her clit before dipping in again. She sighed happily and spread her legs open wide for Eli as he gently pumped that finger in and out of her. He closed his lips over her clit and suckled on it as she slid her fingertips into his hair, encouraging him wordlessly.

She slid her hand down to her mound and held her outer lips open with her fingers, giving him easier access to lick her as he added another finger and pumped into her over and over. The added friction sent a ripple through her pussy, and she began to move with him, rocking her hips. His warm tongue sent shivers of delight through her as he laved her clit and suckled it, gradually building her arousal to a sweeping crescendo. He added a third finger, and the added fullness sliding into her brought her orgasm crashing down on her. She came with a low, soft, panting moan. When she was through, Eli came to lay by her side, licking his fingers like a little boy with a special treat.

Resting his head on his hand, Eli he stroked her abdomen. "Good morning, my angel," he said in a soft, husky drawl.

She chuckled softly. "*I'll say*. Did you sleep well?"

"Much better than I did the last two nights." He smiled as she stretched contentedly. "How do you feel this morning? Are you sore?"

"Yes, I'm sore, but I wouldn't trade last night for all the coconut cream pie in the world."

"All the—" Eli began to say then got a mischievous little gleam in his eyes. "Coconut cream pie, huh?"

"Mmm-hmm. My *favorite*."

"Oh, the possibilities. Let me get you some ibuprofen." Eli helped her sit up and frowned when she groaned a little, but she smiled at him as she stood and stretched again. He pulled her into a warm, gentle embrace, and his hands on her body felt too good for words.

* * * *

Eli took them all to breakfast at Taquería Gomez. Elijah and Kelly were already packed up and ready to leave for home early that morning. They talked outside in the parking lot for a few minutes before getting on the road. Eli walked Rachel to her truck, opened the door for her, and thought that she was moving slowly as she carefully climbed into the driver's seat. Gazing into her loving blue eyes, he experienced such pride and satisfaction that his woman would give herself to him in every possible way, but also felt remorse to be the cause of the pain she must be in. He pressed his lips against her cheek and nuzzled her, breathing in her clean, womanly scent.

Her hands strayed over his shoulders and into his hair as she intuitively reassured him, "Not for all the coconut cream pie in the world, Eli. I promise I feel fine," she said to him softly

"I'm working tonight, so you'll have a chance to rest."

"I will. After I come up and spend a little time with you at the club. I'll be fine, Eli," she assure him. "I expected to be this sore after the first time. It won't always be this way." He opened his mouth, about to say there might not be another time, and she pressed her fingertips to his lips. "I'm making you supper tonight at my place. I love you, Eli."

He kissed her, feathering his tongue over hers as his hands slid down to her hips and squeezed gently. "I'll see you this afternoon. I love you, too."

* * * *

"Knock, knock."

Rachel looked up, smiled, and rolled her eyes at Bernice's smirky little grin as she poked her head in the doorway. "Hi. What's up?"

"Something arrived for you," Bernice said in a sing-song voice as she walked into Rachel's office.

Rachel had been working from home for a couple of weeks and was glad to be back at her desk. She had spent the day working through the stacks of paperwork that had accumulated during her medical leave. She'd come straight into work from breakfast with Eli, Elijah, and Kelly to get an early start on the day.

In her hands, Bernice carried a large vase filled with roses. In contrast to the first bouquet, which had met its sad end in her apartment fire, these were a deep, vivid red except for one flaming orange rose nestled in the center. Bernice placed the vase in front of her on her desk blotter, and Rachel removed the card from its holder, pleased to note that the envelope it was in was still sealed.

"Are they from your fiancé?"

Rachel slipped the card from the envelope.

I think the best kind of love grows from friendship first.
Thank you for trusting me.
        Love—Eli

"Yes, they're from Eli," Rachel replied softly, enjoying the beautiful aroma of the roses.

Things sure had changed a lot since the last time he'd given her flowers. Bernice sighed dreamily. After the receptionist returned to her desk in the lobby, Rachel took out her cell phone and dialed his number. That man needed to write a book for other men on how to romance a woman. *Chapter Ten: How to thank your woman for letting you take her ass.*

"Hello, angel."

"Hi, yourself, handsome."

* * * *

Eli opened her front door and inhaled a delicious aroma. He grinned as his empty stomach responded with a growl, and his mouth watered. He could hear a noise but didn't see her. He called out as he closed the front door and thought he heard a muffled response from the kitchen. He noticed her roses sitting in their vase on her kitchen counter and grinned when he found her on her hands and knees, rearranging the interior of a cabinet. Her winsome little heart-shaped ass was stuck in the air as she reached deep in the cabinet.

"Hi, baby!" she said in a strained, muffled voice. "How was your day?"

Eli leaned against the counter for a few seconds to enjoy the pretty sight. Her snug jeans accentuated her shapely ass and her strong thighs. A deep growl in his chest accompanied the possessive feeling he experienced on a regular basis when he was around her.

Mine.

"It's a damn sight better now." He squatted down beside her, wondering how she'd felt during the day. She backed up from the cabinet, wiped a lock of hair from her face, and smiled serenely at him.

"Hi, handsome." She leaned toward him and kissed him then began to back away from the cabinet to stand. She had a glass lid in her hand. He stood and helped her to her feet.

Rachel smiled up at him sweetly when he wrapped his arms around her and laid a warm, so-happy-to-be-home kiss on her lips.

"How are you feeling, angel?"

"Much better. I got a massage this afternoon. It helped with my sore muscles, and I'm feeling better *everywhere else*, too."

"I'm glad to hear it. Something smells good."

"Supper will be ready in a few minutes. It's in the oven right now. I hope you like King Ranch Chicken."

"I love it. I hope you made a bunch."

"Enough for leftovers if you want them."

"Come sit with me."

He pulled her by the hand into the living room. She followed him and climbed into his lap after he sat. He cuddled her to him and gently squeezed her, enjoying the way she melted against him and rested her head on his chest with a soft, happy sigh.

He strummed his fingers over her ribs. "I want you to rest tonight, okay, angel? *Okay?*"

He wanted to carry her to bed, strip her, and tuck her in under the sheets and blankets. Then he wanted wrap himself around her and watch over her as she slept. The caveman approved of his plan. She brought out all his territorial instincts.

Giggling softly, she said, "Eli, it's not that bad. I mean, I don't plan on asking for anal sex again for at least a week or so. But if you insist, we can lay off for tonight."

"Tell you what," he said, hiding a grin, because he knew damn good and well he'd give her whatever she wanted. "You be a good girl, and we'll see."

She rubbed her cheek against his chest and stroked his pec slowly. "What if I'm not a good girl?"

Damn, he loved when she used that whispery seductive voice on him.

"Well, I think we've established you might need to be punished. I wouldn't spank you right now for obvious reasons, but I could tie you down with your new bondage sashes and have my wicked way with you."

"Well, I guess I'll just have to take my chances and make it worth the punishment if I misbehave."

If. Yeah, right.

There was no *if*, and Eli knew it. It was more like *when*. She'd called him that afternoon to thank him for the roses and mentioned that she'd been thinking about what they'd talked about the night Joseph Hazelle had been in the club. She'd also hinted that now her arm was out of its cast and healed up nicely, perhaps she'd like to play a little. Her exact words had been, "I'm feeling rather naughty these days."

Eli growled, imagining all the ways she would find to be naughty, and said, "No misbehavior tonight. Right now, I'm fighting the urge to go tuck you into bed and feed you supper there. I'll do anything you want to, but not tonight."

"I promise to be good and rest tonight. I don't like to see you so worried about me," she clasped her fingers with his and gave him a wicked little grin, "but I'm intrigued that you've been thinking about my new bondage sashes. Will you tie me up sometime soon?" she asked keenly.

He couldn't suppress a chuckle at her eagerness. "Would you like that?"

"Like it? I *need* it!" she said enthusiastically.

"Well, angel, I am all about meeting your needs."

* * * *

After Eli left for work, Rachel cleaned up the supper mess and delivered leftovers to Eli's refrigerator then changed clothes and dolled herself up. After fixing her makeup and hair, she put on the little black dress Eli liked so much then slipped on the new shoes she'd found the weekend before. He hadn't seen the shoes yet, but she thought he was going to like them, *a lot.*

Looking in the mirror, she liked what she saw. Yes, the dress fit her well, but she also liked the twinkle she saw in her eyes and the glow in her cheeks. Rachel was happy, and it showed on her face and in how she carried herself. She slipped into her soft fleece leopard print coat and put her wallet and lipstick into her evening bag.

When she pulled up to the parking lot, she was surprised by how many cars were there for a Monday. She found a parking space and walked across the lot to the sidewalk along the front of the club. Rachel was excited, she felt beautiful, and she couldn't wait to see Eli. It had only been an hour since he left, but she already longed for him. Her phone vibrated inside her evening bag, and she stopped on the sidewalk to check it. It was a text from Kelly with a picture of Matthew in his little baby bath seat, soap bubbles piled on his head. The message said:

> *Hiya, Auntie Rachel!*
> *See me in my bath?*
> *I love you!*
> *Matthew*

As Rachel took a few seconds to reply to the message, several men pushed open the club door and stepped out. She looked up briefly as they walked toward her. They must have come in straight from work because they still wore their work uniforms. One of them looked familiar, and she automatically looked down at the name *Reese* embroidered on his work shirt. Lowering her eyes to her phone, Rachel felt her heart jump into her throat. She did her best to not react visibly. She wouldn't give him that satisfaction.

One of the other men said, "Mmm, maybe we should've stayed. Look at that, would ya? Like to get me some of that." *Wow. Charming and smooth.*

She gritted her teeth as Reese snickered repulsively and said plainly so she could hear him, "Had me some of that a few years back, Tommy. How you doing, Rachel, honey?" Chills and gooseflesh raced over her skin as she stood frozen to the spot. He snickered. "Nice and fresh, too. Did her a favor and popped her little cherry for her."

The others laughed, and Rachel watched them look back at her speculatively in the reflection of the window before her. She closed her phone, her heart pounded and icy, cold chills raced over her skin. She tried to swallow the lump in her throat and couldn't because her mouth had gone bone-dry. The door was less than ten feet away. Taking several slow deep breaths, she forced her feet to move as he continued his nasty story. She reached with cold fingers for the door. Inside the club, she didn't feel so exposed, so vulnerable. Her friends were here and this was Eli's territory, so to speak. Pausing inside the doorway, she braced herself against the wall for a minute. She tried to calm her breathing and slow her heart rate.

Chapter Thirty-nine

Rachel felt his big, protective presence beside her and looked up into his handsome face. His knuckles grazed her chin, and he peered at her with concern.

"Angel? Are you all right? Mike said you were out here. He said it looked like something was wrong. What is it, angel?" He pulled her to him and then said seriously, "Rachel, you're trembling hard. What happened?"

The strong, independent nature in her wanted to keep this to herself. She'd already dealt with it, gotten over it, and moved on. No good could come from involving Eli. It was old history. Since falling in love with him, she was learning that dependent was not all bad, nor was independent all good. Balance had changed her perspective. She could admit that she loved having a freaking huge alpha male for a fiancé, one who made it clear he'd fight battles for her. A tiny primal cavewoman spark flared inside of her, and the shaking stopped.

Reaching for him when he leaned to her, Rachel wrapped her arms around his neck and hugged him hard.

"Did something happen just now?" he asked, confusion and worry showing on his face.

"Yes, but you're working, and I don't want you distracted with my issues. Later tonight will be soon enough. Right now, I need a stiff drink and to hold on to your hand for a little while. I'll tell you all about it later, but for right now, just be with me?" she asked, her heart beating with intense love and passion for the man standing with her. "I love you like crazy, Eli Wolf."

"I love you, too, angel. Let me see you," he said appreciatively as he released her and looked her over.

Untying the belt on her coat, she allowed it to slide down her arms. She draped it over a forearm and modeled for him. He gave her an admiring grin and said, "You look beautiful tonight."

His eyes trailed down to her feet, and she gave herself a mental fist pump when she saw them open wide at the sight of her high-heeled black pumps. What was it about that school-girl style combined with five-inch heels that drove men wild? She didn't get it, but she felt victorious nonetheless at the little beads of sweat that popped out on his upper lip.

"Holy shit, you have no idea how hot you are in those heels," Eli growled. She did a little turn and modeled for him to give him the full effect.

"A woman loves knowing she's dressed in a way that affects her man so...viscerally." She moved close to him and brushed her abdomen ever so slightly against his bulging cock, which was becoming more noticeable by the moment.

He growled low. "You're playing with fire, little girl."

"I might get burned?"

"You torture me."

She shook her head and murmured, "I love you."

"Let's get you that drink before I nail you right here in the entryway." He grinned at her, but she could tell he was a little concerned for her by the look in his eyes. He was patient with her, though, and did not press her for any more answers.

Eli ordered her a mixed drink from Quinten, and she sipped it slowly while she quietly visited with Eli and Mike. Eli talked about the hunt and told them that Ethan planned on roasting both pigs, one on a spit and the other one Yucatan style, in an in-ground pit. Ethan came and visited with them for a while and chatted enthusiastically about digging and arranging the pit for the roast.

Rachel saw a lot of people she knew and asked Eli if he would mind if she went and mingled for a little bit. He drew her to him and embraced her gently then smiled and told her to go have fun. She took her purse and made a stop in the ladies' room first.

Besides all the lewd gossip she usually heard in the restroom when the club was busy like tonight, there were a few stray remarks about the handsome hunk working the door. She rolled her eyes and gave herself another mental fist pump when the talk didn't faze her all that much. Now, if one of the bimbos put her hands on Eli tonight, Rachel was liable to lose it, but they could talk all they wanted. She was the one he would come home to. Two women were talking over the bathroom stalls to each other about him, not even trying to be discreet.

One of Rachel's friends looked down the counter at her and rolled her eyes. Rachel smiled and shrugged as she refreshed her lip liner. She didn't comment at all but saved her energy for anyone who acted on what they talked about.

Rachel left the bathroom to mingle and visit with friends. Rosemary showed up during the evening, and Rachel gave her an enthusiastic hug. "You look like royalty dressed like that, Rosemary."

Always one to spit in the face of convention, Rosemary was dressed in all white tonight. From her polished white cowgirl boots to her jeans and white silk western top. The contrast with her long, curly black hair made her stand out in the crowd even more. Her ivory complexion, violet-blue eyes, and dark red lip color reminded Rachel of a china doll's.

"Why thank you, Rachel. You're not so bad yourself. How are wedding plans coming?"

Rachel chuckled easily. "Kelly and Grace have taken the reins. My dress is supposed to be ready this week sometime. I sure did enjoy the lingerie shower last weekend."

"Mmm, me, too! Such *excellent* service we had, huh?" She winked at Rachel.

"Stellar, and so thoughtful, too."

They spoke for a few minutes, and then Rosemary went in search of Bernadette and some other friends who were meeting her there. Rachel wondered if Wes and Evan would put in an appearance tonight.

Rachel mingled through the club and caught up with other friends she had not seen since before the accident. A little later in the evening, she encountered Adam and Jack talking to Ace Webster and Rosemary's friend Kathleen Stevens, who must have come in recently, as well. Jack saw her coming, and the men stood to greet her.

"Hello, Rachel. You sure are lookin' pretty tonight," Jack said and kissed her cheek.

"Thank you, Jack. You're such a sweet talker. Hello, Adam." She hugged them both. "Everyone is looking forward to the bonfire and roast this weekend. Rosemary told me she and the boys will be there."

"Oh, good. Grace was hoping they would come over," Adam replied. "Grace was looking for you when she came in, but she brought supper for Ethan, so they're in the office at the moment. She should be out in a bit."

"Ace and Kathleen are going to be at the house this weekend, too," Jack added.

Rachel smiled at Jack's reference to them as a couple. More of Grace's work, no doubt. "Good! The more the merrier."

"We may have to add a third pig by the time Grace is done inviting people." Adam grinned indulgently.

"Will you tell Grace I'm looking for her when she comes out of the office?" Rachel asked. "I need to go check in with Eli. I've been wandering around for a while, and I don't want him to feel *neglected*," she said teasingly.

"We can't be having any of that, now can we?" Jack said with a crooked smile. He gestured with his dark head toward the front of the club. "He looks like he's got his hands full right now."

Eli was surrounded by a small group of big-haired blondes. They were flirting and talking with him, and Rachel could hear the giggling from across the room. They must have just come in. She didn't recognize any of them.

Rachel smirked at Jack and Adam, and they promised to pass the message on to Grace. She stopped at the bar and asked for a Coke from Quinten, who also slid her a shot of tequila for Eli and winked at her.

"On Ethan," he said softly and wiped down the bar.

She thanked him and lifted the glasses and made her way to her poor beleaguered sweetheart. She caught his eye as she sauntered toward him, moving slowly, allowing him to look his fill. The heat and love in his eyes did her heart good.

There were only four of them this time, so she had no trouble wading through the group. She placed her glass and evening bag on Eli's table and then turned to him to give him his shot. Three of them looked like nice enough women, but she noticed one of them looked her dead in the eye and slid the back of her hand over Eli's biceps in an inviting caress.

Eli ignored her touch, reached for Rachel, and gave her a loving, wet kiss. As he did so, she maintained unwavering eye contact with the forward blonde and slowly slid her hand up the same arm and over his biceps. Her right hand stopped and caressed the spot the woman had touched. Her engagement ring sparkled in the light.

Eli said, "Girls, this is my fiancée, Rachel."

Rachel continued to stare at the other woman until she averted her eyes and backed away slightly. Rachel turned to one of the other women, a petite blonde, who behaved more circumspectly, and said, "I love your dress. I noticed that table of guys over there was checking you all out a few seconds ago. They're all single. The one with the white hat is a nice guy and a good dancer, if you came to dance." Then she turned back to the other blonde, who was staring daggers at her, and continued, "But if you've come to 'horn in' on couples, I gotta tell you, this isn't the place for you."

The woman had the decency to blush, so Rachel turned back to the blonde she'd addressed before. "*See?* He's looking right at you. I'll bet he's going to ask you to dance. He's kind of a hero to the ladies around here, but he's a little shy."

The blonde smiled at Brice Huvell, and he smiled back then excused himself from the table of men where he sat and approached the front as the women watched. The little blonde blushed a little and glanced uncertainly at Rachel.

"Brice is very nice. He'll treat you like a *lady*." As she said the word lady, she glanced back at the other blonde pointedly, before checking Brice's progress crossing the club. "Oh! Here come two more. Looks like your dance partners have arrived," Rachel said, winking at Brice, Andy, and Vince as they made their way over to help Rachel extricate Eli from the friendly women's attentions. What good guys.

Eli introduced Brice to the sweet little blonde whose name was Corina Scott, and he asked her politely to dance with him. Within the minute, they were all gone, including the pushy blonde, who sauntered over to the bar partnerless to get a drink while all her friends danced.

"Angel, you are a force of nature." Eli chuckled and kissed her cheek.

"Thank you, honey. I just made three new friends. That other one? *Meh*," she said with a shrug and a little wave of her hand.

"You handled that with real class, angel." He nuzzled her throat. "Are you having fun?"

"Yes, did you see Rosemary Piper when she came in earlier?" Rachel asked happily.

"I think the safer question would be to ask who *didn't* see her. Even if she weren't dressed all in white, she would be glowing, judging by the smile on her face when she found her men over at their table."

"They all look so happy together. It's sweet. Do you get a break tonight?"

"Yeah, I was fixing to come carry you onto the dance floor."

"Don't worry, big man. I'll go willingly anywhere you want me to," she said with a suggestive arch of her eyebrow.

He cleared his throat and told Mike he was taking a break.

After he had her in a close embrace on the dance floor, he whispered, "I don't know what it is about those shoes, but every time I look at you in them, I get hard as a freakin' rock."

"I noticed that you seemed to like them," she murmured. "Wait until I dance for you in them." Encouraged by his low growl, she added, "Maybe I'll wear them the next time you fuck me." Sliding her fingers into the hair at the nape of his neck, Rachel stroked tenderly, and asked, "Does this qualify as bad behavior?"

"Nuh-uh. This is good behavior, just bad timing. I want you to rest tonight," he said firmly as he led her in the dance.

"I won't tease you anymore, Eli. But remember I can have these shoes on and be ready and waiting in two minutes." She smiled and held up two fingers, giving him a naughty little grin.

"Bad girl," he drawled and squeezed her to him.

Brice and Corina twirled by and looked lost in a little world of their own as they gazed into each other's eyes.

Rachel nodded toward the couple. "That looks promising."

"He and Ethan have been talking a lot the last few weeks. I think some of Ethan's charm and manners may be rubbing off on Brice."

"Good for him," Rachel said, genuinely hoping this was the clean slate Brice needed in his life. It was hard to change a person's image in a small town when everyone knew them.

Eli's hands slid up to her shoulder blades and then down over her hips to the upper swell of her ass and squeezed her gently. "I love you, angel. You make me a very happy man, you know that?"

Rachel tilted her head up to him as he leaned down and kissed her tenderly on the lips, stroking her tongue gently with his. A delicious burn began in her clit, a fire kindled by his hands on her and stoked by his kiss and sweet words. He stroked her hips and waist, and his thumbs slid up the sides of her abs lightly in that tickling touch that drove her crazy. Her shuddering gasps against his lips made him smile in satisfaction, and he squeezed her tightly to him when her hips tilted reflexively and pressed against his stiff cock inside his leathers.

"I love you, too, Eli," she murmured dreamily when he released her lips. "You make me feel so…"

"Beautiful? Desirable? Hot? Wet?"

"You have such power over me. With just a look or a touch, you've got me panting and ready," she said softly, her cheek pressed to his chest as they moved smoothly over the dance floor.

He traced his warm hands down her lower back to the top of her ass, and he held her against him securely as they danced to Thompson Square's "Are You Gonna Kiss Me Or Not." His cock grew very rigid against her abdomen and Rachel looked up when she heard him groan faintly.

"What are you thinking about right now?" *As if I don't already know.*

He tilted his head to her and whispered, "I'm fantasizing about you wearing those shoes while we fuck."

To the others it would look like they were having a quiet conversation as they danced in a close embrace. Rachel hoped they maintained that appearance because she had a feeling he had more than a few words to share about his fantasy and his sexy voice already had her pussy clenching.

"I want you to wear those shoes and the G-string with the little ties on the sides. I'm going to light candles and put them on the back deck late one night so we can enjoy fucking outside."

Oh, yes, please tell me more.

"I'll lay back in one of the loungers and watch you come to me with that sexy walk of yours."

His splayed fingers pressed on her ass, his leather clad thigh slid easily over the smooth knit fabric that covered her mound, and the ache in her clit increased.

Rachel rewarded his efforts with a soft moan she hoped only he could hear. He timed his words well as the dancers transitioned into the next song, "Who Are you When I'm Not Looking" by Blake Shelton.

Eli's lips brushed her temple as he spoke softly to her. "You're going to straddle the lounger I'm lying in with your back to me, bend over and give me your pussy to play with. I'm going to put you on my lap, with your legs spread wide outside of mine, and your back to me, and slide my cock into your sweet cunt and let you ride me while I play with your clit until you come."

The tip of his tongue stroked the outer shell of her ear, and he whispered, "But I'm not going to come yet."

Maybe not, baby, but I'm about to come right now!

"I'm going to pull out of you and turn you so you face me on the padded lounger. I'll slide my cock into your little pussy, in one hard stroke." For a second he pressed her to his erection firmly.

Rachel knew it was impossible, but she felt it just as he said it.

"Then, I'm going to take the vibrator you've brought with you and slide it into your luscious, tight ass." He slid a finger down the her cleft and every nerve ending in her asshole fired to life. "Then, while I fuck your hot wet pussy, I'll pump the vibrator in and out with my strokes until you scream and come for me."

He pressed again as he spoke,

"I'll let you ride me until you climax once more because I love hearing all those sweet sexy sounds you make." His thigh brushed her mound again. The mention of how much he enjoyed listening to her nearly had her coming right there on the dance floor.

"I'm going to fill you with my cum and watch it drip from your pussy in the candlelight when I pull out of you. Then I'm going to take you inside and start all over again."

Oh, yes, please more!

"So now you know what I was thinking about," Eli said with a sexy chuckle.

A low, erotic moan slipped from her lips. "Oh, Eli." She laid her head against his chest as her body throbbed with desire. "You're amazing."

"I could say the same thing about you, angel. I could feel the tension in your body build up as I held you. You want to come really bad right now, don't you?"

Her pussy clenched in affirmation and she nodded against his chest and sighed.

"I love listening to the little aroused sounds you make, angel. So quiet, so sexy and intense. When I get home, I'm going to make you come so hard you see stars." Eli squeezed her to him and groaned. "Damn, you feel good."

Rachel wanted to do a jiggling happy dance as she noticed his earlier declaration that they should lay off for tonight seemed to have been laid aside.

"So do you." Chuckling, Rachel couldn't help but notice the erection currently pressed against her abdomen as they danced. It was a good thing the club was dimly lit, otherwise everyone there would know what Eli was thinking about.

After the dance, they mingled around the club for a few minutes, talking with friends. Rachel was distracted the whole time by the way her body tingled and hummed all over. When they came near the restroom, Rachel excused herself for a few minutes.

Boy, did Eli have the ability to strum her body to a screaming fever pitch. His words and touch had left her soaking wet with her juices, and aching to be fucked. While she was drying her hands, Corina Scott and one of her friends came giggling into the restroom. Corina had a pretty glow in her pale ivory cheeks.

"Oh! Hey, Rachel! I am so glad you introduced me to Brice. He's waiting for me outside right now. I think he's so handsome." Corina blushed with pleasure.

Rachel smiled. "You're welcome. He's a nice guy and I'm glad he's being good to you. What about Andy and Vince?" she asked the other girl.

"Oh, they're out there, too. We're having fun dancing with them, but Brice only has eyes for Corina. It's about time that life dealt you some happiness, sweetie." That comment made Rachel wonder about Corina's story. Looking in her eyes, Rachel had the impression that Corina had been through a lot in her life. Though she was young, there were bluish hints of dark circles under her eyes and she seemed a little fragile, physically.

"He told me I was pretty," Corina said dreamily and another pink blush stole over her cheeks.

"Well, you are, and your face is glowing," Rachel told her honestly.

"Listen, Rachel," Corina said, watching the door. "Our co-worker, Sandra, the one who put her hand on your fiancé? She's not really a friend. She overheard at work that we were coming out here and invited herself along."

"Oh, that's okay. I've gotten used to dealing with persistent women where Eli is concerned. I'm glad you like it here. I have a friend I want to introduce you to later. I think you'd like Grace a lot."

Corina said she'd watch for her. Rachel stepped out of the restroom and spotted Eli talking with Brice. Eli smiled when he caught a glimpse of her. For a night out that started as one of the worst on record, it was shaping up very well.

* * * *

Eli looked up from his conversation with Brice Huvell, as Rachel reentered the hallway from the ladies' room, and admired her as she closed the distance between them. Her eyes twinkled as she slipped her arm around his waist, and Eli said, "I was just telling Brice how to get out to the Divine Creek Ranch. He got an invite from Grace for him *and* a date."

"Oh? You should ask Corina, Brice. She's sweet and pretty, too, don't you think?"

"I sure do, Rachel." Brice nodded and looked down as if he didn't know if he should say more.

"Well, I guess we'll see you on the dance floor, Brice." Eli took Rachel's soft hand, nodded to Brice, and led her toward the front of the club.

He squeezed her to him. "How are you doing?"

Rachel's face was radiant as she gazed up at him and tilted her cheek into his caressing palm. "I'm heavenly."

Eli's cock twitched in response to the sexy tone of her voice. *I'll say.*

"Wow, that good?" He smiled with satisfaction when she said nothing more, only nodded and burrowed closer to him. Eli enjoyed the feel of her womanly, soft, fragrant body pressed closely to his. He looked down at her in his arms and noticed her lip trembled. "You're my whole life, angel."

"Aw, you two are just the sweetest things," Grace said as she walked up to where they stood at the front. "Have you been *having fun* on the dance floor?"

"Lots of fun," Rachel said, glancing up at Eli and giggling, before asking her, "Have you put in a song request?"

"Two songs, back to back. Ethan is up in the booth right now." Grace pointed to him and waved when Ethan looked over at her. He blew her a kiss and put his hand over his heart. She kissed her fingers and waved back. "Can I borrow her, Eli?"

"Sure, Grace." He kissed Rachel's temple and whispered, "Did you tell her what we were talking about on the dance floor?"

Rachel smiled suggestively and replied, "No, of course not. But I think she has radar. You can imagine *how* she might know. She says Ethan is a *wonderful* dancer. What? TMI?" She snickered and said, "*Ooops!* I promised to be good, didn't I?"

"Oh, you're *good* all right." He kissed her again. "Dance for me, angel."

She looked at him with pure lust in her eyes and gave him a sexy smile. "*Only* for you."

Chapter Forty

"Hillbilly Bone" by Blake Shelton and Trace Adkins began to play. In fascination, Eli watched her hips sway as she walked away in those killer shoes. She looked back at him like she knew he'd be watching and glanced down at the fly of his leathers.

Damn. He could feel the heat of her gaze on his crotch, and his eager cock pulsed in response. The heavy beat and raunchy guitar rhythm had both women swinging their hips as they stepped on the dance floor, where they were joined by other couples and individuals.

He would be hard-pressed to explain why the sight of her pretty little feet perched so high on those sexy heels had such a visceral, primal effect on his libido, but they did. All Eli could imagine was the scene from his earlier-spoken fantasy with her holding the arms of the lounger on the back deck, straddling the frame of the chair with her long, luscious legs spread wide and her pussy presented for him, ready and waiting. The thought made his erection throb for her soft warmth to sink into. And she hadn't even begun to *really* dance yet. Damn, but she had a way with him.

He noticed several men, business-suit types, at a table near the dance floor nudge each other as Grace and Rachel began to dance. Rosemary bounced out onto the dance floor with them, and then three of the little blondes from the scene at the door earlier came and danced with them, too. He watched the men and read their body language and the looks of lust on their faces. Slowly moving through the groups at the tables, Eli took a position midway to the dance floor and near their table. There were other couples on the dance floor, but all the girls with Rachel and Grace danced together in a group.

His eyes were drawn to the hypnotic sway of Rachel's hips as they moved to the slow, driving beat of the song. She slid her hands down her ribs, over her hips and around to her ass.

Tonight he could tell she *truly* didn't care what anyone else in that club thought of the way she danced. Rachel's eyes were closed most of the time when she wasn't watching him playfully across the room. He always felt protective and watchful when she danced, but he knew tonight she needed him to watch over her and protect her so she could have her fun.

Rachel smiled when she saw he had moved closer through the tables toward her side of the dance floor. She shimmied and dipped down, rolling her hips. She slid the backs of her fingers over her ribs and the sides of her breasts upward into her hair. That was a move he was particularly fond of, and he knew *she* knew it, too.

He was distracted by movement from the table of men, who he could see were enthusiastically enjoying the girls' dancing. One of them was even waving a dollar bill. The girls ignored them, and one of the men rose from his seat and began to make his way toward the edge of the dance floor, *toward Grace*. She hadn't noticed him yet. *Shit.* A split second before Eli made his move, he saw Ethan step up to the man.

Eli hadn't even realized it when Ethan came to stand near him, watching over the girls also. Ethan wanted his customers to have a good time, but not *that* good, especially where *his* woman was concerned. The poor guy had come to within a couple of feet of Grace when Ethan clapped a hand down on his shoulder and spoke in his ear. The man threw his hands up immediately in a gesture of surrender and backed away at the look in Ethan's eyes. Eli grinned, relieved he wasn't the only one with a fucking Neanderthal residing in his psyche.

The men at that table settled down when they realized they'd been mistaken in thinking the girls were dancing to entertain them. Ethan approached the table and shook hands with a couple of them, pointed at the group of girls, then gestured at the other territorial looking men positioned around the dance floor.

Every one of those girls was being watched over by the object of her affections and was not available for their enjoyment. Ethan hailed a waitress and ordered them complimentary drinks to soothe any feelings of disappointment. Eli smiled, thinking how smooth Ethan was at his job because none of the girls was ever aware of what could have become an ugly scene if the men had touched one of them. He thought Grace might have had an inkling as she glanced over at Ethan, then at Eli. He smiled at her, and she went back to her fun.

The other men relaxed visibly and went back to watching their ladies but moved protectively closer to the dance floor. The girls were safer than if they'd been inside Fort Knox. The final chorus thumped, hips were swaying, and shiny curls bobbing as Eli reached the edge of the dance floor. The girls laughed and blew kisses at their happily tortured men, ignoring the others who watched appreciatively.

Another song began as Trace Adkins's grinning face appeared on the video monitor over the bar. The girls all cheered for Ethan, who had a knack for picking songs for Grace to dance to. They began to dance to the slightly faster beat as "Honky Tonk Badonkadonk" played good and loud.

Rachel put her hands on her hips and shook her moneymaker, edging slowly through the group until she was directly in front of Eli. She danced right up to him and even brushed him with her breasts as he stood perfectly still. His cock pounded against his fly as he watched her tempting erotic movements. Rachel shimmied all the way down facing him, eye level with his cock, then moved slowly back up, brushing against him again as if she were a professional exotic dancer.

His woman was incredibly beautiful and sensual in her movements and his throbbing, insistent cock was negotiating with his weakening resolve like crazy. Moving like this, she *had* to feel better. She was so tempting in that dress, and he noticed the shoes again, and *fu-huck* his determination truly began to crumble. How she even stayed upright with her heels perched so precariously high, her legs looking ten feet long, was beyond him. *Damn!*

Rachel turned her back to him again and shimmied her ass within inches of the erection she'd made eye contact with moments earlier when she'd dipped for him. Eli stood through the song, hands on his hips, watching her and tightly reigning in his control.

As the last chorus began to play, she became bolder, smiling at him and giving him a come-hither look over her shoulder. She allowed her luscious ass to *accidentally* bump against his thighs as she dipped again. She turned without ever rubbing against his erection, because she wasn't *that* cruel, and faced him. Placing her hands on his abs, Rachel and her hands up and over his pecs as she moved with the beat.

She dipped and rolled her hips again, sliding her hands over his shoulders. Of their own volition, his hands reached for her hips and stroked over them, grasping gently as she swished them in front of him. His fingers slid over her ass as she moved. *Fuck*, but she was hotter than hell tonight!

As the song faded, she smiled up at him, and her fingers trailed down to his hips, her movements slowing until she breathlessly allowed him to pull her into his arms.

He growled in her ear as the club cheered the girls' efforts. "You are the *hottest* fucking thing in this place, Rachel. You're not leaving my side the rest of the time you're here. I don't want to have to kill anyone tonight. Damn, but you're beautiful. You and the other girls are going to have to stay near your men tonight, or there are going to be fights breaking out all over the club."

Rachel's eyes glowed with blue fire as she looked up at him. "You're not mad, are you? That I danced so suggestively for you? I really let go."

"I *know*, and, *no*, I'm not mad at you. But any man comes near you and he's liable to lose a limb or worse." He gently pulled her to him, and they walked back to the front. Eli ordered her another Coke after he helped her into her chair and smiled down into her radiant face. "Now, how am I supposed to let you leave by yourself tonight?" he asked, hands on his hips, standing in front of her.

"Don't think about it right now. I'm not leaving for a while. It's only nine o'clock," she said, checking her watch.

Not for the first time, Eli wondered how his jobs and his odd hours would affect their lives. He enjoyed working for Ethan and Ben a lot. Most of the time, Eli felt like he worked *with* them and not *for* them. Rachel never complained about his hours as a bouncer or the challenges inherent to that line of work, trusting in his abilities. If anything, she seemed to have more of a problem with the tower climbing work. Maybe down the road changes in work would come, but for now, he didn't want to rush into more. The next item on their agenda was a change of address.

Rachel had cleared a little time off on Wednesday afternoon, and they made an appointment with a friend of Rachel's who was a real estate agent. She had a list of properties to show them, some with houses and others without that they could build on. This was where the tower work came in so handy. He charged premium rates for climbing, and that money would help make building a home of their own a reality that much quicker.

Rachel leaned against him as he sat next to her, and he kissed the top of her head, breathing in her beautiful womanly scent. She looked up at him and smiled. "I finished the novel today."

"You did? Congratulations, that was fast!" he said admiringly as he kissed her forehead and hugged her.

"It literally flew from my fingertips once I got started. After I re-read it and check it for errors, I'm going to submit it for publication and see what happens from there."

"My wife, the bestselling author," he said, looking down at her proudly.

"That sounds heavenly coming from you. Calling me your wife like that. No one has ever called me a writer, either."

Eli didn't pretend to be interested in her career as a writer. He did care and loved seeing her live out her life-long dream. He laced his fingers in hers, and they chatted with Mike about his wife and kids and the wedding.

* * * *

Across the club, Ethan looked on with amusement as he kept an eye out for Rachel's approach while Grace and the girls planned a bachelorette party for her. Grace had her phone to her ear, brainstorming with Kelly. Rosemary, Kathleen, and even Corina, who Grace had taken under her wing because of Brice's clear interest in her, sat together at Grace's table all in cahoots with each other. Ethan considered Brice his friend, and so for Grace it was only natural to go ahead and claim the little sweetheart who had caught his eye as one of *the girls*.

Grace looked at Ethan speculatively then winked at him and blew him an air kiss. "I don't know. He's right here. I'll ask. No, I can't ask Mike. He's over talking with Eli and Rachel right now. Let me ask. Hold on."

Ethan drew closer to her, and she asked, "Are there going to be strippers at Eli's bachelor party? Kelly says no strippers for our party if you aren't hiring one for Eli."

Ethan shrugged and looked at Adam and Jack. "What do you think?" He didn't want to get crossways with Rachel, but he knew they'd keep Eli out of trouble. "What if we went to a strip club instead of hiring a specific stripper?" he asked.

She returned the phone to her ear, repeated his question, then nodded and looked up. "What if we took Rachel out to Morehead and did the same thing? What would Eli say?"

Ethan thought about it for a second. He somehow doubted Eli would have a problem, but on one condition. "What if one of us went with your group and one of you went with our group, sort of as chaperones? Plus, that way, you would have a man to watch over you and keep you safe. We could hire a limousine, so none of you had to drive."

"I like that idea!" Grace said with a twinkle in her eye. "But how do we choose? All of us want to go to the party." She didn't like the thought of anyone missing out on the fun.

"Oh, I think whoever goes as a chaperone will be shown a good time, but we could draw straws," Ethan suggested.

"No need. I'll volunteer to go with them," Adam said, grinning at Grace as she smiled devilishly at him and then winked.

Ethan had a feeling Adam was willing because he wanted to watch over Grace as much as Rachel and not because he planned to enjoy the bachelorette party. Although, Grace did have a way of making *everything* fun. Shit, maybe he should have volunteered for chaperone duty.

"Good," Ethan said. "Then you pick someone from your group to come with us. We'll keep her safe and make sure she enjoys herself, too. She can keep an eye on Eli for Rachel while Adam watches over Rachel. Fair enough?"

Grace repeated the idea into the phone and then nodded at them. "Okay, I'll call you with a date. Yes, I'll get Erin to babysit for you. What?" She listened and looked up at Ethan, fighting back laughter, and asked him, "Were you going to let Erin come to the bachelorette party?" At his bulgy-eyed look, she snickered. "I thought not. Um, no, Erin won't be in on all the hot stripper fun. I'll call her and arrange it. Love you, too! Bye! All right," she said to the group, "all we have to do is pick one of the ladies to go with the guys to the gentlemen's club. I think I know who fits that bill *perfectly*, too." She chuckled and tapped her fingernail on the screen of her phone again.

"Hey, Charity, ever been to a gentleman's strip club? Wanna go? I thought you'd say that, you kinky thing!" Grace rolled her eyes and laughed. "Yes, you can wear *whatever* you want!"

* * * *

An hour later, Eli walked Rachel out to her truck in the parking lot. There was a light chill in the air, and he drew her close to his side when she shivered. Glancing around for anyone lurking in the parking lot, he unlocked and opened her door for her. He helped her into the truck and smoothed his hand over her silky, voluptuous calf.

"You were something else tonight, angel." He drew a fingertip under her bottom lip before he leaned down and kissed her soft lips lightly. Her warm little tongue flicked out playfully and licked his bottom lip then sucked on it gently when he returned for another kiss.

"Thank you for watching out for us while we were on the dance floor." She slid her fingertips over his biceps. "I always feel safe with you, Eli."

"The pleasure was mine. Thank you. You feeling safe is my job and my pleasure."

"We didn't mean to cause a problem."

"That wasn't for you to worry about. All of you were spoken for in that group, and it was our responsibility to watch out for you so that you could have your fun. If you'd been aware, it would have spoiled it for you. It's *our* job to keep you safe."

During the course of the night, he'd made a point of speaking with Brice, Andy, and Vince, making certain that they knew they would need to make sure Corina, Lisa, Michelle, and even Sandra made it back to their vehicle in the parking lot safely when they left. He knew all the other women who had danced with Grace were leaving with the men who brought them. He'd been pleased to note that the three men had stuck to the women and made sure nobody bothered them once the girls made it clear they welcomed their attention. It was a win-win situation for all involved.

"I love your alpha male sensibilities. It's a huge turn-on, Eli," she said softly, and her warm gaze made him feel about ten feet tall.

"I'm all about turning you on, angel. And, yeah, you definitely bring out the alpha in me."

"I *love* that guy." She chuckled as he nuzzled her lips with his.

"Will you tell me what happened earlier tonight after I get home?" He'd tried to focus on the moment while she'd been there, but whatever had happened earlier had never strayed very far from his mind. She seemed to handle herself well tonight, but whatever it was had really upset her earlier and that didn't sit well with him. The alpha male in him wanted to make whatever it was *right* for her.

She smiled up at him and said without hesitation, "Yes, it hardly even matters to me now, but I'll tell you everything. I probably should have told you about it before today. I'll be waiting for you."

"In my bed?" He growled softly.

"Yes, in your bed." She giggled and kissed him again.

"Good. I'll see you in a little while, angel. Drive safely, and remember to text me when you're in the house so I know you made it home all right."

"I will. I love you."

He stood in the parking lot and watched as she backed out, waved to him, and drove out of the parking lot.

* * * *

Later that night, Eli leaned against the bedroom doorframe and drank in her appearance. She was fresh from her shower and dressed in her black lace nightgown. Her hair was soft and brushed out, and he imagined it smelled clean like the shampoo she used. The lamp was on beside the bed, but she'd also lit the candles around the room for when he eventually turned the lamp off. Her computer sat open in her lap, indicating what she'd been doing while she waited for him to get home. He leaned over the edge of the bed and kissed her lovingly.

"I'm going to take a shower and then I'll join you."

"I'll warm the bed for you," she replied softly, shut down her computer, and laid it on the bedside table.

He showered and returned to the bedroom, wearing his robe. She'd turned off the lamp, so only the soft, warm candlelight flickered around the room. He slipped the robe off and turned to her as she lay on her side, watching him appreciatively. Her eyes moved over his body like a warm caress. No matter his words or his resolve, the look in her eyes confirmed

Rachel would have her way, whatever it was, and he would not object. His stiff, erect cock twitched insistently and volunteered for duty.

"Will you tell me now?" He lay down, pulled her to him, and gently caressed her arms and shoulders. She climbed over him, straddled his hips, and laid her supple body over his. He groaned in bliss at the silky, warm contact.

"In a few minutes. Let me love you now." She joined her lips to his and caressed his cheek.

Rachel received no argument from him and smiled as she slid down his body, kissing a damp trail along his torso as she went. She pressed her breasts to his cock as she slid lower until she reached her destination and smiled up at him. She flicked the tip of her warm tongue out and licked the head of his cock. He hissed softly and arched his back at the warm touch of her velvety tongue.

She licked her lips and slid them over the underside of his cock, tonguing him and swirling back and forth until she reached the base of his cock and proceeded through his crisp curls to the sac beneath.

Eli's hips flexed, and he shuddered and moaned, relieved he could make as much noise as he wanted to. His balls drew up as she licked and suckled them gently with her warm mouth, and he moaned again. He slid his fingers through her silky hair and breathed out words of encouragement to her. She gently sucked one ball into her mouth and caressed it with her tongue and paid tender attention to him there for a minute and then moved back up.

Laving his cock with her warm wet tongue, she pressed her lips against the throbbing head. Sliding between her full soft lips into her mouth was second only to sliding into her pussy. The way she sucked his cock for him, tugging gently to mimic the way her pussy tugged him when she gripped him with her inner muscles, sent icy-hot chills up and down his spine. He couldn't help but move with her. When he encouraged her to suck harder, and she did, there was no other feeling like it. Rachel always took her time with him and he loved that the most about having her lips on his cock.

She sucked his cock lovingly for a few minutes, responding softly as he whispered to her how much she pleased him, how much he loved her. After another minute, she suckled him one last time and climbed back over him. She lifted her nightgown, revealing the satiny-smooth beauty beneath as she pulled it over her head and laid it aside.

Stroking her pussy with his fingertips, Eli could feel the slick evidence of her desire. She moaned softly and moved against his fingers when he fingered her swollen clit and then lay down on his torso and straddled him again above his hard cock. She kissed his lips, and he lost himself in her eyes as she lay over his chest and slowly slid down until the big head of his cock made contact with her slick, wet entrance.

Eli loved the feel of her soft, resistant flesh as his head pressed for entrance against her quivering, slippery-hot opening. He flexed his hips, pressing for entry into those tight muscles. She inched back a tiny bit more and groaned softly in delight when her resistance subsided, and he slid inside her warm body. He groaned in ecstasy as her wet heat tightly engulfed his shaft and wished he could stay inside her like this forever. She looked down into his eyes as she squeezed him with her pussy muscles. A strangled, gasping moan escaped his lips, and he fought the urge to release right then.

"Angel!" he growled in ecstasy as she swiveled her hips over his cock.

"I love you, Eli."

"I love you." He wrapped his arms around her warm, voluptuous body.

She continued squeezing him rhythmically then tilted her hips to give him a different sensation. He lay still for her and allowed her to play as long as she wanted, giving her the control over this beautiful moment. Her sexy body draped over his was sweet torture he gladly submitted to.

Rachel's breathing roughened, and she slid down another notch and welcomed more of his aching cock into her hot, lush wetness. She continued squeezing him and rocked over him in wet, sensual grace. She played like this over him, whispering to him of her love and desire for him, until her arousal flamed into a fire around him, and she rose over him, her blue eyes glittering with lust.

Bracing her delicate hands on his chest, Rachel slid down all the way on him in one luscious, sweeping plunge to the hilt. Her soft, moaning gasp was music to his ears. The sound of it alone made him want to come.

She remained motionless for a second then opened her eyes and steadied herself. She flung her long, fragrant hair over her shoulder, sat upright and lifted off slightly, and rocked her hips as she slid back down over him. He thrust against her, wanting to be as deep inside her as he could be.

Her soft lips parted on a moan, and her eyelids slid closed in bliss. The backs of her hands slid up her rib cage in a perfect copy of her dance move from earlier in the evening, her fingernails straying over her tight, erect nipples, and then her hands slid up into her hair. Her back arched, and her head tilted back. He felt the ends of her hair trace in a tickling touch over his thighs.

He experienced a moment of something like déjà vu, remembering the moment he'd seen her face on the dance floor as she danced with Grace the first time he'd laid eyes on her. He'd envisioned her like this, astride him, her back arched, soft lips parted in ecstasy as she rode his cock in rapturous abandon.

Back then, he knew he desired her body. Now, he knew *her*. He knew the color of her eyes, the depth of her love, the goodness and gentleness of her soul, and he was reduced in that moment to a man hopelessly enslaved to his woman. He was overcome with the strength of her love for him, her desire for him.

Eli threw his head back in blissful surrender as she rode his aching, throbbing cock to a blistering, red-hot orgasm, both of them crying out in unadulterated joy. They rode every single pulse together as his cum jetted from his cock, and her pussy clenched like a vise around him. When the pulses stopped, she toppled limply over him as a quivering, sated sigh escaped her lips.

He held her as she trembled against him and traced his fingers over her silky back. As she lay over him, her flush swept over her, and it filled him with primal male satisfaction to feel this visible, tangible proof that she had experienced such great pleasure with him. Her soft breathing wafted over his chest, tickling the smattering of chest hairs there. She sighed deeply and touched his face.

Softly, he asked, "Are you all right? Any pain?"

"No. Making love with you was beautiful, pure pleasure. No pain at all. Thank you for letting me have my way with you. I loved it. Do you feel good?"

"Hmm, do I feel good? I feel like I died and went to heaven. I feel like I'm still there." He tilted his hips slightly, feeling his cock lodged in her tight, hot depths. They both moaned softly. "That's heaven, angel."

After a few minutes, she rose and allowed him to pull out. He held out his arms to hold her against his chest. After she laid her head on his shoulder and relaxed, he said gently, "Tell me what happened before you came in tonight." He tried to brace himself for whatever she might say.

She told him exactly what happened in the parking lot, blushing hotly, and he held his reaction in check as well as he could and listened.

Chapter Forty-one

"Reese McCoy," he grated out under his breath.

She could hear the indignation in his voice and feel it in the tense muscles under her palm.

"Yes. You know who he is?"

"He works for an outfit that subcontracts with the electrical co-op in this part of Texas. I've worked with him at some of the electrical sub-stations in the area on their wireless Internet antennas. I remember seeing him come in the club this evening."

"We dated briefly right after I moved out on my own. I was restless and testing my new independence. He took me out a couple of times, and I didn't realize he was only after one thing. One thing led to another, and...you know. It hurt horribly, and he wasn't gentle at all, like he didn't care it was my first time. He seemed to make a game out of how hard he took me, like that was how he wanted it, with no thought for me. I never heard from him again after he got what he wanted."

Rachel felt the tension in Eli's body increase. She stroked his chest and kissed him there. She wondered what went through his mind. She gave him time to process, and he asked. "Did he know you were a virgin?"

"Yes, when it looked like we were going to have sex, I told him. I thought he had a right to know beforehand that I had no experience. But I also hoped that he would take his time and be gentle. It was like I poured gasoline on a lit match." She knew it was a strain for him to hear those things when she felt a rumble in his chest under her hand and heard a soft growl. His body vibrated with tension for a moment. "I couldn't get him to stop. I couldn't get him to slow down. He didn't even bother with a condom."

"I'd gotten on the pill, so I never lived through the fear of wondering if he got me pregnant, but I felt so stupid. Before that night, I never would have thought that if I told him I was a virgin he would take pleasure in doing it so roughly. I bled like crazy and cried afterward. He was…triumphant. When I continued crying, he slapped me and told me to get a hold of myself and deal with it. It was over and I wasn't a virgin anymore 'thanks to him.' That was how he put it." She sensed the tension in Eli's body and the quickening of his heartbeat, though he still stroked her gently. "I *never* told him I wanted to get it over with. Those were his suppositions. I took the first opportunity that presented itself. I paid hard for my foolishness. The bleeding didn't stop until the next day. I waited a few days to recover, and then I went to a doctor and got all the tests they recommended. I was never more ashamed of my own stupidity than I was in that moment."

"But he hurt you, and then revisited that pain on you again tonight."

"The shame I felt is for being nonchalant about giving up a part of myself that was sacred to someone so *foul*. I was blind at the time and naïve. I—I can't believe I felt this way, but I wanted to get it over with. I never *once* told him that, but it was how I felt before he…did what he did."

"Did the doctor ask you if he'd raped you?"

"Yes, but I told them no because, in essence, I had asked for it. I went willingly, to a point. I couldn't call it rape because I consented to be with him."

"He ambushed you."

"Yes, he did. But pressing charges against him, with the circumstances being what they were, I'd have been raped over and over again going through the proper legal channels, in the courts, the media, in front of my family and friends. Tell me I chose wrong," she said, mild challenge in her voice. "I do know this. Someday, Reese will get paid back for what he did. It doesn't even matter if I ever hear about it or know it happened. I know he'll be repaid."

"Did you get some help?"

She appreciated him more in that moment than he could realize for understanding that it wasn't something that she could just *get over* without help.

"Yes, I was referred to a support group and went for a couple of years. They helped me a lot. Now, it's just something that happened to me a long time ago. It doesn't affect who I am now. I don't think it has impacted how I relate to you, though my behavior tonight was perhaps a bit over the top," she said with a slight grin. "I have moved on from the trauma, but that doesn't mean I enjoyed encountering him tonight or hearing his vulgar retelling of the incident in the parking lot. I've always been able to avoid him when our paths have crossed before. I don't hide from him, mind you, but I've been able to avoid any face-to-face contact. That's saying a lot, considering the size of this town. I hope someday he'll move away or disappear."

"Does your father or any other man in your life know?"

"Are you kidding? I didn't want to see my dad go to prison or any of his friends or my classmates, for that matter. They all knew something was wrong for a while, but I attributed it to the stress of going to school and being out on my own. I was fairly solitary for a while. Getting out and socializing was very therapeutic, proving to myself I could socialize and enjoy having friends to hang out with safely. They all welcomed me back like I'd never been gone." She paused for a moment before asking, "Did you consider him a friend?"

"No. He's a greasy, lazy son of a bitch. He wouldn't know what a decent day's work felt like if it reared up and bit him in the ass."

She'd noticed that time had not been kind to Reese, though it had only been nine years since that night. "I'm sorry I didn't tell you about this thing that happened to me sooner. You had a right to know that about me."

"Rachel, I want all of you, even the parts that have been hurt."

"If I had kept my head straight, I would have come to you untouched. I regret that now more than anything."

He lifted her chin to gaze into her eyes. "No regrets, remember? Our first time was precious to me. Whether you were a virgin or not, it was no less magical or amazing. I wish I could erase the pain of that memory from your mind."

"You have, you know? You are so gentle and sweet, and I finally understood what making love was *supposed* to feel like. My efforts to get past losing my virginity backfired on me, you see? Because I still didn't know what it was like until I met you and fell in love with you. How do you feel about what I've told you?"

He took his time answering her. She thought he was trying to protect her from the depth of the emotions he experienced. He simply said, "Vengeful, but not foolish. You and I have big plans for our lives, and nothing is going to change that. But I do feel vengeful."

"I'm sorry he's someone you work with."

"He'd actually have to do some work for that to be true. I'm self-employed, so I don't have to work with him."

"What are you going to do?"

"Nothing except hold you, right now. How do you feel?"

"Light as a feather."

"Good. Angel, I'm sorry it happened, and I'd erase it all from your memory if I could. You know you're safe with me."

"Of course."

"Then it will all work out."

She couldn't quite put her finger on it, but she knew he was formulating a plan. That had not been her intention in telling him.

"You're going to do something, aren't you?" She sat up and looked at him.

"I'm not going to kill him, if that's what you're worried about." Eli smiled at her and tucked a stray lock of hair behind her ear. She allowed him to cuddle her to his chest, and she fell asleep listening to the comforting sound of his heartbeat as he stroked her back.

* * * *

Eli had to smile as Charlie took his hat off and scratched his head in embarrassed surprise. Eli and Rachel had just shared a clear conversation through the wall adjoining their bedrooms.

"Well, I'll be damned, Eli! I could see where that might be a bit of a…uh…*problem*. I wonder why none of the other renters said anything."

"Well, Mr. Hardaway was practically deaf, and he never had any visitors except his grown kids. He was always very quiet, and I never heard a thing from over on his side. We didn't discover it until one day when there were people home on both sides of the duplex." Eli spared his congenial landlord the more descriptive details.

Charlie had stopped by on Wednesday to get started on some repairs he'd talked to Eli about before Rachel had her accident. Eli explained to him that they had since gotten engaged and would be house hunting in the area for a place of their own. Eli offered to pay whatever penalties Charlie expected for breaking the lease so early, but Charlie waved off his offer.

"You've have been such neat renters, never give me any trouble, never late with the rent, and you keep the place looking nice. I'm not going to charge you any penalties. But I am glad you showed me this wall. I'm going to have to get some soundproofing in there. When's the wedding?" he asked, and they chatted for a while.

Charlie changed his plans and made a top priority of putting in sound-reducing insulation in the hollow wall. Rachel was at Eli's place more than her own, so she cleared out her bedroom and moved the furniture back to her parent's storage barn until it was needed again.

Her mom and dad never batted an eye about the bed returning and never asked about her sleeping arrangements.

Rachel and Eli met with Jane Jensen, Rachel's real estate agent friend. Jane directed them around the area to ten different properties. They liked a few of the acreage sites, especially the ones that had a lot of oak trees on them. Eli and Rachel both had a dream of having a home amidst oak trees, far back from the road. Several of the properties Jane showed them fit the bill.

There was one twenty-acre ranch that had a nice-sized older house on it. It was more space than the two of them needed, but it offered room to grow and to raise a family. The previous owners had evidently loved gardening because the overgrown flowerbeds hinted that, until recently, they had been lovingly maintained.

The lawn in front of the house had not survived the hot summer and drought the year before and would need to be re-done, but the house and yards were surrounded by woods on all sides. He could see kids running in safety and freedom in the yards and around in the wooded area and playing in the low creek that ran through the property.

Jane kindly turned down the offer for lunch and left them with a shortened list of the properties they liked the best, along with the directions for getting to each, so that they could talk in private about what they should do next. Jane told them she had the key to the ranch house if they wanted to pick it up and go take another look in case they missed something before.

Eli took Rachel to Rudy's, and they sat in the quiet corner booth and held hands and talked.

"You liked the ranch house, didn't you?" he asked, smiling softly at the excitement in her eyes when he brought it up.

She nodded. "I did. Someone took care of that place while they lived there. It's a little rundown from being vacant, but I see a lot of potential. They worked hard on the basic landscaping and all the shrubs and trees around the house."

"I like the long, meandering driveway through the woods and the trees all around the house, but the lawn...Ugh."

Rachel nodded. "I know. We'd have to rip out all that carpet grass."

"As far as the house goes," Eli said, "it needs major updating and remodeling. Replace any rotten wood, paint, and maybe redo some flooring. I can do a lot of that, if the price is right on the house."

"I could help with the paint and other things. I'd like to hire a professional to update the landscaping, and it would be worth it to put in a sprinkler system."

He laughed. "We're talking like we already made our decision."

"Oh, no, not yet. I want to have it inspected first. I'm not getting emotionally invested until we know if it would mean buying a money pit. I do like the basic structure and layout, though. The house itself seems solid and structurally sound."

"All those appliances would have to go, for sure."

Rachel laughed and rolled her eyes. "I haven't seen a harvest gold refrigerator in years! Yes, all new appliances, please! We need to see about the wiring in the house also..."

They talked and laughed through lunch. Rudy congratulated Eli and Rachel on their upcoming nuptials and brought them a complimentary dessert, which they shared before Rachel went back to the office. Eli told her he would be home by early evening after his last service call of the day.

* * * *

Eli sat down with the men at one of the tables, and Ethan brought them all beers. Eli looked around at the group and said, "What I tell you can't leave this room, or this group. Whether you help me or not, you have to promise me that much." Eli wished he could have included Mike and Rogelio at this gathering but they were too close to Rachel's father. Rachel had been very clear on why she hadn't told him years ago and Eli respected her wishes.

Ethan, Jack, Adam, and Ace agreed.

Eli detailed to them what happened to Rachel and that she had received no justice for what had been done to her. He told the story to the best of his recollection, and when he was done, he could have heard a pin drop it was so quiet around the table. Eli looked around the table, making eye contact with all of them in turn.

"Rachel says she's content that someday he'll get what's coming to him, and I think she was a little worried I'd kill him at first. You can imagine how I reacted, right?"

The indignation he felt so strongly was clearly reflected on their faces.

Ace spoke up first. "I could look into his past, into his dealings for you. Find dirt on him. He sounds like a predator. If he did that to her, he's done other bad things that could come to light. He would not fare well in prison. I'd be willing to bet he's got lots of skeletons hanging in his closet. Let me do some digging. Do you have much information on him?"

"Just his name and employer. I work with him from time to time."

"That's a start."

When Jack spoke, his demeanor was calm, as were Ethan and Adam's, but Eli could see the anger beneath. He thought they might feel strongly about what happened to Rachel. "Eli, first, thanks for deciding to call on us about this. We'll do whatever we can to help you. Ace, if you need someone to help watch this bastard or assist you in any way, you let us know. Calling on Ace was a good idea, Eli. He'll help us nail this son of a bitch, but good."

Ethan and Adam nodded.

"That prick won't know what hit him," Adam muttered.

"I promised Rachel I wouldn't kill him, but it's damned tempting."

Ace chuckled and nodded in understanding. "Don't do anything permanent yet. I have a good feeling about this. If this guy gets his jollies doing things like this, he's probably got buddies he brags to. He's boasted about other stuff, too, I'll bet. Let's focus on making him the girlfriend of some seven-foot tall, three-hundred-pound prison inmate. I'll start digging for you this afternoon and contact my guy to watch him."

"Thank you, guys." Eli shook their hands. "Ace, whatever the cost, I'll cover it."

378

Heather Rainier

Ethan said firmly, "There's no way he's gonna to get away with hurting another woman like that ever again. Ace will find something."

Adam spoke up then. "We know how it feels to find out that the woman you love has been harmed and mistreated by someone she trusted. We'll bring this guy to justice, one way or another."

"Thanks, man," Eli said, glad to have their backing.

"Do you know if you'll be working with him anytime soon?" Ace asked as he made notes on a pad.

"No, I only see him on the jobs scheduled at the sub-stations. He works all over the co-op's service area, which would explain why she hasn't run into him more often. The company he works for assigns them randomly."

"Okay, I'll track him down."

"And don't worry, Eli," Jack said. "This conversation won't leave this room."

* * * *

Ethan said good-bye to the others when they left and went to his office. He worked for a while, looking over purchase orders and paying bills. Thoughts of Grace occupied his mind and made it difficult to focus for any length of time.

Ethan could relate to how Eli felt right now. He remembered a time when he'd felt like killing the bastard who had mistreated Grace. He recalled not being able to move fast enough to stop Owen before he'd viciously struck Grace twice in the face. He shuddered at the memory of the way she'd toppled backward against the kitchen counter and then had hit the floor at Owen's feet. His heart throbbed at the memory of the way her body had shaken as he held her tightly in his arms afterward.

They'd made it their mission to begin to undo the negative self-image Owen had sown in her mind and to convince her the woman they saw was beautiful and precious, not fat and ugly. With their love and attention, they'd made a believer out of her, and she made them the happiest of men.

During the previous night, he'd awakened with her curled up beside him in his bed. He'd stayed at the club late and she must have come to check on him and decided to snuggle up under his covers. While he watched her sleep, she'd stirred and cuddled closer to him with her lips pressed to his chest. Later that morning as dawn turned the sky a pale gray, they'd made love. Ethan remembered the way she'd felt, so warm and sleep tender as he held her in his arms and stroked into her sweet, hot pussy, both of them coming with a deep, burning intensity.

Ethan slipped his phone from his pocket. Today was Grace's day off, and when she answered, he could hear horses neighing in the background. She must be out in the barn.

"Hello, my baby." Her voice had a mellow, seductive tone that sent a shot of lust straight to his cock. He knew he'd be hard and aching by the time he was done talking to her.

"Hello, Gracie. What are you up to?"

"I'm out in the barn, brushing down Coraggio. What are you doing?" Grace had a way of asking questions like that. Her subtle, suggestive tone hinted at what she wished he was doing. He answered the question she was *really* asking.

"Wishing I could take you in my arms and sink right into your silky little pussy. The sound of your sexy voice makes me hard enough to hammer nails."

Grace hummed softly in approval. "I wish I were there. I'd let you hammer me instead. After I finish with Coraggio, I'm going to work for a while. I have a hot love scene to write."

"Well, honey, you'd know a thing or two about hot love scenes, wouldn't you?" The throbbing steel pole in his jeans testified to that fact. Ethan, Jack and Adam had watched her blossom into their very own sex goddess since she'd begun writing.

"As well-loved as I am? I should be able to set my laptop to smoldering," she replied with a giggle. "Wanna come help me with research?"

"I'm tempted. I should be done here in another hour or so. I had another reason for calling, though."

"What's that, babe?"

"You haven't hinted to me what you'd like for Christmas."

Ethan already knew what the three of them planned on getting her for Christmas. There was a BMW Z4 on special order for her at the dealership in Morehead. It was going to be a deep, sparkling blue that reminded them of her eyes with butter-soft leather seats and a premium sound system.

"I'll have to think about it, Ethan. The way you all spoil me, I'm hard-pressed to come up with something I need that I don't already have."

"A flat screen TV for your bedroom?"

"My bedroom is *not* for watching television. All the entertainment I need up there walks up my stairs in cowboy boots," she said, chuckling.

"New outdoor furniture?"

"I wouldn't trade that old porch glider for anything. Too many beautiful memories made in it."

"I'm pretty attached to that old glider myself," he replied softly, remembering all the times they'd made love on it with her straddled in his lap under a blanket. It rocked *just right*.

"*I know*," she said quickly, a soft hitch in her voice.

"What, Gracie?"

She paused, breathing softly in the phone. Boy, whatever it was, it was *good*. "Do you remember the night I wore my clit clip for you the first time?"

"I'll *never* forget that night. I've never seen anything hotter in my whole life, especially the way you teased us into discovering it on you. *Yes*, I remember, Gracie."

"Well, you said Clay makes…that kind of jewelry, too."

Ethan growled softly, loving the way her mind worked. "Is that what you want? Maybe something with a little more weight to it? Like solid gold?" At her strained, whispered assent, he knew he had the perfect gift. "Any type of jewelry in particular?"

"I'll leave it all…up to you. I wish you were here." She sighed with need. "You'll be home in another hour or two?"

"Maybe less, if I hurry." He was a newly motivated man.

"Hurry."

Chapter Forty-two

Eli laughed with Rachel when Craig Morgan's "Bonfire" played on the country radio station as he drove them out to the Divine Creek Ranch for the bonfire and pig roast Saturday night. Eli was planning to drop Rachel off and visit for a little while with the men before heading in with Ethan to the club.

His dad and sister arrived with baby Matthew in tow. Grace had talked Kelly into staying over at the ranch so they could talk wedding plans later, and Rachel went with them up to the ranch house to get her settled. His dad was staying in the second bedroom at Rachel's duplex.

Eli smiled when Ace and Kathleen arrived, and Ace showed him the corner of a manila envelope in his jacket pocket and nodded. The man worked fast.

The Divine Creek Ranch hands helped to set up tables, and one of them with the necessary skills helped Ethan get the sound system connected and working so they'd have music later if anyone wanted to dance. Adam had *his* fun earlier in the week, using the rented bulldozer to pile the massive mounds of mesquite they'd cleared the year before into a gigantic pile on the edge of the new pasture. Rachel helped Grace, her mom, and some of the other ladies with setting out the food on the tables.

Eli, Ace, Ethan, Jack, and Adam had a chance to put their heads together. Ace removed the manila envelope from his coat pocket and opened it, saying, "Mr. McCoy was easy to track down and tail. He doesn't go very far afield to hide his activities. This is even more serious than we thought. It made me nauseous, what we uncovered."

Eli and the others waited as he laid out the papers and photographs on the work bench in the first barn where they were less likely to be interrupted. "What do you mean? He's done that sort of thing before?"

"He's a pedophile." The disgust was evident in Ace's tone of voice.

"Oh, fuck," Ethan muttered softly.

Ace pointed to a black and white photograph. "That's a roadside hotel on this side of Morehead where McCoy rented a room on Wednesday night. That girl being escorted into his room is a young prostitute."

Jack groaned, "Oh, no. How young?"

"My guy, Kemp, pulled some long hours this week and matched his photograph to her face on the National Center for Missing and Exploited Children website. She's a fourteen-year-old runaway."

"She's only fourteen?" Eli said, filled with revulsion. The hardened girl in the image looked young, but not that young.

"Yeah. Drugs and living on the street ages you. Kemp had an inkling, and once he found her on the website, he called me, and I contacted the police with the description and license plate of the car that brought her, and they told me they would act on the information immediately."

"Damn," Adam said softly. "Fourteen?"

Ace nodded sadly. "If we'd known, that would have been when he got arrested. If adults want to get together and do crazy stuff in a roadside motel, that's one thing. Start messing with kids and people take action. Another friend of mine hacked into his computer and provided us with his e-mail and Internet contacts, along with archived e-mails. He saves records of his conquests instead of deleting them. He likes to brag. The most recent e-mail is a description of what he did to the girl in the hotel room. I don't recommend reading it. It'll ruin your evening. In the right hands, this information is just cause to search his residence.

"A skilled friend of mine has been to his house and located his hiding place for storing videos and pictures, mostly teenagers, but also some preteens, both male and female. He also found a drug stash that he probably uses when his victims won't settle down for him, or it may be for his own use. The dumb bastard even used credit cards to pay for the motel rooms.

"I'm surprised it was this easy to find evidence for bringing the proper authorities down on him. Have any of you ever heard what happens to pedophiles in prison? He won't fare well. The information is copied and ready to be sent to the FBI, the local police, and county authorities, as well.

"Rachel's name has been left out of the documentation. The young girl in the motel room was the most disturbing part of this for me once I saw the pictures. Kemp got a good enough digital image of her that hopefully it won't be long before they track her down and get her back home, or more likely into rehab and off the streets."

"So what do we do next?" Eli asked, still trying to take it all in.

Ace nodded, almost apologetically. "I have a friend at the FBI who will take an interest in his activities and can get the ball rolling. Eli, I know you wanna kill him, but avoid any contact with him if you can. All his buddies and regular coworkers will probably be investigated, too. Judging by some of his contacts and e-mails, he may work with other men who are involved in the same sort of activities."

"Part of me wishes I could have just two minutes alone with him."

Ace nodded again. "I hear ya, but I'd steer clear of him. I'll be watching him again tomorrow. McCoy appears to be settled at home for the evening watching television tonight, so Kemp is taking a break right now, and he'll check in with me after supper. If there are any new developments, I'll let you know. I know we have enough evidence now, but I feel like it's our civic duty to keep an eye on this asshole."

"Ace? If he..." Jack looked disgusted and hesitated for a second before continuing, "If it looks like he's up to something real bad..."

"I get what you're saying," Ace replied. "If he is on one of his exploits, we'll call the police and FBI immediately and document until they arrive. We won't let any other children be hurt. If it comes down to it, we'll act if we have to."

"Thank you," Eli said.

Ace smiled with grim determination. "Like I said, it's our civic duty to bring this evil motherfucker to justice. He held out a black and white surveillance photo of McCoy to them, which they passed to each other. "This is what he looks like, in case you've never seen him before."

Eli reminded them, "Remember, Rachel can't know about any of this."

"We'd be cool about it," Adam said, and the others nodded.

Eli put out his hand to shake Ace's and the others' and said, "Then I guess you need to contact your friend at the FBI."

Ace nodded and replaced the papers and pictures in the envelope and put it in his coat pocket. "Consider it done."

* * * *

Rachel sat with Grace, Kelly, and Teresa in lounge chairs a safe distance from the bonfire. The sun had long since set, and Rachel and Grace would be leaving shortly to take massive amounts of food up to feed their men and the other employees at the club. Adam and Jack were, at that moment, loading disposable aluminum pans with ribs and roasted pork, potato salad, beans, cole slaw, cornbread, sausage, Ethan's homemade barbecue sauce, and Grace's peach cobbler into Jack's SUV. They were doing it for Grace so she could sit and visit with the other ladies. The only reason they weren't also delivering the food was because Rachel and Grace wanted to see their hard-working men, since they couldn't be there for most of the evenings' festivities.

Rachel chuckled into her plastic cup. "My dad is drunk."

She was drinking Coke and serving as the designated driver for the evening trip up to the club. Grace snorted before taking another sip from her beer.

"How can you tell, Rachel? He's always so stoic and serious," Grace said.

"See how he's all lovey-dovey, getting in Mom's space like that? Ooops! He just *grabbed her ass.* Shit, now I'm scarred for life!" she said dramatically, covering her eyes. "He likes to dance with her when he's drunk. Listen to her giggle, would you?"

"Your parents are the cutest thing," Kelly said. "It's nice to see older married couples like that are still totally into each other. Gives the rest of us hope for the future. I hope Christopher is still grabbing my ass when I'm that age."

"Aw! Look at Brice and Corina. Aren't they sweet?" Rachel nodded to where the couple were sitting on the tailgate of Brice's pickup truck, smooching.

Adam and Jack came over and squatted down beside Grace's lounger.

Jack said, "Darlin', everything is loaded up in the back of the SUV. Make sure and take it slow on the turns."

Grace leaned forward to smooch Jack's nose. "Okay! Rachel's the designated driver for this trip."

"Are you getting inebriated, baby?" Adam asked, quirking an eyebrow at her when she snickered and patted his tanned cheek.

Grace shook her head and replied, "Nuh-uh, but I have had a couple of beers. I don't want to take any chances behind the wheel."

"Good. Thanks for doing that for her, Rachel," Adam replied, smiling over at Rachel.

"You're welcome, Adam. I don't mind." Jack handed Rachel the keys to the SUV, and Rachel said, "We'll be back in a little bit." To the girls she said, "Ladies, keep the party lively until we return."

Rachel had Grace text message Eli as they neared the club. The girls were supposed to pull up to the rear entrance, and the employees would bring the food in through the backdoor and put it in the kitchen. Then they could come and go and eat as they had time. Grace and Rachel set the food up and put out the utensils and paper plates then made up nice, full plates for Ethan and Eli. They came back to take a break and eat while the girls were there. Their men talked them both into one little dance before they returned to the ranch.

It was a good thing the Divine Creek Ranch didn't have any close neighbors. Even with the SUV's windows closed, as they pulled down the long driveway toward the barns, they could hear the music blasting. Rachel parked Jack's SUV next to the screened-in porch, where they were met by Jack and Adam.

"Everything go all right, darlin'?" Jack kissed Grace.

"Oh, yes! They all said they were coming out after they got off at one. They all said thanks for sending the food. The club was busy, but I think we have them beat with our noise level. What are you doing?"

"We're claimin' our dance partners!" Jack laughed as he put Grace over his shoulder and carried her giggling around the barn to the area that had arbitrarily been designated as the dance floor.

* * * *

A while later, Grace reveled in Adam's secure embrace as he led her around the improvised dance floor. Her cheek was pressed against his firm, warm chest, and she held on as they danced a slow, languid waltz together. He squeezed her gently, and she looked up at him then smiled at the twinkle in his pale green eyes.

"Baby, I just realized something." His deep, sexy voice sent a delicate shudder through her, centering in her clit. In his arms, she was never more than a heartbeat away from arousal.

"What, honey?"

"You haven't told me what you want from me for Christmas."

She snuggled closer to his tall frame in the crisp night air. "I already have what I want."

"I'm glad you feel that way, but I want to give you something special for Christmas," he murmured as he stroked her cheek with a callused finger.

"I don't need anything." She held on to him tighter. "Just your arms around me."

Adam sighed. "Are you giving me something?" he countered reasonably.

"Oooh, yes, baby! And it's going to be so awesome!" she said, her cheeks warming as she envisioned the looks on their faces when they opened their gifts.

"So you understand why I would want to give you something? You love the idea of having a surprise for me for Christmas. I want to get you something, too."

Well, he certainly has me there, doesn't he?

She tilted her head up to look at him. "All right. Only I can't think of anything I want right now."

"There's bound to be something you'd like to have or maybe do?"

"Oh. Something we could do together?"

"Sure. Wanna go skydiving?" he asked, grinning at the face she made.

"You *do* know me, right? Do I strike you as the type to leap boldly from a perfectly good airplane?" Grace asked with a chuckle.

"Okay, it was just a thought. How about a swimming pool?"

"That's too big an expenditure for a Christmas gift. You can do that in the spring if you want to, though. Then we could have parties out by the pool. But I do have an idea."

"What is it, baby?"

"I've always wanted to take formal ballroom dancing lessons. You know, the Viennese waltz, the cha-cha-cha, and the rumba? That's what I want from you, Adam. Ballroom dance lessons," she announced happily.

He looked down at her quizzically. "You're sure? You're already a phenomenal dancer. You and Ethan make such good dance partners. Maybe you should ask him..."

She realized taking ballroom dancing lessons to him was like her going skydiving—a bit of a stretch out of his comfort zone.

"He's already decided what he's getting me. I love dancing with him, you, and Jack. But I want to take lessons with *you*. We'd have to go to Morehead, so we'd have the drive over there and the time in the lessons, for *just the two of us*. Wouldn't you like that?" she asked softly, rubbing her breasts against his chest.

Adam squeezed her and chuckled sexily. "Since you put it *that* way, baby, I think dancing lessons would be fun."

"Thank you, honey. I've always wanted to do that."

"If you think of something else you want, you tell me, okay? Maybe something you can unwrap from me on Christmas morning."

"I love you." She sighed happily.

"I love you, too, baby."

Jack walked up and patted Adam on the back. Adam deftly twirled her into Jack's arms.

"Dizzy?" Jack asked with a grin as she giggled and settled in his strong embrace.

"Oh, no. My buzz was short-lived. I haven't had any more beer since we got back. I may get one later, but I'm having fun without it. Are you having fun, honey?"

"Yes, darlin', especially with you in my arms," he murmured and kissed her gently. "I heard you talking to Adam about Christmas when I walked up. Are you going to tell me what I can get you for under the Christmas tree?"

"I do know of something I've wanted to do."

"Name it, darlin'."

"You and me at Tessa's. *Just the two of us* in one of the privacy booths." His immediate smile confirmed that he liked the way she thought.

"What about something to unwrap Christmas morning? Jewelry, maybe?"

"Honey, jewelry *always* works. Now that you mention it, I would like something else. Remember the slave bracelet you all had made for Rachel?"

At his nod, she said, "I liked that slave bracelet and anklet. Can Clay make something to go with my other matching pieces?"

"I'm sure he could. I'll ask him. I'll get you the bracelet and let Adam get you the anklet. Ethan already has another surprise up his sleeve for you."

"But I know about—"

"Yeah. This is something you *didn't* ask for, though. I'm anxious to see *you* in what you asked him for. Naughty, naughty girl." He growled into her ear with his sexy Texas drawl. Her clit throbbed, as Grace realized he was imagining her in her more intimate jewelry pieces. "You are a sweet, hot thing, Grace Warner." She trembled deliciously when he pressed her to him so his stiffening cock was against her belly. "I want you. Right now."

She surreptitiously rubbed against him again. "Tack room, first barn. Give me a two-minute head start." The tack room in the first barn had a lock on the inside of the room. She had no idea why. His hands slid down over her ass and squeezed gently.

He chuckled softly and his next words made her pussy go completely slick. "Two minutes. Bare-assed and over my favorite saddle."

He patted her ass then kissed her and led her from the dance floor. He casually strolled over to the beer keg then looked back at her with secret promise in his eyes. She slipped away into the shadows and made her way up to the darkened first barn. Walking up the moonlit aisle between the horse stalls, Grace paused when Languir nickered faintly at her, and she patted his neck before continuing on to the tack room. She found the key to the outer padlock and unlocked it then slipped inside, leaving the key on the shelf nearby. Moonlight filtered in from the roof skylights as Grace located Jack's saddle on its rack and quickly took off her boots and socks. She unbuttoned her jeans and slipped them off and folded them. As she laid them on a bench, she heard a sound.

"Darlin'?"

"I'm here."

The door cracked open, and Jack entered then turned to lock it from the inside. She slid her fingers into the waistband of her thong, slipped it off, and laid it with the jeans. She silently moved to him and gasped at the feel of his hot hands as they slid around her waist and palmed her ass cheeks. He kissed her hard on the lips, and she wrapped her arms around his neck. His fingers glided down the cleft of her ass and found her hot and wet. His callused fingertips slid into her slick heat, and she was unable to stop the gasp that escaped her lips.

"Darlin', you're hot and ready, aren't you? Eager to play?" His other hand slid over her mound, and his fingertips stroked her clit as well.

"Mmm-*hmm*," she moaned softly as she fumbled with his belt and the fly of his jeans.

Once she had his thick cock free of the denim, she knelt in front of him and, without preamble, slid his rock-hard erection between her lips. His low groan of pleasure brought another rush of moisture to her swollen lips. She worked him in a slow sucking rhythm until he stopped her. Surprised, she looked up. The intense love and lust in his tanned face spoke volumes to her, and he didn't need to say a word.

She rose to her feet and sauntered bare-assed over to his saddle, which sat on its rack at hip level. She looked over her shoulder at him, and crooked her finger. She leaned over the saddle and took hold of the rack underneath as she braced her feet in the corners of the stand. She knew doing so presented her ass in a delicious display that would have his cock screaming to get inside of her.

"Mmm, darlin', that is such a pretty sight. You on your little tippy-toes, this pretty little pussy of mine for the taking," he whispered softly so they would not be overheard if someone came in the barn.

He slid his fingers up her inner thighs and caressed her inner lips. He chuckled at her little moan of pleasure. One hand slid around her hip and down over her mound to play with her clit. Doing that caused her back to arch, and she offered herself to him with soft, panting breaths. She groaned when his thick cock pressed at her entrance and pushed back onto him, crying out softly as his thick heat burrowed inside her.

"Oh, Jack! Oh, oh, honey, I'm already so—"

"Is it good, darlin'? Does my cock feel good slidin' into you?" He gently but firmly grasped her hips, thrusting all the way to the hilt. His other hand strummed her clit as he began to stroke into her, and he tilted his hips as his cockhead slid past her sweet spot.

"Oh, Jack…" Gone was the notion of keeping silent. There was just no way.

Jack growled softly. "You have such a soft, warm little pussy, darlin'. I'm never going to get enough of it."

He pulled out and thrust in again, pressing her firmly against the saddle and thrusting deeply inside her. She loved the feel his thick, hot erection sliding into her. He rubbed her pleasure spot and strummed her clit at the same time. She groaned in happy delight as the little jumping spasms began in her cunt. She arched her back and tightened up around his cock as she gyrated against him.

"Jack, I'm close, I'm…I'm…oh, Jack, I'm coming!" She gasped. Soft little cries escaped her lips as the muscles in her pussy gripped him tightly, and he pumped wildly into her hot depths.

Grace felt his lips between her shoulder blades as he continued strumming her clit and rocked his hips into her. On the heels of her first orgasm, another bloomed, and she tightened her muscles around his cock again. He fucked her with firm, short strokes, ramming to the hilt with each thrust.

Her breasts and hair swayed over the saddle as she turned to look over her shoulder. She watched Jack as his thrusts became more intense, and she groaned in ecstasy as another stronger orgasm rippled through her body. Her hips undulated wildly as she rode his cock with a low moan, uncaring who heard that time. With a final thrust and a deep growl, Jack held her tightly to him and she hummed in approval as she felt his cock pulse deep inside her.

She lay over the saddle, completely boneless as he slid from her and went in search of something she could use to clean up with. Finally, he came back with his clean handkerchief and helped her. After she was re-dressed and he was put back together, he pulled her into a gentle embrace.

"Darlin', you're my every dream come true, you know that? Was I too rough?"

She chortled softly in the dim light. "No, you were rough *enough*. I love you, Jack. I'm so lucky to have you in my life. I love you so much." She looped her arms gently around his waist.

"I love you, darlin'." He held the base of her head in his hands as he kissed her thoroughly but gently. "I'll always love you."

"Our guests may be wondering where we are. We should probably get back."

"You want me to give you a head start?"

She waved a hand carelessly. "Ah, we're married. Anyone here who is shocked needs to be shocked more often," she replied, chuckling softly.

Jack grinned at her and reached in his jacket pocket. Checking his cell phone, he got a serious look on his face and said to her, "Darlin', let me take you back to the party. There's something I need to deal with. It won't take but a few minutes. I need to borrow Adam from you for a few minutes, too, if you don't mind."

Grace noticed the serious look on his face and grew worried. "Is everything all right?"

He smiled warmly at her and kissed her. "It's perfect. I have to make a call, and we'll both be back before you know it."

Chapter Forty-three

Jack walked Grace back to the party and stopped to hold her and kiss her tenderly once more then made his way through the shadows to where his SUV was parked. He sent a text, and Adam and Ace joined him less than two minutes later. Once they were in the SUV and he was pulling down the long gravel driveway, he called Ethan back. Ace sat in the front passenger seat sending a text.

"I can't *fucking* believe our luck." Ethan's voice grated over the speaker phone. "You guys need to get your asses here quick. Eli's holding it together so far, probably only because McCoy hasn't mentioned seeing Rachel here the other day. He's drunk as a skunk and running his mouth non-stop up at the bar. Pull around to the back. I've left the door propped open, and the security cameras are already turned off. Hope you have a plan."

"We'll take care of it," Jack said. "You closing up right now?"

"It's last call. The waitresses and other workers are already cleaning up so they can all get out to the ranch. The timing is perfect," Ethan replied. "McCoy won't know what hit him, or who, for that matter."

Ace said. "Kemp is going to meet us there. Remember, not one word about who this is for or what we know about his predilections. The less said the better. Jack, have Eli tap him on the head before he brings him out back. Kemp will handle the rest. He'll think he blacked out and won't know who beat him up. But not one word about what we know, or he'll bolt if he remembers what you said."

They all agreed as they pulled up to the backdoor. Using a hunting knife, Jack tore off the corner of a heavy cotton tarp, grabbed a roll of duct tape, and gave them to the men. A large, black Escalade pulled up beside them, and a giant of a man climbed from the front seat. The man was built like a tank but dressed in a suit and an expensive leather coat. He nodded at them and spoke quietly with Ace.

Jack left the others waiting in the back and went in. The bar was emptying out as people finished their drinks and headed to the front door. Eli, Mike, and Rogelio were all smiles when they saw Jack. Eli must have let them in on it, considering how close they were to Rachel, though he doubted that Eli gave them all the details.

* * * *

Eli watched Reese McCoy in disgust as he sat at the bar, raving about his days on the Divine High School football team to Ben, completely unaware the lights had come on and the place was closing down. When the last customer was out the front door and the deadbolt lock slid into place, Mike nodded at Eli. Eli looked at Jack, who gestured to the backdoor. Eli approached the overweight, slobbering drunk. A dissipated, degenerate lifestyle had visited its revenge on him in the last few years, and Eli was revolted by even the thought of touching him.

Eli took him by one upper arm and lifted him bodily from the tall chair.

"Hey there, buddy. Come on with me. I'll help you out to your truck," Eli grated out as he steered him to the backdoor.

McCoy was so blindly drunk he didn't even realize he was being escorted out the backdoor. "Aww, shanks, Eli. What a good guy, here's my keesh," he slurred, handing the key ring to Eli.

As Eli pulled him into the dim hallway, he tapped him lightly on the head with his fist, knocking Reese silly. He toed open the backdoor into the alley, where Ace and Adam waited with the blindfold and the duct tape. As they secured the tarp over his face so he could breathe but not see, they gave him a chance to regain his wits. Ace gestured to Eli with a finger to his lips, and Eli nodded in understanding.

For each innocent victim McCoy had ever abused or used, they silently kicked his sleazy, drunken, perverted, and dissipated ass. Justice was almost served. It would be complete when Ace got the incriminating evidence to his friend at the FBI.

After they were done, Ace got Jack's attention. "Kemp would be happy to move him around front to his truck, but he was wondering if he could borrow your duct tape."

Raising an eyebrow and smiling, Jack handed the roll of tape to him and said, "Sure. Why don't you invite him back to the ranch? I know it's late and all, but let him know he's more than welcome."

"Sure. Be right back."

Kemp slung McCoy onto Jack's torn drop cloth on the rear floorboard of his Escalade and shook Ace's hand before leaving to finish his task. He waved to the others, saying nothing else, and Jack drove away from the club with Ethan and Eli following behind in Ethan's truck.

After they returned to the ranch, Eli stopped them and said, "I would have been satisfied with seeing him on the evening news getting hauled into jail. Thank you, guys. That was for Rachel."

Jack replied, "I wish like hell that it'd never been necessary in the first place, but I'm sincerely glad to be a tool for justice to be served."

"We look out for our women," Adam said softly.

"Hell yeah, we do," Ethan added, and the others nodded.

Ace reminded them, "Not a word to anybody. He's got to think he was jumped in the parking lot by thugs."

"Greasy fucking bastard," Ethan said. "I need to wash my hands."

"Me, too," Adam replied with a grimace.

* * * *

Rachel and Grace sat in the loungers by the bonfire, talking with her mom, Rosemary, Charity, and Jack's older sister, Anne.

"I wonder what's keeping the guys?" Grace asked. Rachel checked her watch. It was a little past one thirty.

"The club was pretty busy," Rachel commented. "Maybe they had a lot of cleanup to do. Or maybe Jack's errand took longer than he expected. What was he up to, anyway?"

"I don't know," Grace said with a shrug. "He didn't tell me."

Rachel was getting another cup of beer from the keg when large, gentle hands slid around her hips and pulled her to a tall, hard body. She shivered at his husky voice next to her ear. "You're beautiful with your hair tousled and your cheeks rosy from the chilly air. Do you need me to warm you up a little, angel?"

She turned and smiled up at him, handed him the beer, and replied, "Just feeling your big, strong arms around me makes my heat index rise, big man." She rose on her tiptoes, and he leaned down to kiss her. "We were starting to wonder where you were."

"Mmm, the place was still packed at closing time." He kissed her deeply, lifting her from her feet for a few seconds. "Bonfire's going strong, I see."

"Yeah, as big as Adam piled it, it'll still be going on Monday." She chuckled. "It's nice and warm to sit near it, but I smell like smoke now. Everyone else follow you out?"

"Oh yeah, the whole crew is coming," Eli said, gesturing with a thumb toward the increased noise level near the dance floor. Several newcomers made their way over, greeted Rachel, and visited the beer keg.

It was then that Rachel noticed Eli's hands. "What were you doing before you got here?" she asked softly, tracing a fingertip over a swollen knuckle as she examined his hand.

"Just doing my job," he murmured softly, but when she gazed up into his eyes, she saw something more. More than just him doing his job. For some odd reason, it struck her that he seemed satisfied.

"Oh? Did...someone get out of hand?" she asked softly. A shiver raced up her spine.

"Yeah, he needed to be taught a lesson. He won't be mistreating any more women for a *long* time."

"Oh. Somebody I know?" she asked, pressing his knuckle against her cheek, looking up at him with brimming eyes.

He nodded to her, and she hid her face in his chest as he smoothly moved away from the edge of the crowd into the darkness. "Are you upset with me? I didn't seek him out. McCoy came in the bar and got drunk and...irritating."

"He wasn't worth all this trouble."

"Oh, yeah he *was*," Eli said with deep conviction in his voice. "It's behind us now."

Jack approached with his cell phone. Smiling at Rachel, he beckoned to Eli and held out his phone. She watched as Eli took a sip of his beer and looked at the screen. She snickered as Jack jumped back when Eli spewed what he'd just sipped.

"Does that say what I think it says?"

She thought she heard Jack whisper, "Duct tape *underwear*," as he pointed at the screen. Eli made a disgusted face and handed him the phone.

"Good thing there's no picture," Eli replied.

* * * *

Rachel couldn't hold back a yawn at two thirty, and Eli chuckled when she did the Jell-O-neck-head-bob for the second time in five minutes.

"I think it's time to tuck you into bed, Rachel. Does Dad have the key to your front door?"

She'd given her future father-in-law the key earlier in the evening. "Yeah. Why don't we go say goodnight to Grace and the guys?" She yawned sleepily. She'd wanted to stay for a while once Eli arrived at the ranch since he'd missed the early evening fun.

They said goodnight, and Grace reminded her to sleep well since she was having her formal bridal portrait the next afternoon.

"You should sleep in. You don't want to have puffy, sleepy eyes."

Eli drove while Rachel dozed on the way home and lifted her from her truck and carried her to the front porch. He set her down to unlock the door then swept her back into his arms and carried her over the threshold.

"Good practice," he whispered then kissed her.

They took a relaxing hot shower, and he washed her hair. "When are you going to wear that sexy-as-hell leather outfit for me?" he asked, massaging her scalp gently with his fingertips.

She moaned gratefully at his touch. "When we go out next Saturday night. You have that Saturday off, right?"

"Mmm-hmm. The boots, too? And the slave jewelry?"

"All of it. You're fun, Eli. I love you," she said dreamily as she rinsed her hair.

He then turned off the water and wrapped a towel around her. "That's what you think now. Wait until *tomorrow* night."

"Goody." She giggled then yawned again as she climbed onto his bed.

He got under the covers with her and cuddled her back to his front and drew the sheet and blankets over them. She wriggled back against him, loving the feel of his body heat pressed against her. She decided she didn't mind if he wanted to press some of that body heat *inside* her right now as well.

Eli chuckled and whispered, "Sleep for now, angel. You're tired, and you've had a long day. We'll make love when we wake up."

"I love you." She wiggled back against him on her side until she was effectively sitting in his lap. They were skin-to-skin from her heels up to the top of her head, which rested under his chin on his biceps, when she sighed in contentment. His warm hand slid over her hip and stilled her movements with a soft chuckle.

"You're tempting me. I want you to rest, angel. In the morning, I'll love you good and hard. Right now, we're tired." He kissed the top of her head. "Be a good girl."

"Mmm."

* * * *

Eli made good on his promise later that morning when she awoke to find him poised above her, between her thighs, suckling on one of her nipples and playing with the other. He must have been playing with her for a while because her pussy felt swollen and hot and soaking wet.

He released the nipple in his mouth with a soft pop and said, with a big grin, "Good morning, angel."

He slid into her wet pussy in one smooth, slick stroke. She wrapped her legs around his hips and drew as close as she could to him.

"Oh, Eli! How long have you been awake?" she whispered. Her pussy trembled and tightened around him. She was close to coming already.

"A while," he murmured, flexing his powerful body over her and thrusting his enormous cock deep inside her.

She wrapped her arms around him and stroked his back, feeling the muscles there flexing under her fingertips. He was so massive, so larger-than-life, and she loved the way it felt when he covered her body with his own. "I've been playing by myself for that whole time. I'm glad you woke up."

"Oh! Eli, I don't know how you get me all hot while I'm asleep."

He nuzzled her throat and thrust inside her. He explained in his deep sexy voice, "I'm very gentle, not trying to wake you up, just trying to get you wet and hot for me. Then you wake up when your body can't stand it any longer. I know you're close because your hips were flexing even before you were awake."

"Oooh." She whimpered soft and low, her cheeks flushing with warmth as he gently fucked her.

He wet his finger and stroked her clit gently, growling in approval when she reacted instantly, arching her back and rocking against him.

"Mmm, I love when you move like that, angel. I can't get enough of the way you fuck me and take every inch of me, greedy for more." He placed her heels on his shoulders then gently grasped her hips and lifted her slightly, pumping into her with a slow, steady rhythm. She began to whimper, and her breath came in panting cries.

He pulled out of her, and she groaned in desperation because she'd been so close to coming. "Don't worry, angel. You're going to come good and hard. Get on your hands and knees." He growled in a deep, lust-ridden voice as he helped her. He pulled the pillows away from the headboard and helped her lay over a stack of them to support her pelvis. She moaned in wild anticipation.

His hands kneaded her ass cheeks over and over and she sighed when he placed his cock at her wet entrance.

"Oh, yes, Eli!" she wailed as he slid inside her a bit. Not nearly enough. Not nearly what she wanted from him. His chuckle sounded mischievous, as he teased her with what she wanted so badly now.

"Is my angel ready to be ridden hard? Are you sure you don't want to take it slow?" He gave her another inch before pulling out then slowly, torturously, pumped in, giving her another inch. He held her hips still on the pillows so she couldn't rear back on his cock and impale herself, and the muscles in her pussy tightened, desperate for him.

"Eli!" she murmured in a soft shaky voice.

He leaned over her, his lips near her ear, and said, "Tell me what you need, angel. I'll give it to you."

Rachel knew exactly what she needed. Looking over her shoulder at him, she said, "Eli, I need you to fill me full with your long, hard cock and fuck me till I come screaming. Fill me with your cum and don't stop until I'm overflowing with it."

Chapter Forty-four

Her pussy clenched at the glitter of lust in his eyes.

"Angel, your wish is my command." He punctuated the last word by thrusting his cock deep into her pussy in one slippery, wet plunge.

He stroked her pussy as her rasping cries of ecstasy built to a full-on scream. He fucked her hard like she'd begged him to, the ecstasy building inside her higher and higher. She came with a great wailing cry, and he roared as his release exploded from him.

He gathered her to him, lifting her, so she was upright and her back was against his chest, his cock still hard inside her. He slid a hand down to her mound, the other holding her to him. He stroked her clit as he rocked against her, and she gave herself over to another orgasm, this one milder and sweeter for them both. She reveled in the sensation of him holding her like this and fucking her from behind and imagined what they must look like locked together this way.

While she recovered, he nuzzled her neck and caressed her blushing breasts and stroked her abdomen, his fingers drifting down to the juncture where the top of her thighs dipped to her mound.

"Angel, I…" He sighed, tried to speak again, and kissed her shoulder silently. His hands were incredibly gentle as he stroked her.

"I know, Eli. I feel it, too. There are no words, are there?"

He shook his head then kissed her temple tenderly. "What I want to say, what I feel would sound silly coming out of my mouth. I can't seem to…"

"Then tell me what you feel, Eli. I'd never laugh at what you're trying to express from your heart. Tell me, and I'll bet I won't think it's silly at all."

"No woman will ever be as well-loved as you will. When you ask me for my cock, I'll give it to you as many times as you want it. You're the perfect woman for me, Rachel. There's a fucking caveman inside of me, and not only are you not intimidated by him, you seem to enjoy him as well. The caveman is beating his chest right now, wanting to fuck again, fill you again, and watch my cum dripping from between your sexy thighs after I'm done. Then he wants to curl you up with him and hold you while you sleep with your pussy filled to overflowing. See? It's stupid."

"It's not stupid, Eli. It's beautiful. Cavemen are not politically correct, but I never wanted you to be politically correct. I love every part of you, especially that guy. I like that part of you is wild. You make me feel wild, too. Being with you and having you inside me makes me want to do crazy things with you."

Rachel groaned and arched her back. She rocked against him and knew their words were having an effect on both their libidos as his cock grew hard inside her again, filling her throbbing pussy tightly. She might not get out of bed before noon. "So what does he want to do now, go out and kill a saber-toothed tiger and bring back the meat to feed me?"

He growled and thrust gently inside of her, groaning as his hardening cock slid through the rush of hot moisture generated by their shared fantasy. "That's later. Plus, he'll skin it and make a hide for you to sleep under and stay warm. No, first, after you wake up, he'll want to fuck some more. Because your pussy is the *sweetest* thing he's ever known." He growled. "He'd wallow in bed with you all day if that were possible."

"See, that's something else I love about him. He's tender, sweet, and careful with me. Loving you is beautiful in all its forms, Eli."

He lifted her more upright then placed her hands on the headboard for support, his own hand beside hers, and began to thrust gently but with an increasing pace. He slid two fingers into her hot, swollen slit and tenderly stroked her engorged clitoris, and her head fell back to his shoulder. She moaned softly at the sensation.

She held on and rocked with him, and as her orgasm loomed over her, her hips began to undulate with his rhythm, and he growled, encouraging her to come for him, and she did. She took every pulse greedily, satisfying what she supposed was the *cavewoman* in *her*. Then, whispering words of encouragement to him, she continued to fuck him into his own orgasm as he filled her to overflowing with his cum.

"You're amazing, Eli. You're still hard, aren't you?"

"Fuck yes. You keep me that way."

In an utterly wanton display, she placed her hands back on the bed and lay chest down over the pillows. She arched her back, watching him over her shoulder as he slowly pulled his semi-erect cock from her pussy. She was filled with satisfaction and growled in a soft feminine way at the pleasure that was all over his face at the sight of his milky cum dripping from her tender, well-used pussy. He stroked her pussy lips, which she knew would feel hot and well-fucked. She sighed and moaned in sated bliss at his touch and the male pride in his eyes when he glanced up to see her watching him.

"I can't get enough of you." He lay down beside her. He spooned her to his chest, one hand on a breast, the other in her slit, stroking her lips and her clit, alternating between the two. Pressed back against his warmth, she felt consumed with love and need for him. They were both slightly damp with sweat, and she was very aroused by his clean, manly scent.

"I can't get enough of you." She gasped in pleasure, amazed that he had her turned on again so quickly.

"We're like addicts." He slipped his fingers into her opening and slid them through her slick heat. She whimpered and arched her back to him in offering. Incredibly, *impossibly*, he was hard again against her buttocks.

"Oh, please, Eli. Please." She reached for him.

Sounding doubtful, he said, "If I do, you won't be able to *walk*."

"Yes, I will. I *need* you, Eli!" she whimpered, lost in the erotic bliss of being with him.

* * * *

Eli couldn't take his eyes off of Rachel as they ate lunch at O'Reilley's. They sat and talked at a table for two, and Eli felt like he must be wearing a big sappy grin as he sat there taking in her glowing beauty. She would blush when she caught him staring but said nothing about it, sometimes just pausing to gaze into his eyes quietly.

At one point he asked softly, "What are you thinking about?" He watched in pleasure as her cheeks blushed rosily.

"I was just imagining what it will be like, being married to you, making a home with you and…"

"And what?" he asked huskily over the lump in his throat. He couldn't help but respond to the love in her eyes.

"Waking up to someone who loves as sweet and hard as you do every morning. Raising a bunch of kids with you. Making that house into a home with you."

The sappy grin returned to his face as he imagined it along with her.

Eli was meeting a home inspector later in the week to check out the ranch house they had looked at to determine if the house was sound enough to warrant an investment in the necessary remodel. After they heard from the inspector, they'd decide about whether to make an offer on it or not.

After paying the bill, Eli walked her through the crowded lobby and out to his truck. He lifted her gently into the passenger seat since she was wearing her long denim skirt and buckled her in. She grinned and kissed him as he *accidentally* brushed her breast with his shoulder. This was becoming a habit with him.

He took her back to the duplex so she could drive herself out to her parents' ranch. He helped her load her wedding dress, which was zipped up in a long opaque garment bag, and the tote bag that contained her hot rollers, cosmetics, shoes, and other accessories so she could beautify herself for the portraits Carrie and Raquel would be shooting of her today.

Smiling at her once she was buckled into her seat, he said, "I have a couple of errands of my own to run right now, so I'm going to take off, too. How are you feeling?" He placed a hand on her upper thigh, squeezed gently and felt her body quiver slightly in response.

Her beautiful face radiated love when she looked into his eyes. "I feel super."

"Good. Have fun with the girls." He kissed her tenderly then waved as she backed out of their driveway.

* * * *

"Holy *hot* freakin' hell!" Kelly shouted as Rachel quickly snapped closed the hinged cover on her nude portrait and clutched it to her chest. Grace did the same with the ones she had done for her men. Kelly had snuck up on them as they were taking their first looks at the nudes, which Carrie had brought with her. Teresa and Rachel's mom were outside helping Carrie and Raquel arrange potted plants for an advantageous shot out at the pavilion.

"Kelly! I'm shocked!" Grace said in mock horror. "When Little Matthew's first word is 'hell,' I want to be a fly on the wall when his daddy asks you where he learned it."

Kelly snorted. "Trust me, he'll know." Then she reached out to get another look at the portraits they clutched. "Come on, I'm like a sister, or something, right? Show me?" she wheedled.

"Okay, you can see mine," Grace said, laughing, and laid all three out on the bed in Rachel's old room. Kelly opened them all and gasped, looking over at Grace with new respect and admiration. "Grace, they are going to *love* these. They are so...so gorgeous."

Grace clapped her hands in happiness. "I think they will, too. It's good to have someone else's opinion, though."

"They used the lighting and shadows so cleverly. You are so brave to do these, and I love that they are all black and white. It gives them a timeless quality."

"Thanks, sweetie."

"Can I see yours, Rachel?" Kelly asked nicely. "Please!"

Rachel smiled and relented, cringing when Kelly flipped it open and gasped. Rachel shut her eyes and said, cringing, "Too much? Too much *me*?"

"Nuh-uh. It's perfect! He's going to treasure this. I love how you have your hands in your hair. That does great things for your boobs. He's gonna be *stunned*!"

"Carrie said we could look at the others, but we better hurry because we need to get your hair fixed, Rachel."

They peeked at her mom's first and cooed over it. Her mom looked over her shoulder into the camera, a feather boa framing her lush, satiny shoulders as she gazed at the camera with a come-hither stare meant for Rachel's father.

"Daddy's going to love it."

They looked at Teresa's next. Carrie had captured her demure personality perfectly in the shy tilt of her head and the way her eyes looked up at the camera.

In Kelly's portrait, she was reclining on a chaise lounge, dressed in a white gown and barefooted. Kelly had a twinkle in her eyes and appeared to be slowly drawing the hem of the gown up her legs.

"*Wow*, your husband will love this, won't he? Can you send him a copy of it?" Rachel asked.

"She gave me a disk with the file on it that I can load on the computer and e-mail to him. She also printed me a small copy to mail to him. This one is for our bedroom. He's going to love it." Kelly sniffled and wiped a tear from her eye. The girls hugged her and let her bawl for a minute. She pulled it together pretty quickly, though, and they got started rolling Rachel's hair. Rachel's more risqué boudoir portraits were in the back of Carrie's SUV, otherwise they'd have snuck a peek at those as well.

The portrait shoot went well. The weather held out nicely, not too bright and not too cloudy, but the temperature was a little on the cool side. Afterward, her mom served them a late snack, and they had fun looking at *almost* all of the portraits, including the boudoir portraits. Her mom was giddy with excitement for her father to see the portrait that evening.

Teresa was thrilled with her portrait as well but begged off early. Angel had volunteered to watch Michael for her that afternoon, and she didn't want to take too much advantage of his good nature. The others looked knowingly at each other. Anyone who observed Angel with Michael knew he was over the moon for the little boy. He probably was taking him for a horseback ride around the ranch at that very minute, completely unaware of what time it was.

Rachel's mother invited her to stay for supper, but Rachel declined, since Eli had told her he had already made plans, but promised they'd come over for supper another night soon.

She pulled into the driveway, happy to see Eli's truck parked there. Another familiar SUV was parked behind the motorcycle, and Rachel recognized Jane Jensen, their real estate agent, standing on the porch talking with Eli and Elijah.

Jane was animated, and her pale cheeks were flushed a pretty pink. Rachel waved back when Jane waved at her but sat in the truck observing. Jane was speaking to Eli about something but kept looking up at Elijah and smiling. Rachel climbed from her truck after a few moments, smiling and wondering what was up with Eli's dad and Jane. Elijah was a sociable, easygoing guy and quite good-looking. Jane seemed quite taken with him.

Interesting.

Eli stepped off the porch and came to her, swinging her up into his arms and hugging her.

Elijah spoke several quiet words to Jane. She nodded and handed him a business card. She turned and stepped off the porch. "I have to run. Hi, Rachel, Eli and Elijah can fill you in on the news. I'll look forward to hearing from you soon. Wish I could stay, but I have another appointment to keep." She hugged Rachel, said good-bye to Eli, then turned to wave at Elijah, who was standing on the porch, leaning up against one of the porch beams smiling at Jane. She blushed again and hurried to her car. Rachel looked up at Eli in curiosity, and he cleared his throat and rolled his eyes at her. Something was *definitely* cooking there.

"Well, kids. It's time for me to hit the road," Elijah said as he stepped off the porch. "Gotta get back to San Antonio, but I'm sure I'll be back soon."

"Okay, Dad. I sure am glad you got to come out for the pig roast. I hope you had a good time," Rachel said, walking with Eli over to where he stood on the driveway.

"Oh, I did, I did. I know you have plans, so I'll let you get on with them. I'll catch a quick bite in town and head on out."

"I could fix you some supper, Elijah. I don't mind at all," Rachel replied, not liking the thought of him leaving hungry.

"Nah, sweetie. I should have gotten on the road earlier. Got caught up talking with Eli and Miss Jensen. But thanks for the offer."

"You're welcome. Drive safely, all right?" she said and gave him a hug and a kiss on the cheek. Eli hugged his dad. His dad got in his pickup and waved as he drove out of sight.

"Interesting," Rachel said softly.

"You have no idea," Eli said meaningfully, kissing her again. "I have a feeling we may be seeing more of Dad around these parts, thanks to a certain pretty real estate agent."

"She seems like she is attracted to him."

"Oh, *I'll* say." He chuckled. "And Dad was definitely turning the charm on for her."

"So tell me the good news."

"Jane stopped by to let us know that the current owners of the ranch house are becoming anxious to sell the house so they can settle the estate and pay bills. Taxes are due on the house, and they are hoping to get them taken care of at the time of sale. The county is willing to work with them, but they need to get it sold soon. They are willing to consider any reasonable offer."

"Excellent. Did you tell her we want to have it inspected?"

"Yes. I told her I'd be meeting with an inspector this week. She understood that we wouldn't know anything until then."

"Great, what else is going on?"

"I have a surprise inside for you."

"Oh, goody, can I see it?"

Eli brought her inside, but she didn't see anything out of the ordinary. He convinced her to take a warm shower while he got ready. While she was in the shower, he came in and said, "I've put something on the counter for you. After you have it on, open the bathroom door, and I'll come get you."

When she stepped from the shower, toweling her hair dry, all she found on the counter was the satin blindfold.

With her heart pounding, she dried her hair quickly and tied it on. With her eyes covered, she opened the bathroom door. Deprived of her sight, and turned on by the idea of being naked and vulnerable like this, she waited for him.

He didn't keep her long. She gasped when she felt his touch at her waist. He gathered her to him, and she went with him into the bedroom. Quietly, he helped her onto the bed and positioned her comfortably. He moved to one side of the bed, and she heard fabric being gathered up, and then he lifted her wrist gently and began to tie something soft to it.

Her bondage sashes.

"Eli, what are you—" she began to say until he held something to her lips. Uncertain, she didn't know what to do.

"It's just a grape. Eat it. I know you must be hungry. I'm going to feed you with my hands. Is that all right?"

She sighed happily and nodded, chewing on the grape he slipped between her lips. He went around the other side of the bed and tied her other wrist. Her arms were bound now, but not tightly. She had freedom to move a little. He crawled up on the bed between her thighs and offered her a piece of cheese, which she took gratefully, realizing she was hungry.

As she ate the cheese, he slid his warm hands up her thighs, groaning softly as he touched her. She wasn't expecting it when he lifted her hips and slid her down so that her arms stretched out toward either corner of the bed. He caressed and stroked her hips before offering her a small chunk of freshly-baked bread that had been dipped in a sweet cream cheese dip. She "mmm-ed" over that, and he gave her another as he chuckled before he left the bed and moved down to the foot. He stroked her arch as he lifted her foot. She lifted her head blindly in confusion.

"Wait a minute, I only had two. How—"

"I ordered two more." Amusement filled his voice. He spread her thigh out wide. "Is that too much? Are your muscles sore from this morning?"

"Oh, no. I...I–like it, actually," she stammered as he held another grape to her lips, which she accepted gladly.

He tied her ankle down, and her heart began to pound. She felt so exposed already, but when he spread the other thigh, she knew her glistening wet pussy would be opened for him. Then what would he do?

He placed another piece of cheese between her lips then tied the other ankle down, spreading her till she had to moan with the erotic pleasure of it. More moisture gathered in her opening, and she knew he'd see it, too. He crawled between her thighs and smoothed his warm hands gently over her, gently rubbing down the muscles in her thighs and calves and in her arms. Once when he leaned over her, he groaned again like he was restraining himself.

After he finished rubbing her down, he left the bed again. He returned with something he laid on the mattress. Sliding his hand up her torso from her abdomen to between her breasts, he offered another small chunk of the bread smeared with the cream cheese dip. As he caressed her, he spoke love words to her, telling her he adored her and he'd thought of her as he sat on the back deck that afternoon and played his guitar. All the while, he fed her more grapes, cheese, and bread.

When she'd had her fill, he said, "Now, it's my turn to eat."

"You've fed me, but you haven't eaten?" she asked softly. Her pussy began to throb in time with her heartbeat,

"Oh, I've had the main course, but now I want dessert. I think you will like it, too."

She was startled when she felt a moderately cold touch on her nipple. It was his fingers, smearing something on her. Her heart began to pound, and her breathing turned into panting. He smeared more of the same thing on the other nipple. It was cold, but her nipple felt like it was on fire. His fingers came back with more, placing it on her quivering abdomen randomly in a pattern that led down to her mound, his fingers caressing and smearing the dessert on her as he returned with more and more. He stopped, and her breathing became rasping moans because she knew what was next, and she knew he was looking at her mound, enjoying the view and building her anticipation.

"I'm going to enjoy licking my dessert from you so much, angel. But nowhere more than from *right here*." His warm fingers delivered a dollop of whatever the dessert was to her mound and enflamed pussy. He was going to use her as his dessert platter.

She wanted to moan and scream with delight and agony at the same time. The smearing of the dessert on her had been sheer, torturous bliss, and now he was going to lick it off of her, as well. She arched her back, crying out when he applied an extra-large blob all over her lips and her clit, being very thorough. He spread more over her hipbones and into the dip at the juncture of her hip and thigh. He moved up to her chest and spread the last of it over her collarbones.

"This is how I'd love to always eat my dessert. Straight off your luscious, sexy body. Want to know what it is?" At her panting nod, he said, "Open up, angel, and taste what I'm about to feast on."

She opened her lips and felt two fingers slip into her mouth, a little of the dessert on the ends of them. She sucked good and hard, causing him to groan in pleasure as she stroked his fingers with her tongue. The creamy coconut custard and whipped cream with little flakes of baked sugary coconut mixed in

"Mmm, my favorite. Coconut cream *pie*." She sighed blissfully.

"I think it's about to become my new favorite, as well." He bent down and lapped at her collarbones.

She sighed happily taking a little mouthful here and there from his fingertips, sucking them some more for him. He worked his way slowly down her body, feasting greedily on her nipples as he sucked each one clean and released it with a soft pop.

Finally, Eli reached her mound and growled as he dug into his dessert with real gusto. He laved her hot lips and her clit until she writhed in pleasure. He dipped his tongue into her entrance, getting every trace of his coconut cream pie. He licked her until it was all gone, by which time she was begging incoherently.

"Would you like some more pie? Or would you rather have my cock, angel?" he asked as he smoothly untied the restraints at her ankles.

"Eli," she purred, "I need it, I want your cock." She lifted her knees as he moved into position between her thighs and wrapped her legs around him.

In one smooth, gentle stroke he slid into her slick, pussy, through *her* cream. "Angel, I'd rather have you for dessert than anything else."

She moaned softly as he raised her ankles and spread her thighs wide. "So beautiful. I love to fuck you. You were so sweet, letting me eat my dessert off your little wet pussy. I have a couple of surprises for you. I think you're going to love this new toy I bought for you."

"Oh?" Her heart pounded in her ears, as he shifted around for a few seconds.

Eli pressed something soft and wet against the flesh around her clit. When he released the pressure, a gentle vibrating suction began directly over her clit.

"Oh, Eli!" Her hips began to undulate, finding her own unique rhythm as he encouraged her. Her breathing became rasping moans as he quickly lubed her asshole and positioned something slippery at her ass. "What is it? Eli!"

"It's a plug, like you've been using, but this one has something special about it." He slipped the plug into her lubed opening. She cried out when it began to vibrate inside her ass, in *just* the right spot. She couldn't help but move with it, on him. The vibrations might have had their origin on her clit and in her ass, but the sensations coursed through her whole body. Holding back was not an option and she moved uninhibitedly on his cock, which felt like it had gotten even larger. Being tied down and helpless magnified her need to move.

"Oh, Eli, It's *so* good, all so good! I'm going to come!" she cried out, arching her back, moving in a wild rhythm along with him. "Oh! I'm— I'm...oh! I'm coming, Eli! Yes!"

Her hips ground into him as she screamed and exploded in ecstasy. He looped her calves over his forearms while thrusting into her with his long, hard cock. He pressed on the toy that held her clit in a suction grip and it began to vibrate faster and harder. Her body seized up, and she came with a joyous wail. As she recovered, he released the suction at her clit and turned off the vibrating plug and carefully slid it from her ass. Then he pulled out of her, hard as a bar of steel. Did she miss something?

Breathless, she mumbled softly, "Eli, you haven't come yet, have you?"

"No, I wanted to untie you first and take off your blindfold. I need to hold you while I make love to you and finish while I'm looking into your eyes."

Eli pulled the sashes at her wrists loose seconds later, and slipped the blindfold off, as well. Rachel's body still vibrated from her orgasm as she gazed up into his handsome face. He smiled and kissed her as he settled over her, and she spread her legs wide for him. He slid back inside her slick passage, groaning deeply in pleasure. His arms slid around her, one arm under her hips, the other under her shoulders, and he held her to him tightly and began to stroke into her with long, smooth, agonizingly beautiful stokes, all the way in, all the way out.

She felt captured and consumed, tight in his arms like this, acquiescing to his strength and immense power as he fucked her tenderly, neither fast nor slow, but somewhere in between. Perfectly.

He might be a large, tall, intimidating man to some, with good reason, but to her, he was always her gentle giant. His heart, for her, was as immense and magnificent as the rest of him. His face became serious, and the tension started to build in his body. Her body responded, tightening up like a bow string pulled taut. He began to pump into her with mindless abandon.

His roar broke her tension, and she came again along with him. He thrust deeply, filling her with his cum, stroking her hard, holding her hard, crying out in ecstasy until his head slumped weakly to her shoulder. His ebony hair spread over her chest like a silken blanket.

When she came back to herself, she slowly released her arms and legs which were wrapped around his body, holding on as tight as he had been holding on to her.

"Eli, you are so...beautiful when you come. The pleasure is written all over your face, and the way you sound when you come touches something so deep inside me. I *love* that sound," she whispered. She took a deep, shaky breath as her heart rate began to return to normal.

He raised his head from her shoulder, his pale gray gaze searching her eyes. He smiled tenderly at her, tilted his head, and kissed her adoringly. He stroked her tongue the way his body had stroked hers earlier. She caressed his shoulders and his arms, and then her fingers strayed in his long, black, silken hair. His kisses spread along her jawline and down her throat as he slowly withdrew his cock. They both chuckled when he lifted his body from hers and their flesh stuck together from the sugar in the coconut cream pie.

"Another shower?" She laughed as she touched her fingers to the slightly sticky flesh of her torso. "I appreciate you not getting any in my hair."

"Yeah, I'll go start the shower for us." He grinned as he rose gloriously naked from the bed, lifted the tray that contained all the food, and returned it to the kitchen. He returned to the bed and gathered up the toys to wash them and helped her rise from the bed, where she had been enjoying the view as he came and went.

"Keep ogling me like that, and I'm going to get hard again." He gestured to the long shaft hanging between his legs that already looked like it was taking an interest.

So soon. It takes a licking and keeps on ticking. It amazed her, the lovemaking stamina this man possessed.

She arched a dark eyebrow, saying, "And that's a problem because?"

"Insatiable woman," he growled, coming up behind her and grasping her ass in both hands, making her yelp and giggle as they went into the bathroom.

* * * *

When the movie they put on after their shower was over, Eli lifted her soundly sleeping form from the couch, carried her to his bed, and tucked her in. Removing his robe, he climbed in behind her then pulled the covers over them. She murmured contentedly when he slid her black satin robe from her, needing the direct contact with her warm, sleep-tender flesh. He fell asleep breathing in the clean scent of her hair, mixed with her own womanly fragrance that was a part of who she was. Drawing his knees up behind her, he drew her deeper into his embrace and curled her to him, pleasing the caveman who resided in his chest, near the heart that she had claimed to the uttermost.

Chapter Forty-five

On Saturday morning, a week before the wedding, Rachel's cell phone rang, and she and Eli couldn't help but chuckle. Grace had gotten hold of Rachel's new cell phone and downloaded special ring tones so Rachel would know who was calling based on the ringer. The ringer for Grace sounded, playing "The Stripper." Eli shook his head and grinned at Grace's humor.

Kelly's ringer was "Wild Thing," Charity's was "Friends in Low Places," and her mom's was "Respect." Bashful Teresa also had a special ring tone, which all the girls thought was hysterical, "Rockstar" by Nickelback. There was no telling who else in her address book got a special ringtone. Rachel supposed she'd find out eventually.

"Hello, Grace."

"Now, *see?* Isn't it nice to know who's calling without even looking at the caller ID?"

"Very amusing. I hope you *never* call me while I'm in church."

Grace snorted. "Now that *would* be embarrassing! Hey, listen, we wanted to have a little something for you and Eli up at The Pony tonight, sort of like an engagement party. Why don't you dress in something hot and sexy and come up to the club?"

"I think we were planning to go over there tonight, anyway. What time?"

"Oh, how about…six o'clock?"

"We can do that. And, Grace? Thanks. You've been so good to us."

"I love you guys. See you at six o'clock."

Putting the phone away, Rachel smiled at Eli across the breakfast table. "That girl's up to something."

"Mmm-hmm. Can't wait," he said, taking a sip of his black coffee.

Later that morning, they left to go on their first Christmas shopping trip together. They stayed in Divine and visited all the little small retail businesses that had struggled in the last year to stay afloat. With most everyone on their list taken care of, they stopped at a local drive-in and split a hot fudge sundae together.

He fed her a bite and asked, "You wanna know one of the things I love about you?"

She gave him a crooked grin and nodded. "Sure."

"I love that you don't obsess about your weight and your appearance to me. You don't sit there and simper and whine about how you shouldn't be eating this sundae with me because you might get fat. I love sharing it with you and watching you enjoy it. That tells me that you're happy with who you are, which is the woman I'm in love with."

"Thank you, Eli. Women who do that drive me crazy. It's like they feel they have to make excuses for enjoying life and what it offers. That extreme focus on food, being obsessed with it like so many are, is a sign that there's something missing from their lives. I like chocolate, and if you offer it to me, I'll probably take it. I'm happy with this body, though I know it's not perfect. If *you're* happy with this body, then it's all good."

"Angel, your body is heaven to me," he replied softly and put the spoon to her lips, smiling when she licked it suggestively. "Mmm, heaven."

They put up Eli's artificial tree when they got back home, opting to not get a real one since they would be on their honeymoon most of the ten days between the wedding and Christmas. It would be a shame to come home to a dried-out, dead Christmas tree. Rachel handed him the Christmas tree topper, an angel, and stepped back to look the tree over. She had found the angel at one of the shops that day and purchased it to commemorate their first Christmas together. Soon, it was time to get ready for the evening's festivities, whatever they were.

Eli asked, "Are you going to wear your leather outfit for me tonight?"

"Wait till you see me," she said, giggling as she turned on the shower and collected what she would need. After her shower, her pussy got a little damp as she began to slip into all that soft leather.

She zipped up the knee-high, black patent platform boots and stood up, amazed at the difference in her height looking in the mirror. She rolled her hair and applied her makeup, going for an extreme dark, dramatically shadowed and lined eye and blood-red lips. Her hair she left in wild, loose finger-styled curls, which she sprayed carefully, then stared back at the sexy stranger in the mirror. She threaded the buckle on her collar and positioned the large ring at the front of her throat.

She called out, "Eli? Are you ready?" as she attached the slave bracelet on her upper arm and hung the matching dangling earrings in her ears.

"Hell yeah, I'm ready!" he called from the living room.

She took a few deep breaths to calm her pounding heart. She glanced once more at the beautiful stranger in the mirror and smiled with deep, sexy satisfaction. Yeah, he *thought* he was ready. She hoped he was sitting down. She reached down and adjusted the zippers on the sides of the skirt, a little higher, like she'd seen Charity do. She stood tall, opened the door, and swept out into the hallway, sauntering into the living room, where Eli stood at the bar, replying to a text message. She stopped in front of him and stood there in poised silence, waiting for his reaction.

He was dressed in his black leathers and a snug black T-shirt with his black leather biker boots and his heavy black leather riding jacket. He looked delicious, and she wanted to push him back on the couch and ravish him on the spot. He looked up and dropped his phone and didn't even notice when it hit the floor.

* * * *

Eli was sending a text message when she called out to him. The bathroom door opened, and a cloud of scent floated down the hallway, a combination of the bodywash she used and the perfume she wore tonight. At the swish of her leathers, he looked up and was stunned stupid.

Eli stood there trying to catch his breath. He dimly heard a clatter and thought he might have dropped something. The blood pounded in his ears and rushed with painful force into his rapidly thickening cock.

She stood in front of him, her feet spaced apart in a wide, confident stance, waiting for his reaction. There was no denying it was Rachel. Her midnight-blue eyes, her light olive complexion, and her soft, full kissable lips all told him it was her. But this beauty before him was a whole new dimension of Rachel.

Her eyes were made up dark and mysterious with thick lashes, and she'd painted her lips red. The corset was laced tight up the front, and her lovely breasts generously filled the confines of the bust in a way that made his mouth water.

Eli gulped convulsively and drank the rest of her in. She had on the short leather skirt, which fit her like a second skin, with the zippers adjusted to at least a five-inch slit either side, and then he got a good look at her long, shapely legs sheathed in fishnet stockings and encased in tall, shiny black boots with the platform and ultra high heels. In them she was at least five inches taller, if not more.

He still had not spoken, but she obviously could see his reaction in his eyes because she gave him a sexy, knowing smile and glanced at the front of his leathers, where his erection stood, perfectly hard, screaming incessantly to get inside her. He did the only thing he could do, the only thing he could do that was worthy of her effect on him.

He slid to his knees before her, stunned.

She gasped as he wrapped his hands around her shiny, patent-encased ankles and slid his palms slowly up her calves. She moaned faintly when his hands made contact with the back of her knees. He felt her tremble as his hands paused at her hemline, and he looked up into her face. Her eyes were closed, and her ruby red lips were parted as she panted quietly, her cheeks a blushing rose color.

He slid his hands beneath her skirt, because he *needed* to know, and groaned in tortured delight when he discovered she was wearing fishnet stockings and a garter belt. He traced his fingers up the backs of her thighs, to what lay beneath the garter belt. Her breathing accelerated to a staccato panting rhythm as his fingertips skimmed over her bare ass cheeks then slid to the front, to the smooth, leather of her G-string. Dressed in leather from head to toe, she was a goddess. No, that description wasn't quite right. She owned him, body and soul. He slid his arms around her and pressed his face to her abdomen, his lips at her mound.

He looked up at her, in awe. "My queen."

* * * *

Now it was Rachel's turn to be speechless. On his knees, he called her his *queen*. Her heart pounded an insane rhythm, and she had to reach for the bar to steady herself with a hand as he kissed the knuckles of her other hand. When she'd sauntered out confidently earlier and waited for his response, she didn't realize how profoundly his reaction might affect *her*.

"Oh, Eli." Her lips trembled, and she fought the tears that wanted to flood her eyes. She'd worked too hard on her eye makeup to ruin it now.

He stood in front of her with a positively euphoric look on his face as he placed a little white box, wrapped with a white satin bow, into her hand. "A little something for tonight."

Rachel looked up at him, surprised at his unexpected gift. "Thank you, Eli."

She untied the satin ribbon.

"I hope you like it and that I chose well based on past conversations."

Glancing up at him, she lifted the lid then looked inside. Lying in the box was a heavy, flat, solid silver heart pendant with a lobster claw clasp. Engraved in script letters on the heart was the name *Eli*. Whoa.

"Turn it over, Rachel." On the other side in thick, larger block letters was another word. A *warning*. MINE.

"Oh." She breathed out, fingering the lobster claw. She understood. This was a tag to be worn from the ring of her collar. *He understood.* He knew how this would resonate with her. She claimed to be his, she'd promised she was his, she'd cried out in ecstasy she was his, and now the whole world would know it, know that he owned her body and soul. She smiled joyfully and handed it to him and lifted the ring on the collar. He slipped it on with his name facing up.

"I'm glad you like it." He fingered it above her cleavage as her heart thumped rapidly beneath it.

"I love it," she whispered. "Knowing I'm yours and that you lay claim to me like this, it...feels so *good*, Eli," she finished lamely, unable to find the right words.

"I love you, angel. That tag says you are mine, but it rests there only by your choice, only if you believe it's true. I would never seek to truly enslave you, Rachel."

"I already am."

His fingertips brushed lightly over her cheekbone as he looked at her with deep approval and appreciation.

"It's six fifteen. We don't want to be late. I have your jacket here." He traced his fingers over the slave bracelet on her arm, noticing it for the first time, and smiled softly. He held the jacket, and she slipped her arms into it then turned to him, the fringe swaying with her movement.

"Beautiful," he murmured.

* * * *

Eli helped Rachel climb from the seat of his Dodge, and she smiled wickedly as she treated him to a sexy glimpse of her inner thigh above the edge of her fishnet stocking before boldly sliding down his torso as he set her on her feet.

"How do I look, handsome?" she asked with a naughty grin, giving his chest a light brush with her breasts just for good measure. The sexy rumble that rose from his chest sent a quiver of pure lust straight to her clit.

"I should pop that delectable fanny of yours for teasing me like that before we go into public," he growled, squeezing her ass cheek as she giggled unrepentantly. "You look good enough to eat right here in the parking lot, angel." He softened his words with a gentle nuzzle against her neck that sent delicious shivers all over her body, and her pussy swelled and throbbed in response to his touch.

"You're not so bad yourself, handsome man." She laid her hand over his heart. "I promise I'll be so good you'll have to *beg* me to be bad."

"And what if being bad *is* good as long as you're with me?"

Rachel didn't hold back her sexy chuckle. Her hand slid down over his chest and abdomen to the waist of his leathers as she said, "Honey, you know the old saying, 'When I'm good, I'm very good. But when I'm bad, I'm even better?'" Her fingertips slid an inch into his waistband, right by his fly. "I'll be as bad as you want me to be." *Maybe even badder if it means I get extra licks, handsome.*

"Shit. Let's get inside before I start getting ideas. You're wicked tonight, woman." He took her hand and led her to the club's front entrance.

"Let's see what Grace has up her sleeves, or down her stocking, or wherever she hides her bright ideas," Rachel said, grinning at Eli when he laughed at her comment.

He pulled open the door for her and held her hand as she stepped in. When Mike and Rogelio looked up and saw them, they got twin reactions. First, there was a deep, squinting scowl of non-recognition of the female with Eli, then bulgy, bug-eyed shock as they realized it *was* Rachel with Eli. Mike let out a loud wolf whistle that drew *everyone's* attention as she sauntered confidently up to Mike, and was eye-to-eye with him and Rogelio. She gave them both big smiles and left red lip prints on their cheeks to match the red and white Santa hats they were both wearing. Rachel wondered who sweet-talked them into wearing them but had a pretty good guess. Grace, no doubt.

"Dang, girl!" Mike said loudly. "You're killing me! Wait till your *dad* sees you! You're in *trouble!*"

"My dad is not—" She was interrupted by the tell-tale distinctive throat clearing noise behind her.

"Ahem." It sounded just like her—

"Dad! What are you doing here?"

"Hoping to see my lovely daughter. You do look lovely, princess, if a little...*different* from what your dad's used to." Her dad turned to Eli. "Wolf, was this leather outfit your idea? You seem to match tonight," he said sarcastically as Rachel whapped her dad gently on the arm.

"Dad, there's nothing wrong with how I'm dressed. These were all shower gifts. You should be glad I'm not wearing what *Mom* gave me for a shower gift." She grinned as her dad squirmed a little.

"I don't see any other women dressed head-to-toe in leather, and since when are you so tall? Oh, never mind, you look beautiful." He kissed her cheek as Charity and Justin walked in, dressed similarly to Rachel and Eli.

Grace made it up to the front, surprising them with Kelly in tow. Rachel and Eli hugged her and asked where Matthew was. Kelly explained he was with Ethan's little sister, Erin, at Grace's overnight.

Grace had on a beautiful, red velvet corset, edged with sparkling rhinestones at the bust, with a transparent black wrap thrown over her shoulders. She wore it with a black satin pencil skirt, which ended below the knee. Her pretty, pedicured feet were done up in glittering, silver high-heeled sandals.

Kelly was going for a classic look in a slinky little black dress with shiny, black high heels on her dainty tiny feet. Her hair was styled in whimsical little ringlets all around her face. She looked like a pixie on a hot date. Standing next to Kelly was Elijah, dressed in Wranglers, cowboy boots, and an open-collared white dress shirt.

Rachel turned to Grace and grinned. "Okay, what's going on, Grace?"

Grace smirked. "Come sit down, and we'll tell you. By the way, you are smokin' hot in that leather outfit, Rachel!"

Rachel and Eli followed her to the table they usually sat at. Everybody else was there. Everybody—her parents, Charity and Justin, Kelly, Elijah, Rosemary, Wes and Evan, Kathleen and Ace, Corina and Brice, Ethan, Jack, Adam. Teresa and Angel were there, too.

Rachel greeted them all, a little surprised, and turned to Grace. Grace said two words she hated to hear—bachelorette party.

Then she said two more Rachel hated even *worse*—bachelor party.

Shit.

Her old jealous nature reared its ugly head. A strippers and her fiancé in close proximity to each other. She felt a deep crease formed between her brows, and she turned to Eli, looking up at him uncertainly.

He stroked her back and murmured quietly, "This is a surprise to me, too, baby."

Grace touched her hand and said sincerely, "Don't worry, Rachel. Charity is going with the men as a sort of chaperone. She'll keep an eye on Eli and run wicked interference with any women who get too friendly. Plus, they're going to a strip club, not hiring a stripper to come to them. And if he misbehaves, she'll rat him out faster than she can type WTF."

Chapter Forty-six

"My thoughts exactly, 'What the *f*—'" Rachel zipped her lip, remembering her dad was there.

Then she realized something. It was great that Charity would be there. Then she'd get all the juicy details later, but if her dad was in attendance, Eli would never—*No.* That was just it. Eli, *her* Eli, would never lay a hand on another woman as long as she was alive. Not because she was jealous of other women but because he loved her and wanted only her.

She relaxed, and looked into Eli's eyes. "Go have fun, honey."

Eli did a double take. "But—what?"

She murmured to him, "No regrets, remember? I trust *you*, Eli. Charity will deal with anyone who gets too frisky with you. Break a few twenties so you have one dollar bills for the dancers, but remember," she whispered sexily, "I dance for *love*."

He slid his palms up and down her waist until her dad cleared his throat, and then he returned from the spell she cast over him.

"But that's not all," Grace said. "Rachel, *you're* coming with all the ladies. There are two limousines waiting. The men will go to a gentlemen's club in Morehead, taking Charity with them as escort. The ladies will be going to a ladies' club in Morehead, and Adam will be our gentleman escort, keeping us safe and watching over Rachel. We'll only be a few minutes apart the whole evening. The clubs are that close. Adam and Charity will keep in touch, and we'll rendezvous back here when we're ready. How does that sound, Eli?"

Eli never hesitated. "Go have some fun, angel." Then he added softly, "I'll be ready and waiting for *my* lap dance when we're alone."

She nuzzled his throat, realizing she was going to miss him for the next few hours, but gasped in pleasure and a sudden rush of...delight as his hands grasped the zippers on each side of her skirt and slowly slid the zippers down to the bottom. He made no show of it. Only she was aware of what he was doing as the others prepared to leave.

Folding the zipper tabs down and locking them in place, he growled, "These stay closed while you are away from me, angel." Then he kissed the silver pendant hanging from the ring on her collar and looked into her eyes, checking for her reaction.

She seductively promised, "They'll stay where they are until you unzip them all the way…if you *want* to."

"Oh, I *want* to, all right." He squeezed her ass while her dad wasn't looking and kissed her hungrily.

She went to the ladies' room to fix her lipstick and fluff her hair. Grace came in to do the same. She gestured to heavy silver pendant and said, "May I?" Rachel smiled and nodded. Grace lifted it, read Eli's name, turned it over, and smiled wickedly. "Nice," she murmured softly. "It looks good on the collar, makes it more…meaningful, I think." She eyed Rachel carefully.

"Definitely more meaningful. I love it. Thanks again for the collar."

"You're welcome. Eli is waiting to escort you outside. You may not have realized it, but when you came in wearing this *hotter-than-hell* outfit, you caused quite a stir amongst the male customers. I'm not even sure they've recognized you yet. It's funny, I think I heard Eli *growl* earlier." Grace chuckled. "My territorial men aren't the only ones growling tonight. But check the club when you walk out and you'll see what I mean. It's good for a girl's ego."

Rachel grinned. "You look beautiful tonight. Let me guess. Um…Adam bought this outfit for you, head to toe, including the lingerie and shoes. From…June."

"That's a no-brainer. Did you see Adam tonight? He's very handsome in his suit."

"You make a perfect couple in your evening attire. He looks devastatingly delicious," she added, making Grace laugh. "Speaking of gorgeous, let's get *our* fannies out to the limo."

She exited the ladies' room and stopped at the entrance to the back hall. Eli was across the club speaking privately with Adam. Rachel had to laugh. Adam was probably reassuring Eli how many different parts he'd break off of any guy who got frisky with her.

She smiled and sauntered away from the hallway, trying to ignore the impact she had on the men in the club. Stares followed her, and more than a few men got elbows in their ribs from their dates. Two unfortunate friendly fellows she'd never met approached her before she gotten far.

"Excuse me, beautiful, would you like to dance?"

"Pardon me, darlin', care to dance with *me*?"

A third was approaching and about to speak up when she stopped them and smiled at all of them and gestured to Eli, who was striding across the club. "I'm sorry. I'm here with my fiancé." Caught in Eli's admiring gaze, she sauntered through the crowd to him.

"Hey, beautiful. Ready to go?"

"Ready as I'll *ever* be," she said dryly. What was she supposed to do at a ladies' strip club, anyway?

When she asked that question in the limo, all the ladies stopped talking, looked at her, and burst out in laughter.

Grace replied, "You don't *do* anything, sweet cheeks. They come to *you*."

"Tell me honest and straight what you have planned. No games. No stupid 'suck for a buck' bachelorette T-shirt, and no scavenger hunts. I don't want to be embarrassed."

Grace scoffed. "Aw! I liked the 'suck for a buck' T-shirt idea. But Kelly said it would piss Eli off too much if he found out dancers were sucking LifeSavers off your shirt. So thank her, I suppose, party pooper. Nope, we're just going to enjoy a few drinks and watch men take their clothes off. Lap dances are your option."

Rachel looked over at Kelly and clasped her hands together and mouthed, *"Thank you!"*

Kelly snickered and gave her a thumbs-up signal. Rachel was feeling more trepidation by the minute. She sat next to Grace in the limo, and Adam sat on the other side of Grace. As Rachel watched the others laugh and joke around, a hand gently tapped her shoulder. She looked, and Adam leaned over behind Grace.

"Don't worry, Rachel. We're going to make sure you have a good time without getting embarrassed or in trouble with Eli."

"You won't let them take me up on stage, will you?"

"I have the strictest instructions from Eli that you are not to be taken up on stage or embarrassed in any way. This is supposed to be fun for you, too."

"Is that what you and Eli were talking about at the club?"

"Partly. But even if he hadn't approached me with that specific concern, I still wouldn't let them do that. Don't worry. You're going to have a great time." He patted her shoulder.

Rachel smiled at him and tried to relax enough to join in the conversations. She was caught up in her own thoughts, wishing she'd known about this whole bachelorette–strip club plan to begin with. She'd have done what she did best—research the subject. She pulled out her cell phone and did some quick Internet research on strip club etiquette and what to expect in a strip club. She quickly scanned and found three well-organized articles from several different perspectives—dancers, bouncers, and customers. A lot of the rules were common sense. She leaned over to Adam and got his attention.

"What is the touching rule in the club they are going to?"

"Generally, their policy is 'touch and go,' which means you touch and you go, escorted by a bouncer out the door."

"What about lap dances? How much?"

"Usually about thirty bucks and then you buy the girl a drink. She usually makes half of what the customer pays for the drinks, which are outrageously expensive. The guys plan to keep him at the main stage watching the onstage dancers and tipping them. Out on the floor is where the lap dances happen. After they dance on stage, the girls go around and receive tips from the customers on the floor for the dance. Then if a customer likes them, they buy them a drink and the girl will offer to give a lap dance."

"What are the rules for lap dances there?"

"Hands down at your sides the whole time. Very strict, very big bouncers, very talented dancers."

"Can you tell me what a lap dance is?"

He defined that particular club's version of a lap dance. The dancer sat on the customer's knee, moving to the music, gyrating and pulling the customers face to her breasts if she wanted to. She could touch him anywhere she wanted, but the customer could not place his hands on the dancer, or he was out the door. She might lift her G-string and let the customer tuck the money under the string.

"What about one-on-one rooms or VIP rooms?"

"They have a VIP room. They won't take him in there. As long as the tips flow, the girls will hang around and chat, enjoy a drink, and give a preview of a lap dance. They thought the best place for him would be at the main stage with a thick stack of bills."

"Are they *all* topless?"

He grinned at her. "Not a stitch above the waist where they are going. Even the waitresses."

She was thoughtful for a moment. The limitations they had placed on Eli basically negated any fun time he would have tonight. *Crappity-crap.*

"Thanks, Adam."

She dialed Charity's cell phone number. "Have I got a job for you, Charity. This is what I want you to do..."

* * * *

Eli had a good time talking and laughing with all the men. They kept their stories mostly clean until Charity finally had enough and told the dirtiest joke she could think of. That broke the ice real good, and they'd acted like red-blooded American men from that point forward. He was glad Charity had been on her phone with an important call for the last few minutes because the talk had gotten fairly raunchy.

When they had gotten to the club, Jack tipped the doorman, who found them a large table at the main stage. Eli realized they were insulating him from contact with the dancers once they left the stage and mingled on the floor. Although there was plenty of beautiful bared flesh to look at in the club, none of it did much for him. He could appreciate a lovely pair of breasts and long legs as much as any guy there, and he might even have had wood a time or two, but none of these were what his body was craving. There were beautiful smiles and probably even deep-blue eyes here, too, but none that could compare with Rachel's.

A waitress delivered their drinks, and when she smiled and placed his in front of him, he tipped her and smiled back. Topless or not, this was a job to her. Charity and Justin stood up at the bar talking for a minute before he kissed her and came back to the table and sat down, chuckling.

"You're not gonna believe this."

"What?" Eli looked over at him briefly and then smiled at the dancer on stage. Jack and Ethan looked over at Justin, too.

"The manager offered Charity a job as a dancer. No audition, *nothing*, just liked the way she looked and moved when she came in."

Eli chuckled as the blonde on the stage dipped in front of him and smiled flirtatiously. "I'm not a bit surprised, Justin. Charity is gorgeous, and she's got guts. What did you say?"

"That I'd be her best-tipping customer, and I asked her to reserve her first lap dance for me," he said with a chuckle. "Shit, man. The mother of two half-grown kids, and someone offers her a job based solely on the way she looks and carries herself. No way was I going to tell her no. She knows her own mind."

"In other words, you trust her to make the *right* choice?" Peter asked, admiring the dancer's long legs as she swung over him on the pole.

"No, I trust her to know what she can handle and what she can't. Working nights is hard. I know. I did it for years."

They clapped for the dancer as her song came to an end, and each of them tipped her several more bills. She smiled at Jack, Ethan, and Justin and hooked her finger in her G-string, inviting them to tuck the bills in for her. Then she sauntered in her skyscraper high heels over to Eli, half-squatted in front of him, and hooked her thumb in the other side of her G-string. He slid a couple more bills in under the string. She smiled seductively, blew him an air kiss, and worked her way down the stage.

"They're going to be all over him with that long black hair," Justin muttered.

Eli chuckled and looked back at the bar, where Charity was chatting with the pretty blonde who had just finished her dance. The blonde nodded and smiled enthusiastically. She moved away from Charity to work the room while Charity talked to a petite strawberry blonde with shoulder-length curls. She nodded and made her way to the door that led backstage.

A song started, and another dancer took the stage, this one of medium build with long auburn curls. Her body shimmered as the lights reflected off her body glitter while she danced. She worked her way down the stage and over to their table when the men held paper bills between their fingers.

She grinned and flirted as she danced, blowing his dad an air kiss as she trailed her hair over his shoulder when she spun over him. He grinned and "mmm-ed" but politely kept his hand gripping a bill at the edge of the stage, flirting back. She did it again, slipping the bill from his grasp in the same move. She paid similar flirtatious attention to all the men as the bills kept coming before dancing her way to the other end of the stage.

The club had gotten busier, and they were on their second round of drinks when the pretty blonde dancer made her way to their table. "Hello, boys. Did you like my dance?" she asked flirtatiously, slipping her forearm through Ethan's and sliding her hand over Jack's shoulder. The men commented positively and slipped her more bills, for which she thanked them kindly.

"We sure did, sweetheart. What's your name?" Ethan slipped her a ten as Justin rose from his seat next to Eli and offered it to her. She smiled at him and sat down.

"My name is Charlotta. I haven't seen you here before. Where are you all from?"

"Most of us are from Divine. Can we buy you a drink?" Justin offered when the waitress reappeared. Charlotta nodded and told the waitress what she wanted.

"I understand there's a man among you tonight who's tying the knot soon," she said, looking up at Justin.

Justin slapped Eli on the back. "This is Eli, one of the best friends a guy ever had."

"Well, congratulations, Eli," she said in her smooth-as-honey voice.

Charlotta made conversation with them for several more minutes while she drank her mixed drink as a couple of other girls approached and chatted with the other guys. All of the men were well aware of the rules and did not touch any of the dancers but allowed the women to touch them. Poor Brice had his hands stuck in the pockets of his jeans, like he was afraid he would forget and wind up getting kicked out, but his grin was a mile wide.

A dancer with platinum blonde hair came and sat in Peter's lap and began flirting with him. Cool as a cucumber, he grinned and offered to buy her a drink. He chatted with her as if this happened to him every night and twice on Sundays, but he kept his hands resting on the arms of his chair. Wes and Evan were approached by a sexy little dancer with short, black, spiky hair who evidently knew them from previous visits, calling them by name. She offered a lap dance to them, and when they accepted, she led them to a couch along one of the walls not far away.

Charlotta sat and talked for another minute or two with Eli and Justin about mundane things, telling them that she was student working online toward a degree in psychology. The tips helped to pay bills and tuition.

The next dance song began, and the tiny little strawberry blonde with shoulder-length curls bobbed out on the stage, dressed in a schoolgirl outfit, dancing to Nickelback's "Shakin' Hands." She danced and flirted with the customers from the stage, revealing her tight little tush as she spun on the pole.

Dancing to the hard rock beat, she made her way down the stage to the bachelor party, gyrating and dancing for the admiring men. She winked at Charlotta, who grinned conspiratorially as the little blonde popped her top open in Eli's face, making him grin broadly. She slipped the necktie off and draped it around Eli's neck and pulled him a little closer as his friends hooted and hollered in encouragement. She gave him a crooked little grin and winked then pecked him on the cheek very lightly, and this time her smile reached her eyes when all he did was wink back and nod appreciatively, handing her a paper bill for her efforts.

She spun on the pole at their end of the stage, and the men kept the tips coming, assuring her continued attention. Her top came off to loud cheers, revealing her perfect, full breasts, just right for her small size. As the song came to the final chorus, she stripped her schoolgirl skirt off, revealing the pure white G-string underneath. The only other thing she had on were her little white lace anklets and her white schoolgirl high heels. She returned to their end of the stage and thanked the guys and flirted briefly as she collected the tips they gave her. Eli handed her the tie she'd slipped around his neck and a couple of folded bills, thanking her as she blew another kiss to him.

"That's Cami. She's a little sweetie. Thanks for remembering the rules earlier, you know, not touching?" Charlotta added softly to Eli. "A drunken customer pulled her from the stage one night last week while she was dancing. It scared the daylights out of her. We appreciate the men who really *are* gentlemen. Eli, may I offer you a lap dance?"

She asked so sweetly, Eli imagined that she never got turned down. He smiled apologetically at her and said, "I'm sorry, Charlotta. I wouldn't feel right about doing that. My fiancée—"

Charlotta held up her hand to stop him from apologizing further. She seemed more impressed than rejected by his refusal. "Don't apologize, Eli. I think it's sweet of you, but I did have to at least offer. Well, I need to go get ready to dance again. Would you mind if I stopped by your table again in a little while?" she asked as Eli rose from his chair.

"We'd like that very much, Charlotta. We'll save your seat," Justin replied.

Eli was developing a nice buzz when Cami walked up, bubbly as could be. "Hiya, fellas! How was my dance earlier? Did you like it?" she asked as she smiled up at them. She could not have been more than five feet tall, though her high heels helped. The other men greeted her and slipped her numerous bills, which she tucked in her G-string, thanking them enthusiastically. Eli doubted all of those were ones.

"Could we buy you a drink?" Eli said, offering her his chair and standing to his full height.

"Oh, my goodness you're tall as an oak tree, aren't you!" she said giggling. "I'd love a drink, thank you." She sat in Eli's chair and gave the waitress her order. "So what brings you here tonight? Are you from out of town?"

A couple more girls who'd finished their dances joined the group, making small talk with the men after ordering a drink.

"Bachelor party," Eli said as Jack slapped him on the back. "I'm getting married next Saturday."

"Oh! Congratulations! By the way, I'm Cami. So what do you do...." She hesitated.

"Eli! Sorry, my name is Eli. I'm a bouncer at a club in Divine."

"Really? Divine is such a pretty town. What's the name of the club, if you don't mind me asking?"

He told her, and they talked for a few minutes. They asked her if she liked her job, and she said she did most of the time and the money was good. She asked them if they had traveled much and then revealed why she was working in the club.

"I'm a student right now, but after I graduate in May, I'm taking off for three months to travel through Europe with a couple of friends. I'm dancing three nights a week right now and putting the money I make away for the trip. It's sort of a last hurrah before settling down in a career."

"What's your major?" Ethan asked, hailing the waitress for another round for the ladies.

"Thank you. My major is business management. I'd like to have my own nightclub someday. The hours suit me."

"Ethan here owns The Dancing Pony in Divine," Jack said, joining the conversation after the dancer he had been talking to left to go perform on stage.

As they talked with the girls, they never ignored the dancers who performed on stage, showing their appreciation with their tips. The pace of the conversation was different than in a regular club. The dancers who sat with them allowed them to enjoy the view, spreading the money around, so to speak. Wes and Evan returned to the table and offered the dancer who had just given them both lap dances a drink, which she gladly accepted.

"Charlotta told us about your scare last week. I'm glad you weren't injured," Justin softly remarked to Cami.

"Me, too. I guess the poor guy got too drunk and forgot the rules of the club. By the way, thanks, Eli, for remembering them earlier. Your whole group are real sweethearts, and I appreciate the tips."

"You're welcome, Cami." A few minutes later, when the waitress returned, Eli said, "Buy you another drink?"

"Sure, I have time for another quick one, and then I'll need to get back to work. Eli, since this is your bachelor party, could I offer you a lap dance?" Cami asked, her voice silky and seductive as she leaned into him a little. She looked over his shoulder and smiled. Eli looked up and saw Charity standing behind him with a devious grin, holding out her phone to him.

"A quick phone call for you, sexy." Eli took the phone and put it tightly to his ear so he could hear.

"Hello?"

He smiled as Rachel said, "Hello, handsome! Are you having a good time?"

"Yeah! How about you?"

"None of them compare to you, Eli." Even over the noise, he could hear the sexy tone she used.

"Same here, angel."

"Eli, listen, I want you to have fun tonight. No regrets, right? I trust you. I want you to let Charlotta and Cami dance for you this evening. I want you to enjoy yourself."

"Angel, are you sure? I'm having a good time."

"Let them dance for you, but remember when we get home tonight I'm giving you a *real* lap dance." He growled into the phone at that thought and heard her giggle. "I love you!"

"I love you, too, angel." The connection ended, and he handed the phone to Charity and asked, "What have you been up to?"

Charity scoffed and rolled her eyes and grinned at him. "You weren't cooperating with her *plan.* I had no choice but to call her. I think it made her night when I told her you refused the lap dance from Charlotta."

* * * *

Rachel knew that Eli's bachelor party was not the typical bachelor party. They had not been turned loose in the strip club to sample the delights of all the women who made their living there. Charity had been along to raise the standard of conduct a little and help form a buffer around Eli.

The same basic privileges were afforded to her at the other club. Grace had Adam sit right next to Rachel, and though there were a number of dancers, none touched her inappropriately. Once she made the call and talked to Eli, giving him a green light to interact with the two dancers Charity had specifically hired for him, Adam did the same basic thing for Rachel and found two dancers who were conversational, charming, and willing to work within the same parameters.

No one touched the zippers on her skirt or anything under it, nor were they allowed to touch from the top of her cleavage down, ensuring her breasts were untouched. She had an interesting encounter with one of the two dancers Adam had hired to entertain her personally. He had agreed to the rules, and as he had danced for her, he lifted the silver heart to look at it since it rested well above her cleavage. When he saw a man's name, he gently turned the tag, and she saw more than just the expected smiling reaction in the dancer's eyes.

Later, he gestured to the silver tag on her collar. "For some people, that tag has a powerful message from your fiancé. I take it as an honor to be one of the dancers chosen to entertain you." He sipped his drink and grinned up at Taylor, her other dancer, as he danced for Rachel from the stage she sat next to.

Rachel's curiosity was piqued. "What does it mean to you? I'm sorry, that sounds rude. The collar was a shower gift, but the tag means something special to me. What does it mean to you?" She hoped she didn't offend him with the blunt question.

"It means that you are precious and valuable to your fiancé. It's a way of marking you and warning others off, obviously. It is also significant because you allowed him to display it on you openly like this. You must be deeply in love with him."

Rachel's cheeks tingled with heat, and she said simply, "Soul deep." She missed Eli very much in that moment.

"I can see that."

Grace and the others were blissfully ignorant of their conversation, busy cheering for Taylor and waving bills to get him to come dance for them. Even her mom was busy flirting and having fun. She smiled at Brandon and thanked him. The conversation was a strangely comfortable moment in the midst of in a sea of erotic and, at times, comical interaction between the women and the dancers.

"How's your drink? Are you ready for another?" Brandon asked, once again playing the role of exotic dancer. She had him order another for both of them.

He peered at her and said, "You're looking serious and contemplative. I'm sorry if I ruined the sexy bachelorette vibe you had going."

"You didn't, not at all. But you have given me some food for thought."

"Well, Rachel, it has been more than a pleasure to serve you *and* your fiancé tonight. Make sure and tell Eli I was honored," Brandon said as he rose from his seat. "How about I give you something more...*stereotypical* to think of for a little while. After all, you *are* in a strip club. Ready for another lap dance?" he asked with a devilish gleam in his pretty green eyes.

"Twist my arm, why don't you?" She enjoyed the attentions of both Brandon and Taylor. They were sexy, sensual, and erotic in their moves and dances without carrying it too far. But she felt an unmistakable camaraderie with Brandon.

* * * *

Eli felt his cheeks flush with pleasure that refusing the lap dance meant that much to Rachel.

Charity grinned widely and continued. "Rachel wants you to have a good time. She wanted me to find two beautiful dancers that looked *nothing* like her who would work within her parameters but still show you a sexy, good time."

"She did, did she? What limitations did she give?" he asked, looking at an impish Cami as she giggled behind her hand before answering him.

"Basically, we can touch you anywhere except for your hair and your crotch. Everything else is fair game. I like your fiancée. She's got spunk!"

"You have *no* idea." Eli found it ironic that Rachel's *voice* on the phone had gotten him hard when the sexy little thing wearing nothing but a thong and those high heels hadn't. Maybe the sight of them only affected him when Rachel wore them.

"Well, now you have no worries, right? You know me and Charlotta will be taking good care of you and that we will keep our hands out of your fiancée's private territory. Charity said that you receive a lot of unwanted attention from women who come in the club and that Rachel is the jealous type. We know how that is. We both have boyfriends. At least our bouncers keep most of the customers from touching us. You kind of have to take it, don't you, or lose their business?"

Eli shrugged. "It's not as bad since Rachel and I got engaged. She handles it pretty well now and has even made some new friends that way. Most people are pretty decent that come in there."

"I'm going to talk to Charlotta about visiting The Dancing Pony sometime. It would be nice to go out to a club and keep my shirt on while I dance with something besides a shiny pole," she added, chuckling. "Enjoy your drink, and I hope you take me up on the offer of a lap dance. Charlotta is coming on now and then she'll come sit with you again. You should let Char give you a lap dance. She's smokin' hot!" She patted his chest before leaving their group to mingle with the customers.

Charlotta did a slow, sexy striptease out of a sexy red satin evening gown and gloves to "Santa Baby" sung by Kellie Pickler. She paid special attention to Eli but danced for all the men seated at the stage. Later, she rejoined them at their table, clad in her red satin G-string and red tasseled pasties, thanking all the men as they handed her more folded bills.

Justin ordered Charlotta a drink, and she chatted with Eli, Justin, and Charity. "You're fiancée sounds like a lot of fun, Eli. Are you ready for your lap dance?" The other men happened to hear her question and cheered him on, even Peter.

"Sure," he said, meeting with shouted approval from all the men.

Charlotta rose from her chair and led him to a low bench-like seat located at the end of the stage. She sat him down on the edge. Placing her hands over his on the seat, she said, "Just keep your hands here and let me do the rest, Eli."

She leapt onto his thighs, gracefully resting on her shins. Balancing perfectly, she rose up to press her perfumed breasts into his face and began to dance for him, gyrating to the loud music. She slid down onto only one of his thighs and continued to dance for him, sensual and sexy, but she was true to her promise to Rachel and Charity and never once touched his cock or his hair, even accidentally.

After the dance, she escorted him back to the table and sat in the seat Justin offered while Charity sat in Eli's at his insistence. Charity saw to it that Charlotta had another drink and slipped her an extra tip for executing the dance without breaking the rules.

Cami's next dance started, and they enjoyed watching her shake her tail feathers, this time in a little Christmas Elf costume. She danced to another Christmas song, "I Saw Mommy Kissing Santa Claus" sung by The Ronettes, and playfully slipped a red and white Santa hat on Eli's head and kissed his cheek, Cami threw down her best moves for Eli and his table as the smiling men waved money for her to come and collect. She flirted with them enthusiastically before moving down the stage to entertain the other customers. Charlotta chatted with them a while longer then excused herself to go get ready for her last dance. They invited her back for one last drink afterward before it was time for them to go. She happily agreed and excused herself.

After finishing her dance, Cami returned immediately to their table, clad in her red and white candy-striped thong and stilettos. "Charlotta says we're going to visit The Dancing Pony some night when we're both off for the evening and our boyfriends can get away."

Charity had a twinkle in her eye. "Cami, why don't you call me and let me know what night, and I'll make sure and let the girls know. I have a question for you. Have you ever been asked to give lessons in striptease?"

"All the time. Sometimes the customers bring in their wives, and if the wives are cool, they have a good time. It's those wives that will ask if we give lessons in pole dancing or stripping. None of us are professional instructors, but we can teach what we know. Did you know you can buy your own pole online to use at home?"

"Yeah," Justin said with a big wide smile. "I got her one for Christmas last year."

Charity leaned into him and kissed him. "He sure did. He was very appreciative of my efforts, but I think I'd learn more from interacting with a teacher than I did from watching the video. I'd like to talk to you sometime about that. I'll bet Rachel would fall all over herself signing up for those lessons, too."

"Now see, *this* is what makes this job fun," Cami said to Charity. "You girls get that we do this for a living and that we're not hooker sleazebags trying to steal your husbands. Unfortunately, not all the women that come in with their husbands are cool with it. They want to prove something to themselves, and they get uncomfortable or self-conscious and wind up resenting us, their husbands, or themselves. This is entertainment, and I have no desire to run off with anyone's man."

"Does your boyfriend come in while you work? Is he okay with you doing your job?" Charity asked.

Cami replied, "We have a unique situation, not typical at all. He's also a dancer. Contrary to popular opinion, male strippers are not all gay, nor are they self-obsessed. He stripped during his college days to help pay his tuition because he could make more doing that than waiting tables and had more time for studying. He's working tonight at the club you told me your sister took Rachel to." She patted Eli's chest. "He may be giving her a lap dance right now!"

In an oddly bizarre way, Eli found that both amusing and acceptable. If he'd been questioned yesterday what he thought about *any* man giving Rachel a lap dance, he would have gone ballistic, but Charity was handling things well on this end, and he was confident that Adam was having similar good luck at the other club.

"Really!" Charity laughed at the irony. "What's his name?"

"His stage name is Brandon, but his real name is Jacob. He prefers to not use his real name. A lot of us do that."

"Is Cami your real name, if you don't mind me asking?" Charity asked in a lower voice.

"Not at all. It's short for Camilla. No one's called me Cami since high school, except for here. I like things simple. So are you going to take me up on my earlier offer for a lap dance?" she asked cheekily as she stepped from her chair gracefully and crooked her finger at him. "I promise I'll *mind my manners*. I'd be just as territorial as Rachel if you were my fiancé. Come with me, and I'll make this as painless as possible for you." She grinned wickedly, swinging her hips, her breasts bobbing like little ripe melons as she seated him on the low couch against the wall.

More cheering cat calls came from the men at his table, but he ignored them and grinned admiringly up at her as he sat on his hands. "I'm helpless. Do your worst."

"You know that old expression, right? 'When I'm good I'm really good—'"

He nodded and laughed. "'But when I'm bad, I'm even better?' Yeah, Rachel used it on me earlier this evening. You two *should* meet."

"Your fiancée sounds so cool! Does she like to dance?" she asked as she slid down over his thighs, grinding on his knee.

"The first time I saw her, she was dancing. I was half in love by the time 'Save a Horse Ride a Cowboy' was finished playing."

She looked surprised and said, "Shooey! That was a close call! It was a toss-up what to play for my last dance earlier, and I picked a holiday number over 'Save a Horse Ride a Cowboy.' I wouldn't have wanted to mess that up for you." She smiled sassily as she shook her breasts right in his face, careful to not touch his hair when she gripped his shoulders. "Tell me what she's like," she said, dancing for him but distracting him with questions about Rachel at the same time, bless her, because she was good.

"Tall, beautiful, brunette, voluptuous and perfect. She's self-confident and sassy, like you. She works as a bookkeeper, but she is also a writer. She just finished her first book."

Cami carefully turned in his lap and gave him an up close view of her tight little tush, saying cheekily, "Sorry, Eli, it's not a lap dance if I don't do that move at least once. I don't want management to think you got cheated. What does she write?"

Eli chuckled, thinking she'd probably never had to explain *why* she used that move before. "She writes erotic romance."

She turned to look at him in pleased surprise. "Hot damn! Good for her! I hope I get to read her book someday."

"Me, too."

"I'll bet you're her *muse*, aren't you?" she asked as she shook her breasts in his face again. He smiled but must have looked doubtful because she added, "Trust me, Eli, you are *definitely* muse material."

"Thanks, Cami. You're a real sweetheart."

"Back at ya! I've enjoyed getting to visit with you tonight. That Charity is a real hoot, too. Her sister sounds like a peach."

She climbed from his lap, and he rose from the bench. "Grace and Rachel are close. She and my sister are the ones planning our wedding. She's multi-talented."

Charity cackled, looking at the screen on her phone as they returned to the table. "Shit a monkey! Look at this!"

Justin looked and frowned at Eli. "Dude, it's a picture of Rachel getting a lap dance. You sure you wanna look?"

Eli scoffed and held out his hand for the phone. "Man, the woman trusts and loves me enough to arrange for me to have a couple of lap dances in a strip club, how can I object? Adam is right there with her. He probably interviewed and fingerprinted that dancer before he let him anywhere near Rachel."

Cami held out her hand. "Can I see?" Charity handed her the phone first, and she grinned and laughed as she said, "Guess who that is dancing for her." She turned the phone so he could see.

Eli looked at the picture on the screen. Rachel was sitting in a low, armless chair, her hands in her lap as a male stripper danced for her in a leather G-string. She was smiling and laughing gaily in the picture, looking like she was having a blast. Then he noticed her zippers. They were right where he had left them, zipped all the way down.

"Your boyfriend?"

"Yep! And oooh, Eli! She is hotter than hell in all that *leather*. You two make the perfect couple. Wanna take a picture to send back to her?"

She and Charlotta posed with Eli, and Charity sent the picture to Adam's phone. A text came back a minute later.

Wow! They're pretty!
Ask them if they give striptease lessons for me?
I love you, honey!

He chuckled when Charity showed him the message then showed it to Cami and Charlotta.

"Tell your fiancée we'll *both* give her lessons. You, too, Charity," Charlotta said.

"And Grace, too!" Cami added, giggling playfully when both Jack and Ethan perked up at that news.

"Hot damn!" Jack hollered.

"Hell yeah!" Ethan yelled. "Charity, text Adam back and let him know. Lessons for any of the ladies who want them are on me."

The girls stayed for a little while longer, finishing their drinks. The men talked Brice into accepting the lap dance offered by the sexy little dancer with short, spiky, black hair. He behaved himself like a perfect gentleman, saying only appropriately complimentary things to her, and tipped her generously when she was finished.

The driver arrived at eleven, and the two dancers rose from their seats and thanked all the men for their generosity. They both gave Eli a light peck on the cheek and wished him and Rachel all the best and promised to get their boyfriends to bring them out to The Dancing Pony soon. They told Charity they'd let her know when, after she gave them her number. Charity texted Adam to let him know they were about to leave and return to The

Pony and Adam texted back, saying all the girls were ready to return to the club, too.

Sounding a little nervous, Brice asked, "What are we gonna do when we get there and they smell other women's perfume on us?" Eli had personally heard Corina assure Brice he should have a good time. She'd said she had a friend who was a stripper in college and that she trusted Brice. It was obvious the poor guy didn't want to screw up with his sweet little girlfriend.

"No, the question you need to ask yourselves," Charity replied, "is what *you're* going to do when the women get out of the limo and smell like other men's cologne? You call it even and *let it go.*" She typed on her cell phone keyboard. "Because they're asking themselves the same question *right now.* Pointing at the phone, she said, "See? I just saved you a relationship dilemma. Now let's go dance. I need to *shake* it, baby."

Chapter Forty-seven

Eli climbed out of the vehicle and waited with the others on the sidewalk as the ladies' limo pulled up. The limousines arrived within a few minutes of each other at The Dancing Pony. He reached for one of the door handles and opened the door, holding his hand out to assist the women.

Eli smiled to see them all bubbly and cheerful from their fun evening. Rachel waited and exited the vehicle last as all the couples were all reunited. Eli wrapped his long arms around Rachel's curvy, leather-clad body and kissed her hard. When he released her, she grinned and swiped a gentle finger on his cheek and held it up.

"Body glitter is a new look for you," she said with a sexy chuckle.

"You, too," he replied, wiping a smudge from her bare shoulder. "Aren't you cold?"

"A little, now that I'm out of the car." She gestured to her arms and shoulders. "I noticed when we left that I have it all over my arms. I wanted to clean up in the ladies' room first, so I don't get it inside my new jacket. If my jacket is going to smell like cologne, I want it to be yours only."

"Do you feel like staying and dancing?" he asked as the other couples talked.

"Yeah, I do. Is that okay?"

"Of course. Let me know when you're ready to leave and we're out of here."

Peter, Renata, Elijah, and Kelly all said their goodnights, and the others went inside to dance and hang out together a while longer. As Eli and Rachel strode in, Eli felt the caveman reassert some territoriality in his psyche as he saw how many men stared at Rachel in her corset and miniskirt.

* * * *

Rachel saw Eli watching her as she returned from cleaning up in the ladies' room. She recognized the intense look in his eyes and smiled while she slowly sauntered across the club toward him. Dressed in her leather outfit, she felt like a siren calling out to his body to respond, and respond it *definitely* did. A suggestive smile spread slowly across Rachel's face as she went into his arms and felt the large, hard bulge pressed against her belly. He pulled her onto the dance floor as a classic, romantic song began to play. Keith Whitley crooned the lyrics to "When You Say Nothing At All" as she stroked his back through the black silkiness of his long hair and rested her cheek against his chest, utterly happy.

"I want to tell you something, Rachel. But I don't want for you to think I expect that you had a similar experience, okay? I know you're only human, just like me."

Her confusion must have shown on her face because he forged on immediately. "There were beautiful women everywhere we looked, who were good at their jobs, but not one of them aroused me the way you do. Sure, a well-executed move or a particularly teasing view might have rendered a tingle or two, but I only got truly rock-hard one time tonight. You know when that was?" he asked as she smiled softly up at him and shook her head. "It was when I heard your soft, sexy voice on Charity's cell phone when you called."

He laughed softly. "Cami had on little white high heels just like that pair of shiny black heels you wear with the strap over the top, and even *that* didn't do it for me. All you have to do is walk into a room with those on, fully clothed, and my cock is ready for action."

She felt her cheeks flush and giggled. "Really? And she was topless, wasn't she?"

"Totally. They were both terrific, but they didn't do it for me. Now, here we are dancing and talking, and I'm hard and ready to take you right now. It's like my cock missed you and wasn't considering any substitutes."

She smiled. "A hard man is good to find," she said in her best sexy vamp voice. He threw his head back and laughed with her.

"I'll bet you and Cami would be great friends, given the chance."

"Speaking of Cami, her boyfriend, Brandon, was one of the dancers Adam hired to entertain me for the evening. He pointed her out in the picture Charity sent Adam. He and I had an interesting, if cryptic, conversation."

"Really?"

Rachel nodded, happy to share the exchange with him. "He saw and understood my tag. He knew to look at the back. He made a point of asking me to tell you that he was honored to be one of the ones chosen to entertain me. They were both awesome and never said or did anything to raise Adam's eyebrows. I had fun but never had to worry that they would get too…overt.

"I want *you* to know something else, too. That place was wall-to-wall muscled, sexy bodies, and not a one of them held a candle to the man I love. Their oiled pecs and abs were nothing compared to my man's. It was all fun, and I had a fantastic time, never doubt it. But it was a little like vacationing on the Texas Gulf Coast if I lived in the Caribbean. Probably a lot of fun, but I couldn't wait to get back home. You're my home, Eli," she said, sighing happily when he gathered her to him and lifted her off her feet and kissed her tenderly.

"You're good at putting your feelings into words, angel. You are home to me, as well. And I love *coming* home." He growled, nuzzling her throat. "You're hot, angel. Do you want to take off this heavy jacket?" he asked, peeling her jacket from one shoulder. The cool air felt good against her hot flesh.

She'd been a little warm but had decided that she probably should leave the jacket on for his benefit. When they'd re-entered the club earlier, she'd gotten a lot of looks. She nodded. "But only if it's all right with you, Eli. I know there's a lot of *me* showing tonight."

He growled again. "Mmm, there sure is. I love every inch of it. But you're not leaving my side for the rest of the evening, so I don't mind." He helped her out of it and held it over his arm as they continued dancing. "You are absolutely incredible tonight, Rachel. When I set eyes on you earlier…You *are* my queen. Do you understand that? You give yourself to me completely, but ultimately it is *me* who is *your* slave."

"You see? That's why no man could ever compete with you. I have the same feelings for you. I'm your slave, to do with as you will."

He leaned toward her and kissed her, then said in his deep, rumbling sexy voice, "Well, my slave girl, I want you to dance for me. Were you and the girls planning on dancing for us tonight?"

"Mmm, would you like that, baby?" she replied, radiant with happiness.

As the song ended, they returned to the table where the others sat. He placed her jacket over her chair back and pulled Ethan aside, speaking quietly to him. Ethan grinned and nodded then turned to speak to Grace and excused himself from the table as the others talked.

Grace leaned over to her and said, "Ethan is arranging a good dance song for us. I wasn't sure how Eli would feel about you dancing tonight in your leathers, but Ethan says *Eli* wants a dance song for us. He's asking the DJ to play it next."

"Good, because I'm certainly in the mood." She rubbed up against Eli, smiling when he growled softly. She looked up and caught him ogling her cleavage. "See something you like, handsome?" she asked and bit her lip suggestively.

"I see something I *need*." The deep, wanting way he said it made her pussy begin to warm and throb, desire for him flaring inside her. Desire to be away from this crowd.

She turned to him, looking into his sensual gray gaze. "After I dance for you, I want to go home." She pulled him to her and spoke softly, "I want to go home, and I want you to make love to me. I *need you*." Her voice felt shaky.

He straightened and looked in her eyes with promise in his own. He helped her into her chair and casually put his hands on her knees. Anyone looking would have at first assumed he was caressing her legs, showing her affection. But his fingers flicked the tabs on the zippers at the hem of her leather skirt open. He leaned into her and kissed her tenderly, and her heart pounded as she felt the vibration of the heavy metal teeth unzipping a little at a time until they were locked back in place where she had them earlier.

Oh, boy.

"You're with me now," he said as his fingers gently slid into the slits the zippers created and caressed her inner thighs above her fishnet stockings. Oh, hell yeah she was right with him, *right now*. "Be ready to leave when the song is done, angel," he murmured.

Ethan returned to the table so he could have a front row seat for the show. Grace went to Ethan to kiss him and thank him and whispered in Jack and Adam's ears before kissing them, as well.

Rachel grinned at Grace when they both recognized the song Ethan had chosen for them. Jason Aldean's "My Kinda Party" began to pound over the sound system, and Rachel and Grace moved away from their men onto the dance floor, joined there by Kathleen, Charity, Corina, and Rosemary.

Rachel smiled when Angel non-verbally affirmed Teresa's choice to sit and watch, drawing her closer to him and kissing the top of her head. He didn't look disappointed in the least. Rachel thought the two of them together were brilliant. Angel did not need another Patricia in his life. He needed someone whose waters ran deep and was quiet and stable. Sane sure helped, too.

Rachel turned, rolling and grinding her hips as Eli stood at the edge of the dance floor. She gradually moved closer to him as she rocked and swayed. Rachel slid the backs of her fingertips up her waist, over the sides of her breasts and her collarbones, then into her hair, lifting it off her neck. Her palms slid back down and traced over the leather covering her ass and hips then down her thighs as she ground down as low as she dared before she came back up, turning her back to Eli. Thrusting out her ass in a risqué move, she slapped it, hard. His eyebrows shot up in his only perceivable reaction.

Rachel dipped and swung her hips, grinding in a circle right in front of him, brushing her breasts against the thin knit of his T-shirt. Even through the leather of her corset she sensed his body heat, and her nipples hardened into stinging little points. The beat of the song pounded through Rachel's body and she timed each sinuous movement with its rhythm. Smiling up at him, she winked and shimmied for him as he smiled back at her. Rachel could see the tension in his posture and caught him glancing around the room briefly but didn't spare a thought for who else watched. She didn't give a rat's ass who looked as long as they didn't touch.

Looping her fingers around the front of his belt to stabilize herself, she slowly ground down in front of him one more time, nice and slow, then just as slowly rose in a circling grind, brushing lightly against his front with her breasts, as the song ended. He looked down at her admiringly as she stood against him, her hands clutching his biceps.

The deep timbre of his sexy voice sent a quiver straight to the part of her that was currently very damp and hot. "You're hotter than hell, all on your own, Rachel Lopez. *How* are you going to dance for me after you've had lessons?"

"Oh, I'll be smoother and sexier," she replied, feeling like a goddess as he kissed her. He knew all the right things to say.

"Damn, woman. You could write books on smooth and sexy. Hell, *you* could give lessons. Half the men in here were watching you with their mouths hanging open."

"Nuh-uh, really?" She chuckled as he held out her jacket so she could slip her arms into it. She embraced Charity and thanked her for running interference for her.

"Oh, no problem. I want to go back again and take you and Grace with us. I'm glad you had a good time and that you weren't too upset with us for not clearing it with you ahead of time."

"I would never have agreed."

"I know. Sometimes it's better to beg forgiveness than ask permission."

"Well, you're right. It was a blast. But we are *so* out of here now," Rachel said, laughing.

Charity snickered. "I notice you seem in a bit of a hurry." Eli hugged her, too, after thanking Adam for taking care of Rachel and seeing to her entertainment, as well.

Rachel said goodnight to Grace last. "I can never thank you enough for all you have done for me, and for us," she said, hugging her.

"Seriously, I feel the same way about having you as my friend, Rachel. I'm so glad tonight turned out all right for you, at least I'm assuming it did by the smiles on both your faces and the fact you're in such an *all-fired* hurry to get out of here all of a sudden." She giggled as Eli hugged her, too.

"Smokin' hot, Rachel," Mike said as Eli shook hands with him and Rogelio. Rachel hugged them both, and then they hurried out the door to Eli's truck.

The radio played softly in the truck as he drove them home. A sweet, deep current of desire flowed like a river between them as Eli held her hand on his thigh, stroking her palm gently.

"Rachel, I was jealous as hell when all those men watched you while you danced, but I was also proud that you're mine. I wanted them to see it was me you danced for, me you held on to and brushed up against. The caveman wanted me to throw you over my shoulder and walk out the moment the song ended. Anyone who didn't know you would believe you were a professional dancer."

"Thank you, Eli. Something comes over me when I dance for you. I get this feeling…and I see the appreciation in your eyes. It spurs me on."

"I love watching the way you move." He shifted in his seat beneath her hand.

When they got in the house and Eli locked the door behind him, he led her back to the bedroom, turning off all the lights as they went. Rachel lit a few candles as he turned on the shower and came back to the bedroom. They both undressed, and she watched with open admiration as his proud, naked body was revealed. He undid the catch on the back of her skirt, unzipped it, allowed it to slip to the floor, then knelt in front of her and helped her step out of it. He looked up at her with adoration as she stood in her fishnets, boots, G-string, and, of course, the corset and collar.

"I need to *look* at you for a minute, Rachel. Just take in the sight of you like this." His cock stood completely rigid, firm and stiff against his abdomen. Her hands itched to reach out and touch him, to draw him close to her, but Naughty Rachel tapped her shoulder and told her to *pose* for him.

Keeping eye contact as long as she could, she turned slowly and tilted her ass to him, making eye contact again. She pulled at the bows on the front of her corset and slowly slid her fingers through the laces, undoing them, until it slipped to the floor.

The silver tag reflected the candlelight as she stood before him in a wide, confident stance. He slid a warm hand over the ankle of one of her boots, then up her calf and knee. As he reached her thigh and the fishnet stockings, his movement was slow and unhurried. His warm palm rode all the way up to her hip, where the ties of one side of her G-string were dangling, begging to be tugged free. He plucked gently at one, and the bow came undone.

Rachel's pussy began to pulse and ache, and she hoped he would touch her soon. His other hand slid up the other leg, repeating the process. He reached a single, gentle finger up to the dip at the top of her thigh and slid it under the edge of the leather, tugging gently as it came loose under the garter the fishnet stockings were attached to.

Slowly, he pulled the ties free and allowed them to brush deliciously through her damp flesh. He paused again and looked up at her, his eyes almost worshipful. He repeated his move from the beginning of the evening, sliding both hands around her ankles and up the back of her calves, over her thighs and to her hips, then around to her ass. His hot fingers left a fiery trail behind them.

She moaned as Eli's fingers met just above the cleft of her ass and teased against the ultra sensitive spot there, sending a lightning bolt straight to her clit. Her pussy flooded with even more moisture, and her muscles tightened and contracted, foreshadowing an orgasm of seismic proportions.

He carefully unzipped the boots, placed her hands on his shoulders, and helped her to step from each ultra-tall boot. After they were gone, he undid the garters from her stockings and slid his fingers carefully under the waist of the garter and unhooked it.

Chapter Forty-eight

After their shower, she followed her gentle giant back to the candlelit bedroom. Rachel's heart pounded and felt so full it might overflow. He molded his lips to hers in a searing, yet gentle kiss and stroked her tongue and her lips with his. His hands slid over her shoulders and down her back in a light, tickling touch that made her hips undulate reflexively as he caressed all the right spots. She moaned in pleasure as his hands slid farther, his fingers splaying over her ass as he gently grasped each cheek and squeezed.

He released her and pulled back the covers then helped her to climb onto the bed. She crawled on her hand and knees and could tell that her pussy was soaking wet, and he could probably see her lips glisten as she moved away from him into the center of the bed. She glanced back and saw that he watched and knew he saw it. The thought made her pussy clench again, aching for him to fill her.

She lay down in the center of the bed with her head resting on his pillow and looked at him through half-shuttered eyes. He stood there, gazing at her with adoration and lust warring on his features. Eli was a huge mountain of a man and so incredibly beautiful standing there fully erect and ready to make love to her. Rachel slid her feet up and parted her thighs as she fanned her hair out on the pillow.

Eli crawled over to her, coming to rest on his knees between her parted thighs. She slid them farther apart, opened herself for him, and slid her hands down her abdomen and over her mound, topped by dark curls, into her dripping slit. She parted her wet outer lips, hearing his low growl as her gentle fingers revealed the slick, heated flesh inside.

Under her fingertips, her lips and clitoris felt engorged and hot with her arousal. Rachel's breath came in soft, shuddering pants as she watched his face. Her pussy convulsed as he licked his lips, and she knew with absolute certainty that if she felt his tongue once against her clit, she would come fast and loud.

He seemed in complete control, as she watched with lust pounding through her veins, while he stroked his cock with one hand. Rachel wished it were her pussy stroking him instead. She licked her lips, and he smiled at her and she thought maybe that was his intent.

Rachel spread her legs wider and arched her back as she brushed a finger over her slick pussy lips. She didn't *dare* touch her clit. She was saving that for him. Her finger slid though her juices, making slippery, wet sounds as it slid between her lips into her engorged opening.

Rachel froze, knowing she had pushed herself *just past* the pinnacle as her pussy began pulsing in radiating waves. She looked into his eyes, and her breath began to roll out of her in heaving, high-pitched cries. He understood, and, instantly, his warm, wet tongue sought and found her clit with his first touch, licking and flicking at it expertly. She sobbed out her release as she plunged her fingers farther in her slit, thrusting with each pulse. Eli hungrily licked her clit and her fingers as her honey flowed from her pussy.

Grasping her softly rocking hips, Eli lifted her to his mouth, and he continued licking her clit and her lips as her hands fell away limply to the bed. He teased her gently to another cresting orgasm then lowered her, fit his blunt, thick head to her opening, and groaned loudly as his big cock slid home in one smooth stroke.

* * * *

Eli growled deeply with satisfaction at her responsiveness, happy that she was finding her pleasure on him for herself. When he was deep inside her, he stopped moving. He wanted to savor the hot, silky feel of her pussy gloving his aching cock. He suckled on her breasts and breathed in her subtle womanly fragrance.

Flexing his hips, Eli thrust inside her, pulled out a bit and slid back inside, loving the sweet, sexy way she sighed in pleasure. Pulling out again, he thrust fully into her sweet, satiny heat.

Little muscle spasms rippled through her walls as he continued thrusting. He wanted to be gentle but gradually lost control as each thrust came harder and harder. He fucked her with every inch of his thick, engorged cock. Rachel grasped his wrists in an effort to keep her body from sliding up on the bed. She arched her back and pounded back against him as her moan becoming a wail.

Eli rose over her on his knees, never missing a beat, and grasped her hips. He watched as his hard, red cock filled her, sliding through the cream that dripped from her and coated his cock. He threw his head back when his release signaled its arrival. His spine tingled, and his thighs went rigid as he pumped into her repeatedly. Rachel's pussy became impossibly tighter as her wail grew into a scream of utter rapture. She came in a glorious gushing wave, her hips rocking wildly in his tight grasp, her pussy convulsing on his cock. His spine stiffened, and he came with an animalistic howl.

Continuing to thrust inside her, he tilted his hips and rubbed her at just the right angle. He slid one hand from her hip to her clit and stoked her clit firmly. Her body bowed majestically, and she sobbed in surrender to the ecstasy.

Relaxing over her, Eli stroked her face and felt the heat spread as she flushed for him, a sign that her pleasure had been extreme. He gathered Rachel's warm quivering body in his arms and kissed her tenderly. She held on tight and kissed him back. Her body fit to his so perfectly. He tucked her into the circle of his arms, where she fell soundly asleep, warm and satisfied, like him.

* * * *

The week of their wedding, Rachel worked on Monday and Tuesday but didn't get all that much done. Using every spare moment, she polished her completed manuscript, looking for discrepancies and errors. She tweaked wording here and there and streamlined where the story needed it. As she read the final pages, she cried.

Rachel stored a copy on a DVD and printed one copy. She took the printed copy to the local print shop and made four sets and then used their binding machine to bind them into book form. By Wednesday at lunchtime, she had composed a query e-mail and attached the manuscript to the e-mail. After they ate, Eli sat with her, and she looked up at him, excited and teary-eyed as she prepared to submit her book to a publisher. Eli put his arms around her and kissed her temple as she clicked the send button.

Wiping her eyes with the backs of her hands, she said, "I did it."

"You did, honey. We'll all say we knew you before you were famous. Now we have another reason to celebrate tonight at Tessa's. I've got two more service calls to take care of this afternoon. What are you going to do now?"

"I have a surprise to deliver to three wild and crazy women out at the Divine Creek Ranch. Grace said she, Charity, and Kelly would all be at her house this afternoon. I'm calling her in a minute to let her know I'm coming out, but I'm not telling her why. I printed and bound copies of the manuscript, one for each of them as a surprise."

"Will I be able to hear the screams from my job site?"

"Knowing them? Yeah, probably. It was thoughtful of you to come home for lunch and be here with me when I submitted the story. It means a lot to me that you did. That felt like the big moment, clicking 'send'. My hands are shaking." She held them up to show him as they trembled slightly. He took them in his big, warm hands and kissed the knuckles of both.

"My wife, the bestselling author." He enfolded her in his arms.

When it was time for him to go back to work, she bundled up because it was a little chilly that day and then locked up the house. She showed him the box on the front seat of her truck, which contained the bound manuscripts.

"There's a copy for us, which you are welcome to read, if you'd like. I wouldn't mind having a man's viewpoint on my work for future reference."

"You wouldn't mind?"

"*No.* You were part of my inspiration to write it. It seems appropriate to have you read it."

"Well, have a good time. I'm going to my service call, and I'll see you when I get home later this afternoon. Reservations are for seven, so we should leave around six."

"I'll be ready, honey. Stay warm." A weak cold front had blown through, but the weather was expected to be mild for that weekend. Rachel hugged him tight, kissed his warm lips and climbed in and started the ignition. The heated air blew over them. He closed her door then smiled and waved at her before he walked to his truck and got in. She rubbed her hands together to warm them, experiencing a hunger for him to stay near her that never really abated. She sensed the same reluctance to part in Eli at times, as well.

During a visit with her mother earlier that week, Rachel had asked her mom if her feelings for her dad had changed over the years. Did she still feel the way she had before she married him?

"Well, Rachel, there's no simple answer to that question. After Peter asked me to marry him, he would do little things for me, like call me at work to say hi. He would bring me a flower or a candy bar. I was in awe of him, that he loved me enough to make a lifetime commitment, and I was afraid that I would disappoint him as a wife." Her mom had brought two bowls and a sack of pecans to the table, and Rachel had helped her crack and shell pecans as they'd talked.

"The first few weeks I was nervous all the time, trying so hard to keep things perfect. He never saw dirty clothes on the floor or dishes in the sink. He came home on our one month anniversary with a dozen red roses, a great big Hershey bar, and a pepperoni pizza. I'd planned on making him an elaborate meal."

Her mom had smiled with a faraway look in her eyes as she'd popped a small sliver of pecan in her mouth. "I think he knew I'd bite off more than I could chew because he got home early before I started cooking. He came in the door of our little house, put everything on the table, then took me in his arms and gave me the roses." Her voice had gotten misty and crackled a little, and Rachel had heard her sniffle.

"He sat down with me on the couch and had a heart-to-heart talk with me. I'll never forget what he said. 'Honey, stop trying to please me so hard. You please me when you wake up in the morning and smile at me. You please me when you laugh. I come home to a perfect house and meal that you spent hours on, but you're smiling less often. You don't laugh as much as you used to, and you're trying to be the perfect lover when the truth is you're exhausted.'

"I broke down and cried for a long time while he held me. I felt like I had been released from bondage. We ate the pizza, and watched the Blues Brothers on *Saturday Night Live*. From then on, because I still had a full-time job, when I got home from work, I didn't do anything house-related for at least a half hour. I sat down on the couch and read the paper, watched the news, or listened to music before I ever got up to start supper. When your dad got home, he would come sit on the couch, and—"

"Pat his lap for you to sit in it," Rachel had finished for her, sniffling herself. She had her own memories of her parents' daily evening ritual.

"Yes. I discovered he didn't care whether I did laundry every day as long as he had socks and underwear. And he always helped me with the evening dishes. At the rate I was going, I'd have made us both miserable. He had the guts to risk offending me so that he could have back the girl he'd intended to marry. Don't try to become who you think Eli needs after you're married. Be who you are now because that's who he wants. Let him be strong for you and *allow* yourself to rely on him.

"We did a good job raising you to be independent so that you could take care of yourself. You got your degree, you have your work, *and* you're writing," her mom had said as she patted Rachel's arm. "You keep pursuing that dream because he's fascinated by that part of you. I can tell by the way he looks at you when you talk about it. You have real chemistry together, but you are going to need to be patient with yourself and him as you lay the groundwork for your married life over the next few years. He's a good man, but they're all human."

"Thanks, Mom."

"And change all the locks when your child moves away from home." She'd snickered, trying to lighten the mood a little.

Rachel had laughed, remembering walking in on her parents one day *in flagrante* on the dining room table. "You had to remind me of that *didn't you*? I said I was sorry! I didn't even know you still did that!" she'd added with a full-body shudder that made her mom cackle.

"Honey, we are *still* 'doin' it'! And that's another thing—"

Oh, no! No sex talks please! "I can't hear you, la-la-la-la!" Rachel had cringed with her fingers stuck in her ears.

"But this is important!"

"La-la-la-la! Can't hear you! La-la-la." She'd laughed and knew her face had turned beet red.

Oh, Lord, I'm about to get a pre-nuptial pep talk!

"Rachel Lopez!"

"Okay, okay. I'm sorry. I'll listen." Rachel snickered. *No, please, no!*

"Never hold out on him. Give him what he needs as often as he wants it. Too many women use sex as a tool to manipulate their man. *Never* do that. It will backfire every time. Oh, and *regular blow jobs will make him your willing slave*," she'd added in a rush and chuckled gaily at Rachel's sudden intake of air.

"Mom!"

"What? Did you think I don't do that? That I didn't know what a blowjob is?" she'd asked in a knowing tone.

"I figured that you did. You got married in the seventies, after all. *Everyone* was freaky! But I didn't need that image *burned* into my brain." Rachel had laughed and experienced another full body shudder.

"Then I shouldn't tell you that your father is very good at—"

Rachel had screamed and jumped up from the couch like she'd been shot from a cannon. "Don't! Don't say it, *please*! I got you, okay? I get it. Screw his brains out. *Check.* Blow jobs. *Check*! Eek!"

She and her mother had laughed hard before her mom said, "That bonfire out at Grace's burned bright for two days, but did you know there are still red-hot coals at the base of it? She was out there recently and could smell it burning. Fires like that can smolder down deep for months sometimes. Red-hot love is good, but real love smolders for a lifetime. That's what I want for you. Remember to always hold on to him and let him know how much you need him." In a trembling voice she'd added, "I'm proud of you, Rachel."

"I love you, Mom," Rachel had said with a sniffle.

"Now when do I get my autographed copy of your book, hmm?"

"Mom, it's full of hot sex!"

"Ooh, goody! What? I helped make *you*. I know how it works," her mom had said expectantly.

Holy crap! Want to get away?

Chapter Forty-nine

When Rachel pulled up to the Divine Creek ranch house, she noticed that Grace had somehow found the time to put out Christmas decorations on the front of the house, as well as inside. "Is everything all right, Rachel?" Grace hugged her and led her in. Charity and Kelly sat at the tall dining table, rolling up a large sheet of white paper, which probably had the wedding decorations mapped out. They were supposed to start decorating tomorrow. Charity turned her legal pad over and laid her pencil down.

"I have a surprise for you," Rachel said happily and laid the manuscript box on the table.

Grace peeked in the box, her eyes became huge, and she squeaked and did a little happy dance. Rachel grinned and reached in the box and handed her the copy that was inscribed to her. Grace held it in her hands like a precious little infant.

"Is that what I freakin' think it is?" Charity rose from her chair as Kelly came from her side of the table, and Rachel placed their copies in their hands.

Kelly held it with reverent hands. "*Bella's Bridled Desire*." Ooooh! So you finished it?" she asked as she went to Rachel and hugged her.

"Yes, I submitted the manuscript to a publisher today. Now I just wait and work on the outline for the next story."

"You had these made just for us?"

"You've become my best friends, and I wanted you to be the first to read it."

"We're the first?" Grace asked, a little awed as she looked down at the title page and smiled.

"Yes, I also have a copy for Eli and me. He'll be reading it, too. It's kind of scary, you know? Like showing you what's in my head. You may think I'm a little freaky."

Charity laughed. "Silly girl, we already know that about you. I have a feeling I'm gonna be up all night." She gleefully hugged the thick manuscript.

Grace and Kelly agreed, but Grace said, "Not too late. I'll need both of you awake for tomorrow."

Rachel gathered the box, which contained the last copy of the manuscript. "I'm keeping you from your strategizing."

"Yes, and you have an appointment at Madeleine's to get to, don't you?" Grace said.

Her mother had surprised Rachel with a gift certificate for a massage and exfoliation treatment at Madeleine's Day Spa. "Yes, but I wanted to bring those over to you. I hope you enjoy it."

"I'm going to start mine after we finish our planning session," Kelly said enthusiastically.

"What should I tell the guys if they want to take a look?" Grace asked her.

"That I value a man's opinion of it, as well, but it is an erotic romance. They may not be interested in it."

"Rachel, my men know all there is to know about erotic romance," Grace answered, blushing right along with Rachel.

"I can imagine. Yes, tell them I would love for them to read it. Same for Justin."

Rachel arrived back home after her spa appointment around mid-afternoon, feeling like she was buzzing and tingling from head to toe. The massage therapist had gone deep on her shoulders and her back, which had been knotted and tense, and now she was loose and relaxed. She had plenty of time before she had to start getting ready for their special evening at Tessa's. She tingled with excitement for how this evening might turn out. Complete uninterrupted privacy in the middle of a crowded restaurant. The possibilities were endless.

* * * *

Rachel knelt on the padded seat, panting quietly. "Eli, I'm ready to come right now," Rachel whimpered softly as her pussy pulsed in anticipation.

He kissed her and lifted her hips as she held on to the railing on the back of the private, enclosed booth, straddling his lean hips.

"I'm so fucking turned on myself I may not last a minute," he whispered. "The thought of making love to you with so many people so close by has my cock screaming for you."

The thought had her pussy pulsing, too!

"It's the caveman." She giggled softly. "He wants hot communal cave sex, doesn't he?"

He positioned the head of his cock at her hot, quivering entrance, and they were about to have sex in the middle of a crowded restaurant. She imagined doing it with the drapes wide open.

Rachel looked into his gray eyes, flexed her hips slightly, and smiled at the satisfaction on his face as he entered her. Gripping his cock with the muscles in her pussy, she slid down on him, and a soft shiver raced down her spine as her name slipped reverently from his lips. She undulated her hips, and another whimper escaping her softly as she felt the tell-tale tingling spasms in her pussy that made her long to rock into an orgasm with him right then. Not wanting it to be over so soon, she tried to hold the orgasm off, focusing on kissing his lips and stopped her ascent for a moment.

He held her tenderly in position, giving her a second. "We have time. No need to rush."

When the throb had lessened a little, she circled over him as his cock pressed into her depths. Rachel knew he was working to keep from thrusting into her by the tension on his face. She gripped the railing behind the backrest with both hands and looked at him as she ground on him once and stopped.

"Angel, do that again, slowly." He slid his hands over her abdomen and back to her ass, squeezing gently. Tilting her pelvis forward, she ground on him again, achingly slowly this time, her pussy enveloping another of his thick, long inches inside her.

She stopped to kiss him, trying to relax and ignore the part of her brain that was screaming for her to plunge down on him and ride him to a screaming, gushing orgasm. Holding out would make it all the sweeter, she knew. After a minute, she squeezed his cock gently and smiled at his soft groan, and she rolled her pelvis, lifted off him a little, and repeated the motion.

"Oh, I like that. I love feeling your thick hard cock filling me so tightly. You're huge, Eli."

She ground on him some more, her pussy tightening as her tension built, aching for him to fill her completely, wanting more than just the first few inches. Her hips flexed against him, and she laid her forehead on his as he wrapped his arms around her hips, holding her still.

His breathing was soft panting like hers as she asked, "How much time do we have until the waiter texts you again?"

He glanced at his watch and replied, "Fifteen minutes."

"Hold out for five minutes. Then we both get to fuck until we come."

"Three, baby. I'll never make it five. You have amazing control, Rachel. I thought you were going to come several times, but you didn't."

"You told me to wait, so I'm trying real hard," she whimpered, feeling a fresh rush of moisture to her pussy at his compliment.

"I love you, baby." He groaned softly as she lifted off, leaving only the head inside of her. Then she ground down until he was in as far as he had been a moment ago. Her juices wet his cock, and she lifted again and rolled in the other direction. The look on his face was one of torture, but the best kind, as she took another inch then slowly lifted off. She kissed him, her heart throbbing with love for him even as her cunt ached for the pounding of his cock. She pumped in small, tiny movements, and he moaned quietly.

"Time?" she asked breathlessly.

"One minute, angel." He groaned softly as he tried to focus on his watch.

Rachel leaned back a little and tilted her pelvis forward, holding the rail, and remembered that on the other side of the heavy drape in front of her was a room full of people. Her control began to crumble. At his soft, sexy growl, another fresh rush of moisture came to her pussy.

He muttered, "Thirty."

She imagined that the drapes were opening and they were being observed.

"Twenty."

She bit her lip to keep from moaning out loud. She descended, knowing the best, thickest part remained.

"Ten," he gasped.

She began a slow, unstoppable glide over his silky, rock-hard flesh.

"Oh, angel. Now, please, please, angel. *Fuck me,*" Eli implored almost imperceptibly. In the warm glow of the candlelight his handsome face was beautiful and his expression was intense with passion. He tilted his head back, and breathed quietly.

"Hold me, Eli. Please don't let me scream."

He wrapped his arms around her securely and pulled her face close to his. "You're not going to scream. Put your lips on mine, angel."

Rachel did and exhaled sharply as she ground all the way to the hilt then lifted and began to ride him in a slow hip-grinding dance. Her hips flexed against him. His thickness stretched her lips, and she rubbed her clit against him. With a shudder, Rachel welcomed the rippling spasms that rushed over her. Her control left her as his arms tightened around her. He held her head in his gentle hands as she kissed him, and he quieted her moan with his mouth. Her hips gyrated wildly over his cock, grinding as each pulse shook her to her core, warmth exploding through her spasming pussy.

He released her head and tightened his arms around her hips and began to thrust powerfully, the only sound the soft, wet slip and slide of their flesh as they moved against each other. His head fell back on the backrest, and she pressed her mouth to his. Rachel enveloped his soft groan as he thrust once more and came on a silent scream, thrusting powerfully as he held onto her.

Rachel imagined what it would be like if she opened her eyes and realized they were fucking out in the open while all the restaurant patrons watched them. She ground down on him again in quick succession and buried her face in his neck. Her lips clamped tightly shut as she came again, overpowered by the extreme sensation of waiting so long on the edge of coming, the erotic extreme of his orgasm, and the fantasy of fucking in public. If she had been able to, she would have screamed the roof off, and because she couldn't, it was that much more powerful. Eli's erection twitched and pulsed inside her.

She lay against his warmth, trying to quietly catch her breath. Her quickly cooling body shivered perceptibly. He quietly reached for his coat and pulled it over her shoulders, still breathing a little hard. She stayed like that a few more minutes, sated and resting, before she lifted her head and smiled at him.

She whispered shakily, "Wow."

"My thoughts exactly. Wow."

"How long?"

"About five minutes." She sat up limply and allowed him to help her lift off of him then helped her stand up.

After cleaning up, he helped her put her thong back on. Giggling softly, she adjusted her stockings and garters and slid her skirt back down her thighs. By the time she was done and ready to roll the table back into its original position, he was re-dressed and looking as handsome as ever in his black suit. Rachel turned to him, melting in his gaze as he looked up at her from his seated position. He looked like a man satisfied and in love as he gazed at her wordlessly.

Self-consciously, she asked, "What? Can you tell? Do I look demolished?" she asked, feeling her hair and wiping under her eyes, checking for smudges.

"You look…radiant. I feel like I'm having a vision, angel. And you're *marrying me*. Wow."

"Yes, I am. Thank you, baby. I was afraid that I looked bedraggled or untidy. My face feels very hot." She put her hands to her cheeks as he pulled her down to sit beside him.

He placed his palm against her flushing cheek. "You're blushing beautifully, but if you don't think about it, it'll fade in a few minutes. Are those matches on the table? I'm going to relight the candles then pull the table back. You just sit and relax."

The phone vibrated right on time. "I'm going to ask him for another five minutes." His fingertips moved quickly over the keyboard. "That will give us a chance to cool off a bit more."

She leaned her head against his shoulder. He turned slightly toward her and pulled her back against his chest, wrapping his arms around her. She placed her hands over his and stayed there, enjoying the quiet, satisfied embrace until they heard the light tapping at the entrance. Rachel sat back in the booth as Eli responded, and the waiter entered with another tray. On the tray was one large dinner plate with a generous portion of coconut cream pie, Rachel's favorite dessert, with two forks.

"How has your evening been so far?" the waiter asked as he gathered the other plates and stacked them on the tray.

"Perfect," Eli said honestly, but Rachel knew he was referring to the whole experience and not just the tenderness of his steak. Her cheeks tingled with a blush at his sneaky compliment.

"Please tell Paul and Peter that it was delicious, in every sense," she said, squeezing Eli's thigh under the table, "and that the coconut cream pie looks luscious, as well. Their skills are unsurpassed, and they've made this an evening we'll never forget." Her fingers stole up his inner thigh before he placed his warm hand over hers, stopping her mischievous advance.

"I will, and congratulations on your upcoming wedding this weekend. May you have many happy years together." He bowed to them then refilled their wine and excused himself, allowing the heavy drape to fall closed again.

She took a forkful of the creamy dessert and fed it to Eli then took the bite he offered to her. She put her fork down and placed her hand on his shoulder, looking up at him for approval. He smiled and pulled her back into his lap.

"There. That is so much better!" she said happily, being careful not to wiggle or move suddenly in his lap.

He kissed her cleavage and said, "Mmm-hmm, it sure is."

Taking a small bite from the dessert, she looked directly in his eyes and touched the fork lightly to her cleavage, careful to not touch the chiffon.

"Oops! Look what happened. I spilled it." She seductively slid a finger down the edge of her bodice and invited him in. "You wouldn't want to miss out on dessert, would you?" Eli literally swooped in. His warm mouth and tongue removed every trace of the dessert.

Grinning devilishly, he said, "I love your cream." The look in his eyes and the tone of his sexy voice left no doubt *which* cream he was referring to. "I'm sure I'm going to want seconds when we get home. As a matter of fact, I may want to slip some more dessert between *your* lips once we get home."

"Hot damn!" Rachel giggled playfully. "You can have thirds if you want it." She didn't doubt his stamina for a minute.

Eli put his lips to her ear. "You're wet for me again now, aren't you?"

Rachel's eyes slid shut in bliss at the sound of that velvety, promising voice, and she nodded in delight. She leaned her head against his chest and snuggled as she reached with the fork for another bite and slipped this one between his lips. They shared some more of the dessert, and Eli buzzed the waiter to bring the bill.

After he paid and tipped the waiter, Eli rose from the table and helped Rachel scoot out. Rachel detoured to the restroom, and Eli waited for her by the entry. Eli told Rachel when she returned that Tessa was penciling them into her calendar for next year on their one year anniversary. After greeting Paul and Peter, she asked Eli if he knew that Tessa's brothers were bikers.

"Well, maybe we can get together and go for a ride in the spring," Eli suggested, clasping Rachel's fingers with his.

"We'd like that a lot. Good luck this weekend. We're sorry we couldn't come. Tessa has us packed to the gills that night, back-to-back all evening. What can you do?" Peter said with a shrug.

"Such is life in the restaurant industry. Life and love have to revolve around food," Paul said with a mischievous grin. "I think we have that concept pretty well-developed around here."

Eli chuckled deeply. "I'll say."

* * * *

They had just arrived home from Tessa's, and Eli chuckled quietly, watching Rachel as she came down the hall with the large, flat package in her hands. He could see the anticipation in her eyes as she placed the gift-wrapped box in his hands.

"Who goes first?" he asked, noting she practically vibrated with excitement. Eli knew he was going to like whatever was in this box. She was giggly and giddy with excitement, and she hadn't even opened her gift yet.

"You do! You go first, honey," she replied.

He laid the box on the coffee table and began ripping the paper off the plain cardboard box. Lifting the lid, he found several flat, tissue-wrapped packages on a bed of packing peanuts inside.

"Does it matter which one I open first?"

She touched a couple and pointed to a small one. "This one first."

He patted his thigh. "Come sit in my lap."

Rachel climbed up and watched him open the first portrait. It was a framed black and white photograph of her under a big pecan tree. She was lying on a blanket, on her tummy, dressed in blue jeans and a low-cut T-shirt, barefooted. Her hair was ruffled around her shoulders by a passing breeze, and she had a faraway look in her eyes.

The way she was lying on the blanket, her luscious cleavage was showcased to its best advantage. The necklace she wore in the shot invited the eye there.

"Wow, I love this. Thank you, angel." He kissed her. "When did you do these?"

"About a month ago."

She handed him the next one. He ripped the tissue off and was taken completely by surprise. "Hot damn!"

In this color portrait, Rachel was dressed in the black satin gown and robe he had bought for her, posed seductively on her side, resting on a chaise lounge. The robe was off one shoulder, and the black satin was arranged around her in light-reflective puddles. Her hair was spread out around her on the pillows.

"You know how much I love your hair like that."

Through the deep slit on the side of the nightgown, one calf was bared as well as her knee and part of her thigh. Her head rested on her hand, and she was looking directly in the camera lens with a sexy come-hither stare. The light was soft as if she were surrounded by candles.

"This is beautiful. I want to hang it in our bedroom, if that's all right."

"Of course. That's why I had them done for you. I'm glad you like them...so far," she said softly reaching in for another tissue wrapped frame.

"So far?" He ripped the tissue of the next one eagerly, and his jaw popped open silently.

This time, Rachel was dressed in a short sexy black satin nightie. She was facing the end of a bed made up with an antique ivory quilt. One knee was propped on the bed, and she was standing on tiptoe, stretching her delicate arch and defining her calf muscle.

The front and the back of the nightie were held in place by a drawstring from under her arm down to her hip, where it was tied. The space between the front and the back of the gown was at least five inches wide, so the side of her full rounded breast, her waist, hip, and thigh were all bare.

Rachel was looking over her left shoulder with a naughty little one-sided grin. Dangling by its ties from her hand was the black satin blindfold he'd given her. It was playful but the intent was clear in her eyes. She was ready for some slap and tickle.

He let out a little "huh" sound and looked at her and said, "Are there more?"

She giggled, kissed his cheek and reached into the box again, lifting yet another tissue wrapped package. He ripped the paper off.

"Whoa," he said softly, gazing at it, admiring her more and more.

This was a large one, done in black and white. In this picture, she was posed in front of an open window through which soft light filtered.

She was brushing her hair as she looked out the window so her arms were up above her shoulders. She was dressed in a white corset that laced up the back, the ribbon bows just barely visible. She wore a white G-string and white garters securing her white lace-trimmed stockings. Her feet were shod in sexy white high-heeled pumps.

"Damn, that is beautiful, angel," he said softly, looking at her. "You're one gutsy lady."

"Do you like it?"

"I love it. I love them all! It's unbelievable."

"Do you like them enough to hang them in our bedroom?"

"Of course! But I'm not letting just anyone go in there, that's for sure!"

Giggling, she said, "Understood." Rachel rose from his knee, and he pulled her back, cuddling her to him.

"You're not getting away that quick, naughty girl. I love them, and I love you," he murmured, kissing her tenderly.

"I guess you don't want the last one," she said with a touch of pouty sadness.

"There's more?"

"One more. A special one," Rachel said and Eli noted the twinkle in her eyes.

"Special one?"

Reaching into the packing peanuts, Rachel rummaged through them till she found it, building his anticipation before she handed it to him.

This one felt different as he removed the wrapping. It was a bound leather frame that opened like a book. He flipped the cover back on itself and nearly dropped it when he saw the photo inside of it. An eleven-by-fourteen inch, black and white *nude* portrait of Rachel.

Eli gulped loudly. The light was much softer in this portrait, and she was posed in front of a lit fireplace on a black bearskin rug. She was on her knees perched on her raised heels. Her knees were parted, and her arms were bent, her hands in her hair. Her back was arched, and her breasts were tilted up in an enticing display.

The light shimmered in her hair and her skin was a teasing mixture of light and shadow because of the backlighting. She was turned away from the camera just enough so that only the tiniest trace of the dark curls over her mound were visible. The photo had an old-fashioned, grainy quality to it. The lighting was perfect over the curve of her hip and her ass to the gentle upper and lower swell of her breasts. Even her navel was a lighting masterpiece. Her face was relaxed and contemplative, her eyes slightly downcast, the irises catching the light a little. His fingers traced on the glass over her form.

"You posed nude for me," he said softly.

"I sure did. It took a little convincing, but I did it."

"This is beautiful." Eli looked down at it again and squeezed her close.

She flipped the cover back over and demonstrated its dual function. "The cover serves as a stand. If it becomes necessary to close it for privacy's sake, you flip it closed, put it on the shelf and it looks like a scrapbook."

"I'll display it proudly unless we have company. Angel, you've blown me away with these. Damn! I'm still trying to wrap my mind around the fact you were willing to pose nude for me! You're incredibly beautiful in all of them. You're full of surprises. Speaking of which, it's time to open *your* gift."

* * * *

Rachel ripped the paper off with glee and looked up at him in confusion when she saw wrapped packages similar in shape to the ones he had opened.

He smiled and said nothing, just handed her the first one. She removed the wrapping paper and held the black frame, similar in style and color to the ones she'd had Carrie and Raquel use.

"Carrie and Raquel shot you?"

"Carrie did. She met me out at the lake the Monday after the hog hunt."

"We were *had*, weren't we?"

"Yes, by Ethan and Grace, I believe. Ethan took me upstairs and showed me the outdoor portraits they had made for Grace for her wedding gift. He suggested maybe you might like something similar."

"He was *right*. Grace showed me the boudoir portraits she had done for them that hang in their bedrooms. I decided to do the same thing for you." Rachel was holding the frame facedown.

"Turn it over. See what you think."

She did as he asked. "Oh, *mama*."

It was a black and white of Eli posed in his leather jacket, a white T-shirt, faded blue jeans, and his black leather biker boots. He was sitting on his motorcycle, his long, raven-black hair waving in the breeze behind him. His big, muscular arms were crossed over his chest as he gazed into the camera, the filtered sunlight illuminating the pale gray of his eyes. His smile was devilish and playful.

"Like it?"

"I love it," she said dreamily. "I want more."

The next one was taken down at the cove on Bowie Lake. It was a much tighter shot of a shirtless, tanned Eli. He was sitting down against one of the massive trees that grew neat the water's edge, and he was resting his head against the weathered, gray bark. The look on his face was intense, and his body seemed to vibrate with restrained energy. His pale gray eyes radiated with sexual heat. It was a startlingly honest revelation of his feelings in his eyes, and she released a purely feminine sigh. Rachel recognized this guy.

"The caveman." She laid her hand on the image.

"I was afraid you might not like this one. I thought the look on my face was too…intense."

"It is intense, but I know him. The part of you that is so fiercely protective and territorial. Very *intense*, but also fiercely loyal and protective of me. I love that wild part of you." Tapping the glass with her fingertip, she added, "He makes *me* feel safe."

The wrapping on the next one revealed another black and white image. In this one, he was walking toward the camera through the trees in a mix of sunlight and shadow. The trees were not as thick here, so he was well lit, just a subtle shadow here and there.

Eli was looking off into the distance across the lake, but his thoughts appeared much farther away. His face was relaxed in this portrait, serene, in fact. His eyes were illuminated by a ray of sun, and there was a soft smile on his lips. His arms were relaxed, loose at his sides. He was bare-chested and barefoot, his jeans riding low on his lean hips. Eli's thoughts were obvious in the subtle hint of an erection through the denim of his jeans. In sunlight, it would have been obvious, but with the mix of sunlight and shadow playing over his body, only someone looking for it would see it.

Sighing softly in appreciation, Rachel glanced at the portrait of the caveman and at this one, feeling so blessed and fortunate. This was her portrait of Eli the lover. Both were her soul mates, the caveman and the lover.

She looked up at him, feeling pure wonder. "How did Carrie manage to capture such authentic shots of your personality? There's a different aspect of you in each of these."

Eli shrugged. "She would ask me questions about you, I would answer her and tell her about you, and then she would start snapping pictures. Once I got used to the camera, I let my mind wander until she would ask the next question. That one of me on the Harley, I was thinking about you sending me that naughty nekkid picture mail 'did you eat yet?' when we were on the hog hunt. Bad girl."

"I'll bet I can guess what you were thinking in this one." She chuckled, tapping the glass on the portrait of her lover man.

"Well, the obvious answer is that I was thinking about making love to you. I was specifically thinking about making love with you after we got home from the hog hunt the night before. I was remembering the sounds you made when you came each time. It's a sweet, precious memory."

"That was an amazing night. I like knowing the way I sound when I come has such an effect on you." Her cheeks warmed at her own sweet memories of that night.

"Remember the fantasy I shared with you on the dance floor?"

"Yes, the high heels, the side-tying G-string, and the vibrator on the deck chair in back?"

He reached over and lifted the last and largest picture from the box. "That fantasy was in my mind that morning when we were doing this portrait. I shared it with you later that same night on the dance floor."

"My goodness, this is a *nice big one*," she purred, glancing naughtily at him as he groaned and rolled his eyes. Rachel didn't miss the erection now straining at his zipper, either. She ripped off the paper and took a look. Her eyes popped open as round as saucers.

"*Oh. My. Word.*" Her fingers traced over the glass. She stood it up against the coffee table and looked at it in awe. This portrait was a black and white, not coincidentally matted and framed to match her portrait in front of the window in her white corset.

Sneaky freaking photographers.

Eli was standing in the water to his upper thighs. He was soaking wet, the water sluicing down his body, dripping from his thickly muscled arms, which were bent. His hands were at the sides of his head, like he was slicking his dripping-wet hair back from his face. Water droplets glistened on his torso and his face, sparkling like diamonds wherever the sunlight touched them.

His eyelashes were wet and clung together into little points all around his eyes, which were sparkling with the reflection from the water. Eli looked directly into the camera, his sensuous lips opened slightly as if he'd come up for a breath of air, a playful, sexy smile on his handsome face. His massive shoulders, biceps, and pectorals corded with muscular power.

The weight of the water pulled the waistband even lower on his soaking-wet jeans, and *damned* if the top button wasn't popped open! The little opening revealed a marked absence of undergarments, and the wet fabric left nothing to the imagination about the size and placement of his cock, which didn't seem to mind the cold water at all. It wasn't visible, just the delectable outline of it through the wet denim. She gulped loudly when her mouth started to water.

"Was the water cold?"

"It might have been a little cold, but you can probably guess what was on my mind. I don't remember feeling cold. And just so you know, I buttoned right back up after she took it," he said, kissing the top of her head before she looked up at him, smiling.

"I wasn't going to ask. But I'm glad to know. These are the nicest, finest, most thoughtful gifts I've ever received, Eli. Thank you."

Rachel kissed him as he held her in his lap. His palm rested lightly on her cheek. He tilted his head and deepened their kiss, so gentle and tender it made her heart throb and ache as well as other parts farther south.

When she came up for air, she said, "Eli, I'm so in love with you it hurts."

"Can I make the hurt feel better?"

"No, make it worse," she whispered.

Chapter Fifty

Rachel was at home wrapping Christmas gifts she would be delivering later in the day. They had decided to extend their honeymoon over Christmas and would return home on the evening of the twenty-sixth. She was attaching the gift tag to Rogelio's shirt box when the doorbell rang.

Rising from the breakfast bar where she'd set up shop, she answered the door. Corina Scott stood there looking cute as ever in her Christmas cardigan, T-shirt, blue jeans, and boots. Her hair was done up like usual, and judging by the time, she must be on her lunch break. Corina cut hair at one of the ladies' hair salons between Divine and Morehead.

"Corina? This was kind of far to come for lunch. Are you okay?" Rachel noticed the troubled expression on her friend's face.

"My one o'clock cancelled, and I took the rest of the day off to help with decorations at your mom and dad's."

"That was nice of you. We appreciate your help. Are you all right? Is something wrong?"

"Yes, actually. I know this is not the best time, and I can help you wrap while we talk if you want," Corina offered, gesturing to the rolls of paper and other gift-wrapping paraphernalia.

"I'd love some help! I have quite a few to go. Tell me what's up." Rachel fixed her a glass of tea and offered her a seat at the counter.

"I was at The Pony last night with Brice. While I was in the ladies' room, I met a person who told me she was a regular there. She said she wanted to warn me about Brice. She wouldn't be specific. She said to 'watch out.' She said her name is Barbara James and that I should ask you about Brice."

Rachel groaned and rolled her eyes. Some people just could not stand to see someone happy and had to do whatever they could to bring them down.

"Brice has been nothing but kind and wonderful to me. He treats me like a lady, like you said he would that first night. I know he's not perfect or anything. I decided I would trust what I know and see and ask you about her since she said she knew you. I noticed she sat at the bar the whole time we were there. Brice asked me if everything was all right when I sat down. I suppose he could tell something was wrong. I told him I was fine. I wasn't going to tell him what she said because she didn't say anything besides 'watch out,' whatever that means. Can you tell me what she might have meant? And tell me if I should talk to him?"

"I can tell you what I think she meant, but before I do, I want you to know I think you are the sweetest, freshest breeze that has ever blown through his not always happy life. I know none of it will matter to you because you're right in trusting your instincts."

Corina placed a small box on a piece of paper and began wrapping. Rachel disliked the woman Corina referred to intensely in that moment for causing Corina needless worry like this. "I need to know, Rachel. I think I'm falling in love with him. If he has a history I may hear about from someone like her again, I need to be armed with at least a few facts. I'm a realist but an optimistic one. I know he's not perfect, and I've figured out that his home life growing up was not good, or safe, for that matter."

"You need to know Barbara James is a busybody and a barfly." Rachel wrapped as she spoke, setting the pace by busying her hands, and allowed Corina to settle in and think about what all she had to say. "She likes to be in other people's business, and she loves to gossip. Barbara probably thinks she did you a favor and will talk about you behind your back if you persist in seeing Brice.

"I've seen the way Brice looks at you sometimes, Corina. I wouldn't be a bit surprised if he hasn't already admitted to himself he's in love with you. You're something pure and perfect to him, and I think sometimes he's afraid of scaring you off." Glancing up at the young woman, Rachel asked, "Has he told you he loves you?"

Corina cheeks turned a rosy color. "No, but I think he started to last Saturday after you and Eli left the club. We were interrupted, and then he seemed to lose his nerve. I didn't push him, just hugged him and stayed by his side. Sometimes he's like that. He doesn't need to talk but just sit and kind of 'be' with me."

Rachel smiled, recalling a time when Brice would have said the first thing that popped into his head.

Corina asked, "Can you tell me what Barbara meant by what she said?"

"Up until back in September, Brice Huvell is what you could've called 'socially challenged.'"

By the time she was done telling Corina what she could, Corina seemed to feel much better.

Rachel placed a hand on Corina's delicate forearm and said, "I would disregard anything Barbara said to you. Trust your own instincts. If anybody says anything to you in front of him, could I ask a huge favor?" At Corina's nod, Rachel continued, "Defend Brice. You don't have to condone or excuse past mistakes he's made. But you have a much better grasp of the man he is now than anyone else in this little town. He's worth it, Corina. Believe in him like crazy because that's what he *needs*. And don't worry, I'll bet Brice tells you he loves you this weekend. He's probably waiting for the perfect time, to be romantic, which is what Ethan would encourage him to do."

"Rachel, I'm so glad I came to you about this. I *knew* I couldn't put too much credence in what Barbara was saying. She's so..." Corina said, faltering at last.

"Loud and obnoxious? Yes, you can say it. Try to ignore her talk. Trust what your eyes see and what your heart is telling you about him. Where are Michelle and Lisa today?" Rachel asked.

"Oh, they're at work right now, but they told me they're meeting Andy and Vince at The Pony later."

"How's Sandra?" Rachel grinned mischievously.

"Strutting around the salon with her lip stuck out. Sandra spends more time primping on herself than she does on her customers. She overheard I was coming out to see you. You should have seen her, acting like someone had stuck a corncob up her ass."

Rachel burst out laughing at the vivid imagery. They talked and wrapped gifts for a while longer then Corina took her iced tea glass to the sink and rinsed it out.

"Thanks for the help with my Christmas wrapping." Rachel hugged her.

"Thanks for talking me down off the ledge."

"You weren't that bad, Corina. Your instincts were already telling you what you needed to hear."

Rachel finished wrapping everything else and packed her suitcase for the honeymoon. Eli had gone in search of boxes for her to use for packing up her apartment. All the furniture was already returned in storage with the exception of her cedar chest, which she'd agreed to let Eli take to a furniture refinisher for her. He was in Morehead at the moment, picking up some things he would need for the trip.

Rachel walked over to her side of the duplex and began gathering things, moving them into the kitchen and organizing them into boxes. She needed a little background noise but didn't feel like going back to the other side for her MP3 player. She turned on the television and listened to the noontime news while she went through the rooms and brought everything in and put it on the breakfast bar.

She was removing the contents of a kitchen drawer into a box when a familiar name caught her attention. Rachel left the kitchen and grabbed the remote, turned up the volume, and listened to the news anchor share the story.

"...arrest was made and charges of trafficking in child pornography were filed against a Divine man. Reese McCoy, age thirty-four, was charged and taken into custody on several counts and is also being investigated on allegations of rape of a teenage runaway. McCoy was also charged with narcotics possession and is being investigated for tax evasion, as well. The arrest came as the result of an anonymous tip to the FBI and local police authorities. Extensive evidence was uncovered in his home..."

Rachel stood there watching a belligerent Reese McCoy being led to a police car in handcuffs. He had been rather overweight when she last saw him, but she noticed he walked, or rather, waddled strangely as he was led shuffling to the police car and put in the back. Boxes and boxes of papers and electronic equipment were being taken as evidence out the front door, and she prayed that they had what they needed and that he wouldn't be able to hurt anyone else ever again.

Rachel turned the news off and plugged in her alarm clock radio in the kitchen and listened to music while she worked instead. She sealed each box and stacked them by the door for Eli to come get later. Eli had made her promise she would not try to move all the boxes herself. After they were all stacked, and ready to be moved, she went back over to the other side and carried the Christmas presents she needed to deliver out to the Tundra.

She called to check in with Eli before she left to see how his shopping trip was going and to let him know what she had accomplished. Rachel also told him about what she'd seen on the news that afternoon, and Eli commented that it sounded like McCoy's deeds had finally caught up with him. He asked her how she was feeling about it, and she told him that she was relieved and satisfied that justice would be done now. She felt sorry for his young victims.

Rachel ran her errands, delivering all the Christmas presents. She swung by the ranch and left the gifts for Grace and her men, Kelly, Matthew, and Elijah with Jack, who was at home doing paperwork in his office. She swung by with gifts for Mike and Rosa and the kids then went out to Rogelio's and dropped off his present and a big box of Milk-Bones for Rogelio's dogs.

The sun was setting by the time she arrived home after making all her stops. Eli's truck was in the driveway, and she hurried inside, happy he had beaten her home. She discovered him in the second bedroom, stacking all the boxes against a wall.

"Hello, angel." He squeezed her and kissed her thoroughly. "Pizza and a movie are waiting for us in the kitchen. I thought I'd go ahead and get these moved over while I waited for you to come home. Did you get finished?"

"Yep! I'm done. Now all I have to do is pick up my dress and your ring tomorrow. I volunteered to bring the girls' dresses out to them, and the evil *elf* told me, and I quote, to 'stay the hell away.' The stress has gotten to her, to them all. Crazy people. My dad was the only one who sounded like he was having a good time. Grace has him running errands for her. Mom sounded like she was busy, too."

"I'm not working tomorrow, so we could run those errands together, if you'd like? Will your dress be wrapped up?"

"Should be. If we go together, then we can get both rings at once."

They made a list of the stops they would have to make the next day, she called to check in with Grace while they ate their pizza, and Eli put in the movie. After she finished her call, Rachel came and cuddled up with Eli on the couch.

"Is Grace okay?"

Rachel nodded and rested her head on Eli's chest. "Oh, yeah. I couldn't get a word in with a wedge, but it sounds like she and Kelly had it all completely under control. Honey?" She began, tracing a pattern on his thigh. "There's something I want to do right now. Do you mind watching this later?"

"No, what do you need?"

You.

"To make a fantasy a reality." Rachel smiled invitingly at him as she rose to her feet and went in the bedroom. She gathered all the candles from the bedroom and asked him to take them on the back deck, and understanding dawned in his eyes.

Rachel felt her cheeks blush under his warm gaze as he took the candles from her. "It's a wonderful night tonight. Why don't we see what it's like to make love under the stars? No one will see us or hear us. Everyone is too busy to bother coming over here."

"You're always full of surprises, angel."

"Could you light the candles for me and take my robe and a blanket out there to cuddle up in afterward?"

"Sure, anything else you need?"

"Just you. Nekkid. I'll be ready in a few minutes."

* * * *

Eli lit the candles and set them out on the deck and laid her robe and a blanket on a nearby table. He laid a towel on the reclining deck lounger. Getting harder by the moment, he began to undress outside under the light of the moon and stars.

When he was naked, he reclined in the deck chair. Thinking about what she was changing into right now had him hard as a steel pole. He lay back and stroked his cock and imagined her slipping those shoes on. His cock responded to that mental image and the additional stimulation of being outdoors stark naked, readying for the fulfillment of his fantasy. A fantasy she wanted him to have come true. Rachel was amazing.

The porch light went off, and the deck was plunged into soft, flickering candlelight. He'd made sure and positioned some candles by the door so she would be able to see where she was going and so he would be able to see her. The backdoor opened, and the woman he loved stepped through, even sexier than in his original fantasy.

Moving toward him slowly and seductively, Rachel was naked except for her black satin side-tying G-string. Her feet were shod in her five-inch naughty school girl pumps, just like in his fantasy. She carried in her hand the vibrator that stimulated her G-spot and clitoris at the same time and a bottle of lubricant. Rachel stood in front of him at the end of the chair, her shoulders back, hand on her hip and her feet in a wide, self-assured stance, nothing hidden. The scent of jasmine floated on the air from her dewy skin.

"I hope I didn't keep you waiting long."

He chuckled. "You're a beautiful sight, standing there, angel. Turn for me," he murmured.

Rachel complied, slowly and confidently giving him a nice, slow view of her ass and legs. She gazed down at him with desire glittering in her eyes as he stroked his cock, drinking in the sight of her. He knew that seeing him stroke himself never failed to turn her on.

He spread his legs as he sat up, put a foot on the deck on either side of the lounger, and held out his hand to her. "Come here to me, angel."

She stepped over to his right side, taking his hand.

"Eli, I want you to make your fantasy a reality. Do to me exactly what you told me about. I'm yours," she whispered as she leaned down to kiss him. She arched her back with a gasp when his hand slid up her thigh to palm her ass.

"Thank you, angel. This is only the first time we are making love outside. You, naked in the moonlight, are a vision. Turn your back to me and take my hands. I promise I won't let you fall." She reached back, and he allowed her to grasp his hands securely. "Hold on to me and straddle the chair facing away from me."

Straddling the chair, she leaned forward, giving him a mouth-watering close-up view of her ass. Her stance now was wide but not so wide that she was unstable.

"How's that? Too hard on your ankles?"

"No, my ankles are fine. How is it for you?"

Eli could hear the smile in her voice. He sat back in the reclining deck chair, admiring her ass and pondered her question.

Pretty fucking near perfection from where I'm sitting.

Tilting forward at the hip a little, Rachel braced her hands on her thighs. Eli traced the palms of his hands up the backs of her thighs to her ass, trailing the pads of his thumbs up her inner thigh so that, as his hands met, his thumbs caressed her outer lips through the black satin. He smiled at her sudden intake of breath.

"It's perfect for me, angel. Did that feel good?"

"Yes, Eli. You're making me wet doing that. Oh, don't stop." She whimpered when he slowly did it again, his hands moving slowly as they neared the apex of her thighs. He slid his fingers over her hips, and pulled on the little ties of her G-string. The fabric slipped away, and he laid it aside.

"How does it feel to be naked and outside with nothing on but these heels?" he asked as he slid his hands over the tops of her feet before moving up her calves again.

"Oh!" she whimpered as he made slow torturous progress, building the anticipation.

In the still air around them, he caught the scent of her arousal, and his cock twitched in response to her siren's call.

"Mmm, what will I find when I reach your pretty little pussy? You must like to be naked and under the stars. Are you very wet?"

"Yes, Eli. I love it out here. So open and exposed. Oh! Your hands. I need your hands on me so much." She cried out in pleasure when his fingertips reached her ass and slid to her lips and parted them so he could see her most intimate self. "Oh, Eli!" she whimpered.

He sat forward in the deck chair and stroked her lips, which glistened with her arousal in the moonlight. He could easily see how wet and needy she was. The novelty of being outside in such a vulnerable position, naked and straddling his deck chair with her beautiful ass in his face, was having as pronounced an effect on her as it was on him. His cock twitched with the need to be inside her. Eli's mouth watered for a little taste, and he tilted his head as he grasped her hips and slid his tongue through her opened slit. She cried out in pleasure as he satisfied his desire to have a taste of her pussy. He slid his tongue in her opening and then gently flicked over her engorged clitoris. She trembled in his hands.

"Are you all right?'

"Oh, Eli, yes!"

"Put your hands down on the cushion in front of you." Placing her hands on the cushion he'd put there for that purpose took the pressure off her knees and tilted her a bit more, so Eli had even better access.

Returning his mouth to her pussy, Eli feasted on her honey as she squirmed and moaned. He paid loving attention to her clit, bringing her close to the edge as his cock throbbed between his legs, aching to slide into her. With her back turned, she was unaware when he lifted the vibrator she had brought outside with her. He set it on its lowest setting and gently placed the nubbed head to her wet, parted inner lips, which had swelled and darkened to a deep rose color. She whimpered in raw ecstasy.

"Are you ready for the vibrator? Ready to come for me?'

"Yes, baby." She cried out as the thick, jelly-like vibrator slipped into her slick opening.

He slowly slid the vibrating nubbed head toward her G-spot. When he reached it, the lip of the clitoral vibrator made contact with her clit. He tilted the vibrator, applied pressure to her G-spot, began a slow stroking motion, and pressed the outer vibrator against her clit.

Her pussy dripped with her juices, and he leaned forward for another taste as he continued the short, firm strokes to her pleasure spots. He enjoyed the rising sounds of her ecstasy, which told him he was stroking her just right. He backed off slightly until Rachel begged him to make her come, then he applied steady, direct stimulation.

Rachel was beautiful as her back arched, and she cried out in ecstasy, her hips undulating in a slow, sensuous dance as her orgasm took her. Before she had a chance to come down from those heights, he switched off the vibrator, gently removed it then securely grasped the backs of her thighs and said, "I have you angel, and I won't let you fall, I promise. Bend your knees. I'm going to slide you down over my cock. I can't wait another second do be inside you."

"Oh, yes, Eli." Rachel held onto his arms and did as he instructed, bending her knees. She cried out as her pussy convulsed in hot liquid waves around his cock and came again as he slid deep. The caveman growled in deep approval at her welcome.

"Fuck, that is hot, feeling you clenching on my cock like that."

He lifted her thighs and spread them wide over his, and she placed her hands on the cushion in front of her, leaning forward a bit, so she had some leverage. He was seated to the hilt as she sat down on him, touching the deepest part of her.

"How does it feel?"

She moaned softly and shifted on him. "Like you own every inch of me, Eli. Is it good?"

"Like heaven. Are you ready? I'm going to lie back a little. Hold your balance and let me do the lifting. I want to fuck you till you come for me again. Are you touching yourself?"

"Do you want me to?"

"Yes, I want you to use the vibrator on your clit."

Eli lay back while Rachel turned on the vibrator and he slid his hands under her hips. She had a little leverage to pump on him as he began to thrust into her gently. She applied the vibrator to her clit, and he groaned.

"I can feel the vibrator on my cock, too. Damn, that's amazing," he said as he looked down, lifting her and seeing her cream smeared all over his cock as he pumped into her. "Fuck, I love how your little lips part over my cock like they're kissing me while I tunnel into you."

Her walls tightened around him.

"Oh, yes, Eli! Fuck me harder, please, please, please, yes! I'm...I'm coming, Eli!" She wailed loudly as her hips moved uncontrollably over his cock.

He thought his head would explode trying to restrain himself. In order to make the fantasy real, he had to hold off on coming, for now.

She moaned as he growled deep, fighting with his control but maintaining it. The need to fuck and come inside her was almost insurmountable. Rachel settled back against his chest, and he allowed her to catch her breath and steady herself.

She turned to him, dreamy eyed, and said, "I love you, Eli. I love your fantasy."

"You're my fantasy coming true," he murmured as he stroked her shoulder. "Ready for more?"

"Always."

Helping her rise, he withdrew his still fully engorged cock from her hot, languid depths. It stood straight out from him, demanding he return to the tight confines of her pussy so it could finish what he'd started. Eli took no small delight in her feminine little moan as he slid from her. The sight of her pussy, wet with her cum as she rose to one knee on the chair only served to torture his already painfully hard cock.

"Can you stand, angel?"

"If you'll help me a little." Rachel reached out to him as he rose and offered her his hand to help her up. She stepped carefully, mindful of his bare feet as he drew her to him in a passionate kiss. She giggled when his insistent erection twitched between them, refusing to be ignored.

Stepping away from him, she turned back to the lounger, and stretched luxuriously, raising her arms over her head. She ran her fingers through her hair, sighed sexily, then reached for the arms of the deck chair. She slowly lifted a foot, parted her long, satiny legs, and straddled the chair. Clad only in the high heels, her back arched and her ass tilted up, she offered herself to him. Turning her head, Rachel flipped her hair over her shoulder, gave him a sexy teasing smile and wiggled her ass at him.

"My pussy is begging for your cock again. How about you come here and fuck me, then fill me with your cum this time."

She didn't have to ask twice. Eli straddled the chair behind her, the shoes bringing her up to the perfect height. He grasped her hips, positioned his head at her entrance, pausing to enjoy the sight of her like this. Her strong legs were stretched long and graceful, and her pussy was completely open and welcoming to him, dripping wet and ready to be taken.

This sight would stay buried in his heart as a deeply cherished memory. Not one he'd trot out and share during the holidays with family but maybe with just her. This memory of her making his fantasy a reality.

Rachel panted as he took in the sight of her. She bent her knees slightly and pressed her cunt back against his cock a little bit, enticing him. He growled low at the sensation of her tight wet heat squeezing on his head and said, "Hold on."

Eli impaled her with one solid thrust, grasping her tightly against him as she moaned deeply and flexed against him in powerful waves.

"Slow down, baby," he murmured, and she panted, stilling her movements.

He slid his hands up from her hips to her abdomen and over her ribs, pulling her gently into a standing position. Eli kneaded the delectable handfuls of her breasts gently but firmly, and she reached behind her and threaded her fingers into his hair. She laid her head back, and he tilted forward to kiss her tenderly as he began to thrust into her, looking into her eyes, so filled with bliss.

"Eli," she whispered, "it's so good. It's so right with you. You fill me perfectly." She placed her hands over his as he cupped her breasts, and she rocked back onto him, grinding on his cock. He growled deeply when she did it, and his strokes became firmer as he tunneled into her heat.

"Angel," he groaned, "you are my fantasy come true. You feel so good. You look so good, taking my cock like this." He slid a hand down to her slit and stroked a finger over her clit. Rachel reacted to the additional stimulation immediately.

"Oh, give it to me hard, Eli, please! Harder and faster! Fill me, oh! Eli! I'm coming!" She groaned low, thrusting back on his cock hard and tight, flexing her hips and drawing on him with a powerful womanly strength her soft feminine curves belied.

Maybe his Rachel had a little cavewoman in *her*? Her counterpart to his caveman. Her response to her orgasm had an almost feral, primitive quality to it. Eli loved the hell out of this part of her that took whatever the fuck she wanted when she wanted it, as hard as she could. He howled in ecstasy as his cock pulsed inside her, and her pussy consumed every drop of his cum, milking his cock.

Surprising him, Rachel reached back with both hands, grasped the backs of his thighs, and held on to him tightly. His cavewoman growled and arched against him, daring him to pull out before she was finished with him. He bent over her, wrapped his arms around her and growled back in answer, pounding into her with renewed vigor, giving her what she demanded.

Firmly stroking her clit, Eli trapped her against him and fucked her until her pussy clenched in ecstasy. She threw her head back and moaned rapturously and her body stroked him with her tightening muscles again.

She went limp in his arms, the satisfied cavewoman's grip released, and his sweet gentle Rachel returned.

Sliding his still semi-erect cock from her, he laid her limp form back against him, lifted her, and held her in his arms. Stepping back from the lounger, he turned and sat back down on the towel-covered cushions, cuddling her close to him as she clung to him and her breath hitched.

Pushing her hair back from her face, she looked up at him, her cheeks flushed bright pink. "I'm sorry, Eli."

Flabbergasted, he looked down at her and said, "Huh?"

"Sorry, I was so…forceful with you. I felt like I lost control. I think I scratched you with my long fingernails." She was embarrassed for being his cavewoman.

"Wow, lose control like that as often as you need to. That was fucking amazing. I've only seen a little glimpse of *that* one here and there. But I love *the shit* out of the cavewoman. She's hot and wild."

"Really?" she said with a breathless giggle.

"She takes whatever the fuck she wants and won't be denied. I *get* her. I *love* her."

"Oh! Well, all right, but she's gone now. I think she exploded. It's just a puddle of Rachel that is left behind," Rachel replied, laughing softly as she stroked his shoulder.

"Oh, but see, I win either way because *melting* Rachel is another favorite of mine, the one who needs me to hold her after she comes undone. She's pure sugar and sweetness," he whispered as she repositioned, having gained some strength back.

Smiling radiantly, Rachel straddled him and laid her warm, wet pussy on his now hard cock. She moaned at the feel of his heat against her own, moved forward at his own sharp intake, and did as he had told her in his fantasy. She laid her pussy against the head of his cock, over his abdomen. Eli flexed when she did and both of them whimpered softly when he slid into her easily.

"Are you sore, angel?"

"No. I'm aching for another filling with this magical cock of yours. I'm going to do like you said and slowly work my way down your cock until I've taken all of you inside me. I'm going to grind on you until we both have one more sweet release. Then I'm going to fall into a deep, coma-like sleep."

"Music to my ears, angel. I'm going to slip these off of you so you can be more comfortable." He slid each pump from her feet and left them lying on the deck.

He reached for the blanket on the table he'd moved to within easy reach of the chair and unfolded it over her until they were both under its warmth. He groaned as she moved in a small, sinuous motion against him, fucking the part of his cock that rested inside her tight heat, sliding him deeper by minute degrees. Eli caressed her shoulders and back, stroking her and touching her wherever he could. His hands came to rest on her ass, and her slow, circling grind continued over him.

This part was even *better* than his fantasy as Rachel lost herself to the fluid, repetitive, rocking motion of her hips. He knew the moment when she no longer controlled the motions and they controlled her. She moaned quietly, her cheek resting on his chest, and her eyes closed. Her rhythm remained slow, and the tension built inside them both.

She began to moan and cry out, murmuring his name in an erotically thrilling, intense voice as her strokes became a little longer but no less delicious and sensuous over him. Tears flowed freely from her eyes, and he did nothing to stop her or them for fear of distracting her from this profound moment. Eli watched in awe as she lost herself utterly in the sweetest orgasmic wave he'd ever known, taking him along with her as her gently tugging pussy milked another blissful release from him.

There had been no fucking, no thrusting on his part, just a sinuous draw from her pussy to his cock, coaxing him to fill her one more time. The pulses went on and on, and he felt, at that moment, that she took more from him into her than his seed. Rachel drew his love into her, binding him to her irrevocably. Her cheek rested on his chest, and her breathing was punctuated by hitching sobs of bliss. He closed his eyes, feeling tears flow from his eyes. The ache in his heart was almost painful as he gave himself utterly to her, heart and soul, falling even deeper in love with her. She drifted into a deep, motionless sleep as he caressed her back tenderly, unable to keep from touching her.

Later, he wrapped the blanket around her, rose with her in his arms, carried her in through the backdoor, and tucked her into the bed, wrapped in the quilt. The temperature had dropped since going outside earlier, so he slipped into his robe and went back to collect the candles and blow them out. He gathered everything and brought all of it back inside. After cleaning up, he turned off the lights and slipped under the covers. He untucked the blanket she was wrapped in and drew her gently to him, sharing his warmth with her. Rachel never stirred once, even as he kissed her face and her hair.

Chapter Fifty-one

Eli awakened to the sound of a groan and realized it was himself he heard. Then he was overcome by a warm feeling of utter bliss. Rachel's warm, soft hands were at his hips, and he realized he was moving as he came fully awake and opened his eyes. The warmth was her velvety-soft mouth and tongue on his cock, and the movement was his hips thrusting his cock between her soft, welcoming lips as she sucked his cock under the covers.

He drew off the blanket and found her, hair tousled, sleepy-eyed, and giggling as she suckled on his cock. Judging by its size, *it* had been awake for a while and was glad Eli had finally woken up and gotten with the program. She sighed blissfully and released his cock with a resounding pop.

"Good morning, my baby." Rachel climbed on him and kissed his lips happily. She positioned his cock at her entrance and slid down over him, flexing and grinding on him as he growled deep in bliss. She clasped her fingers with his and rose and plunged down hard onto him.

"Yes," she whispered as she began to rock gently, keeping all of him inside her. He moaned softly at the feel of her tight, wet pussy gloving him so tightly.

Eli kissed her knuckles and murmured, "Good morning, beautiful."

He thrust deeply into her, causing her to topple giggling onto him. He released her hands and rolled her on her back and pulled out until just the head remained in her slick entrance. "I could get used to being awakened like that in the morning." He thrust into her, searching for that spot, knowing he found it when her eyes rolled back and her lips pressed together on a whimper.

"I know what you mean." Rachel groaned blissfully when he did it again.

"I can't seem to get enough of you, my angel," He rose up to look down at the honeyed place where they were joined together.

Biting his lip, he pulled out and lifted her ankles until they were above her and spread them wide, seeing her reacting to this position. She loved being taken in positions where control was given over to him. He held her thighs spread wide, her pussy lips parted and wet with her cream. He positioned his cock at her pussy again and growled at the way it nudged her lips aside, sliding around in her wetness. He loved watching her little lips spread and stretch around him, drawing her clit closer to his cock.

Looking into her blue eyes, Eli saw the glittering desire and her own awareness of how much he loved that sight. He pulled out and did it again, just to see them stretch around him one more time, noticing her clit was swelling as she got even more turned on by the sight of him watching her like that. He pushed in a few inches, engulfed in her heat, and watched as his cock disappeared inside of her then reappeared, coated in her cream.

"Fuck. That is beautiful. Your pussy is so hot. I'm as hard as a baseball bat. Don't move a muscle," he growled as he pulled out and stalked to the bathroom, returning with a large hand mirror. "Look. I want you to see." He lifted her legs, spread them wide, and replaced his twitching, hard erection at her entrance again. She held the mirror, and he said, "Look, isn't it beautiful?"

"Oh, Eli." She watched as he slowly pushed his rock-hard cock between her lips while he stroked her clit. He felt the fresh rush of moisture to her pussy, when his cock disappeared inside her and slid back out, coated in fresh clear honey. "Oh, Eli, it's beautiful. Nothing compares to you sliding into me."

"I can say the same thing about your sweet pussy. You like watching my cock slide into you, don't you? See how dark and swollen you've gotten? I can tell how much it affects you to watch this. Our bedroom will have lots of mirrors so you can watch as we fuck."

Rachel giggled in delighted abandon. "Oh, yes, Eli. I want to watch you fuck me from every angle, and I want to watch up close like this, too."

A thought came to him and he asked, "Have you been using your plugs?"

"Yes." Rachel looked up into his eyes and smiled. He groaned in pleasure as he stroked her with his cock.

"You have?"

"Of course, I wanted to be ready the next time you wanted my ass. You want it now?" Rachel was *perfect*.

"If you think you can handle it."

"I can. I'll get the lube, you fix the mirror."

Eli positioned the mirror on the closet door, Rachel got the lube, and he retrieved the dual clit and G-spot vibrator from last night, in case she wanted to use it, and put them at the end of the bed where he could reach them. She turned and backed to the end of the bed and wiggled her ass at him. He chuckled as he applied lube to her ass and pressed with a finger. She relaxed, and the muscles gave way under the pressure.

"Good, baby. That hurt?"

"No," she growled, thrusting back a little as he chuckled again.

"Eager little vixen, aren't you?"

"For you, yes!"

He applied the nozzle of the lube to her opening and squeezed some inside her then applied more to his hand and slathered his cock with it.

"Ready? I'll go slow."

"Yes, I'm ready." She watched in the mirror as he placed his stiff cock at her opening and grasped her hip gently, pulling her back onto him. His heart began to pound at the pleasure of her ultra-tight passage encircling his cock. He rocked into and out of her in short, gentle strokes, fighting for control not to plunge in. The sensation was unlike anything else he could name.

"Oh, fuck, Eli, it feels so good! So tight and hot!" Rachel moaned and arched against him.

"Ready for the vibrator?"

Enthusiastically, she wailed as she ground her ass against him. "Oh, yes, honey, yes!"

He switched it on low and stroked her clit with it, making her buck violently and moan, and then he pressed it to her entrance. He rocked out of her ass and placed it in position, where it hummed with her movements as well as on his throbbing erection. He clenched his teeth as his balls drew up tight to his body at the vibration against his cock inside her.

Eli grasped her hips and began a smooth rhythm in and out as her pussy and ass began to clench. "You're close, aren't you? Come for me, Rachel."

He strummed her sweet spots with the vibrator as he pumped into her ass. She began to whimper and arch her back, taking more of him, and cried out in bliss as he slid to the hilt. Her ass clenched tightly.

"Oh, Eli, I'm coming!" She wailed as he pumped into each opening. Several thrusts later, his body became rigid as his scorching release exploded in hot streams inside her.

"Angel!"

Rachel's arms gave out, and her upper body collapsed on the bed as he held her in place by her hips. She moaned softly and relaxed against him. Still seeing stars as he caught his breath, he removed the toy and pulled his softening cock from her ass and pressed her to lie down.

"Be right back, angel." He returned with a hot washcloth, cleaned her up, and helped her up to the pillows. "I'm going to shower real quick. Be right back." He kissed her as she lay down to rest for a few minutes. He covered her, took the washcloth and toy with him and left the room.

When he returned to the bedroom fresh from his shower to dress, he discovered her curled up in the bed. She was sound asleep and he didn't have the heart to wake her. He checked the clock and grinned. They had plenty of time. He picked up her phone from the bedside table and carried it with him to the kitchen so if it rang it wouldn't disturb her.

Two hours later, he heard a slight movement from the bedroom and her muted voice. "Crap."

She was sitting up in the bed, her hair wild and disheveled, and turned to the doorway when he chuckled.

"Hungry? I made some lunch?"

She grinned sheepishly at him. "Believe it or not, I'm famished."

"Of course I believe it. Making love that many times for that long is hard work. You *should* be starving, you didn't have any breakfast." Handing her one of his T-shirts, he added, "Stay here, and I'll bring it to you."

He brought her lunch, and she ate hungrily. While she was in the shower, her phone rang, and Eli spoke at length with Jane Jensen. She told him she'd heard from the owners of the ranch and that they were amenable to the offer Eli and Rachel made. Jane hoped to hear something that day and not have to bother them on their honeymoon. As the conversation drew to a close, Jane mentioned that she would be at the wedding the next day.

Eli replied, "We're looking forward to you being there, too."

"I mean I'll be there with your dad," Jane replied, sounding a little uncertain. "I hope that's all right. Elijah knew you'd invited me, but he asked me last week if I might be interested in going as his date."

"Oh! I see." He chuckled.

She sounded genuinely worried. "I hope that's all right with you, Eli."

"Of course it is. It's good to see him...dating."

"Awkward?"

"No, I'm a big boy. Dad deserves to have fun, too."

"Well, I guess we wait to hear from the sellers. Enjoy your day," she said. He chuckled at that thought.

So far, so good.

* * * *

Rachel was seated in front of the vanity mirror in Grace's bathroom. Soft country music played on the stereo in the bedroom. She watched as Grace separated her hair into small sections and rolled each into a hot roller and pinned it down on her head. Rachel had assured Grace that she could do this. Rolling her hair was something she'd done on a regular basis, but Grace insisted that she should relax and allow herself to be fussed over a little.

Rachel was doing her own makeup, but Grace asked Carrie to help since she was going to be here, anyway, taking pictures as the bride got ready. There was even going to be a shot of Rachel in just her heels, lingerie, jewelry, and bridal veil that she knew Eli would *love.* The rollers were in place when Carrie came in and shot a grinning picture of Rachel with rollers and pins all over her head.

"Aren't you nervous?" Grace asked.

"I'm not nervous at all. I'm worried that I'll take one look at Eli at the end of the aisle and make a fool of myself bawling like a baby. He insists I'll be fine, and it'll be the other way around. But we're not nervous at all. No. Just make sure I've got a hanky on me and that we use waterproof mascara and eyeliner."

"Do we know where the rings are?" Grace asked, lacing her into the corset after she had the G-string on.

"Teresa has both of them in safekeeping in their boxes until right before the ceremony. I have to say I'm glad we ditched the ring pillow. I liked your idea better." Rachel smiled as she remembered the rehearsal the night before. To a little boy, a small pillow is just too much like a football.

Carrie did her makeup, Grace finished her hair-do, and they moved on to the stockings and shoes. Then Grace pinned the flowing, lightweight veil into Rachel's hair. Carrie snapped some pictures, giggling when Rachel warned her to quit shooting her ass.

Carrie snorted with laughter and said, "Nah, Eli will be thanking me, honey, for making sure this freaking-hot outfit got immortalized. Maybe I'll put them all in a naughty little wedding album for him to keep in a safe place since I have a feeling he doesn't share well."

"Rachel, why don't you camp it up a bit before we put on the dress? That's *perfect!*" Grace encouraged as Rachel struck a sizzle pose with her fingertip on her ass, and said, *"Tssssss!"*

That few minutes of silliness did a lot to help her jitters about becoming too serious and teary-eyed, and maybe that was Grace's purpose all along. Grace helped her into the dress, which felt like a dream on, not stiff and bulky at all. Because there were several layers of fabric to the skirt, she wore no slip underneath, just her lingerie. Carrie was busy snapping pictures as they talked.

There was a tap at the door, and Carrie opened it when they heard Rachel's father's voice. Her mom and dad had brought the Escalade to escort Rachel back to the Lopez ranch. Rachel stood by the open window and turned as they entered. Both her parents stood there looking at her, a mixture of love, pride, and pain on their faces. Her mom started crying first, and her dad, bless him, shed tears, as well, as they came to her. Carrie was ready for it and shot quietly as they embraced Rachel, and she wiped their tears, fighting tears of her own.

Grace stood back in her royal-blue dress and quietly waited as they spoke softly to Rachel, touching her dress and her hair and her cheek. She smiled and nodded, and they turned to go. Carrie snapped that portrait as they looked up. Perfect.

When they were within sight of the pavilion on the ranch, Grace had Rachel turn away so she wouldn't be able to see it. The sun was nearing the horizon, breathtaking in brilliant colors and the perfect background. The ceremony would start in less than twenty minutes. As instructed, all the drapes and blinds in the large back windows of the house were drawn so she couldn't see out yet.

The bride's party waited inside the ranch house with Justin and Ethan. Eli waited out at the pavilion with the preacher. They all wore admiring smiles as Rachel entered the front door. Kelly helped her with her short train while Grace hurried to put Rachel's things in the Dodge Ram. Grace came in, her cell phone to her ear, talking to Charity, who was overseeing things from the other side of the backdoor.

"Rachel, do you need a few minutes?" Grace asked as Ethan escorted her mom out through the barely-open backdoor to walk her to her seat.

Rachel nodded and took steady, calming breaths for a couple of minutes.

Grace patted her shoulder and said, "You take your time and let me know when *you're* ready."

"How is my lipstick?" she asked, standing to look in a mirror. Grace had done a beautiful job on her hair.

Grace replied, "Your lipstick is perfect."

Ethan slipped back in the backdoor and nodded. Grace held her phone to her ear then looked at Rachel. "Ready to go, Rachel?"

Rachel turned to her and smiled. "I'm ready."

Carrie shot pictures as Grace lined them up in order. Teresa removed the wedding bands from their boxes, tied a ribbon through them, and then looped the ribbon over Little Michael's sweetly tousled black curls so that it hung around his neck. He grinned and stuck his hand in his little pocket and reached for his mommy's hand. He was being escorted by his mommy, who found a dress in the same shade of royal blue so she would fit in with the rest of the wedding party. Teresa would walk him down the aisle, to where he would stand with Ethan and Justin. She would have a seat in the front row so he could join her when he lost interest or when one of the men brought him to her, whichever came first. He was dressed in a black tuxedo that matched Justin and Ethan's and looked as cute as button.

Grace lined them up, positioning Rachel away from the doorway on her father's arm. Kelly went first, a bouquet of deep red roses in her hands as she stepped to the door on Justin's arm. Grace whispered into the phone, and Charity opened the door from the other side, glancing in at Rachel. Her eyes popped wide open, and she gave her the big thumbs-up then disappeared just as quickly. Kelly looked back and winked then allowed Justin to lead her through the door.

Grace joined Ethan at the open door and smiled up at him. Rachel smiled, catching Ethan in the act of looking down Grace's cleavage admiringly. Grace rolled her eyes and hugged his arm, and then she turned and blew an air kiss to Rachel as he led her through the door. They moved closer to the door, and Rachel could hear guitars playing. The basic melody was familiar, but Rachel couldn't place it at the moment.

Teresa smiled down at Michael and nodded then led him through the door. Rachel turned to look at her father. He gazed into her eyes, fighting tears hard, and tried to smile at her but failed miserably. She pulled her hanky from inside her sleeve and blotted his tears and kissed his cheeks as Carrie shot one last image then slipped through the door.

"Your mom and I love you so much, Rachel. You've made us very proud of you. You've found a man of worth, and I hope he makes you happy in your lives together. This is your time, princess. Ready? He's waiting for you."

She tucked the handkerchief back into her sleeve, took the bouquet of vivid red and flaming orange roses he handed her, and took his arm. He led her to the door, and she turned to him.

"Do I look all right, Dad?"

"A little better than all right, princess. Can you see him up there? I'll guide you, honey. You just keep your eyes on him."

Rachel looked up the gentle, smooth slope to the pavilion, awash now in a thousand twinkling lights. She stood still, searching for him as her eyes adjusted to the dimmer lighting outside the door. She found him easily because she need only look for the tallest man there. She couldn't clearly make out his features yet, but she knew the moment he caught sight of her as she stepped out on her father's arm and moved forward into the dwindling light.

Eli's body language changed. He became motionless, focused on her. Other people noticed the change, and guests began turning to watch her. The soft guitar music continued, and she realized that Grace must have speakers set up between the pavilion and the house. Otherwise, there was not much chance she would have heard the music playing from the pavilion, but the music was a perfect wedding processional. Charity adjusted her short train and backed away, smiling at her.

Her father patted her hand and led her forward. Eli stood with the preacher, flanked by the members of the wedding party. Little Michael was perched happily on Justin's arm. Each step brought her closer to Eli until she could clearly make out his features. His handsome face was illuminated by candlelight, and anyone could tell he was a man very deeply in love. It was in his eyes and his sensual smile and the way he held himself. Rachel's lip quivered when she clearly saw his gentle heart in his eyes and prayed for the waterworks to hold off a bit longer.

The area where the ceremony was to take place was surrounded on either side of the wedding party by two long rows of evergreen trees. The sunset blazed beyond where Eli and the preacher stood.

Processing slowly forward on her dad's arm, Rachel was thankful her tears and quivering lip were under control as they moved down the aisle between the rows of guests who now stood for her. The guitar music intensified, heralding her arrival in their midst.

Gazing into Eli's crystalline eyes, she remembered walking to him at the club the night she faced her fears of insurmountable jealousy and dealt with a whole horde of females as they flirted with him. Rachel remembered facing the women again and again, singly and in groups, proving to herself that she could overcome her jealousy and she did have what it took to hold him. Humbled that the love in his eyes was for her, she reflected it back in her own. Her heart throbbed with adoration and respect for him that he didn't try to play it cool for everyone there. He watched her as she moved toward him like she was the only woman in the world and she was his.

Taking a deep breath, Rachel felt her rigid body relax. Her stiff spine, tall and straight as always, loosened. Sauntering Rachel, the woman who moved *for* him, to please him, made her appearance. Whether it was walking away from him while he ogled her ass or walking toward him as he eyeballed her swaying hips and full breasts or dancing for him, Sauntering Rachel smiled at him with a seductive twinkle, and she watched his reaction. She could tell by the glitter in his eyes that he was *liking* what he saw as she closed the remaining distance between them.

Her father stopped with her at the end of the bridal runner as the preacher and Eli approached them. Rachel turned to her father, who was once again fighting tears. She kissed his leathery cheek and looked back at her mom and smiled. Her father responded as he was directed in the rehearsal the night before. Then he backed away and sat in the empty chair beside her mother, dabbing his eyes with his handkerchief.

Rachel looked up at Eli and smiled happily. Love glowed in his gray eyes as he took in her appearance. He led her to the spot where they were to say their vows. As she moved beside him, he looked down at her and whispered, "You're a vision, angel."

Rachel softly replied, "You look so handsome."

The preacher shared a short message with Rachel and Eli and the congregation. He detailed a little of their history for those who did not know their story and spoke about marriage vows being sacred. He asked for the rings.

Justin nodded to Michael and set him on his little feet. He stopped in front of Eli and looked up, and up, and up, and up, until his little head was craning far back. The congregation chuckled. Michael slipped the ribbon from around his neck and handed it to Eli, who squatted down and accepted the rings then held out his hand. Michael slapped his palm with a little cracking sound and returned to Justin, who picked him up again so he could see what was going to happen.

The preacher prayed for them and spoke about the rings and their significance. "Rachel and Eli both wanted to have something special inscribed inside the other's wedding band. They kept the inscriptions a secret from each other until now. They wanted to give each other a part of themselves they could carry inside their wedding band and in their hearts. They communicated the inscriptions to me separately and told me how the words spoke volumes to their hearts even though they were few. After all, how much can you fit inside a wedding band?

"It is my earnest prayer that they keep those words in their hearts and that we would do the same. We should care for each other in such a way that we can say we live with *no regrets*. This is a philosophy they have both developed in their love for each other and in the life they look forward to living. I pray it continues on and believe that it will because they both chose the exact same inscription for each other without knowing it."

Rachel looked up at Eli and laughed with him, not surprised at all. Eli took her hand in his.

The pastor laughed with the congregation and held up his hands, "Whoa, Eli. Can't kiss her yet. I'll get on with it, though."

Rachel exchanged rings with Eli and thought she held it together pretty well as she repeated her vows and listened to him say his. When he was given the go-ahead, Eli gathered her bodily in his arms and kissed the daylights out of her amidst cat calls, whistles, and clapping. Soon, they were surrounded by guests hugging Rachel and patting Eli on the back.

As their guests congregated around them, the rows of chairs were removed and dispersed around the tables. The guests were invited to take a seat so that they could be served while the bride and groom and the wedding party took pictures briefly.

Rachel had a chance to look around and notice all the hard work the girls had put into the decorations. The wind blew softly through the fir trees that surrounded their group, filling the air with their woodsy fragrance. The tables were decorated with candles, which gave the outdoor setting an intimate feeling. Rachel noticed that strands of twinkling white lights which had been strung from the rafters were being illuminated little by little.

Each round table was spread with a royal blue tablecloth. In the center of each table was a tall ivory pillar candle within a hurricane globe so they wouldn't blow out at the first breeze that blew past. Each globe was centered inside an evergreen wreath, votive candles arranged randomly around the wreaths.

She didn't know how she had missed it, but brilliant red poinsettias were grouped at the entrance to the pavilion. The bridal party's table was a long rectangle, spread with a white tablecloth and holding more tall pillars under hurricane globes. Evergreen boughs lined the outside edge of the table. Plates were prepared by the caterer and served at the bridal party's table, and as they ate, all the guests were served.

Rachel noticed Ben and Quentin, Mike and Rogelio, and several others from the bar and leaned forward to Ethan. When she caught his eye, she said, "Who's at the bar?"

Ethan grinned and replied, "Nobody. They are all *here*. The employees *and* the customers. Ben and I figured with so many invited and planning to attend that we could close the club for the evening. We left a sign saying we were sorry that the club was closed for a family wedding."

Her lips trembled as she pressed them together for a second before saying, "Thank you, Ethan. That was sweet of you."

"You're welcome, Rachel. You're special to us, remember?"

She nodded, a little choked up as he patted her hand. She took a deep breath and relaxed, slid her chair closer to Eli's, then said, "Enough of this formal stuff, already."

Rising from her chair, Rachel sat in Eli's lap amidst snickers and chuckles from the guests and wedding party, and they fed each other from their plates. Things loosened up a little then.

After they ate, Rachel and Eli were kept occupied for a while being introduced to family members, cousins, aunt, and uncles.

Eli had been excited to find out that his grandparents on his father's side were in attendance. Rachel was thrilled when Eli introduced them to her and hoped for an opportunity to hear some of the stories these two could tell about Eli.

The DJ from the club had his equipment set up on the other side of the pavilion. The Christmas trees were moved back to line the perimeter and more Christmas lights were turned on, adding more sparkle to the pavilion of lights. Carrie and Raquel shot pictures as Rachel and Eli cut the cake.

Rachel lifted his bite of cake to his lips and grinned devilishly as she slid her fingers into his mouth, her heart flip-flopping when he licked and sucked the icing from her fingers.

The crowd whistled and clapped for Rachel to take a bite. She opened her mouth when he swiped cake and icing with his index finger from the plate and slid it between her lips. Rachel caught his hand, their rings twinkling in the lights, and sucked his finger completely clean. She ignored the outrageous catcalls, whistles, and applause as she flicked the tip of his finger with her tongue before releasing him. At the guests' urging, they shared a kiss at the cake table. Camera flashes went off all around them like a short-lived strobe. Grace turned the cakes over to the caterer to cut and deliver to the guests.

"Mrs. Wolf, I do believe it's time for our dance," Eli said. A thrill rushed through her at his softly spoken words.

The crowd moved to the tables as the DJ announced the first dance and introduced them as Mr. and Mrs. Eli Wolf to applause from the guests. Grace had asked her to put together a list of any songs she wanted played at the reception and asked Eli for a similar list. Grace had told Rachel that Eli picked the instrumental music for the processional and had asked that the actual song be played for their first dance.

She recognized the instrumental guitar music from her processional when the song began again, and the vocals jogged her memory. It was "Just Look at You" by Jimmy Wayne. Eli gently pulled her into a close embrace, and all she could see was his handsome face. Her hand rested on his chest as they moved to the music like they had been dancing together all their lives. He looked so handsome in his black tuxedo, vest, and black tie. She slid her hand up to cup his tanned cheek and he leaned down to kiss her tenderly.

"My husband," she murmured softly.

"My wife," he replied, kissing her deeper this time.

Chapter Fifty-two

They came up for air when Eli felt a tap on his shoulder. He drew back from kissing Rachel to find his father-in-law standing behind him, waiting for his dance with his daughter. Heartland's "I Loved Her First" was already playing, and he apologetically released Rachel into her father's arms and went to Renata and asked her to dance with him, which she did happily.

"Welcome to our family, Eli." Rachel's mom glided expertly with him over the dance floor.

Smiling, he said, "Thank you, Renata. Now I know where Rachel gets her natural grace and dancing skills from."

Blushing, his mother-in-law thanked him. "You are such a sweet talker, Eli. You make Rachel very happy. We're glad she found such a good man. Peter has always thought highly of you, and I have, too. I'll never forget the first time I met you. Do you remember?"

"The hospital." He nodded thoughtfully. He wondered what she must have thought of him. A train wreck.

"Yes. I remember you called us regularly while we were on the road coming home, giving us regular updates about her condition. You met us at the main entrance of the hospital and took us to her instead of waiting for us to come find you. And you never, ever left her side while her condition was so serious. Every mother wants a man for her daughter that loves that deep and knows how to show respect. The love you felt for her was in your exhausted eyes. I was ready to claim you as a son-in-law then."

He felt his cheeks warm a little at her words. "I had already ordered her ring by that time, hoping she would say yes to me when the time was right."

"And here we are," she said as he spun her, the song coming to an end.

Renata hugged him, and he kissed her cheek and walked her to her husband, who was holding a weeping Rachel. Peter looked up at him apologetically as he returned her to Eli. For now, nobody else had noticed, and he hoped to keep it that way. He gathered her to him and kept dancing, knowing stopping would draw every eye to them. Peter and Renata nodded approvingly as he held her and spoke softly.

"What is it, angel?"

"It's Daddy. You won't believe it. I'm not sure I do. He told me he saved money all these years for my wedding, which I already knew, but he didn't tell me he invested it. It's been a *really good* investment. What Grace spent on the wedding and reception didn't even scratch the surface on the little bit he pulled out to pay for all this. There's enough to *buy* our ranch, Eli. Or we can put it all in savings and investments and let it keep growing. Eli, *I had no idea.* He said it was just a lucky break that paid off for the family. He said that was why he taught me to always save my money and handle it wisely, so I'd be able to handle this money after I got married."

"There's enough to pay for the house?"

She whispered the amount, "Two hundred thousand dollars."

Holy cow.

"I wasn't sure what to say for a minute."

"How do you feel about your dad buying your house for you? Be honest, angel."

"He raised me to take care of myself, and I've trusted you to put a roof over my head, Eli."

"I can pay for the house you live in, angel. Why don't we wait and talk about it while we're gone and get your dad's advice later. It sounds like he has some experience with investments and money management. I suppose it's just the pride thing for me."

"Yeah, me, too, but I understand what you're saying. We'll figure it all out. It sure does give us some options, though," she said, her beautiful face radiant despite her tears.

"True. I'm so glad those were happy tears you were crying."

"I'll say." She dabbed gently beneath her eyes with her hanky. "Now, I want to celebrate with you. You know how much I love you, right?"

"Yes, I do, Mrs. Wolf."

"That sounds wonderful." She sighed shakily. "Say it again," she said with a watery giggle.

"Mrs. Wolf, Mrs. Wolf, Mrs. Wolf. My wife, my woman."

"My fantasy come true." She blushed as he slid his hand down her back to just barely above the upper swell of her ass.

"Mine," he growled.

"Mine," she growled softly back.

* * * *

They were joined by others on the dance floor as Tim McGraw and Faith Hill sang "It's Your Love." Rachel was as light as a feather and positively euphoric when Eli pulled her to the center of the dance floor as the song ended. She thought he wanted to dance with her again but noticed Grace and Ethan putting two chairs in the middle where all could see. The guests speculated quietly, wondering what was going to happen.

"Eli, we already talked about this," she said, making a giggling assumption. "No *garter groping!*"

He turned to her and chuckled. "Oh, there *will be* garter groping, but only when we're alone tonight. Then I plan on groping *all* the interesting articles of clothing you have on under this pretty dress, and not just your garters, Mrs. Wolf. This has nothing to do with me sliding my hand up your leg, though I *do like* the way you think." He laughed. "I have a little surprise for you, angel."

"A surprise?" she asked, conscious of the guests pulling their chairs to the edge of the dance floor.

He seated her in one of the chairs and handed her the glass of wine Grace brought to him, placing his glass by his chair. Grace brought another chair, and the DJ turned down the music. Rachel turned and looked behind her when she heard movement. It was Ethan approaching with two guitars. She turned and looked at Eli and smiled up at him as he winked at her. She got comfortable in her chair and took a sip of her wine. Ethan handed Eli his guitar, and they both took a seat before her, Eli directly in front of her and Ethan at his side. They checked tune quickly, and Grace spoke from the DJ's table.

"Ladies and gentlemen, you may or may not know it, but we have some real musical talent in our midst. Eli wanted to do something special for Rachel tonight, and he and Ethan have been working on this for weeks. We hope you enjoy it."

They began to play their guitars in a slow, sweet rhythm that she recognized instantly. "She's Got a Way With Me" by Billy Currington. They must have been practicing on the sly, very faithfully because they were smooth and in synchronization with each other.

She had no idea he could sing. *None.*

It's a gentle touch, but more than enough.
She can stop this ol' world from spinning too much.
It's a natural thing, and I do believe
I've found my reason to be.

* * * *

Eli sang the chorus, gazing into her expressive, brimming blue eyes. The words flowed from the depths of his heart. Ethan's background vocals were dead-on and made the song even better. He was so glad he'd discovered that Ethan had some serious skills. It was obvious Rachel loved this.

I'm not the same man, since she's been around.
There's more to this life, I've suddenly found.
I look at myself now so differently.
It's her love that brings me peace.

* * * *

Rachel felt tears slide down her cheeks as she listened. From the first note to the last, this was not a nervous, uncomfortably performed declaration of love. This was a well-rehearsed, polished, and professional performance. They played together like they had for years, and they could *both* sing. Ethan provided back-up vocals for Eli as he sang the song to her. Eli's voice was like a rich, luxurious caress, making love to her senses. When they were done, the guests clapped and cheered wildly for them.

Eli smiled at her, and so did Ethan as he rose from his chair and took Eli's guitar from him. Eli held out his hand to Rachel as Ethan, and Justin returned with filled wine glasses. Both men raised their glasses and toasted Eli and Rachel then Grace and Kelly joined them and offered toasts as well.

Rachel was still flabbergasted but took a minute to profusely thank Grace and Kelly for their hard work, grabbing Charity and thanking her, too. The girls giggled when Eli picked her up and bodily carried her back to the dance floor in mid-sentence.

She looked up at him and said, "Eli, I had *no* idea you could sing like that."

"There have been so many times when I've wanted to sing to you, especially as you fell asleep. Both Ethan and I were given classical guitar lessons when we were growing up. One night at the bar, we were talking and we discovered that we both could play and sing."

"Your voice," she murmured happily, "your voice *makes love* to my ears."

"Wow! That good, huh?"

"I want to throw myself at you shamelessly right now."

"Well, it's interesting that you mention that because Grace is about to dim the lights for Ethan so they can dance, and I've requested two or three songs for just...that...reason, *if* you're feelin' me?" He growled quietly and wrapped his arms around her waist.

Pressing her body to his, Rachel felt the growing hardness at his groin. "Oh, I'm feelin' you all right." The lights dimmed, and she smiled up at him softly as the first bars of "Let's Make Love" by Faith Hill and Tim McGraw began to play, and a soft sigh left her lips.

Grace had already joined Ethan on the dance floor, speaking softly to him. They began to dance, and he tilted his head down and pressed his lips to her ear. Her eyes shut in bliss, and she turned her face into his shoulder.

Rachel smiled up at Eli. He kissed her, and she tilted her head into his shoulder, his long, coal-black hair shielding her face from view as he whispered in her ear. And his voice really *did* make love to her.

* * * *

After the dance, Eli returned with Rachel to their table. He drew her into his lap and gave her a chance to collect herself and drink some water. She told him she was thankful for the dimmer lights that disguised her spreading blush. Eli playfully fed her bites of cake, and it was a sweet, quiet moment between them before the others began coming up to visit. By the time she recovered, a blissful Grace and smiling Ethan had joined the group. Corina and Brice came and congratulated them, and so did Ace and Kathleen. Rosemary twirled by with Evan and Wes, dancing with both of them at the same time. Somehow, that girl managed to keep both their hands full. Rachel pointed out Eli's dad dancing with Jane Jensen, who was looking pretty in a red satin dress.

Grace returned to the table after dancing with Jack and caught Rachel's eye. She enthusiastically signaled that the girls wanted to dance. Rachel nodded, and Eli grinned, helping her up from his lap. She and the other girls made their way to the dance floor as "If I Die Young" by The Band Perry ended.

"Save a Horse, Ride a Cowboy" started playing over the loudspeakers, and the girls started rocking. Eli stood next to Jack, Adam, and Ethan and groaned, watching the way the gown moved sinuously with her body, her little silver sandals flashing in the muted light as she danced.

Eli smiled over at Jack when he heard him groan, watching Grace grind with them. At the center of the group, Rachel gradually moved closer and closer across the dance floor until she was right in front of Eli. Her eyes flashed in the twinkling lights as she trailed a finger down his chest and abdomen then freaking stuck it in her mouth and *sucked on it*!

Damn! That song ended, but not the torture, as the DJ played "Honky Tonk Badonkadonk" by Trace Adkins next.

* * * *

Ethan stood with Jack and Adam, conversing quietly as he watched the woman he loved dance. Grace exuded happiness and confidence, but he remembered how shyly she had stepped into their lives, not realizing she was about to win the hearts and devotion of not one, but three men. Now, she moved sensuously and gracefully, with joyful freedom, looking beautiful in her blue dress, supremely confident of their love as she gazed at them watching her from the edge of the dance floor.

Ethan spoke up. "Her other gift came today."

"Oh, yeah?" Adam asked with a crooked smile. "She find it?"

"No, I was there when UPS brought it. It's hidden in your closet, Jack. I need to attach an anchor to a beam in her bedroom ceiling to support it."

"Grace will wonder what it's for. She'll talk the surprise right out of us," Jack warned. They all knew full well her persuasive abilities.

"We'll put it in the day before Christmas while she's away from the house. She'll be so busy with Christmas festivities and stuff that she won't even notice it in the ceiling. I'd rather do that because you know the moment she opens it, she's going to want to try it out."

"I like that plan," Adam said then groaned as she rolled her hips seductively to the music.

Ethan smiled and blew her a kiss and put his hand on his heart when she smiled at him. "She loves making love on that old porch glider so much. Wait till she gets a load of her love swing," he murmured, imagining her in it right then. The men smiled and agreed, watching her indulgently as the song came to an end and she moved gracefully across the dance floor to them.

Jack kissed her as she reached for him first. "Darlin', I'd say the wedding is a huge success. Are you tired?"

"Yes, but also very happy. It all turned out perfect, and Rachel was a gem through the whole process. Eli, too," she added as she hugged Ethan. "It was a great idea to suggest the photo shoot, honey. She loved the pictures."

"Well, you did, Gracie, so we figured it was worth a shot. I hear hers were pretty well received also."

She grinned. "Yeah, you know what that's like." To which they all nodded, remembering her unveiling their boudoir portraits to them before their wedding.

Smiling playfully, Grace said, "You have to take opportunities like that when they come your way, right?"

Adam grinned and nuzzled her neck as she hugged him. "Seize the day, baby?"

"That's my motto!" As her men crowded a little closer to her on the dim edge of the dance floor, she caught Adam looking straight down her cleavage. "Is that what you're doin' right now?"

He growled. "Yes, because I'd regret it if I didn't take the opportunity. You're luscious, baby."

"You all say the sweetest things. What were you talking about while I was dancing?"

"Your Christmas surprise," Ethan replied, and eyed her insatiably.

"Oooh! Is it that good? You look at me like you want to eat me!" She giggled softly as they came close even closer.

Ethan growled softly. "That's only for starters. Then we might play a little hide and seek, maybe a little Twister."

Grace pressed her lips together and blushed prettily.

"But eventually we'll be done playin' games," Jack murmured softly so only they could hear.

"Then we'll make love to you," Ethan murmured, kissing her warm cheek.

Adam lifted her palm and kissed it and said, "Until you lose track of who is touching you where."

Jack kissed the knuckles of her other hand.

"Oh, mama."

* * * *

Rachel laughed as she collapsed into Eli's strong arms when the song ended.

"How long before we can leave?" he asked with a deep, sexy growl. She loved when he growled like that. It was a sexy, primal sound that her body always responded to with an equally primal reaction.

His big, strong arms wrapped around her waist and pulled her to him tightly. That move squeezed her breasts up so that they nearly overflowed her gown. He smiled crookedly before glancing around to see if anyone watched. Quickly, he pressed a kiss to the top of each breast then released her. Rachel had to hold on to him breathlessly for a few seconds. Her skin tingled where his warm lips had touched her.

She looked up at him flirtatiously. "A few more dances?"

"With you *in* my arms, yes. You girls were torturing us poor guys standing here watching you." The soft smile on his face told her he hadn't suffered too badly, but the hard cock pressed against her belly hinted at his impatience.

Looking all business with a happy gleam in her eye, Grace came to Rachel and said, "Time for the bouquet toss!"

All the single women in the room crowded the front and jockeyed for position as Rachel looked over her shoulder, giggling at them and making them wait. She tossed it high in the air. Rosemary jumped a split second after Erin, who was taller. Rosemary's well-timed move intercepted the bouquet in the crucial moment. She came down the winner and held up the prize in triumph. Jack and Ace nudged Wes and Evan in the ribs when they saw who had won it. Wes and Evan grinned at her when she returned to their sides with it in her hands.

"Eli wants to know when we're leaving," Rachel said as Grace rejoined her after the bouquet toss.

"I was coming to see if you want me to help you change here or if you want to get to the bed and breakfast and let Eli undress you."

"I'd rather let him since what's underneath is a surprise."

"It's no fun if he doesn't get to unwrap the gift first," Grace quipped. "Your luggage, including your makeup case, is in the truck, which is securely locked. Some of the kids *may* have decorated the outside of the truck, but everything inside is safe."

Rachel scoffed good-naturedly. "Come on, Grace, I saw you hand Charity's kids the bag with crepe paper streamers in it."

Grace hid a gleeful snort behind her hand. "Oh, well! A little bit of decorations on the truck won't hurt. People love that stuff! I warned them they could not use shoe polish, though."

Rachel hugged Grace happily as Kelly joined them. "This was the happiest night of my life. You both made it beautiful and perfect. Thank you, from the bottom of our hearts."

Eli joined them as Grace and Kelly hugged her.

Kelly took Rachel's hands. "Rachel, thank you for making my *brother's* dreams come true." She sniffled and started to cry. Eli laughed and hugged Kelly, lifting her off her feet. "You're the best big brother in the whole world!" she mumbled from inside his big embrace.

"Thanks, sis."

Grace looked at Rachel and said, "I'm so glad you gave him a chance, Rachel. Men of worth are so hard to find. You've married a good one." She turned to Eli and poked him gently in the chest with her fingertip. "And you, you big *galoot*. Take good care of my dear friend."

"I promise, beautiful," Eli said and leaned down to hug her. "Thanks for being such a good friend to us."

Eli hugged his dad and grandparents, and Rachel hugged her mom and dad, thanking them again. The wedding guests lined up and tossed birdseed over them as they ran from the pavilion together. Halfway down the paved walk, Eli stopped and scooped her up in his arms. As the guests cheered, he ran to the truck with her.

Chapter Fifty-three

Firelight flickered around them, the only light in the bedroom as Eli stood behind Rachel and unzipped the wedding dress. Her sweet, womanly fragrance filled his nostrils, and his hardening cock responded with a yearning twitch. The dress fell from her in a silken whisper to the thick rug between the bed and the fireplace. He placed a warm kiss on her shoulder and helped her step from the dress. She turned, and he took a deep breath, sighing appreciatively.

"Well, this looks familiar."

Stepping back, Eli took a moment to enjoy the sight of her. Rachel's hair was brushed out in soft waves, and she was laced into the white silk corset from her portrait. He could see the slightest hint of her rose-colored nipples through the patterned lace of the cups. She wore a white silk G-string, the garters, sheer white stockings, her pretty silver heels, and nothing else. She gave him a graceful turn then presented her back to him, and he undid the bow at the back.

"Carrie shot a series of pictures for you back at Grace's house while I got dressed. She thought you might like that." He heard the quiver of excitement in her voice.

"I would." The corset had hook and eye fasteners on the side, but what was the fun in that? He continued working the laces through his fingers until the corset fell away. She turned to him, slid his tuxedo jacket off his shoulders, and unbuttoned his shirt while he removed his tie and vest. They took their time and didn't rush the moment.

Eli gazed down at her, adoring her, as everything fell to the floor around them. He removed his shoes and socks, stopping her when she would have removed the rest of her clothing. She reached to help him with the button of his pants, and he could hear her soft, uneven breathing.

Finally freed of her clothing, she rested her warm, silken body against his. She sighed as he slid his hand down her back to the waist of her G-string. He led her to the large thick rug in front of the screened fireplace and got down on his knees. He placed her hands on his shoulders so she wouldn't lose her balance and slipped her high-heeled sandals from her slender, graceful feet. He lifted each foot to his knee and slowly slid the sheer white stockings from her long legs, one at a time.

He drew her down to her knees in front of him and gently grasped her warm hips with his hands, kissing her until she clung to him breathlessly. Her hands trembled, and her lips quivered a little as he lapped at her bottom lip with the tip of his tongue. Desire sang in his blood, and his impatient cock twitched persistently at being ignored. He lowered her to the rug slowly and reclined beside her. With one hand, he hooked the waist band of the G-string from her hips and slid it quickly down her legs until she was free of it.

Eli slowly stroked her collarbone and leaned down to suckle a nipple. His hand continued down her trembling torso to a softly rounded hip then over her mound. Her breath caught in her throat as his fingers strayed into her warm, wet lips, glistening with the silken evidence of how aroused she was by his attention.

"Oh, angel," he groaned over her nipple, licking it softly. "So wet already."

Rachel moaned breathlessly as his fingers stroked her clit, gently sliding through her slick honey. She arched and moved with his hands. The muscles in her cunt clenched around his finger when he slipped it inside and stroked her pussy, sliding through all her juices. He gently rubbed her clit with his thumb and added another finger to the first, stroking into her silky, delicate flesh.

Rachel's hand stroked his shoulder. "Oh, Eli." She threw her head back, and her back arched. "Baby, you're so good to me."

She moved on his finger and began to pant and cry out. He began a gentle pumping motion and growled when her muscles tightened on his fingers. She came with a low, moaning sob. Stroking her until she finished, he kissed her gently and nuzzled her lips.

"I adore you, angel," he whispered as she reached for him.

Kneeling between her legs, Eli hooked one of her thighs over his forearm, lifting her hips slightly. He growled low when her silky, wet heat kissed his cock as he positioned the head at her opening.

She looked up at him, love radiating from her eyes. "Make love to me, Eli," she murmured softly when he hesitated for a few seconds.

He wanted to enjoy and remember the moment when he entered his wife for the first time. He smiled at her as his body vibrated with desire, and her breath caught with a deep, impassioned moan as he quite literally slid home.

Epilogue

June, six months later...

"I can't believe I'm really going to do this." Rachel said to herself as she looked in the mirror. At Cami's direction, she applied another layer of liquid eyeliner to her eyelids. Charlotta helped Rachel with her false eyelashes and put the sky-high acrylic shoes by the stool.

"Oh, don't worry. You're going to be phenomenal. I can't wait to see you up there," Charlotta told her.

"You have time to run through your routine once if you hurry." Cami buckled the silver strap on the clear platforms. The shoes put any other pair of fuck-me shoes she owned to utter shame. Just as Cami and Charlotta had taught her, Rachel rose from the stool gracefully, tilting out her ass as she straightened her legs in a classic stripper turn. She adjusted the waistband on the skimpy black and silver cheeky shorts, which revealed most of her ass to great advantage. She checked and adjusted her cleavage in the mirror. Charlotta teased and sprayed Rachel's hair one last time, making it big and wild. She needed to look just different enough from her everyday self for this to work but enough like herself to catch his eye.

"Your music is out at the DJ booth, cued up and ready to go," Cami said, trotting back in the room in her white, ruffled bikini thong and white ruffled bra. Her feet were shod in her white platform school girl style pumps.

"You don't think the Trace Adkins song would have been a better choice? I could do either one."

The girls shook their heads, and Cami said, "You need music that is totally different from what you usually listen to when you're together. It needs to be just different enough that when he hears it, it won't automatically bring you to mind."

Rachel grinned. "And you're sure neither of you danced for him to these songs?"

"I've never danced to either one of those songs, but I may use your routines after you're done, if you don't mind," Charlotta said, grinning.

"Well, you both taught me and helped develop the routines, so go for it. Just not for *him*, okay?"

Cami giggled. "No problem. I used to dance to 'Supermassive Black Hole,' but it's been a while, and I've never danced to 'Bad Things.' That routine is my favorite."

"It's the vampire thing." Charlotta snickered. "Maybe he'll *bite* you tonight."

Rachel laughed and checked her ass in the mirror one last time, running her hand over a dimple that was visible.

"Do I have enough body glitter on?" Rachel asked.

"You look perfect," Charlotta reassured her. "Once you get under the purple neon lights, all imperfections disappear. Your ass looks great. You're going to want to warm up a little."

"Yeah, how long do I have?"

"Twenty minutes, give or take. The appointment isn't scheduled until two o'clock, and it's one thirty now. Jake is meeting him at the door since the front is locked. It's going to be *perfect*."

Rachel was a little nervous, but the girls' enthusiasm helped to build her confidence. She ran through part of her routine under the lights. Her muscles felt warm and relaxed when Charlotta came from the front and waved at her and Cami to get behind the curtain, where they listened and waited.

* * * *

Eli checked his appointment planner and made a quick call while he sat in his truck. He'd arrived early for his two o'clock appointment. When five minutes until two rolled around, he got out of his truck and strode across the parking lot to the door and was met by one of the managers.

Charlotta had given his name to the owner. They were having some problems with their AV system, and the manager had called Eli. Eli had told him it sounded like a signal distribution problem and agreed to come and check it out the following day.

"Thanks for coming, Eli," Jake said, shaking his hand. "Let me show you where everything is. I have a lot of paperwork that I'm trying to wade through right now, so if you need me, I'll be in my office. Charlotta is here working on routines with a couple of the other dancers. If you need me, she can direct you to my office." Jake showed him the problem then exited through a heavy wooden door beside the bar.

"Hi, Eli," Charlotta said as she walked up, dressed in short shorts and a workout top.

He turned, smiled at her, and gave her a friendly hug, saying, "It's good to see you."

"You, too. I'm helping two other dancers refine some routines and practice some new moves. Will it bother you if we have the music up? We don't want to be in your way."

"Oh, no. I'm checking the monitors right now. You won't be bothering me at all. Rachel tells me she has enjoyed taking lessons with you both."

"I'm glad to hear that," Charlotta said in her melodic, sweet-as-honey voice. "She's an excellent student. Some things come naturally to people, and Rachel is a natural at dance."

"*I'll* say," Eli said.

She chuckled. "I'm glad you've enjoyed the fruits of her labor."

"Yep." He carefully pulled the monitor from its built-in cabinet.

"Well, I'll get out of your hair. Good luck finding whatever the problem is."

"'Kay," he said as she walked away. Hmm, that was odd. When he pulled the monitor back, he expected to see a mess behind the TV, but the cables were all fitted properly, the wiring neat and orderly, and all labeled properly. He sighed, thinking he'd have to trace the problem back to the source.

As he double-checked the wiring and connections behind the monitor, music began to pound through the loudspeakers in the heavy bass beat that dancers preferred. He glanced up briefly as Cami and another dancer took the stage, running though their routine. Jake must have hired a new dancer, and Cami was developing a routine to do with her. They were moving simultaneously to Muse's "Supermassive Black Hole."

He went back to work but felt his eyes drawn again. And again. The other stripper was *something else*. He could be a happily married man and still appreciate that fact. She had long, curly, dark hair, and under the purple lights, he couldn't be sure if it was black or brown. Her features were in shadow. She was built perfectly, with soft, smoothly toned feminine curves. She and Cami went through the basic moves of their dance on the stage, and then she turned and leapt for the pole, timed perfectly with Cami. She spun and worked her way up the pole, using her ankle and the back of her calf for leverage.

Guiltily, he realized his full attention was on the dancer and not his job. Even worse, his cock responded. He turned away, trying to ignore her. Now he understood why Rachel had arranged for Charity to find two strippers at his bachelor party who looked *nothing* like her. It made sense, and it also explained why he was responding to this one. She reminded him of Rachel.

To check the theory, he glanced up again over the back of the monitor, and sure enough, she *really did* remind him of Rachel. His cock wholeheartedly agreed, wanting Rachel, preferably *right now*. He realized he was still watching when she looked up from her squatting position at the base of the pole and gracefully rose, swinging her delectable ass way out. Then she grinned at him.

He stood up and banged his head on the cabinet. *No.* He looked away, feeling guilty when a white-hot streak of pure lust shot right through him. The dancer was *flirting* with him, and he was responding. He needed to get done and get the *fuck* out of there.

He cursed at himself for taking this job.

Sure, Jake, I can fix your problem. No, Charlotta, you won't distract me a bit. No, Eli, you're not some horny, over-sexed fucking Neanderthal—

He glanced up as she climbed the pole, in sync with Cami, and somehow held herself there with no hands, arched out over the stage, spinning. Reaching for the pole, she flipped herself then spread her long legs above her head into a perfect ballet-like split before twining them around the pole. She slid back down it fast, way too fast for his comfort. Stopping smoothly at the last second, with just her fingertips on the stage floor, she rotated onto the stage on her back. She rolled and rose on her skyscraper shoes, her knees parted as wide as they would go, and ground her way into a standing—

What. The. Fuck?

His heart lurched, and his pulse pounded in his ears. He *knew* that grind. The dancer flicked her hair and looked over her shoulder, directly at him. Smiling again, she twisted around the pole, lifted her feet off the stage, and spun with her hair sailing around her. Releasing the pole, she danced on the stage, skimming her hands down her satiny thighs. His cock reared up when she caressed her mostly-bare, curvaceous ass then trailed the backs of her fingers over her ribs and the sides of her full, round breasts, up her throat, and into her hair.

He *knew* that move, too.

The beautiful dancer shimmied down to a squat and crooked her finger at him as she rose gracefully, rolling her luscious hips. The song ended, and another song began. Cami left the stage as the dancer transitioned smoothly into Jace Everett's "Bad Things." He pushed the TV monitor back into the cabinet because there was nothing wrong with their system. He knew why he was here.

His cock tingled in gratitude when he slowly made his way out from behind the bar, moved toward the stage, and took a seat, smiling territorially at his dancer. She never spoke or broke character as she turned and grasped the pole again, dancing with it as she swung her ass out, stepping gracefully in the heels that were higher than any he'd ever seen on her before. They made her legs look impossibly long.

Leaping to the pole, she spun as she climbed higher then somehow flipped upside down and executed another perfect split, and the lines of her long, supple thighs and calves made his mouth water and his cock twitch. In a move that made his heart lurch fearfully, she released her grip on the pole and locked her calf around it before she could plummet to the stage.

She slowly slid down and lowered her body gracefully to the stage, her ankles still twined around the pole. She released the pole, stretched out, and came up on her hands and knees. The sweetly arching curve of her back inspired vibrations in his cock that had him gritting his teeth to control his response, as did the sinuous grinding of her hips as she whipped her hair back with her hand. Sitting upright, she ground her hips and pumped up and down in an erotic move that he could've sworn he felt on his cock. Repeating the movement, she caressed her abdomen and slid her hands over her breasts.

She placed the sole of her shoe on the stage and rose on one knee then leaned forward on that foot and smoothly placed the other shoe on the stage.

and rose in a slow, graceful rolling movement, swinging her ass out again. Swinging her beautiful ass out like that was akin to waving a red flag in front of a bull. She danced around the pole then spun around it, climbing again. She rotated upside down and split her legs wide open as she did, one hand above her on the pole and one below, lowering her in the spin until she came to a stop spread wide directly in front of him.

He had no idea she was so flexible.

She came to her knees and executed a roll on her hands and knees that positioned her at the edge of the stage, her ass directly in front of him. She gave him a teasing little shake, which had him grinning and chuckling at the sudden urge he had to lean forward and take a little bite. Rising again gracefully, she rolled her hips, one foot first and then the other. She took the pole in hand and leapt to it, spinning with one calf around it, the other bent up to her ass, and threw her hair around. Spinning, coming back to the stage, she swung her legs out, landing flawlessly.

She continued dancing around the pole, rolling and grinding her hips, swinging her ass out, always in slow, unhurried erotic movements. She stretched out her hips to him and swung her ass around and back again as the music began to fade. She stood upright and released the pole and sauntered gracefully in the skyscraper heels until she stood directly above him in a wide, sexy, confident stance.

Slowly, she squatted and lowered one hand to the stage and then the other. She panted lightly, and her body was covered in a fine sheen of body glitter and sweat. The purple lights illuminated the upper swells of her succulent, full breasts, and she was close enough to him that he could detect her sweet womanly scent, tinged with her arousal.

He'd already glanced around and knew they were alone in the main room of the club. Jake probably had surveillance cameras and monitors in his office so he could keep an eye on his business, which was wise. It was for that reason Eli was relieved that she'd not removed her top as part of her dance. To Jake, they were probably just more breasts, one pair out of twenty or thirty he saw on a nightly basis. To Eli, they were the most perfect twin beauties in the world and not for others eyes, only *his*. He was glad she felt the same way.

"Sir, if you enjoyed my dance you're permitted to tip me." She smiled playfully at him and hooked her finger in the elastic waistband of her skimpy little shorts as if she thought he might actually slip a bill in there, then added, "But why stop at the tip, when I'd really prefer the whole thing?"

There was no stopping the deep rumble that rose from his chest as he stood. He couldn't take her up on the offer here, so he kept the caveman in check. Given his height, he was at eye level with her on the stage. He placed his warm hands on hers and kissed her, gently at first, but his hunger for her deepened quickly.

When he released her lips, she spoke softly. "Did you like how I danced for you?"

"You are one incredible woman, Rachel Wolf."

She gave him a sexy, confident grin. "Why, thank you."

"Why here?"

"It was Cami and Charlotta's idea. They thought you deserved the full strip club experience, and I've been fantasizing about doing this since we first started. I had to do it when no one was around, so they thought of an excuse to get you here. Sorry you had to go through the trouble of messing with the monitors. If I could perform on a real strip club stage, privately for you, then I had to take that opportunity, right?"

"Of course. I loved it.

"No regrets?" she asked as she reached for him.

"No regrets, angel." He lifted her gently from the stage and set her on her feet. He grinned as he looked at her. Rachel was nearly eye level with him in those heels. She slid her hands over his chest and wrapped her arms around his neck.

"I'm probably getting body glitter all over you."

"Mmm, yes, angel. Get it *all over me.*"

He slid his hands over her ribs and down her waist as he kissed her deeply. She moaned when he squeezed her ass cheeks.

"You're bringing the shoes home, right?"

A seductive smile spread across her lips. "Oh, yeah, these are mine."

He growled deeply in approval.

THE END

www.heatherrainier.com

ABOUT THE AUTHOR

Heather Rainier lives and writes in South Central Texas. Her stories offer up the content of her fantasies, with autobiographical humor, triumph and tragedy mixed in.

Heather believes that life doesn't always present love to us in neat little sanitized packages. Sometimes we have to seize the day, live life with no regrets, forget the past, never give up, learn to trust, and dare to live, even in outrageous circumstances.

When not happily typing at her keyboard, Heather is usually busy corralling her kids, volunteering at local schools, or loving on her smokin' hot husband, who thankfully loves to cook.

Also by Heather Rainier

Ménage Everlasting: Divine Creek Ranch 1: *Divine Grace*
Ménage Everlasting: Divine Creek Ranch 3: *Heavenly Angel*

Available at
BOOKSTRAND.COM

Siren Publishing, Inc.
www.SirenPublishing.com

Lightning Source UK Ltd.
Milton Keynes UK
UKOW042205040712

9 781610 342766